ALL THE DAYS OF MY LIFE

All The Days of
My Life

Hilary Bailey

HEINEMANN : LONDON

William Heinemann Ltd
10 Upper Grosvenor Street, London W1X 9PA

LONDON   MELBOURNE   TORONTO
JOHANNESBURG   AUCKLAND

First published 1984

© Hilary Bailey 1984

SBN 434 04595 0

Photoset by Rowland Phototypesetting Ltd
Bury St Edmunds, Suffolk
Printed and bound in Great Britain by
The Pitman Press Ltd, Bath

For Sophie and Kate

The author wishes to thank the Arts Council of Great Britain, and the British taxpayers, who gave her a grant of £3,000 in 1980 to help her write this book.

PROLOGUE

1996

The wheels of Sir Herbert Precious's black limousine came noiselessly (for the vehicle was powered by electricity) up the long, broad drive, with its rows of beech trees on either side, and stopped in the half-circle of gravel in front of a big red brick country house, Allaun Towers. Three wide stone steps, sheltered by a portico, led up to the front door. Yellow and white chrysanthemums, interspersed with clumps of low, green plants, cut back for the winter, stood tall in the flower beds along the walls of the house, like lines of shock-headed boys. On the other side of the car the lawn dropped down slightly towards a shrubbery. Beyond it a silver strip of lake glittered. In the distance lay fields. Far to the left were the misty hills. A late September sun shone over the trees and lake. The walls of the house were ruddy, glowing with light.

Before his chauffeur could reach the door of the car Sir Herbert had half opened it. As the man pulled it fully open and held it for him Sir Herbert got out and walked across to where the butler, who had earlier been at the front of the house, listening for the sound of wheels on the drive, was now waiting on the steps before the open front door. A tall, lean, agile man in his early sixties, Sir Herbert marched up the steps and, going into the house, said, "Hullo, Henderson. No hat. Coat's in the car. I hope you're well."

"Pretty well, considering, Sir Herbert," said the butler, shutting the door behind him.

"It's nice to be back," he said.

"It's a pleasure to see you again, Sir Herbert," said Henderson. "Lady Allaun is in the drawing room. Will you go straight in?"

"Wash my hands first," said Sir Herbert. "Don't worry, I'll see myself in afterwards. Would you just tell her I'm here?"

He cast a glance at the doorway, which led to the drawing room, over which hung a portrait of some ancient Allaun, with pointed toe,

3

one hand on his heart and the other on his long beribboned walking stick. Then he went swiftly across the marble tiles in the opposite direction, through an archway and into the cloakroom – there to pause, relax a little and, somehow, still his own, suddenly fast-beating heart before he had to join Lady Allaun in the drawing room.

"It's the power of the past," he thinks, as he pushes back his cuffs and runs a little cold water over the veins on the undersides of his wrists. "What a turmoil of old memories and old emotions! In the end, recollection has as much strength to disturb us as thoughts of the present when we were young, or our anticipations of the future. And on this particular occasion, how especially disturbing memory is!"

And he dries his hands, pulls his cuffs down, stares, blindly, in the mirror at his thick, brown-grey hair and long, pale face. Not as young as he used to be, he thinks, but he can still outwalk his son. He sees himself smile at his own vanity and turns from the glass. He takes a few long, deep breaths, to calm himself and then, quite collectedly, crosses the hall and goes with a springy stride under the picture of the old, seventeenth-century Allaun, down the short passageway, to where he is awaited.

After the butler's announcement, and while Sir Herbert was washing his hands, Lady Allaun sits in an armchair, her back to the long windows which look out over the garden. She stares into the logs which burn in the wide fireplace. Beside her is a small table on which lies an open, many-tiered rosewood workbasket, full of cottons and silks. An embroidery frame, from which white linen falls in folds, stays neglected on her lap as she gazes unseeingly at the flames. To one side of her, opposite the fire, stands a long sofa, upholstered in the same soft grey as her own chair. On the other side of the fire, facing her, stands a second chair. As darkness comes the room slowly dims.

And so she sits, Lady Allaun, a tallish woman in her sixties, perhaps a little plumper than she used to be. Her hair, which must once have been blonde, is now both a little greyer and a little darker. Nevertheless, her eyes are still very blue in a plump and rosy face.

Outside in the fading light rooks caw and swoop through misty air over the sweep of land beyond the house, over the trees, the lawn, the lake. There is a sound as Sir Herbert opens the double doors of the drawing room, comes in, sees her . . .

Lady Allaun looks up. She cries, "Hullo, Bert." She goes across the room, puts both hands on his shoulders and kisses him firmly on the mouth.

4

"Molly!" says Sir Herbert, holding her at arm's length and staring into her face. "Not a day older, I swear. How long is it now? Five years?"

"Six," she says, surveying him. "You're not so bad yourself. Come and sit down. I've asked Henderson to bring in some tea. It's lovely to see you again."

"Thank you," says Sir Herbert. "Well —" and he looks around the room.

"There seems so much to say."

"We'd better say it, then," says Molly Allaun in a practical but polite tone.

"Things, financially speaking, are going pretty well then?" Sir Herbert asks, equally evenly.

"Can't complain," Molly Allaun says with assurance. "It's rolling in and in — enough to see me out at any rate."

"You've been wiser than me," Sir Herbert sighs.

"Ah — I'm so sorry," says Molly.

"Well, I'm glad to hear you're all right," says Sir Herbert.

As Molly cuts him a piece of cake, he hands her his plate and says, "So you've no financial problems?"

"No," she tells him.

"Then — to come to the point. Why the memoirs?"

"The memoirs," says Molly and grins. "More like confessions —" She stares into the fire and says, after a pause, well, I don't know why I made the tapes all about my life, really. I needed a change. It was something to do, something for me, myself. But I don't think that was it. I never asked myself why I was doing it — not until recently, now I've finished. I started work after Johnnie died — Johnnie Bridges. I think that had a lot to do with it."

"Ah — Johnnie," says Sir Herbert.

"Poor Johnnie." Then she says, "It was cancer — in the prison hospital at Brixton. He never thought to send for me till it was too late. Life's all ragged ends, isn't it?"

Sir Herbert sadly nods.

"Anyway," Molly goes on, "that's what started me off, I suppose. After all, it's not just Johnnie — even at best we two haven't got much time ahead of us and what's to come is liable to be just more of the same. No changes. Ever think about that?"

"Of course I think about it," he replies. "But it doesn't worry me much."

5

"Nor me – much," Molly says. "But I'm getting old now. So are you. We've only got peace and quiet and a bit of contentment to look forward to. That's natural but, face facts, it's a path with no turnings, now."

"What you've so tenderly described is a perfectly understandable exercise in recollection and understanding. But why publish – and why now?"

"I want to tell my story now, while I'm still alive. But it's not to cause trouble, or for the money, or to start a scandal. Really, it's because now's the only time I know. It's different for you. You've got a different attitude – your work, your old family, your farm – they've all got a footing in the past and the future. A feeling of continuity, that's what you've always had – much good has it done you. It's always been different for me. Now's been the only time I've ever known, from a child onward. You ask me to wait – you're asking the impossible. I don't believe in it. I don't believe in the future. I want my story to happen now, the way everything's always happened and always will. And I don't want you, or anyone else, standing in my way. Here's my offer. You take a copy of the tapes and listen to them. It's all there. I've never felt much like writing. I've never been any good at it and it goes against the grain after all these years. You know my motto – never put anything on paper and if you do, don't sign it."

"All too well," Sir Herbert agrees. "That's what I'm worried –"

"Well," she interrupts, "you take those tapes and if you can find one lie, or anything like it, you tell me. And, for the rest, listen hard and give me an opinion and I'll hold everything until you give it. I'll take you seriously, I won't sign a thing, I promise you."

Sir Herbert left next day, towards evening. Only as the car went through the big gates at the bottom of the drive did he settle his long body comfortably into the upholstery and realize how uneasy he had felt as the car swung down between the trees, and how tired he was. He suffered regret at leaving the comfortable life of Allaun Towers, and the company of his friend, and a feeling of deep release as he finally left the grounds. Flashes of the past days came to him – of the candles in their silver candelabra on the table, of the arrival of the great platter of pheasant, of Molly Allaun throwing herself back in her chair and laughing, of their quiet walk round the rose garden at the back of the house where flowers still bloomed, of their talking by the fire in their deep armchairs, late into the night. But all the time, he realized, the remembrance of the past had been running, like an underground river, below the surface of the present. Perhaps, he thought, it was all those memories, not produced for the conscious mind to recognize but there, all the same, like sights seen from the corner of the eye, noises almost out of hearing, waves of perfume evoking a response, but no specific association, which had tired him so much. But he had the tapes, and tonight he would start listening to them.

As the car moved through the countryside Sir Herbert began to think that he need not just sit and listen to Molly Allaun's version of the truth. Surely he could shed some light on some of the events, correct a few of the errors she would almost undoubtedly have made? In fact, he thought, some comment and criticism, some corrections, even some additional information might be extremely useful before the final and, he now thinks, irrevocable, revelations she had decided to make.

He opened the leather case of cassette tapes on the seat beside him and removed the first. Immediately the car fills with the familiar voice.

And tonight, thinks Sir Herbert, and all the next day, Molly Allaun will be raising the dead for him.

Mary Waterhouse

1941

Mary Waterhouse sat on the train. There were six other children in the compartment. She was nearly five and they were all bigger than her. They scuffled their feet on the tops of the crumpled newspaper which had wrapped their sandwiches and was now lying on the floor. They had been squabbling, about who was entitled to the last few mouthfuls from the bottle of Tizer which was being passed round. The girls sat on one side, facing the way the train was going. Cissie Messiter was making a cat's cradle from the string which had been round the newspaper in which her sandwiches had been wrapped. Beside her, Peggy James, her mouth open in her big, fat face, stared across to where Frank Jessop and James Hodges were standing up and bouncing on the seats opposite her. James's sister, Win, in the corner by the corridor, was asleep. Ian Brent was lying in the luggage rack. Mannie Frankel, in the corridor, was leaning out of the window shouting at any house or cottage they passed. "Oy! Cows!" he cried out. "Wotcher! Cows!" The bottle of Tizer landed in the newspapers on the floor, with a thud.

But Mary Waterhouse, in the corner by the window, was alone, staring out at the brilliant sunburnt heath, at trees and bushes and fields, at the long, drying grass and foxgloves growing in the earth and cinders of the railway embankments, which blurred, as the train swept them on, into long streaks of yellow-green and small streaks of dull red. She could feel the heat on her face as the train hurtled forward, and the scratching of the hot, plush seats on the backs of her thighs. Her mouth and the back of her throat were dry, but she did not think about getting a drink. She had never been so fast, seen so much green, so many things growing, so much open sky, such a wide landscape, going on, in its variety of fields, small winding roads, hills and dales and open, fern-filled common land. It was like a dream, or a picture in her book. What could it be like, she thought, to live in one of those houses with gardens full of flowers and things growing, opening into fields? You could get up in the morning and walk straight out into a field, feeling the grass under your feet and the sun on your back. Or, she thought, perhaps you'd be allowed to pick a flower whenever you liked, if it really was your garden outside your house. She felt her arms, prickling full of flowers, and sensed the smell, like passing a flower-seller in the street, right under her nose. No one to tell you to get your hands off. You'd have to be rich, thought Mary, sitting in her flimsy maroon dress with the mustard-coloured flowers on it, very rich to pay the landlord of a house like that, with a garden.

It must be like magic, like turning the pages of her book, going further and further into the picture of the lady in the long dress in the deep forest.

She must have fallen into that four-year-old's daze, awake but dreaming, for Mr Burns's angry voice came at her suddenly, as he shouted "Look at this filthy mess –" and she realized suddenly that all the children had snapped to attention. She had even heard, at the back of her dream, Ian Brent plop down from the luggage rack like a ripe apple from a tree, and land, somehow, in his proper place in a sitting position. Now he sat stiffly, arms folded, eyes straight forward, in the position Mr Burns insisted they assume in the classroom. All the children had their arms folded and looked ahead of them. Cissie Messiter was straightbacked, but right on the edge of her seat; was trying, unobtrusively, to kick the newspapers into the narrow space underneath. Only Peggy James, beside her, had her head turned witlessly towards the corridor, where Mannie Frankel was holding the side of his head and crying.

Beside him Mr Burns, red-faced and sweating, went on shouting into the compartment, "I told all of you, before you got on this train, to behave yourselves. You're not in the slums now. You're going to a decent place, to meet a decent set of people, country people, not pigs, like all of you. If I catch you with your head out of the window once more, my lad," he said, turning to the blubbering Mannie, "you won't have any head left to put out. Is that understood?"

Mannie, conditioned to expect that tone of voice to be followed by a blow, cried all the harder.

Mr Burns bent over him, took his ear in his hand, put his face ogreishly against the boy's and said again, "Understand?"

Mannie Frankel let out an earsplitting scream.

Mr Burns released him suddenly, so that he stumbled backwards.

All the children in the carriage, except Peggy, continued to stare straight ahead of them, not daring to meet each others' eyes. Mary's thumb, as she heard Mannie's walking run along the corridor of the moving train, moved up, slowly and steadily, from her lap into her mouth. She did not know what was going to happen. She felt very frightened. Mr Burns, sweating in his shiny black suit, his collar and tie, at the carriage door, might come in and make them all put out their hands and hit them with his long wooden ruler. He had broken a girl's finger once, her brother Jackie had told her. Just as bad was the loss of her magic dream, like getting a toffee and having Ivy snatch it away, unwrap it and put it in her own mouth. Great big red lips, yellow teeth, pink tongue sucking round her toffee.

"Take your thumb out of your mouth, Mary Waterhouse," came the shouting voice. "You're not a baby now." She took it out.

"As for the rest of you guttersnipes – get this carriage cleaned up. Ugh – it smells. Didn't your mothers give you a wash before you came?" And he disappeared.

"Ivy washed me," Mary said into the rustling noise as the children collected newspapers from the floor. She was remembering the cloth, grey and part of an old shirt, which had gone wet and stale-smelling, round her neck and ears, before she set off for the school, where all the children, with paper bags or brown paper parcels containing their clothes, had mustered in the playground before leaving for the station. She remembered the way Ivy's chest, on a level with her own head, moved in and out in sharp jerks. She panted as she wiped. "Don't move your bloody head," she had cried, as Mary turned away to avoid her breath. "Little madam," she had muttered crossly, but Mary did not know exactly what she meant.

"I don't know what I'm supposed to do with all this lot," said sharp-faced Cissie, standing up, clutching a heap of screwed up newspaper to her bony little chest. "Old Burns just thinks he's better than what we are. Just because he's a rotten schoolteacher. My mum says she remembers him coming to school with no boots on. She reckons he used to live down Wakefield Street and there were eight of them in the family. And they didn't have no blankets in the winter time," she concluded triumphantly and stood there, peaky and small, in the middle of the jolting carriage, wearing a grey, woollen skirt too long for her and a skimpy, faded blouse with flowers on it. "Here, Peggy," she said. "Chuck these out the window."

Peggy, who was still sitting down, stood up slowly and took the papers. The others watched her.

At the window she said, "I might get into trouble."

Mary stood up and, standing on tiptoes, began to help her push the newspapers out. They were whisked off, down the side of the train. Peggy joined her at the window and laughed as the newspapers were half-torn from her grasp.

"Now come and sit down and behave yourself, Peggy," ordered Cissie, the oldest child of a large family. Peggy, the slow-witted child, father unknown, of slow-witted Marge Jones, who lived over the stable in Meakin Street where old Tom Totteridge kept his horse and cart, did as she was told. She said, "I want my mum."

"Oh, my Gawd," said Cissie.

"CARLESS TALK COSTS LIVES," Frank Jessop read, slowly and stonily, from the advertisement opposite him, above Mary's head.

The train went, for a long, dark time, through a tunnel. In the blackness, in the acrid stench of soot, Peggy began to cry. There was a thump in the corridor outside, and a cry of pain.

"It's all dark," said Mary, frightened.

"It's a tunnel," said Ian Brent. "I went through one before – on the way to the seaside."

"Does it stop?" asked Cissie.

"Course it does. It's a tunnel, ain't it." Nevertheless in the banging, snorting, pitch black carriage he was uncertain. "Here! What's that?" he cried in alarm as the thumping started again in the corridor.

"It's me," came a voice, Mannie's. "I'm trying to get in. I can't find the door. Why's it gone all dark? Is it an air raid?"

"No," said Ian. "Here – I'll stick my hand out the door. See if you can grab hold of it."

They were blinded by sudden light. Ian Brent was there with his hand out. Cissie licked her lips. Mannie stood there in the carriage door, uncertain of his reception.

It was Peggy who half shouted, "Wetpants. Wetpants. Mannie is a wetpants," but the others, whose fears had all been increased by the sudden and unexpected darkness, ignored her. They were in no mood, now, to turn on each other.

Win Hodges, who had been up best part of the night, doing her own and her brother's washing, slept on in the corner, pale as a cellar mushroom.

14

"When will we be there?" Cissie asked Ian Brent. An only child, with a father who worked for the Gas Board and a mother sewing part-time in a bakery, he had been away on trains twice before.

"Search me," he said. "Must be getting on for teatime now."

Mary, still blinking a little, went back to looking out of the window. The train drew them through a big pinewood. The great eye of the sun hovered over the points of the trees. Looking down deep into the darkness of the branches, Mary remembered, again, her one book and the picture of the two children holding hands amid the long, dark trunks of the trees, at night.

"Oh – it's about two kids, whose Mum and Dad couldn't feed them no more, so they took them out in the woods and lost them on purpose like so they couldn't find their own way home," Ivy had told her negligently. As she remembered that, Mary's mouth opened. The trees, their tops gleaming with sunshine, which had so charmed her, now made her feel scared. Her eyes filled and brimmed over. Tears began to roll down her chubby cheeks.

"What's up, Mary?" said Frank Jessop.

Mary, remembering more of Ivy's words, "– then they come to a witch's house and she tried to eat them up –" and seeing Ivy's blonde hair streaming down from under a steeple-crowned hat, gave a deep, gasping sob, like a howl.

"Cheer up, Mary. It'll be all right," said Frank. "It's fer yer own good. You can 'ave an egg every day. You can go home when we've beat the Germans."

This did not comfort Mary, who felt she did not want to go home. There, on the one side, was the picture, just like a photograph, of Sid and Ivy standing outside the narrow brick house in Meakin Street, and on the other the picture in the book, showing herself and her brother Jackie abandoned and wandering in the dark forest at night. Lost between the two visions, she went on crying. Gradually, under cover of the sobs, her natural optimism asserted itself. Jackie would always look after her. He always did. Nothing bad ever happened to Jackie. The forest must have an edge. They could walk out of it, away, into the fields beyond. And, just then, the trees gave way to an expanse of fern-covered common land, vast, green, fenceless, hedgeless, intersected by small trodden pathways through the high ferns and gorse, all warmed and lit by the golden light of afternoon, as far as the pastureland, which rose in gentle hills on the horizon. And Mary, rubbing her two grubby hands over her wet cheeks, wiping her nose on her bare arm, ceased to sob.

"When we've beat the Germans –" Frank had said. The children's voices muttered on in the hot carriage. They were tired now.

"Dunno when that will be."

"My Dad," Jim Hodges said stolidly, "reckons we'll lose."

"What?" Mannie Frankel said, looking frightened: "Why? Why'll we lose?"

"My Dad says," Jim Hodges told him, "they've got more men, and more equipment than what we've got. He says anyone can see we're being beaten to a jelly. They're on the doorstep, he says, my Dad says –" and he paused. "He says Mr Churchill's a liar."

"Cor," said Cissie. "What a rotten thing to say. Your Dad's a rotten German spy."

"His friend thinks so, too," said Jim. "They know Winnie's got a plane waiting for him out in the country somewhere, and when the Germans come he'll drive out there in his car and go all the way to America."

Cissie, looking out into the countryside, involuntarily searching for the plane, muttered, "I don't believe yer."

"That's right, isn't it, Win?" Jim said. He reached out and jerked her knee about. "Wake up, Win. Doesn't our Dad know Winston Churchill's got a plane somewhere so he can escape when we lose the war? Here, Win, doesn't our Dad say that?"

Win, waking up, said, "Oh yer. That's what he says. What do you want to wake me up for? I'm tired."

"So you could tell them it was true, what I said," Jim said sensibly. "You can go back to sleep now." And she did. "There – see," he said to the others, "that's what my Dad says. He doesn't care who wins the war."

"He must be stupid," said Frank Jessop.

"Don't you call my Dad stupid," Jim said. "He reckons we'd all be no worse off under the Germans than what we'd be under Churchill. He shoots the workers."

"No worse off with Germans –" said Mannie. "Speak for yourself, then. Me and my Mum and Dad would be worse off, that's for sure."

"Oh – Jews," said Jim. "That's different. My Dad don't care about the Jews. He says there's too many of them anyway, and they've got all the money. My Dad's thinking about the working classes."

"Who are they?" asked Mary, but no one heard her.

"They'd shoot the King," said Cissie, scratching her head. "'Ere, I hope there's no little strangers in the backs of these seats. My head don't half itch."

"They do them over every day with a brush," Ian Brent said. "I know – I seen them. Anythink in your head you must have picked up at home."

"Liar," said Cissie, but without energy. Most of the children, hot, tired and hungry, were losing heart.

"I hope I get on a farm," Jim Hodges said placidly. "I wouldn't half like to see the animals."

"What animals?" said Mary.

"Sheep and cows," said Jim. "That sort of thing."

"I hope the bull gets you, Jim Hodges," said Cissie in a murmur.

"Chickens," said Frank Jessop, leaning excitedly towards Mary. "You know – oh, you know, Mary, they lay eggs and that."

"Lay eggs," said Mary. "What – eggs?"

"Yeah, 'course. What you eat."

Mary had an egg every day. Ivy did not, nor did Sid, nor Jackie.

"Don't you tell nobody about these eggs," Ivy had instructed her, with her face close to Mary's, for emphasis. "If I get to hear you've said one word – one word, mind – I'll lock you in the coal-hole and I won't never let you out. Are you listening?"

So Mary, with the mystery of eggs growing deeper but still inextricably bound up somehow with getting locked up, said, "Oh," and no more. To change the subject she asked Frank, "Is this the country?"

"Course it is," said Frank.

"Don't they have air raids here?"

"Course they don't. Why do you think we come here?" said Frank. "'Ullo – there's Jackie. Wotcher, Jack."

Mary's brother leaned against the side of the door, surveying the seated children. "Wotcher," he said. "Everybody happy?"

"Get out of it," said Ian Brent scornfully.

"Thought I'd just pop in to see what you lot was doing," said Jackie. "I told him I wanted to go to the toilet."

"Who? Burns?" said Cissie. "You in with 'im?"

"Yer," said Jackie. "'E give me one of 'is sandwiches, dinnertime."

"*Never*," said Ian Brent. "What was in 'em?"

"Paste," said Jackie. "You all right, Mare? You been crying, ain't yer? Your face is all dirty. Cor, you don't 'alf look a sight. Cheer up, gel, we'll be there in 'alf an hour."

"I think it was that tunnel," said Cissie. "I reckon she's too young to come away on her own, like."

"Well, she's got me, ain't she?" said Jackie. "Stands to reason – our Mum knows no 'arm will come to old Mary while brother Jack's about. That's right, ain't it, Mare?"

Mary nodded at him gratefully.

"Well, I'd better be getting back," said Jackie. "Now I've paid me call. Can't say I think a lot of the holiday so far."

"Cor – 'ark at you," said Ian Brent. "Cheerful Charlie. Come to cheer us all up, 'ave you?"

"Well – here we are, leaving home for Gawd knows where, to live with a load of swedebashers we've never seen before in all our lives, you don't want to believe all they tell you about fresh air and eggs and milk and that – there's got to be a snag somewhere."

"What do you know?" said Ian Brent suspiciously.

"Only that things don't always work out like they say they will. That's the law of life, chum, take it from me."

"Well, we're here now, so we'd better make the best of it," said Cissie.

"Oh, yer," said Jackie. "That'll get you a long way."

"You can't do anything about it," said Cissie. "You've got to put up with it, same as us."

Jackie smiled. "If I don't like it, I'm going home."

"Garn," said Ian Brent. "How will you manage that, Tarzan?"

"Oh," said Jackie, airily. "There's always a way if you use your brains, my boy. Well – I'd better be going, before he comes looking for me. – Chin up, Mare," he added, "we're nearly there." And, turning round, off he swaggered; shrimpy Jack, four foot six, nine years old, in boots too big for him, long grey flannel trousers reaching to his knees and an old black jacket, cut down from one of his father's.

"Reckons he's clever," grumbled Cissie, when he had gone. "He'll find out."

But he had cheered the little evacuees, for whom the long hot journey into the unknown had come to seem eternal, as if they would never go home and never arrive at their destination. Mary, suddenly refilled with hope and happiness, as if it had been poured in through the top of her head and had flooded through her body, right down to her toes, sighed, altered her position, and leaned back contentedly against the scratchy upholstery. Jackie could do anything. He could drown unwanted kittens in a bucket and climb up to the roof and sit by the chimneypots shouting, "Look at me!" He could cheek Ivy and dodge out of the door laughing before she caught him a smack round the ear. Once he went for a ride on the district nurse's bicycle and left it down the railway sidings and came home, and no one knew who'd done it. Mary loved Jackie. She really felt miserable when she had to eat her egg, in secret, after he'd gone to school, so that he couldn't have a dip of it. She started to think about eggs again.

She was thirsty, though. The great ball of the sun, lower now in the west, still burned down over the moving landscape, a patchwork of small fields, some green with long corn, some pastures, marked off with hedges intersected by little brown pathways across or around the sides. Thick clumps of trees, oak and elm, stood in rises and in hollows. There was no noise now, except for the puffing of the train and its regular clacking over the rails. The children sat quietly. The world outside the windows lay still and glowing under the afternoon sun. The train puffed on.

Suddenly there was a cottage with a little garden hedged with blossoming rose bushes. Across the lawn a washing line billowed with clothes pegged out to dry. On one side there was a garden path leading down from the back door of the house to a vegetable patch at the bottom of the garden. Halfway down the path, her skipping rope sweeping over her head in arcs, a little girl was jumping. As Mary watched, the rope swung and the little girl jumped up and down in the sunshine, her gold hair bouncing.

The train took them past as Mary, turning round with her cheek hard against the window, just saw the kitchen door open and a small black and white dog bound out and race down the path towards the skipping girl. Then the train swung round a bend. Suddenly they were travelling between big embankments of black stones, covered with straggling grass and surmounted by rough bushes.

Mary now turned back to face Frank Jessop, sitting opposite her in the other corner and, with her hand suddenly over her mouth, uttered a small moan of loss.

The train swept them into another dark tunnel.

She sat there, rigid in the dark, feeling her heart thudding in her chest.

"It's a long way to Tipperary," sang the others in ragged chorus.

"It's a long way to go."

"Oh Peggy – get your bloody hand off me – I nearly had a fit," came Cissie's voice.

"It's a long way to Tipperary, to the sweetest girl I know."

But Mary sat quietly, stiff and straight, feeling her heart pound and the blood pulsing in her head. As they came out into the light she said, in a meek voice, amid a chorus of moans, groans, boos and cheers, "Cissie, have you got a comb?"

"What?" said Cissie, pushing Peggy's bulk away from her. "Get off, Peg. You're all right now. What – a comb? What for?"

"I want to borrow your comb," said Mary. "And then will you take me to the toilet?"

"Oh, Gawd," said Cissie. "What with you and Peggy, there's no peace. All right then. Come on."

"I want the comb," repeated Mary.

"Comb it when you come back."

"I want to comb it there," said Mary.

"Whatever for?" said Cissue.

"I just do," said Mary, trading on the knowledge that Cissie was used to the irrational obstinacies of small children. In fact she desperately wanted to comb her hair in front of the mirror she had seen in the lavatory. There was no mirror in the compartment, just the empty wooden space where it had once been. She had a perfectly good reason but she would not say what it was. She knew better than to do that. Instead she squeezed out a few tears and made a low moaning sound. Threatened by this, Cissie said quickly, "All right. Don't start crying. Here's the comb. Come on – I'll take you."

At the door to the lavatory, Mary said, "Now, you go away."

Cissie gave her a straight look and said, doubtfully, "Don't lock the door, mind."

"Give us the comb, then."

Cissie, handing to her half a pink bakelite comb said, "What're you up to, Mary Waterhouse?" Her only answer was the stupid look on Mary's face. She shrugged and walked back along the corridor, calling back, "Don't you dare lock that door."

But she did not say why not and Mary, standing on her toes now, inside the lavatory, scarcely heard her. She did lock the door, leaning against it for support and flipping the metal bar over into the socket with the tips of her fingers. Once the door was locked she pulled up her dress, pulled down her dingy white knickers with the sagging elastic, peed, and pulled the knickers up again. Then she started. The little compartment was dim, for the windows were made of frosted glass but, doggedly, as it rocked to and fro, she stood on her toes and pulled up her dress and wetted the hem under the tap in the washbasin. She washed her face over with part of the damp dress and dried it roughly the same way, for there was no towel, not even any lavatory paper, in the compartment. She washed her hands and then rubbed them, clean but wet, over her face again and down her legs. Seeing the heavy smears of dirt up and down her legs which this process produced, and guessing that similar smears must still be on her face, she jumped on the lavatory seat and, as the tray swayed, looked in the glass. Then she got down, unlaced her black shoes, took off her socks and soaked one under the tap in the basin. She cleaned her face carefully with it. She dried it with the other. She stood on the lavatory seat holding both socks, which dripped down on to her bare feet. Craning forward, she looked again at her face in the glass. It was clean. Bending over in the rocking compartment, staggering from time to time, she washed her legs with the socks. Then she started to comb her fair, slightly unruly hair, which hung down to her shoulders. Oh, the pain of dragging that comb through the knots and tangles as the train tossed to and fro – the pain in her arm as she tugged over and over again at the same knots, shutting her eyes, which kept on watering with agony as she tugged. To think she was doing this to herself, instead of having Ivy do it to her. It seemed like hours and hours she spent there, in the little dim compartment, as the train hurtled them through a countryside she could not see because of the frosted glass in the windows.

But there were two ideas as sharp as arrows in Mary's head. One was that, for reasons she could not quite analyse, she must look like a good girl when she arrived. The other was a notion about a lady with long gold hair, a long white dress and a gold crown, walking through a meadow, full of grass and little white flowers. As she tugged and pulled at her hair, and, staggering continually against the moving walls of the compartment, tried to keep her feet in the small smelly room, her mind ran on these two things – the good girl with the clean face and the golden-haired lady. How often had someone turned to Ivy in a shop, or in the street and, glancing down at little Mary, said, "Oh, look at the little mite with her lovely hair – like a little princess."

By now Mary knew she had not done the top of her head properly. She had not, somehow, been able to reach right up to the parting. But, from her ears down, her hair was as untangled as she could manage. She put on her shoes and reached up to undo the bolt on the door. She was becoming frightened, already, by the massive risk she was taking, involving using up a perfectly good pair of socks. She went cold all over when, suddenly, she thought of the smacking she could get for that alone. Then she found she could not push the bolt up from its socket, and panic took over. Standing on her toes, with her heels out of the black shoes, wrestling with the bolt, she began to breathe hard and fast, on the verge of tears. She was trapped. "Oh –" she said to herself. "Oh –" thinking about Meakin Park, the gritty paths, tired London grass, with its heaps of dog dirt, grubby laurel – and "Oh –" she said again, seeing in her mind the great, green heath spread out in front of her. She fought the bolt, which was getting sticky under her fingers. Would she ever get out? What happened if you couldn't? Would all the others get out of the train and leave her behind?

"Oh, Mary," wailed Cissie, outside. "You've gone and locked yourself in. I'll get the blame, now."

Mary, in a panic with the tears stinging in her eyes, tears which she knew would make her helpless in a moment, cried, shakily, "No – I never," and, fairly leaping in the air, managed to push the bolt up. Her heel came down painfully on to the edge of her battered, dusty, scraped black shoe. She yelped in pain as Cissie pushed the door open, knocking her on the forehead.

"At least you look cleaner," said Cissie, with grudging approval. "There's a good girl. Now, come on back. Mr Burns says we're nearly there."

She stood back for Mary to pass in front of her. Mary, still breathing hard, did not budge.

"Come on," said Cissie, impatiently.

"You go first," said Mary.

"Mary."

But Mary just stood there. Cissie dropped her suspicious eyes slowly to Mary's feet. "What you done with your socks?"

"Washed my face with them," said Mary.

"Washed your face?" Cissie said, her voice getting higher and higher. "Washed your face? You bloody little fool – what were you thinking about? Do I need to watch you all the time – oh, I could fetch you such a clout."

She looked at Mary for a long, hard moment, then said, "Well – where are they?"

"On the floor," said Mary.

"On the fl— oh – you haven't the sense you were born with. Here – let me get past you."

And Cissie pushed in and picked the two dirty, soggy socks off the floor. She put them in Mary's hand. "Get hold of these — you'll have to wear them wet. And give my comb back."

Mary followed Cissie up the corridor and at the next open window, bent over, wiped her shoes over quickly with the socks, and tossed them out of the open window. Then, head down, with an obstinate, but frightened look on her face, she followed Cissie along and sat down in the corner seat.

Cissie, settling back, said, "Get your socks on. Then I'll lace your shoes up. Bloody little fool," she said to the others. "She washed her face with her socks."

"Where are they, Mare?" asked James Hodges.

"What?" screamed Cissie. She craned forward to look at Mary's feet, then Mary. "What've you done with your socks?"

"Will you do up my shoes?" asked Mary.

"Not till you tell me where those socks are."

"We're slowing down," said Ian Brent. "Look, that's a signal box."

"Do them up," said Mary, urgently. "We're getting there."

"Where are those socks?" said Cissie.

Mary was frightened. "Do them up, Cissie. Please. Please do them up."

"First tell me where those socks are," said Cissie. "Or you'll be left behind on the train when we all get out."

Mary broke. "I threw them out the window," she said.

Cissie looked at her. "Now I've heard everything," she began but there was no time for more.

"I hope you're all ready," said Mr Burns, looking in and passing down the corridor saying "Are you ready, Charles Grayson?" into another compartment. And, as Cissie furiously laced up the black shoes on Mary's bare feet, the train stopped at Framlingham.

Later, the coach driver, sitting outside the pub with his pint on the long wooden table in front of him, as a country twilight came down over the silent village street, turned to the postman and said, "I never seen anything like them evacuees when they come trooping through the barrier towards me. Nor'd old George, you could tell that from the look on his face."

"Oh?" said the postman, encouraging him to say more.

The busdriver slapped at a midge and went on, "There wasn't a decent pair of boots or shoes among them. One lad had on a pair of boots you'd have sworn were his father's. And they've that pale and pasty look, you'd think they'd been brought up in the cellar. And the smell of that bus when they got out – I had to open the windows for half an hour after they'd gone. Not a proper smell, just stale, sort of, I dunno – I dunno, bad-smelling. What we're to make of them, I'm sure. I don't reckon they've got any place here. Sooner they go back home the better, if you ask me. They mean trouble, one way or t'other."

"They'll soon settle in," said the village postman, sitting there in his uniform, with his cap on the table in front of him, next to his pint. "Kids is kids anywhere you go – they'll fit in after a bit till you can't tell the difference."

"Not this lot," said the busdriver.

"Well, whichever way you look at it," said the postman, "they've got to stop here. With the whole of London going up like a fireworks factory every night."

"Well – 'tis a pity," said the busdriver.

"We can't turn our faces against them," said the postman.

"What happened to them?" said another man.

"I just drove them to the village hall," said the busdriver. "Left them there to get sorted out."

"I hear old George Twining got hold of a couple of good strong lads for the farm," said the man.

"Good luck to him then," said the busdriver with emphasis. "I hope it keeps fine for him."

Village opinion, slow to take shape but, once set, set as hard as rock, was in the process of formation, in the douce air of the West Kent village where Mary and the other twenty-five evacuees had been sent in the summer of 1941 to escape the bombing in London.

The children sat on the bare boards of the village hall. In front of them, on a platform, were Mr Burns and a thin lady in a green uniform, sitting at a table with a pile of papers and a vase of roses on it.

They were very subdued. They did not know what was going to happen to them. Tumbled out of the bus by a big, florid driver, who looked at them expressionlessly as they walked past with their carrier bags and parcels of clothes, led across the village square, where huge, clumsy birds waddled across the grass from the duckpond, assailed by the smell of warm air full of pollen, unlike the air they were used to breathing, past the twitching curtains of neat houses with hedged gardens, they had been marched into the darkness of the village hall and made to sit down. Mr Burns had joined the vicar and some men and women on the platform in front of them. The lady behind the desk, her pale blonde hair combed up very neatly under her green hat, had stood up and made a speech in a voice Mary vaguely associated with the radio. Mary sat as close to her brother Jackie as she could, with Cissie on the other side.

And then, suddenly, a pair of heavy boots, and gaitered legs, trod past her. A big hand landed on Jackie's shoulder, a man's voice said, "Stand up, boy." Mary saw her brother Jackie stand up. His cocky expression faded, then came back.

"I'll take this lad, and this one behind him," said the voice.

"All right, Twining," said the lady at the desk in her high, very clear voice. "Mr Burns – will you give me the names?"

"Come on then, boys, move yourselves," said the man, and, as if in a dream, Mary felt Jackie stand up and saw Ian Brent stand too, and saw the legs of the man and two boys begin to work through the packed children's bodies. Mr Burns said something to the lady in the front. At the table, Jackie and Ian looked around, quite bewildered. The lady wrote something in the book in front of her. The vicar spoke to Ian Brent. As the man turned to leave, with Jackie and Ian behind him, Mary, realizing the atrocity happening in the hall, jumped up and cried, "I want to go with Jackie!"

The lady called "Twining" and the gaitered man turned round.

Mary, standing up among the other children, stared at Jackie, who was biting his lip. "– can't split up the family," Mary heard the lady say.

The gaitered man looked at Mary. "She's too young," he said. "If that's the case, your ladyship, I'll have to take another boy."

And the lady looked at Mary, in her maroon dress and sockless black shoes, very small and blonde, with her little face all pinched with loss, then glanced at the other children sitting round her and said, "I'll take the little girl. Will you come with me –" and looking swiftly at her list "– Mary? You can see your brother very often. He'll be living on the farm next door." Mary, seeing at once her brother's confused face, the pretty, tall lady with the pale blonde hair and clear-cut pale features, the princess in the field of daisies, and summing up all these impressions with the true instinct she was seldom to lose (demonstrating, for the first significant and perhaps most important time in her life, that tendency of hers always to accept, rather than refuse to say "yes", where another person might say "no"), drew in a deep breath and said, "Yes, yes, please."

And the lady said, "Good," and wrote something in her book.

25

Jackie and Ian were led out into the sunshine. Mary tried not to cry and, failing, hid her sobs.

That night she slept in a bed with a white, rose-sprigged cover in a little attic bedroom at the front of the house which looked out over the lawn, the lake and into the trees beyond, where the rooks cawed as they circled and settled for the night.

It was her first night at Allaun Towers.

"Bit quieter 'ere these days, wivout 'is Nibs 'anging about causing trouble," observed Sidney Waterhouse, in a satisfied tone as he raised his foaming glass (rightly called his, for there was no other glass in the Waterhouse home) to his foaming moustache, and took a deep draught.

"Trust you to say that," observed his wife, Ivy Waterhouse, who was at the sink, rinsing out some smalls. 'You 'aven't got any thought for the poor little sod, miles from 'ome, 'ave you? Or little Mary, either. Oh no, you're thinking of yourself, as usual." She hoisted a pair of woollen pants, closer to grey than white, and then held them up, dripping into the enamel sink bowl, letting the creases drop out. Her mouth, from which the lipstick had vanished, except for the line of red marking a cupid's bow around the edges, was turned down. Her eyes were tired. "These are going home," she remarked, and indeed they were a sad sight, the off-white shorts, with frayed elastic waistband, and the wavering edge around the legs.

"There's a hole here what must make life very convenient for you," she said, poking her finger, then two fingers, then three, through a hole between the legs. Then, seemingly irrelevantly, she said, "Beer, fags and women, that's all you're interested in, Sid Waterhouse, and never mind the consequences. What you do with your pants, I can't think."

"No need for them in this weather, that's what I say," her husband remarked comfortably, sitting there in his vest, his braces dangling down the side of his blue serge trousers. "Anyway, who sees them?"

"I don't know who sees them," said Ivy angrily, turning to face him. "That's what I don't know. I'd like to, I know that."

"You're getting fanciful, love," said Sid, taking another drink. "What you need is a nice cuddle."

"Oh, yes," said Ivy, sceptically, "another mouth to feed – another lot of crying and bawling in the middle of the night and dirty nappies as if the bombing wasn't enough. And where will you be – 'firewatching'.

That's the name for it now, isn't it? Used to be called something else before the war."

She realized he was not listening to her. In her slippers, too heavy in stomach and bust for the scarlet cotton dress with tropical flowers on it, she moved from the sink to the table and, hands on splayed hips said, "One thing's certain, Sidney Waterhouse – from now on you can whistle for me. You can sleep in Jackie and Mary's bed. I'm done with all that lot."

"We'll see about that," he said. "Don't suppose you'll ever change. Not really. Come on love, come upstairs for a bit."

"Pig," said Ivy. "You're a pig, and that's all. I nearly died the last time and what did you care? I could've bled to death – what's in it for me, that's what I want to know? Old Mother Green and her remedies, what nearly kill you, or a houseful of kids, that's the choice. Oh no – you don't get me going in for all that again."

"That's what they all say," said Sid philosophically. "Have a glass of beer." He took a brown bottle from under the table and opened it. "Find us a cup."

Ivy handed him a mug with the young smiling faces of King George and Queen Elizabeth and the royal arms upon it. Sid poured the beer. She sat down opposite him at the kitchen table. She wiped the sweat from her brow and drank.

"Why can't you just take precautions, like other men?" she said, in a milder tone. "You don't want me in the family way again, do you?"

"Anyone can slip up, from time to time," he said uncomfortably.

"What's a slip up to you is years of bleeding work for me," she told him. "Oh – I'm sick of it all. This war's getting me down."

Silence fell in the little hot kitchen where the flies buzzed. On the windowsill beyond the stone sink the feathery leaves of two tomato plants in earthenware pots drooped in the blistering heat. Beyond them was a small yard paved with cracked asphalt where a shirt and a dress hung motionless on a washing line in the burning heat. Then there was a low brick wall and, beyond that, another row of houses.

"She's at it again," Ivy remarked lethargically, turning round to look at the back of the houses opposite. "Upstairs curtains drawn in the middle of the day."

"Not my business what other people do with their private lives," said Sid. "Lucky to have the energy in this 'eat – or the chance," he added gloomily.

The battered kitchen clock, propped up with a matchbox where one of its legs should have been, ticked loudly in the silence. This couple, sitting in their cramped and not-too-clean kitchen, exchanging blunt matrimonial remarks, might not seem an attractive pair. Day and night Sid drove a bus from Harlesden in the West of London to Liverpool Street in the East. At dawn he might be forced to make a detour off the bus route, because it was blocked with rubble, often the remains of whole houses, sometimes the wreckage of half a street. There men and women in tin hats were often still digging out the dead and injured, where people were searching the heaps of brick, creeping beneath their broken walls to find their possessions – their cat, their dog, the remains of a baby's pram or a bicycle which could not be replaced. Thousands had already died, thousands of houses had been destroyed in inner London alone.

By night Sid drove his bus through the blacked-out streets of a city full of ruins where the only light was from skies beamed through by searchlights moving remorselessly to and fro, searching for enemy planes, or from fires burning at a distance. The only noise was the steady drone of bombers overhead. Frequently he stopped the bus to the wail of sirens, and ran, with the passengers, to the nearest air raid shelter. Sometimes, if no shelter was possible they crouched under the bus. When the all clear sounded, he got back in the cab of the bus, the tired passengers got in and Sid Waterhouse drove on, marking, tiredly, which buildings had been destroyed during the raid. At night he sometimes took his turn wearing a tin hat in the belfry of St Stephen's waiting for the drone of enemy planes, seeing their black bodies pierce the searchlights like giant insects, watching their black eggs drop, hit the ground and turn into fire. If the raid was too close he and his friend Harry Flanders would rush down the narrow steps of the belfry into the church and shelter in the crypt. There they would crouch in darkness, hearing the air battle overhead, saving the batteries in their torches in case the church was hit and it took time to dig them out – if they could be got out. If the local bombing became too intense, either Sid or Harry Flanders would race down the belfry steps, duck along a street, bang on a door and shout, "Where's Spot?" After a pause the door would open a crack to let out a black and white mongrel, mostly terrier, with a black patch over one eye. This dog would run beside the rescuers to the bomb site, nose through the still burning ruins and start to dig. Where Spot dug, the rescuers began their work for he always knew where people had been buried and were still alive, in cellars and under stairs. Once he guided them to where a baby lay in its pram, in a cellar, with two lumps of masonry locked over its body, preventing a mass of rubble overhead from falling on it.

Some nights were quiet. Sid and Harry would play cards, chat and doze. But the fatigue of busy days and interrupted nights turned Sid grey in the face. He said he did not know how he stayed on his feet.

Meanwhile Ivy, with her ration books, allowing her and Sid tiny portions of cheese and meat and two eggs a week, queued for an hour for potatoes and up to two hours for a rabbit which was not rationed. At night if heavy raids seemed likely, she took up a pack of sandwiches and a jug of tea and ran, as the sirens screamed, through the streets to the smelly station, where she bedded down on the platform, under blankets with hundreds of others who snored, tossed, groaned, giggled and muttered through the night as the raid went on overhead. Ivy, originally from the East End of London, had an uncle in the docks and useful connections all over Wapping and Limehouse. When she could, she took a bus down to the smashed areas around the docks, and generally came back with some sugar, a packet of tea or a tin of meat which some relative had got while unloading a ship. Oddly enough, the thought of death was further from Sid and Ivy's minds than might be expected – it was sleep and a bit more food they craved.

In that year alone, 1941, without allies except those from the Commonwealth, and with the German forces twenty miles away on the other side of the Channel, Britain, including Sid in his bus and Ivy in her queue, stood alone and waited, as they had waited for a year, for invasion.

Danger and hardship and imminent death broke the normal course of Sid and Ivy Waterhouse's lives. When the battle was over they would be different people. Meanwhile, the clues dropped. It could have been the thought of the rings buried under the floorboards of bombed houses or the bottles of orange juice Ivy collected from the clinic as part of her pregnant woman's allowances of extra food and milk, which reminded her of an infant sister, born dead in the 1920s, or it could have been the cream and gilt rooms of large houses now open to public gaze once the walls fell down, or the tapestried sofa dangling over the ragged edge of an upper-storey floor as Sid passed daily in his bus – whatever was happening, the day was coming when the accumulated effect of little random incidents and observations would result in new ideas for the Waterhouses – they had seen more of the world as it was destroyed than they had ever seen while it was still intact. When the war was over they would want more for themselves.

At Allaun Towers Mary is playing on the lawn, in the sunshine. She wears a clean print dress, white socks and her hair gleams gold. She is skipping.

They couldn't see why I kept on and on, asking about skipping ropes. Nor did I – I just knew I had to have one. I never said nothing about wanting one because with Sid and Ivy that was generally the way of making sure you never got what you wanted. "You can't have everything you want in this world," they used to say.

And finally the housekeeper, Mrs Gates, caught me looking at the extra washing line hung up in the washhouse. She knew straight away, being working class herself, what that desperate, staring look meant. So she hauled down the line out of the washhouse, and sent me inside for the big knife she used for cutting up string and big sheets of greaseproof paper, and then she sat down on the grass outside the kitchen door, and cut me off a bit of that white, thick rope. I'll never forget the look of it, lying there, so clean, on the grass. It was a sunny day, too. She made a couple of big knots at each end and I skipped and skipped and skipped – she said I'd wear a hole in the lawn. Of course, I had to skip outside her kitchen door, on the grass in the middle of the vegetable garden. I wasn't supposed to step on the lawn in front of the house. That grass was special. I did it once though because the grass was springier there. I got up very early, before anyone was up. I remember creeping through the silent house and the trees round the lawn with the misty sun coming up over them and going up and down while I jumped, and coming down on the grass, which was all springy and wet with dew, and feeling all that fresh, chilly morning air on my arms and face – then old Benson, the gardener, crept up behind and caught me by the arm and soon put a stop to me. There must have been a row, but I expect I got off by using my blue eyes.

Sir Herbert, as his car passed a glass-fronted pub, where a naked man and woman danced on a small stage, cut the tape recording and began to speak:

The first paper in that unmarked file which was to become so important to me, that first key to the whole affair which was to become part of the structure of my life for the next forty years, was just a small sheet of my father's old writing paper, headed with our address in Eaton Place. When I first saw it, it must even then have been twenty years old, just as old as I was myself. It was uncrumpled, although marked and slightly roughened by prolonged contact with the cover of the folder in which it lay, on top of the first closely typed page of what looked like a long report. In the centre of the page, in my father's small fine hand, was written an address, no name, just 19, Meakin Street, London. And, in a slightly darker ink, those words were crossed out, and, underneath, in the same hand, was written, Allaun Towers, West Framlingham, Kent.

It looked, somehow, dark as it lay there. Something made me turn from the desk on which the folder rested, with my father's voice still in my ears – "You'd better read all these papers and let me know what you think." I wanted to escape it. I walked over to the window and looked down into the gardens below.

"It must never leave this office," he said. "Nor can I ask you to take over this part of the work unless you wish to. I must have your full and willing agreement – or someone else will have to be found."

"I don't know what it is yet, of course," I said, temporizing. A flight of shrilling starlings swooped over, blackening the sky.

"You'll have to read it first," he told me.

I walked away from the window. It was an April day, nearly evening. The garden below was beginning to grow green. So I walked across to take the file from his outstretched hand. I, a young man, who should properly have been excited and intrigued by a part of my new responsibilities, and proud of the trust I knew my father was suddenly reposing in me, felt, nevertheless, a chill. A second later, the file in my hand, I did feel all the appropriate, dignified emotions, and I remember saying, as coolly as possible, "Then I'll just sit down and take a look at it." I attempted to suppress my enthusiasm, my curiosity and delight, and to sound the proper man I was proposing to become. I remember walking back from the window, sitting down and beginning to read.

I have the file by me now, and the others which followed it. I was curiously reluctant to open it and see again that one sheet of paper, with the two addresses on it. When I opened the file – lo – it was gone! That seems so disappointing, now. There is no mystery – it was otiose, anyway, conveying no useful information: possibly, after all these years, it had either deteriorated to the point where a tidier hand than mine decided to remove it, or had merely dried, or the holes had torn and it had fallen from the file without being noticed. Nevertheless I recall it as clearly as if I held it in my hand now.

The hot days of June 1941 continued and the days at Allaun Towers fell into a regular pattern. It did not take Mary long to comprehend the differences, physical and moral, between her London life and her country one. Her sheets, in the little servant's bedroom, with the faded roses on the wallpaper, were changed once a week by Mrs Gates. Her new brush and comb, which stood on the marble top of the washstand, were washed in the bath with her every Saturday night, when Mrs Gates bathed her. Her few clothes had to be put in the small chest of drawers in the room, or hung in the pine wardrobe. She woke every morning at seven-thirty, when she heard Mrs Gates creak heavily out of bed in the room next to hers. Then she got up and looked out of the window over the stretch of tiles below, where the roof extended, and off into the sunshine on the lawn where the blackbirds flew, settled, pecked at the dewy grass.

"You up? Good girl," Mrs Gates would say, putting her grey head, still tousled, round the door. "Get yourself washed now."

There was a stone sink on the landing. Mary's flannel hung on a brass hook above it. Her toothbrush was in an enamel mug, with Donald Duck painted on it. She would put on the tap and, standing on tiptoe, wash her hands, face and neck with the flannel and a big bar of yellow soap. The water was cold. Then she would go back into her room, wrestle off her nightdress and put on a cotton dress, clean white socks and her new red sandals with the strap with the buckle.

Mrs Gates had stood four-square on the carpet in the drawing room, facing out Lady Allaun who sat, half-turned, at the writing desk. "Only one pair of knickers," she had told Lady Allaun forcibly, "and those hardly fit for dusters."

Lady Allaun, blinking as the sunlight flooded in through the long windows said, a little sharply, "Oh, Good Lord, Mrs Gates. I'm writing to Sir Frederick."

"She's nothing at all to sleep in," Mrs Gates continued remorselessly. "In her pants and vest, she said. Think of that."

"Don't tell me any more," said Lady Allaun, turning back to her desk, on which the half-finished letter lay. Mrs Gates did not move. After a pause Lady Allaun said, "Of course, in the old days Nanny used to –"

"She'd need new clothes sooner or later, your ladyship," said Mrs Gates.

"Her family's responsibility," said Lady Allaun. "But obviously we can't have the child walking about in tatters."

"I was thinking I could take her into Gladly on my afternoon off and fit her out," said Mrs Gates.

"That's a good idea – thank you, Mrs Gates," said Isabel Allaun.

Mrs Gates stood her ground. It was not always easy to get money out of the gentry. Persistence payed. "I have her clothing coupons –" she suggested.

Lady Allaun said, "Yes – I'll give you a cheque to cash in Gladly to cover the cost. About eight pounds should do, shouldn't it?" She took a chequebook from the pigeon-hole in the desk and began to write out a cheque.

"More like twelve would be necessary, your ladyship," said Mrs Gates, "with today's prices what they are." She had no wish to go through this scene again in a few months' time, when warmer clothing would be needed for Mary.

"Damn," said Lady Allaun, making an alteration on the cheque. "I must say I didn't bargain for all this. I hope you'll be as careful as you can, Mrs Gates."

"Of course, Lady Allaun," said Mrs Gates in a neutral tone. "Thank you." She made no attempt to lighten her tread as she stumped back down the passageway to the kitchen.

"Like blood from a stone," she muttered to herself as she shut the kitchen door behind her, all the more annoyed because now there was no kitchenmaid or parlourmaid to grumble with. There was no Rose, no Maggie. They had both been called up for the army. Sometimes Clarisse, on leave, appeared in the back door with her khaki cap set rakishly over blonde hair a few shades lighter than it had been when she was a parlourmaid, and grinning with bright red lips, might say, "Hullo, Mrs Gates. How's the rubbing and scrubbing these days?" And Mrs Gates, feeling the full weight of her fifty-year-old legs, would reply, with feeling, "None the better for seeing you lounging in the doorway, Clarisse. And if you're coming in my clean kitchen kindly take that fag out of your mouth first."

"I wouldn't set foot in this kitchen again for five pounds," Clarisse would return. "I'm off with my boyfriend to the flicks so keep smiling through, Mrs Gates."

Mrs Gates was torn between disapproval of these cheeky young things, with their new freedom and contempt for the long-established village rules, and her pleasure that they had escaped, or so it seemed, into a better-paid, more independent life.

Meanwhile, in the big, scrubbed kitchen, there was only tiny white-haired Mary, reading a book with a glass of milk at her elbow. At least, Mrs Gates thought, she'd got the money.

'Lady Allaun has given me the money for some nice new clothes for you,' she told Mary. "Here – are you reading that?"

"I can't understand some of the words," said Mary, "just the pictures. Jackie taught me some words." She's sharp enough, Mrs Gates thought. These Cockney kids were.

"You'll learn a lot more when you go to school in September," she said.

This was a shock for Mary. "Is the teacher nice?" she asked.

"If you behave yourself," Mrs Gates said. "Anyway, we'll get the bus into Gladly tomorrow and get you some new things. Get rid of them old boots."

Mary looked at her sharply. "What're you going to do with my boots?" she demanded. "You can't take my boots."

"Those boots are going in the dustbin," Mrs Gates said firmly. "There'll be no more boots while you're here."

"What am I going to wear then?" asked Mary.

"Shoes," said Mrs Gates.

"Oh," said Mary excitedly. Shoes were a step up in the world.

The next afternoon, with her hair newly trimmed, so that the blonde curls framed her face, wearing a pink striped dress, white socks and the new red sandals, Mary was taken into the drawing room to thank Lady Allaun. She felt as if she could skip, jump and fly as high as the ceiling. She tried to walk slowly and steadily into the room.

"Mary would like to thank you kindly for buying her the new clothes," Mrs Gates explained.

"Transformed," said Lady Allaun, impressed by the beauty of the child. "Well done, Mrs. Gates."

"Thank you very much, your ladyship," said Mary.

"Worth every penny," said Isabel Allaun. "You look charming, Mary." She picked up her book again. "You might try, Mrs Gates," she said as an afterthought, "to do something about the child's speech.

It's unpleasant to hear such an ugly voice coming from such a pretty face."

"Do you hear that, Mary?" said Mrs Gates. "You're to try and speak more nicely."

"I can speak very nice," said Mary, exactly imitating Isabel Allaun's voice.

Lady Allaun put the book in her lap. She stared at Mary.

"Say that again," she said.

"I can speak very nice," said Mary, just as before.

Lady Allaun, fascinated but not pleased, said, "Quite a little parrot, I see. Well, Mary, that's very good. I can see you're a clever girl."

"Thank you, my lady," said Mary, in Mrs Gates' voice.

"My God," said Isabel Allaun as Mrs Gates led the little girl from the room.

Back in the kitchen the housekeeper confronted Mary severely. "Don't you go putting on them posh airs no more," she said. "That's for the gentry, not you."

Understanding that the posh airs must have something to do with her imitations of the voices, Mary said, in her sharp, Cockney accent, "What's the gentry, then?"

"Rich people. People what's above you," Mrs Gates told her.

"Above me?" wondered Mary.

"You're in the kitchen, now," said Mrs Gates, "and her ladyship's in the drawing room. I work for her, cleaning and cooking and for as long as you're here you're going to have to do it too – God knows, I need some help. That's the difference – that's all you need to know."

Mary pouted and said, "How am I supposed to talk then?"

"Not like a guttersnipe, that's for sure," Mrs Gates said unreasonably. " ' 'Ow am I s'posed ter talk' indeed. In the meanwhile, put them dishes away. You know where they go."

Mary, in the new red sandals, trotted off to the dresser with the dishes, trying not to drop anything.

A year later all the problems had been resolved. All the London children talked in the same slow burr as the village children, except when they formed sides – then the London children would drop back into Cockney, to emphasize their solidarity.

Mary had changed. She had gained weight. Her formerly pale face was rosy with health. The following summer she had insisted on having exactly the same sandals she had had the previous year. She still felt happy, every morning, as she did up the buckles carefully and went down the back stairs to breakfast in the kitchen. It was nearly always the same meal. There was porridge, made with the oatmeal which had stood cooking on the kitchen range overnight and toast and honey and milk which Arthur Twining, illegally, left for them every morning in a churn on the back step.

Meanwhile Mrs Gates carefully conveyed Isabel Allaun's egg into its pan of boiling water. Mary, who had now found out about eggs from her brother Jack, still working on the Twining farm, made no remark. She ate her porridge, not asking for an egg, not even demanding a dribble of golden syrup, in the shape of an M, across her porridge. Mrs Gates disliked it when she asked for favours. Also, she had found out that many children in the village were not as lucky as she. On the whole, though, she felt very secure, more secure, in fact, with the imperturbable Mrs Gates than she had ever felt with Ivy Waterhouse, whose nervy London ways often led to a quick smack when she least expected one, or a sudden hug where a blow might have been much more appropriate.

By and large Lady Allaun, too, had coped calmly with the arrival of this grubby child, with her whining cockney voice – a child who had never slept in a bed, let alone a room, by herself, who had never owned a toothbrush, had never seen any bath other than the kitchen sink, or eaten, it seemed to her, anything but fish and chips, egg and chips or pie and chips, all washed down with cups of tea. But Mary, Lady Allaun recognized early on, was pretty, bright, adaptable and fairly quiet. The house was large and Mrs Gates was fond of the child and very capable. So Lady Allaun was content that she had set the necessary example in taking in one of London's threatened children and had not made too bad a bargain in doing so.

At Twining's farm Mary's brother Jack and his friend Ian worked like dogs but ate like hogs, slept in the beds belonging to the two Twining boys, who had both been conscripted, and one killed, and grew strong and healthy. They even helped to bring Mrs Twining, whose Donald's bones lay at the bottom of the Channel in the carcase of a Spitfire, back to the normal world.

Jim and Win Hodges, too, stepped into the places of the dead, for the Becketts, who ran a market garden a mile from the village, had lost two of their three children from diphtheria the previous winter. The brother and sister became slow and ruddy, in the country style, as they worked between the rows of onions and sprouts in winter and culled the apples in the orchard in summer. Their sharp voices and quick city glances had gone. Like the boys at Twining's farm, they were soon children of the house.

Mannie Frankel, who had also taken to his new life, sleeping in the postman's loft and helping with the mail every day, was wrenched suddenly from a pleasant life by his brother Ben, who arrived while Mannie was hanging over the garden gate and dreaming quietly into the street, and took him immediately back to London. The family had come to the conclusion that with the Germans a bare forty miles away on the coast of Normandy, Mannie was in more danger at Framlingham than he would be in London, if there were an invasion. In London, they reasoned, they could move from place to place more easily and Mannie's distinctively Jewish looks would be less obvious than they were in Framlingham, where the rest of the population had a solid, Saxon appearance.

But as the other London children settled down, or were taken back by their parents for one reason or another, things went from bad to worse for Cissie Messiter and Peggy Jones at the Rectory. Cissie grew paler and thinner. Peggy became slower and slower, and more irritating to Mrs Templeton, who, herself, grew thinner.

Perhaps, out of all the evacuees at Framlingham, Mary Waterhouse was the happiest. She was the youngest, so that her earlier memories erased themselves faster. Her beloved Jack was just a short walk across the fields from her. She had the best conditions – she was, after all, the squire's evacuee. The Allaun fields, including those of the tenant farmers on either side, were hers to play in. There she walked in the late summer among rows of stiff and yellow wheat, plucking off the ears and rubbing them between her fingers, chewing on the hard grains. There were the meadows in spring. The sweet grass was hers to lie in and gaze up at the blue sky. The poppies in the summer cornfields were hers to pick, the shady copses were hers to wander in, the shallow stream at the bottom of the watermeadows was hers to dam, to paddle in, to float twigs in, pretending they were boats. She would lie there for hours wondering how long it would take her to get to the sea if she followed the stream until it became a river and the river until it reached the sea. In autumn she and Jack got the best conkers from the trees on the estate. Sometimes, lying dreaming in a summer field, she would see planes fighting in the sky, in the distance, over the orchards and fields and hills. She would watch them spiral down in rolling columns of smoke but thought little about it, except to have a daydream about capturing a German airman and taking him to the village policeman. Sometimes she would pick up an extra large piece of shrapnel and lug it home for Jackie, who had the biggest shrapnel collection in Framlingham, but this, like the army trucks going up the main street or the burnt-out carcase of a plane growing among the ferns up on the hillside, was just another part of the landscape, no more interesting than the sight of a full moon moving silently among the clouds, or a sickle moon suspended above the oaks and the lakes in the grounds of Allaun Towers. Mary often stayed up at night in order to stare over the tiles at the darkness and the sky. She had to be very quiet or Mrs Gates, in the next room, would hear her. Their proximity, however, ended a year after she arrived, in an odd way.

Mary came swooping up the drive after school one day in September with her deliberately unbuttoned mac blowing away from her in the wind. Jackie had been telling her about Dracula and, with typical egotism, she had instantly assumed the role of Dracula, rather than one of his victims. Leaves from the trees on either side of the drive were blowing round her head as she whirled and swerved. She stopped suddenly when she saw a long, low, black limousine parked in the semi-circle of gravel in front of the house. Looking at the car Mary wondered if it belonged to the mysterious "Sir Frederick" whose visit was expected shortly. They were a funny family, Mary thought. They never came home. Lady Allaun had once gone to see this "Sir Frederick" in London, when he was on leave. Another time she had gone to see her son, Tom, in Yorkshire, where he was staying with his cousin, Charlie. But none of the family ever came here. There's enough room, Mary thought wonderingly, remembering for a moment the four small rooms at Meakin Street, where everyone was in the way of someone most of the time. Perhaps it was just too far to come, from where they were, she decided. But it would be a nice sight to see Sir Frederick in his soldier's uniform.

As she came through the back door she said to Mrs Gates, who was bending over to open the door of the kitchen range, "Is that Sir Frederick's car?"

"No," said Mrs Gates, straightening up with a baking tray of scones in her hands, "but whoever it is he's important. Lady Allaun got a letter this morning and starts on about a proper tea, straight away. With cake – a proper tea, she says. She must think I'm Fortnum and

Mason's. What I had to promise Twining for a pat of butter I daren't tell you."

"Is there a cake?" said Mary eagerly. "Where is it?"

"On the table, in there," Mrs Gates said, nodding in the direction of the drawing room as she put the scones on a rack.

"Do you think they'll leave any?" said Mary. "Can I have a bit if they do?"

"A piece – you should say 'a piece'," said Mrs Gates. "I expect they'll leave some. Have to be fairly greedy to finish it all between the two of them."

From the board above the kitchen door the drawing room bell jangled. Mary's game, when Mrs Gates and Lady Allaun were both out of the house for a little while, was to run all round the house, upstairs and down, pushing all the bellpushes in all the rooms, bedrooms, dining room, drawing room and library, and try to get back to the kitchen before any of the brass bells across the door had stopped vibrating. She had never managed it yet, even though the bell in the big bathroom was broken.

Mrs Gates went out of the kitchen to answer the bell and Mary opened the oven door to see what there was for supper. It was shepherd's pie.

Mrs Gates stood in the kitchen doorway, observing her. She said, without feeling, "I've told you time and again not to open that stove door without asking." Mary looked at her guiltily. "Anyway," said Mrs Gates, "you're wanted in the drawing room for some reason. Take that mac upstairs, put them wet shoes by the fire and go straight up and give yourself a tidy – change those socks, put your sandals on and brush your hair."

"What am I going in there for?" asked Mary.

"I don't know," said Mrs Gates, grimly.

"Will they let me have a bit of cake? Is it chocolate?" Mary asked excitedly.

"They might," said Mrs Gates. "But don't go begging for it, mind. Wait till you're asked." She stood on the flagstones, after Mary had trotted out to get ready, and said, "Something funny going on." Then she started spooning jam into a cut glass bowl. As she did so she tried to work out why the evacuee was being summoned in to tea in the drawing room. At five years old. Perhaps Lady Allaun was trying to prove to some bigwig she was doing her bit for the war effort. But that theory, seemed unlikely and, even with her sophisticated knowledge of everything which might take place in the household, she could not imagine what the answer to this could be. The limousine, driven by a chauffeur in civilian uniform, had come to the house at three. A tall, middle-aged man, obviously, to Mrs Gates's experienced eye, someone of dignity and importance, had come in. Mrs Gates knew that Lady Allaun did not know him. At four the bell had rung for tea. At four-thirty, with a batch of fresh scones and a fresh pot of tea made she had to prepare Mary Waterhouse to go in to the drawing room. Not *The Times*, interviewing the better class of home for evacuees, she thought. Not the police, come to say the Waterhouses had been killed in a raid. Had it got something to do with that letter from Mary's mother announcing the birth of a little sister? Not likely, thought Mrs Gates, that anyone so posh would arrive to discuss the birth of a Shirley Waterhouse, in the drawing room. It made no sense at all.

"So it's a big, front bedroom for you now, madam," said Mrs Gates, who was on her knees, polishing the wood surrounds from the skirting boards to the edge of the faded green and gold carpet of the large bedroom. "Well – get your dusters and give us a hand then."

So Mary went off and got the little pinafore Mrs Gates had made for her, the one with the pink rabbit on the front, and collected her dusters from her own corner of the cleaning cupboard and ran upstairs again to help. She liked the room. It was important. It was above the library. There was a big carved chest under one window. There was a dressing table, made of inlaid wood, for Mary to put her clothes in. There were two little tapestry chairs under the other window. The heavy, faded green velvet curtains had been taken down for a good airing. The dusty grey-green carpet had been vacuumed. She even had her own bellpush.

"I've got my own bell, now," said Mary with satisfaction as she pushed her rag into the polish and smeared some on the floorboards.

"Woe betide you if you use it," said Mrs Gates.

"I might get scared," Mary said. "Why am I moving my room?"

"I told you – it must be to do with Tom coming home," said Mrs Gates.

"Is he nice? Will he play with me?" asked Mary.

"He's a big boy. He goes to school with a lot of other boys," Mrs Gates said diplomatically. "He might think you're too young."

"He can play with Jackie – he's the same age," said Mary as she polished the floor.

"Maybe," said Mrs Gates.

"I'll ask him if I can borrow his puzzles," she said vaguely. She very much wanted the piles of wooden jigsaw puzzles stored in Tom's room, at the opposite end of the landing from hers. She had once sneaked her brother Jack up to the room. Looking at the spotted rocking horse, the train set laid all round the floor, the meccano, all Jack had said was, "Cor – this is like the King of England's place." But Mary was forbidden to touch anything in the room.

Mrs Gates now looked at her dubiously. Hard as she tried to root out lightminded, egotistical and optimistic ideas from the golden head of her charge and to plant instead a few wholesome saplings of doubt, fear and humility she was, like many a gardener, eternally defeated by nature. Mary's soil seemed unable to accept them. If one hope died another automatically sprang up in its place. She sighed as she looked at the child energetically rubbing the boards with a yellow duster, got up and put a sheet of old wallpaper in a drawer, for lining. She had, she thought, seen many such girls in her time and few of them had come to any good. She had even had some, fortunately not much, of that spirit herself, but God knows, it had been quickly enough knocked out of her after she left service impulsively at seventeen years old to marry Gates, a printer. She had borne a baby which died of scarlet fever six months later, which was, perhaps, a blessing in the circumstances for not long after Gates had run off without a word. Luckily the Allauns had taken her back. Luckily she had learned her lesson then. She hoped Mary would not have to learn her own so painfully – married to a charmer, bearing a child he could not be bothered to keep. She finished lining the drawers and bent over to wipe up the smears, which were Mary's mistakes in polishing.

Isabel Allaun's son Tom arrived a few days later. He was brought from the station by old Benson, the gardener, odd-job man and chauffeur now that the other two male staff had been called up. They had saved their petrol coupons for the trip so that Tom would feel welcomed on his first visit home for more than a year. Mary saw him from her bedroom window, sitting in the back of the Bentley with his mother. He was thin, small and very fair. Mary rushed downstairs and shouted to Mrs Gates. Together they took up positions on the front step. The boy who walked up the steps a little ahead of Isabel Allaun had hair so pale it was almost white, and lashes so pale there seemed to

41

be no edging to his very pale blue eyes. He wore a grey jacket, short grey trousers and a white shirt, with a school tie.

"Hullo, Mrs Gates," he said. "Hope you're well." Then, looking past the housekeeper at Mary he said, "Is this the evacuee?"

Mary's mouth went down. The word "evacuee" was never used in a friendly way, even between the village children. It meant intruder, alien, someone who was ignorant and did not know how to behave. Isabel Allaun frowned. She had evidently told Tom to be polite to the evacuee. "This is Mary Waterhouse, Tom, as I told you," she said.

"Sorry, Mary," said Tom, pushing past her into the hall. Mary, with sinking heart, realized that he was not sorry.

The issue came up again at tea. "She has tea with us?" Tom said, his pale eyebrows raised.

"She is a guest," said Lady Allaun.

"She makes a lot of crumbs," Tom said, studying Mary as she ate her cake. "What about dinner?"

"Mary goes to bed early," said his mother. "She does not sit up to dinner. Nor will you if you continue to refer to anyone, however young, who is sitting in the room, as 'she'. Can we have done with this? I don't want your first visit home for so long to start with silly arguments."

"All I can say," Tom Allaun said clearly, "is that it's the first time I've heard an evacuee called a guest."

Isabel Allaun bit her lip but said only, "Your father should be arriving in the next few days. Won't it be nice to be all together again for once?"

Sir Frederick, however, was delayed and Tom, bored without the usual company of his cousin, Charlie, and frustrated by the rain, which poured down all day long, passed the time by tormenting Mary secretly, jumping out on her from corners, pulling terrifying faces at her while no one was looking and, on one occasion, coming into her room after she was asleep, dressed in a sheet and howling like a ghost. Mary was terrified of him and of his faces, his pinches and squeezes on her upper arms and his frightening remarks. When challenged he denied that he had ever been in her room and told her a story about a ghost which had always haunted her room. "I'm surprised you haven't seen it before," he said. "Other people have. That's why no one ever sleeps in it. I expect that's why they gave it to you."

The half term seemed very long to Mary. She grew pale. She dared not to go to sleep at night in case Tom, or the ghost, came in again.

42

When Jackie who, in spite of the rain, had been hard-worked all week by Twining finally made his way to the back door he found Mary very subdued and Mrs Gates surprisingly welcoming. Taking off his cap and wiping his feet carefully on the doormat outside Jack came in and said to Mrs Gates, "What's up with 'er?" He nodded at Mary who was sitting in a chair staring up at the ceiling.

Mrs Gates said, "Want a cup of tea, Jack?" as if she were talking to a grown-up. Jack, like a grown-up, replied, "That's very kind, Mrs Gates. Thank you. Well, Mare," he said, going over to her, "What's up, then, gel? You look as if you'd lost a shilling and found sixpence."

"She's not getting along too well with young Tom," said Mrs Gates.

"Oh – ah," said Jack, understanding. "I'd forgotten about him. I've heard about him before, from Mr Twining. He cut up a live chicken with an axe – right?"

"He was too young to know any better," said Mrs Gates.

"Not what Mr Twining said," the boy told her promptly. "He said it was unnatural and it made him go cold all over. And you should see what he does – Twining, I mean – with lambs and the pigs and all that. He's not exactly lily-livered."

"Twining should keep a still tongue in his head," was all Mrs Gates could manage.

"Anyway, what's he been doing to my old Molly?" said Jack. "Come on, Mare – out with it."

"He keeps on frightening me and pinching me and he says I've got to sleep in the shed with the spiders. They won't send our Shirley here, will they, Jack?"

"Poor little Mary," said Jack. "Course they won't. She's only a baby. I'll see to Tom Allaun –"

"Oh no you won't," said Mrs Gates. "All you'll do that way is cause more trouble for Mary, not to mention yourself. He's going back to school on Monday – just let it be, Jack, there's a good lad."

Jack looked at her. He said, "Yes, Mrs Gates."

"Here's your tea, then," she told him. "Have a couple of these digestives."

"You'd better stay out of his way, then, Mary," said Jack.

"I'll go back to London and live with Ivy and Sid and the baby," Mary said obstinately.

"There's a war on," Jack told her.

"If a little baby can be in the war so can I," Mary said. She was frightened but she would not show it.

43

"You'll stay where you are," said Jack. "Because it's the best place to be." The Waterhouses glared at each other. For a moment they were like two adults. Then Mary dipped her head and said, "All right."

That night Mary awoke to find a spooky head in a sheet, with a torch beaming out of two sooty eyeholes, staring at her. She screamed and could not stop screaming. Isabel Allaun stood in the bedroom doorway in a white nightdress, looking furious. Mrs Gates made hot milk. Mary sobbed out her story about a ghost. In the end Mrs Gates took her upstairs to sleep with her in her own big brass-knobbed bedstead. She was not very surprised, after Tom had gone back to school, to find that she had one sheet too few. Tom had evidently disposed of the evidence. Mary's peace of mind did not immediately return, however, for as he left in the car he managed to put his head out of the window and whisper to her, "I'll be back soon for Christmas. *And* I'm bringing my cousin Charlie with me, ha, ha. Smelly evacuee!"

Mary went back into the house with a white face, feeling the air around her sour with malice. Her terrors diminished during the next two months of rain and early darkness. Sir Frederick came for the weekend and was nice to her. He brought her a doll from Africa. But when they started to practise the Christmas carols at school she became frightened again. While she was worrying about the arrival of the boys, Pearl Harbor was bombed and the USA came into the war.

"Don't see why we shouldn't have them home for Christmas," said Sidney Waterhouse, forking up a piece of meat pie. "They're our kids, after all."

"Maybe," said Ivy. "I do miss them. But what've we got to offer them here? Bombs – rationing – where they are, they'll be killing geese for Christmas dinners. And they're safe, that's what matters."

"They haven't even seen their sister yet," Sid pointed out.

"Suppose they come here and get killed, what will you think then?" demanded Ivy. The baby, which was lying in a basket on the kitchen floor, began to cry. Ivy, stooping down to pick her up and opening the buttons on her cardigan said, "Oh, Christ."

"I don't know why you can't feed the baby properly," Sid said jealously as the greedy baby sucked at the breast. "Why don't you give it a decent bottle, or something?"

"I'd lose that extra pint of milk I'm allocated as a nursing mother," said Ivy. "And that's what goes in your tea, half the time."

44

"I'd have thought," remarked Sid, "that with the government handing out free babies' milk you'd be only too pleased to be rid of all this business."

"You'd better get off to work," said Ivy. "It's getting on for six." At that moment there came the wail of the air raid siren. Sid picked his bus driver's cap and coat off a chair and started for the door. "Don't go now, Sid," Ivy said. "Wait a bit and see where it is."

"I can't stand here waiting for an air raid to stop," he said. There was a whistling sound, a huge explosion, the floor shook and the cups rattled on a shelf. Ivy jumped and the nipple came out of the baby's mouth.

"Whew," said Sid. "That was close."

"Don't go, love," said Ivy, taking no notice of the roaring baby. "You'd be mad to start running about." There was a second explosion as another bomb dropped. "Too late for the shelter," he said, going to the window. "Might as well have a cup of tea. Oh, Christ. It looks like Wattenblath Street. They're trying to hit the flaming railway again." A red flicker was filling the room. Ivy sat down with the baby, saying, half to herself, "I hate all this. What a world to bring a baby into." She froze as the whistling sound of a bomb came again. "Sid," she cried, "Sid – we're going to die –" But the crash came a little further off. "Come away from that window, Sid," she yelled. "Pull the curtains."

Sid, drawing the blackout curtains across the window, said, "Take it easy, love. I'll put the kettle on." He came across the small room and kissed the top of the baby's head. "Be all right," he told her, "they're on the run." He turned on the light.

Ivy went on feeding the baby. She said, "Someone's knocking at the door. Better open up."

Sid went to open the door and came in again followed by a thickset man of about thirty wearing a rough khaki tunic and trousers. He hesitated in the doorway, seeing Ivy feeding the baby. "Oh – excuse me, Ivy," he said. "Just wondered if I could shelter here until it's over. I didn't realize –"

"Can't stand on ceremony in times like these," Ivy said briskly. "Come on in. Sid's just put the kettle on." She gave him a careful look, then rearranged her dress and put the baby back in its basket, where the little girl whimpered and then fell asleep.

Once again the house shook. Sid ran to the kitchen window and cried out, "I think they got the depot. I'll have to go."

"Oh, no, Sid," wailed Ivy. "Don't go – you can't do any good."

Sid was putting on his coat, saying, "It's no good, Ivy. They'll all be in there – Harry, Jim Jessop, all of them. Half of them are coming off shift and the other half's going on."

"You can't help, Sid," she cried. She jumped up and took his coat by the sleeve. "For God's sake think of the rest of us."

"I'm another pair of hands Ivy," he said. "That's what they need. Raid's mostly over, anyway. You can hear the ack-ack guns making short work."

"They've only got to drop one more," said Ivy. "And that's you gone. Think of that."

He said urgently, "Ivy, love, I've got to go – what sort of a man would I be?"

Ivy sighed and dropped his sleeve. "All right. Go if you've got to," she said. He put on his cap and went out. She followed him on to the pavement. The sky to the west was red with fire. A plane droned overhead. There was gunfire. They stood outside the house with their heads bent, as if that would protect them from the bombs.

"Don't leave me and Shirley in the house with that gangster," she whispered. "Anything might happen."

"He's harmless," said Sid. "He's in the army now."

"He's gone AWOL," said Ivy. "He'll be posted as a deserter. He's done time for half-killing a woman, Sid. How can you go and leave me here with him?"

"He never touched a woman," said Sid. "Oh, well – his wife – that's different, isn't it? Listen, Arnie Rose is perfectly all right as long as you know him. What's more, this is just an excuse to keep me back. You were at school with him. You're no more afraid of him than I am. I've got to go. The raid's nearly over. I have to go down to the bus depot and see if anybody's hurt."

The skies were quieter now. The gunfire was more sporadic. Ivy looked up and then across at the red glow along the skyline. She said, "All right, Sid. Look after yourself."

"We'll meet again," he said. He went off down the pavement into the darkness. She heard him call back, "Bye, love."

"Bye, Sid," she shouted after him and went back into the house. She bumped into Arnie Rose in the passageway and jumped.

"Come on in, Ivy," he said. "Don't worry. Old Sid'll be all right. What you need is to warm up and have a little drink of something I've got in my pocket. Let's cheer up and keep the cold out."

Ivy thought that if the raid was nearing its end Arnie Rose ought to be on his way. She thought that a man with any decency in him might have offered to go along with Sid and help at the bus depot. But she suffered Arnie to lead her back into the kitchen where he sat down confidentially at the kitchen table and produced a full half-bottle of whisky from his pocket. "And plenty more where that came from," he remarked. Ivy took the glass he offered and thought to herself, "Please, God – keep Sid safe. Amen."

Sid returned as the first light was coming up over winter streets filled with drizzling rain. He was dirty and haggard. "Sorry, gel," he said. "It wasn't a direct hit – one of the sheds collapsed with a bloke inside. After we got him out I started helping in the houses nearby. We found an old lady in the coalshed but there was two little girls killed. Heat up some water. I want a wash."

Ivy filled a big saucepan with water and put it on the gas. She handed him a cup of tea and put two slices of bacon in the pan. "Poor little girls," she said.

"You're right about not bringing Mary and Jack back here for Christmas," he told her. "I must have been barmy to think about it."

"Get any sleep?" asked Ivy, turning the rashers.

"Best part of an hour in the cab of one of the buses," he said. "I felt too tired to walk home. You look pale. You all right?"

"I never slept much," said Ivy. "Shirley was all right, though." She did not add that she had spent nearly all night evading Arnie Rose. She had been too cautious to ask him directly to leave, or even call a neighbour to help her get rid of him. She thought it would not be a good idea to upset Arnold Rose. She did not want her husband to upset him either.

Sid bit into his bacon sandwich and said, "We could all do with a year in bed, I reckon. I don't know how much more of this we can stand."

"A lot more," said Ivy. "You'd be surprised what people can put up with."

"Can't go on forever, though, can it?" he said. "Families split up. Casualties. Raids every bloody night. Queues – we may not have had much in the old days but at least we had our homes, and a bit of peace and quiet."

"Peace and quiet to starve in," said Ivy. "At least the kids are getting their milk and orange juice and dried eggs. People are being looked after, you can say that. That reminds me – Arnie Rose can get us a big,

47

fat chicken for Christmas — cost thirty shillings, though."

"Thirty shillings," he said. "My God, that Arnie's got a nerve."

Ivy said, "Get to bed, love. See if you can get a few hours' sleep."

"Fancy joining me?" asked Sid wistfully.

"I've got to go shopping early to avoid the queues," Ivy said.

Sid went grumpily up to bed.

Down at Twining's, in Framlingham, Christmas was a jolly affair, in spite of Twining's drunken tumble against Mrs Twining's grandfather's clock when he came home from the pub on Christmas Eve. This caused a crash and some shouting downstairs at midnight but the row was over by Christmas Day itself, when there were cries and laughs, big fires to drive off the country dark, and a fat goose from the farmyard on the dinner table. There was Mrs Twining's mother's famous Christmas pudding — "you could climb mount Everest on it" — there were mince pies and plenty of port, games of cards and drunken songs round the piano. Ian and Jackie, the evacuees, were well pleased with the wooden soldiers and the cricket bat and stumps which had once belonged to the Twining boys. They both fell asleep on the parlour sofa at midnight as the Twinings, Mrs Twining's mother, Twining's brother and his wife, their children and the village postman and his wife, who had come up on bicycles for supper, all stood round the piano singing, "There'll be blue skies over/The white cliffs of Dover/Tomorrow. Just you wait and see."

But earlier on, up at the Towers, in the afternoon, poor Mary had been crouching in the damp shrubbery at the foot of the lawn. She drew big, sobbing breaths and peeped through the damp leaves at the lights in the sitting room, which had just been turned on. As she watched, the curtains were drawn. She wondered if she had time to make a dash back to the house, before Tom and his cousin Charlie found her. She might, she thought, have to stay in these bushes until bedtime.

In front of the bushes lay the second-hand tricycle, freshly painted red, which she had found under the tree this morning, with her name on a card on the handlebars. They had let her pedal it up and down the corridor and round and round the hall. It was while she was circling the hall, in a state of complete delight, that she had seen Tom and Charlie looking at her nastily through the half open door of the cloakroom. She had instantly pedalled past the foot of the big staircase which ran upstairs and back into the corridor which led to the kitchen. There she sat on the tricycle, by the kitchen range, looking very worried. When Mrs Gates asked her what was the matter she said only, "Tom and Charlie are going to hurt me." Mrs Gates had scoffed at her but she knew that she was right. Sure enough, they had chased her out of the house in the afternoon while the adults were dozy with their lunch. Now she crouched, shaking like a robin on a cold twig, in the bushes. The tricycle, her pride and joy, lay just beyond the shrubbery, on the lawn. She could not see how to escape.

"Got you," said Charles Markham, falling on her through the sopping rhododendrons and shaking raindrops all over her. She felt his hard hands on her shoulders. Then, removing one hand he began to pinch her on the inside of her thighs and – oh – pulling down her knickers. "No, no," she cried out. "Let me alone!"

Now Tom was holding her flat on the ground by her shoulders as Charlie pulled her pants down to her knees. "Ooh, look, Tom-tom," he cried in a high voice. "Look at her little bum-bum – and something else besides."

He had very big blue eyes, red cheeks and a mass of brown curly hair. He was eleven. Mary could hear him breathing in and out heavily.

"Dis-gusting," said Tom. "That's disgusting – quick, pull up her dirty drawers so we don't have to look."

Mary, sobbing, felt consuming rage. She would kill them. She would kill them somehow – she knew she would. But Tom was holding her shoulders and Charlie had one big hand on her knee.

"I like looking, though," said Charlie, in a heavy, rude voice. "Little no-knickers evacuee. Did you like your nice little trikie, then?"

A sweeping, surging rage filled Mary's head. Twisting sideways she bit Tom on his serge-clad arm, sinking her teeth in like a dog, disregarding the thick, stuffy taste of the material and just imagining the white arm beneath. She pictured her toothmarks, with blood spurting out of them.

Tom screamed. Charlie suddenly realized what was happening and let go of her knee. Mary leaped up, pulled up her knickers and picked a stick from the ground. Running away was useless, for they were faster than she was. Some inspiration made her shout, "I'm telling – I'm telling what you did," and as Tom stood there, his face twisted with pain and alarm, she began to hit both of them round their faces with the little stick. A moment later Charlie was wrenching the stick from her hand. Mary, shouting, "I'm telling. I'm telling," took to her heels and ran out of the shrubbery, across the lawn and through the back door into the kitchen.

Mrs Gates, cutting sandwiches on the table said, "Mary! Whatever's happened to you?" although, by the time the words were out of her lips, she knew without telling, roughly what it was. The sobbing, muddy child, with leaves caught in the back of her hair, was evidence enough.

"It was Tom and Charlie," said Mary. "They—they pulled down my knickers."

"Oh," said Mrs Gates. Then she said, "Oh," again. "— The villains."

"You tell Lady Allaun," demanded Mary. "You go and tell her what they did to me."

"Not now," said Mrs Gates. It was not just because it was Christmas Day and because there were guests in the house. It was because complaints like this were not made to the gentry about their sons or relatives. The matter would need to be more serious before Mrs Gates would go to Lady Allaun with it.

"I'm going then," said Mary. "They're naughty boys, Tom and Charlie, and I told them I was going to tell." And with that, furious, with the tear-stains making dirty tracks down her cheeks, she opened the kitchen door.

"You can't go into the drawing room like that," said Mrs Gates, holding her by the shoulder. "Let's get you clean first and decide what to do."

"I'm telling. I'm telling," Mary screamed at Mrs Gates, as she had at Tom and Charlie. This new restraint, so like being held down outside in the bushes, was frightening her even more. Then they began to tussle, with Mrs Gates trying to hold her back without hurting her and Mary trying to free herself.

Lady Allaun, hurrying towards them down the passageway in a blue chiffon dress and a shawl said, "What is all this?"

"She's had an argument with Tom and Charlie," said Mrs Gates.

"Really – children on Christmas Day," said Isabel impatiently. "Well—I suppose it's the excitement. I came to ask you when we might expect some tea, Mrs Gates. Sally Staines is perfectly prepared to help you, if you can't cope, you do know that, don't you? As for the rest—I suggest Mary tidies herself before she comes in for tea. In fact, it might be better if she had hers in the kitchen." And with that she turned and walked back. Mary, still gripped by Mrs Gates, said, "They took my knickers down," but either Isabel Allaun did not hear her or did not choose to hear her. She was soon gone. Mary gasped. She looked up at Mrs Gates. "She doesn't care," she exclaimed.

"I don't think she heard you, love," said Mrs Gates gently. "Come along upstairs. I'll help you to sort yourself out."

She helped Mary to wash herself and brushed her hair. She took her shoes off and put her under the quilt in the big, faded, elegant bedroom and sat with her until she fell asleep. Downstairs there was scurrying and questions asked and answered as Lady Allaun and her downtrodden cousin produced tea for the guests. Mrs Gates looked at Mary's pale face, which still, in sleep, bore an anxious expression. From here she was summoned by Charlie, knocking nervously on the door, to get some attention for his cousin's face. There was a long scrape on it and Mrs Gates was careful to wash it ungently and overload it with smarting iodine. She affected not to notice Tom's clutch on his sleeve, where the bite was stinging. She had noticed the piece of serge fluff caught between Mary's front teeth so she had no difficulty in working out his problem. In fact Tom spent the remaining ten days of the holidays in mounting pain as the bite slowly festered. There is no mistaking the marks of a human bite and he could not explain where it came from without awkward questions being asked. He had to wait until he returned to school to have it treated.

Mrs Gates brought Mary supper in bed later on. She read a fairy story and tried to forget the dripping bushes and Tom and Charlie's bullying. Wriggling her hot little body in bed, she read, stumblingly, "Cinderella was as good as she was beautiful. She set aside apartments in the palace for her two sisters, and married them the very same day to two gentlemen of high rank about the Court."

The moral to the tale baffled her:

"It is surely a great advantage
To have spirit and courage,
Good breeding and common sense,
And other qualities of this sort,
Which are the gifts of Heaven!
You will do well to own these:
But, for success, they may well be in vain
If, as a final gift, one has not
The blessing of godfather or godmother."

Later when Mrs Gates brought up some hot milk she asked her to explain this. Mrs Gates, almost as baffled as Mary had been at first, thought about it and then said, in spite of the pain in her legs, "It looks to me as if the man who wrote this knew a bit about the world – you'll understand when you're older. Why don't you get on to an easier bit in your book?"

Mary had already put Isabel Allaun's Christmas present to her under the pillow and was fast asleep.

Meanwhile the war went on. A shabbier, greyer population felt the worst of the danger receding although the streets were still full of uniformed men, the bombing went on, the rationing went on and no street was without its cratered, brick-laden gap, where a house had been destroyed. But the Germans had been beaten in Russia and, the previous year, men and women had been hopeful enough about the future to queue for a government report recommending that a national attack should be made on what it described as five giant evils – "want, disease, ignorance, squalor and idleness." It was as the Allied Forces were preparing for the attack on Sicily that Isabel Allaun led Tom, Charlie and Mary up Scoop Hill to the top of the Common, where the midsummer fair was being held. None of them were thinking about the war, still less the reconstruction afterwards. It was a brilliant day. A skylark sung overhead in a sky of clearest blue. They puffed up the last part of the path and got on to the plateau-like bit of heath, which had been a hill fort in the Bronze Age and a meeting place for the local witches' coven in mediaeval times and had always, through the ages, been the private spot where lovers went to lie down in peace.

The music they had heard, dimly, lower down the path, was louder as they got over the top of Scoop Hill. There were roundabouts and swings, coconut shies, a Punch and Judy, stalls selling lemonade, a rifle range. Beyond the fairground, towards the further edge of the hill were the brightly painted gypsy caravans.

Mary was awestruck by the transformation of the barren stretch of grass and fern. She was struck by the noise, the bright colours of the roundabouts, especially the wooden horses, with their white coats, black spots and red reins. She was impressed, but frightened, by the gypsies themselves – the long sallow faces, the black drooping hair and the bright, long skirts of the women, the swarthy looks and bold stances of the strong gypsy men. One of them, she saw, actually wore gold earrings in his ears. And she thought she would die if she did not have a ride on one of the white horses, going round and round with the music.

"There's a lot here have never heard of the call-up," she heard Rabbity Jim mutter to Mrs Gates, as they stood by the rifle range, watching a tall gypsy keep his hand in by firing at playing cards pinned up at the end of it. The prizes, Mary saw, were pottery dogs and dancing ladies in red and black Spanish dresses.

"What's a call-up?" Mary said clearly.

"Be quiet if you're staying with us," Mrs Gates said sharply. The gypsy grinned round at Rabbity Jim. Jack glared at him. They were in the same trade really – poaching, picking up a country living.

Threatened with dismissal, Mary took Mrs Gates's hand. She had slipped away from Isabel Allaun, and Tom and Charlie, recognizing that Lady Allaun's response to the fair might be chilling and knowing that she would not have any fun going round with Tom and Charlie. After the Christmas holiday they had not reappeared. They had spent the Easter holidays at Charlie's house and had only arrived at Allaun Towers a few days before, in the freshly-polished Bentley. Ever since, Mary had been waiting for trouble. She did not know that after her threats to tell Lady Allaun about them and Tom's difficulty in explaining the festering bite-mark to the matron of the school, they had tacitly agreed to leave her alone. Next time, they thought, there could be even worse trouble. But Mary, on her side, felt utterly unprotected. Mrs Gates had not defended her. She was still not sure if Isabel Allaun had heard her, that afternoon in the passageway. Being a child Mary could accept the fact of things heard, but not understood, facts deliberately ignored and half-truths told, but her nature ran counter to ambiguity. Her fragmentary memories of life in Meakin Street did not include evasions and wilful ignorance – just Ivy noticing all too plainly that Sid was drunk, and accusing him loudly, just rows about the rent and embraces exchanged. Tact, discretion and blind eyes turned were not part of the Meakin Street experience – and even if she had totally forgotten all of it her brother Jack, hater of secrets and hypocrisy, even at ten years of age, would have been a perpetual reminder. However, on that day, the day of the fair, she forgot all this, dodged Tom and Charlie and sank into the bliss of the rides, the lemonade, the blue sky and the organ playing "Show Me The Way To Go Home" and "Just a Song At Twilight". The local people jostled, chatted and threw coconuts at plywood models of Hitler and Goering in order to win a plate with the King and Queen's head on it. They rode

53

on the merry-go-round, ducked into a tent to see the bearded lady, the mermaid or the fortune teller, drank gritty lemonade and, if they were young enough, put their arms round each other, giggled and gave each other pinches.

Mary spotted Jackie moving round and round and up and down to the tune of "Roll out the Barrel." He looked blissful. When it stopped she ran up, got on the horse beside him, gave the man her sixpence and, holding on tight, swooped up and down beside him, seeing Mrs Gates and Rabbity Jim and Isabel Allaun and all the village faces – postman, baker, one of the school-teachers, all blurring and going past her, as if in a dream. She caught the eye of the brawny gypsy in the middle of the merry-go-round, lost him again on the upswing and so went round and round and up and down until – whoops – her little white sunhat fell off and lay, looking like a dinner plate on the dusty grass. Then she began to slip and fell on the neck of the horse, grabbing it but still feeling herself slipping sideways until, luckily, the horses slowed and finally stopped. "Ooh," she said. "Ooh – I feel all dizzy. I nearly fell off." Then, as Mrs Gates came up carrying her hat she said, "Can I have another go – Mrs Gates, please."

"In a minute," said Mrs Gates, helping her off the roundabout. Tom was scrambling on. He gave her a malicious stare from his pale blue eyes. Mary quickly took Mrs Gates's hand and said, "In a minute, then." They bought lemonade from a tall gypsy woman. She, too, had gold hoops through her ears. "Have you got holes in your ears?" Mary asked.

"I have that," said the woman. She gave Mary a funny look and Mrs Gates dragged her away. "Why are you pulling me?" whined Mary.

"They steal blonde babies," hissed Mrs Gates. "They leave their own in the cradle."

"I'm not a baby," said Mary. "I'm too big to steal."

"Too cheeky, as well," said Mrs Gates.

They bumped into Isabel Allaun, who looked embarrassed at being caught ducking out of the fortune teller's tent.

"So silly, really," she said. "Still, they do tell you the most extraordinary things about yourself – not surprising, I suppose. They pick up all the local gossip as they travel." She moved on and then turned back. "Benson's got the car down at the end of the lane," she said. "Do you two want to come back with us?"

"Oh, no," said Mary. "I want another go on the merry-go-round. Can we stay?" she asked Mrs Gates.

"Let her stay, Lou," said the gypsy woman, coming out of her tent.

Mrs Gates looked at her sharply, upset by this use of her Christian name. Mary stared at the gypsy woman. She wore a long, coloured skirt, a coloured blouse and a patterned scarf round her head, with tails on it which went down to her shoulders. Her hair was long and black. She felt somehow warm, from a distance, as if you were standing close to the fire on a cold day. The big gypsy man by the coconut shy was, she noticed, staring at them. Were the gypsies going to steal her away? She felt she wouldn't mind going off with this woman, with her bright clothes and the gold rings in her ears, especially in a caravan with a horse to pull it.

"You'll have to walk all the way home," warned Mrs Gates. Tom and Charlie came up then and stood by Lady Allaun.

"I don't mind," she said quickly.

"I'll hold you to that when you start complaining," Mrs Gates told her.

Lady Allaun, Tom and Charlie walked away. She heard Tom saying, "It's not much of a fair, really, is it?" But Mary couldn't agree: she was so happy she gave a little skip.

"You'll be wanting your fortunes told," the gypsy woman stated flatly. She was not young but her face was unlined. The black hair framed an oval face and large, dark eyes.

"Well – maybe, gypsy," said Mrs Gates.

"You'll regret it if you don't," the gypsy said.

"Wait for me, Mary," said Mrs Gates suddenly, and, with the speed of a watched alcoholic getting into a pub, she ducked through the flap of the gypsy's tent.

Mary, disappointed of her ride, stood bored outside the tent in the grit. Jackie came up, luckily, and paid for another ride on the merry-go-round.

The big gypsy man who ran the merry-go-round did not tell them to get off at the end of the ride. He winked at Jack and said, "You and your sister are good for another go – yes?"

Jack winked back and said, "Thanks, mate." Mary stared at him and wondered how it was that he always knew what to do. After that, she thought she had better go and stand outside the tent again. Mrs Gates had been a long time. Some of the grown-ups and their children were drifting away downhill, towards their tea. The children turned back often, to catch the last sounds of the music. At the same time the older children and young people, left unattended at the fair, began to shout and run between the sideshows. The hilltop began to look more itself – there was the grass, the buttercups and the fern growing between the stationary caravans. There were times, as Mary stood outside the tent, when it seemed the noise, the music of the barrel-organ and the merry-go-round ceased for seconds on end.

Mrs Gates put her head out of the tent and said, "Mary – Mary! You're to come in, the lady says."

Mary came out of her dream and said, "What!" in alarm. She could see darkness inside, and the dim figure of a woman sitting bent over a table. She was not sure this was what she wanted.

"Mary! Hurry up!" Mrs Gates said urgently. "The lady's asked for you special." Her voice sounded rather as it did when Lady Allaun was in one of her bad moods, demanding the impossible and ready to burst out in a rage if she did not get it. This hardened Mary's attitude. "I don't want to go in the tent – it's dark," she said obstinately.

Mrs Gates repeated the gypsy's words, "Get the little girl with the golden hair who is like your daughter but not your daughter, like a child of the house but not a child of the house. Fancy that – I'd told her nothing about you. Now, come in – she'll tell you your fortune and not charge a penny, that's what she said." Mrs Gates's country accent had grown stronger as it did when she was tired or excited. Mary did not like her in this exalted mood. It scared her. So did the dark tent. She did not want her fortune told, whatever that was. She heard a voice speaking from within the tent. Mrs Gates turned her head to hear. She said to Mary, "She asks will you meet her by her caravan?"

"Oh, yes," said Mary, pleased by the idea of getting close to one of the caravans and perhaps seeing inside. Some of them had chimneys on the top so there must be a little fireplace.

"Come on then," said Mrs Gates, emerging from the tent and taking her by the hand. They walked behind the tent and over to the caravans, which stood close to the edge of the hill. "I wonder why she wants to see you," Mrs Gates said as they went along. "You just a little girl, too. Fetch the little fair girl to me, she said – and never set eyes on you before –"

"Lady Allaun went in there before," remarked Mary. "Perhaps she said about me." Mrs Gates took no notice. "The things she told me about myself," she went on wonderingly. "Things I swear have been a secret between me and my Maker for thirty years – things not a living soul knows – and about Gates, too, God give him rest, for she says he's dead, of an accident, she said –"

Mary twisted her hand suddenly out of Mrs Gates's and said, "Do we have to go?" She mistrusted this excitable chat. It seemed to be involving her in a way she did not like. Perhaps the gypsy was a witch and she would be left alone with her. Perhaps after all she did not want to go off in the caravan. Her hand was once more back in that of Mrs Gates. She was being dragged towards the caravan. The woman sat on the steps, smiling at her.

"You stay with me," Mary demanded fiercely of Mrs Gates.

"Of course I will, Mary," said Mrs Gates.

"All the time," Mary insisted.

"That's right," said Mrs Gates.

The caravan, red, with black designs on it, stood back from the fairground, on its own, amid a stretch of trampled ferns. Nearby an old white horse stood tethered, cropping grass peacefully. Larks, too high to be seen, sung their evening song in the sky.

Mary dragged her feet as they walked up to the woman on the caravan steps. But it was not the same woman – this one was very old, with a brown face lined and puckered like a shelled walnut, and grey-black hair pinned up on top of her head, held with two combs made of bone. She wore gold earrings and a long, ruddy-coloured dress.

"Mrs Gates – it's a witch," Mary hissed as they advanced. Was Mrs Gates going to leave her with the witch? Perhaps she had sold her – perhaps it was like Hansel and Gretel. She wished Jack were nearby.

"It's a witch," she said again in an even lower voice. The lark sang on, overhead. Mary was full of fear.

"I'm not a witch," said the old woman, as they came right up to the steps of the caravan. "Don't be afraid of me." She stood up and Mary saw that she was quite a tall woman. She came slowly down the steps and, as Mary and Mrs Gates drew back, she made a kind of stiff, mocking curtsey in their direction. Then she sat down on the step of the caravan again and said to Mary, "Sit down on the grass by me." Mary looked anxiously at Mrs Gates, who nodded and, when she was sitting down, drew close to her. The old woman said, "Give me your hand then, little girl." Mary, again staring up at Mrs Gates, held out her hot, grimy hand. The touch of the other's hand, brown, fine-boned and cool, calmed her fears a little. The old woman looked first at the palm, then at the back. "An impatient hand," said the gypsy. "Here is one who does not look before she leaps. Here is strength and the need to learn judgment." She had a lilting voice, not like the clipped tones of Lady Allaun or the more robust tones of Mrs Gates, not a county voice

57

nor a Londoner's either. It had a strange accent and a compelling, singing sound. It was a bit like music, Mary thought. She did not quite trust the voice. Suddenly a little wind came over the edge of the hill and made her shiver. The silence was broken by Mrs Gates, saying, "Well, come on, gypsy. What else do you see?" She spoke roughly for although country people were afraid of the gypsies, who told fortunes and could curse a woman's unborn child in the womb, they also despised them as beggars and chicken thieves.

"Watch your tongue, old woman," said the gypsy. "For I see you here, in the child's palm." She bent her head over Mary's palm and said, tracing little lines on it with her cool, brown finger. "I cannot see all – some I cannot tell you but this is the hand of an uncanny child with an odd past and a future stranger still." Her voice sang on, "Born of strange blood she will marry strangely, once far off from here a true marriage but short, unlucky, once close to here, but no true marriage and once, alas, true marriage but too close – too close." She fell silent and began again, tracing Mary's palm again with her finger. Mary sat still, feeling as if she could not move. She sensed Mrs Gates, rigid beside her. The old woman began to speak again in her sing-song voice. "I see children but a wrong deed, not done wrongly and a long hard path for you, my child, which you will tread bravely. You," she said, now looking directly at Mary, "will be rich and poor and rich again but never at ease – no, not till you are as old as me and maybe not even then. Close to a fortune, close to a kingdom at the last she will make her own way though the path will twist and turn – someone watches over you –" she said. Her voice trailed off. She looked, now, quite old and tired. Then she said to Mrs Gates, in a normal voice, "A brave hand – impatient, hasty, soft heart and an open pocket –" Mrs Gates stood looking at her, awed and then, fighting her own dread, urged, "Come on, gypsy woman. What do you mean by all this? You've frightened the child and told her nothing."

"She's not afraid," said the old woman and she was right. Mary felt quite excited.

"Is that about me?" she demanded. "About getting married and getting rich and all that?"

"Now look what you've done," said Mrs Gates. "She's over-excited on account of your mystifying nonsense." But the old woman just looked at Mary and said, "She looks forward to the journey, not knowing how many miles she will have to travel without rest."

"Like everybody else in this mortal world," said Mrs Gates and then, as if dealing with a dishonest tradesman over a bill said, "So she marries three times, do you mean to say? And she'll be rich? And what's all this about no true marriage? And how, pray, will she end?"

"As we all do," said the gypsy from her seat on the caravan steps. "In six feet of earth, no more, no less."

Mrs Gates breathed out impatiently and then reconciled herself to getting no more information from the old woman. She fumbled in her worn black handbag and took out her purse. She handed the old woman two coins — half crowns. Mary was startled. It was a lot of money. But the gypsy woman waved the money away, reluctant even to touch it. "No — not for this. No crowned heads," she said.

"No — what do you mean?" asked Mrs Gates, looking at the money in her palm. Then she understood. The coins bore the heads of George VI and Edward VII. "Well — what sort of money do you want, then?" she asked. It was required to cross the gypsy's palm with silver or bad luck would follow. So the gypsies said.

"Nothing — nothing," said the woman. "Put your money away."

Now the fair was stilling. The gypsies were packing up the stalls. Mary, glancing behind her, watched two of them lifting a big, white, black-spotted wooden horse off the roundabout. They began to carry it towards the little group — the old gypsy woman, the middle-aged housekeeper, the little, golden-haired girl.

"You cannot tell us any more, gypsy?" asked Mrs Gates in an unusually humble tone.

"The ending will not be unhappy," said the woman. "Does that satisfy you? And she will not fail you, old woman — does that please you?"

"I suppose it will have to," said Mrs Gates. She said formally, "Thank you, gypsy. Visit me when next you are passing through."

She took Mary's hand and began to lead her away.

"She will be there at your ending — will you like that?" the gypsy called out from behind. Mrs Gates swung round in alarm. "Not soon," said the woman, with a malicious smile, revealing teeth stained and broken like an old dog's, and one shiny gold tooth in front.

"What do you mean?" asked Mrs Gates. Mary felt the grip tighten on her hand.

Impatiently, the gypsy said, "Not soon. You will both die peacefully, in your beds, in old age. Can you ask more than that? Go home."

A small child with a brown face, curly black hair and, Mary noticed, small gold rings in her ears, ran up to the woman, clasped at her skirts and began to chatter in what sounded like a foreign language. The woman bent down to talk to her, then straightened up and stood there looking at them. Behind her the sun was descending behind a landscape of hills and rolling fields.

"Come and kiss me, child," she said to Mary. Mary looked at Mrs Gates, who gave her a secret push in the side. She ran forward obediently and put her face up to the old woman, who bent down and brushed her cheek with dry lips. Looking into Mary's eyes she said, "Aha." Mary ran back to Mrs Gates. 'Goodbye," she shouted. The woman and the gypsy child watched their backs as they walked off, through the bustle of the closing down of the fair, the small knots of youngsters standing about and giggling, and to the edge of the hill. On the way down, sliding on the dry earth and stones of the steep path, Mrs Gates was silent. Once in the lane leading past Twining's farm and so to the track across the fields to Allaun Towers, she began to talk. "Well, well," she said, "to think of all that. And she never took any money for it, either. She told you your fortune for nothing."

"What's a fortune?" Mary asked.

"What's going to happen to you," Mrs Gates told her.

"Is it magic?" Mary asked.

"Like magic," said Mrs Gates. Mary brushed her hand along the lower leaves of the bushes and remarked, "You said there was no such thing."

Mrs Gates said wonderingly, "To think I'd see the day when a gypsy would tell a fortune and not charge a penny for it – and the things she said – enough to make your hair curl – three husbands you're to have, Mary. I wonder if there's any truth in it. Oh, my."

Mary had been startled by the shifting relationship between Mrs Gates and the gypsy woman. At one minute Mrs Gates had been demanding and disrespectful, rather like Lady Allaun in shops and, on the other hand, she was plainly flattered and impressed by the gypsy's attention. For her part, Mary was vaguely disturbed by the whole thing. If the magic was really true, she was not sure she liked the sound of it all. She concentrated on making a mixed bouquet of daisies, buttercups and trailing weeds on the way home. So they walked in silence until they were cutting back over the fields beyond the lake. Then Mrs Gates said suddenly, "I think that woman was Urania Heron."

"Who's Urany Heron?" asked Mary.

60

"She's the Queen of the Gypsies," Mrs Gates said solemnly. "That's who she is."

"Can she do spells?" asked Mary.

"I expect so," said Mrs Gates.

They passed by the edges of the lake, where ducks quacked and began to settle for the night. Mary thought that she would try to forget all about the gypsy. And, as it happened, there was a shock for them when they got back to the Towers, so she never, after that, remembered the fortune-telling episode very clearly.

There was this red-faced man in a major's uniform, stick and all, and he was standing on the Turkish rug in front of the fireplace in the drawing room when we were called in there. When he saw me he just picked me up, spun me round and put me back on the mat. He said, "Well, you can see there's something special here, whatever it is." Then he put his hand in his pocket and gave me a little silver filigree necklace. He must have bought it specially for me in India. There was his hat, too, with the brass on it, lying on the sofa. He let me wear it.

Sir Frederick was nice and funny that weekend. He borrowed a horse and let me ride on it with him. He told me stories. He was so kind – I think I took to him so much because he reminded me a lot of Sid, my dad. That was the last time I saw him happy though, Sir Frederick. It was rotten, really, what happened. It was the times took it out of him, I think. First the war and then the peace. Towards the end of the war Sir Frederick came home for good. They let him out early, I think, because he wasn't well. They must have spotted he'd gone a bit funny.

Sir Herbert, who has passed through the confusing streets of London, reaches the peace of his own quiet home in Kensington. Again he comments on Mary's story:

Curiously enough Mary Waterhouse's accidental encounter with the gypsy, Urania Heron, crops up in one of Lady Allaun's letters to the Ministry of Home Affairs, which passed the correspondence on to my father. These letters were chiefly about Mary's health, which was always good, and about her progress at school. But oddly enough, in one of them, written in 1942, Lady Allaun actually records what she had gathered from Mrs Gates about the gypsy's prophecies. There was no comment from my father at the time but in 1952, when Mary's husband, Jim Flanders, was hanged and the course of her life began to look worrying he must have recollected Lady Allaun's letter. I do not believe for a moment that my father was superstitious, but the old woman's remarks, though vague, must have made him stop and think. Short and unlucky, she had said, of Mary's marriage. No one would have disputed that. At any rate it was his duty to look into the thing and so he did. He gave the mission to me. He sent me off in search of the gypsy. Of course, he explained almost nothing. He said only that there were reasons why the girl, Mary Waterhouse, had to be watched and that her future, which had in part, perhaps, been predicted by the gypsy, was of such concern that it was worthwhile trying to find the woman again, to find out what she knew, if anything, and, perhaps more importantly, how she knew it. He naturally passed the gypsy-hunt off fairly lightly and as far as I was concerned it was just a piece of good luck for a boy of seventeen (the chance of a chase through England during a long, dull summer holiday). I set off for Kent with my schoolfriend, Allan Pimm, in his little black Morris Minor. The trail led us into Dorset and, after a fortnight, back to the south of England again, to Rye, where we had heard the gypsies were camping on the flats near the sea. It was early spring and a dull, grey day when we arrived there. A strong wind was coming off a dark, turbulent sea. The wind tossed the reeds and long grass about as we walked about a mile from the car, which we had parked by the roadside, to where the caravans were sited between the road and the sea. I could not imagine why they had picked this wilderness to use as a camp. Later I learned that the local councils were at this time forever harassing the gypsies in order to prevent them from coming into rapidly suburbanizing neighbourhoods. The gypsies, once part of the normal pattern of rural life, useful and mistrusted at the same time, salesmen of scarce goods and extra hands at times when help was needed on the land, had lost their role. Now they were always on the move, evading the police and local authorities.

The camp looked very tiny as we advanced over these raw flats. Small horses cropped apathetically at the tough and salty grass. As we got closer we saw two women, in flapping skirts, making their way up from the beach, laden with big bundles of driftwood. The caravans, close to, looked less trim than they must once have done. The eccentric red, black and yellow decorations seemed worn and the varnish was cracking on the wooden panels. Two of the horses were in bad condition. I looked at my friend, Allan, and could see that, standing in this flat, grey spot, he felt as depressed as I did. We had reached the caravan site at about the same time as the two women who had been fighting up against the wind from the other direction. They instantly assumed smiles both wary and propitiatory. I went up to them and said, politely I hope, "We are looking for an old lady, Urania Heron. Is she here? We should like to see her."

Both the women looked us over quickly. In retrospect I realize that neither Allan nor I came into that class of girls, or women in middle age, or men with bad nerves and shaky prospects who would normally be seeking out a gypsy in this God-forsaken spot, so as to get their fortunes told. We were a pair of fresh-faced schoolboys, silly, innocent and well-meaning as only schoolboys of that era could be, if the system had not already bruised and corrupted them. Allan and I, new from the playing fields and the study, must have been a mystifying pair. One of the women, still clutching her bundle of driftwood said, "What would your business be with her?"

"My father would like to see her," I said, which was in the circumstances probably the best answer I could have given. At least they could not think, then, that I was from the local authority or the Inland Revenue, come to worry and harass them.

"Give me your name, then," said the woman, "and I'll ask her if she'll see you so you can tell her your father's business with her. She may refuse you — she's old and ill." A sharp gust of salt wind hit us. I looked at Allan who was standing a little further off and bending my head towards the woman, so that he could not hear, I said, "My name is Precious. In connection with Miss Mary Waterhouse."

She gave me a sharp look and said, "I'll ask." Then she crossed the flattened and soaking ground between the caravans and, her long black hair flying in the wind, went up some steps into a large van painted in gold and black. The other woman remained behind, to watch us, I suppose.

The woman came back. She said, "You can come. He must stay outside."

"Sorry, Allan," I told him. "I thought it might come to this. Why don't you go back and wait in the car." Staunch, stocky Allan said, "That's all right. I'll stay here." He wanted to make sure I was all right. I left him standing philosophically on the grass and followed the woman up the steps of the caravan. I turned as I went in and he gave me a smile. He accepted without question that I was up to something he was not to know about. Poor Allan. He died four years later, of blood poisoning, on National Service in the Malayan jungle, one of the last defenders of the British Empire. As I went into the caravan then, though, I was relieved to have him at my back. I was not sure what I was going to find – a crone, mumbling, surrounded by bones and rags or a fat lady crouching over a crystal ball with a teacup of gin in her hand.

The interior of the caravan proved reassuring. It was clean and cheerful, with snapshots hanging on the wall, a little table with a white cloth and a vase of flowers upon it, pots of herbs in sparkling jars on a little shelf and a bright, tiny fire crackling in a miniature fireplace on one wall. In a fairly large bed in one corner, propped up on three large pillows covered in white, lace-trimmed pillowcases, lay an old lady so thin and small that there seemed to be no body at all under the sheet and patchwork quilt covering her.

The younger woman pulled a chair up beside the bed for me. I sat down. Then she went and stood with her back against the door, watching.

The old lady – so old I could not even begin to guess her age, said in a low voice, "Give me your hand, young fellow." She took my big, red hand in her little claw. The sensation was not unpleasant. Then, the weight of my hand being evidently too great for her, she lowered it gently on to the sheet in front of her. This meant that I had to bend towards her. I was not upset or alarmed, for suddenly she reminded me of my dearly loved grandmother who had died the year before.

She looked at my hand and, somehow, seemed satisfied. I said, "My father wishes to speak to you about Mary Waterhouse. I believe you told her fortune many years ago at Framlingham. Some of what you said seems to be coming true. He has an interest in hearing the rest."

"I do not doubt it," she said. "But your father will never speak to me now. I am very near my end."

"Oh, no," I said, trying to reassure her, but she cut me off. "I have little strength now, for telling the future. One thing I do know – I shall never see your father. I know this also – he is watching the girl for a master. She has the power, the girl, to bring ruin to the master. Your father obeys, like a dog."

I nodded rather doubtfully at this. I did not know whether what she said was correct. I did not believe my father was the man to act merely at someone else's bidding. However, I felt it would be wrong to burden this frail old woman with comments or questions, so I said nothing.

She went on in a high, sing-song voice, which seemed to me like a thread which might break at any moment. She said, "He wants to know what will happen to the girl so that he can make his plans to prevent it. But that is nonsense. The future is the future – knowing it does not mean that you can make plans to change it. He thinks he will send her to another country – he will not be able to do that. Better for his master if the girl were dead but she will not die. She will have a long life. Tell him this – tell your father this –" and at this point she broke off and closed her eyes for a moment, as if to gather her strength. "Tell him," she said again, "that he cannot alter the course of things. If he acts, the results will not be what he wants but only what he fears. Tell him – nothing can be changed."

She was tired. She closed lids, fragile as brown rice paper, over her eyes. I felt I could not press her any further for information. In any case I had been sent to find her, not question her.

"Come away," the woman at the door said, in a low voice. So I took my hand from the sheet where it lay and stood up. The old woman, Urania, without opening her eyes, said, "You, boy, are the important person in this business. Do not forget it." Then she added something else, of a personal nature, which shook me considerably. And, telling myself that it was foolish and primitive to have any belief in magic, fortune-telling and the like, I left the caravan.

As I walked across the windy flats, I tried to explain to Allan how little I knew of this business. I did not want him to think I was deliberately keeping secrets from him.

"Don't worry," said Allan, "and above all, don't tell me anything you shouldn't. Business is business, after all – and as far as I'm concerned we've had a good fortnight's holiday at your father's expense. I'm grateful for that." He was a gentleman, Allan, if ever I met one. Perhaps it was better that he died in one of his country's last colonial wars. He never had to discover that his standards were no longer useful or respected, the service he had been reared to give was not needed any longer.

Over dinner that night I told my father of my meeting with Urania Heron. With some trepidation I told him what she had said about his only doing his master's bidding, like a dog. When he heard this he put down the knife he had lifted in order to cut a piece of cheese on his plate, and stared ahead at the candles on the table, burning in their candelabra. And he muttered, "I wish she had not said that."

"Why not?" I asked.

"No matter," he told me. "What else?" I told him, leaving out the woman's parting remark to me, which I felt was private. At the end of my account my father said, "As to never seeing her – she's wrong. I most surely will see her. We'll start early tomorrow. You can take me to the spot. I must admit, I never thought I'd be involved in running a mad old gypsy to ground in the Romney Marshes and, God knows, I'm not superstitious but perhaps for the first time in my life I'm beginning to wonder – the old woman appears to know something – perhaps more than I do. I want to see her. Get an early night, Bert. We'll start at six tomorrow morning."

My mother, who I knew had invited guests for dinner, merely said, "Do you think you'll be back by the evening?"

"Certainly," said my father, with assurance.

And we were back for dinner the next night, but disappointed. To begin with, on the whole wide sweep of this spot in the misty and desolate marshes, we found no gypsies or caravans. We found where they had been. My father, approaching, was particularly appalled by the mess they had left behind. There was broken crockery, scattered, and splintered wood and, in the middle of what had been the campsite a large fire still smoked. The fire had fallen apart untidily. Half-burned books, more charred pieces of wood – the leg of a table, the front of a drawer – and what looked like the back of a hairbrush, lay scattered in the smouldering ashes of the fire which had obviously been abandoned, and was going out.

But, standing in the middle of all this confusion my father and I both saw plainly that this was no ordinary abandoned campsite. It was plain that whole sets of dishes had been deliberately smashed and the fragments lying about were only part of the general breakage. Then my father pointed towards the beach. Near where the sea lashed and roared there was a caravan, half-burnt, its metal struts poking up like the skeleton of a vast animal. A thin plume of smoke waved up still from it and was dispersed by the wind as it hit the pyre in great gusts, throwing up little clouds of ash. We stood together on the deserted campsite, hearing only the crying of the gulls and the sound of the tide, not knowing what to think about the scene. Then, "What's that?" he said and moved beyond where the caravans had stood. I followed him. There, under a scrubby tree, was a plot of freshly dug earth. We both looked down at it. As we stared I heard voices on the wind and two small figures, holding their arms in mystifying positions, began to come towards us. As they approached through the foggy air we saw that they were two ordinary looking men in wellingtons and corduroy trousers. They carried spades over their shoulders. They looked intently at us as they came up. "Good morning," said my father.

"Morning," said one of them.

"Do you know what all this is about?" asked my father. "This seems to be a grave. What's happened to the caravan down there?" At this point I began to feel nervous. Some violence had been done, I thought, and here was my father, alone on these marshes, asking questions in his official-sounding voice. These two men might be the originators of whatever trouble had taken place.

"What's your interest in all this?" said the second man, who was middle-aged and unshaven.

"I'm not from the police, the council or the Customs and Excise, if that's what you're thinking," said my father, who plainly had a better grasp on the situation than I had. "We're here to see one of the gypsies, on very private business. But when we arrived we found all this – and no gypsy camp. Do you know what has happened, or where they might have gone to?"

At this, both men seemed easier about the situation although they still looked as if they might have something to hide.

"Gypsy funeral," said the first man. "Leastways, they burned the body in Rye churchyard. There was more than a hundred present – some of them must have set off before she died, they reckon. But they broke her pots and pans and burned the van. It's their custom, see."

"Ah," said my father. "Of course. Was it the old woman, Urania Heron, who died?"

"That was her," said the first man. "Urania – some called her Queen of the Gypsies, though maybe that was to get custom. They have a fair old number of Kings and Queens, the travelling people. Died a rich woman, so they tell me." The other man was looking at my father shrewdly. He had him placed as some kind of official, in spite of his denials. He said, "If you're from the Inland Revenue, even you can't catch up with her now. And you'll have no luck with the survivors, either."

"Mm," said my father. Turning to me he said, "She said I'd never talk to her."

I just nodded. The two men stood silent. The second one said, "Well – if you want to find them they'll have flown to the four winds by now." It became plainer and plainer they were waiting for us to leave. In the end the second man said, "Come on, then. Let's get on with it."

The other looked at my father and muttered, "As a matter of fact, we're here for the horse." And he nodded at the patch of earth.

Light dawned on father's face, "Ah," he said. "I knew it couldn't be a human grave. This is where they've buried the horse?"

"They normally kill the horse, see," the man told him. "Not that hers was good for much anyway – old as she was, it looked. So we thought we'd come for the carcase – sell it, like. No good to anyone stuck where it is, is it?"

"No," said my father. "Don't worry – I'm not from the Inland Revenue. I came to have my fortune told," he continued boldly. "They say the old woman could tell the future."

Both men stared incredulously at my father. A less likely customer for the crystal ball and mumbo-jumbo of the gypsy's tent could not have been imagined.

"The women reckoned she could," was all the stubble-faced man could say. "I don't go in for a lot of that myself. What's the good knowing if you can't do anything about it, that's what I say?"

"I expect you're right," said my father.

"If you'll excuse us now," he said. "We'll get on. In case by chance they come back. They can get very nasty, them Romany men."

"We'll leave you to it, then," father said. "Thank you for the information."

"You're welcome," they said, and turned to their grisly work.

We walked away from the sea, hearing the gulls' noise overhead and the thud of the spades behind us. We walked across the soggy marshland to the car. "That's that, then," my father said into the wind, "– no fortune-teller for me. Pity."

"I expect it's all nonsense anyway," said I.

"I daresay," he said. "But I wish I'd met her."

1945

The war was over and Mary Waterhouse was sitting on the same train which had brought her to Framlingham four years before. Then she had been nearly five years old. Now she was nine. Then she was with all the other evacuees. Now she travelled with Mrs Gates, who was sitting opposite her. And then she had been a poorly dressed Cockney girl while now she had about her the indefinable air of a nanny's child, sitting up nice and straight in her highly polished brown sandals, very white socks and slightly starched pink and white striped cotton dress, with a small white collar. Her blonde hair was done in two plaits, which ended in pink bows.

She stared doubtfully at Mrs Gates. Then she dutifully picked up the green-bound volume of *Gulliver's Travels*, which, with its companion volume, *Robinson Crusoe*, had been Sir Frederick Allaun's sad parting present to her, and began to read. Mrs Gates sat there like a stone with the waves of semi-formulated resentments going through her head, as they had now for many days and weeks. Why hadn't those shiftless parents of Mary's come and collected her straight away, as soon as they got Lady Allaun's letter? It wasn't good enough to send an ill-written scrawl a week later, saying they were having a street party and couldn't spare the time to come down with the baby – a baby which must be three years old by now, by her calculations. A party, indeed – not to mention the suggestion that Mary should be put on the train, alone, and that they'd meet her at Victoria. What sort of people put a child of nine on a railway train alone, with the trains and streets full of demobbed soldiers and goodness knows who? And the cheeky suggestion that Mary should stay on and come home with the others in the care of a welfare worker. What business was it of theirs to make such a suggestion, when Lady Allaun had told them in so many words that Mary's room was needed for a relative, a convalescent naval officer? They must be a trashy, common lot, these Waterhouses. Advantage-takers, that's what they were. Not that poor Mrs Twining's heart wouldn't break when she had to part with Jack. And his friend Ian, but Mrs Gates had the idea that it was young Jack Bessie Twining was particularly fond of. She was herself, for that matter. Still, what had to be, had to be. She just wondered if these Waterhouses would appreciate what a good and clever lad he was when he got back. Of course, Twining could make the excuse that he needed the lads to stay on for the harvest — she just hoped that when they got to the station this "Mrs Ivy Waterhouse", as she had signed herself, would be there on time, to meet them. They sounded like a badly organized lot, with their parties and late replies to letters. All she could say, Mrs Gates thought to herself, was that if there was any confusion at the station she'd turn straight round, with Mary, and get the next train back. Let Ivy Waterhouse arrive late and she could whistle for her daughter. They'd be on the train back to Framlingham in a flash and home in time for a late tea.

Mrs Gates gave a deep sigh of anger — and found tears in her eyes. Mary looked up from her book and said, "Oh — Mrs Gates —"

"None of that," said Mrs Gates in a firm, cross voice. Mary went back to her book. She was very nervous. Mrs Gates sat up, ramrod straight, fighting her misery at parting with Mary by overlaying it with rage. There was another battle in her breast, too, where old-fashioned loyalty to her employers quarrelled with dislike, even bewilderment. For what Mrs Gates could not quite acknowledge openly to herself was that it had been wrong of Lady Allaun to write so summarily to the Waterhouses, more or less ordering them to remove the child within three weeks. The reasons behind it were shoddy and Mrs Gates also knew that. Who should know better than she, who had begun in service at the Towers when she was sixteen, and Sir Frederick only a child? — she who had looked after them, sick and well, for nearly forty years — who had been one of the only two servants invited to Sir Frederick and Lady Allaun's wedding at St James, Piccadilly? Mrs Gates knew the eddies and currents of the house as she knew her own pulse and the beating of her heart. But she could never truly admit what she knew to herself, even in thought. Servants should not talk of what they know about their masters; good servants are well advised not even to think of what they know. So Mrs Gates, in the railway carriage, trained her mind on the misdeeds of the imaginary Waterhouses to prevent the sadness and disillusion she felt from welling up.

Unfortunately, matching the puffing of the engine as it took them remorselessly towards London, came the word – "Adoption – adoption – adoption," as though it were hissing out of the funnel of the train. For the word had, and she knew it, been mentioned between Sir Frederick and Lady Allaun. An important letter had been written and the reply, which Mrs Gates had not seen arrive, had given support for the idea. The family solicitor had been summoned. Mrs Gates, without listening at a single door or laying eyes on a single letter which had not been put away, knew all this. She knew, too, that Sir Frederick had been strongly in favour of trying to adopt Mary and Lady Allaun not so keen. That squared with what Mrs Gates knew of both of them. She, for her part, had no doubt that the Waterhouses would agree to the adoption and that Mary would shortly be the legal child of the house. So what had gone amiss?

Mrs Gates's thoughts, as the train got closer and closer to London, started coming with a rush. The summerhouse – it was what had happened in the summerhouse which had put a stop to everything.

The summerhouse lay at the very edge of the lawn at the front of Allaun Towers. It stood to the left, where the hedge surrounding the kitchen garden met the rhododendron bushes. If she had not been picking peas at the time, Mrs Gates would have seen nothing. As it was she had just flung a handful of pods into her basket, which lay on the ground, and was straightening up for a moment to ease the pull on her back when she saw, over the hedge, through the rather dirty panes of the octagonal summerhouse, the child, Mary, and Sir Frederick. Mary was sitting on Sir Frederick's knee, that much she could make out, and he was apparently reading to her. The sight was not unusual. Sir Frederick often took Mary out of the house on days when she was not at school – and there had been many of these days, in April, when she had been away for three weeks with an obstinate throat infection. They would walk about the estate or, as now, go and read in the summerhouse, where there was an old basketchair, lodged in front of the doorway, which was wedged wide open due to the condition of its hinges. These reading sessions – in fact, Sir Frederick's association with Mary in general – did not entirely please Isabel Allaun, Mrs Gates knew. Truth was – and that, at least, Mrs Gates was prepared to admit about her employer – Isabel Allaun was one of those women whose jealousy of other women was profound. It was not just a question of disliking women in genuine rivalry with her. It was automatic for her to see any woman, old, ugly, poor or nine years old as a challenge and to

73

look on them with disfavour. So even her husband's affection for a little girl threatened her. In addition Lady Allaun had been jumpy ever since Sir Frederick came back. He had arrived in a strange condition, vague, tired and absent-minded. It was as if he wanted to block most things out of his mind. He slept a great deal, avoided company and read a great many detective stories. He also, as Mrs Gates knew, for she heard him, prowled about the house at night. In the morning she would find he had made tea, eaten a couple of slices of toast and then, presumably, gone back to bed without washing up his cup and plate, which stood on the kitchen table in the morning, witnesses to his lonely night. It was not surprising that Isabel Allaun, who had held the house and grounds, the three tenant farms and the small household together, alone, for five difficult years, was upset. She had looked forward to her husband's return, an easing of conditions and a return to the good old days of trips to Town and entertaining the neighbours. And what had been sent back to her after five years was a weakened man who avoided leaving his own house and grounds as if he were afraid, refused to visit or be visited, continued to leave all the responsibility to her and could not, so Mrs Gates observed, even seem to look his wife in the eye. It was as if he felt guilty towards her, she thought. And well he might, for he knew what was required of him and could not, or would not, do it. It was not good enough to pass all your time reading or just wandering about hand in hand with a little girl. He would not even pay proper attention to his own son — he often found an excuse to leave the room when Tom came in, during the week he spent at home at half term, and this was also wrong, thought Mrs Gates, who privately considered that Tom was a boy very much in need of a father's hand.

Mrs Gates had taken it on herself one morning, when getting the day's orders from Lady Allaun, to introduce the subject of shell-shock. She began by saying that the lateness of the post was probably because the postmistress was having a difficult time with her old father, who had been in the trenches in World War I and had never been quite normal since. At this, Lady Allaun, who knew what was coming, had straightened her already straight back, looked her housekeeper firmly in the eye and said, "How lucky we are that no matter how dreadful this war has been for everyone, that, at least, is one thing we have been spared. There have been no shell-shock cases from this war." Mrs Gates said no more but she knew Lady Allaun understood what she had been trying to tell her. She had been put firmly in her place. There was nothing else she could do. Nevertheless, if it was not shell-shock, thought Mrs Gates, it was something very like it.

Towards the end of the war Sir Frederick had been sent to France just after the Normandy landings. He had fought his way through Germany, ending up in one of the first parties to enter the concentration camp at Belsen, or was it Auschwitz? Whichever it was, small wonder he was like he was, Mrs Gates thought. Maybe only the presence of little, rosy Mary Waterhouse was enough to drive out the memory of the walking skeletons in the concentration camp.

Still, the mystery of what had happened in the summerhouse remained. All Mrs Gates knew was that, just as she spotted the two familiar figures in the summerhouse and, the ache in her back somewhat relieved, was about to bend down again and pick more peas, she had seen Isabel Allaun running down the lawn with an expression of great rage on her face. Mrs Gates, half-hidden behind the hedge, had stood staring in astonishment. Then Lady Allaun had stopped short, about fifteen yards from the summerhouse door and shouted, "Frederick! Come out at once!" She must have been watching them from the drawing room window but what could she have seen, from such a distance, to make her behave in such an uncharacteristic way – like a street woman, Mrs Gates thought to herself. Had she seen something or had she imagined it? Had her husband been giving Mary a kiss or a cuddle or had he really, because that was the most likely explanation for Isabel Allaun's behaviour, actually been interfering with her, molesting her, putting his hand too high on her thigh, or under her little white knickers? That was a horrible thought and Mrs Gates did not believe it. Now she was admitting to the thoughts Mrs Gates examined the situation candidly. She had seen such things before; she knew of things like this, and worse, much worse. But although Sir Frederick was not in his right mind and needed comfort – and pray God, he had not tried to find it in the child – she could not believe things had gone too far. Mrs Gates stole a look at Mary as she sat reading. She did not have the look of a child who had taken part in naughty games with a middle-aged man, but then, with girls in particular, you could seldom tell. Girls learned to conceal things like that from an early age, Mrs Gates knew that. Nevertheless, she was still sure nothing had been too wrong – until, that is, Isabel Allaun started shouting. What a scene for a lady to make. Then Mary had gone white as a sheet as Isabel stood on the grass, shouting, in a cracking voice, uncertain in its pitch, "Come out, Frederick, I tell

you." And, to silence her terrifying voice Sir Frederick had come out of
the summerhouse, over the lawn all dappled with sun, saying something in a low voice, which Mrs Gates could not hear. But she could
hear the bewilderment in his tone and he looked very bent, very old,
twenty years older than he really was.

At that point Mrs Gates had pulled herself together, slipped out of
the vegetable garden through a gap in the hedge, leaving the basket of
peas on the ground, and, trying to look as if she had just come from the
house, went to the summerhouse door, where Mary stood, dazed and
rather frightened, and had said, using as normal a voice as possible,
"Mary – I've been looking for you everywhere. You promised to go
down to Twining's for the eggs."

"Did I?" Mary answered, looking confused. "I must have forgotten." In fact she had not – Mrs Gates had made the story up on the spur
of the moment.

"You must," she had told the child. "Will you go down now, before
lunch? I must have them quickly." At that, Mary had run off, with one
startled glance at Sir Frederick and Lady Allaun, still talking, in low
voices, on the grass, oblivious to the other two, while Mrs Gates had
gone straight back to the house.

After that there were high words in the drawing room. Voices could
be heard right along the passageway and through the kitchen door,
behind which Mrs Gates tried to get on with preparing the lunch. Not
that there was any lunch. Sir Frederick took to his bed with a bottle of
whisky after the row. Isabel Allaun said that she was going out to see
some neighbours. Which, Mrs Gates worked out, must have been
when she took the letter asking the Waterhouses to collect Mary down
to the post office. So she and Mary ate their chops together in the
kitchen. And that was the end of any talk of adoption and the reason
why they were sitting together in this stuffy train, now nearly in
London, judging by the parade of shabby houses and the gaps in the
streets, like mouths with many teeth missing.

Mrs Gates sighed. It was this dreadful war which was to blame.
Without the war Mary would never have come to the Towers. Sir
Frederick would have been the same bluff, selfish fellow he had once
been. Isabel Allaun would have been the same snobbish, not unkind,
country lady, with her bridge and her shopping trips. And now Mary
had to go back to what was most likely a slum. Probably her father
drank, thought Mrs Gates, and there seemed no doubt that her mother
was a slut and a slummock, if you considered the state of the child's

clothes when she had arrived. You didn't have to be dirty, even if you were poor, thought Mrs Gates self-righteously. But all this resentment against the unknown Waterhouses now, as the train got closer and closer to Victoria, had little power to console. If only, she thought miserably, that scene outside the summerhouse had never happened. What could it have been that Lady Allaun saw? And what did that child, reading her book so calmly, really know?

It was very hot that day and the air was sweet with the flowers – I don't suppose I'd have remembered anything if it hadn't been for the sequel – Isabel going mad like that, on the lawn, with her body all straight and stiff and her blonde hair coming down out of the big, soft bun she used to put it in and her eyes all hot. She usually had those pale, cold blue eyes, Ice Maiden eyes, but this time they were blazing. But another bit of me wasn't that surprised. I knew Sir Frederick wasn't the way he should have been. Even a child, or perhaps specially a child, could spot it. I'd seen him before, remember, when he came back home on leave and then he was like Father Christmas, big and ruddy only with a little toothbrush moustache instead of a beard. After his first leave he always brought me back a present. He was always coming into the room, shouting something and picking me up and swinging me round. Those times, too, he'd try to do something about the work that needed doing because there hadn't been enough staff for years. So he'd take me with him to mend the catch on the gate to stop Twining's cows from getting into the grounds, or shoot all the rabbits which had been multiplying cheerfully for years while no one did anything about it. Those times Tom would go too, and be allowed to fire at a pigeon or so. Anyway, the last time he came, after he was released by the army, you could tell he wasn't the same. He wore the same old grey cardigan all the time. He shuffled. He'd sit in a chair in the library for hours on end, staring into space. Mrs Gates called it shell-shock when she was talking to her friends. Really, it was depression – there was less help for it then. "Mad," he sometimes whispered to himself when he thought there wasn't anyone there. "I'm mad." I walked into the library one day with a butterfly – a Red Admiral – in my hands to show him. He shuffled into the top drawer, which was open just as I came in. I pretended I didn't know what it was but I did – throughout the years, sneaking around the house opening drawers and cupboards while nobody was about, I'd been fascinated by the revolver in the top

77

drawer of the desk. It wasn't loaded, of course. I'd tried it. But I think it was that day. I think he was going to shoot himself. Better if he had really. From what I heard years later he never really recovered. The experience made Isabel worse. She was never a big-hearted woman but she must have been a lot nicer in the days when she had the life she wanted.

Anyway, there it was. Frederick Allaun was a wreck – and I was his only consolation. All I meant was a bit of life for him, I think, something to take away the taste of all those deaths. I knew there was something not quite right about it, mind you, there was the funny way his hands were always on me as if it was an accident, but it wasn't. They were big hands, always cold. I did know it wasn't the normal relationship of a child with an adult. I knew he needed me and that made me a bit uneasy, and I knew I felt sorry for him, which made me uneasy as well because, after all, children don't like to feel sorry for adults. It seems wrong to them. But I liked him. I suppose a lot of people would say I was a girl who'd been without a father for a long time. Maybe that was it, maybe it wasn't. But Frederick Allaun never went over the line, whatever it is. Well, it's the difference between big, cold hands on your body and big, cold hands right up between your legs, or worse. In a way we both knew this touching and feeling wasn't right – sometimes I'd make an excuse and shift away from him. Sometimes he'd drop his hands, which might have been round my waist, as if he'd been scalded. So I don't know what Isabel saw in the summerhouse – couldn't have been more than a peck on the cheek or something but whatever it was she couldn't bear it. She never forgave me, I don't think, not for forty years, but she was like that anyway and her own problems must have been terrible, for her to let it all out like that. Cold scenes and silences were more her style, deathly chills she could create, and rooms turning to refrigerators on the spot. But she must have been really upset to stand yelling like that. After that she'd have been so fed up with herself she would have had to get rid of me anyway – probably a hollow victory, because maybe if I'd stayed around Sir Frederick might have got back to normal.

Anyway, there it was – I got the chuck from Allaun Towers. Looking back I realise that Isabel would have manoeuvred it probably anyway. She didn't want me around taking Sir Frederick's attention away from Tom – not that he got it even after I'd gone, but she wasn't to know that. And I daresay she saw me growing up into a pretty girl and then it would have been "Mirror, mirror on the wall, Who is the fairest one of all," with her cast as the wicked stepmother. Poor old Isabel. She must have had very little happiness in her miserable bloody life. She would have done better, when she'd first polished me off, and after that Sir Fred, to have gone and got another bloke. It might have prevented Tom's ruin. Probably couldn't find anyone good enough for her.

Anyway, there I was, catapulted out of the Towers and back to Victoria before I could draw breath – my God, Ivy was a shock to me first go off, and no mistake.

Imagine it – there's me, little miss primknickers, standing on the station, which is full of smoke and absolutely filthy and horrible-smelling to a child who'd spent years in the country. It's crammed with worn-out looking people with grey faces, and soldiers and sailors, and there, suddenly, was this bleached-haired, over-made-up woman of thirty-four standing at the barrier waiting for me with a grubby little girl – or so she seemed to my countrified, upper-class eyes – and the girl's holding out a bar of chocolate to me and in a flash I'm in the arms of this woman, her bright red lips are all over my face, she smells of fags, and all in the middle of this noisy, smelly station. And it was my mother – it took my breath away. There we stood, me in the clutch of this woman, and the people pushing round us and the trains banging and snorting and belching out smoke and this common little girl, my sister, Shirley, is saying over and over again, "Here – Mary – d'you wanna bar o' choclit. Look – I brought you this bar o' choclit." It was like a horror story. Years later, when I was living in South Moulton Street with Steven Greene he put me on to reading Greek myths. One night, late, he read me out the story of Persephone, the girl who was rescued from the underworld by her mother, sort of taken back into the light and fields and so forth. I was thinking all the time, while he was reading, "My God – I remember that. Only it was my mum who took me into the underworld." I could see that station then, as clearly as I saw it when I turned up in London as a child. I can still see it now.

Of course, looking back, I realize how bloody awful it would have been to have become little Mary Allaun, and grown up in that dodgy atmosphere at the Towers. Mrs Gates wouldn't have been the be all and end all for very long. In no time I'd have been exposed to the whole lot – Isabel and her jealousy and snobberies, Tom Allaun and, worse still, Charlie Markham and then there'd have been poor old Sir Frederick . . . I was a lot better off with Sid and Ivy, in the long run, but

I wasn't half staggered at the time, I can tell you. Probably the first of a long series of shocks, I suppose.

Inside the cafeteria tea urns hissed on the counter, behind which a tired woman in an overall dealt out tea and rock buns, snapping at people who asked if there were any biscuits or cheese sandwiches. People sat close-packed at small tables.

"I hope you'll let Mary come and visit us in the holidays," Mrs Gates said, looking Ivy Waterhouse firmly in the heavily mascaraed eye. Then she looked sharply at a couple of drunk soldiers who had jogged the table as they went unsteadily towards the door.

"If she can," said Ivy in a neutral tone.

"I'm sure Sir Frederick and Lady Allaun would be only too pleased to help with the fares," said Mrs Gates, adding tactfully, "you are a big family, after all, or will be, when Jack's home again."

"It depends," said Ivy stiffly. "She'd better settle in here first, before we discuss plans." She was a proud woman and disliked the way Mrs Gates was looking at her. She knew Mrs Gates would have described her as a bit of overpainted trash, if not as something worse. She was not going to have her family's finances discussed by a woman she regarded as servant, which was not a position of dignity, as far as Ivy was concerned.

"I'd be pleased to come and collect her from here," Mrs Gates persisted, "to spare you the long journey." At this Ivy, staring into the healthy, stiffened face of Mrs Gates, thought that this was the woman who had cared for her daughter for a long time. And detected the desire to keep in touch with the child hidden by Mrs Gates's manner. She said, "I think that would be a nice idea, Mrs Gates."

And Mrs Gates, who had now had time to look behind Ivy's heavy make-up and shabby appearance — and also look round her at the others in the cafeteria, almost equally shabby, worn and strained — said, confidentially, "It could be quite a good thing for her — to keep up the connection."

"They sent her back quick enough," said Ivy. "I hope there'd be no more of that. Reading between the lines, I thought there'd been some trouble. I hope Mary done nothing wrong."

"Not a bit of it," Mrs Gates said, a little too promptly. "Results of the war. They had no choice but to send her home. Sir

Frederick told me particularly to say Mary would be very welcome for visits."

"We'll have to see then, shan't we?" said Ivy. "Shirley – stop playing with that biscuit. Eat it or leave it alone. Named after Shirley Temple she was," she told Mrs Gates. "Out of luck there, wasn't I? Look at that hair – straight as a yard of pumpwater."

Mary had been studying the little girl with some horror, as she broke up the digestive biscuit, the last one, given to her as a favour by the woman behind the counter. She was making a little pile of crumbs on the table, and then licking up the crumbs with a finger she put in her mouth before sticking it in the crumby heap. Now she looked at her sister's hair which was, indeed, very straight.

"She's a very pretty girl," Mrs Gates said. "All your children are good-looking, Mrs Waterhouse." And, thinking of Mary and Jack, "thoroughly good-natured."

"Thank you, Mrs Gates," Ivy said. "And I'd like to thank you very much for taking such good care of Mary. She couldn't have fallen into better hands."

Mrs Gates responded, equally formally, "It's been nothing but a pleasure, Mrs Waterhouse."

At this point Ivy, who since Mrs Gates's remarks about her children, seemed to have been thinking, bit her lip, bent forward and was, Mrs Gates knew, about to say something of importance. Mrs Gates sat waiting, with her hands in her lap. A momentous statement was about to be made in that crowded cafeteria. Then Ivy breathed out slightly and leaned back. She had changed her mind about speaking. Mrs Gates betrayed nothing. It would come out in the end, she reflected. Everything did. All you ever needed to do was wait. And so she stood up politely and said, "I must be going now or I'll miss my train back. Don't forget – if ever you need me, or Mary does, I'll be ready for as long as I'm spared."

"For a long time, I hope," said Ivy Waterhouse. "Mrs Gates – thank you again for all you've done." Ivy made as if to stand up but Mrs Gates said, "Don't come with me. You start your journey home," and kissing Mary on the cheek she walked steadily to the door and out of it. Ivy said, to herself, "Poor woman – it must be a blow parting with you, Mary." And Mary burst into tears.

"Eat your choclit," said little Shirley, offering the only solution she knew. "I saved my ration – I brung it all the way."

Mary gave an agonized glance over her shoulder, searching for the invisible Mrs Gates. Now that it had happened she could not believe it. She stared at Shirley as the tears rolled down her cheeks. Shirley was holding out a Mars bar, slightly soiled and softened by its long journey.

"All of it?" Mary said. Only the village children were allowed to eat their sweet ration all at once. Hers was always doled out to her in small portions by Mrs Gates, every evening, before she cleaned her teeth.

Shirley said, "Yer."

Mary took it and said, "You can have half," and broke the bar in two. "I've still got my full week's ration in my book," she said.

"I got sixpence off Dad," Shirley told her. "For coming here," she added tactlessly.

"Didn't you want to come?" Mary asked.

"I wanted to stay and help with the party," Shirley said. She was cramming the sticky Mars bar into her mouth like a famished animal. Mary looked at her despondently. She seemed like quite a nice little girl but she was ever so dirty. She thought of Mrs Gates again. Ivy quickly stubbed out her cigarette and stood up. "Come on, Mary. We're going home."

They pushed out of the station and climbed upstairs on a big, red bus. As the bus began to move Mary's fear began to evaporate. She began to feel excited. The city they passed through was very big. The buildings were huge and dark with soot. They passed the Queen's garden, at the back of the Palace and Ivy promised they could go to see it from the front, soon. There were great, wide streets, there were birds in mobs and clusters on the ledges of the buildings, there were statues of men on prancing horses and the top deck of the bus was full of people. Two of the soldiers, who wore funny uniforms, were all black. There was another one with a turban on his head. And everywhere, as they went along, sitting right in front, there were gaps between the buildings, full of rubble. "That's why we had to send you away," explained Ivy.

"London Bridge is falling down, falling down, falling down –" Mary sang. She was feeling cheerful, though a little frightened. Now they were going to have a party in all the ruins, she thought. "Build it up with sticks and stones, sticks and stones, sticks and stones –" she sang.

The big, generous buildings gave way to narrower streets, tired and battered. "Nearly home," said Ivy. "Mind you, it'll be a bit different from what you're used to, Mary. You'll have to make the best of it."

They had what seemed like a long walk from the bus stop, through some dingy streets with uneven paving stones and small shops with dusty windows. Then they walked up a street wider and busier than any Mary could remember, with a big Woolworths and a huge Home and Colonial and all sorts of shops selling clothes and shoes. In the shoe shop there was a picture of the King and Queen. There was a big Odeon. Mary hoped they would go there soon. She had seen very few films in her life. Then they walked up Treadwell Street, where small houses led straight into a dusty street. And round the corner into shabby, narrow Meakin Street.

"Here we are — home again," said Ivy cheerfully. "Looks pretty, don't it?" But to Mary's eyes it did not. The red, white and blue bunting stretched across the street from upper window to upper window did not look pretty. The twists of bunting round the lamp posts did not look pretty and the Union Jack hanging limply from three or four windows did not, equally, help to cheer the forty houses on both sides of the street. Indeed, the fresh colours only drew attention to the dirty brickwork, the small windows, with cracking paint on their frames, the peeling front doors and the general lack of freshness and openness in the terrace of small, two-storey houses, rushed up eighty years before to accommodate the Victorian working classes. Mary stared, urgently wondering which of the houses she would be living in. Then a great surge of will came over her. She thought, "Well — I'll make the best of it." She felt slightly better.

Two men, one in a khaki battledress tunic and old corduroy trousers, the other in a black suit and a shirt without a collar, were hauling a trestle table along the street.

"Hullo, Ivy," said the man in the khaki tunic, putting down his end of the trestle. "Well, well — you must be little Mary. What a great, pretty girl you've grown into, I must say. Welcome home." He stared round the street, waving like a host. "Not much — but it's home." A pale boy, older than Mary, ran up. He said, " 'Ere, Dad, let me 'elp —" and then stopped and stared at Mary. The starched dress with its immaculate collar obviously caught his attention. "My Dad's back from the Middle East," he told her. "Inne brahn?" Mary could not understand him.

"This is Jim," said the tanned man. "I expect you'll be going to Wattenblath Street School together."

Mary looked at the boy, who, Mrs Gates's training told her, was a village boy. "Well then," said Ivy, "we'd better be getting home and sprucing up for the party. 'Bye, Mr Flanders, keep up the good work. Nice man, Joe Flanders," she remarked, as she and Mary walked up the street, with Shirley running in front. "Couldn't ask for better neighbours. He's a driver on the buses, same as your dad."

Number 19, Meakin Street was the same as all the other houses. The front door, which Sid, in a cheery mood, had painted red in 1938, led straight out on to the pavement. The paint on this door, which was now cracked and peeling, was the first thing Mary recognized from the past. "It's the old door," she thought, staring at the paint, the doorknocker and the tiny iron letterbox. Inside the house was the parlour, which looked out on to the street. Behind it was the kitchen, which overlooked a small yard, where washing was hung to dry nearly every day in the week. In the yard, next to the coal bunker, was a door to the lavatory. Upstairs there were two bedrooms, papered with floral wallpaper. In one bedroom Mary would sleep, with Jack, when he returned, while Shirley would go into her parents' bedroom and sleep in a little truckle bed next to the window. There was no bathroom. The family bathed in a big metal bath which hung on the back of the kitchen door, where it gonged out a note every time the back door was opened or closed. The water for the baths, or more often bath, since normally everyone bathed in the same water, was heated by Ivy in kettles and pans on the kitchen stove. Only Sid did not participate in the weekly bath. He went on Fridays to the public baths, where there was more hot water and the towels were softer. Like pints at the pub, this was a luxury allowed to the breadwinner.

Standing in the narrow passageway, putting her key back in her handbag, Ivy said, "Come on, you two. I'll just put the kettle on and we'll have a bite before the party. I've made some lovely salmon sandwiches for the street, but we'll pinch a few in advance. Go in the parlour, Shirl, and sit down and behave yourself." And Mary followed her mother into the little kitchen and looked out through one of the windows beside the door into the narrow yard. Ivy, putting the kettle on, said, "I'm sorry, gel. Bit riches to rags, isn't it? But think of all the poor souls who haven't got anywhere to live — we should be very grateful."

"I'll have to make the best of it," said Mary. Ivy looked at her and burst out laughing. "You've no bleeding choice, Mary Waterhouse," she told her.

84

Mary had a job eating as they sat round the small dining table in the parlour, which otherwise had in it nothing but a small suite of furniture, two armchairs and a sofa, upholstered in a hard brown material known as leatherette. She gagged on the sandwich, which was filled with tinned salmon on slices of margerined bread. She had a hard job not to pull a face when she drank her tea, which was at once bitter and very sweet, being strong and full of sugar. At Allaun Towers she had never been offered, or wanted, tea. Now, in Meakin Street, she had too much sense to ask for a glass of milk. "There's no cows for miles," she thought to herself. Then she, Ivy and Shirley went out into the street to help with the party – spreading sheets on the trestles, assembling the sandwiches and biscuits, chatting with the other neighbours. For Mary the whole thing took the quality of a dream. This morning she had woken in her bed at Allaun Towers to the sound of calling wood pigeons. Now, this afternoon, she was carrying plates and setting them down incongruously on tables laid out in a narrow, dusty, London street.

Under the bunting the line of trestles was covered with cakes and biscuits and sandwiches. There was Tizer and lemonade for the children and two big enamel bowls in the middle of the table containing an apple and an orange for everybody in the street. On the pavement, under a lamp, was a piano, contributed by the Fainlights at number 21. They were an elderly couple who considered themselves a cut above the rest. The piano was a symbol of this superiority and it was only when accused of a want of patriotic fervour on a day of national rejoicing that they had consented to its being moved out into the street. Now, at the piano, wearing a black hat and with her handbag firmly placed on top, Mrs Fainlight sat playing *Pale Hands I Loved*. And front doors began to open and the guests who were not already running up and down the street on errands began to emerge. With the exception of the babies, the too-old and the sick, the whole street sat itself down, ready for the beano. Mrs Fainlight struck up some selections from Gilbert and Sullivan. Red-headed Harry Smith said cheekily to Joe Flanders, "This is a bit morbid, innit – wot no *Roll Out the Barrel*?" and Joe Flanders had said to him, "Keep your mouth shut, Harry. It's her piano. Any complaints and she'll have us hauling it back inside." Meanwhile the real barrel had already been opened and the bung put in. The men carried foaming tankards about with them, smacking their lips and calling out to each other, while the women and children told them to sit down so that they could all turn to. Up a ladder a thickset man was adjusting some bunting to a lamp post, while down below his mate stood holding a pint mug in each hand with his foot on the bottom rung.

"If you fall," he called up, "for Gawd's sake fall away from me and the beer."

The man up the ladder grinned down, pointing in the direction of Mrs Fainlight, still thumping away, indicating that should he fall he would be sure to fall on her. At this point Mrs Fainlight changed over to *Less Than The Dust Beneath Thy Chariot Wheels*. The man at the foot of the ladder mimed pulling it away.

"Sid!" called Ivy from the table. "Are you mad? What're you doing up a bleeding ladder when our Mary's just come back."

"Gawd!" Sid exclaimed, turning his head sharply. "Well, I never did —" and at this came hurrying down the ladder. "Mary, love. I reckoned you wouldn't be here yet. I'm just coming up the street when they urged me up a ladder. Well —" He hugged her then held her at arm's length. Finally he said, "What a lovely little girl. And aren't we glad to have her back."

Mary looked at him wordlessly. He was still in his bus driver's uniform, red in the face, holding the tankard the ladder-holder had thoughtfully thrust into his hand. He had very blue eyes. She smiled and said, "Hullo, Dad." A sharp voice behind called out, "Mary! Mare — hey, Mary!" It was Cissie Messiter, skinny as a rake, hurrying up as fast as she could come, with a huge, rather dirty toddler clutched to her. "Long time no see," she said over the child's head. "Where's Jack?"

"He's in Framlingham, Mr Twining wanted him on the farm," said Mary.

"Poor old Jack — miss the party," Cissie said. "Here — move over. I can't stand up any longer with this lump. How am I expected to enjoy myself carting this lot around the whole time?"

"Is he your brother?" asked Mary.

"Yes," said Cissie. He's called Arthur — the names Mum's given us are shocking. Talk about old-fashioned — I'm changing my name to Sandra when I get older. When did you get back?"

"In the afternoon," said Mary.

"Oh — in the afternoon, your ladyship," said Cissie, mocking Mary's accent. "You'll have to drop that posh voice now you're back here — the other kids'll bash you if you don't — coo, it's lovely to see you back."

"Thanks," said Mary, touched. "Shall I hold the baby for a little while? You could go and play."

Cissie looked at her dubiously, "I don't think so," she said. "Anyway, I'm stopping here. I want my tea. When're they going to set us off?"

"Waiting for the vicar," Sid told her glumly.

"What for?" said Cissie.

"He's going to ask a blessing. Mrs Fainlight and one of the other women insisted," he said. "Seems a bit unnecessary to me."

"You're a rotten heathen, that's why," said Ivy.

"Haven't seen you in church since our Shirley was christened," said Sid. "Shift up, Arnold," he said to the man opposite Cissie and Mary. "Let me sit down opposite our Mary. It's been too long since I seen her."

Cissie was carrying out a running commentary for Mary. "Look – there's Peg's mum – she's had a drop or two. Lipstick inches thick – swaying to and fro – who's that behind her? It's that GI, the one what gives her the gum and the fags and the chocolate bars for Peg. My mum says that won't be all he gives her if she don't watch out – ooh, there's Mrs Flanders in her new dress. Oh, hullo, Mrs Jones," she said, as a plump woman of about thirty-five came past in high-heeled shoes and a tight red dress. Behind her marched a red-faced sergeant in United States army uniform. "See those nylons?" said Cissie. "Did you hear – no, you wouldn't have – well, old Tom comes in the stables early one morning to harness up his horse and who comes down the stairs from her place but – guess what? – a blackie. I'm not lying – black as the ace of spades he was, said old Tom. His hands and all – what do you think of that?"

"An African?" asked Mary, thinking of the pictures in her book at Framlingham.

"African?" said Cissie. "Oh, cor, where have you been? Half these Yanks are black, didn't you know? They got taken there to be slaves hundreds of years ago and they never let them go home. Dad – Dad," she called out to a thin man passing by. "Did you bring me any sweets, Dad?" But the thin man just walked past on the pavement. "He's well away," said Cissie philosophically. "Believe it or not, he's had six pints already. At least. Look – there's Mannie."

Mannie Frankel came up. He was much taller than Mary remembered. "Mary just come back from the country this afternoon," Cissie explained. "Bet that's a relief after all them fields and cows," said

Mannie. "Here – when are we going to get our tea?"

"Waiting for the vicar," said Cissie.

Mannie said, tactfully, "D'you bring any eggs with you, Mare?"

"No," Mary said, "I never thought."

Two women now dragged a huge tea urn, hissing and spitting, up the street on a baby's pram and hoisted it on to the table. Some men rolled another beer cask past the table and set it on a crate at the other end. On the pavement Cissie Messiter's cousin Dorothy danced, slowly, with another girl, to the sounds of Mrs Fainlight's *Onaway, Awake, Beloved*. Children left the table to play and were called back.

Passing the piano Cissie's dad sang, "Roll me over in the clover. Roll me over in the clover and do it again."

"George!" came Mrs Messiter's anguished voice from the tea urn.

"Hasn't anyone in this street got a gramophone," moaned Mannie Frankel.

"I'm not sitting here a minute longer waiting for the vicar," Sid declared. "By the time he turns up there won't be nothing worth blessing – look, there's flies all round them cakes."

"There he is," said Cissie, pointing. It was Mr Burns, the schoolmaster, in a black suit, coming round the corner with the vicar, in his dark suit and dog collar.

"Let's hope he keeps it short," Sid said audibly.

From the head of the table the vicar gave a short address, thanking God for the Allied victory over the forces of darkness and calling a blessing down on the celebrations of the proud and humble alike. With a grateful "amen" from some of the men and women round the table and a mutter of general agreement from the others, the children let rip with their sticky fingers and, as soon as the vicar had disappeared round the corner, the men called out vigorously for more beer.

"Now then, Mrs Fainlight," Ivy called encouragingly. "Come and have a break and have your tea."

"How about a knees-up?" called out Cissie's father.

"Ignore him," said Ivy. "He's drunk."

"I can see that perfectly well myself," replied Mrs Fainlight, distantly, taking up her bag and going down the table to where Lil Messiter and a friend were filling the big, white china cups with tea. Arthur, the baby, knocked over his lemonade. Mary, now famished, ate three buns before anyone could stop her. Not, she suspected, that anyone here would. Sid, in fact, looked at her approvingly. "That's my girl," he said.

"Nice cup of tea, Mrs Fainlight," Lil Messiter said encouragingly. The tea cups went round the table.

"Thank Christ it's all over," said Sid, holding a cheese sandwich. "D'you know I don't think, till I sat down here, I realized it."

"No more rationing," said Ivy feelingly.

"No more fighting," said Joe Flanders, appearing at Sid's shoulder with a mug of beer.

Marge Jones appeared, still swaying, at the end of the table, with her American. It caused a slight chill. People did not really like English-women to associate with Americans – it was felt to be a minor form of collaboration. But Marge said, "Here, folks. Marvin's got his camera. He wants to take a picture of us all – how about it?"

Finally, after a lot of pushing and shoving and shifting of places and slappings of children, and clearings of debris from the table so that it would look nice and fresh, Meakin Street arranged itself, standing and sitting along the length of the table.

Young Jim Flanders stood on a chair at the top, by the tea urn, solemnly playing God Save the King on his mouth organ and old Granny Smith, whom the rowdy Smith family had only just remembered to haul out of the house, was right at the bottom in her wheelchair. Beside her stood old Tom Totteridge, an elderly man in a flat cap and collarless shirt, solemnly holding the bridle of his horse, Tony. In the middle Ivy and Mrs Messiter stood side by side, like a wedding couple, both holding the handle of Ivy's breadknife, which was posed over the big, iced VE Day cake. As Marvin stood ready on the other side of the street there was complete silence but for Jim, still playing his mouth organ. The shutter clicked and all Meakin Street took up the end of the song "Happy and glorious, Long to reign over us. God save the King." The people who had been on the other side of the table then went back into position and the jolly, often tipsy, street party went on.

Nevertheless, there were sad memories, even though no one referred to them – memories of air raids, of the Jypps, who had lived at number 35, next to the stables where old Tom kept his horse, and who had been blown to pieces, along with the house, during the blitz. There was the gap too, where number 7 and number 9 Meakin Street had once stood, until hit by a doodlebug only the year before. Both families had been out, down at the Marquis of Zetland at the bottom of Meakin Street, so luckily the only casualty was an old lady who lived upstairs who had been flung out into the street when the rocket hit. She was a mass of broken bones when the rescue squad picked her up and she never stopped asking for a cup of tea all the way to the hospital. So there were the gaps in the buildings and gaps in families, too. Mrs Sinclair, a widow, had refused to come to the party. Her only son had been killed at Tobruk. Two other men had died, one on the Atlantic convoys, one in Germany. In spite of the victory, everyone was tired. They all knew the general loss.

As evening came the street lamps went on and darkness seemed to take away the memories. The adults had all had a drink or two, the children ran wild, rushing to and fro and shouting louder and louder. Mary, still a dazed stranger, ran with them, in and out of houses, seeing here a proudly kept room, with glass ornaments on the mantelpiece and well swept grate beneath, there an upstairs room where a whole family lived – beds covered with dirty blankets, a grate filled with uncleared ashes, a pile of clothes in a corner. In one house a baby lay in a cot, screaming himself hoarse. In another a row of three wooden elephants brought back by an old soldier who had been in the Indian army, marched across a table. "Let's pinch them," said bold, ginger-headed Harry Smith. But the others told him not to. In Tom Totteridge's stable on the corner old Tony snorted and shifted on his straw. From upstairs came thumps and whispers from Marge Jones and her Marvin. The children clustered in the doorway turned and fled.

In the middle of the street beer kegs now stood on the tables. The older or quieter residents had disappeared and Joe Flanders had captured the piano – although Mrs Fainlight looked out continually from behind her clean net curtains to make sure nothing was happening to it. Joe was thumping out the old favourites which, as everyone got drunker, swung between sentimentality and cheerfulness:
"If I could plant a tiny seed of love" everybody sang,
"In the garden of your heart,
Would it grow to be a great big flower one day
Or would it pine and fade away?"
There was *Knocked 'Em In the Old Kent Road* and a few choruses of *Maybe It's Because I'm a Londoner*, which brought tears to Ivy's eyes. Joe Flanders, who secretly fancied her, slid his arm round the piano and gave her buttocks a squeeze, shouting out quickly, to prevent a protest, "Come on everybody – how about a knees-up?" The old rallying cry got everybody going. As the door of the Marquis of Zetland swung to and fro the street filled with the sound of singing and

the dance began. Some danced in couples, Sid with Ivy, old Mrs Messiter with old Tom Totteridge, Marge Jones, who had reappeared with Marvin, teaching the steps to the amazed American. Some danced alone, hands on hips, doing the peculiar ducking and bending step which must have been taken from some ancient country dance and was now the special property of Londoners having a good time. Everyone joined in, even little children like Shirley dancing away by herself on the pavement, her face puckered with concentration as she watched the others to make sure she got it right. Even Mary, still in the carefully-laundered dress and little white socks, now very grubby, joined in holding Harry Smith's hand.

"Knees up, Mother Brown,
Knees up Mother Brown –
Under the table you must go,
Ee i, ee i, ee i oh.
If I catch you bending
I'll cut your head right off.
Knees up, knees up,
Don't get the breeze up
Knees up, Mother Brown."
Then everybody shouted "Oi!" loudly.

"One more time," shouted Marvin, carried away by it all. So they started up again but Mary, winded, tired and a bit alarmed by Harry Smith, who was a bad, wild boy, strolled away from the music and dancing alone and was quite pleased to find herself at the top corner of Meakin Street, under the lamp, while lower down the celebration went on. Standing there, opposite Tom Totteridge's stable, she felt a little afraid but, suddenly, quite calm.

On the other side of Wattenblath Street the high wall loomed. Mary crept a little closer to the corner of Meakin Street and peered round it, to see what the other street looked like. There, to her left, outside one of the little houses, she saw the figure of a man in a dark suit. He stood under one of the lamp posts, which tilted slightly into the street. He was standing very still. Mary got frightened and ducked back round the corner. She was about to set off down Meakin Street towards the people when a voice called out, "Mary." She jumped. Her little heart banged in her chest. Biting her bottom lip she took a step forward and peered round the corner again, ready to run like the wind.

"Are you Mary?" asked the man. He had not moved from under the lamp post, but stood there, black and still. The voice was like Sir

Frederick's but steadier and more reassuring. He sounded kind. A little lamplight fell on his face, which was long and mild.

"I'm Mary," she said from her corner.

"Will you come her for a moment? I promise I shan't hurt you," he said.

She hesitated, then went up to him. He put his thumb gently under her chin and turned her face upwards, towards his. She met his eyes, which were blue. He looked quite kind and reliable, the sort of man, she thought, who would know what to do, and do it, if you were in any trouble.

"Are you happy to be back?" he asked, quite gently.

"I don't know," said Mary. In a rush she said, "I think I liked it better in the country."

"Try to be happy here," he said after a pause. "And good," he added.

This encouragement made Mary resolve to try but it also confirmed her view that the return to Meakin Street was no great piece of good luck.

"Well – I shall," she said, in a voice which surprised her by its own firmness.

"That's a good girl," he said. "I know you will."

"I think I'd better be getting back," said Mary, growing suddenly uneasy. After all, it was dark and although this man did not look like Alec, from Craye's farm, who could catch you in the dark and do nasty things to you, there was no way of telling, really, what he was like.

"Yes – I expect you must," he said. Then he bent down and gave her a brief, dry kiss on the cheek. "Run along now," he said.

And Mary ran off, calling out "Goodbye," as she ran. When she reached the corner she turned, quickly, to get another look at him but he had disappeared. Perhaps he had backed into the shadows. Perhaps he had walked quickly off in the other direction. Perhaps he was just moving in the darkness between two lamps. Mary ran back to the party and found Ivy leaning over the piano, singing, "There'll be blue skies over, the white cliffs of Dover –" and she pulled at Ivy's hand saying, "Please – can I go to bed now?"

"'Course, love," said Ivy. "Shirley's been tucked up for a long time." Ivy took her hand and led her back to number 19. After a hasty wash with a flannel and a rummage through her case to find her little rose-sprigged nightdress, Mary was in her little iron bedstead, next to Shirley, who was fast asleep. Her eyes were shutting as Ivy left and went back to the street. Mary, wondering vaguely how the man in the black suit had known her name, grew dozier and dozier. And so, as Meakin Street sang *Keep The Home Fires Burning* under her window, Mary Waterhouse fell into a dreamless sleep on her first night back in London.

It was only years later that my father confessed to me about the visit he had paid to Mary in Meakin Street on VE Night. Of course, he knew he should not have gone and sought her out, or drawn himself so obviously to her attention. He said he thought that his visit would be overlooked in the confusion and that he had not, in any case, meant to speak to her. He was leaving, after having watched her for a little while from the end of the street, when he saw her peeping round the corner at him. The temptation to get a better look at her and say a few words of encouragement evidently proved too strong. In fact all this was rather uncharacteristic of my father's ordinary behaviour which was, above all, correct—too much so, perhaps. He told me that he was standing on a terrace, overlooking a carefully cultivated London garden and hearing, in the distance, the hooters, the car horns blaring, the singing and the cheering, when he suddenly felt that he must go and observe his little charge and see how she was managing in her new surroundings. An ounce of information gained by personal observation was often worth a pound gathered from documents. But I still believe that on that night of high emotion my father gave way to an impulse. He told me that what he saw that night disturbed him. He even partly foresaw what was going to happen – although, as he said, it would have taken a playwright to imagine the full extent of the disaster. After his visit to Meakin Street that night he made the most earnest representations to those involved, urging them strongly to remedy Mary's situation without delay. He said that such a child, with evident intelligence and courage, and the promise of beauty, could not be rescued soon enough from that mean street. He saw clearly that in that context the lack of attributes like brains or looks might be better for her – would probably give her a more peaceful life, keep her out of trouble. But for all his urgings it was decided not to interfere. He had to submit. Of course what happened proved him perfectly right – perhaps it was a mercy that he did not live long enough to see exactly how right he had been. Nevertheless, he told me that the spectacle of that child, in the fresh dress so carefully put on her by Mrs Gates at

Framlingham, standing in a bleak London street, alone, at almost eleven o'clock, with a smear of dirt on one cheek and of jam on the other, not knowing the extent of her own bewilderment, was very upsetting. He even confessed to a strong desire to kidnap her then and there.

He knew the lives of the workers on his own estates, of course, but that was completely different. I imagine that Meakin Street, out in force for a celebration, must have startled him. The idea of Mary, child of the gentry, suddenly dumped down there horrified him.

I'm forced to say, though, that just as he had no idea of the way the country was about to go, so he had no idea about the sort of conditions which help a growing child to become whole. In his day parents barely saw their children and fathers were particularly cut off from their own progeny. My father could comprehend the immediate social aspects of Mary's removal from Framlingham to Meakin Street but he could not understand that there might be ways in which Mary would be better off as part of a poor, but sane, family, than trapped in the frozen web at Framlingham. However this is speculative. No one could have anticipated the real consequences of leaving her in Meakin Street. In the event it was a grave mistake.

1952

Wyckender Street, in mid-February, is deserted. For a long, straight half mile the street lights throw pools of light at intervals on to the frosty pavements and over the ends of small neglected front gardens. There, uneven paths lead up to little houses with darkened windows. In some places there are weedy, brickstrewn gaps, where houses once stood. That is one side of the street. On the other runs a tall, brick wall, nine feet high, which hides the railway sidings where unseen trains clank their couplings restlessly. Occasionally a train rushes through the sidings. Occasionally there is a melancholy, muffled whistle from behind the wall. Now, a cutting, icy wind blows up Wyckender Street, past the wall on one side and the houses, shabby with post-war neglect, on the other.

Up the cold and treeless street come three girls, high heels ringing on the icy pavement. They are huddled in big coats and they turn round sometimes to giggle or shout a remark to the three boys mooching along behind them.

"Come on, Joe. 'Ave a go," cries out the boldest girl in a mocking voice. She stops deliberately under a broken street light on the pavement by the bleak line of the brick wall. Hard light from the unprotected lamp falls on bright, fair hair. The other two girls walk on, a little faster than before. "Well —" says one in a shocked voice, glancing back at the figure under the street light.

"She's getting a thoroughly bad name for herself in our street," says the other. "She's out till all hours with Jim Flanders. Her mum can't do nothing about it." The speaker is Cissie Messiter. Heavy pancake make-up, black mascara and bright lipstick do not quite disguise her starveling's face. Her sparrow's legs are a little bowed and she walks with a short tripping step to keep her shoes on. She buys them from a stall in the market and they are usually too wide for her narrow feet.

Behind them, the other two boys pass the couple under the lamp, who are pressed together, kissing. "Aye, aye," they call. They start whistling. The boy, Jim Flanders, lets the girl go. "Take no notice, Jim," says the girl. Her coat is open. Underneath it she is wearing a pencil-slim black skirt and a tight red sweater. Her head, now thrown back slightly, is covered in little golden curls. Her face, heavily powdered, is rather pale under the street lamp, and her eyes are very wide, fringed with curly brown lashes. Her mouth is wide, soft and, at this moment, parted in pleasure and delight. There is practically no future at the laboratory, the steel foundry or in the lecture room for girls who look like this one. All these places are run by men and no man looking at a girl like this will be able to treat her the way he treats everyone else. She does not really understand, as she clutches Jim Flanders under a lamp in Wyckender Street, freezing in her tight sweater and skirt from C and A Modes and her thin, but voluminous coat, that her face and figure will make her future. But they will.

"Oh, Jim. I do love you," says Mary Waterhouse.

"I love you, Mary," says Jim. The heels of the others have ceased to sound on the pavement now. Jim and Mary are alone in the street.

"Let's go over there," Jim says, nodding at the other side of the street.

"All right," says Mary without hesitation. Other girls might argue, or pretend resistance, have to be half-dragged across the street – but not her. So hand in hand they cross the street, Jim, a tall and well set-up lad with his brown hair slicked down on his head, and Mary, tall, energetic and shapely. They go into the gap where two houses once stood. Spring surges through their bodies, even on this cold night.

Mary lies, half under Jim, on the bomb site. They are right up against the back wall of the garden which once belonged to the shattered house. He can still see her face dimly in the light from the street. Her mouth is soft, the corners slightly lifted. Her eyes are dimmed and blurry with pleasure. Although she is lying in a small hollow where cold earth and frozen grass cover the remains of an air raid shelter, she might model for a cameo of an early nineteenth-century beauty.

"Oh, Jim," she breathes out. She is helpless.

They do not know it, as they embrace, but underneath them in the remains of a fur coat, with a small string of seed pearls round her skeleton throat, lies Mrs Thompson's body, entombed permanently in

98

her own air raid shelter. The rescue team thought she was in Bournemouth so they did not bother to look for her.

Joe runs his hand up under Mary's sweater and feels her breast, in its tight, uplift bra. They kiss, bruising their lips against each other. Mary's hand, clutched in Jim's hair, pulls. Her other hand, tugging out his shirt, runs up his back. As they strain there on the ground, first fighting, then exhausted, panting and staring into each other's faces, muttering, fighting again to find more of each other, as the tide rises again, they are like two animals locked in a death struggle. Jim puts Mary's hand on his trousers, where his hard cock lies. He groans, "Mary – Mary." His hand runs up her leg, past her stocking top to between her legs, feeling the wetness of her knickers. "Ah," she says. Mary unbuttons his fly and, with their hands in each other's secret places they withdraw a little, chilled, frightened, and then return to kissing again, kissing each other's mouths, eyes, cheeks, breathing sobbing, misty breaths into each other's faces. But they, themselves, are not cold now. Across the road carriages are shunted noisily into position and joined together. In an upper window, at the house next to the bombsite, a light goes on. Mary and Jim do not hear the noise of the trains, or see the light shining into the next door garden.

"Somebody down there on the bombsite again," says a fat man in striped pyjamas at the window, to the hump under the blankets which was his wife.

"They ought to fence it off – I've told them," says her sleepy voice. A surge of mixed resentments go through her sleep-fogged brain.

"Some poor, silly bitch getting herself into trouble," says the man.

"He's enjoying it," thinks his wife. "Beast. Peeping Tom." She mutters, "No business of yours."

"They ought to fence it off," he says and crosses the floor, getting back into the bed and making it creak.

His wife, feeling the bed lurch like a ship at sea, rolls over, turning her back on him.

Behind the wall a train whistles and goes by.

Mary's hand is round Jim's hard cock, now, inside his underpants. "I love you so much, Jim," she says.

"It's up to her to stop me," is the thought which goes through his mind. "A man can't help himself." But Mary would not stop and so, wrestling with their clothes, Mary's skirt, which would not go up over her hips because it was so tight, and Jim's pants and trousers, which would not go down without a struggle, and with many breaks and

99

pauses, to fumble with clothing, to kiss and mutter and continue again, the scene continues. All the pauses, breaks, mutters, are points where Mary should make a choice. They are the intervals at which she should decide to call a halt but, after so many embraces at the back of the dance hall, in doorways, on this very bomb site on the way home, Mary is not going to stop. She is tired of partial satisfactions, of encounters which sometimes left Jim spent and gasping while she was still unsatisfied. Without making a conscious decision, she is going on.

And so, finally, Jim enters her. Gasping with shock and pleasure her eyes open and she sees what she will never forget – the bricks of the wall they lie near, the lines of cement criss-crossing the bricks, the jagged crack in the wall, running from top to bottom. Jim takes her as she lies there, sobbing in pain and delight.

When he has finished they lie still and then, slowly, feel the cold around their bodies. Mary grows conscious of rough ground under her bottom, a piece of stone sticking into her back.

They stare at each other in the dimness. "Oh – that was lovely, Mare," Jim murmurs. Mary smiles at him. "Oh – we shouldn't have," he tells her.

"Never mind," she says. "It was lovely." Even at that moment Jim knows it should have been Mary, expressing the regret.

"We shouldn't have," he says again. "Did it hurt?"

"Not much," she says. "But it does now. The ground's hard." Then, totally belying what she had just said, her hand comes round his cock again.

"Better go, Mary," he says.

"All right, then," she says.

They struggle into their clothes and walk off the bomb site, hand in hand, in silence. Now they seem strangers to each other. The act has emphasized their differences. Moreover, they have to part now. Jim has to go to his house. Mary has to go to hers. They reach the end of Wyckender Street. "I'd better tidy myself up before I go in," Mary says. "Ivy'll kill me if I turn up like this." She begins to straighten her stocking seams and pat at her hair. Suddenly she feels awful. She wants Jim to say something loving to her, but somehow he will not, or cannot. What he says is, "Be in bed, won't they?"

"Most likely," Mary says, "but they've got the TV now."

"Keeps them out of bed, I suppose," Jim says. And Mary replies glumly, "It's the novelty of it."

They walk up Meakin Street in silence. On the step Jim says, "Oh, Mary. I love you, you know."

"I love you, too, Jim," Mary says.

"Come round for you after work?" he asks.

"Oh, yes," she says. They embrace and he goes off down the silent street. At the bottom of the street, rounding the corner, he waves to her.

The house is dark when she gets in. She can see through the open doorway of the front room that Jack has not come in. He now sleeps on the front room settee as there is no room for him upstairs. As she gets to the landing Ivy's voice calls sleepily from the other bedroom, "You in, Mary?"

"Yes, mum," she calls back.

Mary undresses in the cold, pulls on her nightdress and gets into bed. Shirley, three feet away, in the other bed, does not stir. She is very tired, Mary, as she lies there, feeling the stickiness on the inside of her thighs, and gazing through her little cold window pane at the hazy stars in the hazy London sky. She wishes Jim were there beside her, warm in bed. But she is happy, just the same.

"So that's it," she thinks languidly. "It's lovely, really. Easy. Natural. So that's what they all go on about. Better keep it from Ivy." Then she thinks, "I do love Jim. I really do." Feeling contented, happy and safe, Mary Waterhouse falls asleep.

"She hated her wedding – got stinking drunk on a big glass of sherry the night before," reports Ivy, standing in the street, with her shopping bag, to her friend, Lil Messiter.

"I loved mine," says Lil. "Thought I was the Queen of England. I soon found out otherwise," she adds, looking down at the bulge below her waist. Ivy's eye follows hers. Neither woman says anything. A fifth child at the age of thirty-eight is no good for a woman, especially one in Lil Messiter's state of health. It is so bad, in fact, that you can't say anything about it. Even in 1952, with better medical treatment and care for everyone under the National Health Scheme, an exhausted and slightly undernourished woman can still have a bad time, even die, in childbirth and both the women know it. Ivy reflects, standing in the hot, dusty street, that in Lil's shoes she would have got rid of the kid, no matter what the cost, just like she did before once, after Jack and before Shirley. In fact she would not have become pregnant in the first place. There is free contraceptive advice nowadays and Ivy takes it. She has got herself a job in a breadshop, and she is buying a television on the instalment plan. But this is not the time or the place to state her attitudes or point out her own, luckier, position. All she says is, "Who'd be a woman?"

"Well," says Lil, shifting her shopping bag from one thin hand to the other, to take the weight off one arm, "Your Mary should be all right in that way, at her age. Does the hospital say she's all right?"

"Yes," says Ivy. "She's healthy enough so I suppose that's something to be thankful for. Silly cow – I told her to stop messing about with Jim Flanders. Now she's having a kid, at sixteen years of age."

"They don't listen to you," says Lil. "Oh, Gawd. I'd better go. They'll be back from school soon, wanting their tea."

Ivy watches her friend, very gaunt and thin, moving up the road in an old, bulging, black skirt and faded blouse. She herself is wearing a new, bottle green rayon suit with the skirt at a long and fashionable length. Her hair is still blonde and her lips are still red. She walks up to number 3 Meakin Street, next to the pub, and knocks twice on the door. After a pause there are feet on the stairs and her daughter, Mary, opens the door. She is wearing a narrow black skirt and a maternity smock covered in red roses. Her hair is still short but the cunning bubble cut is growing out. She is pale, and a little puffy in the face, like a flower which has half-opened and now is beginning to droop.

"Come in and have a cup of tea, mum," she says, glad of the break.

"Thought you might like a few oranges – they're good for you," says Ivy, following her up the stairs to the two rooms in which Mary and her husband, Jim, now live. In the room they go into there is an old, plum-coloured moquette suite of a sofa and two armchairs and that, apart from a small table, is all. The small window looks out on to the backs of the other houses. Mary makes a pot of tea in the little kitchen opposite this room. She brings it in and puts it on the table. Her mother goes and fetches the cups, the milk and the sugar. The kitchen, with its ancient gas stove, small sink and second-hand kitchen cupboard, is clean enough for a hospital but the whole flat, Ivy thinks suddenly, looks bare, as if it had been got ready for letting. There is not an ornament, not a bit of knitting, not a pair of shoes lying about to convince a stranger that anyone actually lives there. It looks unnatural, thinks Ivy.

The bedroom, into which she peeps on her return from the kitchen, is even more discouraging. There is the bed, with its grey blankets, neatly made, pillows side by side, and there is the wardrobe, door shut, and there is the chest of drawers, drawers closed, top well dusted. The corners of Ivy's mouth turn down. Thought so, she says to herself.

"What are you doing, mum?" Mary calls angrily from the other room.

"Nothing, Mary," says Ivy and goes into the little front room. "How are you?" she asks, as she put the cups down.

"All right," says Mary. "It's depressing, all this."

There is nothing left of Miss Mary of Allaun Towers – nothing left of bad Mary, terror of the railway sidings, from Meakin Street, either. There's just Mary Flanders now, sixteen years old and pregnant.

She could have done anything with her life, thinks Ivy, her mother. Instead here she is with Jim Flanders, garage mechanic, with a baby on the way. Just sixteen. Poor Mary. Done for, unless she has some luck, poor little cow.

The truth was that the post-war years had made a difference to the way Ivy Waterhouse thought about life. World War II had in some ways broadened people's horizons. Many of Ivy's friends and relations had seen foreign countries, at the government's expense. Everyone had had the chance to look round the inside of other people's houses, broken open by German bombs. For five years stress had been laid on equality – equal struggle, equal fear and equal rations. Anyone in Meakin Street could see the difference between today's children, bred on allocations of milk, orange juice and dried egg, and yesterday's, bred on the dole, scanty wages and desperation. The war ended and a socialist government was returned overwhelmingly. A massively egalitarian programme of reforms was introduced. This, coupled with a boom in all trades due to post-war reconstruction, meant that working-class people were richer and more confident of their rights. As far as the Waterhouses were concerned the increased wages meant a better standard of living.

The rights meant that they could call in a doctor, free, when someone was ill, that bright little Shirley would be able to go to a grammar school later and learn Latin if she wanted to, that even Lil Messiter, with her poor health and household of children, would have an allowance of money for the younger children, no matter what her husband did with his wages and would get proper medical care when the time came for her to have the new baby.

So it was small wonder that Ivy regarded her daughter, Mary, so gloomily. Things were better now. Girls didn't have to be trapped in an early marriage because there was no alternative. And from what she saw, Ivy concluded that Mary was not even happy in her folly. She'd been better off playing the giddy goat up West, like she had, Ivy thought to herself as she walked back down Meakin Street after her visit to Mary. Better doing time in prison for that matter. Surest way to sentence someone for life, that was, she thought – to saddle them with a husband and kid at sixteen years old. At least she, Ivy thought, had had something before it all started – a couple of day trips to Brighton, staying daringly at a boarding house, wearing a brass ring from Woolworth's and pretending to be married – cockles and mussels and going to the fair, dancing on the pebbles on the beach. And she'd been in love with Sid, too, and from what she saw Mary was not in love with Jim Flanders now, and probably never had been, worse luck for both of them. At this point Ivy suppressed the memory of Mary's sobbing confession, in the kitchen one day when she came home from work, and of her own scream – "You stupid little bitch!" – She also forgot the smacking blow round the face she had delivered, which had sent her daughter staggering back against the wall. Then she had flung on her coat and run up the street to Joe and Elizabeth Flanders' house. She had begun to knock repeatedly on the new doorknocker, shaped like a galleon, on their newly-painted door. By that time heads were coming out of windows. The Smith boys, loitering home, paused on the pavement to stare at Ivy Waterhouse, her coat unbuttoned, flying up the street to the Flanders' house. "Whoops-a-daisy," said Harry Smith to his brother, "Mary's been and gone and done it, now."

"Looks like it," said the other. "Silly cow."

In the meanwhile Joe Flanders had come to the door and was saying to Ivy, "Ivy! Nothing wrong, is there?"

"Not unless you call your son making my daughter pregnant 'wrong'," Ivy cried. "I do – where's his mum? I want to see her." And with that she rushed past Joe in the narrow hallway and burst into the front room where Elizabeth Flanders sat knitting and watching the news on TV. The little grey figures flickered as Elizabeth Flanders looked up, startled, and her husband burst in behind Ivy saying, "Ivy! What are you saying?" But Ivy was there first. Standing in front of Elizabeth Flanders with her hands on her hips she cried, "Mary's having a baby and your Jim's the father. What are you going to do? I hope you'll tell him to marry her."

Elizabeth Flanders looked at her in astonishment and fear. She was small, grey woman and at forty years old she seemed more like someone of fifty. Her aim in life was to live as quietly and inoffensively as possible, never interfering, never being interfered with, never doing anything and therefore never making mistakes. Her father, a fierce police sergeant, who now lived in Deal, bullying his roses as once he had bullied his family, had made sure that Liz Flanders would spend her life trying not to offend. This was why Joe Flanders now put his hand on Ivy's shoulder and said, "Sit down, Ivy, and let's talk this over sensible."

"Hah!" snorted Ivy. "Sensible is it? I'd like to see you being sensible if your daughter was in the family way. It's not sense we need – it's action. Where is he, anyway? Don't you think he ought to be here?"

"He's due back from work any time," said Liz Flanders. "But – but, if Mary's expecting as you say, what's to say the baby's my Jim's?"

"What's to say – what's to say," spluttered Ivy. "He's her boyfriend, isn't he? She says it's him. What are you trying to say?"

"That don't mean –" said Liz Flanders in a failing voice.

"Oh – I see," said Ivy. "You're trying to tell me my Mary's a liar are you? And she's playing about with hundreds of them, eh? Every Tom, Dick and Harry that comes along. Now, see here, Elizabeth Flanders – one more word out of you and you'll regret it, I can guarantee you that."

"Stand behind me, Joe," came Elizabeth Flanders' small, rather childish voice. "She's going to strike me."

"No she won't, Elizabeth," said Joe Flanders. "Ivy's come here in good faith –"

"My Jim's a good boy," said his mother. "I can't believe –"

"How dare you sit there and defend him?" cried Ivy. "And where the hell is he, anyway? He should have come with Mary to tell me himself, instead of me having to drag it out of Mary like I did. He must be a nice coward – he can do it all right but he can't take the consequences. 'Course, he's lucky – he's got a mother to hide behind who thinks her son isn't like every other man in the world – oh, no – her son's an angel sent from God who doesn't know the difference between a boy and a girl. My poor girl," Ivy said melodramatically – and then suddenly thought of Mary's pallor, her confusion, her inability to understand fully what was happening to her – and burst, herself, into tears. Tears for herself, for Mary and for all women.

"Don't take on, Ivy," said Joe. "I think we all need a drink and a talk."

"Never mind the drink," said Ivy. "You go and fetch that boy here instantly." She gave a huge sniff.

"Perhaps if Sid was here you'd be better able to control yourself," said Liz.

"Don't sit in that chair telling me to control myself," sobbed Ivy.

"I'll go and get him," muttered Joe leaving the room.

"Why isn't Sid here?" said Liz in her little voice. "It would be such a help —"

"Ooh," said Ivy through gritted teeth. "Ooh — I'll smash everything in this room if I don't get some sense out of you." With that, she turned and lifted the clock off the mantelshelf and held it over the fireplace.

Liz Flanders' pale face flushed. "That was a wedding present."

"Oh," said Ivy, loudly and meaningfully, "it was a wedding present, was it? Well, that's what we're here trying to talk about isn't it? I mean — you're here with this nice clock on the shelf what you got for a wedding present and my girl's throwing up every morning, expecting your boy's kid and no nice wedding presents there on her mantelpiece at the present moment."

"Please sit down, Ivy. You're upsetting my nerves. I'm too shaken to talk like this."

Ivy sat down but put the clock in her lap. "Right," she said. "Now you're calmer, I hope." There was a silence. "Well?" demanded Ivy. "What have you got to say."

Liz Flanders hesitated. "Can't she get rid of it?" she said. "Wouldn't it be better —"

"Nice way to talk about your grandchild," Ivy observed. "'Can't she get rid of it?' Very nice. Touching. But, as it just so happens, no, she can't. Because it's too late. Because I'm not putting my girl in that kind of danger, getting rid of a kid at the stage she's at, for you or anybody. She's having it — and that's that."

"Didn't tell you in time, then?" observed Liz.

"Two people didn't tell me in time," said Ivy. "My daughter and your son."

"If he's the father," said Liz.

Ivy stood up and was about to hurl the clock into the fireplace when Liz said quickly, "I'm sorry. He's only a boy, Ivy. Don't do any damage."

"I couldn't do as much damage in a week around here as what your son done to my Mary in five minutes," Ivy said. "And as to being only a boy — he's almost twenty-one, Liz. My girl's just sixteen. I want your guarantee, here and now, that they get married, otherwise this clock goes right through that telly —"

As the crooner on the TV set sang, "So won't you hurry home tonight, hurry home tonight," Liz stood up to grab the clock, Ivy pulled it away, Liz grabbed a handful of her hair and, as Ivy twisted away, a chair fell over. At this moment Joe Flanders came in. Behind him, holding hands, were Jim and Mary. Mary still had an angry mark on her face where Ivy had hit her.

"My God!" exclaimed Joe. "What's going on in here? Elizabeth — sit down. Mrs Waterhouse — would you kindly put that clock back on the mantelpiece. It won't help to turn the place into a madhouse."

"I'll keep the clock," said Ivy. "Till I'm satisfied."

"Do as you please," Joe said. "Well, come on in, you two. Let's hear what you've got to say about all this."

"There's nothing to say," said Ivy. "We're here to plan the wedding, and that's that."

"Who says there'll be a wedding?" said Liz Flanders. "I'm not sure that's the best way."

"Perhaps you'll tell me what the best way is, then," said Ivy. "I'd like to hear."

"Joe," said his wife. "Are you going to let this woman come round here, try to break up my home and threaten me and still stand there saying nothing? Where's Sid Waterhouse? Doesn't anybody think he should be here?"

"Sid's glued to the telly as usual," Ivy said calmly. "It don't matter whether he's here or not. Your boy's got my girl in the club, they've got to get married and that's all there is to be said about it. You can get all the MPs in the House of Commons in this room and the facts won't alter so you can put that in your pipe and smoke it."

"Joe!" Liz Flanders cried out.

"Don't seem to me there's any other way," Joe Flanders said. "I've talked to Jim on the way here. He's not saying the baby's not his. He's willing to marry Mary."

"Is this true, Jim?" asked Liz Flanders.

"That's right, mum," the young man told her. "Me and Mary have made a bit of a mess of it but we love each other and we want to get married."

"I'm glad to hear it," said Ivy. She put the clock back on the mantelpiece and added, "Seems to me there's not that much more to be said about it. It's a pity, but there you are. What's done's done and we can't change anything. Mary and Jim can put up the banns at St Anthony's as soon as you like. We'll have a small wedding and a few people round to our house afterwards. Some people would make a party of it anyway but I'm too fed up to turn it into a circus."

"Right-ho, Ivy," said Jim's father. "All right by you, Liz?"

"I suppose so," said Liz Flanders. She bent her head angrily towards the television, where a comedian was telling jokes in an American accent.

There was a silence in the room. "Well, then," said Ivy briskly. "We'd better go and tell Sid."

"Drink before you go?" Joe suggested weakly.

"No, thanks," said Ivy. "We'd better be setting off." She sounded as if she and Mary were about to travel the length of London, not just walk down Meakin Street. In the doorway Jim Flanders whispered to Mary, "Same place tonight, Mare?" Mary just nodded and walked past him. In the street she said to her mother, "I don't want to get married, mum."

"Should have thought of that earlier," was Ivy's reply.

"For two pins I'd run away," Mary said.

"What's the point – you wouldn't be running alone," said Ivy grimly. She felt defeated. She had had hopes for her clever, pretty Mary. She could have married well, got something out of life. Now all she had was an early, forced marriage to Jim Flanders, a nice enough lad, but not the sort to set the Thames on fire. That was it, she thought, you did your best and broke your back and this was the outcome in the end. If Mary had come to her sooner maybe something could have been done – as it was the silly bitch was nearly five months gone when she finally told the truth. There was no way out, now. And there was still Sid to tell. He'd shout the odds and then disappear down the Marquis of Zetland and get drunk. A big help. Feeling very old, Ivy led Mary into 19 Meakin Street. "Get upstairs, Mary," she told her daughter flatly, "while I break it to your father."

Upstairs, Mary sat on her bed in the summer heat and stared at the upper windows of the houses opposite. She felt tired and numb. She could not believe, really, that she was going to have a baby, nor that she was going to marry Jim Flanders. She knew things like that were not supposed to happen to her. Her stomach felt very heavy. Perhaps, she thought, this was how things did happen to people – suddenly, without their wanting them to, without any plans being made.

Numbly, she thought it seemed like a dismal prospect, looking after

Jim and cooking his meals and minding the baby. But other girls didn't seem to mind – the trouble was she had never seen herself like that – there must, she thought desperately, be some way of not being bored and poor and depressed. She asked herself whether she loved Jim and decided it was a stupid question now, anyway. She didn't love him as much as she had before she found out about the baby, or even, really, before she fell for the baby in the first place. She supposed having a baby put you off love and perhaps, afterwards when she'd got it, she would be in love again. Anyway, Ivy said she had to get married so she had to get married. What else could she do? Now Dad was going to go on and on at her and maybe have a row with Joe Flanders in the street and she felt so tired, so tired . . .

It must, she thought sleepily, have been the night of the break-in. They'd all had a few drinks and the boys, on pints, while the girls had Babychams, had got bold and boastful in a pub up West. Jim Flanders had been one of the boldest, she thought, not like he was when she told him about the baby. Then he'd been angry and afraid, thought if they ignored it it would somehow go away. She'd known better, in her heart of hearts, but had gone along with the idea because he was older. Which was stupid. She could see now that it did not matter whether you were older or not. It was whether the thing was growing in your body, or somebody else's. But there it was. He had thought the problem would disappear. She had believed that somehow, miraculously, it would all turn out to be a dream. Nothing would happen in the end. A friend of a friend of Cissie Messiter's, Mary thought, was supposed to have had a baby in the ladies' at Charing Cross Station because she didn't know what it was all about. "Didn't want to know, most likely," Cissie had said. "Hid it from herself, that's what." It had been Cissie who had detected her own pregnancy, in the end. It was Cissie who had told her firmly she must tell Ivy. "A girl's best friend is her mother in this type of situation," she had said. "And Ivy'll make him marry you. You can't pick and choose, Mary. You've got nothing else to do." She had ended her remarks on a typical note, "You've no one to blame but yourself."

Well, it was that night of the break-in, Mary thought, when they had strolled in the darkness down a cobbled mews near Grosvenor Square, where the old stables were being converted into small, expensive houses. "Aren't they sweet," Cissie had said. "I wouldn't half like one of them." Then Harry Smith, from up the street, had said, "Fat hopes, my love. These aren't for the likes of you and me," and had added,

"No – careless, though, aren't they. Look at that – ladders all over the place, scaffolding everywhere and no light but that little one at the end of the street. Asking for trouble, though, aren't they?"

"No lights on in half these houses, the completed ones," Jim had said, going a little further down the mews.

"Quite an opportunity for a likely lad," Harry said, following him.

Cissie, from the far end of the mews, said, "I'd have thought you wouldn't be bothered to think like that, Harry. With your father put away again, like he is." For Harry's father had no sooner been released from the German prisoner-of-war camp than, after being caught trying to open a safe in a house in Knightsbridge, he was back as a prisoner again, this time in a British jail. And that sentence had been followed by another. But red-headed Harry's swagger in the darkened mews, his defiant, "Shut up, Cissie," proved that he had learned nothing from his father's example.

"I'm getting out of here," Cissie called down the mews. She turned to the others with her. "Come on," she said. "That lot are going to get themselves into trouble. Come on, Mary. Don't hang about here."

"Oh – I'm stopping for a while," said Mary casually. She moved forward and stood next to Harry at the bottom of the mews, where three old stables had been converted into elegant little houses.

"No law against looking, is there, Cis?" Harry called.

"Here," said Mary to the red-headed lad. "Look at that up there. He's left his bedroom window open. No trouble to get in up that drainpipe."

"We're going home, Mary," Cissie said loudly from the other end of the mews. "Don't blame me if something happens."

"I won't, Cis," Mary called cheekily, over her shoulder.

"Look here," said Jim Flanders, standing now beside Harry and Mary. "Cissie's right. Let's go."

"No," said Mary in a dreamy voice. "Look at it, though. Ever so easy to get in and take a look round. We won't take nothing."

"What happens if we're caught?" asked Jim.

"Caught, caught, caught," mocked Harry. "Where's your guts, Flanders? Down in your boots?"

"We're leaving," said Cissie. "And Mary – I'm telling your mum on you."

"Tell her you saw me standing in a street looking at a building," said Mary. "She'll be shocked. I should think she'll give me the cane."

Cissie and the others went off grumbling together that no good would come of this adventure.

"Thank Christ for that," Harry remarked.

"Missed your goodnight kiss from Susan though, haven't you," said Jim.

"I can stand it," said Harry.

They stood together on the cobbles, looking up at the open window. Suddenly the sky, as if someone had opened a trap door in it, was full of floating snow flakes. Snow drifted down, quickly covering the cobbles with whiteness. The flakes fluttered round the lamp post in the light.

"Ooh – pretty," cried Mary in delight. She put her arms round Jim and gave him a big kiss. She grabbed his hands and they did a sliding jive in the snow.

"Where's Harry gone?" Jim said, staring round.

Mary realized. "He's over there," she said, pointing to the right, where the scaffolding was. "He's fetching a ladder. Silly fool," she added. "How can we leave a ladder propped up against a window – the cops'd be banging on the front door in one minute. Look – hold me shoes."

"Mary!" protested Jim. But she thrust her high-heeled shoes into his hand and was quickly on to a ledge which ran about three inches above the ground, all along the wall. Pushing herself up high with one leg she grasped the point where two exterior pipes joined, hauled herself up and, standing on one foot on the join in the pipes, reached sideways for the window ledge of the open upper window. Then, in her stockinged feet, she inched slowly up the pipe which ran, at an angle, up the wall. Seconds later she had her knees on the window ledge and was toppling herself in. Her shoulders hit thick pile carpet. The dark bulk of furniture stood round the room. Putting her head out of the window she heard the others whispering,

"Put that ladder back – Mary's in there."

"What?"

She whispered down, "I'll let you in through the front door. Wait a minute."

Mary crept across the carpet, her heart banging. Suppose there was someone in? There could be somebody asleep in the next door bedroom – what would she do if she was collared, as Harry's father once had been, by an ex-serviceman with a revolver in his hand. The man had been so angry he'd threatened to murder Harry's dad. As she opened the door cautiously she thought – so what? Who cares?

There was no light in the hall outside. She crept out and went towards the stairs. The door of the other bedroom was open. She peered in. The bed was made up – and empty. She crept down. There was no light coming from either of the closed doors on the ground floor. She opened the front door and held out her hand for her shoes. Jim handed them to her mechanically. The snow still swirled round and round, landing on the heads of the boys, making little caps on their heads. It was very quiet. Even the traffic noise from the nearby big streets was muted.

"You lunatic," said Jim. "What did you think you were playing at?"

"Anybody in?" whispered Harry.

"Don't think so," said Mary.

"Might as well step inside and get warm, then," said Harry. "We can always say we saw the door swinging open and stepped in to make sure everything's all right."

"You bloody fool," Jim whispered angrily.

"Oh, come on, Yellowstreak," said Mary. She turned, in her black, tightwaisted coat, her blonde curls bouncing, her shoes in her hand, and led the way in.

Harry opened the closed doors. "Nobody here," he said. "Cor – look at this kitchen. Bit of a back door there – I'll just slip back the bolts so we can get out fast if anybody comes."

"You done this before, Harry," Jim told him.

"Might have done," said Harry.

"Mary – I wish you'd come home," Jim said. Mary led them into the sitting room and turned on a lamp.

"Oh, look at this," she said, falling into the depths of a well-stuffed sofa in the small but trim living room. "Wish we had something like this. Look at that – swords – on the wall."

"Twenty-one inch TV and all," said Harry. He lifted the lid off a small box on a carved table and leaped back.

"Musical box," said Mary as the tinkling sound filled the air. She must have half-recognized the tune, which was French. She said, "Put the lid back on. Shut it up." The music stopped.

"I feel funny," she said.

"Ill?" enquired Jim.

"No," she said, throwing off the uneasy feeling. "Here –" and she pranced out into the hall, returning in a curly brimmed bowler hat and carrying a walking stick.

112

"I'm Burlington Bertie,
I rise at ten thirty
And saunter around in the park –" she sang.

"Don't make all that noise," Harry told her.

Tugging at the top of the silver-topped cane she produced a sword.

"Sword stick, eh?" said Harry. It was fashionable for well off young men at that time to wear the curly brimmed bowlers, tight-waisted coats and to carry the swords their supposed aristocratic ancestors might have had. "Well, whoever the owner is, he's quite the squire."

"Let's have a drink while we're here," said Jim, nodding at the decanter on the table.

Mary poured them all a whisky and said, handing Harry his glass, "And you can take that knick-knack out of your pocket what I saw you pop in, Harry."

"Suppose so," said Harry reluctantly, removing a silver snuff box and putting it back on the table.

They crept upstairs and opened the wardrobe in the main bedroom, which had Regency striped wallpaper and a huge bed. Inside were many suits, tweed, pinstripe and a full set of dress clothes. There was one long evening dress and a smart ladies' housecoat in maroon, with black froggings.

"He leads a gay life," observed Harry, finishing his drink. Mary was lying on the bed, which had, she discovered, black satin sheets. "This is the life," she said. "Satin sheets – God!" Her eye had caught the photograph, in a silver frame, on the table beside the bed. It was of a couple, the man in a black bow tie and dinner jacket, the girl in a tight black evening dress with a fashionable red mouth, raised chin and naughtily plucked eyebrows. "She must be a model," murmured Mary, whose eye had been caught first by the girl. Then, taking a closer look at the man she said, "Oh, my Gawd – it's Charlie Markham. I could swear it." He had changed little. His pale brown hair had darkened but he still had the same heavy face, ruddy complexion and bright blue eyes. If nothing else had reminded her, she would have recognized him by the little V of hair which grew down in the middle of his forehead. It was a man's face, now, although it still carried the boyish look of good fellowship. She jumped to her feet.

"Who's he?" asked Jim.

"Relation of the people where I was evacuated," Mary explained. "If this is his place I'm leaving. He was a right bully as a kid. No wonder he's got a sword stick."

"Don't get flustered," said Harry.

"Might as well go now, anyway," said Jim. "What's that?" he said, in a low voice.

There were voices downstairs. "– left the door open," said a man's voice.

"Of course I didn't," said another.

"Christ," said Jim. "What are we going to do?"

Harry looked round him. Although the bedroom window was not very high above the cobbles below it was too high to risk jumping. "Bluff it out," he said, unconvincingly. Meanwhile the voices downstairs were getting louder.

"Someone's been in here – look. There's my hat and stick."

"Anything missing?"

"Doesn't seem to be."

"Why didn't you let us leave the ladder up, Mary?" whispered Jim.

"Oh – shut up," Mary hissed back. "Look – we'll have to try another window."

Downstairs, in the hall, a voice hiding nervousness said, "Don't go charging upstairs to investigate, Adrian. Not without the trusty Purdy from under the stairs."

"You would, wouldn't you, Charlie Markham," muttered Mary Waterhouse, once again the pinched, pummelled child of Allaun Towers.

"What?" asked Jim.

"He's coming up with a shotgun," she told him. "Quick – we'll have to try the other room."

So the three crept along the landing while, below, the two men in the hall pulled something heavy out of the cupboard under the stairs.

"Bloody stupid place to keep a trunk," said the one who was not Charlie Markham. The scraping and banging masked the sound of their opening the door of the second bedroom. Inside the clear light produced by the snow outside showed the shapes of a bed, a wardrobe, a dressing table. Mary opened the window quickly.

"Flat roof below," she whispered.

"Right, Charlie," said one of the men downstairs. He sounded determined.

"Right, old man," said Charlie Markham. Mary recognized the tone. She was over the window ledge and on to the roof below in a flash. The two boys came after her. They all crouched below window level in the snow.

"Over that parapet and on to the next bit of roof," Harry Smith said.

Inside, they heard the door of the big bedroom open. "Light's on," said Adrian in astonishment. "D'you leave the light on, Charles?"

"No. I didn't leave the wardrobe open, either," he said.

"Try the other room," said the other.

"Hang on. I've got to check something," came Charlie's voice. There was the sound of a drawer being opened.

"Come on, man," urged Adrian. Mary, Harry and Jim got over the low parapet on to the next roof and ran to the other side.

"Got to get on that scaffolding," Mary said. She pointed to the scaffolding on the next building.

"We can't reach," Harry told her. The light went on in the small bedroom they had just left. It glittered on the snow of the roof they had just left.

"Hurry up," said Mary. "They'll see our footprints." As she leaned forward to try to reach the bar of scaffolding she had to grip so that she could climb down to the ground she had a clear memory of Sir Frederick firing his shotgun at a rabbit. She saw the rabbit stop on the grass, saw it leap, saw it drop limp on the ground. She felt furious with Harry and Jim — Jim had been excused the obligatory two years military service because he had contracted rheumatic fever as a child and had a heart murmur. Harry Smith had dodged National Service by some means known to the Smith family, whose boys never went away to do their duty. Only she knew firsthand what a shotgun could do — worse than that, only she knew what Charlie Markham was. She threw herself on to the scaffolding and began to scramble down. She whispered angrily, "Come on — he'll shoot you —" and she was on the ground, toppling, because one of her shoes had fallen off on the way down. She found it lying sideways in the snow and rammed it on just as Jim landed beside her. He fell over and scrambled up. She pushed him back into the shadows of the half-constructed building. It began to snow again. Mary heard Harry come off the scaffolding — then push in beside them. Squinting up she saw two heads in the open window.

"They got on to the next roof," said the fairer of the two. The other's head went up. He scanned the mews. It was Charlie all right, Mary saw. Older, of course, but with the same pugnacious jaw.

"Can't see 'em," he said. "They must've done a bunk."

"Go out and scout round for them?" suggested Adrian.

"No fear — not in this," said Charlie. "Nothing's gone. Let's go and have a drink." And the heads went in and the light went out.

"Hang on for a bit," said Harry. "They could change their minds. Could be a trick."

Mary began to feel cold. She shivered.

"Your stupid idea," said Jim bitterly.

"Serves us right for listening to a tart," Harry said. "That's a sure recipe for disaster."

"I enjoyed it," said Mary. "Anyway – I got you out of it, didn't I?"

"Can't you belt her, or something?" Harry asked his friend.

"Some hopes," replied Mary.

"Let's go," said Jim. They walked casually up the mews in the driving snow.

In the taxi home Mary smiled. "What a laugh," she said. "Eh – what a game." She felt elated. The excitement of the rooftop escape was still with her. "And fancy that being Charlie Markham's place. I should've left him a note."

"And that's all," said Harry Smith. "Nice, tasty stuff he had there."

"Oh – you," said Mary, giving him a push in the ribs. She could tell, now, that he wouldn't mind her being his girl. But she didn't want to be Harry's girl and, if she was truthful with herself, at that moment she didn't want to be Jim's, either. She was too excited. She wondered what else she could do to get away from Meakin Street, and Sid and Ivy, and her dull job in a shop. What could she do to get an interesting life, with fewer restrictions and more fun? She'd try for it, she thought to herself. She'd try.

But she never got the chance. When she and Jim got back to Meakin Street they found Jack snoring on his makeshift bed downstairs and Sid, Ivy and Shirley gone. Mary remembered they had gone over to Wapping, to spend the night at Ivy's brother's house. So it must have been that night when she and Jim lay in her narrow bed together, whispering so that Jack would not hear. And it must have been that night when she became pregnant. The next day the King, George VI, died. Ivy cried but Mary took no notice. She was in a daze.

The summer after the exploit in Charlie Markham's flat, and a month after her wedding, Mary sat alone in her two rooms at number 3 Meakin Street. Thoughts of the night of the snowstorm drifted through her head. There was nothing left of the nimble, adventurous girl who had enjoyed climbing into Charlie Markham's house. Now she was thick-bodied, tired, clumsy and numb, as if she had, strapped inside her, a huge parcel she could not get rid of. She often stood up and started to move as if she were not pregnant, only to find herself slowed and impeded by the parcel. She tried, furiously, to walk as if she were not carrying it – only to find herself settling back into a slower, more lumbering walk, still bearing it in front of her. Even if she could forget it for a little while someone – Jim, Ivy, a stranger on a bus – would soon remind her. "Here – take my seat, love. You need all the rest you can get." "Don't start trying to put in light bulbs, Mary – you'll twist the cord round the baby's neck." "A pint for me and a lemonade for the wife." Of course, they'd asked her to give up her job. "The customers don't feel happy being served by a girl in your condition – sorry, it's company rules." Mary had few very clear thoughts about her pregnancy but various feelings and sensations began to dominate her. Like an animal, she was afraid, miserable and trapped. Like an animal, she looked for escape – but there was none.

She stood up. "Better get something for Jim's tea," she thought. She took her shopping bag from the hook on the back of the kitchen door, put her purse and keys in it and went out. In Mrs Hamilton's shop opposite the pub she met Ivy, in a fluster. "I was making a nice casserole for your Dad. He's on late shift. Then I find I'm out of salt. What're you having?"

"Tin of stewing steak in a pie," said Mary glumly. "Few chips."

"Here – have a tin of peaches on me," Ivy said generously. "Let's have a tin of peaches, Mrs Hamilton."

"Got to feed the brute," said the fat woman, reaching behind her for a tin of peaches. Mary looked down at the broken biscuits in the glass-fronted case in front of her.

"Got a fancy for some biscuits, Mary?" Ivy asked her encouragingly.

"No," said her daughter.

"I was a devil for pickled onions, myself," said the shopkeeper.

"It was tinned fruit with me," said Ivy. "I'd've robbed shops to get it. Funny, isn't it? There must be a reason."

Mary thought that now they were under way with their anecdotes about pregnancy and birth she would never get her steak. Rudely, she said, "Any chance of a tin of stewing steak, Mrs Hamilton. I don't want to stop here till the baby's born."

Outside the shop Ivy said, "Really, Mary. You weren't half rude in there. It must be your condition. And it's time you started thinking about what kind of pram you want. Your dad and me have agreed to pay for it. You'll want a nice one."

Mary looked at her. She was being dragged into complicated responsibilities again. Ivy wanted a nice pram so that she could push her first grandchild about in it. What she, Mary, wanted, was a new dress. She had seen the others, girls of about her own age, wearing slippers, old shoes, old coats, because there was no money for new things, but still pushing flashy, well upholstered prams up and down the street. They were pale and worn as if no one cared about them any more, as if they were no longer allowed to care about themselves now they had the baby.

"Mary!" came Ivy's voice, called her to attention. Mary stared round at the small houses, baking under fierce afternoon sun. The pavements glittered. The Smith's shaggy dog peed against a lamp post.

"I don't want a pram, mum," she said dully.

"What're you going to push the baby in then?" demanded Ivy. "A wheelbarrow?" Then she seemed to collapse and said, looking at her daughter's dull face, "Oh, God – I've done my best, Mary. If you can't pull yourself together it's not my fault. You've got a good husband and a baby coming. You ought to be pleased. There's a lot worse off."

"Yes, mum," said Mary and turned round to go across the street. "Here," said Ivy, fishing in her handbag. "Here's ten bob. Why don't you and Jim take yourself out to the pictures tonight? Be a break for you."

Mary took the note. "I'm going now," she said.

"What about Jim? What about his tea?" her mother called after her.

"Sod Jim's tea," she called back. It was the first time she had felt cheerful for many months.

Ivy stood on the pavement looking after her knowing the cry of defiance came from a prisoner. She felt depressed. What sort of a mother was Mary going to make if she carried on like this now? What sort of a wife was she making at present, come to that? Still, she consoled herself hopefully, pregnant women were a bit mad at the best of times. Perhaps she'd sort out when the baby came.

That night there was a row, caused by Mary, at 3 Meakin Street. Jim came back to find an empty flat and no supper. Mary came back from seeing *Moulin Rouge* in a good mood and started doing the can-can round the front room. Jim told her he had been worried and had gone to Ivy's, only to find that she, Mary, had gone off to the cinema without thinking of him or his supper. Ivy had cooked him an egg and bacon and now after going to a film without him, here she was prancing round the room doing silly dances likely to bring on a miscarriage. Mary shouted that she didn't care, that she was fed up with living in the flat, with him, and never having any money to enjoy herself. Even if they did, she added, making bad worse, nothing was any fun with him because he was such a misery. Then she went out and, equally suddenly, came back and went on arguing.

The shouting went on and on until the woman from the flat below came up and burst into the room.

"Look what she done!" she shouted furiously at Jim Flanders. In her arms she held a cat, round which many strands of wool were tangled, and half the fairisle sweater Jim's mother had knitted for him. "Look," she said. "She tied the bottom row round Tiger's neck. She must've pushed him through the front door and trapped the sweater inside. Then the poor creature goes running about in a panic unravelling it and getting more and more frightened all the time. She must be barmy."

"Mean me?" Mary said insolently, leaning on the mantelpiece.

"Yes – I do mean you," said the woman. "I heard you come down earlier on and open and close the door. I never knew what you were up to. I thought you was up here having a nasty row, and that hasn't been very nice to listen to. What I never knew you'd decided was to take out your nasty spite on an innocent animal, as well as your poor, suffering husband. I found this cat trying to tug himself away from the lamp post outside and a couple of kids laughing at him. It's wicked. I don't know what the younger generation's coming to. Father's away too long in the forces, no proper discipline, life's been too easy for you lot, let me tell you that. Now look – victimizing animals – you ought to be locked up." She studied Jim's embarrassed face and said, in a milder tone, "I'll leave you to deal with her. She's probably a bit funny due to her condition."

When she had gone Jim buried his face in his hands. "Oh, Mary," he groaned. "Why did you have to go and do that? What's the matter with you? I know you're fed up. So am I, but we can't get out of it now so let's try to make the best of it."

"You've got your job and your money and your own flaming body, all to yourself," said Mary. "And I've got nothing. Make the best of it? You've got the bloody best of it. I'm going to bed."

She lay in bed, thinking of the can-can and the women's dresses, paintings done by the little crippled man. When Jim came in to make it up with her she turned angrily on her side and pretended to go to sleep so that she could go on half-dreaming of Paris in the 1890s. He came back, hours later, from the pub when she was really asleep and tried to wake her and make love to her. She said, "Go away, Jim. Let me sleep."

"They all tell me it'll be better when the baby's born," he told her loudly. "And I'm telling you it'd better be better sooner than that because I can't stand any more of this."

But as it happened things were not better when the baby was born. They were far, far worse. Jim Flanders was dead, which caused much grief in low places and a great deal of consternation in high and unexpected places. Jim was not just dead – he had been hanged for murder.

At a quarter to eight on December 1st 1952 Mary Flanders lay cold in the narrow iron bed back in her parents' house at 19 Meakin Street. Her head on the pillow was turned to the window, which was curtained by thick fog, as if a yellow blanket had been hung over it from the outside. The air inside the room was yellowish and acrid. Mary's eyes, a cold, pale blue now, like a washed out March sky, looked blankly into the fog. It was very quiet. Traffic crawled blindly through the streets. The fog itself caught all sound and muffled it.

Down in the foggy kitchen Ivy sat on a chair, her face rigid, feeding Mary's baby, Josephine, from a bottle. Shirley ate her cornflakes as quietly as possible. Sid was drinking a cup of tea. The oven door was open to provide warmth. The light was on and the curtains were drawn. Sid got up and pulled the curtains aside. Ivy stared hard at him.

"I'm going to open the curtains in the front room as well," he told her.

"Do as you please," she said.

A man passing the house on his way to work saw Sid pulling back the curtains and nodded at him. The few people passing the house that morning walked quietly, taking care not to whistle or talk in loud voices.

Back in the kitchen Ivy finished feeding the baby and put the empty bottle on the table. She sat with the tiny infant propped in the crook of her arm and stared into space. Then she said to Shirley, without looking at her, "You'd better take her up a cup of tea."

Shirley poured milk and tea into a floral-patterned cup and stirred sugar into it. At the door she said, "Have I still got to go to school, Mum?"

"That's what your dad says," Ivy told her. "He wants us to carry on as normal."

Shirley went up the small flight of stairs to the bedrooms. She was afraid. Her mother's face had suddenly fallen into deep lines. She had never seen her look so old.

She opened the bedroom door timidly and walked in with the tea. Her sister, white as chalk, lay in the foggy room, staring at the window.

"Cup of tea, Mary," she told her.

"What's the time?" asked the girl.

"Ten to eight," replied Shirley.

My father put down *The Times* at nearly eight that morning looking involuntarily towards the large clock, almost six feet tall, which stood against the dining room wall. In its centre it had a panel of glass through which a large, bulbed pendulum could be seen moving. He stared at the big Roman numerals on the clock face for a little while. Then he got up, went to the end of the table, where the teapot was standing, poured himself another cup of tea and went back to his seat again. Even I, a boy of sixteen, eating bacon and eggs and looking forward to the day's entertainments – all the more so, since I had been sent home from school with pneumonia, was now better, out of bed and looking forward to some entertainment – even I could not help noticing how preoccupied he was. I became very much aware of the clock's heavy tick. Looking up from my plate again I was surprised to see him sitting with his head in his hands. Perhaps he was trying to block out the sound of the ticking. Alarmed, I was about to ask him if there was anything the matter when the clock began to chime and his attention to the sound somehow deterred me from speaking. When the chimes ended he said vehemently, "Damn them." And repeated it – "Damn them. Damn their eyes." He was very pale. Because I had seldom seen him obviously angry and he never swore while I was present I simply stared at him in astonishment. He got up, then, and walked straight out of the room. A few seconds later I heard the front door slam. I think after that he must have walked about for several hours – at any rate, the next thing I heard was my mother's protests.

He had evidently returned and was insisting that the family leave London and go to our house in the country for Christmas. Worse than that he was not actually planning any date for our return. My mother was very alarmed by all this and tried to get him to change his mind but in the end we went next day. And we stayed, so that my brother and I both returned to school from the country, with no particular idea about whether we would be returning to London or the country at half term.

They must have persuaded him to come back but after that I think my father's attitude changed in some ways. He had been a man of the old school – somewhat rigid, perhaps unimaginative, unquestioningly dutiful, utterly honest, occasionally wry, or humorously cynical, but never really doubting his own integrity or the integrity of those he served. But after that morning, invisibly, he broke. He lost conviction.

In Meakin Street, just before eight, there was a flurry in the fog. A van drew up. Feet banged on the pavement. There was a loud knock at the door. In the kitchen neither Sid nor Ivy stirred and it was Shirley, coming downstairs with the empty cup, who answered.

"All right to come through?" said a cheerful voice. "We've come to get on with your bathroom."

Shirley was saying, "Oh – I don't know –" when Jackie came out of the front room, dressed for work.

"I'll see to it, Shirl," he told her. "Can you come outside a minute, mate?" he asked the workman.

In the kitchen Sid, Ivy and Shirley heard nothing, until the workman's shocked voice came to them, "Sorry, mate. Wouldn't have disturbed you for worlds if I'd known. We'll come back in a few days." Then there was a pause. He added, "Give my sympathy to all inside." The van door banged and it started up.

After a pause Ivy said, "People are very nice, sometimes." She looked at the clock. It was two minutes to eight.

Shortly before eight Albert Pierrepoint, the public hangman, the doctor, the chaplain and some others entered the condemned cell at Wormwood Scrubs. Jim Flanders downed a large tot of brandy offered to him by a warder and held out his arms.

"Arms behind you," a uniformed officer told him.

Jim put his arms behind him. They were strapped behind his back. He was led into the adjoining execution chamber.

On the scaffold his ankles were strapped together. The hangman then looked into his eyes and placed a white hood over his head. He adjusted the rope, the chaplain said the Lord's Prayer and Pierrepoint walked round Jim to the lever on the scaffold, pulled it down with a sharp jerk – and there was Jim Flanders judicially executed, dying with his feet kicking.

Jim's parents, Joe and Elizabeth Flanders, never really recovered. He had been their only child, a candid and humorous boy, the boy for whom Joe Flanders had tried to survive five years of active service in war time. The marriage had never been a happy one and with Jim gone it seemed to have no meaning. Of course, the manner of his death made matters worse. If Jim had just died, of an illness or through an accident, the Flanders could have endured their grief supported by the sympathy of friends and neighbours, and then, as grief faded, would have picked up the pieces and gone on. As it was their mourning was complicated by their own doubts – had they done something wrong? If not, who was responsible? The situation was made worse by the reactions of those about them. There is no formula for expressing sympathy to a murderer's mother or father. And some did not want to sympathize. The Flanders were disgraced. In some ways they shared the blame with the killer. Others were so indignant on behalf of the murdered nightwatchman that they had no pity for the killer or his parents. The Flanders shut themselves up chiefly because it fell to Elizabeth to construct the life the couple were to lead after Jim's death. Joe was too stunned, for a long time, to do anything and Elizabeth, a proud woman, decided that they were being snubbed and despised and would therefore cut themselves off from everyone. Joe had to return to work at the bus garage where he led a relatively normal life but once working hours were over the pair stayed indoors, rejecting callers and all invitations. They lived, month after month, behind drawn curtains in a busy street in a huge city. They saw no one. Elizabeth Flanders shopped in the morning, well away from the area, sliding back with her purchases, hugging the walls of the houses, just after people had gone off to work and the children to school, but before the early shoppers had got their chores finished at home.

Sid often pressed Joe Flanders to come out for a drink after work but he always refused, saying he ought to stay with his wife. Ivy, once the first shock of Jim's death was over, became enraged. She felt both families had trouble to face down and that they should do it together. Many of the people in the street had been kind — Mary, in hospital after the birth of the child, had been given more flowers than most of the other mothers in the ward. This was because the street knew she might be picked on by the other women, or their relatives, if it became known that she was Jim Flanders' widow.

They sent the flowers to show they were standing by her. On the other hand, those who helped in the crisis soon went back to normal but the backbiters had been saving themselves up for later. Ivy's life in the street was difficult. There was a shortage of greetings when she appeared. The respectable Mrs Fainlight would frequently pretend Ivy was not there as they pegged out their laundry on the lines in their adjoining yards, six feet away from each other. She would do the same when they were both sweeping their front steps. Ivy had to hold her head very high when she pushed the twenty guinea pram with the white wheels down to Meakin Park in the afternoons. It was worse because since she had been obliged to give up her job in the breadshop in order to look after the baby her only society now was the street. With Mary lying in bed all day staring at the wall, with Elizabeth Flanders practically slamming the door in her face when she called Ivy felt desperate. She also thought that Elizabeth should have offered to help with the baby so that she, Ivy could go on working part-time.

Ivy sometimes thought she would go mad. She suspected her daughter was mad. Mary had given birth to Josephine in four hours, had not risen from her hospital bed for a week after that and had refused to give her child anything but the most mechanical attention. The staff had put it down to the strain of the trial, which was not over. She had come back to her parents' house and became worse. She lay down all day, or sat in a chair in the front room. She would not go out and neglected the baby until Ivy, pitying the child, which was fed only after long crying spells, took over the care of Josephine. Shirley was too young to be much help. Jack was always studying these days. Sid had been made an inspector and his friends at the depot, after expressing sympathy and having a whip-round to buy the baby an expensive cot, had chosen to forget the whole business, or at least make it appear that they had. It was Ivy who had given up her job; Ivy who was exhaustedly coping with the night and day demands of a small baby; Ivy who had a deeply depressed daughter on her hands. She had not even the support of Lil Messiter, who was like a zombie after a long, hard labour and could scarcely string two coherent words together because she was so tired.

Life was hell at 19 Meakin Street during the early months of 1953. The baby cried. Ivy shouted. Shirley, Jack and Sid slunk about trying to keep out of the way and not be noticed. But however much Ivy went round the house bawling that her daughter was just a poor girl who had made an unfortunate marriage, and there was no need for Mary, or the innocent baby, or anybody else to be held in contempt for that, the others all knew this was merely noise. They respected her battle to protect Mary's good name and to establish Josephine as a respectable baby in the eyes of the world but they knew two guilts were being denied – Ivy's, for forcing the marriage in the first place, and Mary's, for having made such a poor job of enduring it. Even Shirley knew this. They were all sorry for Ivy but they wished she would give up her struggle.

One evening, as Ivy was giving Sid an enraged account of how Elizabeth Flanders had again turned her from the door, where she had gone in a neighbourly way to enquire if Elizabeth would like a chocolate Swiss roll from Froebel's bakery in the High Street, Sid spoke out at last. "I don't know why you don't give over going there. The Flanders don't want anything to do with anybody, least of all us. It's their decision and it's their loss. If they want to live like that they've got the right. Why don't you let them be?"

"You should talk to Joe, man to man," was Ivy's response. "I've asked you time and again. It's not healthy, the way they're carrying on."

"Nor's the way you are," Sid told her. "Let them sort out their problems the best way they can. You've got enough to look after here."

"People are talking," said Ivy.

"They'll never stop, while all this is going on," said Sid. "You stay home and mind your own business. Half this noise is just your way of ignoring what's happened. But it's happened – we've got to deal with the consequences – Jim's dead. His kid needs care and protection. Mary needs the doctor to see her. You can't just go on spending a small fortune on frills and furbelows for the baby, to prove she's as good as anyone else, and badgering the Flanders. Even Shirley's looking peaky. She hardly dares move in this house for fear of getting yelled at and clouted. You want to pull yourself together, Ivy: concentrate on priorities, get the doctor to look at our Mary —"

"I'm supposed to sort all this out singlehanded?" demanded Ivy. "Why don't I find a cure for cancer in my spare time? What will you be doing while I solve it all? Sitting in that chair, I suppose. You've got a nerve, lecturing me. I suppose all this is supposed to be my fault?"

Sid did not reply. Ivy studied his face and her own face went paler still. Two red spots burned on her cheeks. "You think it is, don't you? You're blaming me for all this. That's always the way, isn't it? Things go wrong and it's the woman's fault — she's got to put everything to rights. Of course, if the kids are doing well the man goes down the pub and boasts about it."

Again, Sid said nothing.

"I know what you're thinking," said Ivy. "And you were as much in favour of it as I was. My God — you men are traitors to the core, every man jack of you. Let a woman take the responsibility — if it turns out right you take the credit. If it turns out wrong the woman takes the blame."

"My job's to put bread in their mouths," Sid told her. "And that I have done and I'm still doing."

"Lovely," said Ivy. "You organize a few buses and I have to organize all the people. I know which I'd choose if I had my time all over again."

"No choice for either of us," Sid said and went off to make a cup of tea. He brought Ivy a cup but, to her surprise, did not immediately sit down in front of the television with his own. Instead he went out of the room and she heard his tread on the stairs, going up to Mary's room.

Her nerves were so jangled that all she thought was, "He'll upset her. He'll make more trouble. He blunders about like a bull in a china shop. He's hopeless." She lit a cigarette and tried to relax until the baby cried again, or Sid made some impossible demand or Mary appeared in her dressing-gown to sit, silent and withdrawn, in front of the television.

"All right — I'll get you a bloody TV," boomed the distorted voice of Jim Flanders through Mary's head. "I'll get you a washing machine. I'll take you to the pictures every night —" Inside her head, flat on her pillow, looking towards the window, she heard the bang, like an explosion, of the front door. She lay there, rigid, with the film of her life with Jim unrolling behind her eyeballs.

Mary's fair hair had grown longer, and duller. Her eyes were blank and pale, her face expressionless as pictures went through her head – of the angry young man leaving Meakin Street in a rage – the door banging, the heels of his shoes hard on the pavement outside. Then came images of a body, like a rag doll at the end of a string, swinging at the end of a rope. She saw Jim getting naked out of bed in Meakin Street and bending to kiss her. She saw him in his Sunday suit, shoes well polished, hanging, with his face turned blue and his tongue lolling out. It had probably not been like that, she knew, but that was what she saw. She saw, then, her own hands twisting in her swollen lap as she sat in court, watching Jim in the dock as he stumbled and faltered under the cross-questioning.

"Better when the baby's born – better be – I'll get you a bloody TV –" came the distorted voice, finally cracking and shouting "– wish to God I'd never met you –" Then the banging of the door.

Tears came down Mary's face, cooling on her frozen cheeks as she lay there motionless. Poor Jim. Dead. And the nightwatchman dead, too. Poor old man, beaten over the head by Jim, as if he had turned on the innocent old fellow instead of his wife, who had nagged and nagged – and the judge had said society could not tolerate these violent young men, deprived of proper parental discipline during their formative years, going about like wild beasts in the jungle, taking what they wanted without thought or mercy. The verdict of the jury would determine whether or not the nation was prepared to countenance the wave of violence and lawlessness sweeping the country. Poor Jim. Poor old man. In the end the jury had decided Jim Flanders was guilty but made a strong recommendation for mercy because of his youth, personal circumstances and his previous good record. The judge had told them they were not entitled to add recommendations of any kind and had sentenced Jim to hang. The jury realized, too late, that they had condemned to death a young man whom none of them wanted to see die. Not that there was any doubt of his guilt. He had been seen running away from the warehouse by two people. Only a few minutes later a policeman had discovered the nightwatchman unconscious, bleeding from the head. He had died shortly after and the weapon, a heavy meathook, found beside him had carried Jim Flanders' fingerprints.

Mary, blurry, puffy-faced and heavily pregnant, had been knocked up at three in the morning by the police. A hastily summoned policewoman broke the news to her. She did not respond at first because she could not believe what they told her. When, finally, they made her understand that Jim had been arrested all she said was, "Find Harry Smith." She knew that Jim alone would never have conceived the idea of robbing the warehouse. Moments later, as the Detective Inspector and his sergeant began to question her closely about Harry Smith, she realized she had made a mistake and refused to say any more. If Harry Smith had been involved he was not going to admit it. If he did, Jim would be no better off. It was no surprise to hear later that the entire Smith family had decamped the day after the robbery. No one knew where they were except Mary, because Harry had confided to her the secret of the caravan in an Essex field which proved so useful as a holiday spot and hide-out when creditors were after them. But Mary, overcome with the horror of what, so arbitrarily, seemed to be taking place, saw no point in sending the police to Essex after the Smiths. She did not react to anything during the rest of the time up to, and after, Jim's death. After the trial a middle-aged woman in a dusty black coat came up to her and tried to wish her, and the coming child, a better future. As the woman stumbled through her thought-out phrases, "No point in dwelling in rage and pain, what's done is done, now we must all get on with the future," Mary merely muttered "Thank you" and walked away. It was left to Ivy to express her thanks to the nightwatchman's daughter for her forgiving behaviour.

Mary's attitude disappointed, and partly alienated, the neighbourhood. At first everyone was ready to be sympathetic to the poor girl, to give her more than her due, in fact, for being the heroine of a drama dignified by proceedings at the Old Bailey. But Mary, refusing to talk to reporters or to sympathetic, if curious, well-wishers, gave no satisfaction to her waiting audience. She would not appeal to their sentimentality as the young, pregnant widow of the hanged man. She would not arouse their self-righteousness by responding to remarks about the strangeness of the Smiths' sudden disappearance the day after Jim's arrest. It may have been dissatisfaction with Mary's general behaviour which led to the mutterings about Jim having been driven to crime by his wife and even suggestions that she, a notorious dare-devil, had actually thought up the plan for the robbery and sent him out to do it.

Meanwhile Mary lay day by day upstairs in her bedroom, hearing her baby cry, Shirley get into bed, the noises of the household, through a fog of despair. She heard Elizabeth Flanders' voice as she left the court, leaning on Sid's arm, "You killed my boy. He died because of you." Tears welled from her open eyes. She looked out into the darkness.

She was startled when Sid said, from the open door, "Here's a cup of tea, Mary. I want you to get up."

"I can't, dad. Not now," she replied.

"Yes, you can," said he, prepared for a long battle.

Mary sighed a long sigh and turned over in bed to look at him. She pulled herself into a sitting position.

"All right," she said. "Never mind the tea. I'll come down and drink it."

"See you in a minute, then," he said.

Downstairs Ivy said, "Go and listen at the foot of the stairs, Sid. I'm afraid she may do something desperate."

"If she doesn't, I will, if this goes on," Sid told her. He added calmly, "Anyway she's out of it, now."

Ivy was almost convinced. "I hope you're right," she said.

Mary washed her face and cleaned her teeth and came down while Sid and Ivy waited nervously. Ivy was afraid she would kill herself if Sid was brutal to her. Sid was bent on having the matter out whatever the consequences. And Mary, although she did not know it, had recovered. During the long months of depression, as she had endured the constant replaying of Jim's departure, the arrival of the police and the horrors of the trial, as she had, like a child, winced and flinched from the vision of Jim's body being eaten away in a lime-filled grave in a prison, she had without realizing it been thinking about, and working out, the life open to her as the widow of a convicted murderer and the mother of a small child. She could easily see what the terms were.

She certainly could not go on living with Sid and Ivy. There was no room for her and the child. It would be a strain on all of them. She would be the shameful creature who is returned to her family to be sheltered and forgiven. But if she was lucky, within a few years she could have a job and a Council flat. If she was luckier a man would come along and marry her and take away the stigma of the past. They could move to another area. She could have another child.

Mary felt she couldn't face her parents. She had to get out. After she had gone Jack opened his eyes and said, "I thought she was coming round."

"Nice to see her dressed for the first time for months," Sid remarked.

"It's like having an unexploded bomb right in the middle of the room," Ivy complained. "I daren't open my mouth."

Jack was more confident than his parents. If it came to it, he was sure he could handle Mary. "Leave her alone," he said. "And stop thinking about her like a cuckoo in the nest. She's doing the best she can. You can't expect too much of her – look at the size of her. She weighs nothing. She's close to being very ill. Is anyone going to pour that tea out?"

Mary came back, looking far from ill and said, "Mum – dad. I've settled with the landlord. I'm taking over the Smiths' house at number 4. He'll pay half the decorating – will you help me clean it up?"

"How are you going to cope with the rent?" Sid asked immediately.

"I've got a widow's pension," Mary told him. "I'll get a little job somewhere. Stands to reason I can't go on living here. There isn't room. You can get your job back, mum."

"You'll live there all alone?" said Ivy. "In the whole house?"

"That's right," Mary told her. "I'd ask you to come, Jack, but I want to be on my own for a bit to see how it goes."

"All right," said Jack patiently, although he had thought instantly that he would be more comfortable if he moved in with Mary.

"You can come and study there, see," she said. "And keep an eye on Josephine some evenings, while I'm working."

"That's all right," he said.

Sid and Ivy, faced with their half-grown children organizing themselves so efficiently, sat filled with misgivings. Sid finally remarked, "I don't see how you're going to cope with the expenses –"

"I'll be all right," said Mary. "I'm moving Monday."

Jack looked at her suspiciously. He knew Mary had been up to something. "I'll help you," he said.

So next day Ivy and Mary marched down Meakin Street with the pram, across which lay a new mop, by way of advertisement. They carried buckets and brushes and got the keys from the woman next door in order to let themselves in. They boiled a huge black kettle on the gas stove to get hot water for the task of cleaning up the house. "Faugh," said Ivy fussily, throwing open the kitchen window and door to let in blasts of icy air. "What a stink. It looks as if they never put a damp cloth to anything all the time they were here. Look at this lino – you can't see the colour for the dirt. Put on that bucket full of water, Mary. We'll need gallons. I can smell that toilet from here."

A pale sun filled the little yard outside, where grass grew in the cracks of the asphalt. An elderberry bush grew from a gap in the broken wall. The women scraped grease from the ancient gas stove, scrubbed floors, tore the dirty, tattered net curtains from the windows. As they threw spirits of salt down the lavatory pan of the outside toilet the sky clouded and sleet began to fall. "It'll take days," said Ivy, who was in her element – triumphant, vigorous, scouring out the stone sink in the kitchen, dragging a stained mattress downstairs and propping it outside for the dustman. Here was her damaged daughter, now moving into her own home, not two hundred yards from her own front door. It might have looked better if her brother had also moved in but you couldn't have everything, reasoned Ivy.

"I'll mobilize Jack and your dad at the weekend," she told Mary. "They can start decorating. There's some nice wallpaper going cheap down the market –"

"Don't worry. I'll get it," Mary said.

"It's your home," said Ivy discontentedly.

She did not approve of Mary's lightly striped wallpaper, nor her insistence on pale paintwork all over the house. She nearly exploded when her daughter had a big bedstead with brass knobs on it delivered by a van. "People will think you're setting up house with a man," she said. Nevertheless, she had to admit, when the house filled with pale, early sunshine, that it was a cheering sight. And by that time Ivy badly needed some signs that things were improving.

What baffled and worried both her and Sid was where Mary's money came from. Finally Sid confronted Mary and accused her of going to moneylenders, who would persecute her if she did not repay. Mary, child of her generation, which had never heard of the tight grasp of the local moneylender on poor neighbourhoods, laughed at him. "If you must know," she told him, "I rang the local pub near where the Smiths are hiding out and I told old man Smith if he didn't send me a hundred pounds I'd let on Harry was with Jim that night when they did the robbery. I know he was because I looked out the window after Jim left and I saw them talking on the corner. Anyway, Harry told Jim about the load of cigarettes they were delivering there and asked him to go out and do the job with him. Only Jim refused. They knew there were two men there that night, and they took fingerprints. It could be nasty for Harry if I said anything – I couldn't be bothered at the time."

"Mary!" exclaimed Sid. "It's blackmail!"

"The Smiths won't miss a hundred pounds," said Mary calmly. "It was Harry led Jim astray – now they can pay for a bit of a home for his widow and kid, that's what I say."

Sid was shocked, not so much by what Mary had done as by her cool and ruthless attitude. But he went on repairing the light·in the hall, muttering, "I hope you're not going to make a practice of blackmail, my girl."

When Ivy came into the house with some shopping Sid told her what Mary had done. Ivy said, "Good for her – I'd have done the same, I hope."

"You women are bloody criminals," Sid told her.

"We've got to be," was Ivy's only reply.

Jack came round to help Mary lay the new dark blue carpet in the parlour. Sulkily pulling his end towards the window he said, "I don't like this, Mary. Tugging this bit of ill-gotten gains about. What do you think you're doing, taking money from thieves?"

"Rather I took it off honest people, Jack?" his sister asked. She pulled her end into a corner and nailed it down. "Don't nail it yet," he said irritably. "It's not straight at this end."

"It would be if you concentrated on getting it straight instead of lecturing me about where it came from," said Mary. "And if you're so fussy why don't you go away? I can do it on my own."

"I don't approve of blackmail," he said. At this point the baby, in her pram in the hall, began to cry. Mary went to pick her up and stood in the doorway.

"What do you expect me to do, Jack?" she asked. "Sit on my bum in mum and dad's house, waiting for something to turn up? I've copped a hundred, that's all, off a gang of thieves who copped it off some other sucker. What are you going to do – tell the vicar?"

"You're starting to get hard, Mary," said her brother.

"It's that or go under," she told him. "I'm not going under and nor's my daughter."

"You don't have to," he said. "You've got your whole life before you. You're a pretty girl. You can find a decent bloke who won't mind about Jim. You can marry again."

"Oh, yes," Mary said. "I'm supposed to sit and wait in poverty until my prince comes along and kindly rescues me. With any luck he'll only tell me a few times a year, when we have a row, how nice it was to take me on, with a baby, a murderer's widow. If I just sit tight and keep my nose clean I can have that, eh, Jack? How would you like it yourself?"

"I wouldn't let yourself get bitter, Mary," he advised.

Mary put the baby, now sleeping, back in the pram, and said, "Thanks for the tip. But if this is the price of getting some help with the carpet I'll skip it. No hard feelings, Jack, but you'd better go home."

"Get back up your end," he said, "and shut up."

They got the carpet into position and started passing the hammer back and forth while they tacked it down. Mary looked up from her hammering and said, "The trouble with me as far as you're concerned, Jack, is that I don't fit into any of the categories you're learning at nightschool. I'm not a toiling proletarian, or a bourgeois or a capitalist, or any of that."

"I dunno," said Jack. "At the moment I'd call you an unscrupulous entrepreneur."

"Sounds all right," said his sister, slightly flattered.

After she had put together her home at number 4, Mary lived quietly. She cared for the house and baby, went to bed early and slept troubled sleeps, where she had nightmares about Jim and all kinds of confused dreams in which there were explosions, fires and sadness. She cared for the baby well enough, but if Josephine wanted smiles and tickles and golliwogs dancing on the edge of her pram and talking in funny voices, then it was Sid and Ivy, or the child's Uncle Jack or silly Auntie Shirley, who could imitate Donald Duck, who supplied all that.

It was generally assumed that grave Mary Flanders, little more than a child herself, was suffering from a perfectly natural grief. This may have been so but it was a condition more like battle-fatigue which Mary experienced. She had fits of the shudders. She went off into impenetrable silences. She was only half-aware, sometimes, of what was going on.

Then she heard in July that the barmaid of the Marquis of Zetland had left suddenly to go and become a dancer in the Middle East. The landlord, Ginger Hargreaves, was finding it hard to replace her.

Mary, seeing the job as a useful way of getting Josephine minded in the evenings while she supplemented her income, went to see Ginger.

Sympathetic to her plight and desperate for a replacement for the missing barmaid he agreed to take her on. "I'm taking a risk, mind," he told her, "because you're too young to be in a pub. But if anybody asks, tell them you're eighteen. And if anybody who looks like an official comes in, get out of the bar." So in return for his kindness he paid her only two pounds a week, less than the other girl had got, and from six until ten every night except Mondays Mary pulled pints and poured shorts at the Marquis of Zetland. She was fast with the change, never took a penny for herself and never accepted or helped herself to a drink. This conscientious attitude to the job, and her low wages, made up for the fact that she wore plain dresses and scraped her hair back unbecomingly from her face and tied it at the back with a ribbon, secured from underneath by a rubber band. She wore no make-up until Ginger said, "For Christ's sake put something on your face, Mary. You look about twelve. I'll have the brewery round my ears for employing you." Nor was she up to the usual pub chat: "Have a drink – well, have a fag then. Well if you don't drink or smoke what do you do? Show me one day?" But in spite of her conservative dress and behaviour she got on well. The neighbourhood was beginning to admire her – until the Saturday evening in September when Johnnie Bridges walked in.

The pub was crowded, smoke billowed through the air, the doors were open, because it was a warm evening and somebody was hammering out *Bali Hai* on the out-of-tune piano. Mary had not noticed the three men walk in, nor had she heard the order one had given until a voice said behind her, as she reached up to get a double whisky from the dispenser, "Hurry up, Mary. We're thirsty here." She turned round with the glass in her hand to see a pair of bold, almost black eyes staring into hers.

"What a pretty girl," he said immediately. "Now why do you scrape all your curls back like that?" And he reached over the bar and deftly pulled some of the hair forward from behind her ears. He quickly did the same on the other side and said, "That's better," as if he had known her for years. Mary stood there with the whisky glass in her hand. All the blood drained from her body. She felt as if she would fall down. The man beside the stranger took his glass from her hand. With a sidelong look at him he pressed the money into Mary's palm and pushed her fingers round it. Then he went down the bar and said, "Hullo, Sid. There's a geezer just come in with Marty Malone who's taken a fancy to your Mary."

"I hope not," said Sid. "What do you think of Villa this season?"

"Get rid of Armstrong," the other replied quickly.

"You'd like to get us a double gin and two whiskies, I suppose," said the stranger to Mary. Mary thought quickly; gin means a woman. And the stranger smiled at her, showing big, white, regular teeth and said, "My mate's brought his wife. She's a devil for gin. I'm on my own – I'm looking for the right girl. Maybe you'd like a gin yourself?"

"No, thanks," said Mary. She turned away to get the drinks. Her hand shook. She put the glasses on the bar. He drank the contents of one at a gulp and said, "Maybe a drink isn't what you need. You look like a girl who could do with a bit of fresh air. Why don't we take a walk by the canal? It's so delightful at this time of year."

Mary, who could no longer hear the noise in the pub or feel her feet on the floor, just nodded.

"Come on then," he said. Mary walked round the bar, dropped the flap in the counter and met with the young man's arm as she started to walk to the door.

"Here —" shouted Ginger Hargreaves, who was coming up from the cellar with a bottle of whisky in each hand. "Here – Mary! Where are you going?"

"I'll be back," called Mary, without thinking at all, and went out of the door with Johnnie Bridges.

"What —?" cried Ginger, quite amazed.

"That was your daughter just going out the pub with that mate of Marty Malone's," Sid's sharp-eyed friend told him.

"Who is this Malone?" asked Sid.

"Works for the Rose brothers," the other man said, in a low voice.

"Known the Roses since they had the arses hanging out of their trousers," Sid told him.

"Well – they haven't now," said his friend.

"What's your daughter think she's playing at?" demanded Ginger, coming up to Sid. "She's leaving a bar full of people on a Saturday night to go out for a walk with her boyfriend."

"He's not her boyfriend," said Sid. "She hasn't got a boyfriend." Then he paused, looking uncertain. "Who was he, anyway?"

The young man in the smart suit, who had come to the bar to get his drinks, leaned over and said, "His name's Johnnie Bridges."

"That Johnnie Bridges?" asked Ginger Hargreaves.

"The very one," said the man, and went back to his wife.

"What about him?" asked Sid.

So the publican and his friend told him what they knew about Johnnie Bridges.

"I'll kill him if he hurts my Mary," Sid told them.

Meanwhile Mary and Johnnie Bridges were walking hand in hand by the canal. As they strolled by the slow and turgid water other couples passed them, whispering in the dusky light.

"This is nice," said Mary.

"Come on," he said, "I'll take you for a duck dinner."

"To eat?" she asked.

"Well – I wasn't going to play with it," he said. "You are a nice girl. What a stroke of luck, walking into that pub and finding you there."

"Stroke of luck for me – you coming in," she told him.

As they had walked from the pub she had said, "Do you really want to go for a walk by the canal?"

"Got to get to know you better," he had told her gravely.

"It's a bit late," she had said.

"Just late enough," he said.

Now he stared at her, took her head between his hands and kissed her. She put her arms round his neck and kissed him back. He held her off, staring at her curiously, then they kissed again. Mary's knees weakened. She wanted this stranger as much as she had ever wanted anything in her life. She decided, moreover, that she would have him. She had the conviction of someone who knows for certain that something is their right. He said, "I'd better take you off for that duck. It wouldn't do for me to forget myself."

So they turned back. Mary looked at him covertly as they walked. He was a tall, well-made man of about twenty-seven, dark-eyed and dark-haired. He carried himself lightly and had an air of physical alertness, as if he were ready for action at any second. He wore a very good, dark suit which looked as if it had been made for him, a very white shirt and a long, thin silk tie. He spoke like a Londoner but, now that they were alone together, she seemed to hear that he spoke more precisely than he had in the pub.

"You'll have to tell me something about yourself," he said to her.

"You won't like what you hear," Mary told him.

"Let me be the judge of that," he said.

Opposite, across the water, was the high wall of the cemetery, overhung with trees and creepers. On their left, behind the wall they were nearest, lay the long open expanse of railway line and shunting yards. Above, along the whole length of the canal, was high, open sky, still visibly red on the horizon with the last tip of the setting sun.

"Pretty," said Mary.

"Like a vision," he said, looking up. "See the moon?"

There it was, a sickle moon, upright in the sky. Mary stared up, keeping her face, now, well away from the stranger's eyes. She did not remember her body having felt properly alive since her pregnancy began eighteen months before, unless she counted the pains of labour when she had given birth to Josephine. Mostly, she had forgotten what it was like to feel completely well, completely at one with herself. Now she remembered. She had forgotten, too, what it was like to want a man to kiss her. Now she remembered that also. It was like being raised from the dead.

As they walked up the slope from the canal to the road they kissed again. She felt his warm lips, gentle at first, and then harder, she felt his arms about her and his body pressing hers and felt herself melting, disappearing, feeling nothing but the warmth of his lips and the strength of his body. He felt her breast and she heard herself moan.

"I've got to tell you —" she said, for she became conscious, suddenly, that this man knew nothing about her. What would he think when he found out she was the mother of a child, the widow of a hanged murderer? She feared that he would respond by making a joke, telling her this was no time for a chat, by grabbing her and trying to get what he wanted. In this she underestimated Johnnie Bridges' common sense or common caution. He drew back and said, "Might as well have something to eat while you're telling me. No point in facing it on an empty stomach." Amazingly, he then stepped into the road, waved down a passing taxi and instructed her to get in. At that point she took a look at his suit and asked, once they were sitting in the taxi, "What do you do?"

"A little bit of this and a little bit of that," he said. So she knew he was a gangster. This did not worry her. In fact it cheered her up. Her revelations would be less shocking to him if he was on the wrong side of the law himself. Unless he thought she was unlucky, would bring bad luck to him – men like that were superstitious. He kissed her ears and said, "Don't worry – it may never happen."

When she saw the restaurant, a smart place in Old Compton Street, she said, "I can't go in there – like this."

"Pretend you're Cinderella and the clock struck," he told her, pulling off the rubber band and hair ribbon, which were already falling off by then. So they walked in, got a table, got a menu and Mary Flanders thought again, "He's got to be a gangster or something. Else where is the money coming from?"

"All right," he said, after ordering them two pink gins, "let's have the confession. I'll guess – your father's a police marksman and he's going to shoot anybody who messes around with you and you're on the game, you're pregnant, you've got the clap and you're a typhoid carrier. All that wouldn't matter only you're also a bloke who likes wearing ladies' dresses. I've met 'em all. I don't think you can surprise me. Thing is I've taken a fancy to you."

Mary took a drink from her glass of gin, then another, hoping it would bring her courage.

"I can surprise you," she told him. "I'm sixteen years old and I'm a murderer's widow. He was hung last December. And," she added, "I've had his baby."

"Ah," he said, considering. "Jim Flanders."

There was a silence. He did not meet her eyes. She stared at his soft profile and her new feeling of life began to drain from her. She sensed the old numbness. Then a feeling of grief too sharp to be borne. He would go away, this man she so desperately wanted. She would be left as she was before, no more than a frozen bird on a twig or like flowers left in a vase without water.

He turned back to her and said, quite naturally, "Have you had a boyfriend since your husband died?"

"No," she replied, startled at the question.

"Well, then," he said, "your only problem is deciding what to eat. Mine's trying to get that poncey waiter over here to take the order." His knee touched hers under the table. He squeezed one of her knees between his own. "What do you want to eat?"

Mary, who had seen the word on the menu and remembered the taste from Framlingham, asked, "Can I have pheasant?"

"Not going to be cheap to take about, are you?" said Johnnie Bridges.

Mary bit the bottom lip of her angel's mouth and giggled.

It must have been in 1955, when I still knew nothing about Mary other than her name, when I picked up a photograph I found lying incongruously among the papers on my father's desk. The picture showed a group of people, three men and two women, at a table crowded with bottles in what was evidently a night club. Or it might have been somewhere like the Dorchester — I don't know. All the faces of these people, elaborately dressed in evening clothes, were turned to the camera. The men all looked as if they might have been a little drunk. Two of them were heavy-set, rather stupid-looking, tough and evidently not much soothed by the effects of the dinner, the drinks and the band, which I imagined somehow as playing hit songs from *Call Me Madam* or some such show. Between the two of them was a dark girl, smiling into the camera, an all-teeth smile you felt she must have learned from Hollywood films. She had tight curls, a very low-cut dress and a lot of make-up. She wore long, dangling earrings. She was the type that, in those days, I'm afraid, I would have called a "floosie" or a "tart". Both the heavy men had an arm round her shoulders as she, oblivious of them, gave the club or hotel photographer her professional smile. And next to one of the men was a very fair girl, looking at a handsome chap. He was also staring into the camera and smiling. His hand was over hers on the tabletop. She wore a low-cut gown, like the other girl, and the same dangling earrings. Her hair curled round the same over-made-up face. Why she looked less shop-worn than anyone else in the group I do not know. Perhaps it was her youth – she can have been only eighteen or nineteen at the time. It may have been her loving look at the handsome man beside her or simply that, gazing up at him, her face bore one of the charming half-innocent smiles you can see on the faces of men and women in some of the paintings of Fragonard. At any rate, she was a beauty, and that was chiefly what caught my young man's eye. As for the others, the two tough men were too tough for me, the dark girl too hard and the handsome, reckless-looking man at whom the girl gazed was a type I recognized from school – the big, already-a-man fifth former, he of the sexual exploits in the holidays, the well hit 87 runs against Stoneyhurst and the sharp, cribbing eye in the examination room. In any case, I was jealous of him for having the attention of the girl. When my father came into the room I was still looking at the photograph. Something made me feel guilty when he saw me with it. I dropped it on the desk and said, "Funny picture – anyone you know?"

"Gangsters," he said shortly.

"What have you got it for?" I asked.

"Part of the job," he said rather irritably. "Part of the job."

My eyes went back to the pretty girl. "This one's got a nice smile," I said, pointing at it.

He leaned over my shoulder and looked. "Not in the next one," he told me. He lifted that photograph up to reveal another. This had evidently been taken just before or after the first. Here, the photographer had managed to command the attention of the whole group. The two toughs stared into the camera, smiling grimly. The two girls had widened their eyes and smiled to show their teeth. Only the handsome man on the right looked the same, smiling evenly, calmly, knowingly. In the meanwhile an intruder, a bearded man in a striped shirt, had slipped his arm round the blonde girl and was saying something. Whatever sly remark he made – and I had the idea it was sly – was making her laugh more widely, with her head tilted back in approved Hollywood style, like a picture of a film star outside a Gaumont.

"Mm," I said. "She doesn't look so nice in that one."

"I'm glad you think so," he said.

"Are they Scotland Yard photographs?" I asked. But the whole subject obviously depressed him. He sighed and said, "Never mind." He crossed to the window and looked out over the square. "I wonder," he said, as much to himself as to me, "how you would have turned out if you had had no advantages? If you'd been born in a cottage on one of the farms on the estate, for example. Ever thought about that?"

Naturally, I had not. Indeed, at nineteen the idea that you have "turned out" to be anything is alien and strangely annoying. I took my own life seriously, of course, but I took my condition for granted.

"I suppose I'd have dug ditches in that case," I told my father, "or driven a tractor or something. There's not much alternative for anyone from a cottage is there? I suppose you just do what your father did before you – country people are very conservative, after all, aren't they? And you did what your father did and presumably I may do it one day – unless," I blithered on, "the bolshies get back in again. Then we may get a stronger dose of revolution than we had the last time in which case, I suppose, they'll hang the Royal Family and shoot the House of Lords and I'll be directed to go down the nearest coal mine." I thought these last remarks to be rather suave and funny but soon observed that my father did not. He responded by squashing me – "Yes, well, try thinking a little bit from time to time – I assure you it won't hurt your health."

I said, "Oh, come on, father. You know what I meant."

"Oh, yes," he said. "I know what you meant. But it won't do, dear boy. It won't do." Then he sighed and told me, "I'm turning into an old curmudgeon – you and I must have a serious talk before you go back to the University –" and at that point the telephone mercifully rang, cutting off his rather confusing remarks. As he answered it I made an embarrassed escape.

We never had the promised serious conversation – at least, when we did it was eighteen months later, and I had taken my degree. The photograph was one of the things he explained to me on that summer evening when the starlings swooped over the big London garden and the course of my life was planned for me, exactly like, when you come to think of it, the life of a boy born in a labourer's cottage who grows up to be a tractor-driver or a cowman on the same estate . . .

Johnnie and his mates had planned this big bank raid. They did it and got away with it and that was when I said I couldn't stand any more of it, the worry and the pain and so forth, I said that he had to get out or else – the upshot was that the next day he went to see the Rose brothers and they agreed to go in with him. So they started this gaming club, Frames, in South Molton Street. Johnnie owned a third of it and the Roses the other two-thirds. Johnnie was going to manage it, and get wages for doing that as well as a third part of the profits. And I said I'd act as a hostess, doing some croupiering when needed. I wound up doing all that, and the housekeeping, too, but that's another story.

I'll never forget Frames. Being in it was the sort of thrill some people get from owning their first home – everything in it was lovely. Basically it was a little eighteenth- or early nineteenth-century house in a little West End street. It had been a posh gents hairdresser's, like they used to have in those days, where they'd shave you with a cut-throat razor, polish up your shoes and rub a silk hankie round your bowler before they hand it back to you. Anyway, the man who ran it went out of business and the Roses got the place cheap on a lease. It was Johnnie who got it done up – he had class, you see. That was one of the reasons Norman and Arnie Rose put him in charge. He could look like a gentleman if he wanted to. If the Roses had been in charge of decorating it the place would have looked like a clip joint. Johnnie had it painted up like a normal house – dark green, with a big carved wood front door and a little sign saying "Frames" in gold above it. There were big windows in front, covered with white net curtains. At night big heavy green velvet curtains were pulled over them. The ground floor had a bar and a roulette room at the back, for the small punters. The next two floors were all panelling and green baize tables and thick carpets. That was where the heavy games – poker, chemin de fer, roulette – took place. Subtle lighting, not so dark you couldn't see what you were doing, or the other fellow, for that matter, but not dazzling neon, either. Some nights around two or three, you couldn't see through the air for cigar and cigarette smoke and you couldn't hear anything but low voices, the odd clink of a glass, the click of the dice and the odd smack of a card going down on the baize. A car or two might pass, but the sound was muffled. If you shut your eyes you might think you were at a vicarage tea party. If you opened them you'd see a lot of well dressed men, leaning or sitting at the tables, passing the odd remark, and maybe offering each other cigarettes from silver or gold cigarette cases. In fact they were playing high, in thousands, even tens of thousands on the odd occasion. Some of them would have staked their wives and kids if they'd been worth anything. I don't understand the impulse, myself, but there it is, some people have got it. Fact is after we opened Frames it got fashionable and successful. I thought it was the most glamorous thing in the world. There we were, me in a long dress, Johnnie got up in a dinner jacket and bow tie, smart as you please. I thought it was my birthday – I had four or five long dresses including the black one, with the sequins on the front and the hem, and the flame-red one with the swirling skirt, made up of layers and layers of swirling chiffon, and the green silk which I wore with the pearl necklace Johnnie bought me out of the takings. Can you imagine how I felt, in love with handsome Johnnie, swishing around all night at Frames in the new clothes – after what I'd been through in Meakin Street with Jim Flanders?

Upstairs in the flat we had the big bed with the white fur cover and the white fitted carpets, the fluffy coloured rugs, the cocktail cabinet filled with every kind of drink – Bourbon, Tia Maria, the lot. Not to mention the big sunken bath with the gold taps. Looking back, I suppose it was horrible but at the time it was a dream come true. Ivy was impressed, in spite of herself. Sid wouldn't even come to the club to have a look. He hated Johnnie, like a lot of men did. They spotted something in him they seemed to recognize, and disliked and half-envied, too. But Ivy was partly carried away by his gentlemanly manner and the fact that he was loading her daughter with goodies. She almost forgot that thanks to him she was now in full charge of her granddaughter – because obviously I couldn't bring Josephine up in a club while I was working all hours. She was better off with Ivy, especially as I could afford to give her good money for taking care of the kid. But as I say, Sid couldn't stand the situation, or Johnnie, and the fact that the Rose brothers were the club's backers made it worse.

The Roses never appeared in public at Frames because they knew they'd be out of place in this well heeled, upper-class crowd. No amount of Savile Row suiting, handmade shoes and manicures from

Grosvenor Square could disguise what they were – mobsters. The fact that they existed behind the scenes was good enough. Because the law won't enforce gambling debts the punters had to feel there was somebody behind the door who would force them to pay up. And the Rose brothers were good at accidents – runnings over, fallings out of windows, surprise assaults by strangers in dark alleys. They must have had about sixty men on their unofficial payroll, some full-time, some part-time. They were always busy, threatening shop-owners in Camden Town and Canning Town who hadn't paid up their protection money, arranging for things to happen to their rivals, paying out money to women whose husbands were in prison due to accidents on the Roses' jobs, catching up with lorrydrivers whose loads had somehow not fallen off the backs of their lorries after the Roses had invested in them, beating up tarts who had handed over their takings to their poor old mothers instead of the Roses' appointed agents, or ponces. They had lawyers, doctors, accountants and policemen on the payroll. By this time they were like investors in crime – they never did any of the jobs themselves. They financed them, they invented them, but if the law came round the Rose brothers always had an alibi. It hadn't always been like that, of course. Sid and Ivy could remember them as boys from Wattenblath Street, picking up a bob here and a bob there, collecting bets and running them to the local bookie (off-course betting being illegal in those days) and generally picking and thieving and taking the money home to their evil old mother. It was the war which started them off, of course. Norman had something wrong with him, or convinced the army that he had, so he never had to join up. Arnie deserted and they never found him. That meant they could both make a good thing out of the black market during the war and after it – crates of whisky, nylons, sides of beef and God knows what went through their hands the whole time. They made a fortune. The old West London gangs had broken down badly during the war because of the confusion – when they came to re-form there were the Rose brothers, young and keen, ready to put up a challenge. And they won. Officially they spoke of themselves as two lads from a poor but good home who had made it in the big world outside. They bought their dear old widowed mother a lovely house at Sunningdales and never spoke of her with anything but respect, in spite of the fact that she'd spent their childhoods looking for trade under the viaduct at Waterloo and laying violent hands on her children. They'd been terrified of her. I suppose they had a start in life you wouldn't wish on anybody. It's probably no wonder they were rotten to the core, which they were, in spite of all their back-slapping and drinks-all-round and the horrible, frightening, meant to be friendly, smiles they gave you, which would curdle your blood if you didn't glance away.

Still, whatever they were like I was in business with them, enjoying every minute of it. And as long as they stayed in the background the punters at Frames could forget about them, or take the line that they were bold, bad chaps, like cowboys in a Western, and not up to any real harm. It was only when you got into debt at Frames that you began to get the message that the Rose brothers weren't all that nice. And in the meantime Johnnie and I were standing in front, with Simon, who we'd taken on as an under-manager, and Johnnie and I had a white Jaguar, I had clothes, jewellery, ten or eleven pairs of shoes – I thought I was lucky, I can tell you. Like anybody young, I suppose I thought it would last forever. And then, of course, I had Johnnie.

"God, gel – you're something special," he had said to her, that first night at Meakin Street. He was lying on his back, smoking a Players, in the big bed with the brass knobs. Mary smiled at him. She thought she had never been happier. They had only met the day before.

After the walk along the canal and the dinner at the posh restaurant he had left her at her front door. Afterwards he said, "I knew I could have had you that night, on your own doormat if I wanted. But I wanted to show a bit of respect." Some time after that she realized that he had had to break with his old girlfriend also. Mary went to bed that night dazed and cheerful and apprehensive at the same time. Suppose he did not come back? Suppose he thought she was too young, or he did not like the idea of Josephine or he just thought she was not good enough? But Johnnie, a romantic, was on her step at eight next morning with roses. She invited him in. He said he had to go but that he would see her that evening. Mary, who had scarcely slept the night before, went through the day in an agitated dream. She managed, however, to get to the hairdresser, buy a pair of shoes and deliver Josephine hastily to Ivy at the time when she would normally be expected at the pub. She knew if she said she was going out with Johnnie, Ivy would question her, tell her to go to work and even refuse to mind the child for her. On the other hand, once she was gone Ivy could do nothing about it. She sat biting her nails at Meakin Street for an hour and a half in case Ivy found out she was not at the pub before

Johnnie came to pick her up. Then she was away, out of the house in a flash, sitting beside him in the car as they swept into the West End. He took her to a basement club in Gerrard Street, where, in the dim lighting, drinking the champagne he ordered, she met the people he knew. There were a lot of them, all known by nicknames – Tommo, Lil, Tic-tac – and everyone greeted Johnnie with some respect, offered him drinks, asked him how he was, talked to him in indirect language she could not understand, about things she didn't understand. She even saw Harry Smith's brother, in the corner, drinking beer. He nodded at her and put his nose back in his glass. On the other hand, though ignorant, Mary had sharp instincts and the normal acquaint-anceship with crime of a girl from a working-class family. "He must be a cracksman," she said to herself. Cracksmen, or safe-breakers, were aristocrats. It was skilled work, clean and on the whole non-violent.

"Poor old duck was terrified, standing there in the doorway in her winseyette nightie," he reported to a friend. "'Don't hurt me,' she says, all-of-a-tremble. 'Get back into bed, dear, till I'm finished,' I tell her. 'I wouldn't lay a finger on you for all the world.' So she goes away and I get on with opening the safe. Before I go I shout out, 'I'm through now, darling. You can ring the law.' She's a game old bird – she shouts back, 'Thank you very much. I will.'"

The other man, and those with him, laughed. Their girls leaned against them, smiling. "Dunno where the staff was," Johnnie added. "They must have been hiding in bed with their heads under the blankets. Still, though, you should have seen her in her nightie. I'm bent over the bleeding safe trying not to laugh."

"You'll be the death of yourself one day, Jonno," said the big man beside him. At the same time he looked hard at Mary, who had been discreetly examined a good deal since she first walked in. The women had appraised her. The men had just stared. Johnnie put his arm round her and said, "Ted – Mary Flanders – Ted Saunders."

"Pleased to meet you," murmured Mary.

"Flanders – Flanders –," said the man, trying to remember. Then he said, tactfully, "Are you any relation to Jim Flanders –?"

"I'm his widow," Mary said firmly.

"Oh dear, oh dear," said the man. "Well – I'm very sorry." But neither he, nor any of the others, looked at her strangely any more. Here, thought Mary, was a place where people did not act as if they were sorry for you when they knew you were Jim's widow, something to be said for bad company, then, she thought.

Later, as the men got more noisy at the bar, a girl came over and touched her elbow. "I'm Susie," she said. "Why don't you come and sit down over there with us and leave them to it." She nodded at the men. Mary followed her. There was a dark girl in a lace dress sitting in the corner. "Mary — Jeanne. Jeanne — Mary," Susie said briefly. "Sit down, love," she said to Mary. "They're getting to the boring stage over there. We're better off talking women's talk on our own."

"Funny how they bring you out for the evening and then spend the whole time talking to each other," Mary said.

"Just as well," said Jeanne. "Who wants to hear what they've got to say?"

"You've got a baby, haven't you?" said Susie. "What is it — boy or girl?"

"A little girl — Josephine," Mary told her.

"That's nice," said Susie. "I'd love to see her one day."

"Well — one day," Mary said. "If you're round our way."

The big man, Ted, came over with three drinks. "Two gins for two ladies and a nice big glass of champagne for Mr Bridges' companion," he said, putting them on the table. "Here you are, girls — drink 'em slowly and remember you're always ladies."

"Champagne," said the dark girl, Jeanne, raising her glass and smiling widely at Johnnie. "How did you come to meet him?" she asked. The broad smile was wiped from her face as she looked at Mary.

"In the pub where I work."

"How long ago?" persisted the girl.

"Yesterday," replied Mary.

"Taken a fancy to him, have you?" asked Jeanne.

"Leave her alone, Jeanne," Susie protested to her friend.

"Have you?" Jeanne asked again, peering at her.

"Yes — I suppose I have," answered Mary.

"Well — watch out for yourself, dear," advised Jeanne.

"Leave her alone, Jeanne," Susie said. "She's happy."

"So far," Jeanne said. "She's a nice girl but she's had enough trouble. She doesn't need any more. You know Johnnie — love 'em and leave 'em, that's his motto."

"You know him better than I do," Susie said sharply.

"I suppose I can love him and leave him, too, if I want to," Mary said boldly.

"Doesn't work that way, duckie," said the dark girl. She got up and walked, swaying slightly, up to the bar. She spoke to the men who took almost no notice. Some smiled at her. She was angry when they ignored her and pulled at Johnnie's coat. He shrugged. The big man took her by the elbow and steered her across the room and out of the door. As she went she said, in Mary's direction, "He'll take you to Madame Renée's, in Tite Street. He's bought so many dresses there they give him a discount. Make hay while the sun shines, duckie."

"Poor bitch," said Susie compassionately. "Take no notice of her – she's drunk." Mary, looking at Susie's face, pretty, blurry and kind, thought that she, Susie, was not altogether sober. But she said, "Did that girl, Jeanne, used to be a girlfriend of Johnnie's?"

"Long time ago," Susie said tactfully. "He threw her over and she couldn't forgive him. But it's not just that with Jeanne. It's everything. She has no luck. She just hasn't got any luck at all."

"What happened to her?" Mary asked.

"Oh – this and that. Women's problems," Susie said vaguely. She put her hand over Mary's. "Look here," she said. "Johnnie's kind and generous and a good sort and a nice looker. He doesn't hang around forever – but who does? He can show you a good time. On the other hand, you're only a young girl so don't get carried away. He's here today and gone tomorrow. Remember that. Don't start having too many dreams. Then you'll be all right."

"I know all that," Mary said, surprising herself.

"Good girl," said Susie.

Nevertheless, Mary's eyes went towards the door. Then back across the room again to where the men were still laughing and joking. Then at the women in their attractive clothes. They were all young, or fairly young. They wore a lot of make-up. Her eyes went back to the door.

Then up came Johnnie. He chucked her under the chin and said, "Feeling neglected, pussy? Come on – we'll go and have some fun."

"Why not?" said Susie. "You're only young once." Staring uncertainly round the club, at the well dressed crowd, at the jovial men, the animated women, and then back at Johnnie, bending over her tenderly, Mary said, "That's right. Let's go." And she stood up and went out with him.

"Back to your house?" suggested Johnnie in the car. And Mary said, "Yes." He drove with his hand on her knee. He said, at the traffic lights at Marble Arch, "I don't want you to think I – Put it another way – did Jeanne say anything to you?"

"She's jealous," Mary told him. "I could tell."

"You don't want to believe too much of what they say," he said.

"I don't," said Mary, which was a lie. She believed what they said but did not care. She added, her voice shaking a little, "I love you, Johnnie."

He squeezed her knee and said, "Christ – they've gone green," started the car and drove off. The lights of the park, the gleam of the late summer trees as they drove up Bayswater Road, made her think she was dreaming. Back at Meakin Street she said, "Coming in?" He nodded and she opened the door. In the hall they fell into each other's arms. He carried her up the stairs saying, "You're a nice armful, I must say." In the bedroom he had taken off her clothes resolutely, but somehow expecting a protest and, as she lay naked on the bed, watching him, he had taken off his own clothes and cast himself on top of her saying, "I can't wait – Mary – I can't," and she, with all the certainty in the world, had put her arms around his naked back, said his name, felt his hard cock drive into her and felt such a great, triumphant joy at having him that she knew nothing but pleasure and happiness until the great waves of sensation swept her up at the end and she heard, faintly, through the sensations which took her, a voice, her own, crying out loudly.

"Oh, love," said Johnnie Bridges, looking down at her and kissing her face.

She smiled up at him. "You frightened me there, for a minute," he told her. "What a noise. Have the neighbours rushing in."

"I nearly frightened myself," she said.

"Never happened before?" he said, unsurprised.

"No," she said.

"Funny how often that happens," he said. "Well, then – I'm your first."

"Seems like it," she told him. "Oh, Johnnie, I love you so."

"Oh, gel," he said. "You're special. You're something really special."

But the next day, after Johnnie had left to pick up some clothes from his mother's house, Ivy was banging on the door heavily. Mary opened it with her coat over her nightdress and there stood her mother, in a flowered apron, with the pram. "For two pins," she declared instantly, "I'd have left this outside your door whether you were in or out, and just walked away."

"Do you want to come in, mum?" asked Mary, knowing that she would.

"No, I don't. But I will anyway," Ivy declared.

She dragged the pram in after her and said, "I don't know where you think you were last night. I was running to the neighbours at eleven o'clock at night when you didn't come back. From one I find out you're not at the pub working. And, of course it's Elizabeth Flanders who has to be the one to tell me she saw you get in a man's car at eight o'clock at night when she's coming back from some meeting at the church. Imagine what I felt! You'd better do some thinking, Mary – I've been awake all night worrying. What about the child?"

In the meanwhile she was looking in the parlour, then in the kitchen.

"Cup of tea, mum?" asked Mary.

"Might as well," said Ivy, satisfied that there was no man on the premises. Then she said, "There's nobody upstairs is there?"

"No," Mary told her.

"I don't want to be unreasonable," Ivy told her. "And you'd better give the baby her egg. I haven't fed her any solids."

In the kitchen, where Mary put on the kettle and the water for Josephine's egg, Ivy said, "I'd better warn you that Johnnie Bridges is a criminal. Where do you think he gets his money from? What do you think you're up to?"

"He asked me out. I went," said Mary, feeling Johnnie's hands warm on her body. She trembled a little, even then, as she stood watching the kettle, with the morning light coming through the kitchen and her little daughter banging her spoon on the empty shelf in front of her high chair.

"Well, I hope you won't go again, that's all," said Ivy. "Look, Mary – he's not just a fellow with an ordinary job who gets his hand on a bit of stuff that fell off the back of a lorry from time to time. Johnnie Bridges is a professional. He's tied up with Norman and Arnie Rose and you know what that means. You'd better get rid of him now, or you'll rue it later on. As for tricking me by leaving Josie with me and acting as if you were going to work down at the pub, all so you could go out with him – well, I don't believe it, Mary. I wouldn't have believed you could do a thing like that. I can see what's happening – you're starting to go down. You'd better pull yourself together straight away or I don't know what's going to happen next."

"I'm seeing him again today. Will you look after Josephine?" Mary asked.

"Are you deaf?" demanded Ivy, putting the egg into the boiling water. "Haven't you been listening at all to what I've been saying? I'm telling you – give him up now, before it's too late. He'll wind up in jail, I'm telling you. Do I have to say it twice – if you think I'm going to look after your baby so you can get involved with Johnnie Bridges you've got another think coming."

"Please, mum," said Mary, pleading. "Honestly – he's not bad. He wants to get out of thieving. That's true – he means it."

Ivy's face sagged. She said in a defeated voice, "Mary – they all mean it. Sometimes. And then along comes another job, another chance to get rich quick. And they take it. I can understand what's going through your head. You're lonely, that's natural –"

"I'll ask Lil Messiter, then," Mary interrupted. "She'll be glad of a few bob extra."

"So that's it," said Ivy, changing her tone. "You've got to have a feller at all costs. As long as he's got looks and a bit of money to flash about you don't ask any questions. You stupid little bitch. You'll wind up as a gangster's moll. First him, then somebody else – then God knows what – you'll be chucking yourself in the river in ten years' time and you'll be one of the lucky ones. They don't last long at that game, I can tell you, not them girls. They fetch up on the streets. Always. Only one way to go once you've started that game – down. You've seen them for yourself, hanging about on street corners and under arches in all weathers, looking for a pick-up. Worn out at thirty. He won't marry you, Bridges, and after that no decent man will look at you. Who'd want a gangster's leavings? And what about poor little Josephine?"

Mary, feeling the chill of the street corner blowing about her said, "I like him."

" 'I like him,' " said Ivy, throwing back her head. " 'I like him.' Oh, my Christ. What am I hearing?"

Mary took the egg out of the boiling water with a spoon. She put it into an egg cup to cool.

"I should have known when you took this bloody place what you had in mind," cried Ivy. "I should have put a stop to it."

"I've had enough of this, Mum," Mary shouted back. "You've got no rights over me. I'm a widow – remember. I'm a gangster's widow already. You can't come here as if I'm a little girl from a convent school who ran away with a big, bad man. And I'll see who I like when I like and it hasn't got anything to do with you."

Ivy looked her straight in the eye and said, "I'm leaving – and don't come to me for any help when you're in trouble because you won't get it."

Josephine began to cry as her grandmother slammed the kitchen door behind her. Mary stood still for a moment, partly sobered. This was the first time Ivy had ever threatened to withdraw her support. Then she set her mouth and cracked the top of Josephine's breakfast egg.

It was a long, Indian summer for her. It seemed that the dark green trees would never turn brown, the air would remain perpetually full of golden light, as if the year would stay pitched between the end of summer and the start of autumn for ever and ever. She and Johnnie took Josephine to the seaside and dipped her toes in the waves. She screamed with delight and struggled to get from Mary's arms. They shopped extravagantly, ate, went dancing and made love for long, warm nights in Mary's big bed at Meakin Street.

Meanwhile Johnnie maintained a home of some kind elsewhere. Mary was mildly curious about this unknown address, half-suspecting him of having a wife tucked away somewhere. How, otherwise, were his shirts always so immaculate, starched to exactly the right degree? How were his suits so beautifully pressed and his shoes so well-polished? Sometimes she saw a West End flat, filled with expensive furniture, presided over by a blonde mistress smelling strongly of scent – but it was hard to imagine this figure toiling over a washtub. Sometimes she saw a passive wife in the suburbs – but he did not give the impression of having that sort of domesticity in his life. And none of this vastly worried her. She was in a dream – what mattered was not where he might sometimes hang his hat or pick up his laundry but whether he loved her, and whether she loved him. And she knew she was so happy that nothing could be really wrong. She was content to see him disappear for a few days and then reappear.

But Meakin Street, and especially the women, hated her. She, sad widow of their unjustly hanged Jim Flanders, was now flashing about in a white car with a fancy man. She dragged them down with her carryings-on. Yet she looked so bonny and happy that they could not help comparing their own position with hers. Mary was not paying the price of sin. It looked as if she were getting rewarded for it. Their hard eyes followed her as she wheeled her pram along the street. They whispered, their arms crossed on their breasts. "Tart – disgusting isn't it? Should've been her what got hung."

Strangely enough, Ivy's attitude weakened. She could see her daughter was happy. She heard her grandchild shouting excitedly when Johnnie appeared in the doorway with an oversized teddy bear in his arms. She found the notorious gangster one day in his shirtsleeves in the kitchen, unstopping the sink.

"He's good to you, I will say that," she said grudgingly to Mary, when her daughter showed her a new coat. In the end it was Sid who maintained his hostility to Johnnie. He told Mary bluntly that he did not want to meet Johnnie and that if he did come across him by chance he would say what he thought about him to his face.

"You're carried away, Ivy," he said to his wife one evening, as they were having a cup of tea before going to bed. "Of course she's happy now. What about later? This is the honeymoon but it won't go on. What happens after? Suppose she has a kid – what then? That sort doesn't hang about for long, even if they get the chance, which half the time they can't. They're in prison. Then our Mary's left there, pale and peaky, maybe with another kid, or one on the way, waiting for him to come out. You're not minding Josephine no more while Mary gads about with him." Ivy had weakened over the question of minding the child after her first declarations.

"Oh come on, Sid," Ivy expostulated. "What's she supposed to do – a widow of seventeen with a baby. She's got to go out sometimes."

"Not with him," Sid told her. "Let her look after her kid. It'll bring her to her senses. Let her live quiet and get a little job and wait for a decent feller to turn up – that'll do her more good than turning herself into a gangster's moll before our eyes. She's got to learn. If she doesn't do it now she'll do it the hard way later." He put his cup into the saucer with a bang. "This is for your sake and mine as well as hers," he said. "Because if it goes on, it's us who'll have to pick up the pieces. Say she has another kid and he gets caught – who'll have to support the three of them while he's inside? Us – that's who."

Ivy picked a time when Johnnie was out and went round to Meakin Street. Mary, sitting in front of the fire with the baby on her knee, began to cry. "It's not fair, mum," she said. "Why do I have to get stuck like this?"

"That's what happens to women," Ivy told her unsympathetically. "Anyway – I can't do nothing about it. I can't defy your father. My life'd be a misery. And perhaps it's for the best. It'll give you a chance to look at it all clearly. He's a crook, when all's said and done. And where does he disappear to when he's not here?"

"I don't care," cried Mary. "All I know is Josephine's spoiled my chances."

"Don't sit there with that baby on your knee talking like that," said Ivy. "Your own child – less than a year old."

"*My* child – oh yes," Mary said bitterly. "What about Jim Flanders? Where's her dad? Bloody dead, that's all – went out and got himself hung, that's all. Oh, mum – can't you mind Josie for an hour while I go out and find Johnnie?"

"If he had anything to him he'd be here with you, now," her mother said implacably.

"Yes – watching the telly," Mary said.

Mary sat with tears running down her face, imagining Johnnie, who had been gone for three days, with Susie or Jeanne. He would never come back – if he did he would not stay, not if she had Josephine with her night and day. She could not afford to pay someone to mind her child all the time. Even if she could, most of their outings were spontaneous. She would not be able to organize it. And now Ivy was against her. Just because she had a child the whole world wanted her to resign from life. She was supposed to live like a nun, tending an altar. And the altar was to be Josephine. It wasn't fair. Not fair. Not fair.

"It's not fair," she said.

"Nothing is," responded her mother.

"I can't put up with it," she sobbed.

"You'll have to," said her mother. "All the rest of us did."

"Oh – oh – oh," cried Mary, sobbing and shouting with rage and pain. "I'll kill myself. I will. I will."

Ivy took Josephine from her and said, "You'll have to start watching what you say in front of this child. She's clever. She understands more than you think. And it's time she went to bed."

While Ivy was upstairs settling the baby Mary thought wildly of grabbing her coat and going round the clubs to find Johnnie. Ivy would have to look after Josephine if she had gone. But the thought of the rows to follow frightened her.

She sat and bit her nails to the quick.

Ten days later Johnnie still had not returned. Mary had lost seven pounds in weight and was pale as a ghost. She was sleeping only a few hours each night and, when she did, her dreams terrified her. She had had the same dreams before, in childhood, but not so regularly, or so frighteningly. There were burning buildings, crashes, which often woke her and often a woman's high voice sang over the sounds of destruction, in a foreign language. It was a voice full of loss and sadness, hopeless, forlorn.

She was lying sleepless in bed, and dreading sleep, when the doorknocker was banged over and over again. It was one in the morning. Mary, her heart thudding, ran downstairs in her nightdress. There on the step stood Johnnie Bridges, red-eyed, his suit unpressed, his shirt open at the neck.

"You'd better come in," said Mary.

Once the door was shut behind them he took her in his arms and began to kiss her. "Come on, girl," he muttered. "Upstairs. I need you."

"Not so fast," Mary said. "You haven't been back for a fortnight."

Then he pulled her unresistingly up the stairs and made love to her like a starving man. "Oh, God. I've missed you," he said.

And this made up for everything. At that moment, Josie shouted. There was a bang. Mary jumped out of bed and ran into the bedroom next door. The child was standing on the floor in her nightdress. As Mary stared she walked towards her. Mary caught her as she fell down. "She got out of the cot," Mary exclaimed. "She can walk!"

"We'll have to take her into bed with us," said Johnnie. "She might do it again and hurt herself."

So the three slept cosily together that night. But next day, early, he was off again. "You can't do this," Mary cried out. "It's not fair."

Bending to kiss her he said, "You'll have to trust me. We'll go out tonight. Pick you up at seven."

Mary, in bed, shed a tear on the baby's dark curls. Then she lay back luxuriously and felt a lot better. The constant pain and the nightmares had gone. She had hope, now.

As she left the house with Johnnie that evening Sid, coming home from work in his inspector's uniform, spotted them from across the street as he trudged home. Johnnie was wearing an immaculate shirt and a new well-cut blue suit, just collected from the tailor. Mary wore a bell-skirted red dress and a white fur cape. Mary's father looked away and walked on.

"He'd have to speak to me at the wedding," Johnnie remarked, opening the car door for her. Mary got in, holding the baby, saying nothing. There were times when she was dying to get married to Johnnie. On the other hand, she had seen what happened to you when you married – the whole world expected you to get out of bed with double pneumonia to get your husband's tea or find his socks. As with a baby, a husband was expected to be something like a religion for a woman – down Meakin Street the menfolk were discussed as if they were gods, the sort of god which needed a lot of human sacrifice and tended to do nasty things for no reason. "I'll have to go home and get His tea now," the women would say. Or, "I'd like to do it but He'd make my life a misery." Then, Mary thought, you had to put up with whatever they slung at you and get old before your time. Look at Lil Messiter, half dead from childbearing, the old man taking his spite out on her when he'd had one too many. It didn't look like fun, even when the man was reasonable and the couple loved each other, as she supposed Sid and Ivy did. In Johnnie's circles, she thought, the story was a bit different, but no better. The wives got tucked away in nice houses somewhere in the suburbs while the men went off to clubs, pubs and the races, taking pretty girls with them. She wouldn't want to be one of the wives but the fate of the girls, like Jeanne and Susie, wasn't much good in the long run as they got older and the presents got smaller and they changed hands more often. Once their freshness was gone – and it didn't last long – they disappeared. But the wives looked strained when they appeared in public in their smart dresses, covered in diamanté, and the make-up heavy over faces which had once been as bright as Jeanne's or Susie's. The choices ahead of her were unappealing – hang around and maybe get jaded and start drinking too many gins – marry Johnnie and get tucked away in Ilford, or Dulwich, in a four-bedroomed suburban house with the kids. She sighed and then threw off the thoughts. She was happy now and that was enough. She squeezed Johnnie's arm as they drove round Trafalgar Square and thought suddenly of the Kentish countryside where she had lived as a child. She thought of Allaun Towers and Mrs Gates. She saw the reeds growing by the unkempt lake, the red brick wall of the vegetable garden, the old green brocade chair in her room at the corner of the house. She saw the fields, and the swell of gorse-covered heath above them. She saw every leaf on the elms beside the drive, the gravel in front of the house, with little green tufts of weed growing among the stones. She saw the two pigeons which had nested in a chimney sitting on the lead guttering below her attic, cooing and fluffing out their feathers. She saw the brook, the watercress growing in the shallow water, the long grass along its sides. Then she realized that she and Johnnie were crossing Lambeth Bridge.

"Where are we going?" she asked.

"Ah — thought I'd satisfy your curiosity about my secret gaff," he told her. "The horrible sordid place I creep into when I'm not with you."

"Oh," she said.

He took her hand as they swung round a corner. "You had a rough time while I was gone, didn't you?" he said.

"It was horrible, Johnnie," she blurted out. "I thought you were never coming back. I was like a madwoman. I had dreadful dreams —"

"All right now?" he asked.

"Oh, yes," she said. "I love you, Johnnie," she said.

"I love you, Moll," he said. He had never told her that before.

She felt empty, suddenly, and the memory, dimly, of those half-realized dreams, about crashes and fires, all overlaid with the sweet, sad voice of a woman singing, came back to her. "I must be going barmy," she said to herself. In fact this ride seemed like another dream. They raced the streets. The baby slept on her lap. Where were they going?

"Is it far?" she asked him.

"No — few more miles," he answered. "Anyway, Moll, I've got some plans. I want to change things. I think I'm going to be able to set myself up nicely."

"What are you going to do?" she asked him.

"You know what they say — never tell a woman anything," he told her.

"Why not?"

"It's an old motto in the business. Most of the time you're better off not knowing. Anyway, while I was away I managed to raise a little capital — which I'm thinking of investing and going legitimate."

"Oh, Johnnie — what a relief," she said. "You don't know what it's like, wondering what's happening." Although she thought to herself that it had not been Johnnie's arrest she had dreaded over those recent awful days — it had been his desertion of her.

Then she realized, as they entered suburban, tree-lined streets full of houses built in the nineteenth century, each with a large garden at the front, that there must be some connection between this trip and his new plans. By the time they drew up in front of one of the houses she had become quite excited. They got out and looked at the front of the house. The garden was well tended. There were roses still blooming.

"Here we are," he said. "The secret hide-away of arch-criminal

Johnnie Bridges." Mary doubled up, hanging on to the baby, laughing fit to bust.

"I don't believe it," she said. "You're having me on."

A large tabby cat walked up to them as they stood on the pavement. It began to rub up against Johnnie's trouser leg.

"This your cat?" she asked.

"Yes," he answered. Mary roared with laughter again.

"Oh dear, oh dear," she cried. She bent over, holding the baby against her stomach like a bundle of laundry.

"Stand up," he said, "you're making an exhibition of yourself."

Mary pulled herself together, although a fresh look at the cat, now walking affrontedly up the garden path, made her start again.

"This is where my mum and dad live," Johnnie said with some dignity. She glanced at him as they walked towards the front door. How handsome he was – how well set-up. He smiled down at her. She melted. She wished for a moment they were in bed in Meakin Street. She did not really want to meet his parents. She wanted him all to herself. A private world of whispering and bodies locked together. But there was a woman of about forty, dressed in a dark pink woollen dress, standing already on the threshold. She held out her arms, "Johnnie." He embraced her, said, "Hullo, dad," over her shoulder to an invisible person in the hall and then stood back. "Mum – Dad," he said. "This is Mary."

"Come in," said Mrs Bridges. She was small and dark, with the same large, black eyes as her son. As they went inside she said, "You're very welcome. I was just taking some scones out of the oven. Why don't you bring the baby into the kitchen with me?"

In the large, very clean kitchen there was a smell of baking. Mrs Bridges put on a flowered apron and opened the oven door. She took out a tray of scones. "Just in time," she remarked. Mary sat down at the kitchen table with the baby on her lap. Josephine struggled to get down.

"She's just learned to walk," she said. "She wants to do it all the time."

"Little love," said Mrs Bridges. "What lovely curly hair. Put her down on the floor and we'll both watch her." She unloaded the scones on to a wire rack. "I'll put the kettle on," she said. "Is there anything you want for the baby?"

"She only wants some orange juice later, from her bottle," Mary said. "I've got that. Can I do anything to help you? Butter the scones?"

"Here's the butter," Mrs Bridges said. "You go ahead while I make some sandwiches." Josephine toddled across the kitchen floor while the two women got on with their buttering. "Nice to have a baby about again," Mrs Bridges said. "We haven't had a baby in the house since my niece came to stay over Christmas."

In a way it felt to Mary like being back in the kitchen at Allaun Towers. It was peaceful. The clock ticked. It was unlike Ivy's mad scrambles around the tiny kitchen at Meakin Street. In another way she felt very uneasy. Why was she there and who did they think she was? Above all – did they know how their son made a living? How could they?

"John's never brought a girl back here before," Mrs Bridges said. "Not since he was eighteen, anyway."

Mary was searching for some answer to this when the tall, thin man she had passed in the hall put his head round the door. "Any signs of tea, yet, mother?" he asked. "The beasts are getting restless."

"Go and wash your hands, Edward," Mrs Bridges remarked placidly. "Then you can help with the things."

And so tea was loaded on to the trolley and the teapot was left on the kitchen table for Mr Bridges to carry in.

When they got into the front room Johnnie was half asleep in front of the fire, with his legs stretched out.

"Take no notice," Mrs Bridges advised Mary. "He only comes here to sleep in front of the fire. He reminds me of the cat."

"The cat's got more energy," remarked Mr Bridges coming in with the teapot in one hand and a fireguard in the other. He hooked the fireguard on to the sides of the fireplace remarking, "Don't want any accidents, do we? John – your mother says do you want a scone?"

"Yes, please," said Johnnie, coming out of his doze. Mary was still wondering if his parents knew what he did and how Johnnie had come to be a crook from a background like this? The sons of homes like this became bank managers, or council officials, not safebreakers.

They ate their tea in the orderly and conventional room, with a rose-sprigged cretonne-covered sofa and chairs, and gate-legged tables in stained oak. A big gilt clock ticked on the mantelpiece. The teapot was silver. Mr Bridges talked about his garden – "Not much to be done at this time of the year but prepare for next year. And keep the vegetables coming for the family pot, of course. No excuses accepted in that direction, I can tell you." Mary and Mrs Bridges talked about babies. "You have to let them have a few tumbles now and again," said

Mrs Bridges. "You can't wrap them up in cotton wool." Johnnie said little, except to argue about football with his father. "Say what you like," said Mr Bridges, "these huge transfer fees are no good for the game." And afterwards the men were set to mind the baby and make sure she got into no mischief while the two women took the trolley out in the kitchen to wash up. Mary stood beside Mrs Bridges with the tea cloth while she handed her the thin, bone china plates, one by one. Mary, who, thanks to Mrs Gates, had never broken a plate in her life, treated them with the proper care.

"I didn't know you were coming till yesterday," the older woman said. "He sprung it on me out of the blue, by phone."

"I didn't know I was coming till today," said Mary. "In fact he never told me where we were going. It was a mystery tour." She felt very embarrassed, a tall girl, the mistress of this woman's son, too young to have a fatherless baby. She put down another plate on the kitchen table and asked, "Where do you keep these?"

"Leave them there, dear. I'll put them away after," said Mrs Bridges. Handing her a cup she said carefully, "You do know how he gets his living, don't you?"

Not knowing how to reply Mary said, "Well – er – he's told me one or two things –" and turned to put the cup on the table. She put out her hand for another cup, which Mrs Bridges withheld. "He's a thief," she said.

Mary said, "I know." Mrs Bridges handed her the cup.

"What do your mum and dad think of that?" asked the other woman.

"Not much," Mary said, with feeling. "'Specially my dad."

Mrs Bridges sighed and said, "Well, I'm not surprised."

Mary, thinking she'd better come out with it straight away, said, "Did Johnnie tell you what happened to my husband?"

"That's right," agreed Mrs Bridges. "Young fool – with a baby on the way. Of course, I said at the time he shouldn't have been hanged. There was a lot of feeling about that. In my opinion they hung him as an example."

Molly, at a loss for words, went on drying up the cups and saucers carefully.

"We don't take any of John's money," said Mrs Bridges. "Not a penny – just Christmas and birthday presents so's to be normal, otherwise nothing. What started him off was the war, I suppose. His father, being an engineer, went straight into the airforce and after that it was posting after posting. He was hardly ever here. John was twelve when his father went away – a bad age for a boy's dad to disappear. He was good at school, but he didn't take advantage of it. He got in with the wrong crowd. You know how it can be. I couldn't control him. There were lads coming round for him at half past one in the morning, – girls, not nice ones, I can tell you. By the time his father came back after the war he was a petty criminal. I couldn't bear it – I couldn't bear to admit it, even. But he was. Of course I thought his father would do what I hadn't been able to but – well, he couldn't. There was row after row. We turned him out of the house once, after the police found a lot of cases of watches here, under his bed. He got probation. First offence." She paused, helplessly, looking at Mary as if she hoped to find support. Mary said, "But didn't you ought to have kept him with you, after he got caught and convicted –?"

"It was when he did it again," she said.

Mary felt annoyed with Johnnie, for the first time. It seemed wrong that he should have upset this nice, quiet couple in the way he had. Mrs Bridges did not say so but it was obvious she must have had some plans for Johnnie – she and her husband must have hoped he'd become a doctor, or a lawyer, something like that.

"We had to accept it in the end," Mrs Bridges told her, in a firmer voice. "We had to accept he was what he was. He came back that time but the next time we told him he had a home when he wanted one – whenever, whatever he wanted – but not for that. We couldn't let him use it as a base. We wouldn't have his mates round. We didn't want that kind of girl in our house – I hope I'm not shocking you," she said suddenly. "You're not very old –"

"I've heard these things before," Mary told her.

"It's a terrible thing when a child, especially your only one, does that," Mrs Bridges said. "My hair went completely grey in four years. This isn't my own colour," she added. "He would have had a brother but he died before the war. Polio."

"Oh, my God," Mary said. "Oh – Mrs Bridges. Oh – that's terrible."

"These things happen," said Johnnie's mother. "Unfortunately."

Mary put the drying-up cloth on the table beside the crockery and said, "Mrs Bridges – can I make you a cup of tea? You're all upset – no wonder."

"Yes," she said. "I could do with another cup."

"Sit down, then," said Mary. She put on the kettle.

Mrs Bridges sat down and produced a battered packet of Gold Flake from her pocket. She offered Mary one. Mary, who had learned to smoke to keep up with the other girls in the clubs, took it.

Mrs Bridges said, "You had to know."

Mary, setting the teapot on the table said, "I don't know whether I ought to say this, but he told me he was planning to go legitimate."

"I hope to God he is," she said, puffing out some smoke. "Because – because –" she burst out. "I've been worried to death. I think he did that Putney bank job. He didn't tell you –"

"They never do – they don't trust women," Mary said. "But I thought something had happened. He turned up yesterday looking as if he'd been pulled through a hedge backwards. When was it – the bank robbery?"

"Wednesday night, Thursday morning," said Mrs Bridges. "They must have hid out until they were sure the police had no leads – then he came to you. Anyway, I know it was him. I always know when he's in danger. I can't sleep – I get this instinct. I pray. Silly, isn't it – praying your son will get away with a crime. But he must have some money now. Best if he puts it in a business. Do you think that's what he has in mind?"

"I don't know, Mrs Bridges," said Mary.

"You don't want him to go on thieving, do you?" demanded Johnnie's mother. Mary, as when she was expecting her baby, sensed the obligation of concerning herself selflessly with another person being placed upon her and felt the resentment of a horse tasting the bit.

She tried to answer truthfully by saying, "I'm not his wife, am I, Mrs Bridges? Stand to reason I wouldn't want anyone to go on thieving, not after what happened to my husband. But some people aren't made to work nine to five." She paused, thinking this was a poor argument. All she meant was that she doubted if Johnnie Bridges would ever submit to it. And then added, "And he's got no training, either." She paused again and said, "It's a hard choice, after you've had the best of everything and never got caught – either hard work and low pay, or going on like you are –"

"And ending up behind bars," Mrs Bridges said bitterly. She was not finding in Mary quite the ally she desired. She wanted a woman who would dedicate herself to the reclamation of her son.

"He could have done anything," she said sadly. "He was clever at school."

"That's why he's not been caught thieving," Mary told her bluntly.

She had noticed that behind her lover's pretended insouciance lay a keen efficiency. She took another Gold Flake from the packet held out to her by Mrs Bridges and said, "Look – I don't know how to say this to you but in the first place I haven't got a lot of influence over him so I can't change his mind for you. And secondly, I don't like all this much as you can guess – but I don't know I could ask him to go into a dead-end job and sweat his guts out for years and years, like my dad has."

"All you young people think like that," said Johnnie's mother. "It was the Labour government. You've got high ideas now. In my day you were glad of a job, any job, to keep body and soul together. I hope it keeps fine for you."

The door opened and Johnnie said, "Oh – ladies' smoking party, eh? Aren't you coming back to join us?"

And there were Josephine's erratic steps behind him and her piping voice crying, "Don! Don!" He picked her up and handed her to Mary. "Here you are, love. And I think we'd better be going, mum."

As they left, Mary turned on the garden path and waved goodbye to Mr and Mrs Bridges, who were standing on the step. She knew they were both hoping that the formally perfect picture they saw before them – son, young woman and baby leaving after tea on Sunday – would somehow one day turn out to be as real as it looked.

On the way back he said, "What was mum saying to you in the kitchen? Hoping you'd get me to go straight, was she?"

"That's right," Mary said.

"And you told her you'd try?"

"No," Mary said stoutly. "I told her I couldn't see why anyone should sweat their life out for the company for forty years and fetch up with a gold watch and a thank you from the managing director. Then the geezer goes home to his council house and the managing director pops off to his club as usual for another round of pink gins."

"That's my girl," said Johnnie.

"I said I didn't want to see you in jail, either," remarked Mary.

"You'll never see that," he told her.

"No, that's right," she said. She loved him.

I suppose if you study what all this meant what I was saying wasn't what your average working-class girl would have told the man she loved. The usual would have been, "Unless you go straight I'll never see you again." I couldn't do that. I knew I loved Johnnie so much I couldn't part with him, no matter what he did. I suppose if I found out he'd been torturing little children or beating up old ladies I would have had to get rid of him. But if he'd been that sort I doubt if I'd have taken to him in the first place. As it was, at that time, he was a crook, but not a brutal one. It was a mixture of greed, which he had a lot of, and high spirits and the challenge of it all – but the truth is that I took him on the way he was and that's the point I became what Ivy feared I would – a gangster's moll. In fact Johnnie always called me Molly and in the end everybody did. Even Sid and Ivy got round to it. By that time I think I didn't seem to anybody like a Mary any more. That's a plain old name. Your average Mary in those days was a quiet girl who didn't get up to any tricks. So I suppose the name Molly fitted me better.

But Mary, or Molly as we might as well call her now, had the secret hope that Johnnie's vague remarks about going straight might mean something. She knew he must have a good sum, from £5,000 to £10,000, tucked away. Even if it was as low as £5,000 he could buy a small business, say a newsagent or little cafe. If it was more he could do better. But during the following few weeks her hopes were dashed. The money went out like water – a few hundred lost in a poker game here, a new fur coat for Molly there. She took the coat because she knew if she did not the bookies would get the money anyway. "I can always sell it," she told herself. Meanwhile, they still had a good time at the races, round the clubs. They had champagne at all hours – and sex, too. There was no time when Mary did not desire the hardness of Johnnie's body, his cock plunging so deeply inside her that she felt completely taken over by it. Susie, at the club, looked at her through the smoke one night and said, "It don't last, you know, Moll. Don't expect it to last." Molly knew it would. She knew that the love, desire, romance, fulfilment she and Johnnie gave each other would never fail in their magic.

As autumn wore on and became winter she began to realize the implications of the life she had entered with Johnnie. In early November a few of the friends she had met with him – cheerful, open-handed, friendly men, she thought them – began to call at Meakin Street. They tended to stay late. Sometimes Molly went to bed before they left. She had, after all, to get up early and look after the child. Gradually she realized that the men, Jimmy Carr, Allan Lane and Fred Jones, were in the house for a reason. They were trying to get Johnnie out on another job. By mid-November he was interested and by the end of the month committed. Molly began to find it hard to sleep, as she lay there, hearing the men's voices downstairs, knowing that in probability once she had gone upstairs they had laid out their plans and their streetmaps on the table she had proudly polished. They would be eating the sandwiches she had prepared and left on a plate in the kitchen for them. In the morning there would be crumbs, empty glasses, ashtrays overflowing with stubs – she, Molly, was servicing this operation, which might deprive her of her lover. But she would never be allowed to know what was going on.

She found out. On her side was the fact that Johnnie loved her, and so was incautious in his talk, that she looked over the streetmap one morning and found the faint markings they had made on it and, above all, that none of them expected her to want to know. Of the four men involved Allan Lane was the driver and Fred Jones the looker. Jimmy Carr had fallen in love with the secretary of a solicitor who had an office next door to a small bank in West Ealing. One evening, weary of the efforts to get her to sleep with him before her parents came back from the cinema – the assault had gone on for three months as she explained she wished to be a virgin when she married and he evaded making a proposal – he got fed up and took an impression of the keys of the office, which she had in her handbag in the hall. By the time she came to see him, ready to yield herself up to him, he had lost interest and was working on the plan to rob the bank. On Christmas Day, when the takings from the shops in the area were in the vaults, he and Johnnie would let themselves in through the solicitor's door, blow a hole in the wall on the ground floor, get into the bank, get down into the vaults and break open the safes. Fred Jones had taken a room above the chemist's opposite the bank. From there he could look out and signal the arrival of the police, if they came. The one real danger was that the noise of the explosion when the wall was dynamited would bring them along.

"Do it at dinnertime," Johnnie said. "It's the last thing anybody's thinking about then, not with the turkey falling on the floor and the kids being sick – they'll think the neighbours have got some noisy crackers this year."

"I don't like it," Jimmy Carr had said.

"There hasn't been a time when you could blow out a wall without getting heard since the Blitz," Johnnie pointed out. "Unless you've got some way to getting the *Wehrmacht* to help us that's what we've got to do."

"Drink to it," said one.

" 'Luck, then," said another.

Johnnie Bridges quietly raised his glass.

Not long after, they all left. Molly was awake when her lover came upstairs. When Johnnie rolled into bed she said nothing. In the end he told her, "This way I can set myself straight for good and all."

She knew the rules – don't quarrel when a job is planned. You break a man's nerve that way. Instead she said, "What'll you do?"

"I don't need to make detailed plans if I've got twenty, twenty-five thousand in my pocket."

"With twenty-five thousand in your pocket you'd be broke in a year, the way you spend," Molly told him.

"On you, darling, on you," Johnnie said brusquely. "Look at that coat."

"I don't care about the coat or the money," cried Molly. "It's the danger, Johnnie –"

"Don't you worry about little Johnnie Bridges," he said. "He'll be all right, never you fear."

And he was asleep. Molly lay awake in the darkness. They got used to it – women pleading with them to stay out of trouble, then asking for a fur coat or new bikes for the kids or a holiday in Spain. How many women must have said, "It's the danger, Johnnie," and had to be content with the same devil-may-care reply. How many of them had believed it? And did it have to be like this, with her making the tea and them planning the strategy? And hadn't he gone off her since all this began? Look at him now, snoring like a pig while she lay awake, worrying. How long was it since they'd made love together? Five days? Four? It felt like a million years, thought Molly, not daring to wake her lover with a kiss and make him desire her, just in case he told her to shut up and let him sleep.

A fortnight before Christmas Johnnie's tensions were worse. He and Jimmy Carr were in conflict over everything. Jimmy, who saw himself as a robber in the old style, carrying everything off by flash and bravado, complained about Johnnie's meticulous attitude. Johnnie even made them go to the solicitor's office early one morning to make sure the keys fitted, to check the thickness of the wall between the office and the bank and find out anything else he could. Worse than that, he put Molly in the street to look out and listen.

"Don't want a crowd of blokes hanging about at this hour in the morning," he said. "Moll can just pretend she's coming home after a dance. Dance dress – high heels – trotting alone – who'd suspect her?"

"Oh my God – a woman. That's all we need on this job," groaned Jimmy. "Tell all your business to a tart and it's the surest way to get caught. No disrespect intended, John. Molly's a nice girl but how long could she hold up under interrogation?"

"She won't be under interrogation," Johnnie told him.

So in the end they did let themselves into the office. Molly, in a dance dress, a stole, which kept on slipping, and stiletto heels, tapped up the street. As she approached the office she pretended her heel had broken, took it off to examine it, put it on and hobbled past lamely.

When they met in a side street further off Johnnie demanded as they got in the car, "Did you hear anything?"

"Were you banging on the wall?" Molly asked. "I heard some thuds."

"Bloody hammering," Jimmy Carr told her. "I've been arrested doing a job in my time but I've never been arrested before I done it. I thought that was going to happen this time."

"Better than turning up with all the gear, finding the keys don't fit or we'd have to push six heavy filing cabinets out of the way to get to the wall, or it's six feet thick and reinforced with steel," Johnnie replied. "Haven't you ever heard of reconnaissance?"

Jimmy was about to speak but said nothing. He was showing a lot of patience with Johnnie, whose talents he could not deny but whose nerves were punishing everyone about him.

There was another row that night when Jimmy found out that Johnnie had bought a souped-up van for the getaway. "What's wrong with Allan's car?" he asked. "It goes like the clappers and he's used to it."

"It's registered in the name of his brother-in-law, that's all that's wrong with it," bellowed Johnnie. "They can trace us through it if anybody gets the number."

He was right, of course. Jimmy stared at him as if he could kill him and said, "OK. But you're paying for the bleeder. And I should advise you to get Allan out into the country in it for a little bit of practice before we put our lives in his hands."

"Do you think I hadn't thought of that?" demanded Johnnie.

"You've thought of everything, John," Jimmy replied quietly. "But I think I'll go home now."

Johnnie stared at him. "What's that supposed to mean?" he asked.

"I'm just going home, that's all. I'll see you in a couple of days."

After he had gone Johnnie raged, "Steps out on me at this stage for a few days off. Nice, isn't it? Lovely! Leaves it all to me." He punched the sofa twice and said, "The stupid berk – what does he think he's doing – playing cowboys and Indians?"

Molly sat down heavily in a chair and said, "It's the way you're carrying on, Johnnie. They all know you're right most of the time. Only you're like Hitler. They can't take it."

"That's what you sound like when you're working with kids from a kindergarten," he said.

Molly said, "I'll be glad when this lot's over, I can tell you."

"Thank you. Thank you very much for your support," said her lover vindictively. "I expect you'll be glad to spend the money when I've got it, too."

"I don't care about the bloody money," cried Molly, "I'm fed up with having Jimmy and Fred and Allan draped round the place drinking whisky all night long. I'm responsible for the place. I'm trying to bring up a kid and all I've got is all these men sitting about – no one ever thinks to offer to carry a scuttle of coal for the fire. And your nerves are in a state –"

"There's nothing wrong with my nerves," Johnnie said.

"Johnnie – you twitch all night and toss, and throw yourself about."

"You shut your mouth," said Johnnie Bridges. "And remember how you sleep is according to who you sleep with."

Molly stood up and told him, "This is still my place and I'll say what I like in it."

"Oh, you bitch," shouted Johnnie. "I need peace and quiet and some support. Not your constant nagging."

"You've had all the support you'll get from me," cried Molly. "Now go away and leave me alone. What good are you anyway? You'll be in the nick by the New Year."

"Don't you say that to me," roared Johnnie. He got off the sofa, took two swift paces across the room and hit her, with all his force, flat across the cheek.

Mary staggered and not even feeling any pain, shouted, "Get out, Johnnie, or I'll kill you! I'll kill you I swear it!" Then she fell down in a chair and, with her hand across her aching, stinging face, began to sob. She heard him walk out of the room, go upstairs and start banging about collecting his things. "He'll wake the baby," she thought, in agony. He came down. Even then she thought he might come in and say he was sorry he had hurt her. But he did not. The child began to cry. The door banged. Mary cried. Then she went wearily upstairs bent as an old woman, still weeping. Wiping the back of her hand across her eyes she went into the child's room, sniffing, and tried to soothe her back to sleep. In the end she took her into her own room and lay across the bed, holding her weakly and trying not to look at the open drawers, the scatter of her shoes on the floor at the front of the wardrobe and the bedroom door, gaping open.

Josephine slept. Mary held on to her to make sure she was properly sleeping and muttered, in a choking voice, "Just before Christmas, too. Just before Christmas." And she cried again. She felt guilty, too. The threat that he would get caught and go to jail had been like a witch's curse to him. She knew that. He and his kind were like primitives – in awe of female power, dreading its increase over them, just because it was so strong. And now, since she knew everything, he would do the job not knowing if she had been to the police.

And at the same time she knew that the love affair was over. There was no point in continuing anything once the man had laid violent hands on you. It never got any better after that, only worse. You wound up continually bashed about, wearing a black eye at the corner shop, doing your housework in pain, with your ribs strapped up – if he let you go to the hospital in the first place. You told lies about your injuries which people soon stopped believing. If you were married and had children you might not be able to get away. Even if you had a family, and they would take you in – and sometimes they would not – who would keep you? You had to stay and watch your kids getting more and more afraid of their father, who usually started on them when he had finished with you. You could only survive by getting more and more numb, to kill the misery, like someone serving a long gaol sentence. You could get killed, too. Molly knew all this. She got up and put Josephine back in her cot and lay down again, completely helpless, moaning, "It's over. It's over. It's all over." She did not sleep at all that night.

And in the morning Ivy came round and asked if she could take Josephine for a walk.

"You got a bruise on your face," she remarked.

"Fell down the stairs. Lucky not to drop the baby," Mary said shortly. It was a ritual. Ivy knew quite well what had happened. Mary indicated that she did not want to talk about it. Ivy, uncharacteristically, perhaps, did not insist. She said, "I'll get you some of that white make-up for erasing lines on your face when I go past the chemist."

Mary said, "Thanks, Ivy."

In the hall Ivy, as she loaded Josephine in to the pram, said, "Oh – I forgot. Here's the usual card from Framlingham. Well, this time it's a letter."

"I hope nothing's happened to Mrs Gates," Molly said dully. The memory of what had happened the day before kept sweeping over her like a huge wave.

"I hope not," said Ivy. "Here – open it up straight away."

Mary read it out. " 'Dear Mary, It was only recently that we pieced together the story and realized that you had been in great trouble and were now a mother as well. You must think us very stupid for writing so late after the terrible tragedy you have experienced. We simply did not realize that you were now Mary Flanders – but we're so sorry about your problems and, in short, I am writing to ask if you would like to come and spend Christmas with us here. It would be lovely to see you again and Mrs Gates is dying to see your new daughter. It will be a quiet Christmas as Sir Frederick has not been particularly well but Tom has managed to get a fortnight's leave from his regiment, which is, alas, on active service in Cyprus and so he will be with us. I'm sure you remember him as a boy' – how could I ever forget? muttered Mary – 'so you will be amazed to hear that he now sports a large moustache. I am so sorry to be inviting you rather late but do come if you can – Mrs Gates is waiting eagerly by my side so that she can speed this letter to the post. Even if you can't, do drop us a line very soon to tell us all how you are getting on. With all my love,' Mary read out in astonishment, 'Isabel Allaun.' Wonder what brought that on?"

"Like she said," Ivy offered, "they put two and two together somehow and worked out you were Mary Flanders. Then they felt worried about how you were. It's normal even from them. And Mrs Gates must have badgered them."

"Probably hoping I'll help her out in the kitchen," muttered Mary.

"Why not," demanded Ivy. "You could do with some country air and so could Josephine. It's kind of them to ask you and I think you should accept. Write off now. I'll post it."

In the end Mary wrote two letters. The first said that she would be pleased to bring Josephine to Framlingham at Christmas. The second, to Johnnie, took her longer. "Dear Johnnie," she wrote. "I'm sorry it had to end this way. I can't forgive you for what you did but I hope time will heal all wounds," and here she sniffed, and sobbed again. "I'm wishing you the best of luck," she continued, "and I promise you I will never do anything to hurt or injure you." She dared not be more open in case the letter fell into the wrong hands. She was sure he would understand that she did not intend to betray him to the police. She paused, still crying aloud now and wrote, in a shaky hand, "I will never forget you, Johnnie. Thanks for the good times so let's forget the bad. Yours, Mary." Then she addressed the letter to Johnnie's parents' house. She posted both letters immediately and then went back into the empty house. It felt like a void.

During the next week she miserably, and automatically, prepared herself and the baby for their stay in Framlingham, buying new shoes for Josephine and new nightdresses for herself. She also, doing those things, realized that she should be thinking about money. But, since she cared about nothing now that Johnnie was gone, she did not worry about her finances either. "I'd sooner be dead," she said to herself as she packed. But Ivy, watching her put her clothes carefully into her case, rejoiced. Mary was strong, she thought. One way or another she was getting her luggage packed and into a train. Bridges was gone – so much the better – but her daughter had weathered out the death of her husband, and her confinement, and now the departure of her lover and she was still, however shakily, on her feet. She was strong, thought Ivy, and thank God, because she'd need to be. Mary, catching her mother's approving glance, could not understand what was going through Ivy's head. A week and a half after Johnnie had departed, she was on the train to Framlingham.

So at last I saw Mary Waterhouse. By chance, because I was spending that Christmas with the family of my closest friend at Cambridge, Sebastian Hodges, who knew the Allauns well. He had been the only boy in the neighbourhood whom the Allauns thought suitable to associate with their son, Tom, so he was often hauled over to the Towers, although, as he said, he was not only two years younger than Tom Allaun and had plenty of friends of his own among the local boys, but hated spending the day with Tom because he loathed him. He hated Tom's cousin Charlie even more and said that when they were together the two of them bullied and tormented him so badly – often, it seems, in the notorious Allaun shrubbery – that he used to have nightmares about it.

Sometimes, before one of these occasions he was caught sleep-walking about his own house out of pure nerves. He could explain none of this to his parents who, in any case, apparently knew he did not like going there and often made excuses for him – but they could not always prevent the invitation or its acceptance for fear of upsetting their relationship with one of their few neighbours.

So there we were that Christmas, two big young men of twenty or so, too old to enjoy the excitement as young children can, too young to enjoy it on their behalf, as parents will, so we accepted Isabel Allaun's invitation to a drink on Christmas Eve with alacrity and, the older people in the house being too tired or preoccupied to go, we took their excuses with us over the three miles to Allaun Towers. And found no lights at the front of the house when we arrived. It was Sebastian who connected the flickering light from behind the house and the strengthening smell of burning with the famous Allaun bonfire – at first we wondered if perhaps the house was on fire.

"That's it," he said. "The Fire. It used to be an old custom round here – tenants' bonfire on Christmas Eve. Apparently the Allauns kept it up – they were what was known as parvenus at the time, I think. So they clung to the custom." It was Sebastian's mother, something of a local historian, who explained to me later that the Allaun family had arrived in the neighbourhood around the middle of the nineteenth century with a baronetcy which had something to do with Benjamin Disraeli and a lot of cash earned in Lancashire. Whereupon they joined the local gentry, more numerous in those days, and added to the house conservatories, bathrooms and waterclosets and other luxuries which had not been possible for the old and bankrupt family which had previously owned the house. The vigour they showed over all this apparently undermined the old, and evidently unsound, seventeenth-century foundations. And in reconstructing and repairing the foundations it seems that the two small but pretty towers which had originally stood at either end of the roof began to lurch and lean. In the interests of safety they had to come down. But the Allauns had bought Allaun Towers and they were not to be deprived of the house's name at this stage. They had two tinier towers, only about six feet in height and in the same breadth, constructed on the roof. Now, according to Sebastian's mother, the cold and damp were creeping in – the little rooms were abandoned and left empty. She told me all this rather wryly and I was left to draw my own snobbish conclusions, as I did. In the meanwhile, the old mediaeval tenants' fire burned at the Allauns as it had in the days of their predecessors. As we knocked unavailingly at the front door we heard the village band strike up *Lily of Laguna*. Realizing no one could hear us we strolled round to the back where, on a rough bit of lawn about half an acre in size, we found a big bonfire, a lot of the local people and Lady Allaun, in a sheepskin coat, standing on the paved area which ran the length of the house, doling out punch from a huge bucket set on a tripod over a small flame. On the trestle table in front of her there was fruitcake and sandwiches. The light from the fire cast itself over the grass and into the small wood beyond it. It lit the faces of the people standing round. Children ran to and fro. The band played.

Isabel Allaun greeted us and she ladled out some punch and handed us a glass apiece. She looked consciously jolly but gave the impression she would rather have been back in the house by her drawing-room fire. "I'm not sure where Tom or his father have disappeared to," she told Sebastian. "If you find them could you ask them to come and give me some help. Happy Christmas, Mrs Twining. I hope you're better after your accident," she said to a stout woman standing at the trestle. "Now – let me pour you some of this – it's just the thing for a cold night."

Meanwhile the housekeeper, Mrs Gates, and a man who must have been the gardener, came labouring up with another tub of steaming punch.

"Good Lord," said Isabel Allaun. "I thought we'd had it all."

"Why don't you let me take over," Sebastian offered. "We'd love to help, wouldn't we, Bert?"

"I must say, I think some people have had enough," observed the hostess. There was now some fox-trotting going on over by the band. The children were hopping and skipping in time. From down by the wood raucous laughter came out of the darkness.

"All the more reason to hand over to these young men," remarked Mrs Gates. "You go inside, Lady Allaun, and leave them to it. You look quite tired." She seemed a kindly woman, very much the old kind of reliable upper servant.

"Well, it has been a long day, Mrs Gates. If you don't mind –" she said, turning to us. When we said we would like nothing better than to take charge she walked in through the French windows behind her and closed them. As she went there was an outcry as a man fell in the fire and was pulled out and put out.

"Drunk," Mrs Gates observed. "Serves the silly fellow right."

It was then that I left Sebastian, who claimed to be an old hand at the Allaun Fire, to ladle the punch and drifted over to the edges of the fire. And there, while the band played *Dance Little Lady*, somewhat out of time, I chatted aimlessly with the Hodges' gamekeeper who had turned up for the event under an ancient right, no doubt, since the fire was meant for the tenants, servants and general fiefs of the Allaun estate. He assured me in the traditional manner that there was no game now or ever would be due to a poor breeding season, bad weather, poachers, foxes and hawks and was adding to his list of reasons why there was no point in bothering to go out with a gun the fact that the Allauns were careless managers of their estate when I looked across the fire and saw standing there one of the most beautiful girls I have seen in my life. She was Mary Waterhouse. Molly.

It is hard to explain precisely why she made such a deep impression on me. It was not so much, perhaps, her actual features or colouring, but more the expression she wore, tranquil but gay, absorbed in her child's pleasure at watching the fire. As she stared, partly at the flames and partly at the face of the child which she held, I was completely stunned. In retrospect I believe that one of the things I noted most about her was her good humour. She did not look sulky. She did not look self-absorbed – perhaps it was that I appreciated. That, and her beauty for she was quite startling. She had the eyes and mouth of an angel in an Italian painting. She wore a plaid skirt, a jersey and over this ordinary clothing a flashy white fur jacket. She caught my eye through the flames and smiled at me. Small wonder that I, an impressionable, inexperienced young man of only twenty, made my way over to her. I do not mean to say that I hoped for romance. Evidently she was a mother, which meant that she must be a married woman and in those days that put her completely out of bounds to conventional young men like myself.

"Hullo," I said, "I'm just going to get some more punch. Can I fetch you one?"

Her voice, when it came, startled me. I had expected a country accent or the voice of someone of my own class. Molly was a cockney. "No thanks," she said. "I've got to stay on me feet to look after the baby. I think I've had enough to drink."

But the child set up a clamour at the very mention of the word. "D'ink! D'ink!" she cried.

When I understood what she was saying I asked, "Shall I get something for her. Some milk? Or some water?"

"Well – if you don't mind," Molly said. "Though I think she's trying to stay out of bed – she's a rascal and Mrs Gates has been spoiling her rotten."

I brought back the water but by that time the baby had gone. "Mrs Gates has kidnapped her again," she said. I asked her, jokingly, for a dance and she said, "Delighted."

We waltzed on the rough turf as the band, which was getting worse as the musicians drank more punch, blared the *Blue Danube* waltz out of time. "I'm sorry," I said, as I stepped on her toe.

"Not your fault," she said. "It's the drunks in the band. Oh – whoops – the conductor's down."

The conductor had, indeed, measured his brass-buttoned uniform on the turf. The band silenced itself in ragged chords as the musicians realized what had happened. "Time for the *Last Post*," the girl said with a grin. "Wait a minute – there's his deputy coming in." And, as two trombonists carried the old conductor away a skinny man appeared in front of the band. Laying down his cornet he began to conduct. The waltz began again. We danced on.

"I've been on better floors," she told me. "You need wellingtons for this ball." Then she broke into a jive step, kept to it for a little while and came back into my arms again. I felt as if I were in love. My heart raced. I wanted the dance to go on and on. And at the same time I was disillusioned. This was not the blonde madonna I had seen from across the fire. She was a sharp, rather comical girl and, to put it plainly, she was common. She was married and a girl from the London streets but I wanted to go on dancing with her all night and into the next morning if I could. The band stopped. I thought I would hold her in conversation until it started again. I would try to find out more about her.

It was hard to work out what she was doing at Allaun Towers. I concluded that she must be a relation of the housekeeper's. Then the music began again and we danced a little more – or she jived, most of the time, while I stood still waiting for her. Then Lady Allaun, who must have found out about the collapse of the conductor, and must equally have been becoming more and more irritated by the ragged music, walked across the grass and talked to the new leader of the band, who nodded. They struck up *Silent Night* and followed it by *Good Christian Men Rejoice*, which was well beyond them at the state most of them had reached. Molly and I stood with some of the others watching them until they began to pack up their instruments. It was over. I thought that once she had stopped dancing she had become melancholy. That pretty face seemed sad in the growing darkness. Then she shivered and walked over to the dying fire. I followed her. "Do you feel like some more punch now?" I asked. "It's getting colder."

"Thanks," she said.

I went over to where Sebastian was still loyally ladling out the drink. He said, "Thanks for all your help, Bert. It was great fun running the canteen while you danced in the darkness with that pretty girl." He handed me two cups and I took them over to Molly.

Sebastian came up behind us and said, "Actually, Bert, that stuff's stone cold and old Benson's volunteered to pack everything up – why don't we go inside and have a drink by the fire? Sling it on the grass. It's only fit for weedkiller anyway."

By now the band was drifting away and only a few young couples stood about talking. As we walked back to the house I said, "This is Sebastian Hodges. I'm Herbert Precious – I should have mentioned my name before, I suppose."

"Same here," she said. "I'm Mary Flanders. I'm staying here over Christmas. I lived here during the war when I was an evacuee."

"I remember you," said Sebastian. "You hit me with your skipping rope – stood behind the toolshed and caught me as I came past."

"I don't remember that," said Molly. "I'm ever so sorry."

"You thought I was Tom – he was chasing you," explained Sebastian.

"That sounds more like it," Molly said as we went in.

We had our drinks in the long sitting room. The curtains were drawn. We all kept close to the fire.

"I hope they're staying off the lawn," said Isabel, as we heard the retreat of some of the guests. "Benson has tantrums when he finds wheel marks and big scuffs on it. He burst in last year just before Christmas lunch and made me apologize."

"The trouble is," said Sir Frederick, "that this wonderful old custom originated in the days when there were a dozen servants to prepare and clear up afterwards."

He looked very tired and stooped. Glancing at him as we talked earlier I had already realized that my hopes of a bit of shooting on the estate over Christmas were doomed. I could not imagine a jovial invitation being issued by this man. It looked, too, as if the Allauns were unprosperous. Indeed, Sebastian had told me as much. "This place," he had said, as we stood in the garden looking at his house, "is kept up pretty much by some neat investments of the old man's in Kenya and Rhodesia. But the Allauns haven't got that, short of capital, that's the problem, my father says. They should sell, says Dad, but they won't." He had added, "Sir Fred's not what he was. He used to be a big, burly swine, like Henry VIII. Very hospitable and jolly, a fast evictor, as landlords go, hard rider, big spender, that sort of thing. I don't remember his being any different from the way he is now, myself."

At any rate, whatever he had been, Sir Frederick was now obviously nervous and careworn. He looked like a beaten man and as his wife moved about the drawing room his eyes followed her, rather like a child's.

We talked country talk for a little while, although Molly was mostly silent, sitting in her chair, sipping a whisky and looking from face to face. Eventually she stood up and said, "I'll be off, now. Excuse me but the baby gets up so early."

"I hope we'll meet again before the holiday's over," I said.

"Hope so," she said. She sounded warm enough not to be positively rude and that was enough for me.

As we walked quietly down the drive in the dark Sebastian said to me, "Quite taken with her, aren't you? I don't blame you. She's very lovely. I wouldn't try it on though. Tom did, apparently, and came to a sticky end. He told me what happened. He seems to have caught her in a cupboard, where she was sorting out some sheets – tried to play the wicked squire and got an ugly answer for his pains. From what he said it's only luck he isn't singing soprano in the village choir. Serves him right, of course. Quite honestly I was amazed he had the nerve to tell me his squalid anecdote."

"I'm amazed he had the nerve to do it," I said indignantly. "I mean – for God's sake –" I was full of chivalrous rage on Molly's behalf.

"Well, you never know how much encouragement she may have given him," Sebastian said placidly. "But whether she did or whether she didn't, Tom Allaun's a very funny fellow. There are a lot of stories about him."

"What sort of stories?" I asked.

"Stories not quite funny enough to repeat," Sebastian told me. "Of the *News of the World* variety. Of course, you can't believe everything you hear." Then he fell silent, not wanting to say more.

"I mean to say – she's married," I persisted.

"Widowed," Sebastian told me. "Or so Isabel says. There's something funny about that, too."

"Poor girl," I said. "What an oaf Tom Allaun must be."

"Plenty of 'em about," Sebastian remarked philosophically. Then he said, "Sh!" and stopped in the dark lane. I stopped too.

"Fox! Fox! Tally ho!" he cried and made a trumpeting noise. We chased the fox a hundred yards down the lane before it cut off through a hedge into a field. Then, still laughing, we trudged the last two miles back to the house. I still remember the fresh, crisp December air as we went through the wood, shining torches to show the path. The torchlight glittered over frosty twigs and leaves. We swung the lights round to catch the frost on the bare branches overhead. It was very still. I thought about the girl and, as we came out of the wood to cross the last field, the bells of Framlingham church began to chime in the distance.

"Midnight. Happy Christmas," said Sebastian as we began to climb up the field to the house.

"Happy Christmas," I said, still thinking of that lovely face in the firelight.

Meanwhile, in her old room on the first floor Molly lay in the same bed in which she had slept as a child, staring through the dark windows at the sky. Far away, over the black hills, shone a sickle moon and stars, clear in the cold air. Inside the room she could hear Josephine's light breathing in the cot, which stood beside her. There was no other sound. No wind stirred the trees. The sheep were silent in the fields. Not so much as an owl hooted in this Christmas Eve stillness. Once she thought she heard distant laughter, then that ceased and she lay awake in the darkness, worrying, but somehow half-asleep, as if the deep calm of the countryside had caught her. It was as if the world had ceased to turn, though she knew that in London the traffic would still be moving, hooters would sound at midnight, tipsy men and women would be getting turned out of pubs. In Meakin Street there would be footsteps, a cry as someone bumped into a lamp post, the odd shout, a snatch of song – and Johnnie, at Jimmy Carr's house, probably, would be checking over the equipment behind drawn curtains while Jimmy's wife produced bottles of beer and sandwiches, making an effort to be calm and thinking of her two children upstairs in bed asleep. She would know that on Christmas Day she would be alone and on Christmas night would get either a knock on the door, policemen asking where her husband had been all day, or footsteps on the stairs, Jimmy bursting in with a bag full of fivers and tenners, tipping them on the bed, saying, "Here you are, gel. Told you we could do it, didn't I?" Faced with ten years to be spent virtually as a widow, bringing up the children while Jimmy was inside – or fur coats and new toys and jubilation all round. She'd be biting her lip, all right, Mrs Carr, thought Mary, while the gang downstairs made jokes, checked the pickaxes and wound the blades round with rags to stop the noise, counted the detonators, fuses, snapped the torches on and off – and Molly lay in the silence, thinking, thank God I'm out of it – and still wishing Johnnie was there with her. She missed him all the time and wished she had stayed in London, where she could be sad alone and did not have to pretend to be all right. But knew that would have driven her mad – and so she slept, as Christmas Day arrived.

She woke later in a dull mood and, refusing Mrs Gates's offer to look after Josephine while she went to church with the others said that she would stay behind and look after the dinner, as it baked, simmered and boiled over the gas on the kitchen range. She basted the turkey and roast potatoes, put water in the saucepan containing the Christmas pudding, made over a year before and left in a dark cupboard, gaining in fruitiness and alcoholic strength during another winter, spring, summer and autumn. She prepared the brussels sprouts, basted and put nuts and fruit into bowls. She slipped another spoonful of port into the stilton, which stood, huge as a pramwheel, in the larder. She fed the dining-room fire with logs, and dodged Josephine who was delightedly trundling about with a doll propped in a small wheeled cart which had been piled with bricks. She smacked Mouser, whom she had left, with many tears, as a small ginger kitten and who was now a huge scarfaced creature, clever as the Devil and hungry as a dog.

As she put the ham he had dragged from the table back on its plate and began to knife off his toothmarks she heard the phone ring. She put the ham in the larder and went to answer.

It was Johnnie.

"We done it!" were his first words. "Done it fast. Home and dry!"

"I don't want to talk to you, Johnnie," she said. "I'm glad you're OK but I don't want to talk to you." She felt so unhappy that her voice broke and, hearing it, he grew confident.

"Molly," he said. "I've got £25,000. Look – I'm sorry I hit you – I know I shouldn't've. It was the strain, gel. You must realize."

"It's not that, Johnnie," she said desperately. "But I've got to get out. I can't stand the life – there's Josephine –"

There was a thump from the kitchen. Josephine cried.

"I told you," he said. "I'm going straight. I've got something lined up. Please, please come home. I love you."

"I've got to go," she said.

"I love you," he said desperately. "Molly – don't go –"

"I love you, Johnnie," she cried out and she could hear the despair in her own voice as she said it. She put the phone down and ran to the kitchen. The evil cat had opened the larder door which she had forgotten to catch. He and Josephine sat on either side of the ham. They were both gnawing it. Molly, her own voice ringing in her ears, saying, "I love you" as if she'd said, "Don't kill me," screamed "No!" at Josephine and the cat and frightened them both . . . Then she began to laugh, drove them away from the ham, restored it, put more water in the saucepan containing the pudding, basted the turkey, the beef, the parsnips, the potatoes, threw another log on the fire in the dining room, brought the red wine from the pantry and uncorked it, washed Josephine's face and began to feel wonderful. Johnnie loved her. He was going to go straight and by the time Mrs Gates came back she was singing.

"Well, then, Mary," said Mrs Gates, coming in through the back door and taking off her hat. "You seem cheerful. Why don't you go into the drawing room for a drink with the others while I take it from here?"

"I'll stay by you, my dear," said Molly Flanders. "But while we're at it we'll sneak a glass of master's port – that's what you have to do, isn't it?"

"It's been done," admitted Mrs Gates.

"Just like feudal times round here," remarked Cockney Moll, pouring two glasses of port and putting them on the kitchen table. "Happy Christmas, Mrs Gates," she said, lifting her glass.

Mrs Gates raised her glass and with a curious look at her, said, "Happy Christmas, Mary, love." Then gazing down to where the cat paced by her leg, purring and looking up at her with ferocious love, she said, "That cat's been up to something, of that I'm sure."

The lunch was sedate but greedy. The pudding caught fire beautifully and Josephine, in her high chair, was so impressed that they lit it again, for her, before serving it. After dinner the others – Tom, Sir Frederick and an elderly couple called Hardcastle and their son –

went into the drawing room leaving Mary, who was helping to clear the table, behind with Mrs Gates and Isabel Allaun.

"Come and sit down for a moment, Mary. I've something to ask you," said Isabel.

While Mrs Gates stood by the table, looking at both of them, Molly sat down and said, "What's it all about, then?"

"We're very fond of you here, Mary, as you know," Isabel Allaun said and although her face retained its normal cool expression, although the grey-blonde hair piled on her head still looked immaculately placed, the long hands on the white tablecloth did not move. She went on, "It has been a great pleasure having you here. Mrs Gates has loved it, too. I know that. And Josephine is so sweet – well, to cut a long story short, we wondered if you would like to stay on. This was your home for a long time and seeing you here again has made me realize how much a part of it you were. As you'll see, this isn't a kindness on my part. Sir Frederick is failing, that must be obvious to you. The burdens on me are greater. And none of us here are getting any younger. If you could stay and help Mrs Gates and me we would both be so delighted. We could offer a small wage. You would have Josephine with you – it might suit everyone." And, for such a determined woman, she looked at Molly quite shyly.

Molly was dumbfounded. She said, "It's very kind of you – very kind. It's such a shock – I can't make up my mind. Can I have a few days to think?"

"Of course," said Isabel Allaun. "I didn't expect you to make up your mind on the spot. You see – you could even get a part-time job. Mrs Gates would love to look after Josephine." Mrs Gates nodded. "I'd love to," she said. "In the end it would be like having you back when you were a child, Mary."

Mary sniffed and said, "Well – I feel all over the place. I don't know what to say."

"Don't say anything then," said Isabel Allaun. "I must go into the drawing room. Come along when you're ready. I'm pleased that at least you're thinking about it."

After she had gone, Mrs Gates, picking up a pile of dessert plates, said, "Nice thing for you, Mary. A fresh start. It can't be easy in London with everybody knowing what happened to your husband."

"Yes," said Molly Flanders. "A nice thing." But she knew already she was on her way back to Meakin Street as she followed Mrs Gates along the corridor to the kitchen. She had to decide between a quiet, hard-working life in the country and the challenges, adventures and variety of the city, between a life for herself and her daughter among people who loved her and her handsome gangster, about, he said, to go straight. And there was no choice. Two days later she had turned down Lady Allaun's offer and was hoisting Josephine and herself aboard the train for London.

Three hours after that she and Johnnie were locked together on the sofa in Meakin Street while Josephine hammered on the door to get in, wailing, "Umm. Umm. Umm." It was no use waiting for the child to go away. Johnnie had pulled the curtains together and seized her. Mary, laughing, had let him push her back on to the sofa and had torn at his clothes while he tore at hers. She had cried, "Johnnie. Johnnie. Johnnie," as his hands touched her body, as he finally entered her. Afterwards he said, "I'm back, Mary. I'm not going away any more." And she said, "I know you're not." For a moment she looked into his eyes, into his head. She said, "Oh, Johnnie. I'm happy now. I feel so bad when you're gone." Then she got off the couch and let in the little girl.

"Can't let the kid see this sort of thing too often," remarked Johnnie, pulling on his trousers.

Molly said, "I love you."

That night, sitting in the crowded club while Jimmy, Allan and Johnnie flashed their fivers about – the money, mostly from shops and market stalls, had been in used notes – Molly, tiddley by now, with a strap from her dress falling down over her shoulders, laughed and joked with the rest, even Arnie Rose, whom she usually ignored as much as possible, because she was so afraid of him. This time, in a dinner jacket and black tie, he was making an appearance – something like that of a boss at the firm's Christmas party – obviously the Roses had funded the bank robbery. He and Johnnie were clapping each other on the back and swapping jokes and Mary joined in. As she sat there he put his hand on her bare shoulder and, peering obviously down the front of her dress said, tightening his grip on her shoulder, "Oh, I like the feel of this. This is very nice this is." Molly thought he sounded as if he were sitting down to a couple of pork chops. Trembling internally at his touch she said, "Please don't squeeze me till I'm yours, Mr Rose," looking saucily up at him through the smoke and itching to shrug his hard, damp hand from her flesh. In a moment, she thought, she would flinch, too obviously, from the grip of the man described a few weeks earlier in *The People* as 'London's King of Crime'.

"Got to check the goods before buying in this world," Arnie Rose said expansively, waving the big cigar he held round the room. A blob of ash fell on the table. "But judging by sight and feel – Molly – you're a prime bit of stuff, you are."

A silence fell around the table. Susie and Jimmy Carr glanced automatically towards the bar, where Johnnie was buying drinks. He pushed through the crowd, saw Arnie's hand on Molly's shoulder and remarked, setting three glasses down, "Hullo, Arnie. I hope you're not trying to sign her up for business. I've got exclusive rights."

Arnie looked at him mildly and told him, "As if I'd dream of it, Johnnie. A beautiful girl like this – so much in love with you. But if it wasn't for you I'd be courting her with flowers, and that, my boy, is a fact."

Johnnie ignored the challenge, and the threat. He said, "Take your hand off her shoulder, Arnie, and guess what's coming your way." And he took an empty glass from Allan, who came up with a bottle of champagne in one hand and a fistful of glasses in the other.

Arnie Rose took his hand from Molly's shoulder and accepted the glass, which Allan filled. "And now," he said to Johnnie, "I suggest we go upstairs and talk about our little bit of business."

"Delighted," said Johnnie. They weaved through the crush and went out.

Susie leaned over the table and said, "What's it all about?"

"Don't know," Molly said. She felt depressed. If Johnnie was going straight why was he talking business again with Arnie Rose?

"You're lucky with Johnnie," the girl said wistfully. "He thinks the sun shines out of your eyes – you can tell, the way he looks at you. Blimey, though," she added in a lower voice, "it looks like Arnie's interested – he's a devil, you know, and he don't give up easy." By now she was sitting next to Molly, talking into her ear.

"My mum used to know him as a kid," Molly remarked.

"Don't say nothing about it," Susie said. "He can't stand anybody saying things about him unless he told them first. Here," she said, taking off a long glove, "See this – solid gold. Look at them stones – real rubies. A thousand quid if it's a penny, this."

She took it off and handed it to Molly. Molly envied her. She wished Johnnie would give her something like that. But she thought that Susie was a bit like her sister Shirley, who was now twelve. She also showed off her new trinkets – although Shirley's all came from Woolworths – wanting you to ask who had given them to her and acted, like Susie, all frightened about Arnie Rose, shivering and shuddering as if he was a ghost. What was Arnie Rose anyway, she asked herself? Nothing but a great big bully, always one jump ahead of the law and always looking over his shoulder in case a policeman came round the corner. But she exclaimed over the bracelet and listened to Susie's tale of how she had come by it.

Susie, glancing to the bar said, "Don't look now but who's looking daggers? She still can't get over the loss of her Johnnie – silly cow." It was true. The dark girl, Jeanne, over by the bar was staring at Molly. As Molly gazed she dropped her eyes. Molly stared round the club. The women, glamorously dressed, heavily jewelled and made up, were all glancing at each other. Before she could work out what was going on Arnie Rose and Johnnie were back, smiling into each other's faces, both smoking big cigars and grasping arms when they talked to each other. This public display of bonhomie made Molly even more uneasy. How could Johnnie go straight with Arnie involved? Arnie reminded her of Charlie Markham, suddenly – the same broad smiles and still making her life a misery day after day with his punchings and pinchings and habit of leaping out at her unexpectedly. And she knew neither she nor Johnnie would be safe if Arnold Rose became unhappy with them. Temporarily she even disliked Johnnie for so enjoying Arnie's approval. But now Arnie was saying, "And I'm sure neither of you ladies will refuse another glass of fizz?" He waved at the barman, who came towards them. "And another," said Johnnie, waving two five pound notes about.

So the corks went on popping, champagne bubbled over the edge of the glasses, the girls giggled and the men guffawed and the girls dabbed the corks from the champagne bottles behind their ears, scenting themselves with the drink. After that a party wanted to go on somewhere else but Molly persuaded Johnnie to take her home.

"He's rotten," she told him that night in bed.

"Oh – he's a villain through and through," Johnnie said complacently, sprawled across the bed with a cigarette in his hand. "There's no doubt about it. He's a real villain." He was flattered by the attention Arnie Rose had paid him and the backslapping, the cigars.

"I said he was rotten," said Molly. "He's evil, Johnnie. Bloody evil. You'd better remember that if you're going to get mixed up with him."

"I know all that," said Johnnie. "But he's made me a very fair offer and I'm thinking it over. We sorted out a few details tonight."

"What offer?" said Molly. "Smashed kneecaps?"

"Now then, lovely," he said, kissing her. "None of your business, is it? Your business is something else. I can deal with Arnie – you got to deal with me, see. Here – aren't you lovely? Say, 'I'm lovely.' "

"You're lovely," said Molly, as his warm weight came down on her.

But as it happened the deal between the Rose brothers and Johnnie became her business. She was part of the deal. Johnnie at first did not agree, but when it looked as if Arnie would back out he had to let Molly work there. And so it was that when Frames, the gambling club, opened for the first time and soft-faced debutantes, hiding schoolgirl faces under the heavy paint and hauteur of top models, and their almost-as-young escorts, and men with the small mouths and distanced looks of gamblers, and minor aristocrats, film stars and starlets and MPs, company directors, jockeys, owners and crooks, even a princess, mingled in the high rooms on the opening night, drinking free champagne and having their pictures taken, it was Molly, in cream satin, with her hair on top of her head, who acted as hostess. She concealed her high good humour and satisfaction for the occasion and tried to speak and act like a younger version of Isabel Allaun. Even the Roses were impressed. "I don't believe it, Molly," exclaimed Norman through his cigar. "Arnie told me you were good, had a bit of class, as you might put it but – you look like the real thing. What do you say, Simon? Like your own sister, ain't she?"

Simon Tate, who had been at Oxford and had been taken on as manager, remarked gallantly, "I haven't a sister but if I had I'm sure Molly would make her look as if she ran a whelk stall down Petticoat Lane."

"Think I'm overdoing it, then?" Molly asked him.

"Not a scrap," he told her. "You're fine. The boyfriend's a bit flashy, though. I'll have a word with him."

Molly flushed at hearing Johnnie criticized. "I'm here to see to these things," he told her. The Roses, no fools, had hired him to advise on who was good for what money and do what the Roses described as keeping up the tone – keeping out the riff-raff.

"I don't want to come in here one night and find anybody like me on the premises," Norman Rose had told him genially. "If I do, I'll sack you."

Simon was energetic. The night after the opening he was at the club at nine, saying to Molly, "You must get rid of the woman you've got running the ladies' room as soon as she comes in. Get somebody else — she's got to be something like a trained nurse or a retired housekeeper. She has to look extremely respectable and be quite unshockable. She must be able to produce anything from an aspirin to French scent, not excluding a calming brandy or gin. She must have a list of telephone numbers including doctors, solicitors and the House of Lords. We must look after the ladies or the place will turn into a snooker hall."

"How am I supposed to find her?" moaned Molly. "And it's not my job."

"You'd better ring some smart employment agencies," he told her. "And if you think your job at this club is going to begin and end with standing about in a low-cut dress doing an impression of the Honourable Miss Tinyfeet then think again. You're the only person here, other than me, who can cope. What are they paying you?"

"Fifteen pounds a week," muttered Molly.

"Get cracking, then," he advised, "and then ask them for twenty when you get established as Madame."

This advice did not seem real to Molly, any more than anything else at Frames seemed real. Night after night the clients came into Frames, to see and be seen or to gamble. The hard core of gamblers slightly bewildered her.

"It's the excitement that gets them," Arnie Rose said to her one night as they stood at the small, hidden window in the office upstairs, gazing down at the tables. A young merchant banker stood watching the dice roll across the green baize. His face was quite expressionless, though very pale. The dice halted. He spoke to the croupier and walked away.

"That's him done for," remarked Arnie. "We've got markers off him for a quarter of everything his dad owns. It's the excitement, see. People'll do anything to get it. Drink, drugs, dirty women, trying to break land-sea records, exploring up the Amazon. You show me a bored man and I'll show you a mark, a punter, a sucker."

Again, the reality of the banker's actions did not really strike her. That sort of thing happened at Frames. It meant nothing to her.

"Fancy a gin?" asked Arnie, turning away from the window.

"All right," said Molly. "But I'd better be getting down there soon," she said.

"Good girl," he told her. He handed her the glass and asked, "What are you after, then?"

"After?" she asked.

"Yes – I mean to say, everybody's after something, aren't they? Stands to reason. Take your average bank clerk – he's after security, isn't he? Ask him to rob his bank and he won't. He'd rather have his pension. But you tell him his pension's threatened and he'll do anything. Anything at all," Arnie repeated. He looked hard at Molly. "Nobody's honest," he said, "not when it comes down to it. So there's money, power, safety, excitement – what do you want? What would you do anything – anything at all – for?"

"It's a bit depressing to think like that," Molly told him.

"'Course – you're a woman," he said. "You're not supposed to think." She realized now that he was a bit drunk and became afraid. He stood swaying and peering at her intently. He came closer and put his arm round her. "Maybe with you it's kids and security. You've had a rough time, poor little Molly."

"I'd better get down there, Arnie," she told him. "Celey's looking at her watch. I told her I'd take over on the baccarat."

"Good old Little Molly – always on the go," said Arnie Rose. As she left he said, "Think about what I just said, though, gel. It's kosher – everybody's after something. Even you."

Going fast downstairs on her spikey heels Molly thought, Phew. What was all that about? But the conversation had upset her. Perhaps it was true that everyone wanted something. Certainly, in Frames you saw how much it was possible to want something as silly as a couple of bits of pasteboard with the right pictures or numbers on them. But her real uneasiness was about Johnnie, who was out on unexplained business so much, who seemed not to love her as much as she loved him. And threatened love will take any conversation, any portent, any remark overheard in the street and try to make it a clue to the mystery. Fixing on her smile, she went to the baccarat table, greeted the people she knew and took up the cards.

Not long after Simon Tate arrived and took over the table. He muttered, "Get up to the ladies' room – fast."

In the pink, scented atmosphere she found a woman of thirty in an expensive scarlet dress stretched out on the couch under the mirrors.

"Oh, Christ," Molly said, looking at the pale face. "What's the matter here? Just a minute – she's Alexander Fraser's wife, isn't she? Oh, God, what's the matter with her?"

"Not married," said the other woman, Mrs Brown plump and middle-aged in her pink uniform. "She's married to Perry Elmond, Lord Antony's son."

She lowered her voice, "I think Mr Fraser ditched her tonight. She's been taking pills to calm her down – probably phenobarbitone."

"We should get an ambulance," said Molly.

"No scandal," Mrs Brown said firmly. "Get Mr Fraser."

Molly had seen the woman earlier, leaning over Fraser's shoulder, trying to attract him. She said, "I don't know where he is. He dropped a packet tonight and left. What about her husband – or her mum?" She was desperate.

"Her mother never leaves Scotland," said the woman. "We'll get her into the Sloane Clinic. You stay here and I'll phone them from the office."

"Well, hurry up," said Molly. "Because if there's any delay I'm getting a hospital ambulance."

"She's not too bad. I've seen worse," said the woman.

Molly sat by the woman, whose face was pale and sweating. She moaned and said, "Beattie. Beattie, come here."

Her sister? A dog she had owned in childhood? A nanny? Molly bathed her face, wondered if she ought not to be walking her up and down as you saw people do in films. She prayed she would not die and that no one would try to come into the ladies' room. Frames needed no high-class scandals for the Sunday papers Sid enjoyed after his dinner.

The woman came back into the room and said, "Here – help me carry her down to the front door. Try to smile a bit and make it look as if she's drunk."

And so the two women, with the semi-conscious one between them, half-dragged her rapidly down the stairs. Molly smiled a little in a well-we're-all-human-aren't-we way at anyone who looked anxious or curious. They held her between them on the pavement while they waited for the car from the clinic.

"She had everything," muttered Mrs Brown.

"People always want more, don't they?" Molly said. "If they didn't we'd be out of business, for a start." They bundled the sagging woman into the car and went back inside. "Someone should be told," said Molly. "I wonder who?"

"Ask Mr Tate," advised the woman.

Simon Tate was in the bar. When Molly told him what had happened he muttered, "Stupid bloody woman. I'll go up and try to track down Fraser. After that, her father. Can you stay about and see everything's all right? Johnnie should be here but he hasn't turned up."

By half past four the club had emptied and Simon and Molly were sitting in the office adding up the takings. The door of the safe stood open, ready for the money. Molly's shoes lay thrown in a corner. She curled her aching toes under the table and checked a pile of notes. She jotted down the figure.

"No sign of Johnnie?" Simon asked.

Molly shook her head.

Downstairs the weary croupiers were packing up dice and cards, turning out the lights in the smoke-filled rooms. They were like actors after a performance. One by one the lights over the tables went out. The house was quiet. Molly and Simon finished counting the money. Simon clipped together a small pile of markers with the debtors' signatures on them, shuffled the cheques together and clipped those together. He put the stacks of money and the other bundles in the safe, shut the door and swizzled the knob with the combination lock.

"Shall I make a cup of tea?" asked Molly. She was tired but she wanted company because Johnnie had not returned.

"I'd like one," Simon said. As she made it he said firmly, "This is the second night this week that Johnnie hasn't showed up. And last week he did it once. And the week before. I don't mind covering for him sometimes but I'd like to be asked and I'd like it less often."

"I'll talk to him," Molly said. But she already had and he had already promised to telephone if he got held up and could not come to work. When she asked him where he was he said "Went to a film" or "With some friends." She dared not challenge him in case he lost his temper. Now, Simon said gently, "Is there anything wrong?"

She shook her head and put the tea tray on the table.

"There is though, isn't there?" he told her. "And it's not just another woman."

"There must be one," Molly said. "I rang his mum once when he didn't turn up here. She sounded funny on the phone – sorry for me."

"Look," said Simon, leaning back in his chair, "I must know more." He was long and lean and fair. He had big blue eyes. "I mean, I hope Johnnie isn't having an affair with another woman but it isn't just that, is it. You've been cooking the books. I was looking through the bank statements. Then I compared the evening figures we do together with what has been going to the bank the next morning. Sometimes you take in more than we collected the night before and sometimes less. I'm sorry to say I wondered if you were on the fiddle – perhaps you had a sick parent or – well, you know the sort of thing people get into trouble for – but when I added up the takings here and what was going into the bank over a period of a week to ten days there was no discrepancy. So what are you doing? Borrowing and putting it back again. If you want more wages why don't you say so? I know you're honest and you know you're honest but what happens when the Roses send round that shifty little man they call an accountant and he spots what you've been doing? You know what he's like – if he finds anything fishy, he'll start sniffing and sniffing until he tracks down what's happened. I don't want to be involved."

"I'll stop doing it," muttered Molly.

After a pause Simon said, "Like to tell me why you were doing it in the first place? If you need some help –"

He got up, went into the kitchenette, took a packet of chocolate digestive biscuits from a wall cupboard and came back, eating them.

Meanwhile, Molly said nothing. He held the packet out to her saying, "Have a biscuit." Molly shook her head. Simon took two and ate them both together. Then he said loudly, "Johnnie! – All this is something to do with Johnnie, isn't it? He's gambling – I mean, he's gambling somewhere else, on the horses or something, and you're covering his losses when he loses, and putting it back – no – doesn't work – whoever heard of a punter who could put back his losses so systematically, borrow one day and pay back one, or at most, two days later? So what is it?" He walked to the window, looked down over the back of the house and ate another biscuit. He turned round, "Come on, Molly. I'm curious now. This must be something to do with Johnnie and it means you take, say a couple of hundred off tonight, hide it away somewhere and then, tomorrow or the next day, you pay it in. But, seriously, you must tell me. As I say, we're all involved –" Then his face changed and he scowled. He said, "Ah. I think I'm beginning to see. Well, that's not funny, Moll. Not funny at all. The sums have been getting bigger, too, you know that."

He opened the safe and took out the red book in which they wrote down the night's takings. From the bottom shelf of the safe he took the folder containing the bank statements. He carried both over to the rota on the wall which listed which of the staff were on duty each day. Molly watched him until she was sure what he was doing. Then she said wearily, "All right you get your coconut – I'll save you the sums."

Simon faced her. "You've been evening up the takings so no one would notice they were lower when Johnnie was in? That's right, isn't it?"

She nodded. "He always carries it up the stairs himself on the nights we're on together. That'll be every other night or maybe every two nights. But I came to notice when he was on we were always down and never up – I asked him and he admitted it. He said he was a partner and he needed expenses. So I told him I'd even it up for him. All I had to do was take a bit off the top when I was on duty with you, or whoever, and just take the rest to the bank. Then when Johnnie was on I'd add it on to the money I was paying in at the bank next day."

Simon blew out his breath. "Phew," he said. "What a woman will do for the man she loves. Look here – you've been clever and you've been loyal to Johnnie. But you're putting the rest of us in danger. If the Roses think we've all been helping you, or we knew about it, we'd not just get the sack – we'd get tied up in it and dumped in the Thames. My impulse is to grab my hat and run for it. It's only because I like you that I'm not on the phone now to Arnie or Norman, telling them I've just caught you out in a fraud so they won't blame it all on me. And I'm lucky, Molly Flanders, because I've got reasonably well-off and enquiring relations and the Roses know it. You're in worse trouble. They could really take you for a one-way ride."

"They wouldn't do that," Mary said with assurance.

"Oh, why not, pray?" he enquired.

"Well, I'm a woman," Mary explained, "and I did it for a man. They expect that kind of thing. *And* Arnie wants me. *And*," she concluded triumphantly, "my mum was at Wattenblath Road School with both of them."

"Oh, well," said Simon. "Congratulations." He looked nervous. "Phew," he said and stood up. "I need a drink. We must talk about this, Molly. I think we'd better go up to your flat and work out what to do. If Johnnie comes in so much the better. I'd like a word with him. Very much so, in fact."

And they went upstairs to the lavishly appointed flat, where Simon sat down with a glass and a bottle of brandy. He said, "All you have to do is stop covering up for Johnnie. If you just pay in the takings as they stand from now on you're in the clear. If the accountant catches Johnnie out that's his problem, not yours. And you must tell Johnnie he'll get caught. I'll do the same."

"It's his money," said Molly. "He's a partner."

"He's a third partner. A third of it's his money. After the profits have been added up – he's not entitled to help himself."

"The trouble is, he's taking more each time," Molly said.

"Yes," Simon said gravely, "that is the trouble. And that is why you have to stop covering up. You're working in hundreds now. Soon it might be thousands."

Molly sat there in silence. It was after five in the morning. Simon looked at her sadly. She might have been a tired child. She said, "He's never stayed out all night before."

"I'm sorry," Simon said. "Perhaps if you talk to him – God, what a night. Fraser gone bust. Judy half-dead in the ladies' on phenobarbs. Johnnie's been pilfering and you've been fiddling the books – is it worth it? Is it really worth it?" He paused, then said, "You don't think he's run for it, do you? In case the Rose brothers find out."

"I'll look in the wardrobe," Molly cried. She hoped desperately that Johnnie had really run away. It would be better if he feared the Roses than if he just did not love her. But each of his suits hung there and, in the chest of drawers, all his shirts, pants and socks lay in piles, exactly where she had laid them. It was while staring down at the pile of fifteen or twenty laundered shirts of all colours and kinds that she felt anger. Tears came to her eyes. She went back and said to Simon, "Everything's there."

"You're sounding a bit better," he said. "Grim." He poured himself some more brandy. "Now start thinking. He's been drinking champagne with debutantes while you've done the accounts and picked the dead bodies up in the ladies' lavatory. Yet still, inspired by the spirit of the slums – let him black your eye on Saturday night and tell the neighbours you slipped downstairs – you've been covering up for him. Helping him diddle two of the most frightening men in London."

He leaned forward. "I've decided what to do. There's no point in your agreeing never to cover for Johnnie again. Maybe you'll keep your word and maybe you won't. Men like Johnnie can make women do plenty they don't want to – I can't afford the risk. If the Roses' accountant finds out I could, without any warning at all, find myself in serious trouble. I'm sorry, Molly, but I've got to tell the Roses what's going on."

"No!" she cried out, but he continued, "I've got to. Of course I'll tell them you didn't benefit by what you did. And you're right – they'll forgive you because you're a woman and your cunt is ruling your head – no offence, Molly dear, but it's true – and then I'll go out and join my brother in Kenya as fast as possible and the Roses will go out and get Johnnie. And I should advise you to disappear, too. Just go home, or wherever you do go, and keep your head well below the sandbags."

"Why have you got to do this?" demanded Mary. "You said they wouldn't hurt you."

"They could," he said, "if they wanted to."

She looked at him contemptuously. He said earnestly, "Look, Moll – I'm a homosexual, a deviant, a nancy boy and to you, queer as a nine-bob note. If the Roses take against me they don't need to lay a finger on me. They can get some of their friends in the police to discover me *in flagrante*, to put it politely. It doesn't matter where I am, even if I'm at home in my own bed, I'm committing a crime I can get two years for. Do you understand why I'm afraid?"

"Oh, God," groaned Molly, looking at him. "Oh, Simon. I'm sorry. I didn't know."

"I don't advertise," he said. "But now you see. I've no alternative. I don't want to be a martyr for Johnnie Bridges."

"I must warn him," Molly said instantly.

"All right," said the tall, thin, young man. "I'll ring them up in the morning. That'll give you some time, so you'd better tell him now or by lunchtime they'll be stamping all over his beautiful hands."

"But how can I –?" she asked.

"Try Amanda Walton's little house at 21 Bruton Mews," he said. "I'm sorry. It's been going on for a long time. She's a long cheap streak of spite, as it happens –"

But Molly was in her coat and at the door. She stared at him wildly. "Goodbye," she said. "Good luck."

"And to you, poor little thing," said Simon Tate, behind her back.

She clattered through the streets on her high heels, her coat thrown over her shoulders. She passed a policeman and stared at him furiously. He would not stop her. Of course she had seen the women making up to him in the clubs, brushing their powdered shoulders against his jacket, kissing him on the cheek and calling him "Johnnie" in teasing voices. He had laughed at them for it and said these posh debutantes like a bit of rough trade. Perhaps there had been a little spite in his laughter. But he'd gone and got one now. "I can't stand this. I'll kill her," Molly cried to herself, tearing through the narrow streets. And all the while she'd known nothing, while Simon knew – and how many of the others? And she'd been doing all the work for fifteen pounds a week and thinking she was so clever – while he'd had one hand in the till and the other up an upper-class tart's skirt. She, Molly, had lain awake for him while he touched, kissed, covered the body of another woman. And lied to her later, about being with friends.

She arrived, sobbing, at the entrance to the mews and ran down under streetlamps beginning to pale as dawn came. She hammered, sobbing, on the brass door knocker of the white-painted front door. She banged and banged, unable to bear the thought that inside her lover lay asleep with another woman while she stood in the chilly dawn, on the step outside.

A window went up at the house next door. "What on earth are you doing?" came an indignant voice. Mary did not even look up. She went on banging on the door. The sound filled her head.

"The people you want are obviously not there," said the voice, a woman's. "Will you please stop that noise?"

Molly, now hysterically fascinated by her own rhythmic knocking on the door, began to shout, "Open the door – I know you're in there. Open the door you bastards – I know you're in there. Let me in. You've got to let me in."

Behind her a man's voice cried, "Shut up! If you don't stop immediately I'll call the police."

"Open this door, Johnnie," Molly shouted. "Open this door!" She was banging wildly and still shouting when it opened.

"What are you here for?" said a woman's voice. Molly shouldered in. Amanda Walton, who had backed into the small, square hall as she pushed through the door, was tall, with dark hair swinging loose on her shoulders. She wore a white nightdress with a lace top and a kimono over it. She smelled of sex and this, for some reason, sobered Molly.

"What do you want?" she asked. She was a girl, very little older than Molly.

"I want Johnnie," said Molly.

"Johnnie isn't here," said the other.

"I'll look," said Molly, starting up the stairs. The girl caught her arm. "Where do you think you're going? This is my house."

"Oh – sod off," cried Molly, throwing off her hand.

As she started to gallop up the small flight of stairs Amanda, her voice shaking, called "Johnnie!"

Johnnie appeared on the landing wearing a paisley silk dressing-gown. His face, above the girlish material, was heavy and sullen. He had obviously just woken up. Molly stopped and stared up at him. He stared expressionlessly back at her.

"What's the trouble girls?" he asked. "What are you doing here, Molly?"

Molly suddenly realized that he had been through many such scenes before. She had not and nor, she guessed, had Amanda.

"You ponce," she said. "You bloody ponce."

"Tell her to go away, Johnnie," Amanda cried. "She's been beating on the door. She's woken everyone up. I want her to go."

"You come down here and talk to me," said Molly angrily to Johnnie.

"Look, Molly – I was asleep," he told her.

"In *her* bed," shouted Molly. But there was something about the weary Johnnie and the replete, well cared for Amanda which made her feel shoddy, grubby, and exhausted.

"Well, I should say that was his business,' said Amanda loudly. "And now you've seen what you came for will you please go away? You've no right to be here."

"I've been slaving for him," said Molly in a low voice, feeling all the more at a disadvantage. What did this girl know about work, about relationships hinging on work and wages, on paying the rent and caring for the children? A wave of horror came over her. She felt sick. She looked up at her handsome Johnnie, no longer hers, and tears came to her eyes.

"Johnnie –?" she said, in a wavering voice, still expecting comfort and reassurance.

"Go home, Moll," he said despondently. "Please go home. I'll talk to you later on."

Then she remembered why she had come and said in a low voice, "I came about the club."

"What?" he said, now sounding annoyed. "What about the club? Can't it wait?"

"I'm going into the other room," Amanda said clearly. "And I want this woman out of here straight away. All this is too ridiculous." She turned and began to go through the doorway. Molly said to Johnnie. "There's trouble."

Johnnie, about to protest again, pulled the dressing-gown further round, retied the belt and started to come downstairs. He knew it was serious. He asked Amanda, "Do you mind if Molly and I go into the kitchen to discuss something?"

"I do, as a matter of fact," replied Amanda. She did not move.

"I don't think you're going to want her to hear this," Molly told her.

He looked at her angrily.

All he could reply, in embarrassment, was, "Don't be stupid. Tell me what it's all about."

She said quickly, "I've been adjusting the payments to the bank day by day so it didn't look as if you —" She glanced at Amanda and said, "So you didn't seem to be making deductions before it was paid in. Now Simon's caught me. He says he's got to tell the Roses, so they don't think he did it because — well, because they'll get back at him." She paused and told him, "I've come to warn you."

"Warn me what?" cried Johnnie. "Do I own that club or do I not?" But the vainglorious claim, made for the benefit of Amanda, who was now leaning against the wall with her arms folded, deceived none of them. Both women knew Johnnie was frightened.

"What are you going to do?" she asked.

"Go home, Molly," he said pityingly. "Get some sleep. I'll talk to you at nine o'clock."

But it was all bluff, she knew. He was afraid and when nine o'clock came he would be far away. It was cold on the way back to the club and she began to stagger. Sobbing, she walked among the empty tables, over the carpet, where cigarette ends lay. She breathed in the stale air, looking at the panelling and the pictures of which she was proud. She hauled herself up the stairs to the flat and lay down on the big bed, with its headboard in the shape of a vast, golden shell. She thought of the early days at Meakin Street with Johnnie, and then, still in her clothes, fell asleep for a few hours.

Morning brought her a sick headache and more, sudden memories of how it had been with her lover when they had first met. How they had laughed and made love, how Johnnie had been a man, then, and not somebody in a dinner jacket, flashing smiles at flighty upper-class girls. He went straight and he went rotten, she thought to herself. At least before, when he was thieving, he'd had to use his brains and he'd risked getting caught and sent to prison. Here, at the club, it was easy. Money from the punters, in goes Johnnie's hand and whoops-a-daisy he's down the street with his pockets full of cash.

The phone rang. It was the wine merchants, asking for payment and saying they would have to stop further supplies if the account was not paid. Johnnie's job, she thought, to pay the drink bills. Wearily she told them to send another account, this time to the Roses. It rang again. This time it was Simon Tate. He said, "I thought I'd better ring to tell you I telephoned Norman Rose half an hour ago. He forgave you. He just called you a stupid tart and things like that. But he's furious about Johnnie. Did you find him last night?"

"He was where you said he'd be," Molly told him.

"I'm sorry," said Simon. "Anyway, Norman asked me if you'd warned Johnnie and I said I thought you might have done. He didn't seem surprised."

"What did he say?" Molly asked.

"He said, 'We'll find him, don't worry.' He sounded perfectly calm."

"Of course they'll find him, sooner or later," Molly said bitterly. "They have to do these things to show they're still in charge. Otherwise people would think they'd lost their grip and start taking liberties."

"I wouldn't be in Johnnie's shoes," remarked Simon. "Still, it serves him bloody well right. You take off, forget him, forget the Roses and the whole seedy business. I'm off to Kenya – I'll come and see you when I get back. Where will you be?"

"Try 19 Meakin Street," said Molly. "I think I'm going back to my mum and dad and my kid."

"Maybe you're not so unlucky," Simon said. He sounded very tired.

And so, saying goodbye to the others and explaining what had happened, Molly Flanders, née Mary Waterhouse, took the bus back to Meakin Street.

Ivy was partly distressed and partly pleased to see her wan daughter back on the step with her cases beside her. "Mum, I've come home," was all Molly said. And Ivy, who had always predicted that no good would come of a West End life with a handsome no-good lover, just told her "Come in."

Little Josie, now two, ran to greet her. "Nice to have you home, love," Ivy said. "Cup of tea and tell all about it?"

Of course, I've got to tell you the other beautiful part of the situation because, naturally, no sooner was Johnnie well away than I fell for a baby. I was stupid. I still thought he'd help me – it's funny how you go on trusting some men whatever they do. I suppose you can't believe all that passion and strength of feeling could ever go. You're like some victim of the KGB – they've kept you awake and tortured you and kept you awake and tortured you until you're programmed. You're like a slave. I reckon pleasure can do that, too, and love. You get conditioned. You can't believe really they've changed. So, of course, when I started feeling rotten and I didn't know what to do who did I get in touch with – Johnnie's parents, who else? I left a message it was urgent. I wished I hadn't. He sent a shabby-looking geezer down to Ivy's with a message and I went to meet him in a cafe in Brixton Market. Full of steam and the smell of frying chips, horrible and rancid and no good to me in my condition. He looked bad himself, for Johnnie, that is. Shoes a bit scuffed, shirt not too fresh – I knew he couldn't go back to his parents for long just in case the Roses turned up there. Whatever they would have done to him wouldn't have been pretty and the place could have been smashed up accidentally as well.

So we sat there and he bought me a cup of tea. The market people sat around having cuppas and sandwiches and I remember the fat woman behind the counter kept on looking at us. Johnnie kept looking round, too, staring out of the window at the housewives with their shopping baskets.

First thing he said when he put the tea down was, "I can't stop here long."

"I guessed as much," I said. "What's happening?"

"They'll put me in hospital, or worse, if I don't hand back the money, that's what's happening," he said. "Razors, they said," and he touched his cheek with his hand. You saw a lot of people about then with razor scars on their faces – if you had any sense when you saw them you looked the other way. I imagined Johnnie's face with a deep scar down his cheek from his eye to near his lips. That would be if he was lucky – those old-fashioned cut-throat razors could take your nose half off. Johnnie was horrified at the thought of losing his looks, I could tell. Also a razor scar was like a brand. Once you had one people could tell who you'd been mixed up with.

I said, "How much?" and he told me two thousand. Not bad for a few months' work. Then he asked me for it – the two thousand, I mean. "I know it's the limit, Moll," he said. "I know I haven't done you any good. But I love you. I never loved that upper-class slag. She bored me rigid, as a matter of fact. And I don't know how much longer I can hold out with no money and nowhere to go."

And he looked me in the eye and gave one of his famous smiles. He thought he was talking to Molly Flanders, girl in love and great romantic, I suppose. Who he was talking to was a pregnant girl in a Brixton cafe. I looked him in the eye and the smile faded like the

Cheshire cat's. It's hard on men, really. First the fun and the love and the good times – then you're pregnant and what you really want is a decent bloke who'll make you a cup of tea when you ask him and bring in some steady wages. And someone like Johnnie really isn't like that and can't be – so when they turn on the charm it falls flat as a pancake. Anyway, I didn't have two thousand pounds or anything like it. Admittedly I'd been sending a lot for Josie because Arnie did raise my wages when I asked him, like Simon told me – and I used to get big tips, sometimes a tenner or twenty quid a time, from the big winners – but all there was left was a few quid that Sid had put in the bank for me. But I wasn't going to tell Johnnie that because I could see now I was going to need it, need it badly. I just said, "Johnnie. I've got no money and you know it. I can't help you, I really can't. And there's something else –"

He looked at me like he really hated me. I was afraid, although I knew it was a baby's look on a man's face.

Josie used to look like that when you refused her something she'd set her heart on – because she'd think you could give her anything, only you just wouldn't. But on a man's face that expression can scare you. He said, "You must have put something away –"

I said, "Johnnie – I'm pregnant."

He burst out, then. He said. "Oh – you stupid, bleeding cow. I don't need this. I don't need this at all. Why the fuck didn't you think?"

"What am I going to do, Johnnie?" I said. I was nearly crying, partly because I knew I was daft and it was hopeless to ask him for anything. He wouldn't do anything. He couldn't anyway. But what he could have done was been nice to me – and he wasn't going to do that either.

"What do you think?" he said. "Get rid of it. What do you expect me to do? Marry you and buy a house? What can I bloody well do, Moll? I can't help myself, let alone you. Why in Christ's name did you have to do it?"

I've noticed fatherhood is optional from the word go. A bloke can say "We're having a baby" or "She's having a baby" but no one can ever say "He's having a baby" without knowing it's a bit of a joke. It stays a joke like that forever after, too. But at the time, sitting in that fat-smelling cafe with my stomach churning and a terrified man in front of me, it was a joke I couldn't see.

I said, "I didn't do it on my own, you know." I must have muttered but a woman sitting at the next table overheard. She was a market trader. She was wearing a big apron with a front pocket for the money.

And she shot me this look which said, "Poor cow – he's not going to be much help to you, is he?" Then she put a fag in her mouth and went back to staring at the formica top of the table.

I just stood up and said, "Well, thanks a lot for your help, Johnnie. Do the same for you some time, I hope." He looked at me hopelessly and I was leaving when something struck me and I asked, "Won't your mum and dad get you out of this trouble?"

"Dad won't," he told me. "It's all right, Moll. I'll have to borrow it off Nedermann."

"Congratulations," I said and left, angry as I've ever been in my life, I suppose. So he had an out, after all. He'd asked me for money when all the time he knew he could borrow it. But he didn't want to because he knew Nedermann would make him pay it back, one way or another. He'd rather borrow from a woman, because debts to women aren't serious. They don't come down on you hard if you don't repay. And after I'd been angry I felt numb and sad and finished. What choice had he, after all? Either take money from Ferenc Nedermann or let the Roses mark his pretty face – and worse. Nedermann would let him have the money. He was building up at that time. He'd started just after the war, buying up old slum property and letting it out to people desperate for housing. The building rate had never caught up with the effects of the bombing and the post-war baby boom made sure places were needed. At that time you could get hundreds, even thousands, of pounds just to get into a flat or a house and now the immigrants from the West Indies were beginning to come over Nedermann was doing even better. People didn't want black tenants so he could get any price he liked for cramming families into single rooms.

What he did to get the old tenants out of his houses wasn't too pretty either. But one thing was certain – whatever Johnnie got from Nedermann there'd be nothing for me. I don't know what I wanted when I went to meet him, whether it was for him to go down on one knee in the cafe and say he was desperate to marry me or whether I just wanted a few quid towards the cost of the abortion. Or maybe just a "sorry" would have helped. But whatever I'd wanted I'd got nothing, not even the "sorry", and when I left the place I walked and walked, feeling my feet were made of lead and my head full of cotton wool until finally I realized I'd be better off in a taxi.

On the way back we went through Soho and, because it was getting dark there were all the girls out on the pavement already, in the drizzle, leaning up against walls and lamp posts, taking slow strolls up and down their bits of pavement and the usual swarthy chaps in good clothes standing at a distance and watching. And sure enough, as luck would have it, I spotted Peggy Jones there, walking up and down outside a restaurant. She was heavily made up and I knew why she was there. Next I saw a man go up and say something to her. Then she went round the corner with him. I leaned back against the seat in the taxi feeling as sick as a dog. I remembered her as a backward kid in Framlingham staying with the vicar's mad wife. I remembered her from Meakin Street. Then they'd condemned Tom Totteridge's stable as unfit for habitation and the Jones's, mother and daughter, had disappeared. I thought, My God, she's hardly any older than I am. And I thought, look at your life, Mary Waterhouse – one kid at sixteen by a chap who got himself hanged and now you're in the club again by the likes of Johnnie Bridges. You'd better pull yourself together, I told myself, or there's nothing to stop you winding up on the pavement beside Peggy. There's not too much standing between you and a beat in Soho.

So that was how I fetched up in a back room at Mrs Galton's on the other side of the High Street. I had to lie on the floor on the usual sheets of newspaper while she injected the usual syringe of soapy water, or whatever she used, into my womb – and then I had to hobble home. While she did it I thought, oh, you lie in the bed in your delight with your legs up and then you're on the floor on sheets of newspaper in the same position. See what I mean? The two things are similar? Then you, the wild rover, cripple off back to mum. Afterwards, of course, you wait for the famous "something to happen". Ivy was very good about it and Sid didn't say anything, although I knew she'd told him. He looked pretty grim, though. What I didn't know was that a few months before a girl had collapsed and nearly haemorrhaged to death on a bus he was on. She was going home from a backstreet abortionist's. Luckily the conductor of the bus was a woman and she'd spotted what was happening and made the driver go off route to get the girl to the nearest hospital. But Sid had seen the blood everywhere, and the girl stretched out on the floor, white as paper. No wonder he looked pale himself when he heard what was happening to me. He must have been terrified. It had to be getting on for Christmas, too.

Arnie Rose, master of good timing, turned up after my second flaming appointment in Mrs Galton's back bedroom. The syringe hadn't worked. "You're the sort that hangs on to them," she remarked philosophically. I thought to myself, get out, you little bastard and leave me alone. I was very fierce about that kid. I didn't want it. I'd have jumped in the canal before I'd have had it.

Anyway, there was Arnie, standing in the front room doorway, smoking a big cigar and saying "Well, well, well," and there I was lying on the settee, staring at him in horror, and wearing an old candlewick dressing-gown.

"I was going to suggest you and me going up West for a drink and a bit of dinner," he said. "Just to show there's no hard feelings about that other business."

"Nice of you, Arnie," said Ivy, appearing behind him in the doorway, with a tea tray. "But as a matter of fact Mary's not well." Behind her Shirley peered round to crane at Arnie, with his gold watchchain and cigar. Something to tell the girls at school in the morning. Ivy sent her upstairs to do her homework and gave Arnie a cup of tea.

"I can see she looks a bit peaky, Mrs W," Arnie said. "What's the doctor say?"

Ivy broke all the rules which said that these things were women's secrets and never revealed to men. Some men never even knew their wives were pregnant or had had an abortion even though every other woman in the street knew it. But Ivy just said, "There's no doctor in this. Mrs Galton's the doctor here."

I daresay Arnie had had some dealings with her in the past. He looked embarrassed, then incredulous. He said, "No –"

"I could kill that Bridges," Ivy said fiercely. "I won't be at peace until he gets what's coming to him."

Then I could see what she was up to when she told him.

"You'll be at peace soon enough, then, Ivy," Arnie told her. "Quite a few of us have got scores to settle with him." Then he looked at me and said, still embarrassed, "Well – I'd better be off and leave you to – er – here –" and he got his wallet out of his jacket pocket and pulled out a handful of fivers. "Take it, Ivy," he said. "I'd like to help – plenty more where that comes from."

Ivy was shocked. There are rules about who pays for abortions – and Arnie was not the father of the child, nor a member of the family: What he was, or had been, was a man who had paid for plenty of abortions for the girls he ran. So this gesture, which included me among Arnie's business girls, put Ivy right off. She refused and said Sid could look after me. So Arnie handed over a fiver before he left and said to get something for little Josie and this time Ivy took it.

As the door clicked behind Arnie, she tucked the money behind the clock on the mantelpiece and said, "A nice thing – gangsters coming to call on you. I don't know what people must think."

"They'll feel all right if you tell them who paid for the doll's pram," I told her. I was leaning back feeling horrible and wondering when the pain would start. "They'll all say, oh, well, for all his way of life, Arnie's got a heart of gold when it comes to little kids. Kind to his old mother, too."

"I'd like to be a fly on the wall when they catch up with Johnnie," Ivy said vindictively. But I was too depressed to see it like that. The pain had started now, and like all pain it was made worse by my feelings – here I lay on the settee while the man who had helped to make the baby I was getting rid of had let me down.

It happened that night, with Ivy trying to comfort me and putting newspaper under me to absorb the blood. I won't forget the look on her face when it was over – oh, Christ, the look on a woman's face when she's seen her daughter suffer the consequences of being a woman needs to be seen to be believed. Generations, thousands of years of them have looked like that, passed it on to their daughters, who pass it on to theirs. That face is full of pity but it tries to will a bit of courage into the girl. It says, that's the way it is, but you don't have to let it ruin you, girl.

Of course Johnnie had rejected me when I needed help, but, of course, he turned up when I was all right. Some people are like that – the exact opposite of the person who's always there when you need them. They're the sort that are never there when you just fell off the bus and always around if you won the pools. He ducks in, looking all round like a kid who's been nicking sweets from Woolworths and sits down to talk about marriage and love and a better life when he's got things straight with the Roses. I said, "Go away and leave me alone, Johnnie," because Ivy was in the room but, do you know, if Ivy hadn't been in the room I'd have fallen on his neck, just as usual, and agreed to anything he said. Like I said, I'm sure half of it's like a relationship between a torturer and the person he's torturing. It's that, and of course that you always hope to wipe out the past and set the record straight and have everything back the way it was before. But Ivy wasn't having anything to do with Johnnie and she told him now he'd seen I was all right he could go. He didn't hang about arguing when she pointed out Josie's fiver still on the mantelpiece and told him who it came from and wasn't Arnie kind to drop in and see how I was keeping. Johnnie flashed out the door like greased lightning. Even I had to see the funny side – Ivy and me laughed so much I had to tell her to stop me. I thought I'd do myself a mischief, the state I was in.

1955

It was in February, as Molly stood in the park pushing her daughter on the swing, that a thickset man of medium height came up to her and asked, very politely, "Mrs Flanders?" She looked into an ivory face, with very black, slightly slanted eyes and said, after a hesitation, "That's right. Who are you?" His eyes then turned to the swing, where little Josie was bending herself to and fro to try and keep it in motion, now that Molly had stopped pushing, and he said, almost absent-mindedly, "My name is Ferenc Nedermann." In his thick black overcoat, middle-aged and rather shy, he did not give the impression of being the notorious slum landlord he really was. She said, "How can I help you, Mr Nedermann?"

"I wondered," he said, in his slightly accented English, "if you would be able to tell me where Johnnie Bridges is?"

She shook her head and told him, "No. I wouldn't know where to find him. I haven't seen him since before Christmas."

"You haven't got any idea where he might be?" he said. "At the moment the matter is desperate. He's borrowed money from me and I now need it badly."

"Oh, God," said Molly. She felt sick, tired and depressed suddenly. She never wanted to hear of Johnnie or his complications again. She had still not recovered from his refusal to help her. Meanwhile Nedermann went on staring at Josie, who was now turning her head of brown curls towards Molly and crying out, "Push, mum. Push."

Nedermann, after a pause, said, "It was five thousand pounds. He swore he had a way of paying me back by the middle of last month. At another time I would not mind the delay. But at the moment I need to call on every penny I have."

"Five thousand," Molly said. "He told me it was two."

"To pay off the Roses," Nedermann agreed. "Then he borrowed a further three."

"Why did you lend him so much?" said Molly. "A man who'd already cheated the Roses. What made you think you'd do any better?"

Nedermann shrugged, then moved forward to push the swing – a little push, so that Josephine would not fall off. He turned his head to look at Molly. "He did me a small favour," he said. "And his plans for getting the money to return to me seemed sound."

"You mean you lent him the money to go out and do a job," Molly said bitterly. "And then it failed and he disappeared. That's the story, isn't it?"

"More or less," agreed Nedermann. "People told me Johnnie Bridges never failed."

"That used to be true," she agreed. "Have you tried the police stations?"

"He's not in the hands of the law," Nedermann told her. He gave Josephine a large push, to keep her swinging, and stepped back to look at Molly. "You've no idea where he is – not a clue?"

"I'm telling you the truth," she said. "I don't know where he is."

Josephine then fell off the swing and began to cry. Molly ran to get her, picked her up and returned to Nedermann who said instantly, "Is she hurt?"

"Just a graze," Molly told him and then said bluntly, "Mr Nedermann – I don't want anything more to do with Johnnie or the Rose brothers. And I can't help you." She thought that she wanted no more to do with him either, although she felt sorry for him. He seemed a lonely man. He had been cheated by Johnnie. She had heard of his evictions, his West Indians crammed together, whole families to a room, paying inflated rents and unable to complain because they might not be able to find anywhere else to live. She had heard of his houses run as brothels, the fires caused by faulty wiring, the damp, his practice of doing what they called "putting the schwartzes in" – letting flats in houses to West Indians, who would have noisy parties all night long and wear down the old people who lived there so much that they left. She knew all this but still she thought he was a sad and rather pathetic man.

"I must go now," she said hastily, "and give my little girl her tea."

She let herself thankfully into the little house. But the brief meeting with Nedermann had brought a whole crush of memories back to her mind. She ironed Sid and Jack's shirts and Shirley's school blouses. She put a chicken in the oven. And remembered walking with Johnnie along the canal, and the clubs and Frames and, reaching further back, had a vision of Allaun Towers at Christmas – the long, old building, the old rust-red bricks, the lawn, the bare trees, the big fire at the back of the house – and then, Johnnie again, bending over her as she lay in bed, smiling at him. She felt his body, which she had tried hard to forget. She stood at the sink with a potato in one hand and a knife in the other. Tears of misery and boredom began to drip from her face.

Josephine said, "I lost golly," four times. But Molly did not hear her until at last she looked down into the child's face and said, "What am I going to do?" and burst into tears herself.

"I lost golly. Find golly," demanded her daughter. Molly sat and cried. When Shirley came in from school Molly went upstairs, saying she was unwell, and sat there by herself as the noise of the others coming in began. Nineteen Meakin Street was now badly over-crowded. Although Jack was living with a family near the docks, where he worked, there was not room for Josephine's cot in the bedroom, so she slept in Shirley's bed and Molly in the other, while Shirley had taken up Jack's old position on the front room settee. At weekends, especially if Jack was there with his girlfriend, there was no room in the house at all. Ivy, who had got back her old job in the breadshop, was tiring under the strain. Molly, still living on what the family had saved from her wages and tips, knew that she would have to leave. It would mean getting a job which paid her enough to cover the rent and the cost of a minder for Josephine. That might be difficult, but would not be impossible to manage. The worst thing was her sudden craving for some movement, some excitement, a bit of life. She saw nothing ahead but a Council flat, if she could get one, and a job in a shop or perhaps an office. She did not know what she wanted but she did not want that. She was nineteen and a half. She had a small child to look after and few choices. She went downstairs and sat in the front room while the family had their supper.

Simon Tate walked down Meakin Street that evening, finding it narrow and depressing. A thin and malignant dog barked at him through mist laden with drizzle. A woman walked past, heavy-legged and bowed down with shopping. He knocked on the door of number 19. It was opened by a tired woman in her late thirties, with coarsely dyed blonde hair tied back and held with a black velvet bow at the nape of her neck. She looked at him with the alert, slightly sceptical expression which he recognized as Molly Flanders'. Behind her a pretty two-year-old with round, brown eyes and curly hair stood clutching a grubby doll.

"I'm a friend of Molly's," he said, "from Frames. I brought these." He presented the bunch of roses he had in his hand. The woman looked at him and said, "Come in, then. She's in the front room."

In the small parlour Molly sat with her feet on a stool, smoking and watching TV. She looked up apathetically and then her expression brightened. "Simon!" she cried.

"Here you are, Molly," said Simon. "Hope you're feeling a lot better."

"Excuse me," said Ivy, now satisfied that the visitor was welcome, "we're just eating our tea. Fancy a cup of tea, later?"

"Thank you," said Simon. "I'm just back from Kenya – thought I'd look in."

Simon sat down and said, "That's what it's all about. I've come with a proposition from the Roses. They called me back – found out where I was from the man I used to share the flat with. They've offered me extra wages and they want you back too. They've been trying to run the place with other staff but it hasn't worked out. I'm here to say, how about it?"

"All right for you," said Molly. "They want you because you do your job well. But my worry is that Arnie Rose wants me for other reasons. I mean, I could do with the work but I don't want it on condition I take on Arnie Rose."

"Well, it was Norman who asked me to ask you," he said. "He told me you were attractive, confident and efficient and honest, and you knew the job. Arnie didn't come into it, as far as I know. You'd get more money."

"The other problem is, who would look after Josephine?" Molly told him.

"What about your mother –" Simon suggested.

"She's got a responsible job managing a breadshop. And she likes it," Mary said. "Why should she have to give it up?"

"Up the ante on the Roses. They've offered you twenty a week," Simon responded. "Say you'll do it for twenty-five. With your tips you could afford to make it worth your mother's while."

"Why shouldn't she have a life of her own?" Mary said impatiently.

"Who?" demanded Ivy, coming into the room.

"You, if you want to know," her daughter told her.

"I thought I had one," said Ivy. "Too much of it, most of the time."

Simon looked at Ivy and decided that she was the sort of woman who made up her own mind. So he put the matter to her. And Ivy said that she would take Josephine over during the week, that she would book her in to a state nursery in the mornings and take her to work with her in the afternoons. She added that Mary had to collect Josephine every Friday night and return her at a decent hour on Sundays. She added that all this was subject to Sid's approval but it seemed to Simon this was only a nod to convention.

"Done, then," said Simon, standing up. "It'll be good to have you back. But do you think you're fit enough?"

"Fit for anything," declared Mary. "But is the flat still going? I've got to find somewhere to live. No point in you having the weekend off without Josephine, mum, if I come here with her. And she won't know what's going on."

"Flat's gone," Simon said laconically. "Arnie let it to a bloke called Greene. He's a slightly dubious doctor – unqualified, specializes in looking after society gentlemen and ladies' bad backs – and other things, too. He also draws their pets – dogs and horses and the like. He's the kind of versatile chap they used to keep about the courts of Europe in the old days – could be relied on to produce a love philtre, play a few relaxing songs on the guitar when the king felt out of sorts, and generally help out on any and every occasion." Mary thought there might be more to Greene's talents than he was prepared to say in front of Ivy, but at that moment she was more concerned with her own predicament.

"I'll have to go to an agency and find a flat," she said despondently.

"I think Sid told me the Tomkinsons were moving out of number 4, where you used to live," Ivy said. "He works at the garage but they've got the deposit for a house, now."

"Oh, Christ, mum," Mary said. "Not there. I can't go there." In that house she had weathered out the time after Jim Flanders was hanged. In that house her romance with Johnnie Bridges had begun.

"The rent's low, if the landlord'll let you have it. If you go to an agency you'll get some tiny rathole for twenty guineas a week – and it won't disturb Josie so much –"

Mary groaned. "Have a word with him, then," she told her mother. "Tell him I'll pay half the price of having a bathroom installed if he'll pay the other half. That'll convince the mean sod. I can't be running up here for a bath all the time like I used to and Josie's too big to bathe in the sink any more. All right Tate," she said, rounding on him. "Now you can go home with a Balkan Sobranie drooping out of your mouth after a nice evening witnessing the problems of the poor."

"I was admiring your velocity," remarked Simon. "Goodbye, Mrs Waterhouse. Goodbye, Molly. Monday night at eight?"

And he was gone. "Nice man," Ivy said. "That's the sort you should be setting your cap at from now on, Mary."

"Thanks a lot, mum," said her daughter drily.

The next day Molly put on her old fur coat, mittens and a woolly hat and took a heavily bundled up Josephine out to the scruffy little park.

The sky overhead was livid and dark as they arrived. "It might snow," she told Josephine, who jumped up and down, crying "Snow! Snow!" Molly looked down at her. She was a tartar, and no mistake, she thought. Half the time she clung wordlessly to Ivy's skirts, or sheltered behind Sid. Seconds later she'd be rattling away, nineteen to the dozen, getting hold of a neglected can of paint and painting the back of the house red, sternly counting the milk bottles in front of the milkman, as if checking the delivery, rushing and tearing everywhere. There were times when Mary loked into the bright, huge brown eyes and feared for a child of such emphatic character.

As the first flakes of snow floated down on to the shabby grass and leafless trees of the park, Josephine's round eyes glittered and her little round face was transfigured. She ran across the thin coating of snow on the grass and studied her footprints, she held out her palm and caught the flakes.

Molly watched her, shivering slightly. Back to Frames, she thought. Well, why not? Back to number 4 Meakin Street – again, why not?

In the deserted park, where Josephine was now scraping thin snow together to make a little snowman, she found a man beside her.

"She's a nice child," said Ferenc Nedermann.

Molly looked at him, startled. What was he doing here again?

"She's never seen snow before," she told him.

"It reminds me of winters in my own country," he said.

"Where's that?" she asked.

"Poland," he said. "On the German border."

"That can't have been nice," she said and moved away. She stood by Josephine saying, "There's not a lot of snow here, Josie. Not really enough for a snowman." But the child had seen pictures of snowmen in books, with pipes in their mouths and lumps of coal for eyes.

"A little one — I have a little one," insisted the child. Molly knelt down on the snow to help her. She called back at Nedermann. "If you're still looking for Johnnie I can't help you. I'm not hiding him."

"I know where he is," Nedermann said. "The Roses found him."

"Oh, God," Molly said, squeezing the tiny snowman near the top, to make a head. She sat back on her sopping knees and said to Josie, "Run and get two very little stones for his eyes." The child trotted off. "What did they do to him?" she called.

"They made him pay up — then they beat him up a little bit," he told her.

"What about the money he owes you?" she asked.

"I didn't get all of it."

She looked at the stones Josephine held out. "They're a bit big," she said. Nedermann was beside her. In his leather palm were some small pieces of gravel.

"Thanks," she said, taking them as he crouched beside her. Very carefully, she put them on to the snowman's tiny face. They stuck. Josephine laughed. Then she wandered off, kicking up the snow as she went. Molly put a little piece of brown twig into the snowman's face. "There's his pipe," she said with satisfaction.

Then she looked Nedermann in the face and asked, "Well — you found him. What do you want now?"

"Oh," he said calmly. "I was near here and I wondered if you'd be back. I have to go now. I've got the car. Do you want a lift home?"

"Not a chance," said Molly, who saw that Josephine's friend Sally had arrived in the care of her big sister. "That's her friend," she said. "She'll want to stay until it gets dark now."

"Children should enjoy as much as they can," he told her. "There is no such thing as too much pleasure for a child. Childhood is short."

"You're right," said Molly. She felt uneasy and wished he would go away. She did not know what he wanted. His face was always expressionless and his voice flat. It was the voice of a man in despair. And she wondered what the children of his tenants were doing now. Playing round dangerous oil heaters in their crowded flats? Lying on mattresses damp with the moisture coming into the rooms from leaky roofs and running walls?

"I expect we'll meet again," she said. "I don't know if you're a gambler — I'm getting back my old job as a croupier at Frames, in South Molton Street."

"I shall come and see you," he said, and left her courteously.

Watching the little girls play she wondered if they had marked pretty Johnnie's face. It would make a big difference to him if they'd scarred him, she thought. He would mind that more than anything.

The next time I saw Molly it was with my father. At Frames. The affair began in a peculiar way, with my mother coming to me in a great distress, almost as soon as I entered the house. I was going to spend the weekend at home and go back to Oxford on Sunday. But, no, she said, if the occasion demanded it, I would have to stay.

Matters must be sorted out. She was, in fact, dreadfully upset. She had discovered a bill from Frames in my father's suit when she was emptying the pockets before giving it to the cleaners. Worse than that, this was the second bill she had found. The first he had left on the dressing-table one night and she had come across it in the morning. I'm sure she would not have been nearly so upset by this evidence of a new interest in gambling and fast living by my father if she had not been the youngest daughter of the famous Arthur Udall, "Flash" Udall, who travelled with the fast set surrounding King Edward VII and had, before my mother's childish eyes, brought a family of five daughters to ruin before the First World War. He'd done this by the old means of wine and women but the chief cause of his downfall had been a readiness to bet on anything, anywhere, at any time, from a racehorse to relative speeds of two flies crawling up the wallpaper. So my poor mother had seen her mother's tears and half the property sold off before the old reprobate eventually died in his sins, keeling over on Derby Day just as the horse he backed crossed the finishing line in front. He left his wife nearly penniless with five daughters, four unmarried. Small wonder the little Udalls were forbidden to play cards, or wager over their Racing Demon even with matchsticks or hairpins. Small wonder my mother looked on gambling as man's worst form of weakness. She was naturally even more upset that my father had not confided in her. This secrecy seemed to make his visits to a gaming club more sinister still. So, in a state of great agitation, she asked me, the eldest son, to discuss the matter with my father. And I, feeling the whole thing was rather Victorian and ridiculous, agreed to do so.

The old-fashioned scene took place in his study after dinner. My father burst out laughing and then sobered a little when I told him how genuinely upset my mother had been. "Well," he said, "there are several reasons why I didn't tell your mother what I have been doing, one of them being her sensitivity on the subject. But I assure you none of those reasons involved a sudden excess of gambling fever. In fact, I've spent two dull evenings at Frames in the last month and tonight I shall spend another one – piously hoping I shall never have to cross the threshold again. In fact, partly to cheer me while I'm there, and partly to impress on you the fact that of all men's ways of passing the time gambling is the dullest and least profitable, I now invite you to join me in an outing after dinner. Personally I'd rather go to King's Cross and watch the trains go in and out."

"I wouldn't mind," I said, rather excitedly. "I've always wanted to go to somewhere like Frames. But what shall I tell mother? She'll think I've been bitten by the bug, too, and we'll both be dragged down into hell together. Anyway, what are you doing, going time after time to a place you hate?"

"Part of the job, my boy, that's all," said my father. "I'd better not tell you any more. I'll speak to your mother – at least I can tell her that after tonight I'm giving it up for good. I can blame Tubby Atkinson. I always make him come with me." And at this my father chuckled and went out of the room to find mother. I, who lived on the same staircase as Tom Allaun, had often heard from him and his cousin Charlie wild tales of high stakes, perilous games and fortunes won and lost at Frames. I was excited – although I sincerely hoped not to run into either of them. But even as we walked through the discreet front door in the quiet West End street I was still wondering what on earth my father was coming here for.

We came into a kind of lobby. The wallpaper was restrained and the lighting fairly low. Beyond this lay a bar where several men and some women stood drinking. My father spotted Tubby Atkinson with relief. Tubby bought us both a whisky and said glumly, "So this is to be our last night of pleasure, eh? Just as well. I dread the idea of getting carried away and staking my life on the turn of a card."

My father, equally unenthusiastically, said, "Chemin de fer, then. Finish your drink." A laugh went up from the other end of the bar where the group had thickened. Then one of them detached himself from the group and came towards me shouting, "Bert! Torn up your Band of Hope membership card?"

Embarrassed I saw his big form approaching me. I said, "Hullo, Charlie. Father – this is Charles Markham. Charlie – my father."

"Oh," said Charlie, unabashed. "Good evening, sir. And here

comes Tom —" Introductions were made. Tom Allaun was polite enough but I could tell my father disliked the pair of them. There was something about the combination of Charlie's large, ruddy-complexioned presence and Tom's pallor and slender body which together made each of them seem worse — as the bear pointing up the fox's cunning, so to speak, while the fox emphasized the brute strength of the bear. At college I would hear modern jazz coming from Tom's rooms. On the staircase I would meet friends of his going to visit him — they all tended to look like him, withdrawn, remote, sometimes older than the average undergraduate. He had a way of looking at me without expression as if waiting for me to commit myself to some foolish statement. I always felt he laughed at me behind my back. I have never quite known why I disliked Tom so much, but I did. Living in the same building with him I observed that he stayed up late and rose late, but that otherwise I had no idea of his habits. Charlie, on the other hand, was a celebrated university hooligan. This was no more endearing. His jokes often had a cruel side. Taken in combination Tom and Charlie gave the impression of being like the two Nazi interrogators — the pale Gestapo intellectual who trips you up in your mistakes and then hands you back to the big one for a spot more beating up or torture.

We all strolled up to the main room, which was very quiet and long, with reddish carpet and velvet curtains. And, of course, the green baize tables. And standing at one of them, croupier's rake in hand, there stood my princess, the girl I had seen at the Allauns the Christmas before last. She was, in fact, just like a princess, in her pale satin dress, with her longish blonde hair falling round that spectacularly pretty face. The rake she held might well have been a mace. All she lacked was a crown.

She looked up and caught my eye. I went straight over to her.

"Mary," I said. "It is you, isn't it?"

"The very same," she told me. A tall young man in evening clothes walked up to her and she said something to him. He nodded and took the rake. The game continued and she came over to us.

I introduced her to my father and his friend. My father seemed surprised, which I thought was merely because he did not expect me to know a croupier in a London gaming house.

He was studying her deeply and after we had chatted about the circumstances of our meeting he asked, "Will you come and have a drink with us at the bar? I don't feel like playing just at present."

"Well – " she said. "I'm really supposed – but never mind. Yes – I'd like to."

So we all trooped back to the bar again. My father turned his full attention on Mary and began to ask her about herself. I watched him in awe. To begin with, she evidently liked him and felt at ease with him, so much so that I began to think my father was starting a suspect middle-age phase and might now abandon a hitherto blameless life to take up gambling and go about with pretty girls. In spite of my horror at this prospect I was lost in admiration of his technique. If he asks her out to dinner, I thought, lost between jealousy and admiration, she'll accept. She'll go.

"No, I don't live here," she was telling him. "I live in a little house in the same street as my mum and dad. I've got a small daughter who lives with my mother during the week and comes to me at weekends."

"A respectable girl, really," said Charlie Markham, who suddenly seemed rather drunk, and had his hand heavily clasped round the upper part of Molly's arm.

Molly flinched and a look of fear came into her eyes before she pulled away her arm and said, "Not really. Maybe a bit more respectable than you are, though."

"No – I insist," said Charlie, and he pushed his face close to hers. "You've got a heart of gold, Molly. A heart of gold, that's what you've got. Didn't I always say that, Tom?"

"You certainly did – and do," responded Tom Allaun.

"Surely the tables are calling for you young men?" said my father. "Perhaps you should go upstairs and take the first bet of the evening. Are you going, too?" he asked turning to me. And I had no option but to leave, dragging Tom and Charlie reluctantly behind me. As I went upstairs Tom, from behind, said in a low voice, "Pater often take up with pretty girls in clubs, Bert?"

"Only when the moon's full," I told him, itching for the moment when I could get away from them.

And finally, after losing fifty pounds I could not afford, while Charlie watched my face as I lost and Tom egged me on, hoping, no doubt, that I would start to gamble feverishly without caring what happened, I got out from between their elbows and left them to it. By then their faces had both taken on a steady stare as they watched the dice, the cards and the croupier's rake taking the chips. They barely said goodnight once I had told them I was leaving. But, "You must call your old man into the study before he goes to bed," Tom remembered to say. "You'd better have a serious talk to him about his life."

I found my father in the bar alone, gloomily drinking a glass of whisky and dry ginger. There was no sign of Molly. "Tubby's gone," he told me. "Have you had enough?"

"More than enough," I told him.

In the taxi he asked, "Are they special friends of yours, Allaun and Markham?"

"Certainly not," I said. "Tom lives on my staircase and Charlie's his cousin, that's all. I met them over Christmas when I was staying with Sebastian. They're neighbours, or rather Tom is. But as a matter of fact, I don't like either of them much."

"I'm glad of that," muttered my father.

"Did you enjoy your chat with Mary?" I asked him and he picked up my tone immediately.

"She's a very nice girl," he reassured me, adding, "Although I'm sure I don't know how." And after a pause he said, "Or for how much longer."

For several months Molly Flanders went to work, took a cab back to Meakin Street in the early hours of the morning, slept late, did her household jobs and sometimes picked up Josephine from the bread-shop in the afternoons and took her to the park. For a time she was happy with this routine. She needed to recover from the shocks of the previous few months but, as spring came on and the evenings grew lighter, she became restless. There was nothing she particularly wanted to do but she was bored with what she was doing. So when Ferenc Nedermann turned up at the club one evening and invited her out to dinner she accepted, rather than say no to yet another invitation. She was too wise to do more than flirt with the more enterprising visitors to Frames and the truth was that she felt no interest in any of them. Johnnie had spoiled her for men. She did not trust them. She knew, too, that most of the men at Frames would see her as nothing more than fair game for them – something like an air hostess or a pretty nurse, not to be taken seriously. Nedermann, on the other hand, was middle-aged and sad. He did not want sex, or romance or a good time with a pretty girl – all the things she could no longer give. In the end he sent a big car for her to take her to the Savoy Grill. The driver of the car explained that Nedermann himself had been delayed. Molly, full of childish pleasure, settled down against the leather upholstery and enjoyed the ride.

Nedermann was waiting for her outside. When they had settled in the restaurant he said, "How pretty you look tonight – the prettiest girl in this room. I feel proud to be seen with you."

Molly smiled. She said, "Thank you." But she thought that if Nedermann was going to court her she would have to tell him she was not interested. He, however, gazed at her with his narrow black eyes and said, "I know you are upset about Johnnie Bridges. I only wished to tell you that you looked nice. Few women object to that."

"It's kind of you," she told him. "I'm sorry – I still feel unhappy about the past. I'm sorry if I'm not much fun."

"I don't ask you to be funny," he said. "Do you want to hear how he is?"

"I suppose so," she said.

"Then I'll tell you. I found him. I no longer needed my money so much but I became obstinate and I thought, I'll find you, Johnnie, because you evade me and you owe me money. So I thought, he'll be somewhere – I'll be the detective and find him. It was a challenge, you see, and I must say that I am like the Roses. I don't like to be cheated. If he had come to me and explained he could not pay I could have accepted it. To hide like a child – that was too much."

Molly pulled a face and said, "I wonder if I want to hear any more."

"Better to listen," he advised. "Listen and learn. Shall I go on?"

Molly drank some wine and said, "All right. So – you pulled on your deerstalker and –"

"Deerstalker?" he enquired.

"Like Sherlock Holmes," she told him.

It was quiet in the restaurant. There was no noise from the busy traffic outside in the Strand. "Yes. Like Sherlock Holmes," he agreed. "As you know these people never go very far, in the end. They hide – then they drift back to the pubs, the clubs – so I looked around there but no one had seen him. And after that I thought, where else do these spoilt boys go when they're in trouble and want a bath and fresh clothes and a sympathetic face? Why – back to their mothers, I thought. And after a short search I found the big criminal at home in South London, in front of the fire, eating crumpets like a little prince. And outside, as I'd suspected, the big white car. These heroes will never get rid of the car, whatever they owe. Because how else will they impress women and keep self-respect? That car is them, as they see themselves – fast, flashy and expensive. It broke his heart to part with that car. I had him away from the fireside and at the garage in no time. The man handed him the money in cash and I put my hand out straight away. His face was like at mother's funeral."

Molly burst out laughing. Nedermann's sobriety as he spoke, and his oddly accented English, made the story even funnier. Seeing her laugh, Nedermann's face split into a wide, boyish smile.

"He should have known better than to take on an old Pole," he told her. "And yet," he said, "I envied him. No wonder women love men like that. They have all the cleverness and ingenuity and innocent selfishness of small boys. Yet they are men. They are irresistible. Later, of course, it will become plainer that he never intends to grow up. Peter Pan. It may seem less charming later." He paused, "Better to grow up – in the end," he said.

"You sound as if it's painful," remarked Molly, intrigued in spite of herself, although she thought the conversation slightly odd.

"You know – you have made a beginning. You are older than Johnnie now."

"Eat your dinner, Ferenc," she said, pointing at the plate he had in front of him. "I'll talk about lovely subjects while you get on with it."

"I don't mind about the dinner," Nedermann said. "In such company, food is far from my thoughts."

"Well, it shouldn't be," she said firmly. And she told him anecdotes about the club – the Chinese who had taken £10,000 from a man and given it back to him on the pavement outside the same night; the midget who had been playing roulette standing on a chair at the table until they found he was leaning on it slightly in order to help the ball into the right hole; the contretemps in the ladies room when a man the attendant knew to be a celebrated transvestite tried to gain entry and use the lavatory. "She cries out," reported Molly, " 'I know you well, Lord Brawn, and I hate to think what your mother would have to say at all this.' I was coming upstairs with Simon at the time and we couldn't believe our eyes. Simon caught on fastest – he just stepped forward and said, 'Let the lady in just this one time, Mrs Jones.' He's very sophisticated – Simon." But, she said, seeing that Nedermann had eaten part of his dinner, "What I don't understand is why you lent Johnnie that money in the first place. You're not a fool, you must have known what would happen."

"It didn't matter to me at the time," answered Nedermann. "And I didn't want to see the Roses get him. They are dogs."

"I thought you might have been trying to get him into a position where he had to sell you his part of the club," she said bluntly.

"Oh no," he said, surprised. "I don't want the club. I don't want the complications of pandering to the rich. A man in my position, an emigré, a refugee — it is simpler to deal with the poor."

He's barmy, thought Molly suddenly. That's the answer — he's barmy. I'll eat up and go, that's the best thing to do.

Nedermann contemplated her placidly. "And I get what I want," he said. "Johnnie's working for me now. That way he can pay back the remainder of the money he owes me."

"What?" exclaimed Molly, too loudly. She lowered her voice. "He's dishonest — you know that. Why give him a job?"

"He's very capable," Nedermann replied. "I need an assistant with some brains — the others — hooligans, stupid people. They ruin the business and rob me as well. I need a man to help me with the confusion. Johnnie can sort it out. If he robs me — well, he robs me. I can get rid of him."

He poured more wine for Molly, who suddenly realized that he had barely had any of his, while she had swigged off three or four glasses. He stared at her and then, as the plates were removed said, "Would you like this?" and took a box from his pocket. Molly looked at it. She took it wordlessly, dreading what she would find inside. She realized that Nedermann had been assessing her throughout the meal. She opened it. He watched her, rather as Sid used to when he took something in a bag for her out of his pocket on Friday night. Inside the box was a watch, the face surrounded by small stones, probably diamonds. The strap was made of platinum. Instinctively she knew that if she even took the watch from its box the deal would be struck. And knew he knew. She shook her head, "I'm sorry," she said. "It's too expensive."

"Are you sure?" he asked her, seeing that her eyes were still on the pretty watch.

"Oh, yes," she said. Unobtrusively he took the box from the table, closed it and put it back in his pocket.

"I was hoping," he said, "that you and the little girl would come and live with me. Sometimes I dislike my house when it is full of people. Sometimes I dislike it when it is empty. Sometimes I think I was richer before the war, when I was a poor man."

"I — I — don't want to make any changes just at present," Molly told him with embarrassment. "For the time being – I want to bring up my child, earn my living. Do you understand?"

"More than you do," Nedermann said. "Now then, you have a menu in your hand and at your age, no matter what middle-aged refugees say to you at dinnertime you should still be able to enjoy a nice dessert – chocolate mousse, perhaps?"

And Molly, a little piqued by his placid acceptance of her refusal, had to admit that she wanted some chocolate moussé.

He ate a pear, looked a little sad and told her some jokes about a firm of builders he employed. Molly laughed, even though she knew his builders were hired to patch up decaying houses cheaply so that Nedermann could get high rents from people with no alternatives. Afterwards he put her into the big car and told the driver to take her home. He walked off coolly down the Strand, alone, in his big, black coat.

Back at Meakin Street she thought, "Platinum straps on diamond watches – he's like Rabbity Jim with his pocketful of snares." But the odd thing was that she fell asleep like a baby and woke cheerful.

But proposals, like troubles, never come singly. On Saturday Ivy arrived early in the morning with Josephine. They were having a cup of tea in the kitchen when there came a loud banging on the front door. "Postman," muttered Ivy and went to answer the door, coming back into the kitchen with a black look on her face, followed by Johnnie.

Molly had not seen him now for nearly six months. She had thought about him often but had actually partly forgotten what he was like. Now he seemed to fill the room.

She had, for months, loved and hated him by herself. Now she was confused.

"Hullo, Molly," he said. "I wanted to find out how you were."

"Cup of tea?" she offered.

Ivy stood up straight and said, "Don't give him anything, Molly."

"Oh, come on, mum," Molly said quietly.

Ivy sniffed and said, "Do as you please. But I sincerely hope you'll be gone when I get back from work, Johnnie Bridges."

"It's all right, mum," she said.

After Ivy went he gained more confidence. He sat down at the kitchen table and looked at her, saying, "I had to see how you were. And Josephine. Ferenc said he'd gone out to dinner with you. I've been worrying about you."

"Not a word for six months and then you arrive at eight in the morning," she said. "I'm all right, as you can see. How are you?"

"I'm working for Ferenc. Reason I'm here at this hour is because I've got an early call to make a mile away. I had to see you, Molly, but I was afraid —" He pulled a box out from his pocket and held it out to her. Molly thought the situation was becoming ridiculous. She opened the morocco case and saw a gold bracelet, with a green stone in it.

She passed it back to him saying mockingly, "I can't take it, I'm afraid. It's too expensive. A lady can only accept chocolates and flowers."

"Please, Molly," he said, "I want to make it up to you for everything that happened."

"Nothing to make up for," she told him. "Or anything there is can't be paid for in bracelets."

She stood looking out of the kitchen window. She had put some tubs of earth out in the yard. The crocuses were already out. The daffodils were on the point of blooming.

He came up behind her, put his arms round her waist and pressed against her. That move, which had always meant her turning and going into his arms, and then to bed, made her want him again. She felt very weak, as if she might fall down if he did not go on holding her. But she moved away and said, "It's no good, Johnnie. I've had enough. You let me down." She sat down at the table and put her head in her hands. "You can get out of here with your smiles and your bent jewellery. I don't want any more pain and suffering."

"Molly — Molly," he said, bending over her. "Don't cry. Please don't cry. Things will be different, I swear it. I'm out of trouble now, can't you see that?"

"I'm not going back to all that," she said, sniffing. Still staring at the grain on the table she said fiercely, "You had your chance and you were too bleeding greedy. Greedy as a kid. Now leave me alone."

With his arms around her shoulders he said, "Look at me, Molly, look at me. I've changed —"

"Yes — for five minutes. Soon as you've got what you want you'll change back."

"I want to marry you, Molly," he cried.

Now she looked up at him and, her voice trembling, said, "Bugger off, Johnnie."

"Where there's two gifts there's bound to be three," she said to herself later that day. It was no surprise when a man outside Woolworths that afternoon pressed half a crown into Josephine's hand and disappeared into the crowd of shoppers on the pavement. "Watches, bracelets and half crowns," said Molly to herself as the child stared at the money in her palm. "He did it because he's a kind gentleman who likes little girls," she said, in answer to Josephine's dazzled, "Why?" In spite of her depression about having to send Johnnie packing, for she knew she still loved him in a disastrous way, she could not help grinning. "What are you going to spend it on, then?" she asked.

"Chocolate," Josephine said, dragging her into the sweet shop.

It's my idea nobody's going to want to hear about me until I get to the juicy bits. Not that I care. I'm doing this for myself but the real row on the landing is going to come when I get to how my private affairs collided with public affairs. That's why I've kept very quiet about doing these memoirs at all. I don't want the death threats and subtle bribes to start before I've finished the story. So here's the bit where the Official Secrets Act has to come out and good old Bert Precious (who's bound to get dragged into it somehow) will have absolutely nothing to fear – for a while, anyway. What I'm coming to is the story of Steven Greene, and Wendy Valentine and Carol Rogers and a full supporting caste of peers, Shakespearian actors, High Court judges and cardinals, all caught with their knickers round their knees.

What I remember about meeting Steven Greene for the first time was just walking down South Molton Street with Simon Tate on a chilly evening in late winter, early spring, or whatever. We'd had a bite to eat before I did my first night back at Frames, to set me up, so to speak, and I was droning on about Ivy, how she'd got niggled when Jack's fiancée, Pat, told her that she and Jack were saving for their own house and how I was certain that Ivy would take all the money I gave her for Josephine, feed the child on scraps, pawn her boots and put every penny towards the deposit on her own semi-detached in the suburbs. So I'm carrying on in this working-class way, partly to hide my nerves, and just as we're going into Frames I'm saying, to Simon, "Her only fear is I'll take up with some geezer and give him the money. It's not my welfare she's thinking of, or the morals of the thing, just the cash. Not that there's much chance of that – I'm right off it –" when out booms Norman Rose's voice from the bar, "Sorry to hear you've given up sex, Moll. You'll be a sad loss to the intitootion," and there he was, bounding towards me with a bottle of champagne in his hand, looking affable. Both the brothers were standing there, bulging out of their Savile Row suits. There was only one other person in the bar, a man. And before I knew where I was, I was quaffing champagne with the Roses, grateful but wary, because they suffered from mood changes, like bad dogs – it was like a coming-out party and God knows they were used to giving them. Still, it was a nice gesture, even if I had the idea we all thought I'd done a lot of porridge. In the meanwhile the quiet man at the end of the bar, who was dressed in a grey suit, a striped shirt and a blue silk tie, came up to us, smiling. He was tall and thin, and fairly insignificant, really. He had mouse brown hair and a shyish sort of manner and it was only when he got up close that I realized he had amazing eyes – large and green, with hazel flecks in them. They were fascinating – the moment you saw them you forgot his ordinary-looking face, and his sort of characterless nose – it was like being hypnotized. I really doubt if Steven Greene ever realized what a difference those eyes made. Mind you, he knew about the results of having them.

"Come on, Steve," said Arnie. "Have a glass and meet Molly. She's just come back to us after an absence." (You can see what I mean about all of us vaguely thinking I'd been doing time.)

"Not what you think," I said to him, to set the record straight.

"You look far too fresh for me to think that," he said, in his middle-class voice. So – what was he doing here as a boon companion of the Roses? Clap doctor, was what I thought.

"Meet Steven Greene," said Arnic to me. "Celebrated osteopath – ai, ai – to the famous, internationally celebrated artist, and fortune teller – get him to read your stars sometime – and the man who cured Arnie Rose of his dodgy shoulder. That was the one I got off Randolph Turpin in the Black Cat down in Sunningdales." This story of the fight between himself and the black boxer was one of Arnie's favourites – Steven told me later the bad shoulder was a touch of arthritis. And incidentally, added Arnie, "He lives upstairs."

"How do you do," said Steven Greene. Oh, God, there was a cool but amorous eye, and green as an apple as well – "I've taken over your old flat. You must visit me when you feel like it."

"Don't go," advised Norman. "He's like Rasputin. Goes round to say a few prayers with the Duchess and before you know it – Bob's your uncle. He's a danger to all women, aren't you, Steve?" And he nudged him.

Steven took it well and just said, "Take no notice of him. But if you feel like a drink or a cup of tea —"

"I'd be delighted," I said. I said it in a posh voice because in those days I used to talk the way I thought the person I was with wanted me to talk. In any case, I couldn't have worked at that club if I was effing and blinding and dropping my aitches all over the place. It was only later I thought, "Sod it. I'll talk the way I want to." So Arnie slops a lot more champagne in the glass I held and says, "Take no notice of Lady Muck. She's only one of the locals from the low-class area I come from."

"An area," Steven said, with a kind of bow to me, "from which all seemed destined to rise."

I couldn't help laughing at him. The truth was he was a devil with women, and he knew it and he knew I knew it. Not that I was interested, because what I'd told Simon was right — I hated the idea of love and sex, and all that. Johnnie Bridges had taught me my lesson. But by this time we had to open the club. The barman appeared and the Roses prepared to leave. But before he went Norman turned to me and said, "I want it clear I don't want to see Bridges in here ever — not if he's dying."

"I doubt if he'd come here if he was dying," said I. "He knows you don't like him."

"I want your promise," Norman said bluntly. "I know what you slags are like — no disrespect, Moll — but you can't trust a woman when there's a man in the case. They'll go back to any bloke, even if he beats them, even if he drinks away all the money — they'll do anything for him. The worse he is the more they love him. Honest to God," he said to Steven Greene. "They're not like us. Not like us at all."

"I'll give you my promise, though you don't need it," was what I said. Well, I thought it was true. And Arnie said, in a sentimental way, "He done you wrong, Molly, and that's a fact."

I put on a soupy expression, as if I appreciated the thought, but inside I had the creeps. It was Arnie's girl Sally who had died of septicaemia caused by an abortion she had after Arnie threw her out. He never went to see her once in hospital when she was dying. And why? Because the night he threw her out she was drunk and Arnie Rose, as he said, "couldn't stand to see a woman drunk." And the Roses were making a small fortune out of prostitution all the time. And here was Arnie making out I was the Virgin Mary — it was sinister. With all their horrible brutality they had to believe in "good" women.

And I was one of them, like some kind of pet. Woe betide you, Molly Flanders, if you ever destroy their illusions, I thought to myself. They'll have you for breakfast if you ruin their dream by stepping down off the top of the Christmas tree.

So I said, "Well, let's get going, Steven. – Do you fancy coming upstairs for a minute and pretending to be a crowd playing chemmy – encourage the paying customers?" He agreed but as we went upstairs I couldn't help wondering why the Roses wanted to have him about. Arnie's shoulder couldn't be the only reason.

We stood by the table in the long, empty room and he said, "Where do you live?" So I told him, and how I had to take a taxi back every night because the public transport was shut down at that time. And he offered me the spare room in the flat, to use during the week so I didn't have the bother and expense of going to and fro all the time. "I assure you it's a platonic offer I'm making you," he said. "And I'm not the sort of man who says that hoping it will be untrue in the end, or even the sort who thinks that's what he means but just isn't admitting he hopes for an affair."

I believed him. The Steven Greenes of this world know these things instinctively and, unlike many men, they don't lie to themselves or women. I just wondered why he made the offer.

"Just an impulse," he told me. But later I worked it out that he didn't want the girls, Wendy and Carol, trying to move in, or spending night after night there, sleeping till all hours and leaving the kitchen in a mess. He was fussy, he liked his privacy and he didn't want involved parties to know everything that was going on. He was a man with secrets. He liked things in neat compartments. He thought that someone with another home and a job with regular hours, even if they were funny hours, was the best way of filling the space without complications.

I said "yes", and that way got into quite a bit of trouble and found out a lot more about the world.

That evening Molly went to chat to Mrs Jones in the ladies room after the club shut, a habit of long standing. It was a relief to put her feet up and have a cup of tea. It was useful to find out what the women had been talking about during the evening and often a good way of finding out about potential bad debtors. In the ladies room, too, she was safe from demands from the rest of the staff and, above all, only there would she never find Arnie Rose suddenly at her elbow.

Mrs Jones said, tactfully, "I was looking round the flat after you left and I found your earrings. I tucked them away for you safely." And she handed Molly the earrings with the little emeralds set in them. Molly guessed that Johnnie had come back and cleared out her jewellery box before he went away.

She said, "Thanks, Mrs Jones," and instantly put them on.

"He cracked up after you left," Mrs Jones went on. "I was cleaning that morning and when I told him you'd gone with a suitcase he had to put his hand on the side of the door to steady himself. He looked ready to drop to the ground."

"He had his chance to get respectable," said Molly. "He couldn't take it when it came."

"Looks, brains, a bit of charm – he had the lot," said the woman. "All he lacked was character. There's thousands of them about these days. It must have been the war. They missed a father's hand."

"Plenty like that among the clients," remarked Molly.

"Oh, yes," she said, "and one in the flat upstairs."

"Here –" said Molly. "What is osteo-whatsisname?"

"Osteopathy," said Mrs Jones. "It's backs and bones and things – like they use for runners and athletes when they get injured. But there's another name for what *he* does."

"What is it?" asked Molly.

"I wouldn't care to say," Mrs Jones told her.

"Oh," said Molly. "And how did he get acquainted with the Roses?"

"He's been introducing them – people like Mr Arnold and Mr Norman like to meet people from other spheres of life," said Mrs Jones delicately. "And those people like to meet gentlemen like Mr Arnold and Mr Norman. I think that Mr Greene helped with the introductions."

It was true that Arnie and Norman Rose were becoming fashionable among the more daring intellectuals and with some of the upper classes. They enjoyed having gangsters at their parties and the Roses, especially Norman, took a pride in their connections with film directors and titled ladies.

"He helps a lot of people with a lot of things," said Mrs Jones and, bending forward, added in a low voice, "I wouldn't have too much to do with it if I were you, dear."

But Molly was tired of going back to her empty house by cab in the early hours of the morning. After the night at the club it felt bleak and lonely. It made her miss Johnnie even more and she could hardly bear it.

That night, when she went upstairs, she found Steven Greene, in a maroon silk dressing-gown, shirt and trousers, sitting on the sofa, which had been re-covered, she noticed, in cream. Beside him sat a girl. When Molly came in he was looking into her eyes and telling her, "That's bad. I'll sort it out in the morning with a couple of phone calls."

Then he looked up and said, "Hullo, Molly. Come in and have a drink. I hope you don't mind what I've done to the flat." It had indeed changed. The walls were cream, the carpet a gentle fawn, the uphol-stery and curtains pale. There were watercolours of flowers on the wall. Molly, a bit nettled by the changes, had to admit it, the room was now more restful.

"I suppose it was a bit common, really," she said. "The way I had it, I mean."

"Come and sit down, take your shoes off and meet Wendy," he said. "Wendy – this is Molly. I told you about her. Molly – Wendy Valentine."

Molly sank into a chair, kicked off her shoes and studied the girl. She was pretty, with long, dark, hair and slightly protuberant front teeth, which made her look strangely defenceless. She wore a black sweater, a tight, black skirt and slightly scuffed black pumps. One of her stockings was laddered.

Greene gave her a drink and settled back on the sofa.

"Well, girls," he said. "This is cosy." He smiled at Molly and she was taken, again, by the warmth of the green eyes. He loves women, she thought placidly. He loves them in droves, the more the merrier. He's like a boy with a bag of juicy pears. But the truth was that she did not feel very cosy. The calm atmosphere masked a tension she did not recognize. She looked at the girl, who seemed to her like a poor cold kitten with all its bones showing, mewing against a closed front door hoping that someone would let it in. Her white mac lay flung over the back of a chair. The girl, Wendy Valentine, shut her eyes and seemed to go into a daze.

"Look – go off home now and see if you get a phone call," Greene said. "And I'll speak to the man we were talking about in the morning. When I've done that I'll phone you and then you can tell me all the details."

"All right, Steven," said the girl, standing up. "But you won't forget?"

"Of course not – would I let you down?" he told her. He followed her to the door and Molly thought she heard the sound of paper money changing hands. "Thanks," came the girl's voice. "You won't forget to phone?" He muttered something and closed the door.

Molly's eyes also were shutting. When he came back she opened them and said, "It's all right. I'm going to bed. Long night, you see."

"I do see," he said. "Don't worry about me – I'm a nightbird. I'm an early bird, too. I don't sleep well. I like to have someone to talk to. Another drink?"

She said she would for it was easy to sink into the undemanding comfort of the room.

"Down? Depressed? Blue?" suggested Greene. "Love – it usually is. What's a pretty girl like you doing without a host of suitors, consorts and victims? It's against nature."

"The same old story," Molly told him.

He asked her questions and Molly told him everything. She ended by saying, "I thought the club would be a fresh start but I think he saw it as an episode – just another jampot, like a bank job, to stick his fingers in and pull out as many strawberries as he liked. He's just dishonest I suppose."

"You're a capitalist at heart," said Greene. "And he's a criminal – easy come, easy go – instant gratification."

"My brother says I'm a latent bourgeois," Molly said. "He doesn't like it."

"Communist, is he?" said Greene, interested.

"His fiancée's the proper Communist," Molly explained. 'But Jack's very left wing. He's trying to go to college in Oxford. He was working down the docks – my mum's brother got him in – and now he's getting married to this girl Pat who's got five big docker brothers, all fiery Reds. So during Christmas we went over for a game of cards and you couldn't hear the bidding for the dictatorship of the proletariat. What's an educated man like you doing in a place like this anyway?" she demanded. "What are you doing now?" He was scribbling on a pad.

"I'm drawing you," he said. "I like the shadows under your big, tired eyes."

"You're a sod," said Molly. "But what are you doing here?"

"Ever heard of Aleister Crowley – the Abbey of Thelema – Do What

Thou Wilt Shall Be The Whole of The Law?"

Molly had not, so he told her. She was unimpressed. "Doesn't sound very close to what I know," she told him.

But to her none of this seemed a very good explanation for Greene's presence at South Molton Street. He showed her the sketch. She exclaimed, "That's very good. Aren't you clever."

"I'll get it framed," he told her. She left him in the big, pale room, still drawing, and went to bed. She slept restlessly and, when she got up, was so drowsy that it took her a few moments to take in the fact that Wendy Valentine's white mac was back on the sofa. When she passed the open bedroom door she saw three heads on the pillows of the big bed she had shared with Johnnie. She stared in. There was Greene. There was another head she could not see and, facing her, a pale-faced, brown-haired girl, Wendy. Molly fled and on the stairs outside, shrugging into her dressing-gown, said to herself, "Oh, blimey – that's a bit thick."

Mrs Jones came round the bend in the stairs, on her hands and knees with a stiff brush. She looked up at Molly, rushing downstairs with her dressing-gown open. "You on fire?" she asked.

"Out of milk," Molly lied. "I'm going to make a cup of tea in the office."

Simon Tate was in there, at the desk, paying bills. He said, "Honestly, Molly, we're going to have to check all these. While the cats have been away –" Then, looking up, he spotted the dressing-gown and said, "Look here – we can't have you roaming about like that. Go back and put some clothes on."

"Not 'til I've had my breakfast," said Molly firmly, going into the kitchenette and putting on the kettle. She put some bread under the grill.

"What's up?" called Simon.

"I'll tell you when I've had my breakfast," she said. Then she put her head round the door and said, "Do you know, he's up there in bed with two women. *Two*," she repeated.

Simon seemed unsurprised. "It's been known to happen," he remarked.

"I know that," she said. "I wasn't born yesterday. It's just I don't expect it when I know people. I mean – he's so nice, Steven Greene. He's a nice, kind man."

"I don't suppose he's nasty to them," Simon said. "I don't suppose they'd do it if he were. What are you going to do – move?"

"I don't know," she said. "I'll have to see how it all works out. I mean – I've got a free room, and it's convenient and if you look at it like a sensible person – well, it doesn't matter to me if he gets into bed with a gorilla and a dwarf."

"Just as long as you aren't with them," Simon told her.

But for a month or so after that there were no more events of the same kind. When Molly came upstairs in the evenings Steven Greene was often out. When he was not he was alone, or with Wendy or another girl, Carol. She would hear them talking long after she had gone to bed. The phone often rang and he would have short conversations with the caller. There were parties Greene went to, people he met, services he agreed to render, but it all seemed casual and although she always had the sense that there was movement afoot she never found out exactly what was going on. His finances were erratic – sometimes there would be a brace of plover on the draining board of the kitchen when she went in, sometimes a can of beans stood half open on the top of the fridge. Bills would lie unopened on a table for months – then suddenly disappear. Mary was not particularly interested. She enjoyed chatting to Greene, early in the morning, when the club emptied. She dimly recognized that he was for her rather like her brother Jack. He saw things in a broader context than she was used to. He seemed to come to conclusions she had not been able to reach. He gave her advice. He said of Johnnie, "You'd have him back like a shot if he turned up here. And you will." He also said, "I smelt bad debts when I came up the stairs tonight. You're over the limit. The clients are in too deep. I can feel the desperation."

Molly thought about the dim rooms, where men and women stood and sat at the tables. Often it was a night out, like going to a dance or the cinema. But in a gaming club at least half the clients are serious gamblers, men with a kind of control in their movements as they gamble, like hunters stalking prey. And women with faces bearing little expression. It was late at night, or early the next morning, when the serious gamblers operated, quietly, at the tables where high stakes were the rule, where you could win or lose a few thousand pounds in a minute or two. Next night she studied the faces at her own table – John Farley, the only son of a steel manufacturer in the Midlands, Theo General, middle-aged son of a big landowner in Wiltshire, playing at banking and waiting for his father to die, Sally Weiss, bad daughter of a Swiss millionaire with her lover, Lord Coveney. They were too grim, some of them, she realized. Either they were playing too high or the whole atmosphere of the club was, as Greene had told her, getting desperate.

She woke in the morning thinking, despairingly, of Johnnie. "Get yourself another bloke, Molly Waterhouse," she told herself. But the bad, empty feeling persisted as she went downstairs. She made up the wage packets quickly and went to the safe to take out the money which ought to go to the bank as fast as possible. But on impulse she left the cash and cheques in the safe and took out only the cashbook and the markers, left by gamblers as IOUs for money they did not have at the time. There were £450,000 in outstanding debts. Most of the markers had been re-signed for larger and larger sums over the previous six weeks. She realized how often she had called Simon over to her table and asked him to sign markers for one of the clients, without considering whether she should ask him, instead, to caution the would-be creditor. If the other croupiers were doing the same a bad situation could have developed. Examining the receipts book she saw that she was due, today, to take only £10,000 in cheques and cash to the bank. April was plainly a bad time of year since so many people were away. Even so the debts still amounted to six weeks' takings. You had to give credit at a gambling club but this was too much. When Simon came in, he looked at the pile of markers in front of her, then at her face and said, "I was going to check that today. How bad is it?" She told him.

He sat down and put his head in his hands. "Christ – I've been a bloody fool. What are the Roses going to say to this?"

"What's been going on?" Molly asked.

"My fucking life, that's what's been going on," he told her bitterly. "It's simple – I've been getting done over by a tart ever since I got back from South Africa. Pretty boy – nowhere to go. I took him in. My friend, my old lover really, Geoffrey, moved out when he saw what was going to happen. I fell in love – he pretended he loved me – I go into hock for him, buying silk dressing-gowns and gold watches – all, mind you, to please him and see him smile. Then, gradually, I begin to think he doesn't love me. The pain begins. This morning I woke up with the bone-setters. You know, every bone in your body is broken and today's the day the doctor comes to wrench them all back into place? He hadn't come home, you see. He came in about ten this morning. I was awake, of course, had been since dawn. He said he'd been staying at his brother's but I'd been with Doctor Lovecure since six – I had four hours of agony behind me. So I said, 'I don't believe you,' and he said boo-hoo, how can you doubt me, etc, etc. On the other hand he didn't suggest I telephone his brother. On the contrary, when I said I wanted to he said, again, boo-hoo how can you doubt me, the suggestion is hurtful, horrible and insulting —"

The telephone rang and Molly answered it. She handed it to Simon cautiously, afraid of the effect of the call on his stretched nerves. He said, "I don't think there's much point, Bassie. I think I'd be happier if you just got out. Perhaps I am but I'm very busy and I can't go on like this. I may be, later, but I doubt it." Then he said, very loudly, "Well my dear, I suggest you go to your brother's," and banged the phone down. He turned to Molly with a tired smile and said, "Of course, after I left he decided if I really doubted him I should telephone his brother, even though it might be rather humiliating for him. I suppose he checked and made sure that his brother would say he'd been there. So I've had to throw him out," he said tightly. "Pity, isn't it?"

"Yes," said Molly. "Why don't you phone Geoffrey?"

Simon was not listening. "Serves me right, I suppose," he said, "for taking up with the house tart. He was at the next school down the line from us — he was famous for it. Used to stand on the sidelines fluttering his eyelashes while we played matches with them. He was known as La Grande Horizontale."

"What's that?" asked Molly.

"Famous tart," said Simon.

"Why don't you ring Geoffrey?" asked Molly again.

"He can't help it, I suppose. He just gets what he can and leaves when it looks as if supplies are running out."

"Simon — Geoffrey will help. Please ring him," Molly pleaded.

"He's rubbish, I suppose. I used to come in at four and find him in his dressing-gown listening to jazz and smoking reefers. Nasty habit, that. But so pretty —"

"Geoffrey," said Molly over the phone. "Simon's had a bust-up with some nasty bit of work. Can you forgive him, can you come and see him and, above all, Geoffrey, can you put him back in his right mind because the business is in a mess?" The voice at the other end spoke and she said, "Yes. I am in charge. I've got to be until Simon gets over all this. Please come, Geoffrey —"

She looked at Simon and said, "Come on, Simon, please. Geoffrey's taking you out to lunch at one. We must do something quickly —"

"It's all my fault," he said.

"It's everybody's fault," said Molly. She went out and yelled over the banisters, "Mrs Jones – can you send someone over to the hotel for hot coffee and chicken sandwiches." A voice shouted back. "Well," yelled Molly, "go yourself, then. Do it, for Christ's sake, or we're all out of a job."

"So refreshingly common," Simon murmured to himself as she came back into the room.

"Just as bloody well," Molly told him. "And don't drag class into it. Fact is, you've had a shock and I'm sorry. But we're up the creek here. If it goes on –" The phone rang again. She answered it.

"Arnie," she cried, sounding delighted. "Well – nice to hear yours, too. Yes – yes – oh, of course you have. Well, look here – do you think we could have an extra couple of days, just to make sure the books are in apple pie order – you know, we're so busy – Good. All right then, look forward to seeing you –" She put the phone down and said to Simon, "That's Arnie. He's coming in with the accountant in a week's time for a routine check. He says routine – he can probably smell trouble."

Mrs Jones came in with the tray of coffee and sandwiches. She looked at the pile of markers on the table and put the tray down. She was walking out, full of silent disapproval, when Molly called her back. "Mrs Jones," she said, "you've been trying to warn me, haven't you? So why don't you sit down and have a cup of coffee and tell me whose markers are good and whose are dodgy?"

Mrs Jones did. She ruffled through the markers rapidly delivering comments Molly took down. "No problem there – mother's an American heiress, Chicago meat packers, only son. No problem there – eldest daughter of a bishop, can't afford a scandal. You'll never see that £20,000 again – he just left for Argentina, owing everybody, Whoops-a-daisy. Whatever were you thinking of – no other house would take this one's marker for ninepence." When she finished Simon stood up silently and handed her five pounds, which she tucked in her apron pocket before she left, remarking, "Well – half of them'll cough up, at any rate."

Later, Simon said, "I'd never have thought of that one. Asking the attendant in the ladies lav."

"What do we do next?" said Molly.

"First the polite note, then the phone calls, then the phone calls designed to cause embarrassment, to workplaces, parents' houses, and so forth. We hint a bit about spreading the word about but the really hardened cases don't usually care – the trouble with gambling debts is that they're slightly distinguished. Mark of a gentleman to owe bookmaker, tailor and wine merchant, you see. As a last resort we can threaten to tell interested parties, Mr Arnold and Norman Rose. I've never had to do that yet – it suggests a lack of class I'm not prepared to risk. We'd probably get the money and lose the clients.''

"It all sounds a bit long-winded to me," Molly said. "All that'll take a month or more."

"More like three," Simon told her.

"We'll have to speed it up a bit," Molly told him. "We've got to get half those markers redeemed before Arnie Rose turns up. And that's only a week. We'd better cut out the polite letter for a start."

Simon looked doubtful. "All right," he said. "But if I move too fast this place is going to look like a bucket shop. You can't hurry the upper classes where money's concerned."

"I'll cut upstairs and re-check this list with Steven," Mary said. "He knows a lot of gossip – we can see where levers can be tugged, who's engaged and wouldn't like the rich in-laws to find out before the ceremony, where people are at the moment. You're due for lunch with Geoffrey now at the brasserie. If you could get back at three you could start phoning then. I'll get a sort of dossier together and give it to you before you start. I'd do it myself but it's no good – I'm too common. I don't know the cliches to show I mean business but I'm a lady, really. Anyway, they'd take no notice of a woman."

Simon, startled, agreed. Molly rushed out saying, "I've got to catch Steven before he starts out to fix the old dowagers' backs, or whatever he does." She added over her shoulder, "No boozing and not too much crying and sobbing over that horrible Bassie."

Upstairs, Steven Greene came out of the bathroom wrapped in a large towel. "Spare me half an hour?" Molly asked.

"For anything you like."

"Keep your towel on," she said. "It's information I want."

While they were talking over the names on the markers an agitated ring on the doorbell brought in a tall and beautiful blonde girl in a black suit, with a white fur stole round her shoulders. She kissed Steven, looked at Molly, decided she was harmless and demanded, "Did you get it?"

"In here," he said, pointing into the bedroom. She came out, seconds later, looking less worried. After she left he said, "Poor girl – couldn't pay the rent. I had to lend it to her."

"Very sad," Molly said dryly, not believing him. Before they had done with all the names on the list the phone had rung twice. Each time he answered the speaker in his usual brief and cryptic way. "If he tells you that, he's not being exactly truthful, and you should ask him again," he said. And, "There are limits to my powers, you know, and also to my funds." After the calls he would come back to Molly's side, quite unruffled and say, "Tonia Thompson – don't bother to try. She's in the South of France with Onassis. Dirk Frogett? Never heard of him. Someone's having you on. Ah – Joe Templeton – fifteen thousand. I'm amazed anyone signed that. Hint you'll tell his mum – he's terribly Oedipal. Gordon? You'll have to ring Inverkyle. Sir A – what? – Milligatawny – oh, Mulvaney – no trouble there, he's a rich racehorse owner. Try this one, Pat Jamieson, and say next time you'll ring him at the bank. He won't like that and he can easily afford to pay." When they had finished he leaned back and said, "Don't forget – I had no hand in this. It wouldn't suit me to become known as a man who couldn't keep his mouth shut."

"Thanks, Steven," said Molly, rushing out. "I owe you a favour."

"You do, dear, but try not to sound too much like the Rose brothers," he told her.

In the afternoon the phone calls were made. The evening was quiet. The word was out and the customers were discouraged.

"I hope this isn't the end of the business," remarked Molly, coming into the flat and kicking off her shoes. "After all the trouble we've all gone to."

"Probably temporary," Steven Greene told her. He was lying on the sofa reading a book. "Pour us a drink and have a rest. In a minute I'll run you a nice, hot bath."

He did. When Molly went into the bathroom she found he had poured scent into the water.

"You're so kind," she said, when she had bathed and got into her dressing-gown.

He put his book down. "I shouldn't be. It only corrupts me, probably. What do I want, in fact? To be liked?"

"You help people and they have to help you," Molly observed. "That's your system."

"Sharp girl," he said. "You should read more – you're too intelligent to be so ill-informed."

"Yes," she said. "I should get a book. It'd take my mind off all these problems. Can you recommend one?"

"Have a look over there," he told her. "That item against the wall is what is commonly called a bookshelf. On it you will find books. Look at them and see what you can find to read."

"Sarcastic," murmured Molly and went to the shelf. She looked at the books, then said, suddenly, "I'm haunted by the thought of Johnnie Bridges."

"Let him haunt you, then," Greene said, his eyes still on his book. "It'll end. Unless you're neurotic – which you aren't. In the meanwhile, try improving your mind."

"I'm not the sort," muttered Molly. "I'm going to get a television and put it in my room."

"Molly Flanders," he said. "I'm telling you something for your own good. Carry on as you are, and you'll in the end be a pain in the neck to yourself and everybody else. Endless confusion, rows, scenes and arguments – spinning around doing this, that and the other – no contemplation, no inner life, no nothing. You know what becomes of women if all that goes on too long? They get thoroughly tiresome, and disappointed."

Molly realized he might be telling her a truth. She also spotted the male desire for peace and quiet when faced with female urgencies. She had seen Sid and Ivy driving each other mad like that often enough.

"Where is he anyway?" she said angrily. "Shacked up with some floosie, I daresay."

"You can find out, I expect," Greene said coolly. "I'm advising you, before you take him back, as you undoubtedly will, do try and find out something about yourself first. What do you want?"

"I don't know – Johnnie," Mary answered.

"Just 'Johnnie' isn't a good enough reply. 'Johnnie' won't suffice for a lifetime, nor will any number of Johnnies. As I say, either you find some kind of course for yourself, or others, usually men, will come along and suggest one for you. You'll follow that course until it doesn't work any more – then again, and then again, getting tireder and tireder. It's a case of think now or find out the hard way."

"Oh – very clever," said Molly. "And what about you, then? What's your course you're following? Tell me that?"

"I'm like you, dear Molly," he said. "I go where the wind bloweth, like a girl, but I suspect you're firmer-minded than I am. Now – would you like to come to bed with me?"

"Don't be disgusting," Molly said, looking at the title of a book and putting it back on the shelf.

"Well, I've done my best. I've offered the alternatives of a well-stocked mind or a satisfied body and you've rejected both –" he said and, finding his place in his book, began to read again, looking up only to remark, "I'm on your side, you know. I don't recommend reading to all the pretty girls I'm acquainted with – I think your course may be a complicated one, Molly, and you're going to have to steer it yourself. I'm trying to help you save some time and agony."

"You said you'd do my horoscope," Molly grumbled.

"Your horoscope's a dog's breakfast," he told her. "Someone must have invented your birth certificate from their imagination. It made no sense, so I gave up."

"That's nice," said Molly. "So much for black magic."

He went on reading. The doorbell rang. A young man Molly recognized as a client of the club stood there, holding an envelope. "So sorry to disturb you," he said. "I rushed round as soon as I could – Simon Tate said you were calling in a few markers. A woman let me in but I couldn't find anybody so she said I should come up here –"

Molly was amazed and grateful. She had begun to imagine that none of the defaulters would pay up without many phone calls and hints of blackmail. "Thanks," she said, taking the envelope. "You're very prompt. Would you like to come in for a drink?"

He hesitated, "I'm with a friend," he said.

"Bring them in," she said expansively.

"This is very nice," said the young man, whose name, she recalled, was John Christian. He called down, "Charlie – I've been invited in for a drink. Do you want to come?"

"I always want to come," said a voice and Charlie Markham came round the bend in the stairs and up the steps two at a time.

Mary was horrified. Charlie Markham seldom came to the club now. When he did he tended to come up too close to her, to make dubious remarks and offend her. Because she worked there she had to endure him. Sometimes Simon Tate protected her. Sometimes she clenched her teeth and put up with it. Once, when he came too close and put his hand on her breast, she had hacked him in the shins and hissed, "Leave me alone, Charlie."

He had winced and then recovered, saying, "Sorry, Moll. Just a joke – I'll be careful in future, especially as you're a special friend of Arnold Rose's." He was always well informed. Now, it seemed too late to back out so she had to invite them in.

"Thought I might bump into you, Moll," he said, sitting on the sofa with his glass. He was already rather drunk, she noticed. "Anyway, poor old John got windy about coming here on his own. Thought he might be greeted by one of the Rose brothers' friends, I imagine."

"Steady on, Charlie," said the other. "I didn't think anything of the kind."

"Well, I did," said Charlie. "Their interest in the club isn't exactly a well kept secret. And I thought – well, help a friend to face it out and, who knows, perhaps the charming Molly will be there."

"Any news from Allaun Towers?" demanded Molly, attempting to change the direction of his thoughts. But he just sat lolling in his chair, grinning at her.

"Remember our *rencontre* in the bushes, eh, Moll?" he said. "You and me and cousin Tom? A boy's dream came true."

"I hope there's been more in your life since taking my knickers down in the bushes when I was four," said Molly rudely. She surveyed him. "Though, now I look at you, maybe there hasn't."

John Christian snorted, then said to Charlie, "Come on, Charlie. We'd better be going."

"No need to rush, old man," said Charlie. "What could be nicer than this snug spot. An old friend – and her friend –" he added, looking askance at Steven Greene. "I ask you, what could be more pleasant. I'm at a loose end, Moll," he told her confidingly. "I left the army after a disagreement – just avoided being sent to Cyprus to be shot by some unsavoury gentleman of Mediterranean appearance. Now, here under a cowslip's bell I lie, wondering what to do with the remainder of my life. Any suggestions?"

"Long walk off a short pier," Molly suggested agreeably.

"Cockney wit – so delightful," he said to Greene. "No wonder you love having our Molly in your flat. No," he said to Molly, "actually I think I'll be forced to enter the family business. I forget what it's all about but it's something to do with money so it can't be too bad." He turned to Greene and said, "I hear you're the Queen of the Gypsies? Any chance of getting my fortune told while I'm here? No – on second thoughts I'd rather you didn't."

Greene said coolly, "I think I know your fate already."

"What do you mean by that, oh Queen of the Gypsies and Prince of Ponces?" Charlie said, getting to his feet.

Steven Greene also stood up and said, "I don't need to be clairvoyant to tell you that in the long term you'll go on bullying women and people weaker than yourself as much as you can – or that, in the short term, you'll be standing in South Molton Street in two minutes' time, unless you happen to be on your back on the pavement."

John Christian seized Charlie by the shoulders as he tried to pull towards Greene. He said, "I'm not letting him get away with that –"

"I don't want a row," Greene said.

"Come along, Charlie," said John, getting annoyed. Charlie got free of him and took a step towards Greene. "Don't be bloody stupid," said his friend.

Charlie turned round and started for the door. "Perfectly right, John," he said. "You're so right. Makes no sense at all standing and arguing with a pimp. That's rule 1, after all, don't argue with tradesmen, no matter what they deal in."

Molly slammed the door behind them and sat down angrily in a chair. "Horrible Charlie. Horrible Charlie," she said.

Greene laughed. "Was it true about the bushes?" he asked.

"Oh – you're horrible yourself," she said. "I suppose all men are horrible. Charlie gives me the creeps. He really does. He makes me go all gooseflesh."

Greene, lying back on the sofa, said, "Do you have to sound so common? I love you dearly but it's a great strain on me, having to listen to you. I sometimes think you do it deliberately." He stood up and put on a record. Mary shouted furiously against a Chopin sonata, "Do you have to sound so queer? If you think I sound common I think you sound like a cream puff half the time, if you want to know. I expect you are. And what do you expect me to sound like or behave like? I'm not twenty and I'm the widow of a convicted murderer and I live in Meakin Street and I work at a club owned by gangsters. This isn't Buckingham Palace is it? I'm not the Queen? I'm like I am because of what I am, just like she is. And come to that, Steven Greene, who gave you the right to criticize me? I might come from a rough and ready home but my parents are honest and so am I. Can you say the same?" She stared at him, then said, "All right if I go to bed now, your high-and-mightyship?"

"Don't go, Moll," he said, "I'm sorry. Stay a little while – after all, I nearly got in a fight with that hooligan on your behalf. He'd have murdered me, I can tell you that."

"Bugger off, smarmychops," said Molly, although she had to admit he was telling the truth. Nevertheless, "Common!" she thought, as she undressed and flung herself into bed in a rage. "Common!" What a cheek! What a sauce! Then a wave of depression and loneliness came over her. She was tired and jaded, bored and angry. She needed more but did not know what she wanted. She thought of Johnnie with longing, in spite of what he had done. She thought of Charlie Markham and shuddered. She had not had a holiday or an outing since Johnnie left. Now Steven Greene told her she was common. She was weeping with exhaustion and hopelessness when Steven Greene came into the room in his pyjamas, got into bed and put his arms round her. "You're a valuable girl, Molly," he told her.

A lot of people assume that when you go to the bad, as it used to be called – nowadays I suppose they call it indulging in promiscuity – you do it out of lust and high spirits, in a sort of devil-may-care, pleasure-loving spirit. But most of the time it comes from despair, not knowing what to do with yourself, casting around for a solution, a future or a bit of reassurance. So I've never resented Greene for putting me within an inch of the streets, the Maltese ponce and the clap doctor. It was what I wanted, I suppose, at the time. Anyway, Steven wasn't what Charlie thought he was, not in any direct way. That's to say, he never made a penny at the game. Half the time he was out of pocket. He just brought people together – ignorant millionaires who wanted to buy posh paintings and the dealers who had them in the shops – young, fast aristocrats who wanted to meet a real-life gangster, and gangsters, like the Roses, who enjoyed the connection. The same kind wanted cannabis – Steven knew the black dealers. And half his deals were in information. He got it and he traded it to other people for more information. I'm not saying he didn't get ten percents from time to time, or a crate of champagne delivered at the door. He had to get those things, or how could he have lived? But mostly it was hand-to-mouth stuff and once I found out what was going on I could see the financial set-up was more like Meakin Street than anywhere else – ten bob borrowed till payday and "Excuse me, Mrs Waterhouse, mum says could you kindly lend us a cup of sugar." Wendy Valentine never had the rent, which was only five pounds a week and Carol always had ladders in her stockings so he was always pushing a note into her hand and telling her to go out and get new ones. The position was that among the people Steven brought together were us girls, and the people who wanted us girls – his posh friends and flowers of the gutters, like us. I swear I heard him on the phone using those very words – well, half these deals are in romance, aren't they? It's not what you're getting – it's what it means to you. Some crazy aristo must've fallen in love with the kitchen maid at the age of ten – so yours truly becomes a flower of the gutter. In fact I was the only one of the three of us who was. Wendy and Carol were both the kind of girls who'd spent from ten to fifteen years old dreaming about film stars on some estate in Dagenham or Gravesend. Then the big world presents itself in the shape of some teddy boy who knocks them up outside the local Roxy dance hall – then there's the baby which has to be adopted because the parents can't stand the shame, then they drift to the big city and become amateur prostitutes, only with glamour. The punters are all in the Cabinet, or diplomats, or prime ministers' grandsons. I think that was what saved me from going too far in the game – I knew what was what and if I'd ever had any girlish dreams they'd been knocked out of me. Apart from anything else I was still getting back to Meakin Street to see Josephine over the weekends, though not as often as I should have done. But with what I knew, and a lot of Ivy's horrible sense of reality behind me, I couldn't go for the dream quite the way the other two did. I never even thought I'd get a lot of money out of it because I think both of them, Wendy and Carol, had the idea that in the end Prince Charming was going to come in with the diamonds and the big house with swimming pool in stockbroker Surrey. And I didn't have the real nightmare either – they both thought that if this didn't keep up they'd have to go to work in the only places their neighbourhoods had to offer a girl – somewhere like a boot factory or a bread factory – somewhere like that. The spectre of the white overall and the time-clock haunted them, the way it didn't me. But I think Steven was in on the dream too, half the time. His was a bit different, but it was all glamour – Steven Greene, friend and companion of the great and the man they could trust to get what they needed when they needed it. Also, god of love, though pretty tatty love, you must admit. A lot of the time he couldn't see one side of the deal was naughty girls and the other side was bent sods. They all were, one way or another, why would they have been looking for girls like us? So Steven helped them out, like he treated their old mums' backs and drew their beagles and found another doctor for Aunt Winifred, who'd come by a habit in Berlin in the '30s and got twitchy when the old quack died – yes, he helped but he wasn't their friend. He was a convenience. Poor bugger. They dropped him like a hot potato when he got into trouble – I'll bet the phones ran hot that day. I'll bet the smoke from stuff being burned in the fireplaces would have made a full grown horse faint dead away. I was just a pawn in the game – a silly, depressed girl working in a hothouse atmosphere who'd had two men in her life so far. Jim Flanders, topped for murder. Johnnie Bridges, criminal. And in spite of all that – the hard work, the dodgy past – I suppose I still wanted some fun whatever sort it was. And it was fun, too, going to these parties and country house weekends in the summer, never knowing who you were going to meet or what was going to happen. I saw the world and how it worked – at the time it worked because everybody was a cousin of everybody else. And funnily enough, while I was living with Steven in that flat, he did broaden my mind. He wasn't stupid, whatever else he was. He made me read books. He talked to me. The world got a lot bigger. That's why I'll never hear a bad word said about Steven Greene. And also, as I've said, I was a bit mad. I couldn't have gone on just croupiering and helping Simon to run Frames, and then, if I had any time over, sitting up late chatting with Steven. I was too young and energetic – I wanted to get on the merry-go-round and I did, and stayed on it laughing till the music stopped.

It began on my own initiative when I took on a date with Charlie Markham and I won't say Steven encouraged me. When I set out in my high heels and spotted nylons and the little black dress with the cleavage he told me, "I hope you know what you're doing." But I was on course for ruining myself. I wouldn't be surprised if there wasn't some masochism lurking somewhere – that's what the likes of Johnnie Bridges do to you. You lose all proper sense of yourself. You'll go for anything that might make you feel real for a minute. All I said was, "What do you mean?" And he said, "I don't know but I should be careful." The word careful meant nothing to me in those days – so I went out to dinner with Charlie and then back to his flat, which was all cut-glass and crossed swords over the mantelpiece until you got to the bedroom, which was meant to be seductive but was really dark and gloomy, with dark red walls and black paint and mirrors on the ceiling and a huge fourposter with dark posts and red velvet hangings – it was more like a torture chamber, really, like the spare room at Death Abbey, the one with the flickering candles and the ghost – the mad monk, which was Charlie, who was what they sometimes call inventive. How I got through that night with my nerves, let alone my skin, in one piece I'll never know. I seem to remember falling back on my cheerful cockney sparrer act, giggling when I could and giving uninhibited working-class-style screams when I couldn't help it, especially when he got the cane out. I should have left but I thought, well, I came up here in the first place and, anyway, I thought at any moment he'd stop. Course, the truth was he couldn't get it up without feeling he was hurting and scaring me and the more I fought back, trying to make the best of it, the longer it was all going to take. So I spent the night running round the room. Finally I'm lying there wearing a lot of costume jewellery and a mask, letting him beat me on the bum with a pillow on it (the pillow was my idea) and screaming and begging him to stop only half-acting and I think after that he actually managed it. I was so pulled and pushed about by then I couldn't remember what happened, though I remember feeling nostalgic about Johnnie and thinking about him just lying there with me and making love like a normal, loving person. I got away about six and straight into a taxi. Steven was up when I got in – he'd obviously been out all night himself. He was a bit drunk – he roared when he saw my face and then laughed his head off when I told him what had happened. He managed to make me a cup of coffee while he fell about the kitchen. What he was laughing at was my outrage, as well as what happened. "He's been thinking about you ever since he first frightened you in the shrubbery," he said. "He muttered something like that," I said. I was amazed. "A lot of people are like that," he told me. "Somewhere along the line their bodies and their imaginations get into a fatal knot." I moaned. Believe it or not during the morning round comes a great big bunch of roses, signed "Love, Charlie" and after that a phone call. Charlie, asking me out again. I couldn't believe it. After a night of love like that, more like interrogation by the Gestapo, I couldn't think of anything more horrible. I laughed and said no. After that his voice went a bit funny. I'd made an enemy and the day came when I regretted it. Not that it made much difference in the long run.

After that night I think Steven realized he was on to a good thing as far as I was concerned. So the next night he invited me out to supper with this famous actor, Sir Christopher Wylie, from the Old Vic, a very handsome, vain, middle-aged man. And at least he didn't want me to pretend to be tortured or any kind of horrible fantasy. Being in the trade he probably couldn't stand bad performances. His problem was he just didn't want a normal relationship. He wanted someone to fuck without strings when he felt like it and I didn't mind that. The next was Lord Clover, who had relations in the Cabinet, the Army, the Navy, and the Foreign Office and had this big country house, Lowton, in Sussex. He was something in the Cabinet himself – not a minister but something or other. His wife lived abroad and I commuted between Lowton and Grosvenor Square, where his other house was. He wanted a passive, always naked, woman. I never had to speak or do anything but drift from the bath to the bed. He talked to me incessantly, and if I'd been a spy I could have got pay from the Russians. He actually told me about discussions about defence in the Cabinet and even I could see that was wrong. But if I said a dicky bird to him – he'd hit me. Straight up – I once asked for a cup of coffee and he belted me one round the face. I used to lie there, wishing he kept a diary.

When the scandal started I got a cheque for £2000 from a company, and a phone call after it was delivered telling me to keep my trap shut. Which I did, having no desire to cause any trouble, although I almost think I ought to have done, after what happened to Steven. But I was ill, anyway, at the time.

So it went on – I'm in taxis, limousines, first-class carriages. I'm eating in all the best places and both the blokes are buying me dresses and shoes and I don't know what. I wasn't happy but I wasn't unhappy either. Ivy was unhappy, though. Because of course I never, or hardly ever, saw Josephine and it was hard on Ivy to have her all the time. She used to cry when I left and Ivy said she'd ask every day, five or six times a day, if I was coming. And, of course, I hardly ever did and when I arrived it was Fanny's Return, smelling of scent, all fur coat and no knickers and a fair performance at motherhood. I still feel rotten when I think about it. My whole life was a performance anyway – you don't get any gold bracelets for being your natural self in that game.

Steven kept me going. He would have made a fortune as a ponce if he'd put his mind to it. Flatter and charm, a little threat here and there and I think the little white tablets he used to slip me when I got a bit down helped too. That, and providing a place where you could let your hair down and chat – you get like a tired actor and need the relaxation. And the taking care – he was good at making you a cup of tea, he'd massage your feet, he'd even remember Sid's birthday. It's the taking care you need, after a hard day on your back, making sure the client's satisfied, relaxed and happy when you go. Oh – he was a genius, Steven. When you're blasted out with surrendering everything to keep someone happy – like a slave, really – you'd go to the ends of the earth for a man who asks you how your leg is, or what games you liked to play when you were a kid. Of course, these men weren't that different from half the men in the world, anyway, taking it for granted you were there to serve them. Sometimes I'd go to bed with him, Steven, but not often. In a way I felt as if my sex had somehow gone stale, like an old bun with mildew on it. I used to wonder why Clover and Wylie never noticed there was anything wrong with me. Probably there was something worse wrong with them, that was why they couldn't tell. So I couldn't face going to bed with Steven, or anybody, most of the time. He was very sweet and consoling when I did but it wasn't enough.

Meanwhile the phone calls went on and, honestly, the money situation in that flat was a shambles. What with my wages at the club and the presents I should have been rich but it all dribbled away in bills and buying three pairs of shoes at a time and giving two to my sister because they didn't fit. Shirley was a comfort to me at that time. She was very clever, very kind, especially to Josephine, and if there was one thing she loved it was the wages of sin. She'd go to the pictures with her mates in twenty guinea shoes, smelling of Arpège and burn a hole in a Hartnell blouse with a Woodbine. She'd sing under her breath, if Ivy bawled me out for a neglectful mother and no better than I ought to be:

"See the little country cottage
Where her aged parents live
Drinking the champagne she sends them
But they never can forgive."

It got on Ivy's nerves shockingly but for some reason at that time Shirley was a real friend to me and it wasn't because she thought my life was wonderful either. She could read in Latin. She was heading towards the university. This drove Ivy mad too. I was a trollop and Shirley was practically an intellectual and Ivy couldn't work out which was worse.

Anyway, like all things, good and bad, it came to an end. It was human nature that brought me down. Human nature and bad organization. I was walking into the Dorchester one day, where I was due to meet Clover and a couple of big-wigs for lunch (that was what was happening, on top of everything else – I was getting into a famous little socialite, pretty and enchantingly common, witty and sharp as a tack and, quite honestly, fairly handy as an after-the-event commentator on the scene as it presented itself – I would say whose face had fallen when a certain name was mentioned or who hadn't been too pleased when so-and-so walked in. And in spite of being very ignorant in a lot of ways I had a good sense of what was happening. The problem was to know when to be smart and let on I knew something and when to be our old friend, the sexy blonde who makes two short planks look like Einstein. Never mind – it all came in useful later on, when I was working for myself. At the time it seemed like another little job for tired Mary).

So there I was, that day, done up in a dark red Hartnell suit with a tight skirt and waisted jacket and a little hat perched on my head, same colour, with a tiny veil, moving through the foyer, heading for the restaurant, thinking of nothing but lobster, when who should I bump into but my old friend, Johnnie Bridges, also very well dressed. And beside him none other than Ferenc Nedermann. I hadn't seen either of them for about eighteen months. The truth is that after that terrible date with Charlie Markham I'd spent over a year hardly knowing what was going on. It was autumn now, autumn 1957, and I'd hardly noticed.

The funny thing was, I wasn't surprised to see him. He stopped dead when he saw me, though. I walked up to him and said, "Hullo, Johnnie," in a calm way. "How are you?" I said. "Bit of trouble with the face?" To look at us, all poshed up in hundreds of quids' worth of clothes, standing on thick carpet in a big hotel, you wouldn't have guessed who we were. But Johnnie put his hand to his cheek, sort of defending it. There was a razor mark down one cheek. I'd thought the Roses had finished with him but perhaps they hadn't. Or the mark had been made by someone else.

"Accident," he told me. "I'm getting a plastic surgeon to attend to it next week." He was annoyed that I'd mentioned it. Which was why I had mentioned it, to make him feel he looked rotten. He recovered a bit and asked, "How are you, Moll? You're looking very well."

"Well off, you mean," I told him. "And how are you, Mr Nedermann."

"As well as ever," he said, looking at me rather mournfully.

"It's lovely to have run into you both again," I said to both of them. "We must all get together some time – just for now I've got to hurry off. I'm late for lunch." And with that I swept off, all court train and tiara, feeling satisfied with my coolness, carelessness and smart clothes. Until, of course, the needle started going in, after the soup, and I began to brood about Johnnie and wonder what he was doing.

Then, funnily enough, I began to worry about Josephine, who I hadn't seen for a fortnight, and before I knew where I was I'd got up, saying I wasn't well, and buggered off back to Meakin Street in a taxi.

I daresay by that stage I was ready for a change. I'd have done well to have got out and stayed out, stayed in Meakin Street from then on, before the whole thing turned into a catastrophe. Truth to tell, I was tired out. It was no joke working at the club from ten or eleven at night until three or four in the morning, lending Simon a hand with the organization during the day and then squeezing in all these dates with Clover and Wylie and pretending to be keeping each of them a secret to the other, although I think they knew really. And by that time both of them were putting pressure on me to spend more time with them. I started wondering if Clover even had the idea that with a little French polishing and a fresh set of papers he couldn't get rid of his wife and set his little rough diamond up as the new Lady C – a born optimist. Anyway, with that and Johnnie turning up, too, there's no doubt I should have stayed at Meakin Street from then on and kept out of trouble, but, no, I had to let it get complicated. I was a glutton for punishment in those days. When Johnnie rang me at the club and asked me round to dinner at his new flat off Grosvenor Square, I said I'd go. Needless to say, I went telling myself I'd have a good boast about where I'd been, what I'd been doing, and who with, since he left me in the lurch and then, when I'd impressed him with my new life, my cheerfulness and my enormous beauty I'd let him make a pass and then, as they say, spurn him like a dog. And what do you think I did? Took him back of course. Which left me with a job which kept me up all night and half the day, two peculiar lovers who weren't supposed to know about each other and a third who really had to be kept a secret, especially from Arnie Rose. Small wonder eventually the balloon went up. My God, the things you do when you're young.

It was the music – Johnnie put on this recording of these French cabaret songs. I think he did it because my boasting and sophisticated air of poise and beauty were really taking him in. So he had to rattle me and get me in the mood. And it was that little, sad song, in French, the one I sometimes heard in my dreams and didn't know why, that was what got me going. Perhaps, without that, which was like a trick played on me by a past I didn't know anything about – well, perhaps I'd have stayed clear of him that time, got up and gone home like a lady. Or perhaps not. But the music softened me. I fell for it. The fox had me again. Once again it was the same old tale – the soft skin and the hard prick – by this time I knew he was rotten but the tragedy is that a lot of rotten men aren't like that in bed. It's when they're on their feet that they get evil or seedy or corrupt. That's what a lot of men don't understand when they see a woman hanging around with a bloke who'd sell his old mother for ninepence and throw his little brother in for free – they don't know that while they're with a woman, for that hour or two at night – they're innocent.

I staggered back to the club at ten the next morning and there was Steven, in his dressing-gown, looking daggers at me.

"Where the hell have you been?" were his first words. "Wylie was here at nine saying you'd arranged to go shopping. And Clover rang at nine-thirty, asking for you. I didn't know where you were. I told them both you were at Meakin Street. Were you?"

"What's it to you?" I said to him.

"I don't like being put at a disadvantage like that," he told me, so I told him, "You're just a snob, Steven. You wouldn't be worrying if two dustmen had come round asking for me."

"It's irresponsible to say you'll go somewhere –" he said and then he peered at me. "*Were* you at Meakin Street?" he asked. "No – if you'd been at Meakin Street you wouldn't be back here at ten. Anyway, from the look of you, if you were there I was at midnight mass in Westminster Cathedral last night. What's going on?"

I just thumbed my nose at him. To tell the truth I felt uneasy about all this but I was buoyed up by sheer sex, I suppose. And Steven saw it all. He said sharply, "Bridges. It's Bridges again, isn't it? You stupid bitch – don't think I'm going to cover up for you with people I know."

"You know them," I said, just as sharply. "But don't forget, Steven, if you ever get in any trouble, they won't know you."

And he flinched as if I'd hit him. Then he pulled himself together and said, "Don't forget you're due at Lowton at the weekend. They're counting on you." Then the phone rang. He went to answer it. There was an urgent conversation. It was something to do with some photos of Wendy Valentine and someone in the Foreign Office. The kind they call compromising. And a third party was threatening to show them to the papers, so they had to be bought back but the snag was how to raise the money. Fact is, poor Steven was losing his grip on the situation by that stage. The empire was starting to topple. The weekend at Lowton was cancelled quickly, for example. For no special reason. Poor old Steven had put the girls into some funny spots – Wendy Valentine was knocking off a Russian diplomat and an MP at the same time and, for light relief, this dodgy West Indian drug dealer, and everybody was starting to get interested. That was why Steven's old friends started creeping back into the woodwork and why there weren't going to be any more invitations to country houses.

Anyway, after this call Steven had just poured himself a brandy — at ten in the morning, and he was never a hard drinker, when there's a knock at the door and in come the men from the Special Branch. You could always recognize them in those days by their white belted macs. They're harder to spot now but at that time they always looked like army officers off duty just strolling along to the club. And Steven had a quick word with them in the kitchen and they disappeared. Just like that. My turn to ask, "What the hell's going on here?"

Even then he didn't realize the extent of the cop-out going on around him. He said, "A little local difficulty. A mistake, really. I've told them who to see."

"Special Branch," I said. "What's it all about?"

He said, "Lord Clover wants to set you up in a flat."

"Give up the job?" I asked him and he told me Clover wanted me to live in a flat overlooking Highgate Woods and he'd pay me £3,000 a year, which was a lot of money. And I said no.

Steven was furious. He told me it was a wonderful opportunity and I was stupid to refuse it. And I told him no one was going to bang me up in a flat in Highgate with no job and miles away from my child. I told him, "If I wanted to live in a harem I'd go to Arabia." He had another brandy and then I spotted what was going on and I asked him, "You've made a deal with Clover, that's right isn't it? I have to be got safely out of the way so I won't talk."

"Clover very much wants this," he said.

I said, "Well — it's serious for you, isn't it? Because if I refuse he may get angry and that'll ruin your friendship?"

"Worse than that," said Steven Greene. He meant Clover would take away his protection, as well as his friendship. I didn't know how bad it was all going to get. I just thought all he'd lose was a few perks and a friendship with a man I knew as a short, fat man in his shirttails, going on and on about Cabinet secrets while I lay motionless on a couch with nothing on, pretending to be a famous picture, the Rokeby Venus. So to save him a small loss I was supposed to sign on for countless months, even years, of being something like a slave. So I said no, again.

"You're a bloody little fool," he told me. Even he didn't know completely what the outcome would be for him.

I was back with Johnnie again, so I wasn't thinking straight. We spent the morning pottering around that flat, with the phone ringing all the time and neither of us had any idea what other calls were being made from studies and panelled offices all over town, or who was having a few words with who else over the steak and kidney pie and claret. Levers were being pulled all over the place and Steven was going to get caught and mangled in the machinery. It didn't happen all at once, though. In fact the first thing that happened was at night, the same night, like a French farce. Steven was out and Johnnie and I had gone out and had a bit to drink and come back to the flat in South Molton Street, sneaking up the stairs hoping not to be seen. And we were asleep when the bedroom door opened and in came Clover, in a dinner jacket and cries out, "To think I was going to give you everything – and now this!"

Johnnie struggles up in bed and said, "Who the fuck is this?" I struggle up and say, "I can explain. Let's try to –" when, oh dear, oh dear, in come the Rose brothers. First thing Johnnie does is leap out of bed and put on his trousers. Everyone's shouting. Clover was the first to leave, seeing an undignified scene in progress and not wanting any part in it and then, needless to say, Arnie Rose evicts me, sacks me and, for good measure, evicts Steven Greene, who comes in on the scene innocently, saying "What's going on?"

Looking back you can see it was a set-up. Only the Roses could have seen me go upstairs with Johnnie and then let Clover follow on up, with a key supplied by them. A minute later they burst in and get Steven and all of us out of the flat. The truth is, someone had told them it would be safer to get Steven off their premises. That Johnnie was there, and there's a triangle involving Clover and that Steven was involved with all of us was not the real reason for asking him to go. They'd been tipped off that having Steven about might bring trouble down on them and they had too much to hide. They couldn't afford publicity, investigation and speculation too close to them. I think the chance is that whoever manoeuvred the Roses into evicting Steven hoped that he would just go and disappear. But it was too late. Already the foreign papers were on to Wendy's fun with the Russian agent and the parties Steven had been arranging for people in high places – the ones with the whips and the masks and all. He hadn't said much about that to me, not after I'd been so amazed by Charlie Markham's antics. But by now too many people were curious and Steven showed a lack of tact and *savoir faire*. He stayed instead of going. He had offers of country cottages in Ireland and a studio in Paris – but he hung around and that was his downfall. I'm still surprised I got so little interference. As I say, Clover found me later on in the flat where I was living with Johnnie and then sent me money to shut up. It was funny – he'd always looked like a comic figure to me but when he came to the flat I suddenly saw somebody with power, the landlord, the lawmaker. He just sat there talking and Johnnie listened, not saying a word – like I say, it was funny.

About that time they were trying Wendy Valentine's West Indian for something or other and I thought – just get out, Clover, and leave me in peace. It was frightening in a way because I had the idea that if I looked as if I might start talking something nasty would happen to me. I was glad when he left saying I could call on him at any time. Then I got the shakes. I thought it was nerves but it was the start of pneumonia.

It was my father who managed to keep Mary's name out of the affair, added Sir Herbert. Fortunately she could be represented as a person living at the flat in South Molton Street because she worked at the club downstairs. And Clover and Wylie had both been careful to keep their relationships with her reasonably discreet and I gather a short meeting between the pair reassured each of them that the other was no keener to publicize the story than he was himself.

When Steven Greene's trial, for procuring and living on immoral earnings, came along in January Mary was well out of the way, like so many others. At the same time my father joined the Labour Party. He told my mother one night at dinner. She was perfectly amazed. She looked at him as if he had gone mad. She asked him why. He said he had no idea. It was an impulse. Fortunately, my mother's family had had its share of eccentrics. There was a great uncle who had fought with the anarchists in Russia during the Revolution, another uncle, a bishop, who had turned to Rome, and the usual less public madmen most families contain when you look closely. She therefore took my father's conversion to socialism in her stride and wrote to me in Oxford that she had much enjoyed having Aneurin Bevan to tea. "I was completely charmed by him," she said in her letter. "He is so like a big, well-fed pussy cat, with well-sheathed claws. And he was so very clever. But of course I am still alarmed by your father's eccentricity and I am afraid that if he becomes more extreme there may be difficulties ahead." I imagine she thought he might take to singing The Red Flag in the House of Lords or meeting Soviet agents on Hampstead Heath at night. In fact he did nothing more than canvass during the following General Election and remain close friends with Bevan until the politician's death a few years later.

It was after that important meeting where he offered me a chance to join what I suppose I must call the family firm, that he told me what had happened around the time of Greene's trial. By that time I had, with great astonishment, accepted the offer and was undergoing my real initiation into the job, which included instruction in the long-running serial he drily called *L'Affaire* Waterhouse. "It cost me something in terms of calling in moral overdrafts, and the asking of favours to keep that silly girl out of court," he told me. "And the worst of it was that before and during the trial I discovered I was washing my hands more frequently than necessary. Even I, with no faith in psychiatry, couldn't avoid seeing the significance. It also confirmed your mother's suspicions that I was going off my head. But it was just as well she was in hospital with severe pneumonia during the trial – Mary Flanders, I mean – because God knows what she might not have done if she had been let loose."

"What's she doing now?" I asked him.

"Living with a man who buys and sells houses," my father told me. "She won't marry him, of course, won't settle down and have a family like a normal woman. I'm sure of that if I'm sure of nothing else."

His tone was so comically discontented that I laughed and quoted, "Spirited but uncertain-tempered," which was the auctioneer's description of a mare we had once bought, but re-sold because she bit, balked in order to throw her rider into hedges and ditches and broke her stall to pieces one night.

"Not entirely her fault, I suppose," my father went on in the same depressed tone. Looking at the files in the case always had a bad effect on him. "Nevertheless, I doubt if any good will come of it."

"You can't be sure," I told him.

"Oh, this isn't the end," he told me. "This affair has been bungled from the first – year after year has passed while we all hoped we'd seen the end of the story. I doubt it. I'm beginning to wonder if any of us will come out of this with a whole skin."

Of course, we spoke in the summer of 1958, when the sensational events of the previous year were still fresh in all our minds. Admittedly, it had left behind a lingering feeling that many secrets had not emerged and many people had been unfairly protected. By then one MP had resigned and one man had committed suicide, but no one thought the whole truth had been told and many thought that more might leak out. Small wonder my father was thinking at that time in terms of further discovery and revelation.

The arrival of Clover and the Roses to find Molly in bed with Johnnie turned out to have taken place on Guy Fawkes' Night – 'Indoor fireworks' as Molly remarked later. Next day she moved in with Johnnie Bridges about half a mile away from Frames.

The flat, in a tall block, was luxuriously furnished. There were soft sofas from Heal's, expensive flock wallpaper and a great deal of cunning lighting fixtures and many mirrors. Johnnie's tenancy, which had lasted several months, had already put a stain on the carpet here and a burn on a table there. Nevertheless, Molly felt she had gone up in the world.

For Molly, jobless and without her two persistent clients, it was a holiday, a honeymoon. The catastrophe at the club had been a blessing in disguise. Jaded by a sex life as gruelling as a forced march and always short of sleep, now here was love, luxury and leisure. For a few weeks the London streets, misty, foggy and damp, were springlike. And Johnnie, lying about the flat in his dressing-gown or going with her to shop, or to restaurants, or to the cinema, was happy, too. He had, at last, dissolved the partnership with the Roses and been paid back his share in the club. He said he had not been happy since they had parted and she knew that, in a way, it was true. He asked her to marry him. She said that she would, after Christmas, and knew that he was disappointed. He wanted her to say she must marry now. But as she had told him she would marry him she had looked over his shoulder, to where the fog swirled outside the long net curtains and heard an ambulance wailing in the street. She was afraid. She loved him but she did not trust him.

As soon as she could she went to see Steven Greene. He was now living with Wendy Valentine in a small two-roomed flat in a tall house in Bayswater. As she came in he shunted her quickly into the bedroom, but not before she had seen a very beautiful woman sitting on the sofa in front of a low table in front of the gas fire in the sitting-room. Her shining black hair was pulled back from her face and held at the back with a velvet bow. She had pearls round her throat. She sat tapping long red nails on a tarot card and staring at the others, which were laid out in a circle on the table. Mary sat on the unmade double bed in the other room looking at herself in the dressing-table mirror. While Steven was in the other room, talking to the woman, she lay back – and fell asleep.

She dreamed of fire, again, and the French tune and then of Allaun Towers. She dreamed she was running across a meadow full of green, half-grown corn. She woke to find Steven Greene sitting on the end of the bed. There was some murmuring from the other room. "What's up?" she asked. "You hiring the place out to fortune tellers?"

"Something like that," he told her. His face was pouchy, and his eyes, which had some fresh lines round them, were dull.

"You look bad," she said frankly. "You're only thirty-two and you look forty. You need a break. Why don't you get out of London for a holiday? I came to ask if you wanted a loan. Johnnie's flush and I've got a bit of money off selling a necklace. You can have a couple of hundred, if it helps."

"I've got enough, thanks, Moll," he said. "If the smarter elements are staying away for a while we can always keep going on fortune-telling and low sex."

The murmuring stopped in the other room. The front door closed. "Steven, I'm leaving," called a woman's voice.

Steven and Molly came out of the bedroom. The dark-haired woman had her coat on, "Thanks for the use of the room," she said. "I suppose you'd like your fortune told, dear," she said to Molly.

"No thanks," said Molly. "I don't believe in it."

"Please yourself," said the woman. Looking at Molly she said, "Funny – most girls like a reading, especially if it's free."

"I don't like the idea we can't do anything about things," declared Molly. Her eye caught Steven Greene's and she said, "You've been at it, haven't you? And you don't like what you heard? You should give it up. This is what you sell to the punters."

The dark woman was annoyed and told her, "You'd be surprised if I mentioned the names of some of my clients. They have confidence."

"I didn't mean that," said Molly. "Anyway, it's none of my business." But after the woman had gone she looked at her friend and said, "You're a fool, Steven. You don't want to go in for all this mumbo-jumbo. You've had a setback, that's all. You don't have to sit here with the curtains drawn frightening yourself to death with tarot cards. A load of your posh so-called friends have dropped you. They're more scared than you are, you can bet on that. For one thing, you've

256

got the goods on them – you could get a fortune from the *News of the World* for your revelations about sin in high places. You could blackmail them half to death – there's a lot you know they wouldn't want their wives, innocent daughters, shareholders or fellow aldermen to hear about."

"I couldn't do that," he said.

"No – because you're supposed to be a gentleman. How do you think they got to be gentlemen – because somebody in the family did a few murders, or betrayed his king, or sold him his daughter – that's how they got there and that's how they're prepared to stay there. Very convenient for them that you practise what they preach." She added, "In the meanwhile you're doing them a real favour by sitting there like Christ taking a break from carrying his cross. Stops you from rushing about causing trouble – means the Special Branch and everybody else knows where to find you. I bet this house is watched."

Steven Greene sat by the flaring gas fire and said nothing. "Come on, Steven," she said, "take the money and go to Morocco or something. Have a break and get them worried. You're acting like a girl who's been given the chuck – sitting around hoping they'll see their mistake and come back to you. Why don't you disappear and give them a run for their money?"

"I feel too – disappointed," he told her.

"Well – don't say I didn't warn you," she said. "But I think you could be in trouble, soon. You know too much." Then she said, "Anyway – here's the big news. Johnnie and me are getting married."

At this he said, "Why are you looking so miserable, then?"

"Miserable?" she said. "I'm not miserable. It's you that's miserable. Aren't you going to say 'congratulations' or something?"

Steven shook his head. He said, "I'm broke, I've been deserted by my friends and I can't see my way out so I deserve one luxury – saying what I think. And that is that you're not happy and quite right too, because Johnnie's no good – sorry, Moll, but I've got to say it."

Molly shrugged uncomfortably, "Better not talk about it then – but it's going to happen so make up your mind to it."

"What's he doing now?" asked Steven.

"Johnnie? He's working for Ferenc Nedermann."

"What as?"

"I'm not really sure."

"Why don't you find out," Steven said. "Go and see what he does. A wife should take an interest."

"All right," Molly said. "I will." She knew the suggestion meant that she would not like what she saw.

Suddenly it was as if the fog and the silence outside and the cramped atmosphere of the little flat had exhausted them. Molly asked, "Is there anything to drink here?"

"Not till Wendy gets back," he told her. "Times are hard."

"I'll go," she said.

When she came back with a bottle of whisky and some cheese and ham he opened the door and stared at her like a man who has had a bad shock. She stepped in, saying, "I'll make you a sandwich," then, struck by the atmosphere, "What's happened?"

"They're charging me with living on immoral earnings," he told her.

"Oh, God," she cried, putting her bag on the floor. "Oh – no. How do you know?"

"A friend in the police just phoned and told me," he said. "How could they?"

"You've still got time to get out," Molly said. "They can't charge you if you're not here, can they?"

"Yes, they can," he said. "I'll just have to face it when I get back."

"They warned you so you'd leave," she told him. "Go to New York and don't come back. You can get a living anywhere – you might go down well in the States."

"No time to get a visa," he replied.

"Look," she said. "There's been a decision. Some of your former posh mates want to get rid of you, still. The others have decided they want to punish you – get you discredited – turn you into a criminal. That's what this is all about. You want to get to the first lot. They could get you a visa to the moon in four hours."

"You're talking nonsense," he said.

"Oh, God, Steven," Mary cried. "You've lived among these people. You know all about them. You fixed their orgies. Didn't you ever see them pull a string or two? I don't know where your brains are."

"Better think about your own skin, Molly my dear," was his reply. "If they want to prove I'm a ponce you'll be called to give evidence."

"Glad to do so," Molly said stoutly. 'I'll tell them everything." She wailed, "Oh God, Steven, why don't you get out?"

"I've got nothing to be ashamed of – I'm not guilty," he said. "I wish I had a quid for every pound I've handed over to Wendy Valentine, for a start. She gave my TV to her mother and father."

"As if all that matters," Molly said impatiently. "They'll make it stick, Steven, no matter what you do or say."

He sat down suddenly and said, again, "How could they?"

Molly went into the kitchen and made some sandwiches. All she could see, as she angrily tore holes in the new bread while trying to spread butter on it, was that Steven Greene hoped to rely on the truth to prove his innocence. And, now hacking at the cheese, she muttered, "As if that ever made any difference in court." Over the whisky and slab-like sandwiches she told him, "Sid said never go to court. He said do anything, say anything, pay anything but never go to court because from the moment you step through the door you start losing."

"Molly," he told her patiently, "I'm innocent. A fair trial will still prove an innocent man is innocent."

"I hope you're right," Molly said. "But Sid says the most innocent thing in the world can look guilty in court."

"Well, it's lovely sitting here and listening to your father's opinions about the law," Steven said.

"Phone your solicitor," Molly said firmly. "Do it now."

Steven looked at her and said, "You know, one of these days you're going to turn into a firm-minded woman."

"Be sooner than that, if I have to go on dealing with people like you. You feel betrayed, don't you? You feel let down by friends and now they've put the law on you? And you still can't believe it's true. You still think it's a bad dream and you'll wake up and it'll have gone away. Don't let it happen to you, Steven. Do something or you're for the chop."

"Better go home, Molly, and work out your own story," he told her.

Molly said wearily, "All right. But I'll be back." They ate their sandwiches sitting side by side on the sofa, with their arms round each other's shoulders. After her brief honeymoon she felt very tired again, as she had before.

When she got back to the flat she found Johnnie there. She told him about the coming charge of living on immoral earnings. He said only, "Pack it up, love. I'm worn out with all this. Steven Greene's been walking on the edge for years. Now it's caught up with him and I can't be expected to cry in my tea about that. I've got problems of my own." And Molly sighed and went into the kitchen to get the dinner.

The next day she found out that Steven had been charged. Being unfamiliar with legal processes she went to West End Central police station, which had executed the warrant, and asked the desk officer to go and find a detective.

"In connection with what, miss?" said the policeman, intrigued by a beautiful girl with a cockney accent, standing there in a fur coat, demanding a detective. It was yet another day when the fog was creeping into buildings and swirling in rooms. If she had been connected with criminals, he thought, she would have known better than to set about her business in that way. If she was not, how did she come to be so well dressed and self-assured? Most working-class people were more hesitant in their dealings with the police.

Molly said to him, "It's in connection with Steven Greene."

The policeman looked at her and understood. There were already stories circulating about the high-class orgies arranged by Greene. Wendy Valentine's black lover had been arrested on a drugs' charge but had disappeared before standing trial. Foreign newspapers were mentioning the names of Cabinet ministers and senior members of the clergy who were supposed to have been involved. The British newspapers kept silent but the buzz of gossip was everywhere. And so, "One of Greene's tarts – an amateur," thought the policeman. He went off and fetched a man in plain clothes, who took her into an office and said that a senior officer would soon be coming. For five minutes he tapped his fingers on the desk and looked at her from time to time. Molly said, "I want to make a statement."

"Well – that might be possible," was all he said. "I'm afraid you'll have to wait."

Finally a detective inspector in uniform arrived. Molly said, "My name's Molly Flanders and a friend of mine, Steven Greene, is in trouble. I want to make a statement to help him."

The detective inspector said, "Well – are you sure a young woman like yourself wants to get involved in what might turn out to be a rather unsavoury case? I have to say this to you, in your own interest."

Molly was bewildered by his apparent lack of concern. She said, "I used to live with him – I was his tenant. I know what went on. He never took any money off women – half the time they were taking it off him. It seems to me I could help him by saying what went on."

"Do you know what it's like to stand in the witness box, Mrs Flanders, and have the prosecution badgering you with questions to try and break down your story? It's not very pleasant. And nearly all of us have got little secrets we'd like to hide. There's no hiding anything in court." He looked at her paternally. Molly burst out, "There's nothing

I want to hide. If things about me come out in court that's all right. Why do you want me to keep quiet?"

"Mrs Flanders," said the policeman reproachfully, "we don't want you to keep quiet. If you've got anything to say to help your friend, then you go ahead and say it. I'm just warning you – they'll ask questions about your past. And they'll make a point of asking why you, a good-looking young woman, married, by the sound of it, decided to go and live in a flat with Mr Greene. It's a bit unusual isn't it – sharing a flat with a man? They may dwell on that a bit in court."

"I didn't live there all the time," Molly said. "I just stayed there some days because I worked late in the club below."

"Don't work there any more, then?" asked the policeman. He was a big, thickset man, too big, it seemed, for his own uniform. The large silver buttons on his jacket bulged.

"No. I don't work there any more," replied Molly.

"Any particular reason? Quarrelled with the boss?" enquired the detective inspector.

"I did, as a matter of fact," replied Molly, now on the defensive. "But that's got nothing to do with why I'm here." She began to think the policeman knew everything – that she had slept with Steven Greene, all about Lord Clover, Christopher Wylie and the way her husband had died – "I'm here to speak up for a friend, that's all," she said.

There was a silence. Then the policeman leaned over the desk, his big hands folded and his eyes sympathetic. "Mrs Flanders," he said. "We all appreciate your motives in coming and I respect them. You want to help. But I'd like to do you a favour – nothing easier than for me to take down what you say, get you in court and let you deal with all the nasty insinuations the prosecution throws at you, all the publicity – what are your parents going to think about all this when the neighbours read about it in the papers? – like I say, nothing easier than for me to go right ahead and drag you into all that. But instead, because you're a young woman and I'd like to give you a chance to think it over, I'm going to suggest you go home and talk it over with somebody – your husband, your mum and dad, somebody like that. Then, if you haven't changed your mind, come back here and we'll take down what you have to say."

Molly, suddenly imagining Sid's reaction when he read about her and saw her photograph in the *News of the World*, was almost tempted to comply. The policeman had frightened her. But she drew a deep breath and said, "Thanks. I appreciate the thought. But I'd rather do it now." The policeman's kindly expression changed. He stood up. "All right," he said. "If that's what you want to do – I'll hand this one over to you, George." He left the room and the plain-clothes man sat down behind the desk.

"All right," he said wearily. "Fire away, Mrs Flanders. Let's hear all about it. Give me the date when you first took up residence in Mr Greene's flat."

And so Molly told her story, interrupted by the other officer when he wanted dates and further details. He took it down slowly in longhand. At the end he read it over to her. It sounded, even to Molly's inexperienced ears, flat and unconvincing. All she seemed to have done was deny that Steven Greene had ever taken any money from women. As she signed it she said anxiously, "You'll come to me if you want to know anything else, won't you?"

"We'll be in touch," was all he said in reply. "You may be called to give evidence."

Later that day Steven Greene, lolling, rather drunk, in a chair by the gas fire at his flat told her, "They didn't want you, Moll. They tried to warn you off with their you-don't-want-any-nasty-publicity-a-nice-girl-like-you routine. I wonder if that statement you made will ever reach their files. It could go in the wastepaper basket tomorrow."

"Oh – I don't think so," Molly said.

"Don't think so?" said Wendy Valentine, who was lying on the sofa with a glass of whisky. She wore a silk dressing-gown which sometimes lapped open to show her slip, stockings and suspenders. The room was looking untidy. There were a lot of newspapers about. Wendy said, "I'm telling you, Moll, I was walking down Gerrard Street this morning minding my own business when a police car drew up beside me and they asked me to step in. I was at West End Central for two hours, answering questions. And half of them about Steven. They're collecting evidence."

"The evidence to convict me," Steven added.

Wendy looked across sharply at Molly. "Have you got someone influential on your side?" she demanded.

"What do you mean?" Molly demanded.

"Because I think you're being protected," Wendy said.

Molly thought about the idea. Then she shook her head. "Who'd look after me?" she asked.

"Clover," said Wendy. "Or the Roses."

Molly shrugged. "They can't stop me from giving evidence if I want to," she said.

"They'll offer you money," said Steven. "Take it if you like. I won't hold it against you."

"I don't need money," Molly said.

"No, but Johnnie does," said Wendy Valentine quietly. The phone rang and Steven answered it. He came back and sat down. "Johnnie," he told Molly. "He wondered where you were – says to come back quickly."

"In a minute," Molly said.

"He didn't sound very pleased," warned Steven.

Molly was tired. She roused herself from her chair and went home. There was a row. Johnnie told her to leave Steven Greene and his troubles alone. Molly refused. Johnnie shouted. Molly wept. Johnnie threw a vase at the mirror and broke both. A middle-aged man came from downstairs and complained about the noise. That night Molly lay beside her lover anxiously wondering what had gone wrong.

The next day she stood beside Johnnie in a glass-scattered street in North Kensington. She looked up at the five-storey terraced house. Plaster on the portico had come off in large lumps. The window frames were unpainted, the front door peeling. Curtains were drawn, or tacked over some of the windows. Old, limp net curtains hung at others. One of the panes was cracked and the line of the crack had been mended with sticky tape. Beyond the broken iron railings, on the trodden earth of the small front garden a dog nosed through the contents – papers, tins, scattered tea leaves – of an overturned dustbin. Up the cracked front steps Johnnie was hammering on the front door with his fists. "Mr Pilsutski!" he was calling. "Mr Pilsutski! It's Mr Bridges." Molly walked up to join him, hoping that there would be no answer, that they could go away. "Stupid bugger," Johnnie said, turning to her, "I sent him a postcard saying I was coming." Inside the house a baby cried. Johnnie started hammering and calling again. Then there were slow footsteps and the door was opened a little. A black woman in an apron stood there. She opened the door wider. Through an open door to the left the heads of four black children appeared at different heights.

"Yes?" said the woman. "Who you want? Pilsutski?"

"That's right," said Johnnie.

The woman looked contemptuous. "Downstairs – the basement," she said. Molly, in the meanwhile, looked up and saw an elderly, grey-haired woman coming slowly down the stairs, holding on to the banister.

"Downstairs – thanks," Johnnie said to the black woman and led the way along the passageway to a small door on the left, under the stairs. As he banged on it and went in Molly heard the old woman say, "Mrs Higgins – my sister is ill. The children are being very noisy. Do you think –"

"This way," Johnnie said brusquely to Molly and went down the stairs inside the small door. Upstairs, Molly could hear the black woman shouting.

At the bottom of the stairs an old man in carpet slippers stood on the worn linoleum. "Mr Nader's friend," Johnnie said loudly. "I sent you a postcard."

"Mr Nader?" the man replied, in a strongly accented English.

"Not Mr Nader," Johnnie said, in the same loud voice. "I'm Mr Bridges. Mr Nader's associate. Can I come inside? We don't want the whole house to hear, do we?"

This seemed to produce a response. "Ah," said the man. "No – no. In private. In private. Come this way."

Opening a door he led them into a small, tidy room, containing a three-piece suite and a table covered with a very white lace cloth. On one wall there was a crucifix and underneath another, smaller table, also covered with a white cloth. A fat, middle-aged woman came in.

"Sit down. Sit down, please," said the man. "Maria – make some coffee." She went out.

"My fiancee," said Johnnie, waving at Molly. "I hope you don't mind me bringing her along, Mr Pilsutski."

They sat down. Peering at Molly, Pilsutski said, "How could anyone mind such a pretty face? So you are to be married?"

"That's right," said Johnnie. "Anyway – to business. I hope you don't mind me coming to the point but you realize I've several other properties to see."

Pilsutski nodded. "Well then," said Johnnie. "My colleague Mr Nader would obviously like to see the tenants' rent books. Any chance of making them available?"

"Rent books – ah," said Pilsutski slowly. "Well, you must see, Mr – er –"

"Mr Bridges," supplied Johnnie.

"Yes, Mr Bridges," agreed the old man. "Rent books are not always possible in premises like this. With the comings and goings and the defaultings — and if I supply them, the tenants lose them. So — we manage without them."

"Of course, of course," Johnnie said comprehendingly. "I can see your point of view. But obviously, with the property for sale, my associate Mr Nader would like to have some idea of what the place is bringing in."

The woman appeared with coffee and a cake on a plate. As she served them Pilsutski said, "I wouldn't be parting with this property, like I told Mr Nader, but the doctor told me, 'Mr Pilsutski, the worry of that house is making your wife ill. The best thing you can do is sell it and go and live quietly somewhere in the country, or near the sea.' A man's wife, Mr Bridges, is more precious to him than any business — have some cake, miss," he said to Molly. "It's very good. Not like that," he said to his wife, who was offering Molly the milk. "The lady hasn't got three hands. Pour it in for her." He said something sharply to her in a foreign language. She poured milk into Molly's cup, took her own and went off to sit by the window.

"Yes," Johnnie said sagely. "Property's no joke these days. It's all worry. Interference from this one and that. Worse if you live on the premises. That way you get all the tenants coming to you with their complaints."

"That's right," said Pilsutski. "Every little blocked toilet, every little dispute between them — and there they are banging on the door. Day and night, night and day. You are supposed to look after them like babies in their cradles. It's not worth it. Money is good but not as good as health."

"You said it," said Johnnie. "You just said it. I couldn't agree with you more. Now — I'm afraid I have to ask you some personal questions. We haven't got any rent books. I don't suppose you keep receipts —"

"Well — I'm a busy man —" said Pilsutski.

"Very understandable," said Johnnie. Molly was puzzled at first, then realized that without rent books or receipts no tenant could prove he had paid rent, or even that he was a tenant at all. This made eviction easy. She listened to the two men as they talked.

"So — ground floor," said Johnnie. "Black family — man and a woman and plenty of children. Anybody else?"

"His brother — bus conductor," Pilsutski said.

"How much for their room?" asked Johnnie.

"Seven pounds ten a week," Pilsutski replied.

"Hm," said Johnnie, noting it down. Molly absorbed the information. Sid and Ivy paid five pounds a week for the house in Meakin Street.

"The other doorway on the ground floor?" Johnnie was asking.

"Ah, that," Pilsutski told him. "An old man. Controlled tenant. Now then – upstairs –"

"This old man," interrupted Johnnie. "How much does he pay?"

Reluctantly, Pilsutski told him, "Ten shillings a week."

Johnnie tutted. "Disgraceful, isn't it. Another trial for the landlord."

"The landlord is paying them to live in his house," Pilsutski said. Then, rage conquering discretion, he said, "Upstairs – more bloody control' tenants. Two rooms, first floor, best rooms in the house – big rooms, big windows – old lady and her sister. Do you know what they pay? Two pounds a week. Two lousy pounds."

"You could be getting twenty," Johnnie said. "Or more. They got a bath?"

"Toilet," responded Pilsutski. "Plenty of room for a bath. It could be a luxury flat. But, no – two pounds a week."

"Ladies in good health?" enquired Johnnie.

"The sister's sick at the moment," he said. "But she'll recover. You know old ladies. They –" looking at Molly he changed his mind about what he was going to say and fell silent.

"Never mind. Never mind," Johnnie said. "Perhaps things look better upstairs. How about the second floor? What's that like?"

"At the front – three Irishmen – workers," said Pilsutski. He shrugged. "Three – four – five – I don't know. I ask no questions. Eight pounds a week, they pay. They give no trouble."

"Get drunk and act a bit noisy sometimes, I expect," Johnnie suggested.

Pilsutski looked at him cautiously, then saw the point, and nodded. "Terrible, sometimes," he said. "Falling upstairs, shouting, banging doors. Sometimes fighting. You can hear them down here."

"Very unpleasant for the old ladies," Johnnie said.

"They complain," said the landlord, "but what can I do?"

"Nothing," Johnnie said.

"At the back there," Pilsutski went on, "small room, very quiet man, very clean, works for the Council. Pays three pounds."

Molly sat quietly, drinking her coffee, as the two men, leaning forward towards each other, went on with the inventory of tenants.

Finally Johnnie, with a doubtful face, made a calculation and said, "Well, then. Something in the region of thirty pounds a week? Not a lot, really, is it Mr Pilsutski. Your main problem is these controlled tenants. Without them you'd be getting double."

"Don't I know it, Mr Bridges? Don't I know it?" cried Pilsutski. "But there it is, that's life, what can you do?"

"What indeed," said Johnnie, standing up. "Now perhaps you'll show me round."

"With pleasure," answered Pilsutski and led them up the stairs, back along the passageway and then, after a rapid knock on the door, into the room the black woman had entered. The room was full of beds and small children. A pot steamed on a double gas ring in the corner. The woman, holding a toddler up at the sink while she washed the child's face, swung round when the party trooped in. "What you want now?" she asked Pilsutski sharply.

"Just taking a little look around, madam," Johnnie said smoothly. "See if there's anything we can do for you."

Behind him Molly smelt the odour of the room where about eight people slept, lived and ate. It was a combination of children's urine, stale cooking and sweat but it added up to more than all that, helped, she thought, by lack of ventilation and damp walls. It wasn't the woman's fault that things were like this. She suddenly remembered Ivy's patches of weariness and despair, when she would come home from school and find no tea ready, the washing up not done and everything in a muddle, while Ivy sat at the kitchen table, smoking and drinking cups of tea and saying, "It's no good. It's heartbreaking. I can't cope with any more." And she thought for the first time that if Jim Flanders had been alive she herself might be stuck in the same two rooms in Meakin Street, with several children, and that her life might not be unlike the black woman's. She now stood with her hands on her hips, looking hard at Johnnie and Pilsutski and saying, "This room is damp and the ceiling coming down in the baby's carrycot. And if you," she said turning to Johnnie, "are thinking about buying this rotten house I advise you now, go and look in that toilet in the hall – the pan coming away from the wall. It don't flush. Then you go and ask that woman on the top floor how many pans and buckets she have to put out when the rain come flooding through his rotten, leaking roof. You going to do something for us?" she said to Johnnie. "Don't make me laugh."

"Thank you very much, madam," Johnnie said smoothly, ignoring the hostility as if he were used to it. The toddler went over to an old carrycot on an iron-framed bed and poked the baby inside. The baby wailed. As they all went out the woman, going to the carrycot to comfort the baby, shot a look at Molly. It said, too plainly, that she, the black woman, despised her for her association with the other two – that she, a woman, should know better than to get mixed up with them. Molly, embarrassed, followed Johnnie and Pilsutski down the passageway.

"Poor old man," confided Pilsutski as he hammered on another door. "Only one leg – the other one's no good now." He banged again shouting, "Mr Harris! Mr Harris! It's Mr Pilsutski!"

"Got quite a temper – the lady back there," Johnnie said.

"And the husband," Pilsutski said. "You should hear them some nights, screaming and banging. And the children crying. Still," he said philosophically, "it's the way they live, isn't it?"

"Really noisy, then?" enquired Johnnie.

"Oh – noisy. You couldn't imagine."

"Hm," said Johnnie, sounding almost impressed, as if some special feature of the house like a new bathroom, or a recently papered ceiling, had been pointed out to him.

"Mr Harris! Mr Harris!" Pilsutski called, turning the handle of the door impatiently. "Locked – locked," he said, turning to Johnnie. "The times I told him. 'What if there's a fire,' I say. 'There'll be a tragedy one day –'" He banged on the door again, saying, in a lowered voice, "My opinion is, he's finished. He got a certain look. I can tell – I seen plenty in Poland, during the war."

"Dear, dear," said Johnnie. "Looks as if he's gone out, though."

"Out? Out?" said Pilsutski. "He can't go nowhere – sh – I can hear him coming."

There was a shuffling, scraping sound from inside the room. The door opened slowly. A very old man, his face grey and his eyes red-rimmed, looked round. He was leaning on a crutch.

"What do you want?" he gasped.

"Looking round, looking round, Mr Harris," said Pilsutski.

"Third time this week," said Harris, turning on his crutch so that they could follow him in. The others moved behind him slowly. As he advanced into the room Molly, from behind the others, could hear his breath wheezing in and out of his lungs. There was a tumbled bed, with grey blankets, a table, on which stood a loaf of bread on a breadboard, and a block of margarine, a pot of jam, a packet of tea, a milk bottle, half full. The floor was covered with old linoleum, red and cracked. An old armchair with wooden arms stood beside a small, hissing gas fire. Mr Harris faced Pilsutski and Johnnie, hanging from his crutches. He had no left leg. The other ended in a carpet slipper. He wheezed, waiting for them to speak.

Molly could bear it no longer. She said, "I'll wait in the car, Johnnie." He did not hear her.

"Nice size of room," he said to Pilsutski.

"Give me the keys," she said more loudly, but all he said was, "Make a nice double bed-sit."

Molly turned and left the house quickly. She banged the door behind her and stood on the steps breathing in the relatively fresh air. The tall houses opposite her, with their cracked and broken plaster mouldings, broken window ledges and fallen railings, had almost all the same air as the house she had left. Here and there was a tended garden, fresh paint, neatly curtained windows, but on the whole all the houses were as derelict as this one. Ten children were swarming over abandoned cars in a turning opposite her. She ran down the steps quickly determined not to wait for Johnnie. She'd get a cab, or a bus, she thought. But behind her she heard the sound of a window being pushed up. "Hey – lady," called the black woman. She had managed to shove up the window of her room and was calling down the steps. Molly reluctantly climbed up and heard her say, "What happening? Is your man buying this place?"

"Thinking about it," said Molly. Behind the woman a girl of about four was grinning through the open window at her.

"Who he, then?" asked the woman.

"None of your business, is it?" Molly told her. The little girl poked out her tongue.

"Why not?" the woman said. "We got to live here. The landlord is our business. I have four children. I should know what's going on here."

Molly hesitated. She said, "He works for a man called Ferenc Nedermann –"

"Oh God, oh Lord," the woman cried out. "Nedermann – he the worst, the wickedest landlord in this place. He push us in the street. Pilsutski, he bad, but Nedermann make him look like an angel. Look," she said fiercely to Molly, "You get that man of yours to leave us alone. This house is rubbish anyway. Rubbish," she repeated. "If Nedermann gets his hands on this place – oh, my God, we finished."

Behind her the little girl was looking round her mother's head to study the expression on her face.

"Finished?" Molly asked numbly.

"Out in the street, I'm telling you," the woman said emphatically, trying to make Molly understand. "And that poor old man with one leg – the old ladies – don't you understand? He raise the rents on the ordinary tenants and he get rid of the controlled ones, like the one-leg man. He do anything – frighten them with big dogs, send men with guns, put men in the house to terrify them. Anything so they leave and he can have the place and charge more rent."

Molly stood there, staring into the big, black face of the woman. Behind her the little girl had unconsciously taken on the same earnest, energetic expression.

"Nice girl like you can do a lot," the woman said encouragingly. "Tell him to say the place in worse condition than it is and all the tenants are controlled – that way Nedermann will go and get another house. All you have to do is make your man say the house is no good." An idea struck her. "He can say, too, there a lawyer living on the first floor. That way Nedermann think he get too much trouble whatever he do."

"I can't do it," said Molly. "Johnnie won't take any notice of me."

A child began to cry in the room. "Then you got trouble, too," said the woman and banged the window down. She lifted the girl from the chair she was standing on and turned away. Molly saw her walk into the middle of the room and bend over an invisible child. Molly walked blindly down the steps and up the street. The pavements were uneven and sprinkled with broken glass.

She found there were tears in her eyes. So that was Johnnie's wonderful new, honest job. It was from this work that he came home in his hand-made suits, his impeccable shirts and the shoes he had made for him by a cobbler in Covent Garden. It was after treading through the wreckage in these houses, buying slums for Nedermann, threatening and evicting the tenants, that he returned looking so prosperous and respectable. This job was his idea of going straight. "But it's worse – far worse – than safe-breaking," she thought, realizing she had thought the same about his frauds at Frames.

On a corner she opened the expensive crocodile handbag Johnnie had given her. She found her purse and realized she had not got enough for a taxi, just her bus fare back to the West End. At the same time she remembered that he had not given her any money for weeks. Standing at the bus stop she looked for her post office savings book and realized how little money she had left. It was just as well Steven Greene had refused the money she had offered him. If he had accepted she would have had to sell one of her last two remaining pieces of jewellery. Apart from that she had five pounds. She had unthinkingly bought food and drink for herself and Johnnie, paid the rent on the flat from time to time and now she was broke. Other, worse, thoughts came to her as she stood waiting for the bus. The black woman had seen what was happening to her. She had looked past the expensively piled-up hair, like a golden beehive, and the fur coat and the expensive bag and shoes. She had seen a woman who had no power to persuade her lover not to buy the house – not to do anything. Why not? Because, Molly supposed, he did not love her. Or, if he did, and she supposed in some ways he did, then it was not the love of people who share their lives and pay real attention to each other's thoughts and feelings. Not like Sid and Ivy, for example. She had her hair done and drank champagne and went to clubs but she was disregarded when it came to anything important – must be, or she would have had some idea, by now, about the sort of work Johnnie did. She was Johnnie's ornament, the focus for his romantic feelings, his lover. But she was worse off than Ivy, who had her say, often loudly, about everything involving Sid or herself.

Behind her she thought she heard one of two middle-aged women, with shopping bags, mutter, "Bit of brass." Molly, pretending not to hear, thought to herself, "That's about right. That's about the truth." Self-protective resentment arose. She thought that if she'd been rich she wouldn't be discussed behind her back at bus stops by worn-out old bags. But a fur coat on a girl like her was still the price of surrendered virtue. Decent women had children and worries and bad girls had fur coats, that was the rule, as it always had been.

Once inside the bus, which smelt of cold, and damp, and stale cigarette smoke, Molly lit a cigarette and brooded. She told herself that you couldn't have everything. Did she want to be tied to a sink, a husband who might turn out to be rotten, a gang of children, all her life? So that, with any luck, when she got to nearly forty she'd be able to go out and get a job in a bread shop, like Ivy, and get herself a few new clothes and start saving up for a spin drier? Johnnie was handsome and sexy and generous. She had a posh flat – what more could anyone ask? Then she remembered what he had done when she was pregnant, remembered how she had covered up his thefts at the club, remembered his girlfriend Amanda. And now, she thought, he was living on the profits made out of slums. It seemed worse, she thought, because he was really only an employee. He was like Nedermann's overseer on a slave plantation – he went about evicting and bullying because someone else was paying him to do it. She decided that Johnnie didn't really understand what he was doing. But it was with a shock that she realized Johnnie had never really been poor, as the Roses had, or Ivy, who could remember being given rice puddings made with water to eat, or Sid, who could recall a winter when he and his brothers had gone to school without shoes on their feet. Even she and Jack and Shirley had seen a few plates of chips in front of them without an accompanying fried egg or sausage. She didn't think Johnnie's mother had ever given him a plate of chips for tea or that he had ever shivered through nights when there not only weren't enough blankets for the beds, but not enough overcoats and jackets to pile on them either. Had Johnnie's mother ever sat in the house with her children telling them to shut up about food until their father came home with the wages and she could dash to the fish and chip shop and buy them some supper? She doubted it. And perhaps that was why he didn't worry about those broken-down houses, or the coughing babies and old ladies dragging themselves up and down damaged staircases.

Suddenly, as if to console her, the vision of Allaun Towers, long and low, built of old red brick, weathered to russet, came into her head. She was a small child, standing in the drive on a summer afternoon, with the canopy of branches overhead making patches of brightness and darkness on the ground. She was looking towards the house, where a setting sun threw light over the roof tiles, turning them brilliant. The whole house glowed in the light. She recalled the sound of her feet on the drive, walking through the dapples made by the light, and the silence, the sound of the birds going to roost, the strangeness of coming from under the last trees at the edge of the drive, into the crescent of gravel in front of the house.

But that was yesterday, she told herself, as she sat on top of the bus. And this was now. She was supposed to be getting married after Christmas. And now she would have to sell the gold bracelet Lord Clover had given her and take some money to Ivy and tell her that she was about to marry Johnnie Bridges. She could imagine what Ivy would say. Which would be worse because she would have to tell Ivy that she could not have Josephine with her. Johnnie did not want her. He had offered to take in Josephine but so reluctantly that Molly knew it would never work. So Ivy would be faced with a daughter who was marrying a man she hated and a granddaughter she would have to continue to look after indefinitely.

Again, her mind switched to the stream, the fields and the dusty country paths in summer. And saw the clouded air and wet pavements of Oxford Street, the people struggling on the pavements to do their Christmas shopping, the lights and glitter of commercial Christmas. "Why does it have to be like this?" she thought to herself.

From the back of her mind somewhere a hard voice told her, "It doesn't have to be like this." She ignored the voice and went on feeling the same.

In the event it was a month after Christmas, and two days before the beginning of the trial of Steven Greene, when pneumonia solved Molly's problem.

Molly had been ill for a week but her feeling of physical weakness had been masked by distress. She had tried to tackle Johnnie about working for Nedermann but he brushed off her arguments and said, all too truly, that she was living well on the proceeds of his work. But he had not liked the challenge or the criticism. He had become brusquer, less generous and less affectionate. And yet he was still eager to marry, although from the way he behaved Molly sometimes thought he disliked her. Because she was so uncertain she suggested they leave the wedding until April, when the weather would be better and they could have a honeymoon in Paris. "Be nice," she had said to him eagerly, hoping to placate him. But she saw him begin to sulk at the delay. It was hardly a surprise when he started coming home late, saying he had been with friends. Perhaps if she had been feeling better she could have coped with this more cheerfully. As it was she wept, felt ill and believed that her depression was causing the sensations of sickness. She began to realize this was not so one day in the flat. That night Johnnie did not come home at all and it was the following morning, as Molly was trying to telephone the doctor, that the doorbell rang. Molly put down the phone and crept along the wall to the door. She got it open to find Ivy there. As Ivy launched into recriminations, "Tracked you down at last!" she said. "No point in expecting a visit from you —" Mary fell. Ivy managed to catch her, dragged her inside and put her on her bed.

"Where's Johnnie?" Molly moaned in delirium. Ivy phoned the doctor, who came and diagnosed pneumonia. Molly would have to go to hospital, he said. "Where's Johnnie?" moaned Molly because women in these situations always call for the men in their lives and, the worse the villain, the more desperately they call, perhaps because he is almost never there. She had a temperature of 104°F and her left lung was very badly affected. "Where's Johnnie?" she called as they put her in the ambulance. Ivy clambered in. "Fetch Johnnie," she said. "All right, love," said Ivy gently, "I'll try to find him later." She caught the ambulanceman's eye. He shook his head sadly. Ivy sighed.

Three days later the trial of Steven Greene began. Mary was in hospital, still almost too weak to move. Johnnie Bridges had gone back to the flat at last and was just asking himself where Molly could be when the doorbell rang.

He did not know who the men were who hit him. The punches, and later the kicks, as he lay on the hall floor, were delivered by three strange men, who circled him viciously. They did not speak to each other and the business was all over in four minutes. It was only as they were leaving, and he lay bleeding and moaning on the carpet, that one turned and said, "That's a present from Jack Waterhouse. There'll be another one if you go near his sister again." It was only then that he realized he recognized the grim-faced man who had kicked him remorselessly as he lay on the floor. Even Ivy had not known that Jack and his two docker brothers-in-law were going to beat up Johnnie Bridges. She was not told about it afterwards, either. She heard the news from a cousin of Lil Messiter's who worked as one of Neder-mann's builders. She was with Sid in the Marquis of Zetland one night when the man said, "Nasty business about Johnnie Bridges' accident."

She had replied automatically, "Don't mention that man's name to me —" when she broke off, recognizing the neutral tone of someone looking for a reaction and said quickly, "What accident? What's happened to him?"

"Got beaten up by some fellers," said Lil's cousin. "Thought you'd have heard about it."

He was asking if she knew who was responsible and Ivy, immediate-ly suspecting the perpetrator was her son Jack, said, "No – no – I had no idea. Was he badly hurt?"

"It didn't do him any good," said the man.

"Here, Sid," Ivy called to Sid, who was coming back from the bar with some drinks. "What's all this about Johnnie Bridges? Have you heard anything about it?"

"I heard something about him getting his nose broken," Sid re-marked, putting the drinks down on the table. "Not surprising, I suppose. A man like that's always got a lot of enemies."

Ivy knew immediately that Sid had known about the attack on Johnnie and that Jack had been involved. She took a drink from her glass of gin and lime and said, "Been mixed up with all kinds of people, Johnnie Bridges." And Lil's cousin knew better than to say any more.

Molly's hopes that Johnnie would come to see her in hospital gradually dwindled. It was Ferenc Nedermann who came to see her several times, bringing flowers, after she was over the worst of her illness. When she asked he said that Johnnie was away on business. Still hoping he would be back when she arrived home, she was brought from the hospital by Nedermann. Ivy opened the door and bustled her off to bed. There were roses in a vase in the room but, by now, she was too wise to imagine they had been bought by Johnnie. Ivy came in with a tray of tea and demanded efficiently, "Do you want to sit up?" Then she plumped up the pillows behind her daughter, poured out her tea and said, "You'd better thank Mr Nedermann, Molly. While you were in hospital he paid the rent. He said not to tell you but I said you'd want to know so you could pay it back."

Molly, still weak and shocked by having had a serious illness, replied, "What? The rent? I don't understand. Where's Johnnie?"

"I'm sorry, love," Ivy said. "I'm really sorry." She looked pityingly at Molly.

"Well – what happened? Where is he?" asked Molly. Her head was spinning now. She thought she could not bear any more.

"He's scarpered," Ivy told her. "He's done a bunk. I'm really sorry, love. His clothes aren't here any more – I've looked. Jack and his wife's brothers gave him a good drubbing before he went."

"Oh, Mum," moaned Molly. "Who asked them to interfere? I could kill Jack, I really could."

"You could have died, Molly," said her mother. "And all the time Johnnie was living with a woman in Shepherd's Bush – some kind of a tart, calls herself a model. You'd been in that hospital a week and he never came near you. Jack found out what was going on and lost his temper. What Jack did made no difference – but you knew what he was. You'd had plenty of experience of it before," she added remorselessly. "Now – you drink your tea and thank Mr Nedermann when he comes in. He's been really helpful."

Molly, who had been preparing herself, although she did not realize it, for this moment, hauled herself up on her pillows and said, "My God – I'm penniless. What am I going to do now?"

Ivy sat down on the edge of the bed, looking approvingly at Molly.

275

She said, "I'm relieved you're thinking like that. What we thought was that you'd better move back into number 4. Permanently. You'll have to take Josephine on yourself. You can get a little job. I can't go on working and looking after her forever and, anyway, me and your dad are saving up to move to a nicer place – Beckenham, or Bromley, we were thinking. It'll be easier for you now Josie's going to school. And it's time you took on some of your own responsibilities."

Molly looked at her mother and nodded, wearily. She would have to do what Ivy suggested. Ivy had mothered her child because she had been too young to mother Josephine herself. Ivy had given her a good run. And now Ivy was tired of it. And she, Molly, was broke and had to do something.

"You might as well stop here," her mother told her. "You're all paid up until the end of the month and the landlord's putting in a bathroom. He'll be finished in a fortnight."

"Make a change from bathing in the sink," Molly said gloomily.

"It seems hard at the moment," Ivy said. "But it's swings and roundabouts, isn't it? You have to take the rough with the smooth."

Molly shut her eyes and nodded. She thought resentfully that all her life Ivy had been dedicated to proving that there was no way but hers – husband, children, Meakin Street and poverty. Here she lay, weak, abandoned and broke, the daughter who had tried to escape and failed. She had lost. Ivy had won. A few angry tears crept down her cheeks.

Nedermann knocked at the door and came in. Seeing the tears he said, "Come on, Molly. None of this. So the future looks bleak – it sometimes does. At these times we need courage."

Molly tried not to show how angry she was about all these pieces of philosophy. Instead she sniffed and said, with as much gratitude as she could muster, "I hear you paid the rent. It was very kind of you – I'll pay you back, of course." And bang goes Sir Christopher Wylie's Victorian ring, she thought, hoping that the stones in it were rubies and not garnets.

"You don't need to," Nedermann told her. "I took the money from Johnnie's wages when I fired him last week."

Molly stared at him. "His old tricks," Nedermann explained. "I knew it was happening but he had sorted out a lot of problems – income tax, trouble with councils – he even straightened out some of the accounts. I had to thank him for that. So I let it go on. Maybe when the right time came I would have warned him and kept him on. But then he got careless about coming to do his work –" He looked round questioningly at Ivy, who said, "She knows all about it."

"Well, then," Nedermann said, "I'm sorry but you know the reason – the woman was paying – Johnnie relaxed. Next thing – Johnnie's here on Wednesday but where is he on Thursday? I can't stand that. Also – he got a little greedy. A few hundreds – yes. But thousands of pounds and always increasing – I can't do the sums but I can feel the blood leaving my body like any man can – a coloured woman came to me and told me that Johnnie was all set to get me to pay £6,500 for a house worth £4,000 and then split the difference with the owner. That way they would both make over a thousand pounds from me."

"Was that Pilsutski's house?" asked Molly.

"That's right," Nedermann said. "What do you know about this?" For a moment she knew he suspected she was involved in the fraud.

"I went there with Johnnie one day. I met the woman," Molly said. "Did you reward her?"

"I gave her a bigger flat in the house," Nedermann said. "Two rooms – own toilet on the landing – the same rent. That's my policy – I can be generous to people who are loyal. The rest – let them run for a little while, then –" He made a chopping gesture with one of his big, stubby hands. Mary hoped that the black woman's reward had not been the flat of the two old sisters. "The trouble with Johnnie is," Nedermann went on, "that he betrayed me for so little. I paid him well. If he had been honest I would have given him more than he could ever have taken. They're all the same, these soft boys. But," he said, looking at Molly's face, "you're tired – and I think you still have a little weakness for him – yes? You should be careful of that. He has hurt you twice – how many times? – now? Once is an accident – twice, it looks like masochism." Molly did not recognize his heavy foreign pronunciation of the word, which she had seldom heard anyway. She said fiercely, "I hate his guts, now."

"Be careful of that, too," he said.

After he had gone Ivy cooked some lunch for Molly. She told her where everything was and added that the woman in the flat across the hall would help her if she needed it. As she left she said, "I don't like leaving you but you can't live at number 4, with half the walls out, and there isn't much room with Sid and me. I think you're better off here. It's quieter. I'll be back tomorrow." And she put her coat on and left. "Shall I get you a paper and drop it in?" she called from the hall.

"No, thanks, mum," called Molly, wondering why her mother thought she would want a newspaper.

She lay back on her pillows unhappily. Back to Meakin Street – again, she thought. It was like a nightmare – every time you thought you'd escaped, there you were, back again. But if Ivy was handing back Josephine she had no choice. She'd have to live narrowly and get an ordinary badly paid job with short hours, and bring up her child. Without Johnnie. It should have been a relief that he'd gone but, somehow, it wasn't. You're like some stupid tart, she told herself, pining after some pimp who mistreats her and lives off her money. Not only that, but he'd wanted to marry her and she'd hesitated – probably just as well he's gone, she thought. Probably just as well you have to get back to Meakin Street. Like a butterfly when the summer's over. And with that thought she went to sleep. She heard a high clear voice singing in what she now knew was French. She heard birds singing. There was an old, grey stone building and, somewhere, a clump of willows with grey branches hanging down, like long hair.

The phone rang in the other room and she got up and went to it. She thought it was Johnnie. It was not. It was Wendy Valentine.

"He's dead, you bitch. He's dead," she cried, through her sobs. "Why didn't you help him like you said?"

"What? Wendy?" Molly said in confusion. "Wendy – who's dead?"

"You're a cold bitch, aren't you, Molly Flanders," Wendy said. "When it comes down to it you aren't there, are you. Now he's dead – poor Steven – poor Steve." Her voice broke again.

"Oh my God," Molly cried. "What's been happening! Are you sure he's dead? I don't believe it. I just don't believe it. There wasn't anything wrong with him."

"Didn't have to be, did there," Wendy shouted. "He killed himself, that's what he did. Killed himself." There was a long silence. Wendy, horrified at the meaning of the words, just cried. Molly stood on the carpet in the living room, holding the phone. It must be true. Wendy must be telling her the truth. Then Wendy said, more calmly, "I just want you to know I'll never forget this, Molly – never. You said all these things about turning up in court to speak for him and you never did, did you? And when I ring the flat, over and over again, there isn't anybody there, is there? Left town, hadn't you? Not getting involved. Who paid you, that's what I'd like to know? And I hope you spend the rest of your life wondering if it was worth it."

"You'll have to tell me, Wendy," Molly said desperately. "You'll

278

have to tell me. I've been in hospital. Wendy, I don't know –"
Her voice broke and she said, in a low voice, "I can't – if only I'd
known –"

But Wendy was too full of rage and pain to listen. "I've been in
hospital, Wendy. If only I'd known, Wendy," she mimicked. "You just
shut your trap now, Molly Flanders. You've got nothing to say any
more. But if I ever see you again I'll see you don't forget it. That's a
promise, Molly. You just wait." And the phone went down.

Molly rang Frames and asked if Arnie Rose was there. She still did
not quite believe what Wendy had said. She might be hysterical, mad,
on drugs – anything. Arnie Rose came on the line, sounding friendly. It
seemed he had decided to overlook his grudge about the night when he
had caught her with Johnnie and thrown her out of the club. "Hallo,
Molly," he said expansively. "Heard you hadn't been well. Glad to see
you're back in action again."

"It's Steven," Molly burst out. "Wendy Valentine rang up and said
he was dead. She blamed me."

"Stupid cow," Arnie said. "What could you have had to do with it?"
All Molly knew was that his words confirmed that Steven was dead.
She said, "He is dead, then? What happened?"

"Topped himself in his cell," Arnie told her. "Nasty tragedy. He
didn't have to do that. He'll be a bad loss. Shocking thing, though, isn't
it?"

"Why?" Molly half-cried. "Why did he do it?"

"He was started on a two-year sentence for poncing, wasn't he?"
Arnie said. "He couldn't face the thought of it, a man like him. So
while he was still in Brixton, waiting for transfer, he hung himself. I'm
sorry, Moll. I know you were fond of him. We all were. But I still think
it was a stupid thing to do. Two years, with remission – he'd have been
out in eighteen months. Not as if it was fifteen or twenty years, is it? I
mean, if a man's faced with that you can understand him doing
something desperate."

"He felt everybody had let him down," Molly said sadly. "Even me.
I didn't stand up for him in court. I was in hospital. I didn't know
anything about it."

"Doubt if you could have done anything, Moll," Arnie said. "This
whole business wasn't normal. Cases like this, police evidence is
everything – who the coppers saw going in and out of a certain address
and how often – who gave what to who on a corner – that's the form.
Practically all they had here was Wendy and Carol trying to remember

if one of them lent Steve his rent or he lent it to them. It was ridiculous –
a travesty. Somebody somewhere wanted Steven Greene done, so they
did him. You or I or the Archangel Gabriel couldn't have saved him."

"Didn't they ask you anything?" Molly said.

"No – that's the other thing. First thing you do with a case like that
is ask the landlord what he thinks is going on. Landlord here's a friend
of mine – you know – but they never come near him. Not that it would
have been nice if they had but, the fact is, nobody asked him to dance.
Not a whisper. Same with you – no papers, no subpoena, no nothing.
Because –" he paused. "They didn't want to know what we had to say.
We knew he hadn't done it, that's why. Or, if he had, not a lot of it, so
to speak. See what I'm getting at, Molly darling. If you'd known about
it and you hadn't been in hospital gravely ill, you'd have had a hell of a
job getting anyone to listen to you. They had to smear him, that's my
opinion. He had to be shown up a real swine, living off women.
Because why? Because then, whatever he said, nobody would be
listening. Take the word of a convicted ponce? Good heavens, my
dear," mimicked Arnie, "who could believe a man like that?"

Only part of Molly could believe all this. The picture of the world it
presented was too harsh. She said, "I don't know, Arnie –"

"Take my word for it, Moll," he said. "That's the way it was. He
knew too much about the bishop's knickers. And not just that – I think
there was more."

"Mm?" Molly said.

"Those geezers from the Special Branch have been like flies around
this club," Arnie said. "We even had a burglary. A burglary!" He
snorted. "I ask you, is it likely? Who's going to come round and burgle
the Rose brothers? No normal villain would come near this place.
He'd know what would happen to him if he did. So I'm supposed to
think, when they tell me the flat upstairs has been turned over, 'Oh
dear, oh dear. A naughty burglar has gone in my upstairs flat and tried
to steal something.' I'm supposed to get on the phone to my insurance
company – anyway, they made a dog's breakfast of the place, trying to
make it look like a robbery but I know the trademark of those boys like
I know your pretty face, Moll. Greene knew more than the colour of
the Lord Chancellor's knickers. He'd been dabbling in a little bit of
espionage, stands to reason. He got a few contacts with people in the
government – then there was that Russian diplomat who was knocking off Wendy Valentine. So one side or the other gets in touch with
him – and that's why the flatfoots are nosing round the premises.

Course, they're hopeless. I'd rather send my old granny out to do a robbery. Greene never had anything mind you – he wasn't the sort." Molly still said nothing. Arnie's voice tailed off and he said, "Well, Moll. A rotten business. We'll all miss him."

Molly sniffed. She said, "That's right, Arnie. Thanks for telling me, Arnie."

She spent a bad night, imagining the feelings Greene must have experienced before taking his life in a prison cell. She saw the rope – but would it have been his tie? – round his neck, the swollen eyes bulging, his suffused face. These visions were endless. She got up and swallowed a glass of whisky, which only made it worse. Now, the horror of Jim's death confused itself with that of Steven Greene. She was quite alone in the flat. There was no one she could turn to and as the night went on she thought she might go mad. The horror of her imaginings was bad enough. What made it all worse was the guilt. If only she had been told about the trial. If only she could have appeared to defend Steven. If only she had been sensible enough to see his solicitor in person and insist on giving evidence, instead of believing that the police would call her when she was needed. Perhaps, she thought, she had been called to give evidence, but the letter was lost. At two-thirty in the morning she was searching the flat for a letter which might have been mislaid or put away by Johnnie when he came to collect his clothes. And at six-thirty, unable to bear the thought of another night alone in the empty flat, she packed her clothes and took a taxi to Meakin Street. Never mind the state of the house, she thought, she would collect Josephine and move in immediately. For good. But this was not what happened.

It comes back to me very vividly, almost like a scene from a well-remembered film – the day of Steven Greene's funeral. It was, in fact, rather like that – the leafless trees all round the cemetery, the tombstones, white marble or black slabs, the grey sky and the sombre clothing of the mourners were all reminiscent of a scene from a spy film. The fact that I was keeping my distance from the mourners – virtually skulking about at the back – only added, for me, to that impression. Needless to say, I had not wanted to come. My father had not even suggested it. But the newspaper publicity around the affair and the fact that we both knew that Molly was involved, meant that one of us ought really to attend. My father did not want to ask me. I knew that if I did not go he would. I decided that rather than allow an elderly man to stand about in a graveyard in mid-winter I had better volunteer. He had covered me with a story that I was from the Home Office. Nevertheless it was hardly in my interest to press forward and join the other mourners. To begin with, my story was untrue and, if it had been, it is not likely that I would have been a comforting or a popular figure at the funeral of a man who had hanged himself in custody. It was a gloomy day, in a gloomy place, and I was far from happy about being there.

Greene's poor father, who actually was a clergyman – and that, I suppose, was how Greene out of perversity came by his peculiar, Crowleyesque philosophy – had not been able to face burying his son in his parish in Dorset. Indeed, the church authorities might not have permitted the church burial of a notorious suicide. Nevertheless, he bravely conducted the service at the graveside, in the sort of biting wind which leads the mourners on such occasions to remove their guilt at still being alive by saying that after standing about in such weather they'll probably get ill themselves and be back in a fortnight to bury each other. Not that there was very much of that kind of mournful jocularity on this occasion. Indeed, the shockingly few mourners were heavily outnumbered by photographers and reporters, which was another reason for my skulking at the back, among the tombstones. I had no wish to appear on the front page of a newspaper. Among the few genuine attenders of the funeral I saw Simon Tate and some girls I did not recognize. One of them called Carol, I believe, had come unsuitably dressed in a tight, black suit, black stockings and high heeled shoes. She also wore a little black hat with a veil. It was not her fault, I'm sure, poor girl, that she had come dressed like the classic French widow accused of poisoning her husband. She certainly looked unhappy enough, in spite of her clothes. Wendy Valentine looked ill. She wore old shoes and an untidy fur coat. Her hair was ruffled and her face thin and pale. Martin Pellman, Greene's defence counsel, was there and the Rose brothers. Meanwhile the Greene women – mother and sister – stood at the grave's head, near Mr Greene, and well away from these others, people they did not know and whom they obviously suspected of being part of the London life which had led to Greene's death.

What impressed me most, in fact, was the arrival, rather late, of Lord Clover. By attending the funeral he must have known he was branding himself as a user of Greene's dubious services. I had heard myself that he was part of the conspiracy to nobble the man and get him sent to jail – yet, at the last moment, when he saw how much further things had gone than the conspirators intended, he must have felt remorse and decided, however futilely, to appear at the funeral, publicly associating himself with the dead man, a convicted pimp and, now, a suicide. He stood unflinchingly through the flashes of the cameras pointed in his direction. His photograph was in every British newspaper next day and in plenty of Continental ones too. It was a gesture which put a stop to his further political advancement, but it may have shamed many of his friends, who had not seen fit to come to the funeral of the man they had used. In fact, hiding away from the cameras as I was, I also felt slightly ashamed.

Clover stood beside Molly whose head was bowed almost all the time. It was a depressing scene. The mourners round the graveside consisted of the dead man's family, including a clergyman and a lawyer, the manager of a gambling house, some gangsters and some whores. It was like a highwayman's execution – it was the Beggars' Opera. The last character from that sort of scene is, I suppose, the landlord. And the man I did not recognize, standing opposite Molly and Clover at the graveside, was, of course, that – Ferenc Nedermann, in a thick black coat and a black silk scarf.

I was standing too far off to hear the service but I certainly heard the earth falling on Greene's coffin and the outbreak of sobs from the women when they heard that final sound. When that was over the group broke up uneasily. I saw the Rose brothers step forward together to shake the Reverend Mr Greene's hand and offer a few, no doubt well chosen, words of consolation. I had every confidence in their good behaviour. Formalities like this are taken seriously by men like the Roses. They are accustomed to saying the right thing in circumstances which might make the rest of us feel tongue-tied – where the departed might, perhaps, have died in dubious circumstances or have led a life which will not stand much examination. I don't suppose the Greene family, who were being assured how the Rose brothers had liked and respected their son, were aware that they were with the most feared criminals in London. I don't suppose they were aware of anything, except that they were burying their son and brother and that cameras kept flashing in their direction. After that they were borne away by Martin Pellman. Clover, having spoken to Mr and Mrs Greene, also disappeared. The rest of the party, who, after all, knew each other well, went to a nearby pub. I should not have gone, since there was a danger I would be asked who I was, but by that time I was, frankly, in need of a drink. I sat in a corner while the mourners talked to each other, and the reporters, in another group, made forays towards them to try and make contact.

They were refused every time since some had no desire to talk to the press and others had been signed up exclusively by one paper. Finally I saw Norman Rose say a few words to one of the newshounds. He went away and told the others. From then on Greene's friends were not pestered. I watched them all but mostly I watched Molly Waterhouse. When I saw her talking to Ferenc Nedermann I had no idea that it was her and then, in the pub after Greene's funeral, when she struck her deal with him. If I'd known what the beautiful and still comparatively unhardened girl was doing I think I would have set light to the public house to prevent it. On the other hand, if she had not gone with him I doubt if she would have been the woman she is today.

"I don't know what you mean," Molly said, half-conscious of an argument further down the bar between the landlord and a photographer who wanted to take pictures of the mourners. She had heard from Johnnie months before, that Nedermann was known never to go after women, although he visited a prostitute in a flat in Gerrard Street on Tuesday and Thursday afternoons. She was wondering why he had again asked her to move in with him, since he had not wanted to live with a woman for many years. She was even more baffled because he gave her no impression that he desired her. She was stunned, too. Everything seems unreal after the burial of the dead. Nedermann was looking at her intently. "I'm making you the offer," he said in a low, but firm voice. "You move in and I'll look after you. You and the child."

"Josie?" Molly asked.

"Who else?" he said. "The child. I want the child."

Molly, in search of something which might be real, since the conversation with Nedermann, coming so soon after the burial, seemed like a dream, searched the length of the bar for some reality. She scanned the reporters, the group at the bar, where the laughter kept rising, and then hushing itself when the party thought of why they were together. She even stared, sightlessly, at the tall, thin young man in the corner, with his cowslick of fairish hair falling over his eyes. He looked at her, then looked away, as if he did not want to meet her gaze.

Still confused, Molly held out her glass to Nedermann, who leaned over the bar and tried to attract the barman's attention. While he was occupied in this way she tried to work out why Nedermann made such a point of asking that Josephine should live with them. Had he told her something about his having a wife and child? That something had happened to them? With her eyes on his broad back she thought, using a phrase borrowed from Steven Greene, "He's one of the walking wounded."

She took the drink from Nedermann and swigged from the glass. She didn't want to think about moving in with him now, not after a funeral. But perhaps if she did not decide quickly he would withdraw his offer. And it was worth considering. On one side of the argument lay Meakin Street, the part-time job, the neighbours enjoying the fact that she had come down in the world. There lay the work, the straightened circumstances, the limitations to life for herself and Josephine. On the other hand, life with Nedermann meant security for herself and the child. Josephine would have a better life. And this time, she vowed, she would save money and, when she had served it, hang on to it. There would be no more Bridges, or his like, no more rash spending. But the problem was that she did not love Nedermann. In some ways she felt she did not even like him. She certainly did not like the way he made his living. If she shared his money she would share the way in which he got it. Yet she was sorry for him. She could feel his desperation — he would not lightly take up with another woman and walk out leaving her ill and helpless.

It may have been this last idea, for Johnnic Bridges had damaged her badly, worse than she knew — which led her to say, still in a voice lacking her usual decision, "Yes, I'll come." Nedermann leaned forward and kissed her on the brow.

Further up the bar the Roses, the girls, even Simon Tate, were getting drunk. They were recalling now, some of Greene's most famous exploits. Wendy was saying, "So he leans forward and picks them off the floor and says, 'I believe these are yours, my Lord Bishop.'" They all roared with laughter. "Oh, Gawd," spluttered Arnie Rose. "The Bishop's undies — oh, he was a lad, old Steve."

"When?" Molly asked.

"— down at Bray when he caught me floating in the pool in my birthday suit, playing doctors and nurses with that big, black African," came the voice of a girl. "And he says —"

"Today, if you like," Nedermann said.

"— now you've proved you haven't got any racial prejudice how about something for the folks back home."

Mary said, under the laughter, "All right." Glancing at the others she said, in a low voice, "You have to remember he was kind to me. He talked to me. He gave me books to read. He wasn't just a sex machine, like they're making out. He did drawings. He knew about art. They're carrying on about him as if what they made him out to be in court was true. They'll forget what he was really like soon. He'll be just a label stuck on a lot of dirty stories."

"Come on," Nedermann said. "We'll go for the child."

Some might say — some did — why go off like that, with a man you didn't love? It must've been money. Though I've seen a lot of women do a lot of things like that for money, and a few men, too. Sometimes they can stick a coat of whitewash over it — a wedding, or an attack of true love covers the situation nicely. But there's often money at the back of it though the people involved don't say so, sometimes don't even admit it to themselves. When I told Josephine about it, when she was older she said practically no working-class girl of my times had the idea she could look after herself. No wonder, she said, what with the faulty contraception and rotten jobs — I'd lost my only chance when I never bothered with my education. Not like Shirley. Of course the other difference between Shirley and me is that I was the good-looker. Shirley was a pretty girl but I couldn't sit down on a bus without one of the men starting to get into conversation, asking me out or whatever. It wasn't too easy to tread the boring straight and narrow when fellows kept on offering tempting alternatives. Like Nedermann. He offered me a good life, protection for me and the child — and love. Love — it was more like devotion. I could tell it though I didn't really know the reasons for it. That came out later. But Josephine says she's never forgotten that day when she watched her dolls' pram, all piled high with her toys, being hoisted into a Rolls Royce by a man in a peaked cap. She was only five and I had to stand beside her telling her over and over again that we were going in the car, too. She had this suspicion the car might start up suddenly and drive away with the pram and all her toys. She was in her best red velvet dress and patent leather shoes. She wouldn't put her coat on because it hid her dress. She had all these brown curls flying about and her great big brown eyes were open wide with all the excitement. Ivy was standing there looking doubtful and holding Josephine's coat. Ferenc had impressed her. I knew that. It was because he was older, and looked respectable and, probably, she could sense that he would love Josephine. I can still remember how she took a flying leap into the car that day and began to wave out of the window like the Queen. Ivy was stuck between approving and disapproving, and crying a bit now Josephine was really going. She didn't know what to do with herself. She handed Josie's little case in and said, "Come back soon, Josie." Josie didn't give a flicker of emotion. She just said, "I'm going to live in a big house. I'll have flounces round my dressing-table." She was obsessed with frills and flounces at the time, Josephine. I was so embarrassed that she hadn't said goodbye properly to Ivy that I hit her as soon as we moved off. I must have said something nasty to her, as well. I'll never forget the look on Ferenc's face when he saw Josephine start to sniffle. I might as well have hit him. That was what it was all about, of course.

Ivy was horrified when Molly came back to visit her a week later. While Josephine was out, taking her new doll to show to a friend, she and her daughter sat in the kitchen, talking.

"Oh, God, Molly. I don't know," said Ivy. "You mean you're standing in for his dead wife and baby? That's why he wants you? Molly – it's unnatural."

"I know," said her daughter.

"Here – give me one of your cigarettes," said Ivy, who was supposed to be giving up smoking. She lit up and puffed. "I don't know," she said. "Nothing's ever straightforward where you're concerned." A thought suddenly struck her. "Here," she said. "Where did you spend last night?"

"Orme Square, of course," her daughter told her.

"*Where*, I asked," Ivy said remorselessly.

"In the spare room," Molly answered reluctantly.

Ivy puffed out more smoke and said, "I thought as much." There was a silence. Then she said, "Well – it may work out, I suppose he's better than Johnnie Bridges."

"Josephine's got ruffles on everything," Molly said. "I'll say that. If you could get ruffled shoes, she'd have them. There's nothing Ferenc won't do for us."

Ivy looked at her. "There's something he won't do for you," she told her daughter.

1958

The spring of 1958 seemed to Molly a long time in coming. For months after she moved in the grass in Hyde Park, opposite the house, stayed coarse, dull and tussocky. The trees remained skeletons against a dull sky. She collected Josephine every day from the smart school in Knightsbridge she now attended and brought her home across the park. The little girl, in her green coat and hat, with a green and blue band on it, skipped ahead of her. Mary followed in her smart fur and high boots. Then she would let them both through the park gates, across the main road to the well appointed house in Orme Square. She would make a snack for Josephine and start to cook dinner. By watching the cook Nedermann, who was fussy about his food, had hired to come in on three evenings a week, she was beginning to learn how to cook. She found out how to use wine, garlic and spices in the food she prepared. Nedermann took her shopping. She began to select furniture, curtains, even her own clothing, with more taste than she was accustomed to employ. In the meantime, Josephine, another fast learner, was intoxicated by her new school, and the smart uniform which went with it. She took ballet lessons, talked in an upper-class voice and became what Molly privately described as a proper little madam. Ferenc Nedermann was delighted with the progress of his woman and child. Molly, keen to please, was happy he felt satisfied, but the knowledge that she was a symbol of security and regeneration for him, not a woman, made her feel impoverished. There were times when she would see a couple walking hand in hand in the park and think, "It doesn't matter if they're married to other people or she's pregnant and doesn't dare tell her parents or even if they're going to get married, but he'll knock her about. None of that matters because now, this minute, they've got what they've got – and I haven't." Nedermann gave her a bank account and put money in it for her. Molly took some out and hid it in the Post Office. As a precaution, without telling him, she kept up the rent on the house in Meakin Street.

One day she opened Nedermann's safe in the study – she had not been Johnnie Bridges' girlfriend for nothing. The amount of money in there startled her. There must have been three or four thousand pounds, all in dirty notes thrust into used envelopes or done up with rubber bands. There were also many documents which she did not stop to examine. What she, without knowing, was looking for was the clue to the mystery, a brown envelope on the bottom shelf – an old photograph of a woman of about her own age. The woman held a little girl by the hand. She wore a black coat with a fur collar. Her blonde hair was scraped up in a bun at the back of her head. Her long, unmade-up face bore an expression of kindness and patience. The child, also in a long coat, was thin and also blonde. She looked rather like her mother.

Molly stared at the photograph. She checked the back of the photograph and found an address in Prague. So this must be Mrs Nedermann and the child. Yet the woman was unlike Molly. She was small and slight, her legs looked a little bowed, her teeth protruded. She had a modest, even apologetic air. She was more like a woman from Meakin Street, thought Molly, a woman like Lil Messiter, who has come from a large family where there has never been enough to eat, a woman weakened by over-work during her growing years, the kind who is always tired, always slaving for others, and feels her only right to life is earned by service. The child in the photograph seemed to share the timidity and lack of strength. They wouldn't have lasted long in a concentration camp, Molly thought.

Later, she became indignant, after she had put the picture back in the envelope and shut the safe. She was sitting in the living room, with its pink-shaded lamps and the large chintz-covered sofas and chairs from Heal's, when her pity ceased and her rage grew. It was the rage of the rejected, the anger of a sexually frustrated woman. She had embraced Nedermann, she had even crept into the large room where he slept alone and been told, wearily, that he was tired. She had tried to talk about the situation.

He had only said, "Molly – Molly. I want you as you are. I want nothing more. I want nothing from you." She had not been able to make him understand that she wanted him to make love to her. Somewhere he had learned that sex was a burden for women and bought from those who were selling the favour for money. Molly, in her indignation, began to think that perhaps he had not acquired that thought during hard times as a penniless emigré in Britain, but from the life he had led with poor, crushed Mrs Nedermann.

She found she was drumming her feet angrily on the dark pink carpet under her feet. She had spent two months in this house, she thought, learning how to be a posh man's wife, not knowing the woman she was impersonating had never existed. Czech or English, Molly knew an old coat, an undernourished face and the humble expression of the poor when she saw them. Nedermann, she decided, in one flash of intuition, had been making her be, not the wife, probably dead, whom he had once had. She was trying to be the wife he wished he had had – the bloody sod, she said to herself. Never mind Josephine's ruffles, we're leaving tomorrow. I'll have it out with him tonight.

It was at this point that the doorbell rang. Simon Tate stood on the step. "Moll," he said. "Just passing. I thought I'd call on the offchance – is it inconvenient?"

Molly was very pleased to see Simon's long, thin figure, his pale face and beaky nose.

"Come in," she said. "Don't stand in the cold."

"Phew," he said, after she had taken his coat and led him into the living-room. "Very nice." Then, approaching a picture which hung on the wall he said, in an impressed tone, "*Very* nice. Where did this come from?"

"Ferenc took it in settlement of a debt," Molly explained. The picture was a small portrait of a woman of the eighteenth century. She stood in parkland, with a dog at her feet.

"Not bad," said Simon Tate. "Not bad at all. Well, Moll," he said, swinging round. "Aren't you going to offer me a drink?"

Molly, knowing that Ferenc, who mistrusted alcohol and its effects, would disapprove of this afternoon drinking, said gleefully, "Right you are. How's tricks? What's happening at the Club?"

"Same as usual," he said. "Fortunes made and lost – no soap in the ladies' – gentlemanly disputes on the pavement. I see you fell on your feet again, Moll."

"Courted at the funeral – I might have known the rest would be the same," Molly said disconsolately.

Simon regarded her sulky face and said, "Moll – aren't you rather looking a gift horse in the teeth?"

"Long story," was all Molly said. Trying to be cheerful, she asked Simon for more news of the Club and, finally, unable to help herself, demanded if there was any word of Johnnie Bridges. Simon, looking as if he had hoped she wouldn't ask, said, "Sorry, Moll. He's on remand. I think it's going to be all up with handsome Johnnie for about a year. Just as well, perhaps. You wouldn't want him coming round here making approaches to you now you're so well set up." What he meant was that he knew she might succumb to Johnnie again, if only from boredom.

"What's he done?" asked Molly. "Another robbery?"

Simon hesitated. "Sorry again, Moll. Poncing. He was really doing what Steven Greene was supposed to have done. He was running a few girls in the West End – Marylebone." He paused. "From what I hear he wasn't a bad thief but I suppose that's an easier life than thieving if you're what's known as a bit of a ladies' man."

Molly was shocked. But she said resolutely, "He never did really like women. Just pretended to. No man who *liked* women could treat them like that."

Simon, pouring two gin and tonics and handing one to her, said: "We've been friends for a long time, Molly – you don't look happy. What's the trouble?"

"Nothing," Molly said. "They won't be too nice to Johnnie in jail."

"No," agreed Simon.

"Have you seen Bassie at all?" she enquired.

"He's living with a writer in Morocco," Simon told her. "Come on, Molly – all I see here is a bored housewife. Tell the truth – what's wrong?"

"I'll have to get out, that's what's wrong," Molly suddenly declared. "I'm pining to get back to Meakin Street, horrible as it is. This place is a nightmare. He doesn't – take any interest in me. I'm a hostess and a furniture polisher. I'm just here to impersonate his dead wife, that's all, and Josephine's being given the sun and the moon and the stars as well because he wants his dead daughter back. So I'm like a ghost – and it's worse –" Then she told him about her robbery of the safe and the photograph of the woman she was replacing. "We weren't even the same kind of woman – never could have been. I feel rotten because I know while they were starving to death in concentration camps I was eating currant cake in the country – but I can't stand it any longer."

Simon referred to what she had not directly told him. "You must be using the wrong scent, or something," he said. "If you had a more normal life none of this would matter. You don't love him of course, that's a hindrance. You loved weak Johnnie Bridges. You'd better be careful of that tendency. That sort'll always drag you down. The Queen of England couldn't afford them."

Molly put her head in her hands. "I feel a fool," she said. "It looked all right at the time. I'm fond of Ferenc. I don't like how he makes his living but I am fond of him, whatever you think. But while it's like this I can't go on. Now I'll have to drag back to Meakin Street after two months. My poor mum and dad – how can they explain me away? Supposing it was Josephine doing all this? I'd send her for mental treatment."

It was partly the news about Johnnie which had depressed her. The knowledge that she had invested so much time and passion into a relationship with a man who later found it possible to take money from prostitutes – and Molly knew that meant treating them with a subtle mixture of brutality and faked love – was discouraging. It threw as much doubt on her as it did on Johnnie. He must have offered her the same bait that he later offered to his girls and she, like them, had taken it.

"It might help to get a job," Simon suggested. "Perhaps things would look better if you had another interest."

"Ferenc wouldn't let me get away with that," Molly told him. "He thinks a woman's place is in the home. Anyway, I'm not that bored – I'm learning all these new dishes and so forth. It's no more monotonous than standing in that club night after night saying '*Faites vos jeux*,' and shoving bits of celluloid around with a rake."

"Gets lonelier, though," suggested Simon.

"That's a fact," Molly agreed, but knew that half the loneliness she felt came from living with a man who did not love her.

"I don't know what to do," she confessed. "Unless it's Meakin Street. Perhaps I'd be better off in the country. Once I'm back in Meakin Street I'll decide whether to see if that job at Allaun Towers is still open."

"Tom Allaun's not improving," Simon said. Molly looked at him sharply. His tone had been edgy and she guessed Tom had upset him badly.

"What's he done?" she asked.

Simon, about to tell her, changed his mind. "Just this and that," he said.

After he had gone Molly was rather drunk. She sent a taxi to get

Josephine from school and sat her in front of the television. And by the time Nedermann came home, earlier than expected, she was seated in front of the open safe, crying, with the photograph of his wife and child back in her hand again. She looked up at him, startled, but without her usual fear of his criticisms. She knew, now, she was leaving. The reopening of the safe and the taking of the photograph were like a private farewell. But instead of bursting into exclamations and reproaches about the burgled safe and the exposed photograph Nedermann stood still just inside the door regarding her gravely. Then he said, in a low voice, "You understand – it was a long time ago. I asked you to come here, and Josephine. I wanted to get back the old days. But the longer you and Josephine have been here, the more different you seem. I am sorry – it was selfish. Stupid, also. An old dream."

"We'll go," she said, from the floor. "I plan to go. Tomorrow. We've both made a mistake. I shouldn't have opened your safe –"

"I always thought you might be able to do that."

"Did you think I already had?" she asked.

"Perhaps," he said. "It's an old safe. I guessed you might have learned –"

"You trusted me with all that money?" she asked.

"I didn't think you'd rob me," he said, as if that were the least of his worries. "No – I didn't worry about the money," he added sadly.

He took off his black overcoat and his gloves. He folded the coat neatly and put it over the back of a chair. He stood, a short, thickset, middle-aged man in an open doorway and said, "I love you." Even then there was something unnatural, Molly felt, about his declaration. It did not spring from him, as it might have done from a younger man. It was as if he stated a grave fact. Then he groped for a chair he could not see and fell into it, weeping. His shoulders heaved, he buried his head in his hands. Molly went to him, to comfort him.

That night they slept together for the first time. He was a tentative lover at first, shy, almost afraid of damaging her or letting himself go. As she lay beside him that night Molly felt little satisfaction. But there was something in his bulk and in the sad candour of his love for her which made her feel at once protective towards him and protected herself.

True to form, she was back at Ivy's a week later brandishing a large diamond ring and saying that she was getting married. She expected her family to be pleased that she was marrying a successful man and providing a father and a good home for Josephine. They were not.

"Can I be a bridesmaid, Moll?" asked Shirley.

"Not with them spots," her older sister remarked cruelly. Shirley rushed out of the room in tears. "It's in a registry office anyway," Molly called up the stairs. The reply was an incoherent, angry shout.

"I hope you're more tactful than that when Josephine's fifteen," Ivy remarked. "Honestly, Molly, I should think it over."

"Don't do it, Molly," said Sid, who had been on an early shift and was sitting in his uniform having a cup of tea. "Live with him a bit longer until you've made up your mind. It's not the same for you as it was for us. We had to get married to get a bit of privacy –"

"We had to get married, full stop," Ivy broke in. "But your dad's right. You can take time to consider – you've got Josie to think of, now."

"Marriage is no joke," said Sid. "Next thing – you'll have another kid. Then you're committed."

"No chance of that," Molly told him, although she suspected that Nedermann badly wanted a child by her. "Anyway, I can't think what you're all on about. You acted up enough when I took up with Johnnie without marrying him. Now you're telling me not to get married. It'd be nice if people round here made up their minds."

"Circumstances alter cases," Sid told her gravely.

"What alters what?" Molly asked. "You must all be barmy. I'm better off doing what I want and not listening to you."

"When did you ever do anything else?" demanded Shirley, coming back into the room.

"You can mind your own business, too," said Molly. "When I want the opinion of a spotty teenager I'll ask for it."

"Sorry I spoke," said Shirley. "I ought to know better than to say anything in this house." She went off again, banging the door.

"It's these O Levels," explained Ivy. "She's working ever so hard at her books. They reckon she's got real brains."

"Might make up for her horrible nature," Molly said sharply. she was still annoyed by the reception of her news. She added, "Still – you can all relax for a bit. We can't get married until Ferenc's proved officially that his wife's dead. He heard she was from somebody but that's not good enough for the authorities. He's got to get the proper documents."

"Be a pity if she turns up suddenly," Sid remarked.

Molly stared at him with dislike and, about to marry a wealthy man unacceptable in her own home, swept off in a taxi with the diamond ring glittering on her finger.

In the event, proving Mrs Nedermann's death was a lengthy and painful business. It meant getting a marriage record which might or might not now exist from a bureaucratic and unsympathetic government. It meant checking the death rolls and lists of survivors of the camp in Poland where Mrs Nedermann and the child had been sent. The applications, the replies, the agents' reports cast a pall over their days. Nedermann was obliged to relive the anguish of the post-war years, after others had told him the details of his wife's death of pneumonia in the winter of 1942 and of the death from gangrene, not long after, of his daughter. Molly privately thought that life would have been simpler if he just forgot about proving himself a widower and declared that he was single. But Nedermann, a former refugee, who had lived on sufferance in Britain for many years before achieving nationality, had a terror of infringing regulations. He believed that if he stated he was single at the registrar's a jealous or vindictive compatriot might denounce him, jeopardizing not only the marriage but his status as a citizen.

A year passed before official proof of Nedermann's wife's death arrived.

The photographs of the old documents, with their crumples and their bent-back corners dark on the page, lay between them on the table one morning seeming, somehow, like the proof of their own crime. There was something accusatory about the old typewritten Gothic script, the alterations in a spikey foreign hand, the sheet of paper recording the deaths of thirty-seven people.

Nedermann stood up and picked up the evidence. He left the room silently. A few seconds later Molly heard the door of the safe close. And that evening he handed her the deeds of two houses, numbers 11 and 13 Baldry Place, in Notting Dale. She took the deeds, wondering if she could do something to rescue the houses and their tenants from decay. As she did so, Nedermann remarked gloomily, "Take care of them. My affairs are becoming complicated. It will be all right but these houses are for you, in case anything goes wrong."

Nedermann now owned more than fifty houses in London, half a bingo hall in Leeds (given in payment of a debt) and half a row of back-to-backs in Middlesborough, a swap as part of a deal involving three houses in Edgware. In London most of his houses were Victorian slums, some having been slums since they were built and others having been formerly substantial, now decayed. He had been buying up these properties since the end of World War II and the post-war shortage of housing and the waves of immigrants coming into Britain in the 1950s had made them highly profitable. Indeed, as he told Molly, the profits on his smart block of flats in Mayfair, inhabited by colonels' widows, rising young barristers and single girls whose well-to-do parents paid the rent, were no more than those he drew from his collapsing houses in Notting Hill, Kilburn and Shepherd's Bush. In these buildings, with their unsafe staircases, leaking roofs and poor sanitation, tenants lived crowded together, afraid to complain about the condition of the houses in case they were turned out.

Nedermann himself operated from a couple of ramshackle offices in Bayswater, with a staff of about ten men, ranging from bright young men in smart suits to thugs whose heavy bodies and battered faces indicated to the tenants what they could expect if they made a fuss. They collected their rents accompanied by Alsatian dogs. They were not above showing Nedermann's tenants a glimpse of a revolver if they proved awkward in their complaints or slow with the rent. And yet, like many tyrants, Nedermann was capable of acts of kindness. He had the child of one of his tenants driven in his own car regularly to and from a hospital for treatment. He could give a flat at rock-bottom prices to a homeless stranger he took a liking to. But when Molly complained about the rats in the basement of one of his houses he only said, "What can I do about it? The people who live there – they should kill the rats. Am I ratkiller? No, I'm a businessman. I run my business. I work hard so I don't end up like some of the human vermin living in my property. If they worked like I do they would be living next door to me in Orme Square. Instead they sit and whine about the rats. They are weak. Let them kill their own rats or move out – it's their choice." Molly found all this chilling, but she said nothing. She was having a hard time keeping up with Nedermann's demands on her. She had to be the perfect cook, hostess and mother – three roles in which she had not had much experience – as well as a bright, well-dressed and gay companion when they were at parties and clubs together. But while he wanted her to cause envy in other men he became furious if she drank too much or flirted more than he thought right. On one occasion, at a party at the house of a Member of Parliament, he had told her firmly that they were leaving and, when she hesitated, had dragged her out of the room by her wrist. He had forced her into the car and, slamming the window which separated them from the burly chauffeur, who also acted as a rent-collector, he shouted, "Can't you control yourself? Do you think I can take you to decent places with decent people when you behave like a whore off the streets?" Molly, who had been flirting with a racing driver and given him a little kiss, shouted back, "At least he was paying me some attention. What am I supposed to do? Stand around all evening while you talk about the Leasehold Reform Bill? I keep house all day long and in the evenings I dress up and stand beside you while you talk business. You talk business, you think business – I bet you even dream business. What do you want?"

"A little love – a little loyalty," he replied shortly.

"Like him," she said, nodding at the figure in the driver's seat. "Someone who says yes sir, no sir, three bags full because you're paying him to do it."

"I don't know what you mean with your three bags full," Nedermann said. "I know a woman who has everything she wants should support her husband and not act like a street woman."

"I'm not married to you yet," she reminded him. Underneath his frenzy she could sense the chronic anxiety of the refugee who arrives with nothing but the knowledge of how terrible life can be. It was the fear of being hauled back into the world of deportation, exile and poverty which drove Nedermann. This was also the source of his callous attitude to his tenants – he had suffered once as they did now, he reasoned. If they didn't like it they should do what he had done – escape.

Molly sighed. "I'm like a horse," she complained. "No wonder I feel like a bit of fun from time to time. How many are coming tomorrow?"

"Ten," he told her.

"Oh, Christ," Molly said. "What did you do before you had me? Why can't you get a caterer in? You need six women, not one."

"A woman should look after her man," he told her. "Only the lazy ones complain."

Molly had been bred in the old tradition of women who stand in the street in curlers and slippers, grumbling to each other about their demanding husbands and disorderly children as if these chains were all that prevented them from following their true vocations as film stars or the matrons of London teaching hospitals. She said sourly, "So only the lazy ones complain, eh? What do the good ones do – die at the age of thirty-two with grateful smiles on their faces?"

"My mother has been up at six o'clock every morning of her life," he told her stiffly. "And she is alive and in good health and respected by her children."

Molly groaned. "Bet she wishes she was bloody dead, though," she muttered.

Ivy, who had, again in the traditions of Meakin Street, spent many years calling her daughter a slut, was shocked when she visited Orme Square. "Spit and polish everywhere," she remarked disapprovingly, looking round the sitting room. "It looks lovely, I don't deny it – I don't mind hygiene but you feel you ought to clean your shoes and have a bath before you come in. Who keeps it like this?"

Molly, pouring tea from a silver teapot into bone china cups said, "I do."

Ivy was astonished. "You do?" she said. "I used to have to scream for a week to get you to make your bed. You do all this?"

"Every bleeding bit of it," said Molly. "From washing the tins before I put them in the dustbin to hoovering under Josie's bed – every day."

"Oh, my good God," said Ivy. "Well – hand us that cup, unless you think I'll break it." She got up and wandered to the window. "Nice view," she said, looking over the pretty square beyond. "Pity about the main road."

"Park's opposite – that's a compensation," Molly said.

"Oh, it's very nice, you can't deny it. And our Josie looks as if she'd been washed, starched and hung out to dry."

Josephine was sitting on the rug, reading a book. Her socks were clean, her shoes brightly polished and her brown curls had been pulled back to form a neat bunch at the back of her head.

"She's quietened down," observed her grandmother. "She used to be a real handful. Off in a flash and all over the place. I used to tell her I was going to buy a chain and chain her up." Josephine flashed her grandmother a saucy grin and turned over a page.

"Ferenc says a little girl should behave like a little girl," Molly said.

"I could never see much difference," Ivy observed. "It's hard work to make a normal little girl into a nice little girl. I never had much success at it. I suppose he thinks a woman should behave like a woman, too. All this charring and so forth. Still," she observed in a more rational tone, "I must say he's looking after you well."

"That's a fact, mum," Molly told her.

"Be married soon, I daresay?" questioned Ivy.

"That's right," Molly agreed.

The only other visitor of whom Nedermann approved was Simon Tate. Simon always refused invitations to meals, pleading that his work at the club kept him busy at those hours, but he frequently dropped in during the afternoons to see Molly when she was alone. He insisted on having drinks. As he gazed around one day he observed, "Well, Molly Flanders, you're doing very well. Very tasteful. Nice clean modern lines and just enough of the traditional to add solidity and hint at some links with the past. Who's this?" he asked, gesturing at a portrait in the alcove. "Would that be Graf von Nedermann, member of Bismarck's cabinet? Or could it be the ninth Lord Water-house?"

"Oh – don't be such a snob," Molly said.

"Sorry," Simon told her. "It all looks very nice and I'm enjoying it. Did you arrange the flowers?"

"Who else?" said Molly. She was trying to be lighthearted but Simon noticed she was gulping her gin. She stood up to get another one.

"The only thing baffling me is the reading material," he told her, pointing to the books on the floor.

"Better get rid of them," Molly said, scooping them up. As she bundled them into a sideboard and turned the key on the cupboard door she added, "Ferenc can't stand me sitting about with a book in my hand."

"So you spend the afternoons secretly reading Graham Greene and the collected works of Bernard Shaw?" asked Simon, who had spotted the titles.

"Not bloody likely," grinned Molly, still knocking back the gin.

"What's it all about?" Simon asked.

"Well, if you really want to know," Molly told him, "I remembered what Steven said about how I should take an interest in things and improve my mind. He said once without that I'd end up nothing but a burden to everybody. I started getting bored in the afternoons. There's only so much haute cuisine and going to the hairdressers you can do without going mad. To tell you the honest truth I thought I was getting depressed. So I thought, well, if I read one book and understand it Steven will know, wherever he is, if he's anywhere, that somebody once took him seriously. So I got this book, about a highwayman and a girl in a low-cut dress, and I read it. But it was rubbish – I mean, all that can't have been that different from what I've seen, even if it was years ago, and I never noticed anybody like Arnie Rose in that book and you can be sure that whenever it all happened there'd be an Arnie Rose in it somewhere. Anyway, I knew really that kind of book wasn't what Steven meant. So I joined the library and I took out a few books and I got quite interested in reading, I've been reading these thrillers by Graham Greene – they're good. The Shaw book's just a joke. Steven use to tell me about Professor Higgins while he was trying to turn me into a lady. He even took me to the play, so I thought I'd read it – *Pygmalion*. But plays are too hard to read."

"You'll stand for Parliament next," Simon said.

"You shouldn't laugh at me," Molly said seriously. "It's people like you laughing at people like me that holds us back. Well, you go and laugh at Ivy and Sid – that's all right because they're used to it and they know they can't do anything. But don't try it on with Jack or Shirley, because they've had more chances and they're always passing exams. That's how I know I can't be that stupid – because of Jack and Shirley being bright. That's the difference between you and Steven Greene – whatever else he did, he had a bit of respect for other people."

"Ferenc wouldn't like it if he heard you talking like that," Simon said.

Molly shrugged and stood up again. "Another drink?" she asked.

"You're knocking back the gin a bit this afternoon," he said. "It's not like you."

"Bored housewife aren't I?" Molly said shortly. "Are you having a drink or not?"

"Thanks," Simon said, holding out his glass. "Actually, Moll, if I'm spiteful it's because I'm embarrassed. I'm getting on badly with Norman and Arnie and I'm bored to death with the Club. Could you put in a good word for me with Ferenc? I fancy joining the organization."

"Oh Christ," exclaimed Molly, turning round with the drinks in her hand. "You wouldn't last five minutes. You'd throw up if you had to work for Ferenc. It's a rotten game – all rats, and evictions and rotten bloody fires through overturned oil heaters. You couldn't stomach it, not for a second."

Simon looked round, at the copper bowl of flowers on the elegant table under the oil painting, the water colours on the walls, the thick-pile carpet. He stared at the crystal glass in his hand and put it down.

"That's where all this comes from?" he asked.

"Where did you think? We haven't got a private gold mine in the back garden," snapped Molly. She added, "You might as well finish that drink. It's poured out now and if you don't have it it'll only go down the sink." She hesitated. "Look," she said, "I know I'm a kept woman, living on dirty money. And when we get married it won't be better. It'll be worse because I'll have agreed legally that I don't mind." Pausing again, she said, "Change the subject – what happened to Johnnie?"

"He got two years – it might have been less but one of the girls was under age. I don't think he knew that, though."

"I don't envy him in jail," Molly said.

"That's right," Simon agreed. He added, "Well, I'm sorry to have asked you, Molly. If what you say's true it's obvious I'd better stay put. I'll think about something else. I just can't stand the Club, the punters or anything about them. Also, I'd like to see daylight more often and get weekends off like normal people. Tom Allaun and Charlie Markham are back – they dropped a thousand each last Saturday night and Sunday morning. While other people are out at parties I'm having to absorb spite from men like that – it isn't good enough. They're rotten winners and even worse losers. And Charlie can call on the family firm to make good his loss but I don't know what Tom's going to do."

"His father'll sell off another farm," said Molly, whose connection with the property market had taught her a good deal. Then she stood up, swayed, murmured something about Mrs Gates and a gypsy – and fell down.

Simon rushed over and picked her up just as she regained consciousness. "Molly," he said in a concerned voice. "Are you all right? When did you start drinking?"

"Not the gin," she said weakly, as he ladled her into a chair and went to get her a glass of water. "Not the gin – I'm in the club."

"What about the club?" he said, returning and handing her the water.

"Not that club," she moaned. "The other club – I'm pregnant. I thought as much. I can't get stuck like this." She drank the water, while Simon stared at her in bewilderment. "I can't get stuck like this," she said more emphatically. "I won't have it. I won't have this baby."

Simon stared at her. "You'd better think it over," he advised.

"How long for?" demanded Molly. "Nine months? This isn't anything you can afford time to think about. You'll have to help me."

"What? How?" asked Simon, still startled.

"Ask around," Molly said desperately. "Find out who women go to and how much it costs. I want a posh abortionist and no fuss. And Ferenc mustn't find out."

"Do you think this is quite fair on him?" Simon asked. "He'd be a devoted father —"

"Fair on him?" Molly half-shouted. "What about fair on me? I'm not even bloody married. I've had one fatherless kid. I'm in the running, now, for another. Do you think I want to go through all that again?" Her voice dropped to a threatening whisper. "You just ask around, Simon, and find out what to do. Is Mrs Jones still in charge of the ladies'?"

"Yes," Simon said gloomily.

"Then you ask her," Molly demanded. "She's the one to ask — she's bound to know. Say it's your sister. Do it today." She was nearly shouting again. Simon was alarmed. He said, in a low voice, "All right, Moll. I'll do it." He added, on an inspiration, 'I'll do it now." He was looking for a chance to leave immediately. An embarrassing conversation with Mrs Jones seemed a small price to pay to get away from this hysterical woman who, it seemed, might do anything at any time — throw a glass at a mirror, faint again or begin to scream.

Molly spotted his game and said sulkily, "You do that, then. Go now."

Simon went to the door. "All right," he said. "Are you sure you'll be all right on your own? Would you like me to get Josephine from school for you?"

"I'll get Josephine," Molly said grimly. "You just find Mrs Jones. Then ring me."

"All right," he said.

"But listen," she told him, springing upright in her chair. "If you ring and I say — what shall I say? — yes, if I say "I'll drop in tomorrow and collect it from the club," you shut up. That'll mean Ferenc's here."

"Right," Simon said and, guiltily, left. In the end it was he who drove Molly to Wimpole Street for her interview with the smart abortionist who had two psychiatrists sitting in his basement rubber-stamping the documents asserting that his clients were so unstable that the birth of an unwanted child might cause them serious mental damage. This meant that the abortion, when carried out, was perfectly legal. A few days later Simon drove her to the clinic just outside London where the operations were conducted and came back in the evening to collect her. In the meanwhile Ivy had telephoned Ferenc to tell him that Molly had fainted while on a visit to her house and that she had been put to bed upstairs as a precaution. Molly did spend the night at Meakin Street, after the abortion, and returned next day to Orme Square.

It was a week later when the grey photostats proving the death of Mrs Nedermann arrived. This was perhaps why, as they lay beside the silver coffee pot and the cooling rolls, heated by Molly in the oven every morning, they seemed so much like the evidence of a contemporary crime. Nevertheless, she felt no direct remorse about the abortion of Nedermann's child.

I wasn't happy, not really happy, with Ferenc but I was content, which is something to be grateful for, I suppose. I wasn't flogging Lord This or sucking off Sir That. I wasn't selling aspirins in Boots and trying to make ends meet for me and Josephine. And Josephine got her education off to a good start at school. The private school was better than Wattenblath Elementary School, or whatever they were calling it by that time. And I liked Nedermann and I was sorry for him though I can't say I loved him, whatever that might mean. The truth is he was so repressive I felt irritable with him half the time. He had these high domestic standards and he banned practically everybody I knew from the house. He had to put up with Ivy because she was my mother, after all, but when he came home after she'd gone he used to prowl about the room, saying her cigarette smoke was too strong and opening up the windows and fussing about like an old hen. I couldn't really complain too much – after all, he was paying for everything, including Josephine's ballet lessons and the posh school and the uniform and all that. Still, I suppose I wouldn't have stayed if I hadn't been fond of him – I often used to think of life in Meakin Street, even if it was a bit rough and ready, it would have been a damn sight easier and more fun than living with Ferenc Nedermann. And it wasn't too easy to forget how he got those funds – he had us, Josephine and me, as captives and he had those poor bloody tenants of his in the same state. He was a natural jailer, that was the truth. He got his security from knowing he had everybody under his thumb. There were times when, seeing him carrying on like the Mayor of Scarborough, all watch-chain and haemorrhoids, I felt just like screaming out loud. But there you are, he was kind, he needed me – I couldn't see for crying when he died. They shuffled him off to his grave in the end. He would have died of horror if he could have seen his own funeral. It preyed on my mind for years and in the end, when I had the money, I got everybody together that had known him and I had a great big ceremony, in the cemetery where he was buried, with a proper address by a rabbi and, afterwards, a big party. Then I had a huge, marble tombstone put up for him. Well, I thought it was the least I could do for the poor old bugger.

Anyway, things went from bad to worse. I was lucky in a way not to be married to him. Because if I had, when the crash came he'd have tied me up in the firm as a nominal director of all these banana republic companies he had, I'd have been technically the owner of half his slums – it would have taken years to get out of it and I'd have come out with a business name like Dick Turpin's.

I don't know why I never married him. At first I used to make silly excuses, then he seemed to lose interest in the idea – and there were times, over the last eighteen months to a year, when he wasn't thinking about me, he was too worried. When he did he was usually angry and ratty, out of pure nerves. It was about that time I tried to help sort things out – but it was no good. He wouldn't stop doing what he was doing and he wouldn't take any notice of me. Instead he listened to the others – and they were all out for themselves . . .

The truth is that Nedermann, apart from his weaknesses as a business-man, was out of date. The election of a Labour government, which my father and I had anticipated for at least six months beforehand, put an end to his racketeering. There was a general sense that people were no longer content with corruption and shady dealings on the margins of the law. That all seemed to belong to the post-war period, when commodities like foodstuffs and clothing were still rationed and nearly everything else was in short supply. It was an atmosphere conducive to petty crime and corruption – the purchase of black market nylon stockings or bottles of whisky, cans of paint smuggled out of the back door of a factory, the sweeteners to the Council officials for ignoring unlicensed building work on properties, bribes to renting agencies for tip-offs about flats, "key money" paid to landlords for allowing tenants to move in. Nedermann thrived in that atmosphere. He was providing housing at a time when it was very scarce. That was probably one of the reasons why he was tolerated. Housing author-ities, public health and safety officers, even the police, appeared to take little notice of complaints made against him. He must have been paying some of these blind eyes to stay closed. Then the time came when everyone grew tired of this. At that moment he ran out of control. The situation became alarming. He bought and bought, trading one mortgage against another like a child playing Monopoly. He would buy a house with one payment and agree to pay off the rest on a mortgage, often privately raised at high interest, sometimes as high as 25%. After that the affair would become a question of scrambling to keep up the payments on the place, using the rents from one building to pay the mortgage on another. Almost all transactions were in cash and half of them were never recorded. Gradually his affairs became more complicated and at that point he began to sell off properties to his subordinates, who often took the rents and left him with trailing responsibilities in terms of mortgages or dealings with increasingly vigilant local councils. As the housing regulations began to be more applied many of the tenants took to appealing to local rent tribunals, who had the power to reduce rents considered to be unfair. But as the empire collapsed many of the tenants became less and less certain who their landlords were – one way of evading the law was to register the property in question with a company in the Bahamas or somewhere else. The buildings people lived in could change hands as often as once a month. There was no one to go to in cases of grievance and, worse than that, after months of not collecting rents the invisible landlords could evict them on grounds of non-payment of rent. The whole situation had become an open scandal. Nedermann was no longer useful. His day was over.

Quite what happened that November night I don't know. What is certain is that it is just as well Ferenc Nedermann died then. My impression is that he could not have coped with the combination of financial disaster and disgrace which threatened him. He was probably too proud, and too insecure, to have borne both.

Nevertheless, you can imagine the horror for us as it became plainer and plainer that Nedermann was about to be ruined . . .

It looks inevitable now but then, things do afterwards, don't they? Many a business thriving now has gone through patches where it's only managed to stagger on by a miracle. If it had collapsed then everyone would have said the crash was inevitable.

Basically, if it hadn't been for the police, it wouldn't have mattered about the Roses. And if it hadn't been for the Roses the police wouldn't have mattered. And if Ferenc hadn't got so wound up about everything over the previous year I daresay he could even have survived both attacks. As it was the police had decided to get him for being the landlord of a brothel – he always claimed he had no way of knowing what was going on in his houses but I was never sure if that was true. So the police were coming to arrest him. The other bit of the story is complicated but I think it went like this. He bought two blocks of four houses each, from the Church Commissioners. To get the deal through he'd used a proxy – an old whiskied-up colonel he had on the payroll. Colonel Devereux. That was because he thought the Church Commissioners might be fussy about who they sold to. Now to get even the deposit on these houses together he'd had to mortgage Orme Square. And even then there wasn't enough so then he mortgaged two houses which weren't even paid for, though the bank didn't know he'd done it. And even worse – you'll never believe it – he'd sold one of the houses the week before for cash, to a man called Gerry Armstrong. I don't know whether he thought he could get away with all this for the time being and make good the loss afterwards – I think by that stage his memory had begun to go. He never put anything on paper unless he had to, on account of the Inland Revenue – they were after him then, too, needless to say. And the real clincher to all this was that Armstrong found out that the house he'd paid cash for was already mortgaged – there was about £5,000 owing to the previous owner. Then he found out about the other mortgage. Then – here's the horror story – Ferenc found out Armstrong was a nephew of Norman and Arnold Rose. He's their only sister Marie's boy. I was terrified when I heard this. The general idea was that if you stood accidentally on the foot of a neighbour of a second cousin of the Roses, it was a good idea to apologise on the spot and make sure to send flowers next day. But Ferenc wasn't very worried. When I said I was frightened he told me we'd take the car out that night and go round the clubs and find them and tell them the whole thing had been an accident and we'd soon make good the loss. At the time I thought I believed him. Then I found I was on the phone to Ivy, saying what had happened, and when she advised me to put Josephine in a cab straight round to Meakin Street I went ahead and did it. Ferenc was furious again, when he found Josephine was gone.

That was when I tried to talk some sense into him. I said the best thing was for him to clear out and I'd try to straighten up the books with the accountant while he was gone. The accountant was a quiet little man who let Nedermann have his way because he was afraid of the bullying. I thought if I gave him some peace and quiet he could start a sort-out. That taught me one thing anyway – not to employ an accountant you can frighten. Anyway, Ferenc refused. We began this horrible car-ride, looking for Norman and Arnie. We did the pubs and clubs, asking for them, but it got plainer and plainer nobody wanted to know – in fact they wanted us to go away. That was when I got really scared. Ferenc tried to pretend he wasn't until we got to the Prospect of Whitby, in Wapping. The barman behind the bar didn't have to be asked. He just handed us the drinks we'd ordered and said, "If you're looking for anybody, Mr Nedermann, don't worry. They're out looking for you."

So Ferenc said politely, "Thank you."

And the barman replied, in the same quiet polite way, "But – excuse me, Mr Nedermann – the boss would be grateful if you and the lady could just finish up your drinks, in your own time, of course, we don't want to rush you, and – and, well, go home." He added, to palliate the bluntness of the final part of the message, "I'm sure you understand. It's nothing personal."

"I understand," Ferenc told him. "We'll do what you say."

"Thanks, Mr Nedermann," said the barman. "There's no charge for the drinks, of course. On the house." And he retreated to the other end of the bar and pretended to take an order from a customer who wasn't ordering.

Ferenc's face seemed to collapse after that. He had plenty of nerve, though. He drank his brandy as if he had all the time in the world. He and I even managed a bit of cheery conversation, like two people who had come out to enjoy themselves. We said goodnight to the barman and left like the King and Queen.

Then we didn't know what to do. We drove the car up beside the docks and sat there, watching some boats go up and down the river. It was getting foggy and the hooters of the ships were sounding up and down the Thames. I said, "Look, Ferenc. Why don't you disappear for a day or two? I've known Arnold and Norman since I was small. I'll go to them and explain. Maybe they'll listen to me."

And he told me, "All three of us are businessmen. We can meet and talk and arrange matters between us."

"Please," I said. "Please, Ferenc." But he wouldn't listen. Then he told me that if I was frightened I should leave. I refused. Then he ordered me to leave – that was when I knew he was frightened. I still refused to go but all I could see in my mind's eye while we were sitting there on the dock was two weighted sacks being heaved off the end of it and sinking to the bottom of the river. Arnie and Norman had been known to dispose of people that way – some of them weren't even dead when they hit the water.

Finally I managed to convince Ferenc that the Rose brothers would never harm a hair of my head, no matter what. I wasn't sure myself. You can never be quite sure what people like that are going to do. And we went back to Orme Square, went to bed, made love and, believe it or not, Ferenc Nedermann, with the Rose brothers looking for him, said, "Goodnight, darling," put his head on the pillow and fell into a dreamless sleep. Like a baby. I'm sure of it. I ought to have known because while he was lying there peacefully snoring I was lying awake listening for Norman and Arnie's friends. They weren't going to come and knock on the door politely. They'd send blokes in over the roof if they felt like it. You wouldn't know what happened to you till it'd happened. So I'm lying there with the house creaking and groaning round me, the way they do when you're scared, when the phone rings. Ferenc didn't move. I was out of bed and across the floor like a cat on hot bricks. At first I didn't know who it was, let alone what the voice was saying, but then I managed to make out that it was Colonel Devereux, dead drunk as usual, ringing from some club he used to go to in Pimlico. Mumble, mumble, mumble – I nearly went mad. I was going to put the phone down when I heard him say, "Tell Mr Nedermann. It's important."

"What's important?" I'm yelling. "What's important?" And still Ferenc didn't stir which I suppose was a sign. But I didn't think about it then because the next thing is that somebody, a man, had taken the phone from Devereux. A voice I didn't recognize just said, "Tell Mr Nedermann the Vice Squad has entered number 14 Routledge Square and discovered it to be a brothel. They're on their way to Orme Square now to arrest him." From the voice, I guessed a policeman. He must've been on somebody's payroll besides the Met's but there you are, by that stage he could have been anybody's.

Anyway, the long and short of it is that I went over to Ferenc where he was lying in the bed and I shook him a couple of times to wake him up. Then I shook him a couple of times more and called his name. But I knew, really, he was dead. And it's not to my credit but at that particular moment I never shed a tear. I'm surprised how fast my brain worked – all I thought, straight away, was that I had the cops coming in from one side and the Rose brothers from the other and that I was likely to get caught in the middle. Ferenc had escaped – but I hadn't.

I'm still amazed I was so hard, after living with him for nearly six years, and he was lying there stone dead. I'll be honest, while I was dressing at top speed I was opening my jewellery box and stuffing the jewellery in my handbag at the same time. There wasn't too much of the good stuff left by then. I'd pushed it all at him on odd occasions when he needed ready money fast. I've never had much of a talent for hanging on to the tom. Some women never part with a ring or a brooch they've been given. Look at Isabel Allaun. She hung on to her rings through thick and thin – she'd have seen a baby starve before her very eyes rather than part with the gems – still, there it was, I grabbed what was left and then I got the bunch of keys off the dressing-table, ran downstairs with my shoes in my hand and I opened the safe, grabbed all the money in it and stuffed that in my bag, too. I'd handed back the houses he gave me during another crisis and a few hundred was all I got out of the safe – then I took my coat and sneaked out of the house, looking round all the corners and I'm off, creeping through the mist, into Bayswater Road, in a panic, because I was conspicuous, walking around like that at three in the morning and then, thank God, along came an all-night bus. I'm on it, with my bulging handbag, still dry-eyed, still not taking in the fact that Ferenc was dead, and paying my fare to the black conductor like someone who's been out to dinner with a few friends and stayed a little later than usual.

What a performance. It's amazing how cold and callous you can be when you're in danger. I suppose not stopping to mourn the dead in a crisis is what's kept the human race going over all these millions of years. If we'd all stopped to cry over Uncle Harry we'd have been caught in the sabre-toothed tiger's second strike, when he came back wondering if there was any more to eat. Still, it makes you feel rotten afterwards when you know you behaved like that.

I'd just got my change from the conductor when I looked sideways and I saw this long black car sneaking up the other side of the road. In it, large as life – of course Arnie and Norman Rose, Norman driving. And I thought that they might find me and try and get the money back. They might even take reprisals. So I decided not to go back to Meakin Street until I'd seen what they were doing. I couldn't decide where to go. Then I remembered my sister Shirley. I thought, they'll never think to try and find me in a semi-detached in Greenford. I thought I'd spend a few days there until I'd sorted something out, got over the shock, and found out what the Roses and the police felt about me. But it wasn't a good idea. I could tell that the minute Shirley opened the door.

Shirley was up when Molly rang the doorbell. She came to the door in a faded blue candlewick dressing-gown. She had a feeding bottle in one hand and a baby in the other. She looked at Molly in alarm. As Molly walked in she said, "Sh! Don't make a noise. Brian's asleep. The baby's been fretful all night."

Shirley had been studying physics and chemistry at Imperial College for six months when she met her husband, also a student. She had married at nineteen and given up the course. Her first child had been born a year later.

Molly stepped over the very clean lino on the hall floor and went automatically into the kitchen. She sat down heavily at the small formica table. Meanwhile Shirley put the kettle on. She sat down opposite Molly. She put the feeding bottle in the baby's mouth. He sucked a couple of times and then spat the teat out.

Molly felt uncomfortable in the sparse kitchen faced with her pale, blank-eyed sister. Her handbag, bulging with loot, lay on the kitchen table, next to the baby's bottle.

"Oh, God," Shirley said. She got up and opened a tea caddy. She was scraping a few last spoonfuls from the tin when Molly said, "Why don't you give me the baby?"

Shirley turned and put the baby in her arms. He lay there looking up at her with red, rheumy eyes. There was a thump from upstairs. Hastily pouring boiling water into the teapot Shirley dashed out saying, "That's Brian Junior. I'll get him up before he wakes his dad."

Molly thought, in surprise, it's only four in the morning. Shirley came down with a pale-faced three-year-old. He stared at her from watery blue eyes.

"Would you like to go to sleep on the settee in the lounge?" Shirley asked persuasively. The baby, the boy, and, above all, Shirley, all looked exhausted. There were huge circles under Shirley's blue eyes. Her pale brown hair was slightly dirty and pulled back in a bunch secured by a rubber band. Molly felt embarrassed about having come here in the middle of the night — not that the middle of the night here seemed to be any different from the middle of the day. She now realized that Shirley's position, and state of mind, were much worse than hers. There was a lot she didn't know — she reflected guiltily that she had hardly seen her sister since she got married. She did, however, remember the row at Meakin Street about the engagement.

"You withhold your permission," Molly had yelled at Sid. "She can't marry until she's twenty-one if you don't agree. Make her finish her studies before she gets married. Then she'll have something to fall back on if it doesn't work out."

"She's in love," said Ivy. "And Brian's a decent chap and he'll be the one with the degree. And his parents have got grocers' shops all over West London. They're going to buy them a house as a wedding present."

"Oh, mum," Molly said. "Look at me – if I'd had some qualifications I'd have gone a different way after Jim Flanders died. What's the good of his qualifications to her?"

"I don't know what you're talking about," Ivy told her. "And I can't fathom out why you come here and expect us to take your advice about our Shirley's wedding."

"Shirley's found herself a respectable bloke and she's going to marry him," Sid told her solidly.

"Why can't she get married and go on with her studies, then?" demanded Molly. "It's been done."

"Well, we thought of that," said Ivy, "but Brian's parents didn't fancy the idea. They thought it would be better if she settled down and became a proper wife to Brian – that way he can concentrate on his studies undisturbed. After all, it's his qualifications which'll keep the family."

"What the bloody hell is going to disturb his studies just because his wife's studying, too?" cried Molly. "She's not going to start banging and shouting, is she?"

"Well, Brian's parents thought it would be best if she concentrates on the house and he concentrates on the university."

"Oh," said Molly, angrily stubbing out her cigarette. "It's Brian's parents this and Brian's parents that – what's the matter with you both? You've got as much right to say what happens to your daughter as they have to say what happens to their son. What are you doing – selling her to them as a servant for their Brian?"

"What's important is that she gets a husband and a home of her own," Ivy told her. "A degree in science isn't going to be much help when she's got a family."

"Well – I don't approve," said Molly, standing up. "And if you think I'm coming to the wedding, I'm not. I wouldn't mind betting our

Shirley's brighter than her Brian. That's why the parents want her off the course before the race begins."

"You malicious bitch," Ivy said.

"Bet I'm right, then," Molly said. "And if you look any more relieved about me not coming to the wedding I'll come anyway, just to spoil it for you."

"Not much to look forward to," Sid remarked gloomily. "They're Baptists. Teetotallers."

"Oh, Christ," Molly said. "You should stop this lot straight away. She'll only be unhappy."

Sid looked at Ivy who looked implacably back at him. Ivy said, "We've already seen what happens when daughters go their own way."

Molly, offended, shouted, "She is going her own way. If you want to start being strict parents, tell her she's got to wait to get married." She walked out, still shouting, "She'll be unhappy, I'm telling you."

She asked Shirley round to Orme Square next day but Shirley, over the phone said, "I can't come, Molly. Brian wouldn't like it. Anyway, we're going to a Christian Union meeting." Shirley, on arrival at Imperial College, had become a Christian. This was where she had met Brian. Molly, guessing that Christian fervour and romantic love had got confused in her sister's heart, said, "All right, Shirl. But don't forget that I'm praying now you use your brains and put off the wedding till you've got your degree. Do you think God wants you to sacrifice yourself for Brian?"

"You don't understand, Molly," came Shirley's quiet and convinced voice. "It's not a sacrifice – and if it is, I make it willingly."

And now, she reflected, as weary Shirley put her boy to bed on the sofa, it seemed too late.

They drank a cup of tea and Molly said, "Maybe I shouldn't have come here, Shirl. What I wanted was a few days to hide out, pull myself together and work out who's doing what to who."

"You know I'd like to help you, Molly," said Shirley. "But it's Brian – the disturbance."

Molly thought of stringy Brian, with his thatch of ginger hair and discontented expression. She had been right about the relative abilities of her sister and brother-in-law. Brian had dropped out of the honours degree course after his first year and had not even completed the general degree at another college. It had been said that his father was getting older and needed his son's help in the business but Molly

315

believed he had backed out rather than fail his examinations. Now she said, "I'll push off, then. No point in causing problems in other people's homes."

"Where will you go – mum and dad's?" enquired Shirley.

"Don't be daft," Molly said. "I've kept the rent up at number 4 Meakin Street. If I wanted to go to Meakin Street I've got my own place to go to. Josephine's there now."

Shirley's eyes glinted. "What's up?" she said, with a mixture of her new timidity and a little of the old Waterhouse interest in life's events, however sad and sorry they might be. Molly got a sudden mental image of Brian, Brian's parents and Brian's parents' friends all sitting stiffly behind net curtains avoiding trouble and evading joy.

"It doesn't matter," Molly said. "I just want to stay clear of Meakin Street for a bit. I'll go to a hotel."

Shirley nodded. "Would you like another cup of tea?" she asked.

Molly said, "Look – the baby's asleep. Why don't you creep up and put him back in his cot."

"He'll only wake up again and disturb Brian –"

"I don't see it," interrupted Molly. "Does this happen often? Do you spend many nights creeping the kids up and downstairs so Brian doesn't wake? How do you get any sleep?"

"They don't always do it," Shirley said. "But it's not too bad when they do. I can either doze off on the settee with Brian Junior or else I get on with the books. They're always behind. It gives me a chance to catch up."

"Books? What books?" demanded Molly.

"I do the firm's books," Shirley explained. "The accountant was making a mess of it so I took it over about a year ago. But you have to keep it up or it gets on top of you."

"Oh," said Molly. She took out a packet of cigarettes. "Want one?" she asked. Shirley, who looked frightened, said, "All right – but don't tell Brian."

"Shirley, my gel," Molly told her sister. "When he gets up I won't even be here. I'm just waiting for the tube station to open."

"I'm sorry, Moll," Shirley said.

"Nothing whatever to be sorry about," Molly told her. "What can you do when your sister who's a moral degenerate through no fault of your own turns up in a taxi in the middle of the night. Obviously on the run." She grinned, reached across the table and patted Shirley's arm. "I'm going to Brighton," she said. "But you can do me one

316

favour. Give Ivy a ring tomorrow when you're out shopping. Say I'm all right and I'll get in touch in a couple of days." She paused. "You'd better tell her Ferenc's dead, too."

"Oh – oh dear," said Shirley. "How did that happen?"

"Another day," Molly said.

"I'm worried – why can't you go home? Are you in real trouble?"

"Not really," Molly said. "Take my word for it."

She looked at her sister's anxious face and added, "I haven't done anything wrong."

Shirley's face was still anxious. Molly realized sickly that her sister was more worried about a scandal than she was about her. She said, "Don't worry – it won't get in the papers." Then she hesitated and said, "At least, I don't think so."

"I hope not," Shirley said. Then she looked ashamed of herself.

"Might be something happening down at the tube station now," observed Molly.

"It's still dark," Shirley said.

Molly stood up carefully and handed the baby to her sister. Walking to the tube station along tidy suburban streets in the first light she wondered which of them, the two Waterhouse sisters, was the more wretched on this cold November dawn of 1964.

Once in Brighton she booked into a small hotel on the front and put the jewellery in a safe deposit at a bank. Obeying an instinct she kept back a ring containing a large diamond and left it at a different bank. She walked back to the hotel along the misty road beside the sea. Cold waves lashed the pebbles on the beach below. She wondered if she should have come here. The trouble was that for her, as for many Londoners, the rest of the country barely existed. For them, there was only London and the few towns on the South Coast where they took their holidays. And of these towns, Brighton was the one most like home, almost an extension of the city. At this time of year, though, with the arcades half-shut and the weather gloomy, it depressed Molly. Over the next few days she slept, and had uneasy dreams about Nedermann. She woke sometimes from a seemingly dreamless sleep with a terrible sense of loss. She walked along the gloomy promenade, watching the big grey waves coming in and thought, I didn't love him enough. He wasn't happy enough.

As the gulls flew and cried over her head, she stood on the beach and thought, "I'd better ring Sid and Ivy." She did not want to. This miserable limbo was beginning to suit her. The shock of Nedermann's death and her own flight had drained her. However, she phoned Ivy who told her that Sid's friend in the police had discovered they were not interested in seeing her. On the other hand, she said, Arnie and Norman had sent round a tough-looking man to ask if she or Sid knew where Molly was. She thought he had believed her when she told him they did not know.

"I suppose I'll have to meet them sooner or later," Molly said. She was frightened now.

"I wouldn't," Ivy advised. "I wouldn't go looking for trouble."

"I can't go on hiding forever," Molly pointed out. "And then there's Josephine."

"Sid's friend, the copper, he says you should go to the police and tell them everything. You could get police protection," Ivy said.

"Question is – will the police be more on my side than the Roses'? A lot of them are getting paid off."

"That's the trouble," Ivy said. "Oh, God, Molly. I don't know what you're going to do. And I don't know what can have persuaded you to go to Shirley's. You might have known there'd be no comfort there."

"Nobody told me what it was like, mum," Molly said drily. "What's happened – the glamour of the Baptist grocers wearing off a bit?"

Ivy was plainly too unhappy about the situation to defend herself. She just groaned and then said, unwilling to admit that Molly had been right about the marriage, "I'd like the day to dawn when I'm not worried about both my daughters." She added, with more decision in her voice, "Your best bet is still to come back and go to the police. Sid'll come down with you to the station and back you up."

"I don't want to involve him," said Molly and went back to the hotel feeling depressed and frightened. She realized that if she wanted to avoid the Roses she would have to leave Brighton. She could not make up her mind whether to seek them out and face them or keep on running away. And if she kept on running where could she go? And how long would she have to stay away? Even Framlingham was not safe. She might have to go further – she might have to get Simon Tate to give her the name of someone to go to in Kenya – just to get away from the Roses?

She fell asleep, with the sound of the sea in her ears, dreaming, uneasily, of the Roses pursuing her, of Ferenc Nedermann's ghost. She was trapped in one of his terrible houses. There were patches on the walls which grew and expanded, the windows were broken, she ran across rotting floorboards – she awoke, saying aloud, "He wasn't happy enough."

And, "Who wasn't happy enough, Molly?" asked a familiar voice.

She sat upright, terrified. Arnie Rose was sitting in a chair by the window, looking at her mildly. Molly's heart thudded.

"Who let you in?" she cried.

"Lady downstairs," he told her. "I said you were my wife – we'd had a little matrimonial disagreement. She seemed happy to help."

"You paid her," said Molly. "What do you want, Arnie?"

"You know what I want, Moll," he remarked peaceably. "Neder-mann robbed my family. You robbed Nedermann – had to be you, didn't it? All I want now is what rightly belongs to us. You know I can't let you off the hook. It's discipline. You know," he said in a different tone. "You aren't half a restless sleeper. Tossing and turning all the time. You need a bloke in that bed to quiet you down."

He was not as frightening as she had thought he would be. She said, "Arnie – I've got nothing –"

"Come on, Molly. You done the safe. You forgot to close it after you. And there has to be a lot of jewellery. I'm not one to take away a lady's ornaments but, like I say, it's got to happen."

"I only took what Ferenc would have left me if he'd made a will," claimed Molly.

"Well, it wouldn't have been his to leave, would it, my dear?" Arnie replied.

"How did you find me?" she asked.

"Found your sister, Shirley, in some Baptist Chapel singing hymns in a little beret. She looks shocking these days, Moll. She used to be nice-looker. It must be the hymns and that ginger streak of misery she's married to. Anyway, she didn't want an argument in front of the neighbours –"

"Oh – Shirley," Moll moaned in despair. "Oh – Shirley."

"She didn't enjoy it," Arnie told her. "In fact, do you know, she's the sort you could tear the fingernails off of – if you weren't a gentleman, I mean, and she wouldn't say a dicky bird. Swear to you, Moll, she'd lay down her life for you – only thing she couldn't stand was getting into trouble from that po-faced lot down the chapel. Take my word for it. That's true. But you see," he said in the same reasonable tone, "none of this is getting us any further forward in the little matter we have under

319

consideration. The situation is – I won't mince words – that I have to know what you took out that house in Orme Square and make a deduction. So first you have to tell me where it all is. I give you to the count of five – then I have to turn the place over. Then if it's not here I have to ask where it is. And if you don't want to tell me I have to go on asking – know what I mean?"

Already Molly saw a look in his eye which meant that, now he had begun to think of how he would get the information from her, he was beginning to relish the idea. His talk of Shirley's fingernails had frightened her too.

She said, "All right, Arnie. There's £200 in the bottom drawer of the chest of drawers. It's all I got. And out of that I'll have to pay the hotel. There's some jewellery at the Midland Bank – not a lot. I gave half of it back to Ferenc when the business started going bad." She looked him in the eye and tried to make him believe her. She had not mentioned the diamond ring or the deposit at the other bank. Arnie glanced at her rapidly, decided she was telling the truth and said, "OK, Moll. I believe you. On the other hand, if I ever hear anything that makes me think you haven't been telling me the truth –"

"All right, Arnie," Molly said briskly, getting out of bed. "We'll go to the bank and get the jewellery. Now get out so I can get dressed."

"Sure you don't want me to stay?" he said, as he looked her over.

"Not with poor Ferenc hardly cold," Molly told him. "Have a bit of respect."

"Oh – come on, Moll," he said and Molly smiled the smile she had offered Lord Clover and Sir Christopher Wylie – and submitted to Arnold Rose. He was a slow and slightly brutal lover, a smacker, a hair-puller, a neck-biter. Molly's only surprise was that he was not worse. There was, in any case, no point in worrying about it. The Roses always got their price. "You're a lovely girl, Moll," he told her afterwards. "Never seen a finer and this just proves it more. I hope we're going to see a lot more of each other."

"Ferenc –" Molly murmured.

"I can see that, Molly," he replied. "But you can't go on mourning forever." A couple of days would be nice, though, Molly thought to herself. Fortunately, at that moment Arnie declared, "Well, then, to business. We'd better get ourselves down the bank and see what they've got."

"Good heavens above," he said later, as they sat in a shelter on the windy promenade, looking at the contents of the brown paper carrier bag in which Molly had put the jewellery. "Oh dear, oh dear – this wouldn't improve the look of the Christmas tree much, would it?" He stared her in the eye and asked, "Are you sure you've been telling me the truth, Molly?"

There was nobody about. Mist hung low over the promenade. Molly, knowing she had the ring tucked away in another bank, decided that she would not give it up. She launched into details of what Ferenc had given her and how she had later given it back. "By the time the mortgage had to be paid on Chepstow Villas there was nothing to pay it with – it was a private mortgage, from Arthur Simpkinson and he kept on ringing up. So bang went the diamond earrings – Ferenc kept trying to make me have them back. In the end I nipped down to Asprey's myself and sold them, and a string of pearls, and gave him the money, in cash. After that," she continued, "there we were with hundreds of houses and thousands of pounds of rent coming in and still nothing for Josie's school fees – what could I do? Something else had to go – this time the bracelet –" Arnie interrupted her and shook his head, "Tsk, tsk, tsk," he said. "What a silly girl you've been. Didn't Ivy teach you never to part with the jewellery?"

"Can't say she did," Molly replied, pleased that he had not found out about the ring.

"Well, take my word for it," Arnie told her. "In hard times jewellery's all a woman's got. Diamonds are a girl's best friend." He patted her knee and told her, "We'll have to see about replacing some of the tom, then, at a later date, won't we? Let's get out of this wind and have some lunch."

At a large restaurant on the front they ate oysters and drank champagne. Molly discovered she was quite enjoying herself. The past few days had been terrible. Now Arnie had taken the jewellery and left her the £200 in cash, which was a relief. He spoke well of Ferenc Nedermann so the occasion was respectful. She couldn't help thinking that Arnie and his brother had helped to push Nedermann into his heart attack but it was consoling to be able to speak of him at all.

He said, "Basically I liked Ferenc, very much. He was good company, Ferenc, and a clever businessman. All right, he made some mistakes but there's nothing to say that he couldn't have sorted all that out, if he hadn't died so tragically early. How old was he?"

"Forty-eight," Molly said.

"Forty-eight – I ask you. No age at all. In his prime," Arnie said. "There it is – I suppose none of us knows when we're going to be taken." He put a large piece of steak into his mouth and chewed. "Course I'm sorry I had to go after him like that but I had no choice. I couldn't let him get away with robbing my sister's boy, could I? Course not. If he'd only come to me like a gentleman –" he mused. "Still, water under the bridge, Moll, that's what it is."

Molly nodded and said, knowing he was about to start pressing her, "I can't get over it. One minute he was all right – the next, there I was trying to wake him up. My one consolation is that he couldn't have felt any pain. I don't think he knew anything about it. I'm wondering when they'll release the body after the autopsy –"

"Don't worry about all that, Moll," Arnie said. "The firm'll take care of the arrangements."

"He was a Jew," Molly said.

"That a fact?" Arnie said in surprise. "Should have guessed I suppose. Anyway," he persisted, "that's not what you should be thinking about just at this moment. You have to think of the future – you've got a kid to bring up. Now, I don't want to offend you. You're sensitive and at a time like this – never mind, some things have to be said – I want to tell you what I think about you, Molly. As I see it, you've got a lot of class, a lot of class – and a lot of personality. Now – I respect your grief, it's only natural and right, but a woman can't go on grieving forever and there you are, a good looker, a good dresser and all the rest – you need a man to protect you. What's a woman without a man, when all's said and done? And I could be good to you, Moll."

Molly smiled at him and said, "Arnie –" He went on, with some anger, "I'm good to women. Look at what I done for that slag Wendy Valentine – I don't like speaking ill of women but, let's face facts – she was a right little scrubber. But never mind that, while I was with her she had the best of everything – big cars, fur coats, plenty of sparklers – the lot. And that was for little Wendy, a real Blackwall Tunnel, to put it crudely – sorry, Molly, I'm not a crude man usually, but we all know about her. Not that there was any of that while I was about, of course, but before and after – oh, my God, what a careless girl. Gone right down now, I hear. Black, white or yellow, she doesn't bother. On the skids, good and proper – but, like I say, if I done all that for her, you can imagine what I'd do for you. Because I respect you, Moll. You've had a hard time and done your best for the kid and that's what a woman's judged by in this world – how she treats her kid. And you've always done right by Josie." He paused. "How about it, Moll?" he said. "I'll treat you well. I guarantee it."

322

An idea shot into Molly's head. She captured it rapidly and pinned it, like a butterfly to a board. She realized she was twenty-eight and wanted to do something for herself. She did not want another man, for the time being at any rate, having a hand in shaping her future. She saw that if she took up with Arnold Rose, or anyone else for that matter, she would never be able, as she put it, to call her soul her own. She was also horrified by the idea of Arnie Rose, the man and his life. On the other hand, she was afraid of offending him. She put her knife and fork together on the plate and told him, "I'm very shattered, Arnie. You're right. I'm sensitive. Perhaps I'm oversensitive. But I do need some time, maybe even a month or two, to put my heart together again. You're a fine man, but at a time like this, I haven't anything to bring you."

Pouring some more wine into her glass, he said, "Fair enough, Molly. I thought you might say something like that. Only right – I respect your feelings." He patted her hand with his own large one. There were black hairs growing on it. He had a diamond ring on his little finger. Molly squeezed the hand in reply and said, "That's very understanding of you."

"How about some sweet?" he asked. "And – why not – a little drop of pink champagne to help it down."

"Thank you, Arnie," Molly said, glad to be off the hook, but knowing that it was only a temporary escape. He drove her back to London and dropped her in Meakin Street.

1964

That night, in the now-neglected house at the end of the street Mary lay sleepless in the brass-knobbed bed where once she had lain in joy with her lover, Johnnie. She was thinking hard.

She had two hundred pounds under the mattress and one hundred in the Post Office and, all too soon, Arnie Rose would be coming courting in Meakin Street. It was inadvisable to refuse either of the Rose brothers what they wanted. Arnie's sentimentality could turn easily to violent rage, as if he were a child. She was reasonably safe for a time, while she kept up her pose as a grief-stricken widow under the protection of Sid and Ivy, whom Arnie and Norman's system of loyalties forbade them to offend. Moreover she had, that afternoon, applied for a place for Josephine at the local grammar school. She would get in, Molly guessed, but more money would be needed to pay for the uniform.

She lay there, with a tangle of financial and emotional ideas running round her head. Here was where she had first slept with Johnnie in the days when they had both been more innocent than either of them seemed to be today. Perhaps she should have married Ferenc and obtained some legal right to anything left over when the confusion was sorted out. But then, she thought, would she feel justified in taking it? She had had his child aborted. He would have died a happier man if she had been a proper wife to him, and undertaken to bear him a child. And, she thought, she had known, by now, too much death – Jim, Steven Greene, even Ferenc, had died before their time.

Finally, Molly slept and then awoke, from a nightmare about Ferenc's death, where she could have brought him back to life but could not remember what to do. In the yard outside there was a funny noise. Inside her head a voice said, "Take a shorthand and typing course." She got up to investigate the noise and, on the way downstairs, saw the advantages of the scheme. Firstly, she would be qualified for a better job if she could do shorthand and typing. She saw herself in a white coat, in an office, acting as a doctor's receptionist. Secondly, while she was taking the course she would be out a lot of the time. When she was in she would be studying. This, she thought, would deter Arnie Rose from making unexpected visits and put him off while he was in the house.

By this time she had reached the bottom of the stairs and was opening the kitchen door cautiously. She saw herself, a severe figure in hornrimmed glasses, behind a pile of books. It was dark in the yard outside and she could not at first see where the squeaking sound was coming from. Then she jumped back with a scream – something had touched her foot. She looked back into the lighted kitchen. On the floor by the stove a skinny little black and white kitten sat, with its tail curled round it, mewing up at her. Mary bolted the kitchen door and gave it some milk. She watched its small pink tongue lapping at the milk and said, "All right, Tibbles. Stay if you like. Time I got a nice, little cat to go with my nice, new little life." The cat, she reflected, as she went upstairs, would cheer Josephine, who had been whisked off to Ivy's at a moment of crisis, which she plainly understood, and was now going to move into the humble and untended house. Nedermann, who had given her everything else, had refused to allow her any pets. Even goldfish, he had declared, were unhygienic. There would also be a percentage in turning her new life into something very ordinary and boring. In a small house, with a gangling twelve-year-old child, a secretarial course and, now, a common black and white cat, Molly felt she would be too unglamorous for Arnie Rose to bother with. She decided she would, to deter him further, make sure of a few nights' work a week at the Marquis of Zetland. The money would help, too. So, imagining Josephine happy, a new career in view and Arnie Rose getting into his big, black car and saying farewell to Meakin Street, Molly, finally, went contentedly to sleep. The cat, dissatisfied with a cushion in the kitchen, came upstairs, nosed into the room and slept beside her, with its head on the pillow.

In spite of the cat and in spite of paying a secretarial college more than half her store of money for a four-month course in shorthand and typing, Molly had not reckoned with the fact that, at twenty-eight, she was if anything better-looking by far than she had been at eighteen. Her face had lost its childish roundness, giving it more definition. Her blue eyes still sparkled and her wide mouth, even in repose, still smiled, but her carriage now expressed maturity. All this only intrigued Arnie Rose more. The pretty girl he had once made automatic advances to now had some distinction. "She can't take up with rabble no more," he reported gloomily to his brother Norman. "She'll soon find that out. All I got to do is wait." To this Norman replied, "So you say, Arnie. So you say. But I'm telling you – a bird'll do anything – anything at all."

Arnie called at Meakin Street two or three times a week. Each time, Molly had to let him in. Any other contenders there might have been were soon warned off, by the landlord at the Marquis of Zetland, for example, who had only to mention that Molly was being courted by one of the Rose brothers to see the flirtatious customer immediately back off when Molly returned to the bar.

"It's hopeless, mum," she wailed to Ivy Waterhouse one day. "I'm doing all I can to make it plain I'm trying to be independent. I even tell him I have to start my typing practice after Josie's in bed. Nine o'clock I start rattling on the machine but he still hangs about with his bottles of champagne and I don't know what. Then, I have to go out for a meal with him sometimes and the story's wearing thin – about how I can't get over Ferenc's death. He turns up at the pub of a night and puts the customers off. Now Ginger's beginning to complain – he says he's turning away trade. The boozers can't relax while he's sitting there. And he's going down to the school and bringing Josie home in the car. What am I going to do? I can't refuse him outright but I'm scared if I don't give in he'll take it out on all of us."

"You're cornered," said Ivy. "That's the trouble. I think in the end you might just have to tell him it's no good."

"Even you don't know what he's like," Molly told her mother. "Think of everything horrible anyone could do to anyone and then double it – then you've got Arnie."

"Sid and Jack'll have to speak to him," said Ivy.

"Then Sid has an accident on the way to the depot and Jack falls off the dock," Molly told her. She said glumly, "It's your fault I was born so beautiful, mother." For some reason, Ivy flinched.

That evening Arnie called again and sat under the Christmas tree in the little parlour in Molly's house. The cat prowled between the two motionless figures in the lamplight. Josephine was in the kitchen, doing her homework. Molly sat quite still, like a hunted animal, hoping its enemy will think it gone. Inwardly she was screaming the scream of a woman courted against her will by a man who will not go away.

"I don't know why you don't get rid of that scruffy, nervy thing, Molly," said Arnie, looking at the cat. "Why don't I get you a nice poodle – a pedigree."

"I couldn't look after a dog properly while I'm taking this course," replied Molly. The cat sprang on her lap and began to purr. "Anyway," she said discouragingly, "these houses are running with mice."

"You don't have to live here if you don't want to," Arnie told her. "I thought I'd made that plain." His tone carried some menace. He had come to the conclusion that grief for Ferenc must end. "I expect you let him in the bedroom at night."

"He's company," Molly remarked. It was the wrong remark.

"No need to be alone, darling," Arnie replied. "I can think of better answers than an unhygienic cat. They can give you diseases, you know."

"Opening time," said Molly, getting to her feet. "I'd better go – Ginger's complaining because I'm always late."

"Sit down, Molly," Arnie ordered. Molly looked at him. His face was expressionless. Thinking of Josephine, still doing algebra in the kitchen with the oven door open to provide some heat, she sat down. "See here Molly," he said. It upsets me to see a girl like you in a rathole like this when she could have something a lot better. It upsets me to see you mourning over Ferenc like this. It's time you pulled yourself together and made a few decisions. I've made my offer and I'm beginning to think you're keeping me on a string. I don't like that. I don't like it at all."

Molly stood up. She went close to him and made her eyes go very big. She kept her face very still. She said in a low voice, "I'm afraid of myself, Arnie. You might think I'm superstitious but I'm afraid I could be a bringer of bad luck. Look what's happened to the men in my life – Jim Flanders – hanged. Steven Greene – suicide in a police cell. Ferenc Nedermann – dead in his forties with the coppers after him. What would you think if you were me? You might start to wonder if you didn't carry something bad with you." She dropped her voice even lower and said, "Like a kind of curse."

The room was lit only by one lamp. Arnie gazed up into Molly's large, unblinking eyes. He looked away and said, "That's nonsense, Molly. You're brooding, that's what you're doing. It's unhealthy. It's just a coincidence, that's all."

"I expect you're right, Arnie," Molly said, in an unconvinced, melancholy voice, "but I can't help thinking these things."

She knew that like many criminals Arnold Rose was superstitious. In a world where chance plays an important part, being lucky, or unlucky, mattered. He saw her to the door of the Marquis of Zetland with a thoughtful look on his face and did not come in for a drink, as he often did.

So far, so good, thought Molly, going into the pub and taking her old shoes out of the cupboard below the bar. But it won't work for long. Then what can I do? I'll have to go, but what about Josephine? What about me? Whatever can I do?

After the pub shut officially she was washing glasses in the sink behind the bar when Lil Messiter said, from her corner, "Not your usual smiling self tonight, Moll." Her voice was slurred. Molly, seeing her glass was empty, filled a pint mug with Guinness and took it over to her. She set it in front of the half-drunk woman and said, "Here you are, Mrs Messiter." Then she went back to the washing-up. The landlord often let Lil Messiter stay behind in the pub after closing time. He gave her a free drink, too. Everyone in Meakin Street knew that Lil had had a hard life. She was forty-eight and looked sixty. She had something wrong with her womb. Her husband, who had been a violent man, had died ten years before, leaving her with two children still at school and the other, George, still a toddler. Cissie was then a student nurse at St Thomas's hospital, Edna had married and Phil had run away from home and was living in Scotland. There was no one to offer help or money. Lil had gone out to work as a charwoman to keep her children. Now two of the boys had joined the navy Lil lived alone with her youngest child. She was tired, much older than her years. The older children now sent her a little money. She worked when she was able, and was drunk as often as she could afford. A brutal husband, poverty and five children had broken her. Now she sat in the corner of the Marquis of Zetland with her pint, small and shrivelled up and as happy now as she would ever be.

Molly, still washing up vigorously, looked over at her and told her, "I don't seem to feel I've got a lot to smile about, Mrs Messiter. But we've all got our problems, eh?"

"Life's not easy for a woman on her own," Lil said, shaking her head, "even if she has got lovely golden hair."

"That can make it worse," Molly told her as she wiped down the bar with long sweeps of her arm.

"Don't fancy Arnie, then?" asked Lil, looking automatically at the door of the pub, to make sure that it was shut. "It takes a man to get rid of a man," she added. "As long as you're there on your own he'll keep on prowling round."

"Have another half, Mrs Messiter?" asked Mary. "It's all right – I can't go home till I've swept up."

"I'll have another drop," Lil replied. As Molly brought the glass over Lil looked up at her with bleary eyes. Her grey-brown hair was tangled. She put a skinny hand on Molly's arm as she picked up the used glass and said, "Get rid of him, Molly."

Molly said in an undertone, "What can I do? He's dangerous."

"Find someone who can tackle him," said the woman.

"The Brigade of Guards couldn't do it," Molly told her.

She went behind the bar, got the broom out of the cupboard and began to sweep the floor.

"You'll have to kill him then," Lil said, beginning to laugh. "Take the carving knife to him." She drank from her glass of beer and went on cackling.

"Keep your voice down, Mrs M," Molly warned, as she swept.

"Drop something in his tea – murder him," said Lil, enjoying it.

Molly hastily swept up the dirt and cigarette ends and went out to the dustbins at the back with her dustpan. She emptied it, rinsed out the drying-up cloths and hung them on the sink to dry.

"All finished, Mrs Messiter?" she asked. "Come on – I'll see you home."

She took her by the arm and helped her up the street. It was eleven-thirty but her half-grown son, George, was still up.

"Put her to bed, there's a good lad," she said. "She's had one over the eight tonight." Then, studying his anxious face, she pulled out her purse and said, "Here's half a dollar for you – take it to please me."

He grasped his mother round the waist with one arm and took the money with the other. "Thanks," he said. "Come on, mum – time for Uncle Ned."

What a fucking awful life for that boy, thought Molly, crossing Meakin Street in the drizzle. Not too good for any of us, at the moment. "Oh Christ!" she muttered when she spotted the figure in the darkness pressed up against her front door. Lamps made shiny patches in the puddles in the street. There was no one else about.

'Hullo, Moll," said the man in her doorway.

"Who's that?" she asked, approaching. But of course she knew.

"It's Johnnie, Moll," he said.

Now she fished in her handbag for the doorkeys, saying, "What a surprise."

He followed her in. In the passageway he took her round the waist and tried to turn her round and kiss her but she pulled away, saying, "What are you doing here?" She put out her hand and turned on the light. He smiled at her, almost as if he mimicked his old, carefree smile, but now he was thinner, his face sallower and the smile seemed more like a rictus. "Something wrong?" she said. "Is that why you're here?"

"You've got hard, Molly," he could not resist saying.

"I'm older and wiser," she warned him. "Do you want a cup of tea?"

"What sort of a welcome is that?" he asked.

"Best you'll get – better than you deserve," she said. "I've been on my feet all evening at the pub and I'm tired."

He stood too close to her in the kitchen as she put the kettle on and put out the cups. Trying, Mary thought angrily, to see if she would respond to him as once she had. Using the body with which he had controlled several whores, one less than sixteen years old. And she asked again, "What are you doing here – are you in trouble?"

"A little bit," he admitted.

She poured him a cup of tea and told him, "Then you'd better take yourself and your trouble elsewhere." She lit the oven to warm up the small kitchen and offered him a cigarette.

He wore a pale woollen suit and a black roll-necked sweater. There was a gold watch on his wrist. "The point is, Johnnie," she said, "I'm busy at the moment, and tired, and I've got a girl of twelve. There isn't much room for trouble here."

"I heard you were back here," he told her, "and I was a bit surprised. I thought Ferenc would have left you in better nick. What happened to Orme Square? Didn't he put something aside for you so you'd be all right?"

"Things were in a right old state when he died," Molly said. "And, after all, he wasn't expecting to die. He'd never had anything wrong with him."

"Dodgy ticker, they told me," Johnnie said. "Too bad – it must have been a shock for you."

"It certainly was," Molly said, "especially with Arnie and Norman Rose coming after him from one side and the coppers from the other. I expect that's what killed him. If you've anything left over from what you took off him, Johnnie, I could do with it now."

"Not even any jewellery?" he asked, ignoring her.

"No, not even any jewellery," she told him. "You sound like the Inland Revenue."

"Nice to be back," he said, looking round the kitchen. "When I think about it now I realize how happy we were here. There wasn't ever anybody like you, Moll, and I don't suppose there ever will be."

She poured herself another cup of tea, feeling very tired. "You don't bleeding well change, do you?" she said. "Something goes wrong and there you are, looking for a woman to lean on. What do you want, Johnnie? Let's hear it now and get it over and done with. If it's money you can forget it. There isn't any here."

Putting down his cup he said, "A few weeks' kip, that's all. You can call me a lodger. Money's no problem – if you like, I'll pay rent."

Molly shook her head. "I don't think so," she said. "I've told you – I don't need any complications. There's something at the back of all this and I don't suppose it smells of roses." A thought struck her then and she added, "Talking of roses, Arnie's here a lot and I don't suppose you fancy running into him." She looked at him sadly. "It won't work, Johnnie. Not this time."

He looked at her wearily, "I thought you'd say no," he said. "Fact is, Molly, I got disturbed on a blag with Bones Ferguson – butcher's over in Finchley – with the whole week's takings in the safe at the back. So – there's an intervention by the law – they get Bones and I get away. Now they're looking for me. I can't go anywhere. I need a few weeks, somewhere quiet, until the excitement dies down. Then I can move off."

Molly was horrified. "This is a bloody stupid place to come," she exclaimed. "It's like Piccadilly Circus round here. Hundreds of people – half of them know you and none of them like you. Are you barmy, Johnnie, or what? You need some caravan in a field somewhere, or get up to Liverpool, anywhere but here. And, you're involving me. Think that's fair? Harbouring a fugitive, that's what it's called." She stood up. "Piss off, Johnnie Bridges," she said. "I won't get in trouble for you."

"One night," he pleaded. "I'm tired, Moll. I haven't got anywhere else to go."

"What about all those women?" she asked. "Can't any of them take you in?"

"What women?" he asked her wearily.

She stood up. "One night," she said. "On the sofa – I'll chuck some blankets down the stairs. I'm going to bed, now. And you'd better get out early, the back way, before anyone's about. Watch out for Arnie – he's always on the prowl."

"Not for a week or two," he said.

Halfway up the stairs she asked, "Why not?"

"They say the Roses've been advised to take a holiday in Spain. There's a few serious enquiries being made – they heard it would be better if they weren't around."

"That's one good thing then," Molly said, throwing the blankets down the stairs.

"I won't sleep a wink," she declared to herself. "Not with Johnnie in the house, a wanted fugitive." Almost before she had framed the thought she fell comfortably asleep.

Later he slipped naked into bed beside her saying, "Mary. My Mary." And because it had always been true that their bodies knew each other, had always known each other and, in spite of everything else, would always be friends, Molly and Johnnie Bridges came together unhesitatingly. The brass-knobbed bedstead was their joy, their delight and their home. They soared from it together. They came back to it together.

Then Molly said, "You leave tomorrow, though, Johnnie, in spite of all this."

"OK, Moll," he said. "I don't want to get you into trouble." She lay with her head on his chest. There were questions she could have asked – about what he had been doing, about the prostitutes, about his time in jail – but, just now, she did not want to. She knew that in the years since they had parted life had become seedier, more selfish and more hopeless. She did not want to remind him of it. She did not want to hear about it. All she said was, "That right about Arnie? He's had to leave the country?"

"That's right," Johnnie said. "They went too far this time. The Barnett kid."

"Oh – good God," Mary said in horror.

"Go to sleep, love. Don't think about it," he told her.

She awoke at six in the morning to find him getting into his clothes. She cried, whether it was for his troubles, or because he was going or just for what they had lost she did not know. In spite of the good suit he looked worn. His time in prison had beaten him, as it beats many men. The effects had not quite left him and perhaps never would. "Good luck, Johnnie," she said.

335

"Thanks, darling," he replied. She heard the back door close and knew he was hopping the walls of the yards of the houses in order to get into Wattenblath Street. Then she relaxed. It was not just that she had been worried about harbouring a wanted man. He now made her nervous. She had come to associate him with pain and trouble. She did not want him too close, too often.

She was peacefully cooking breakfast for herself and Josephine, feeling happy that Johnnie was gone and relieved that Arnie Rose had been forced to disappear, when there was a knock at the door. Anxious in case Johnnie had, compulsively, come back, or that the police had found out where he had been, she opened the door. The shock was actually worse than if it had been either Johnnie or the police. It was Arnie Rose, holding a huge bunch of yellow roses in one hand and a flat packet of papers in the other.

He was beaming. Molly could not control an expression of horror. She had thought he was abroad. She now knew he had been involved in the death of a boy of ten, Kenneth Barnett. Realizing she was staring at him in fear she masked it by saying, "Well, well, you're an early bird this morning – you'll have to take us as you find us – Josie's got to get to school and I've got a shorthand test at the college."

She walked rapidly down the passageway and went back to the grill. Turning over the sausages she tried to look as frowsty and tired as possible, while quickly reviewing the state of the house to see if she could remember any traces of Johnnie Bridges which might be lying about.

"Help yourself to a cup of tea," she told him. "Josephine – get the milk in off the step."

"No time – no time, Moll," he said. "Thing is I've got to go away. Should have gone yesterday but I couldn't leave without seeing you. Here I am – turn round and see what I brought you."

"I'll put them in water, Arnie," Molly said but she knew from her years with Nedermann what Arnie was delivering.

Arnie was walking the few paces it took to cover the kitchen, up and down, up and down. Josephine took her plate of sausages wearing a contained expression on her face. As she put the plate on the table she glanced up at her mother, signalling doubt. Molly stared back, willing her to feel confidence. Meanwhile Arnie was saying, "It's not the flowers I'm talking about, Molly dear. I want you to take these papers – legal title to a smart little mews house off Berkeley Square, 99 year lease, all drawn up in your name. But I haven't got time to mess about

336

any more – I want a quick decision and I want it now. You can get in there while I'm gone – talk to Morris about what you want –"

She flung her arms round Arnie and said, "Oh – you're so good to me Arnie –" As she spoke she knew that she would have to go down to Brighton as soon as Josephine left for school. There she could get the ring back from the bank and, on the proceeds, she and Josephine would have to disappear.

Arnie's threatening mood evaporated. He kissed Molly and said, "Now you're talking. I thought you'd see it my way. High time you got out of this rathole."

"Wash that ketchup off your mouth and get off, Josie," Molly said.

In the doorway her daughter looked at her and said, "I don't have to live with him, I'll stay with grandma –"

"Put your hat on and get off," Molly hissed. "I'll sort it all out. Don't worry."

She was about to go in when she saw Lil Messiter coming up the street with a bottle of milk. She paddled up in her old raincoat and called, "Nice change you had last night, eh, Moll? Better than Arnie Rose –"

"Yeah – raining again, Mrs Messiter," called Molly and shut the door.

"Did I hear my name?" asked Arnie, standing in the kitchen doorway.

"Lil Messiter," reported Molly in a panic, "she rambles on something shocking these days. She's had a hard life and she takes a drop too much – doubt if she's ever really sober, as a matter of fact. Oh – all this is such a shock, Arnie. I must go and sit down for a bit."

It was true that she felt as if her legs were giving way. She was terrified that Arnie would find out that Johnnie had been in the house. If Arnie got angry with her he might do something to hurt her daughter.

She walked into the parlour with her heart thudding. Behind her came Arnie saying, "Better to have a lie down, Moll. On the bed upstairs." He's like an ogre in a book, she thought. He'll push me till he gets his way. The worst part of it was that she had not made the bed. If Arnie came upstairs with her he would spot there had been two people in it the night before. Oh, God, thought Molly, now she was for it. Already she could feel the blood and snot running down her face from a smashed nose. Her face felt raw, and unprotected. He took her round the waist just as the door went.

"Don't answer it," he said.

"It might be mum," she told him. Only Ivy, as her mother, and as an old schoolfriend of the Roses, had the necessary influence to stop Arnie in his tracks. She had the impulse to run straight past anyone – postman, gasman or neighbour – who might be standing on the step and just keep on running, away from Arnold Rose.

Fortunately, the caller was Ivy. She stalked in grimly saying, "I hear there's bad news." Lil Messiter had seen Johnnie coming in and had told Ivy that he was there. Molly, shaking her head at her mother and pointing at the parlour door, stopped her from saying more. Ivy, looking at her panic-stricken face said, "I just thought I'd pop round for a chat." They both knew that if Ivy stayed too long the girl behind the counter at the bread shop, Renée, would spend all morning humming *Love Me Do*, wrecking the till roll and ruining next day's orders but Ivy, guessing the situation, opened the parlour door with a determined air. "Well, Arnie," she cried. "Fancy! I haven't seen you for months."

"You're looking very well, Ive," Arnie said gallantly. "More like your daughter's oldest sister. How do you do it?"

"Don't be silly, Arnie," Ivy said. "And me with three grandchildren."

"I expect you could do with a cup of coffee, Mum," Molly said, and ran upstairs quietly. She started to make the bed. Ivy was suddenly on her, surveying the tumbled bed and hissing, "What's going on in this house? Are you mad?" Nevertheless she grasped the bottom of the sheets and blankets and tucked them in swiftly.

"Get this," whispered Molly, throwing her the end of the counterpane. "Just stay here till he goes, mum. He's got to leave soon."

Ivy pulled her end of the counterpane straight, then she stepped back carefully, so as to make no noise, looked at the bed, searched the room with her eyes for other betraying details and nodded.

"Go downstairs and make out you've been in the kitchen," she said in an undertone. "And I'll go and pull the chain up here in a minute or two."

Molly nodded and went swiftly downstairs.

She made the tea and took it into the small sitting room, saying, "Here we are."

"I'm looking forward to our little mews flat, Molly," Arnold said. Just then a car drew up outside.

"I'll answer it," called Ivy coming downstairs. At the door they heard a man's voice. Ivy came back into the room and said, "Gentleman at the door for you, Arnie."

"Ask him to step in," Arnie said.

A thickset man stood in the doorway. "Geoff," Arnie said angrily. "How many times do I have to tell you – don't disturb me when I'm here."

Molly's nerves twanged worse than before. She was used to Nedermann's bully boys but the sight of Geoff shocked her. He was six foot four inches tall. He had shoulders like a brick wall and his face was brutal and mindless. She tried to look calm as the man replied, "Something's come up, Mr Arnold. Mr Norman said I had to come and get you." He bent his huge bulk over Arnie Rose and muttered in his ear.

Arnie looked annoyed for a moment and then put a good face on it. He remarked to Molly, "Well – there you go. Private plane waiting down in Kent and I've got to get on it. I'm sorry to be leaving in a hurry, Moll. See you when I get back. Over in Berkeley Square. Don't forget now – ask Morris for anything you want." He stood up and put a fat roll of notes on the table. He leaned over Molly and kissed her. "Back in two weeks at the latest," he told her and walked out, followed by the large man. The door closed behind them.

"Get up and wave out the window," instructed Ivy. As Molly hesitated she hissed, "Do it!" And Molly did. She waved the car off and then walked into the middle of the room.

"Sit down," Ivy told her. "Have you got a drop of brandy in the house?"

"I'm all right," Molly told her.

"You may be but I'm not," said Ivy. She went into the kitchen and came back with the brandy and two glasses.

"I've got a shorthand test today," said Molly.

Ivy swallowed her brandy. She was very shaken. "You know what he's done, don't you?" Ivy said in a panicky voice. "Why he's got to disappear? It's to do with that little boy. He and Norman must've arranged for him to be kidnapped – then the poor kid died of asthma on the floor of the barn where they put him. That's why they're looking for the Roses. Somebody told on them, at last." Ivy was angry. "Think of that poor child's fear. Dying like that. It's time they were stopped. Perhaps now they'll do something about them."

"They'll wriggle out of it," predicted Molly.

Ivy drank some brandy. "It makes you realize," she said. "Makes

339

you see what they're all about. You can't have him here any more, Molly. He's not fit company for a dog – and there's Josephine – that little boy was ten years old. It's frightening."

"I was going down to Brighton today to get some money I left there," Molly told her. "I was going to get away, with Josephine."

"It's not fair you should have to," Ivy said. "But it seems the only way. Look at that big thug he went out with. You couldn't get enough protection against that lot, not by police or anybody. Nobody'll be safe till they're inside. And look at you, you silly cow – you've not only picked him up and can't drop him but you're messing about with that Bridges too. It makes my blood run cold."

"It was only the one night," Molly told her. "He's on the run, too. I had to take him in."

"You horrify me," said Ivy. She leaned back in her chair. "Molly – you horrify me. One's a gangster and the other's on the run – and he's the one you sleep with. You've encouraged him, Molly. He won't go away. He'll hang about here until the police get him – probably in your bathroom. Then you'll be an accomplice. You'd best leave Josie with me and get away for a few months. I don't know how you managed to get mixed up with this mob in the first place."

"Oh, God – Josephine," Molly groaned in despair. "What sort of a mother am I?"

"No point in crying over spilt milk," Ivy said. But she looked very old. Molly sighed and thought that she wasn't much of a mother, or a daughter either.

Ivy's next remark made matters worse. "You can't even get to Brighton," she said. "There's a train strike."

Molly felt even more trapped. Then she said, "Jack's out on strike, too. He can take me in the car."

"Not till the end of the week," Ivy said. "He's on a course."

Molly looked at Arnie's money, lying on the table. With it she could hire a car to take her to Brighton.

"I wouldn't touch that," Ivy told her.

"I don't think I could," Molly said. She knew if she attacked her savings she could still afford the car but also thought she should leave the money behind for Ivy. She decided, "I'll wait till the strike ends or Jack can take me. Arnie's not going to be back in a hurry. I've got a few days. And in the meanwhile," she stated firmly, "I'm going to see if I can get to the college in time to take that shorthand test."

"I'll ring Jack from work and see if I can get him to do it quicker," declared Ivy. The two women stood up and, shaken, left Meakin Street to go about their business.

Ivy came back in the evening to report that Jack could drive Molly to Brighton the day after next. It was too late. By then Molly was hopelessly trapped.

You can afford a bit of bad luck if your judgment's been good. Likewise you can afford a bit of bad judgment if your luck's in. What you can never afford is a bit of each – stupid decisions and then a calamity. Which is what happened. I've done all my if-onlys about it – did them in Holloway for a year where there wasn't anything else to do. Blamed Johnnie, blamed myself, thought about it over and over again until I nearly sent myself mad. And the banging of the heavy doors and the jangling of the keys and the other women – well, all you can say is that I half-survived it. I don't think anybody ever really gets over that.

What happened is that Johnnie came back. He came at one in the morning and climbed in through the bedroom window, at the back. I had an argument with him then. It went on for hours. He got quite nasty at one point and acted as if he was going to hit me. I couldn't do anything, even if he had, because Josephine was in the house. There he is, dragging me out of bed, calling me a bitch and I couldn't do anything. Anyway, the upshot was that he spent the night on the sofa downstairs. Anyway, he'd refused to go, which meant the only way I could get rid of him that night was to call the police, which I wish – wished over and over again – I'd done. But somehow I didn't want to shop him. So I told him he could sleep downstairs, that if I saw him any more I would tell the police and then I went to sleep, thinking that even if the police arrived that minute I could just about make out he must have got in without me knowing about it. I went to sleep hating him and in the morning he was gone. And I worked out that Josie could go to Ivy's after school, I could dash down to Brighton for the ring – then I'd have the money to go up North for a few months, get a job, send money back to Ivy, write to Arnie saying I was still grieving for Ferenc and had gone away to find my fate or some such rubbish – and then I'd be back, none the worse for wear, in the spring when things had quietened down.

The whole country was buzzing. There were plenty of jobs, quite a lot of fun. I really thought, then, I could get back to London, get a decent job and – and I wind up in Holloway.

I've had some bad moments in my life but one of the worst was when I came back from the college about five in the afternoon and found the house full of policemen. There must have been ten of them, uniformed men and plain-clothes men as well. And Josie's there, in her school uniform, looking as if she's going to faint.

I knew there was something wrong when I came up Meakin Street. They were all out there, round the door – Lil and George, the woman from the corner shop, old man Fainlight. There were a couple of people there I didn't even know.

The other if-only was always about why I didn't turn round at the bottom of the street and run – but how did I know it wasn't an accident? It could have been a gas explosion or a murder, for all I knew. It could have been to do with Josie. And by the time I'd got close enough to ask, the coppers were close enough to find me. "Mrs Flanders?" says an inspector pushing his way down the hall.

"You all right, Josie?" is all I said. The poor kid just nodded at me dumbly. She'd only gone back to get a few books after school and then she opened the door and there they all were. Apparently they pushed past her and she didn't know what was happening. Then there's Ivy and Sid, who'd noticed the crowd at the house. "What's going on?" Sid asks the inspector. He turns to me and asks the same thing. I couldn't answer. Then another policeman, in uniform, edges down the hall and whispers in the inspector's ear. And he looks at me and calls me by name and charges me on the spot, in front of my mother and father and daughter, not to mention half the street. Harbouring a fugitive and receiving stolen goods, those were the charges. The first I couldn't deny and the second staggered me. I'm standing there startled when he hits me again. "Have you got a firearms licence?"

I just stood there. I don't know what I said. The next thing I know I'm in the car on my way to the police station.

The long and short of it is that I got eighteen months. It would have been more but I had no previous criminal record and they reckoned like they usually do, I'd been deceived by a man – and this time that was all too true.

I found out later that Arnie might have left the country but he'd put a man to spy on me. This man must have seen Johnnie either going in or out. He'd phoned Arnie in Spain and Arnie had lost his temper and shopped me. I'm glad it wasn't worse – he could have taken his spite out on my family. But that's small consolation when you're in a cell six feet by eight with two other women.

In all those smells and out of sight of day and pushed around and bullied all the time – and the feet on the corridors, and the clanging of the doors and the rattling of the keys – oh God, it's horrible, wicked, a prison.

Needless to say Arnie made sure they got Johnnie, too. At least he owned up that it was his stolen goods and his gun he'd put under a floorboard in the front room while he was meant to be sleeping there. He got seven years, for doing the robberies and having the gun. And he had a record, too.

I only did fourteen months in the end but it finished me. When I came out I didn't know what to do, I didn't even know who I was.

It's the noise I can remember. The clanging, the footsteps, the echoes, the way the women sometimes, for no reason at all, would begin to shriek and break things. So did I. It was like a madhouse. I was mad some of the time. I used to dream brilliantly coloured dreams, hearing a woman singing, in French, then breaking off into a long, terrible scream. There were days when that song would go through my head, every day, all day. I thought I was haunted. I told one of the women, a French whore by the name of Madeleine. She said, hum it, so I did. And she joined in. She sang me some of the words but she couldn't remember very many – it was about love escaping like the wind and cornfields, sentimental stuff like that. She told me it was an old song that had been popular round the clubs in her mother's day. I was surprised to find that it was a real song and wondered how I knew it but, the funny thing was, as she remembered more and more of the tune and the words I felt worse and worse and in the end I had to tell her to stop singing. I was getting desperate and you can't afford to get like that – not in there. Madeleine was kind – some were, in there, and she stopped and gave me a cigarette – but after she'd gone, I could remember more of the song, myself.

In the end the noise, the confinement, the pressure of the other women, prisoners and guards, was gone. I got out. But I couldn't go home.

1966

Molly Flanders, née Waterhouse, now nearing thirty years old, sits on a bench under trees on the Embankment at two in the morning.

Behind her, on the other side of the road, stand the big buildings of the lawyers and their small, carefully tended lawns. The pavements in front of her are wet. It is quiet, apart from the sound of an odd car passing and the distant banging of a train going over a bridge. She can even hear the sound of the water lapping at the Embankment wall opposite her. It is Spring and the water is high.

She is wearing an old brown skirt, brown shoes, and a large grey jacket. Beside her is a plastic carrier bag containing her flannel and toothbrush, a nightdress, some underclothes and a sweater. There is a chilly wind but the air is fresh. Her eyes, as she sits there, have a vague look. She is not in the real world. Mary Waterhouse, like the crisp packet slopping against the embankment wall or the twigs going down in the currents of the river, she is drifting . . .

In May she is sitting in the same clothes, this time on the stairs of a burned-out warehouse lower down the river, near the docks. Through the open door she can see an expanse of concrete and an abandoned car.

The man sitting beside her offers her a drink from a bottle of red wine. She puts it to her lips. He is decently dressed in green corduroys and a navy blue pea jacket. Unlike the couple crouching in a far, dark corner of the warehouse he is not a derelict. The others, in their huge, ragged overcoats and broken shoes, are sharing a drink from a long, dark bottle. From the stairs Molly and her companion can only see their huddled figures. One of them has a bad cough. But this pair, Molly and her companion, are different, many stages behind the other

347

two. Molly herself looks no more apathetic, no dirtier, than she did a month ago. Her plastic bag is still the same size – she has not taken to collecting stray, talismanic items, or things which might be useful another day. She is still outwardly respectable. If the police approach her she can still say that she is on her way somewhere, and be believed. There will be no more prison for Molly Waterhouse. Or not yet. But below them as they sit on the stairs, they can hear the coughs, the scuffles and the mutters of the others, holed up in the warehouse like rats. Below is a thousand square feet of empty space. Light from the full-length windows falls on the shapes of the tramps, sitting alone or in groups with their bottles, their bundles, their blankets and their old suitcases tied up with string. Occasionally noisy, meaningless quarrels break out. The rows soon die away and one is left shouting an incoherent phrase – "It was my sister that did it. My sister, I tell you, my sister."

"You always say that. That's what you always say."

"I think," says the man in the pea jacket to Molly, "I think I'll just step over to Kilburn to see if a friend of mine's in. D'you want to come? He's got a flat."

Molly shakes her head. She knows the likely outcome of the trip – they will end up in the wrong neighbourhood, or the wrong street, looking for an address which never existed or has been forgotten. Or the friend will have left many years ago. The whole warehouse is full of such dreams – of useful friends and welcoming relatives. Dreams repair ruined childhoods and reclaim ruined pasts. Reality has got lost, or is too hard to face.

The man in the pea jacket gets up and sets off on the long tramp to Kilburn, leaving Molly alone on the stairs. Her memory of how she came to be here is not very clear due to slight malnutrition and permanent fatigue. She seldom sleeps for very long in the same place. After she left Holloway with her brown paper parcel of clothing under her arm Ivy and Sid had expected her to go back to Meakin Street, where they had kept her house on, although it meant forgetting about their savings for the new house they wanted. They said a job as a clerk in the Civil Service had been fixed up for her – someone, they told her, had asked mysteriously not just for any discharged prisoner but specifically for her. The job had been in a museum. But they told her, as she stared at her parents' faces on visiting day, if she did not want to take the job in the museum, then Lady Allaun had written saying that she would like Molly to come down to Framlingham to help Mrs

Gates, who was too old to manage without assistance.

All Molly had said was that she would decide what to do when she left prison. She was now very dazed all the time but had enough rudimentary cunning left to write to Sid and Ivy giving her release date as the 18th, instead of the 13th. She thought that this deliberate mistake would escape any censor's eye and, indeed, it did. When Sid and Ivy came to meet her, she was gone – well, it was freedom she wanted, wasn't it? Freedom. She says the word aloud into the empty space of the warehouse. Down below, there is a loud, mad, laugh.

So it goes on. Molly does the drift, sleeping sometimes in hostels, with the restless, rootless women tossing and turning all round her, and sometimes in derelict houses and sometimes, on fine nights, on patches of waste ground. She gets money from the Social Security (someone has given her a birth certificate in the name of Maria Lane, from Birmingham). She eats eggs and chips in cafes or sandwiches and coffee from snack bars and stalls. Her appearance deteriorates because she can only bathe or wash her hair at the public baths, because her shoes are worn with walking and her clothes have become dirty and damaged by sleeping rough. She hooks up with a couple of mates, a young girl in an Indian dress, who wears no shoes, and an older man who this girl says is her father, although it seems unlikely, for he wears a shiny suit and speaks with a strong Irish accent. They wander together, drinking and taking pills when they can lay hands on them, planning their daily journeys, telling each other long contradictory tales about who they are, have been and will be. Lines of weariness carve themselves on Molly's face. She loses the bottom of a front tooth when a boy throws half a brick at the group while they are sitting round their fire on a patch of waste ground near Commercial Road.

In this way she drifts through the summer of 1966, awake at night, awake at dawn camped on rough grass behind a wall, sleeping on benches and on the ground, restless, nightmare-ridden in sleep, half-awake during the day, hearing her companions talking to each other, "Give us a puff of your fag, then," "the ugly bugger," "get the train to Aberdeen." "Look at him over there, will you, what does he think he is?"

At this point my father said, "We tried to get her a decent job – Do nothing – she's on her own now." I was unhappy about this – I'm unhappier now that I know the facts were even worse than I supposed. I was the person who had to explain how Mary had refused the job, and disappeared. There was considerable consternation. She had, to be frank, been more or less forgotten. The knowledge that she had vanished brought her back to mind. In short, I had been continuing in my duties like some conscientious functionary of a failing empire, who continues to mark the rolls in some distant, barbaric outpost with no idea that events at the centre are causing his efforts to be ignored. No attention was being paid to my continuing labours, which had been organized at a time when they seemed important. Time had dulled all interest in them – indeed, after a brief flurry of concern at her disappearance, it was agreed to let the matter drop and I was left with the sad feeling of someone who finds the work of many years discounted. At that point, keeping an eye on Molly was no longer my responsibility. Yet it remained a minor obsession. I was fascinated. I was, at this time, sorry for Molly, although impatient with her. And there was perhaps, even then, more to it than that. At all events, I still wanted to follow what was happening to her as much as I could but, obviously, at this stage there was no trace of her. Obviously she had something like a nervous breakdown in Holloway. After all, in the space of a few months she had seen her protector, Nedermann, die, had tried to reconstruct her life in spite of being pursued and terrified by one of London's worst gang bosses. She had almost succeeded until the unexpected arrest, trial and imprisonment. No wonder these blows and struggles, followed by the shock of prison, had exhausted her. On her release, she must have wanted to escape everything she knew. The danger was that the dreadful life would drag her down and make permanent the separation from a normal existence she was trying to achieve. She might have gone further and further down until she died perhaps, of self-neglect. The prognosis for her was good – she was young, strong and basically intelligent. Yet even these things are not always enough to save a man or woman. Bad luck and wrong circumstances can destroy the strongest of us.

Molly sat at a long table in a big, institutional room, green-painted to knee height, and dull white above that. She was eating her bowl of soup in the company of tramps, vagabonds, unemployed labourers looking for work, and a couple of blank-eyed hippies in jeans and bright shirts.

Two men entered the silent room, with two others behind them. In front came the vicar of St Botolph's, whose mission this was. Beside him stood a stocky man of medium height, wearing a black suit and a red tie. His stance implied energy. His bright, blue eyes went round the room quickly, taking in what was to be seen.

Molly, sitting between an old lady with bird's-nest grey hair and no teeth, and a young boy who had evidently been thrown out by his parents, took no notice of the party, which was in charge of investigating the extent to which private charities supporting the poor should be subsidized from public funds. Very few of the eaters looked up from their plates, in fact. Some two months earlier a man had been thrown down the stairs of a doss house nearby and kicked to death. The coroner had called it murder. The culprits were either the inmates of the hostel or the staff in charge. Witnesses had scattered fast after the event but the dead man had, it turned out, not been so detached from society as many others – two brothers, one a bank manager, and two sisters, both married to policemen, were keeping the subject of their brother's death on the boil. In consequence the arrival of the vicar and three men in suits was taken to mean further investigation and no one in the room wanted to be involved.

So even when Molly noticed the group in the doorway she pretended to take no notice. She went on eating her bread, which was hard, and ignoring the pain when she bit down on her damaged front tooth.

The man in the black suit and the red tie habitually moved fast. He was at Molly's side very quickly, holding out a large hand and saying, "Hullo. I'm Joe Endell. Who are you?" Molly paused before she realized she was meant to take the outstretched hand. Formal introductions had not been part of her experience for a long time.

"Mary Flanders," she said, taking the hand.

"Are you here often?" he asked.

Molly looked into the bright, blue eyes and told him, "Quite often. The floor's not too good but the band's terrific."

Joe Endell's eyes glittered a little but, short of time and spotting someone who could respond quickly, he merely asked in an undertone, "Have they done it up recently?"

"Cleaned it up a bit – changed the knives and forks," Molly told him in a low voice. In a few seconds she seemed to have left the daze of poverty, fatigue and depression she had been walking through for months. It could have been a spontaneous remission. It could have been the lively glint in Endell's eyes. And so, resuming, more loudly, her mendicant's whine, she said to him, "It's lovely here. One of the best cribs in London." Then, on a lower register, "There's a funny room upstairs where they put blokes who get out of control. I don't think the vicar knows too much – back room, third floor."

She startled herself by her own responses. Fighting them off she looked down at her plate again.

"Thank you very much for talking to me," Endell told her. He moved away to talk to some of the others while she picked up her hard bread, stood up and walked out. She ate it under a big tree in Hyde Park, later, and then fell asleep. In the meanwhile Endell was persecuting the staff at the mission mercilessly, looking into every room and asking questions, while his assistants chafed to get away, thinking they had seen all they needed. On the third floor, since he had seen every room, every lavatory and every bathroom, he could not be refused permission to see inside the small room at the back. The vicar was surprised to find the door locked and the key apparently missing.

"Must be somebody here who can pick a lock," Endell suggested boldly.

At this point a key was hastily produced and the door opened. The party gazed at concrete walls, mysteriously stained, a tiled floor, a mattressless bed. They smelled disinfectant and vomit. Under that, the scent no one can plainly smell but all can detect – fear. The vicar turned to a subordinate to ask a question. Endell made a note in his pocketbook and said, "What's this room for?"

"I shall be finding out," the vicar said firmly.

"I shall be interested to know," said Endell. Endell's companions, now seeing the point of the exhaustive survey of the mission, indicated agreement. Then the party broke up, the barrister to return to his chambers and the civil servant to his ministry, Endell himself to stroll on foot, back to the House of Commons. As he walked beside the river the picture of Molly's frowsled blonde hair, her wide pale mouth, with the chipped tooth, and her weary blue eyes came back to him. "The band's terrific," he said to himself with a grin. He realized that what made her memorable was the way she had spoken to him as an equal. In places such as that, as in many other places, a man such as himself would seldom be spoken to informally. Nor, because of that constraint, would he hear about the little rooms of various kinds on various third floors throughout the country. The people elected you as their representative, thought Joseph Endell, MP, walking through the gloomy high halls of the House of Commons, and then, half the time, they respected you too much to tell you anything they thought unsuitable for you to hear. If the saucy young vagrant had not spoken up, he and the others would never have discovered that sinister room at the mission where the staff must treat awkward customers in any way they saw fit.

Meanwhile Molly, beneath her tree, dreamed of Endell buying eggs in the corner shop in Meakin Street. Then her dreams took on the confusion of the homeless, rootless, lost.

A week later, Joe Endell left the House of Commons at midnight. As he walked along by the river in the intense, late heat which follows a hot, close day in the town he saw a woman sitting at the base of one of the pineapple-topped columns of Lambeth Bridge. She looked, in fact, as if she had been standing against it until she had suddenly slid to the ground. Nice to be in the country, Molly was thinking, as she sat on the pavement. Perhaps, she dreams, she will go to Framlingham and talk to Mrs Gates. In fact she was really heading towards a quiet, cool bed in the vetch and long grass of an old graveyard in the City of London.

As she rose to her feet she came nose to nose with Joe Endell. "Oh," he said, and, a true politician, remembered her name, "Mary Flanders."

Molly was kicking herself for having given him her real name. She said muzzily, "Can't remember yours – what is it?"

"Endell," he told her. On impulse he said, "Can I buy you a meal somewhere?" He told his agent, Sam Needham, later, that he wanted to ask her more about the workings of the hostels, soup kitchens, shelters, even the social services as they might be seen by a homeless person. This was the point at which Sam started to laugh.

However, Endell indeed began to question her as they walked up wide, empty Victoria Street under a full moon.

"How long have you been living rough?"

"Since the Spring," Molly told him.

"This Spring?" said Endell, thinking that she had not yet been reduced by trying to live rough through the winter.

"That's right," said Molly. "What do you do?"

"I'm an MP," Endell told her.

"Oh," said Molly. "Where for?"

"Kilburn West," said Endell.

Molly hesitated. The constituency he named included Meakin

353

Street. She did not want to think about Sid or Ivy or her daughter and she knew that if she told Endell she knew the area he might start trying to arrange something for her. She was probably a responsibility of his. In fact, he probably knew her brother Jack. Endell noticed the silence and filled it. He told her, "I'm Labour. I do some journalism, too. I'm from Yorkshire."

"Labour got in, didn't they?" Molly asked vaguely.

"That's right," Endell said. "This'll do, won't it?" He led her into a small cafe down a side street. They sat down at a formica table.

"This is nice of you," Molly said. "Why?"

"You did me a good turn," he told her. "If you hadn't tipped me off about that little room at the mission I wouldn't have believed it. There were clues in the reports I was reading but I needed to see the real thing. It was pretty horrible."

"Sausage, tomato and chips," said Molly to the man who came up in a stained white apron. "And I'll have a cup of tea."

At a nearby table some lads were lounging, making a noise. Then one of them got up and put some money in a jukebox. The sound of the Rolling Stones beat into the hot atmosphere.

"We'll be watching for that sort of thing in future," Endell told her.

"Good," Molly replied. Through the blur she was conscious of a man sitting opposite her who did not want anything. In the life she was leading nearly everyone wanted something – little evanescent desires, for a cigarette, or a few bob or a pair of shoes, flowed like a current between one and another. And here was someone who was not wondering if she had any money or pills, or a few cigarettes, on her. She took it for granted that he would not want from her what men want from women. She was tired and dirty. She was wearing plimsolls and an old coat. She wore a brown beret over her hair and, as a final touch, she lacked half a front tooth. She was well disguised. She had given up being a woman, perhaps because it had given her too much trouble and pain.

Endell, naturally polite, did not question her about how she came to her present situation but, as they ate, told her about himself. "I'm lucky – they couldn't give me a constituency up North but I was selected for the one in London. There's no travelling so I can spend more time there – in fact, I live there. I've got a lot to learn about the constituency and the people. I couldn't manage without the agent there. He's local and he knows everything and everybody. My parents still live up North, though. My father's a doctor and my mother's a teacher. I've got a brother and sister, too. Have you any brothers and sisters?"

He had delivered all this information in a fast, flat voice with a slight Yorkshire accent. Molly, in the daze of the rough-sleeper and rough-eater, lulled by the food and the heat in the cafe, barely took in what he said. But dimly she recognized in Endell's voice something which was not dulled, like the people she spoke to normally, nor full of masked impatience, like the officials with whom she had to deal.

"I've got a brother and sister, too," she told him.

"Another cup of tea?" he suggested.

"I'll have coffee," she surprised herself by saying. He went to the counter to get it and she became suspicious. Perhaps he was after her – some kind of pervert who picked up tatty women in the street. He could be a murderer. It was not unheard of for men to lure people on the tramp, men or women, to bits of waste ground and kill them. When he came back he carried two coffees. As he drank his he said, "That's better – I had one too many at the bar before I left. It's a hazard."

"Easy to get separated from the kind of people you're meant to be talking about," observed Molly.

"That's right," Endell agreed. "And you – where are you going now? Any plans?"

"Me? I'm just staying out of trouble," Molly replied. It was no use trying to explain. Her life had been too much for her and she could not even find the words to express this. She did not want to. She was done up and glad of it. She could not try any more. She felt a sort of rage against Endell because he could not understand. He might even be trying to draw her back into the world she had left.

He was trying. He looked at her closely. To evade his keen eyes and his friendly expression Molly stood up. "Thanks for the grub," she said. He could still be a murderer, she thought. Better get out. She said to him airily, "I might be going down to Kent. I've got friends there who'll help me."

He nodded at her gravely. After she had gone he sat on. The man in the apron, drying cups behind the bar, said humorously, "Girlfriend gone and left you, then? Better run after her – she could take up with some other bloke."

Endell looked at him. "Ever seen her before?" he asked.

The man shook his head. "Not round here," he told him and went back to his cups.

The months wore on. September was warm but in October the

pavements began to cool under Molly's feet. Sleeping rough became a matter of tossing under sacks and blankets in corners, sleep was thin and wakeful and her body was stiff in the cold dawns. Then it began to rain. She was obliged to sleep in shelters every night, which cost money. One morning a thought came into her head and she set off from the hostel, without thinking, for the House of Commons. By now it was November, dank and chill. When Endell arrived in the Central Lobby to see her he was shocked. She was in a worse condition than when he had last seen her. She wore old shoes and no stockings. Her face was not clean. Her legs were grimy. The hem of her old earth-coloured coat was coming down. There was a big scab on her hand. He sat beside her on a bench under the eye of a policeman. As she spoke, pouring out the words, he became more and more depressed.

"I need twenty pounds," was what she said. "I can't go home like this. My mum would die if she saw me. I've got a little girl, well, she's a big girl now but I can't go on like this. It's getting colder and wetter. I want to change my life and look after my little girl. And I've got the means, see. I've got this valuable diamond at a bank in Brighton. Worth thousands. If I can only get it but I haven't got the fare. And they wouldn't believe it was mine, not looking like this. I have to have the fare and a decent coat and shoes. I can't go home. I've got nobody to turn to – will you help me?"

Endell, horrified by this whining scene, played out publicly in the visitors' hall at the House of Commons, regretted, as the honest citizen will, that he had ever extended the hand of friendship to this down-and-out. He told her firmly, "Look here. I'm not green – you can't expect me to hand over twenty pounds on the strength of a story like that."

Realizing that she was in a public place, talking to a man who had some connection with the outside world, pulled Molly round. She said, "I'm not a liar. I'll ring up the bank and you can talk to them." She took a deep breath. "And you'll find my family at 19 Meakin Street. That's in your constituency. I'm a constituent of yours and that's why I'm here. Name of Flanders, born Waterhouse. You check up – you'll find I'm telling the truth."

Endell reflected that it was this trick of turning from the mendicant to the sane and, indeed, quick-thinking person which baffled him. Deciding quickly to trust her a little he told her, "All right. There's no point in ringing the bank. They wouldn't give me information over the telephone. But if your family are constituents of mine I'll try to help you. If I give you some paper and a stamp will you write to the bank to get confirmation of your story? Get it sent here, care of me. And I'll check —"

"Oh — just give me the money," said Molly impatiently. Her life had conditioned her to getting small items quickly, or not at all. "Just give it to me and I swear, as God's my witness, I'll never trouble you again."

"It's a funny story," Endell said doggedly. "You know that as well as I do. I must look into it and I will. Now — let me give you a few bob for paper and a stamp —"

Molly began to cry, whining, "I don't know what I'm going to do — I don't know which way to turn."

Endell, spotting the falsity, said, "Shut up. Don't let yourself down like this. Take this money, write off and come back next week."

Molly, suddenly bitter as the grave, stood up, ignoring the money he held out, and left the House of Commons.

It was this gesture which made Endell begin to believe she might be telling the truth. But when he looked in the electoral register there was no Waterhouse and no Flanders. "You nearly got taken there," he said to himself.

Molly went on the tramp in November, when most dossers were coming back to the city for the warmth and the extra facilities. She walked straight out of the House of Commons and headed, furiously, over the nearest bridge. She crossed the Thames and started walking south, towards the coast.

She walked doggedly through South London on that rainy morning, still clutching her two carrier bags. She walked through the affluent suburbs with their long lawns and large, neat houses. By afternoon, as the dark was coming down, she was on a long road, under trees with ferny common land on either side. She might have picked up a lift from one of the cars or lorries which swept past her on the road but a kind of obstinacy made her trudge on without stopping. She slept, when she felt she would drop down if she walked any further, beside a tractor in a farm building. She got up at dawn, when she heard a cock crow in the farmyard, and walked on. Later in the morning she bought some rolls in a small bakery in a little place she passed through. She spent the next night in a large park on the outskirts of Brighton. It rained. She was sitting, damp and filthy, on the steps of the bank in Brighton when it opened in the morning. The cashier, reluctantly, called the manager when she explained what she wanted. The manager was calm. She had only the papers they had given her when she left prison to prove her identity. Nevertheless he listened to her story, took several specimens of her signature and asked her to come back later in the day.

Molly sat on the beach, looking at the cold waves and recalling that it was two years since she had last been here. That was when she had deposited the ring. That was before the combination of Arnie Rose and Johnnie Bridges had got her sent to prison. She ought to have been worried about not getting the ring back but she was not.

"Everything seems in order," the manager told her, when she went back to the bank in the afternoon. "In any case," he remarked, giving her the documents to sign, "I recognized you. I never forget a face."

Molly said, "I don't look the same now."

"No," he said, "but I never forget a face."

"Congratulations," Mary replied and, seizing her ring, rushed off to find a jeweller who would buy the ring. After a call to the bank manager he offered her three thousand pounds. She took some in cash and the rest as a cheque. Along the front she threw her bags into the gutter. She raced on. Then she turned back and gazed at the newspapers, old clothing, scarves and the battered hairbrush which lay by the kerb in a heap. She bought some jeans, a sweater and a coat, some soap, shampoo and a toothbrush and managed, with some difficulty and by paying in advance, to book herself into a hotel. Next day she returned to Meakin Street, to find Sid, Ivy and Josephine.

Back at the House of Commons, in his office, Joe Endell was getting a surprise.

"Waterhouse," said Sam Needham, his agent. "Course I know them. Sid Waterhouse was a paid-up member for twenty years. His son's a big union man down in dockland. He's a councillor – chairman of the housing committee – Poplar, I think. I don't know why the Waterhouses aren't on the register. They must have moved out." He pulled down an old copy of the electoral register from a shelf, as he spoke. "One of the daughters was a naughty girl – ah – that's right – Mary." He turned over a page. "There you are – three years back – and – Sid and Ivy Waterhouse, no 19 and – no 4 – Flanders, Mrs Mary. Oh, blimey, that's it, of course. Mary Flanders. Her husband was hanged for murder. Did in a nightwatchman during a factory robbery. He was only a kid. No criminal record but the judge decided to make an example of him. And this girl, his wife, was Sid and Ivy's daughter. It's all coming back to me now. She had a kid just after her husband got topped. After that, she got into trouble."

"Oh, my God," said Endell. "I turned her away. I'd better try and find her."

"Don't do it," Sam Needham said firmly. "And don't reproach yourself. You can't go handing out money to every tramp who comes asking for it. Mind you, she was a lovely kid. I can remember her round the polling station with Sid when she was about ten or eleven. She was like an angel. I bet she's changed now."

"She has," said Endell.

"Better take that wistful look off your face, Joe Endell," warned Needham. "She's the sort that means trouble. I mean – what happened after her husband died was she took up with God knows who. I think she was working in a club. It had something to do with Norman and Arnie Rose, I do know that. And Ivy had to look after the little girl she had. And finally she fetched up with that property racketeer, Nedermann, you know – the one who was rack-renting half your constituency – the one at the back of half your housing cases, even though he's been dead for two years. That lady you're so sorry for lived high, wide and handsome on the profits of his slums and his brothels. That's where the famous jewellery comes from. Don't you bother with her – save your sympathy for those that need it more."

Endell grinned, "All right, Sam."

"I reckon," said Sam, "that little bleeder can still turn the trick, even covered in flea bites and carrying all her worldly wealth in an old carrier bag."

"Sam – I was sorry for her," Endell said.

"I hope that's all you were," Sam told him. "You should get married and suffer like the rest of us."

"I've been married," Endell said. "Now – perhaps we can get back to the sewers in Treadwell Street."

Nevertheless, dining with his girlfriend, Harriet Summers, he could not help mentioning the matter of Molly's appeal to him for help and how he had not been able to prevent her from leaving without it. "She's muddled and despairing," he said. "She doesn't know what she's doing. She might have been on the point of restoring herself – I might have been the man who prevented that."

Harriet, like Sam Needham, told him that he had no need to worry. She added sharply that a woman like Molly Flanders always knew how to look after herself. But, like Sam, she felt an undercurrent of suspicion about Endell's attitude to Molly. The next day, at the *Daily Mirror*, where she worked, she set to work on the files. The information she obtained, together with the memories of the reporters in the newsroom, and in the pub at lunchtime, made up a useful profile of Molly Flanders. She told no one why she was looking in case an enterprising feature writer decided that this gangland heroine turned down-and-out might make a useful piece of copy for the paper. And, being no fool, she did not tell Endell. She just went on burrowing away.

———

In the meanwhile Molly, who had found a dentist in Brighton prepared to replace the broken end of her tooth at short notice, was on her way, cleaned up and respectable, back to Meakin Street.

In the afternoon she knocked on the door of number 19. She was already disconcerted when the door opened. The brass knocker in the shape of a fish did not look like Sid and Ivy's doing. Nor did the brown paint on the front door. Nor did the ivy-trailing window boxes on the ledges outside the front window. Meakin Street was going up in the world. But where were Sid, Ivy and Josephine?

The woman who opened the door was wearing jeans and carried a small baby. Behind her, in the passageway, stood a red tricycle. The woman looked at Molly cautiously. She must still have carried some smell of the streets. She said, "Waterhouse? – Of course. Mrs Waterhouse left an address. She was very insistent – now – where did I put it? Wait there."

Molly waited. She came back with an address book and read out, "20 Abbot's Close, Beckenham."

"Thanks," said Molly and walked back down Meakin Street through the rain. She grinned. Ivy had got her wish at last. The Waterhouses of narrow, poor Meakin Street had become the Waterhouses of suburbia. Then she saw two large, black cars stopping outside number 4, the house which had once been hers. People got out and started to go inside. A tall boy in a black suit stood by the car, staring at the house. Molly ran across the street shouting, "George! Georgie!" The boy, a gangling teenager, with pale brown hair and a long, pale face, stared at her. He looked very drawn.

"Oh, George," she said, realizing the cars were from the undertaker's and Lil Messiter must be dead.

"Molly!" said a surprised voice. "Molly! What are you doing here?"

Molly looked towards the doorway and there stood Cissie, Lil's daughter, short and thin, wearing a good grey suit and well-polished black court shoes.

She said, "I was just coming past. Is it —"

Cissie nodded. "Mum," she said briefly. "Pneumonia. She left it too long. We've just had the funeral. Would you like to come in?"

Molly nodded. She put her arm round George and drew him in with her.

Two children stood in the hall. Inside Mary noticed, with astonishment, her own sofa, her own blue carpet, now stained and gritty, and even her own net curtains hanging dirtily at the window. Cissie, pouring her a glass of whisky, said, "I couldn't do very much — I was at a conference when it happened. We thought a quiet funeral — just family —"

Molly saw only three adults in the room.

"Very strange — you being in the street at the very moment —" Cissie said, handing her the glass. "I'd better go back in the kitchen. I've made a few sandwiches and there's a cake — it's not been done right," she added, violently, "I know that."

'I'll come and give you a hand," Molly said, rising. Cissie's brother-in-law, Ron, also got to his feet, went over and poured himself a whisky from the bottle on the table. The two children ran upstairs. Soon their feet began to sound overhead.

In the kitchen Cissie tutted. "Useless lot," she said, referring to the trio in the other room. "They've left it all to me. Poor old mum — Phil and Artie couldn't even come, worse luck. Phil's the best of them all but he's on a ship to New Zealand. Artie's up in the Firth of Forth, on a nuclear sub." She sniffed. A tear fell on the plate she was picking up. "She had a rotten life," she said.

"I know," Molly said. "I can't understand why Mum and Dad aren't here. Didn't you tell them?"

"Your dad's got flu — didn't you know?" Cissie asked.

"I've been away," Molly said.

"But I thought —" Cissie said.

"No — not that kind of away. Prison — I got out months ago," Molly said bluntly.

"Oh, God," said Cissie. "What's it all about?"

"Well, you're doing well, Cis," Molly told her. "Conferences and so forth. Your mum must have been pleased."

"That's right," said Cissie. "I've avoided what she got."

Molly thought that she was not happy, not at this moment. She had organized her life so as to evade her mother's fate – the poverty, the bad husband, the large family – and now the sufferer was dead. Cissie sniffed again and carried in two plates of sandwiches. Mary followed with more.

They were back in the kitchen again. Molly washed the jug and filled it with water. She took it in. The others, halfway down the whisky bottle, were talking about Lil Messiter. "She should have stood up to him more," Ron's sister said in a blurry voice.

"Not easy in those days," said the bearded brother-in-law.

"I'd lie there at night," Cissie's sister murmured. "Hearing it go on and dreaming of killing him."

Back in the kitchen Molly said, "I forgot to ask – why did she move here – your mum?"

"Old Soames, the landlord, died. His children wanted to sell off some of the houses. They reckoned mum's was so horrible they'd better get it fixed up before worse occurred. So they offered her this and did the old one up and sold it. There's a TV producer living there now."

"Get away," Molly said, impressed.

"In Meakin Street," said Cissie. "A TV producer. We used to think that Mr Fainlight was posh because he had a desk job at the Gas Board."

"I think I'll go and get your nephew and niece from upstairs," Molly said. "I bet they're rummaging through your mum's things."

"You're an angel, Molly," said Cissie. "I suppose they'll want a cup of tea in there."

"Tell them to get it themselves," Molly said. "As a matter of fact, they're my cups and it's my furniture they're sitting on." And she went upstairs and found the boy and girl, who were both about nine, in a litter of Lil Messiter's old cardigans and tired dresses. They were dressed in two of her old slips and tottering about on high-heeled shoes.

"Take that lot off and get downstairs," Molly said unceremoniously. She stood threateningly over them as they struggled out of Lil's old petticoats and kicked off her battered shoes. It seemed like a final outrage. As she followed them sadly downstairs, she noticed the stains on the carpet Lil must have made as she slopped wearily up to bed with her glass still in her hand. What could you say about Lil Messiter's life

— that she had six children, never hurt a fly, died as uncomplainingly as she had lived?

Re-entering the front room Molly sat down next to Cissie. Ron had his arm round his sister, a pale girl who giggled. Molly thought she was probably stoned. Cissie's sister, Edna, looked at her sternly. George, Lil's youngest child, sat in a corner, reading a magazine with a dismantled bicycle on the front.

"What's happening to George, now?" she asked Cissie.

"Going to live in Wimbledon with Ron and Edna," Cissie told her. "Luckily they've got a spare room. It's the only answer. Phil and Artie are at sea, I live half my life in the hospital." Cissie added in an undertone, "The trouble is that George's school wants to put him on a special engineering course, part-time. He's good at it, you see. But if he has to go to Wimbledon he'll have to change schools."

"Oh dear," Molly said.

"Where are you, now?" Cissie asked curiously. "Must take a bit of sorting out when you've been in prison."

Molly grinned. "Say that for old friends," she remarked. "They don't mince words. Well, Cis, I'm nowhere. I've just pulled round after a long time on the tramp. I broke in pieces while I was in Holloway. So now I'm going to go back to the secretarial course I was taking before it all happened."

"You'll be able to get a good job," Cissie said. Molly nodded.

"I just sold a ring I got from Ferenc Nedermann, the property developer," she said candidly. "That'll pay for a place to live. When I've finished the secretarial course I'll get a job and save the rest. Nest egg."

There was a roar of laughter from Ron. His sister looked embarrassed as a whisky stain spread on the sofa.

"I'd better go," Molly said.

"Have another drink," Cissie said. "I want to talk to you." Molly looked at her back. It was straight and energetic. She knew instinctively, because she had known Cissie as a battling, determined child, that she had made her mind up about something. In the meanwhile Cissie's sister Edna came and sat beside her.

"Molly, isn't it?" she said in a high, plangent voice. "It must be years since we've met. But I'm always hearing about you."

"Well, I expect you are," Molly said, knowing that Edna must have enjoyed the details of her scandalous life.

"No wonder, really, is it? I mean, they all say, when Mary Waterhouse is about something always happens," Edna told her with satisfaction. Molly sensed an attack. She changed the subject, "I hear George is moving in with you," she said.

Edna told her, "Ronnie's being very good about it. He says, all in all, blood's thicker than water." But Molly reflected that Edna herself sounded unhappy about the prospect of having her young brother in the house. She felt sorry for George, who was exchanging life in Meakin Street with his poor, wrecked mother for what looked like a cold home with his sister. The boy, in his corner, reading, looked weak, overgrown and incapable of bearing very much more.

Cissie, standing in front of Molly and Edna said, unceremoniously, "Come in the kitchen, Molly. I want to talk to you." Her sister, as Molly stood up, looked at Cissie with dislike.

In the kitchen Molly stared at Cissie, standing, small and straight, with her back to the door which led into the yard. "What's on your mind, Cis?" she asked.

"It's like this, Molly," Cissie said. "You can see what a bitch Edna is. And her husband's not just narrow-minded, like she is. I think he's brutal, as well. I think he hits Edna." For a moment she seemed to lose her firmness. Her small face sagged and she sighed, "I don't suppose she's got over her childhood, any more than any of us have."

"You're all right," Molly told her reassuringly.

"Almost," Cissie said. "Anyway, that's not the point. The point is, I can't take George and nor can the others and we're the only ones who'd help him. What I'm asking you is – if I give you this place to live in, will you have him as a lodger? That way he can go on and take his engineering classes."

"Phew," Molly said. "The problem is, if Josie comes here where will everybody sleep? There's only two bedrooms."

"George can sleep in the front room, if he has to," Cissie said firmly. "I'll pay for one of those settees that turns into a bed. I can fix up a grant for you, for looking after him. We'll pay for his clothes. I don't want you to think I'm asking you to keep him – but I want him taken care of properly. He's had a rotten childhood. I don't want him in Edna's house, getting bullied by that man. I don't want him to lose his chance to do his engineering, either. He's amazing, Molly, he really is. He can fix anything, make anything –"

"I need somewhere to live," Molly said.

"Give it a try, that's all I'm asking," Cissie pleaded, with all the desperation of the oldest child of an uncertain family. "I'm saving to gct my own house and I'm trying to change my job so I'm not on call all the time. It wouldn't be for too long. All I want is for George to go on with his course until I can take him – the thing is," she said, as if she were suddenly weary, "I can't say I approve of everything you've done but you're trying and at least you're goodhearted. I've got confidence in you. Otherwise off goes George, like a homeless dog, and God knows what'll happen to him. I've got the tenancy here. They'd have a job getting you out, especially if George was here with you –"

Molly made up her mind. "Done," she said.

"Thank God," said Cissie, suddenly drinking from the glass she had poured out for Molly. "That's a big weight off my mind."

Molly smiled. "Well – I'm back, it seems," she said, looking round. "Same old gas stove – same old sink."

Cissie said, "About the rent –"

Molly told her, "Can you take care of George till I've seen Sid and Ivy, got things straight here, and all that? Supposing I give you a ring tomorrow evening –"

"All right, Molly," Cissie said.

"Leave it to you to break the news to the family –" Molly told her, disappearing through the door.

The decision to take over the house in Meakin Street and its occupant seemed to clarify Molly's thoughts. As she walked from Beckenham Station she reflected that – yes, she had failed as a daughter and – yes, she had been a terrible mother and that having got herself stupidly trapped by Johnnie Bridges she should at least have had the decency to come straight out of prison and try to reclaim herself. Nevertheless, she wanted no more shame and guilt. Sid and Ivy might not like her when she turned up but she would just face them, offer her daughter a home and, if the reception was too bad, just turn round and go away again.

Despite everything, as she walked up Abbot's Close, she could not help smiling. With its trees planted in little squares of earth in the pavement, its neat little houses, built in the '30s, its tidy gardens and wooden fences, here was everything Ivy had always wanted. In the long years at Meakin Street, where window panes rattled, where the kitchen was dark and inconvenient and where you could put your fingers into the big crack running down the back wall, Ivy had talked about her dream home passionately, inventively and obsessively.

"There's nothing like owning your own place — nothing," she had declared. "Look at this place. Do you know when they put it up — to house the men who built the Albert Hall, that's who! It's a hundred years old. What I want is my own home, with a modern kitchen, easy to run, a bit of garden, some fresh air, not like this stuffy atmosphere. This place is making an old woman of me — I've given half my life to it. A thankless bloody task if ever there was one —"

Twenty, Abbot's Close was semi-detached, with a bow window covered by net curtains. There was a garden, with chrysanthemums in the borders and a neat lawn. Roses had been pruned neatly. Molly, now very nervous, yet delighted at the prospect of at last seeing her parents and daughter, rang the doorbell. Chimes inside the house reproduced the sound of Big Ben.

Ivy answered the door in a smart navy blue two-piece. Her hair had been set recently. She fell back, clutching her heart. "Mary! Oh Mary!" she cried. Molly stepped forward and hugged her. Her decision to face the family out, let them accept her or reject her as they willed, fell apart immediately. "Oh, mum," she wailed. "I'm sorry. I'm sorry I stayed away so long."

"We've been sick with worry," Ivy said, "sick." Drawing away she shouted, "Sid! Josie! Come and see what the cat dragged in! Hurry up!"

Turning back to Molly she said, "You could at least have sent us a postcard, Molly, saying you were all right. It's been terrible."

"I was all washed up, mum," sniffed Molly.

Sid stood in tears, unable to move, outside the living room door. A fat girl with brown curly hair rushed past him and pulled up short a few paces in front of Molly. "Mum!" she shouted.

"Sorry I stayed away so long, Josie," Molly said to her daughter. Josie gave her a kiss and said, "Well — you're back now."

Sid shouted, wiping away the tears on his sleeve, "We heard you were sleeping rough. We thought you might be dead. What sort of a bloody game do you call that?"

"I brought a bottle of champagne to toast my own return," Molly told him. "And a drop of whisky. I'd like to be invited in."

"Half a mind to turn you out," Sid said, angrily. Molly half-believed him but "Take no notice", advised Josephine. "I don't," her mother said. She walked past Sid, kissing him on the cheek as she went. There was a patterned carpet, a floral three-piece suite. An electric fire made of imitation logs burned in the fireplace. Molly wrestled with the champagne and the cork popped. "All over the carpet," mourned Ivy, as Molly poured the wine into glasses.

"Welcome home, Molly," said Sid, lifting his glass.

"I never thought you were dead," Josephine said. "Did I, Ivy? Didn't I say mum was alive?"

"She did," confided Ivy.

"Nice place," Molly said, looking round. "All new – better than Meakin Street."

"She says it isn't," Ivy said, nodding at Josephine. "Would you believe it – she misses that dirty old street."

"I'm at boarding school now," Josephine said. "I got a scholarship. I only come home at weekends and in the holidays."

"That's very clever of you," said Molly, impressed. "Do you like it?"

"Ooh – I love it," declared Josephine. "They've got horses."

"Horses," said Molly.

"It's only about ten miles from Framlingham," Ivy said. "She ran away once and went and dumped herself on Mrs Gates. Mrs Gates made her go back."

"She would," Molly said.

Sid interrupted. "Well – where were you?" he asked. "And what have you decided to do now, that's the question?"

"I was on the tramp, dad," Molly said. "I'm sorry, but there it is. I think I'd had enough trouble and prison was the last straw. When I came out I couldn't face coming back to you in disgrace. I couldn't face making any decisions." She sighed. "It must have been like a horrible holiday really."

"Probably a crisis point," pointed out Josephine. "You had to sum up your life and work out a fresh course."

Molly looked at her daughter. "Taking psychology, are you?" she said. "As well as riding?"

"I'm entitled to speak, aren't I?" asked Josephine.

"I don't know anyone who ever stopped a Waterhouse from speaking," Ivy said. "I've tried hard enough but I've never succeeded. That reminds me – Jack's a prospective candidate."

"What for?" asked Molly.

"Parliament, of course," Sid told her.

"Blimey," Molly said. "Everybody seems to be going up in the world." She sat down. She remembered Joe Endell's blue eyes. She said, "The long and short of it is that I'm moving back to Meakin

Street." She told them about coming across the party back from Lil Messiter's funeral. She told them of her plans to take up the secretarial course again. She added, "I don't see why Josie can't come to Meakin Street and here alternately. George can sleep in the front room when she's there and they'll be company for each other."

"What's he like?" Josephine asked.

Molly told her, "He's crushed. He's had a rotten life and now his mother's dead. You'll be lucky if you can get him out rockin' and rollin'." She added, "He's clever though. He could help you with your maths."

"Don't need any help," Josephine asserted.

Sid, holding out his glass, said, "Pour us another drop of whisky, Molly." As she did so he told her, "I don't know whether all this ought to be discussed with Josephine in the room."

"She's a bit too old to be sent out to play," Molly told him. "We might as well talk in front of her. It isn't as if she's been brought up in a convent, is it? What you're going to say is that it all sounds all right but you don't trust me – you can't have Josephine coming to a house stuffed with stolen property where her mum's hanging around with a gangster. Well, that's over. There won't be any more of that."

"What I don't like is the glint in Josephine's eye when she thinks about it," Ivy said. "They're all mad, these days, the girls. I don't want her getting adventurous and bold when she's supposed to be doing her exams."

"I'm sure she won't," Molly told her mother. "Course, if you think I'm too unwholesome to be allowed to see my own daughter –"

"That's up to you, really, isn't it?" Ivy said tartly.

"Steady work – that's the best way," Sid remarked sententiously.

"Looks like the only way at the moment," Molly told him.

"I can't say I'd fancy moving back to Meakin Street," Ivy said. "Can't you find a nice little flat somewhere?"

"It's cheap," Molly said flatly. "Anyway, those old houses have got a bit of character."

"Got a nice lot of leaking roofs, too," Ivy said. "And outside toilets and badly fitting windows and doors. They're subsiding, you know."

"I miss them," Sid remarked. "Not that I'm unhappy here – but we had some good times –"

"It's the pub you miss," said Mrs Ivy Waterhouse. "You hardly ever had to unplug that outside toilet when it blocked or cook dinner for five in that cramped kitchen. That place was a hell for women – look at poor Lil. It killed her. Don't talk to me about Meakin Street. I never want to hear of it again."

"You can always come over with Josie and go to the pub," Molly said to Sid. Standing up she said, "I'd better go – I'm talking to Cissie tonight and I'll probably be making a start on the place tomorrow. It's in a bit of a state."

She was relieved, as she walked back to the station, that the meeting with her parents had not gone worse.

A quiet Christmas in Meakin Street, she thought, walking through the November dark. Thinking of the cells, of the bomb sites and warehouses she thought, it could be worse. It could be a lot worse.

1967

And, indeed, it could have been worse. The Waterhouses all spent Christmas packed into Jack's house in Wapping. With Jack and his wife, the two West Indian children they had adopted, Molly, Josephine and George Messiter, Sid and Ivy and two of Jack's brothers-in-law, their wives, their children and Jack's mother-in-law. Two turkeys and three Christmas puddings later, as the rest of the family were in the living room, mocking the Queen's speech, as was customary in their circles, Pat, Jack's wife, made a scene in the kitchen over the washing up. Turning from the sink she said, "I'm fed up with them – I'm fed up with all of them. I've been brought up on the rights of bloody man and look at us – all the women, still in the kitchen washing up. What have they ever done for us? We've seen them through strikes and made their sandwiches for hunger marches and backed them up – up and up, all the time. And we still haven't got proper jobs, or pay, or conditions – they'll strike for men but they won't think about women. Look at us – all women – all standing here clearing up all these dishes while they sit there – I can't stand any more of it. I can't. We still don't count – these big humanitarians don't think about us. We're like the paper on the bloody wall, or this bloody sink here. I'm sick of it. Jack won't listen to me. Rights of man." She gazed into the sink and began to sob. "What about the rights of woman?" she cried suddenly and, smashing the meat plate into the crockery in the sink, she ran from the room. After a horrified pause, "Overtired," said Pat's sister-in-law. And "That's right," agreed the other women. "I'll make her a cup of tea," said her mother. "She'll feel better after a nap," Ivy said. As Pat's mother put the kettle on she said, "She's right though." The atmosphere in the kitchen thickened. There was a silence. Then Pat's sister-in-law said, "Better see if anything in the sink's survived the attack." Molly saw

Josephine fold her teacloth neatly, hang it on the rail by the door and quietly leave the room.

Pat came down later, after a sleep, and the day went on cheerfully. Shirley and her family were spending Christmas with her husband's family. "Poor girl," said Ivy, with one of the black toddlers on her knee. "It won't be much fun for her with that lot." Then they all started singing.

How little fun Christmas, or any other time, had been for Shirley came to light in late February.

By this time Molly was almost at the end of her secretarial course and worried about money. She had given Sid and Ivy half the proceeds from the sale of the ring. After all, they had been keeping Josephine for two years. She had spent some of the rest on restoring and repainting the house in Meakin Street, the rest went on taking up again her shorthand and typing course. She found it odd to be living with George and often with Josephine, who came frequently, but the experience was not unpleasant and to her surprise Josephine became fond of dreamy, withdrawn George whose only conversation was about engineering. They played long games of chess. Josephine, who was in the habit of making satirical faces, indicating a state of dulled gloom, at George behind his back, told her mother, "Well, at least he isn't always grabbing me like the boys in Beckenham – and that stuff about machines and cogs is quite interesting." She also questioned her mother about her past. Answering, Molly found it surprising that this flashy character, the former Mrs Molly Flanders, was now practising shorthand in the evenings in front of the television, worrying about the price of fish, letting the cat in and out, and producing large meals for the improbable appetites of two teenagers. She should, she often thought, consider meeting a man, loving him, perhaps marrying him.

The doorbell rang one Sunday afternoon, just as she was giving skinny George Messiter, who had just put down two plateloads of roast beef and Yorkshire pudding, a large slice of apple pie to follow. As she went to answer it she heard a crash. The cat, which had been taken to Beckenham by Sid and Ivy, had evidently trudged all the way back to Meakin Street, and lived as a stray until Molly reappeared. This had destroyed his manners. Now he had leaped on to the stove and grabbed the meat. George was sitting at the table looking astonished. He had no ability to anticipate ordinary domestic events. As Molly ducked down and seized the meat from the cat, the bell rang again. "George," Molly called back at him as she hurried to answer, "You're an idiot." She still held the plate, with the meat on it, in her hand. On the step stood her sister Shirley, with the two boys, Brian and Kevin. Two-year-old Kevin still had the same red-rimmed eyes he had once had as a baby. Both boys were thin and looked anxious. Shirley had a large suitcase and a shoulder bag over one arm.

"You'd better come in," Molly said, with the meat plate still in her hand. As they walked into the front room Shirley started to cry. The doorbell rang again.

Molly decided it would be Shirley's husband but instead found herself facing a tall man in a suit. He carried a clipboard.

"Mrs Messiter in?" he asked, staring at Molly and the plate of meat.

"Not here any more," Molly told him in the accepted style of Meakin Street when faced with strangers making enquiries.

"Oh," he said, still staring at her. "She's down on the electoral register."

Molly could hear thumps and bangs from the front room and guessed that her sister was sitting there in bewilderment while her nephews wrecked the room.

The man recognized her.

"You're Mary Waterhouse aren't you?" he asked.

"And who are you?" said Molly. "Look, you'll have to excuse me —"

Now there came a sharp crash from the kitchen. Molly turned round and shouted, "George!" She turned back and said, "Mr – er." She turned back and said, "George – can you please keep an eye on that bloody cat. What's he done now?"

George, gangling in the kitchen doorway, told her, "It wasn't the cat. I was working on my dishwasher when some plates fell off the table."

Molly said to the man in the doorway, "It's like living with a mad professor." To George she said, "Make us a cup of tea, love. My sister's just arrived."

"You're living here now, are you?" the man asked. He added quickly, "I'm from the Labour Party. I knew your dad – and you, when you were a little girl. I think you met our member, Joe Endell?"

"Oh," said Molly, recalling the scene at the Houses of Parliament. "I remember him."

"He'll be glad to know you're all right," Sam Needham told her.

"Tell him if I vote I'll vote for him. But I'm busy just now," she said.

"Goodbye," said Sam Needham to the closing door. A man in whose face many doors had been shut, he put a note on his clipboard and went on his way, thinking. Mary Waterhouse, even holding her meat plate and yelling about the cat, was lovely. He wondered if Endell had spotted that, under the dirt and old clothes. I bet he did, Needham thought cynically. He worried about Endell, unmarried in his mid-thirties, and wished he would settle down and have a couple of kids. It looked better in an MP and it cut down the chances of a scandal.

Meanwhile Molly had hurried back into the living room and was asking, "What's it all about, Shirl?"

"I've left," Shirley said despondently. "I think there's something wrong with him – Brian."

"What?" Molly asked.

"I can't say, in front of them," Shirley said. She nodded at the two boys, who were jumping on and off the sofa.

George came carefully in with a tray. He had assembled odd cups, a milk bottle and a teapot.

"George Messiter – Lil's boy. He lives here," explained Molly.

The older boy, Brian, reached up and handed the clock to his brother. Molly ran across and took it. She put it on a shelf.

"We want something to play with," he told her.

"Try to stop your brother fiddling with the TV," she said. "Look – I'll turn it on."

"We don't like TV," he said.

Shirley was sitting in a chair, looking into space. Molly poured out the tea. She gave a cup to George. She gave one to Shirley.

"We want something to drink," Brian told his mother. Shirley looked helpless. George said, "I'll get you some water out of the tap."

"Don't like water," said Kevin.

"I'll get you a biscuit, too," George said. Molly stared at him gratefully. For once he seemed to have assessed a situation and worked out how to cope with it. "Come with me," he said.

"Mind their hands on all those broken crocks," warned Molly. When they had gone she turned to her sister. "So you've left," she announced.

"Who wouldn't," Shirley asked. "They're awful, Molly. You can't imagine. His dad was trying to corner me in the kitchen – my own father-in-law – can you believe it?"

"Yes," Molly told her. "I can easily believe it."

376

"And mean!" Shirley exclaimed, "I was getting seven pounds a week housekeeping – and that was to cover everything, including the boys' clothes and shoes. And they're making a fortune from those shops. And muggins here is doing all their accounts for nothing, and for all their creeping Jesus act they're not above a false declaration to the Inland Revenue, just as long as they won't get found out."

"Straight out of Queen Victoria's time, that lot," said Molly. "All hard work, thrift and tabernacles and underneath they're working orphans to death, and putting their hands up the scullery maid's skirt. Honestly, Shirl, I don't know how you stuck it. A month of that and I'd've been off in my bare feet if I had to."

"It's the children," said Shirley. "And then I believed it, you see, for a long time. I was committed. But the nastiness underneath – you wouldn't believe. Brian ended up wanting me to dress up – and him. Are you shocked?"

"Dress up as what?" Molly asked, ignoring the question.

"Well I had to dress up as a tart – you know, corsets and high-heeled shoes," Shirley said, in an undertone. "And he – he –" She paused and said, "He had to dress up as me, in my clothes. That's Saturday night and on Sunday we're in the chapel, singing hymns as usual."

"Oh, dear, oh dear," Molly said. "In Greenford, too."

"And that horrible dad of his – having a go at me, all hands and quoting the Bible to prove it's all right. They're mad, Molly. I think they've driven me mad, too."

"It'll soon wear off," her sister said.

"And it's these pills," sobbed Shirley. "I got them for depression. Brian sent me to the doctor. But I'm crying more. And I think they only make me feel more confused. I asked the doctor but he said to keep on taking them, they'd work in the end. I think I'll give them up."

"You'd better," Molly said. There came another crash, this time from upstairs. She ran up. George said, surveying the mess in the bath, "The big one, Brian, said he wanted to go to the toilet. He must've climbed up."

"There'll be nothing left of this place by Monday," Molly said, turning on the taps and flushing the mixture of shampoo, bath salts and cologne down the drain. She was fishing the broken glass out of the bath and throwing it in the waste bin when George said, "I'm sorry for them really. They're disturbed."

"I'm sure you're right," Molly told him, cutting her hand on a piece of glass, "and so are we now. You're being very nice about this,

377

George. I'll sort something out in a minute. Can you watch them a bit longer?"

She went downstairs and told Shirley, "A few bottles in the bathroom."

"Oh," said Shirley apathetically.

Molly said, "Shirley – I'm sympathetic. But you can see for yourself there isn't much room here. And I'm taking my final tests for my diploma in a fortnight. This place isn't even mine. I've moved in because Cissie Messiter's got rights over the place. But I don't want to attract the landlord's attention. So stay a little while till you get fixed up but you can see the problem."

"Oh, thank you, Molly," her sister said. "I didn't know where to turn."

That night Shirley slept in George's room, with the boys on a borrowed mattress beside her. George slept on the sofa in the front room. This was his usual bed when Josephine came to stay. "Just for a few days," she told George.

At the end of ten days she was desperate. There was too little room at Meakin Street for herself, George, Shirley and the boys. Shirley remained lethargic. An effort to give up the tablets the doctor had given her failed. The more removed she became, the worse her children behaved. Molly would come home from the college tired, and hoping to practise for her tests, to find Shirley watching the TV and expecting her to cook supper for the five of them. Her drawers would have been turned out on to the floor, the kitchen would be in confusion and the cat hiding in the yard behind a tub of flowers which had all been torn up by the roots. Molly began to realize what had turned Ivy into the demonic figure from her childhood, and why she now clung so passionately to the featureless little house in the dull suburb. Waves of fatigue and irritability washed over her. She became obsessed with the importance of passing her tests and getting her diploma, even though she could take the tests again, even though without them she could still secure a good job. She worried about money. Shirley and the boys were costing a lot to keep. But she had not the heart to be too hard on her sister – she was so evidently bemused, trying to understand what had happened to her, trying to fight off the effects of the pills she was taking and lacking any money at all. Nevertheless Molly, coming back from college one day with a shopping basket full of food and the knowledge that she was down to her last fifty pounds, was resolved that she would speak seriously to her sister.

Inside the house Shirley lay comatose on the sofa. She could hear the two boys making an uproar in the yard. It was raining and Molly wondered if they were even wearing coats. George, at the kitchen table, was eating a cheese sandwich and blotting out the noise by reading an engineering magazine. Glancing out of the window Molly saw the two boys coatless, pulling bricks from the garden wall. Kevin still had his bedroom slippers on. She could have screamed.

George went on reading. The doorbell went. Answering it she found Josephine, wearing a lot of black make-up round her eyes, on the step with a small bag. "Josie," she said, "we agreed you weren't coming this weekend –"

"It's my friend's birthday party," Josephine told her. "You and Ivy didn't listen to me."

"There's nowhere for you to sleep –" Molly said.

"I'll go on the kitchen floor –"

She came in with the bag, but before Molly had shut the door the bell rang again. Harold Soames, the old landlord's heir, stood on the step in his navy suit and blue striped shirt and white collar.

"I'd like to see Miss Messiter," he said.

"She's out," said Molly, just as the two boys raced up the stairs, leaving a trail of muddy footprints. Molly saw eviction looming. She had no proper rights as a tenant. "Can I give her a message?" she offered doggedly as one of the boys fell over the cat, who was sneaking downstairs because he could hear them coming up. "I'll give it to her when she gets back."

Shirley came groggily out of the front room and, ignoring Molly and Soames, plodded upstairs after her children, who were now doing something noisy on the landing.

Soames stood staring at Molly, waiting for an explanation. When none came he said, "I don't like what I see." The noise continued upstairs, while Josephine stood staring in the passageway with the make-up standing out on her childish face. The cat streaked along the passageway with what Molly recognized as a chop in its mouth. Brian, coming down, fell down the last two stairs. As he opened his mouth to yell, Joe Endell stepped past the landlord and handed the chop to Molly. At that instant, although no one noticed, a flashlight went off in the street. He said, "I hope I'm not interfering with your way of feeding your pets."

Molly took the chop automatically, failed, for a moment, to recognize him and then seeing the point of humour said with relief, "Oh, Mr

Endell. Mr Endell – let me introduce Mr Soames, my landlord. Mr Soames – this is Mr Endell, our local member of Parliament."

Soames took a deep breath and said, "Well – how do you do, Mr Endell – well, I must be running along. Perhaps you'd tell Miss Messiter to get in touch with me Mrs – er. We landlords have our duty to do," he said to Endell. Endell nodded.

Molly, seizing the advantage, said, "I think perhaps it'd be a good idea to write to her suggesting an appointment."

He smiled at her uneasily, said goodbye and left.

"Do you want to come in?" Molly asked.

Once Endell was inside she began to laugh.

"What's happening?" Shirley said, coming downstairs.

"Eviction, that's what," she said with some relish. "Looks as if we'll all have to find somewhere else to live. A drink, Mr Endell? I think I need one anyway."

She pushed open the door of the front room with difficulty, for at some point the boys had moved the sofa close to it. There were toys, bits of puzzle and a half-made model of a plastic dinosaur lying on the carpet. She handed the chop to Josephine and said, "Put that under the tap and then back in the fridge."

"Shall I make some coffee?" asked Josephine, alarmed by her mother's grim good humour.

"That sounds like a good idea," Endell told her. He had the idea he should say what he had come to say and leave. Sam Needham, who had resolved not to mention Molly Flanders to him, had succumbed to his great weakness – the love of gossip – and had blurted out the story. He had said, to satisfy his conscience about the lapse, "Better stay away, though – that sort means nothing but trouble. She's got a track record, Joe." And Endell, visiting a block of Council flats a mile from Meakin Street, had found himself, nevertheless, driving there.

"Sorry about the mess," Molly said, putting on the electric fire and stooping to pick up some of the litter on the floor. "My sister and her two boys are here temporarily and we're a bit overcrowded."

Shirley came in and sat down. "Josephine said she'd give the boys some baked beans," she said. "You can't mean you're going to be turned out."

"Well, Shirley," explained her sister. "That man was the landlord, Soames. Now I'm here because Cissie said that she'd let me have the place to help me out – also because she didn't want George to have

380

to leave school and go to live with his sister. But that means she's subletting the house to me, which she isn't entitled to do. And I don't think Soames, after what he saw today, is going to believe that I'm not living here. Or everybody else in London. Awkward questions are going to be asked," she said firmly to Shirley. Almost immediately she felt sorry about her pleasure in giving her sister a shock. She remembered the cheerful schoolgirl, singing *She Was Poor But She Was Honest* at her in the kitchen in Ivy's house. She remembered the day they had celebrated her gaining the coveted place at Imperial College. She even remembered, suddenly, the dirty little girl who had offered her squashed chocolate at the station when she first came back from Framlingham. Shirley had never been like this before – she had been warped into the wrong shape and Molly knew she need not stay like it. She said, "Never mind, Shirley. I'll think of something. It could even work out for the best."

Josephine came in with the coffee. "My daughter, Josie," explained Molly. "And Shirley – this is Mr Endell."

"Call me Joe," said Endell to them. 'I'll call you the same," he said to Josephine. The doorbell went again.

"Don't let anybody in," ordered Molly. But after Josephine opened the door there were voices in the hall. "What did I just tell her?" murmured Molly.

"I thought," Ivy said aggressively as she came throught the door, "that if my old family except for Jack and his wife were all crowding back to Meakin Street I might as well come and see what was going on. As for you, miss," she said, turning to Josephine, "I don't suppose you told your mother I told you not to come here."

"I haven't exactly had the chance so far," Josephine told her sulkily.

"Well," Ivy began angrily. Her voice trailed off as she saw Endell.

"This is Joe Endell," explained Molly.

"Oh," Ivy said flatly. Then, realizing who he was she said, "Oh – that's right. The MP. I think I've heard my son Jack mention you. My husband, too."

"You're Jack's mother?" Endell said. "Pleased to meet you at last, Mrs Waterhouse."

At that moment the two boys came into the room, holding cakes in their hands. They began to charge about. A toy gave way on the carpet with a crunch. Kevin, the younger, dropped his cake on the floor. His brother ran over it. Ivy, who had begun to look more agreeable, narrowed her eyes. She glanced at Shirley, who was standing by the window. Her back straightened.

Joe Endell, the tactician, suggested to Molly, "I'm wondering, if we're going to discuss this matter of the tenancy, whether we shouldn't go over the road to the pub and talk?"

Molly hesitated. Ivy said, "If you've got any problems with that ruthless Soames, take advantage of Mr Endell's offer. And," she added, "I could do with the room while I lend Shirley a hand."

"All right," said Molly, glad of the chance to get away. "Will you be all right, Josie?"

"I've got a bone to pick with her, as well," Ivy said.

Endell took Molly by the arm and said, "It seems to me that with Mrs Waterhouse in charge you need feel no anxiety. In fact we might be better off if she was running the country."

"That's right," agreed Ivy. "By the way, there's a photographer lurking about across the street. Is that anything to do with you, Molly?"

"No," said Molly, looking questioningly at Endell. He shook his head. "I thought a flash went off when you came in," Molly told him, remembering.

"Maybe Sam Needham fixed something up with the local paper and forgot to tell me," Endell said.

In the street there was no sign of a photographer. "It looks as if my mother's started on a sort-out," remarked Molly. "I don't give much for the boys' chances."

"They look as if they could do with a little of granny's hand," replied Endell. At that moment a photographer dashed round the corner of the pub. There was a flash. "Oi!" cried Molly. "What do you think you're doing!"

Joe Endell ran after him as he walked away. "Who are you from?" he demanded.

"*Mirror*," said the man.

"What's it all about?" asked Endell.

"Dunno, mate," the photographer replied. "I was just told to come here."

"Is it me, or him?" Molly asked, coming up. She had been photographed at sixteen, the stricken, pregnant widow of a man condemned to death, she had been photographed at Frames, in a low-slung dress, and at Nedermann's funeral — the flashing of cameras had bad associations for her.

"4 Meakin Street. Blonde lady – that's what they told me," he said. "That's you, isn't it?"

"What for?" Molly asked indignantly.

"I've told you – I don't know. You'll have to take it up with the features editor," he said, turning round.

"That's exactly what I will do," Molly shouted after him. They went into the pub. "You look like a gin and tonic to me," Endell said.

"How did you guess?" Molly replied.

"Hullo, Molly," shouted Ginger. "I just saw Ivy going past – she didn't half look in a bad mood."

"That's why I'm here," replied Molly. "Hiding."

"Any news of Sid?"

"He misses this place. Planning another pilgrimage."

Endell handed her a glass of gin. He himself had a pint.

Molly said, "I'm speaking to that features editor first thing tomorrow morning. I know what they're doing. 'Where are they now – the villains of yesteryear?' That sort of thing. Next thing, there'll be a picture of me in my dressing-gown, taking in the milk. It's not fair, just as I'm trying to get my life straight, get some qualifications, pay the rent –"

"Mm," said Endell, keeping his own council in case his girlfriend Harriet had a hand in this. He remembered Harriet's odd reaction to his tale of how Sam Needham had found Molly. Her face had become guarded, and she had said, "I told you – that kind always survive," and had then changed the subject. Endell, not a subtle man in such areas, did not quite understand. But he did know that she had again started talking of the future and was at least acute enough to know that she wanted to marry him. However, he was not sure whether she wanted him for himself or for the life-style he could provide as a young MP who was being watched by senior members of the party.

Harriet had abandoned a well-off family, professional soldiers in the main, because they were too stuffy and conservative for a young woman of the '60s. But he suspected that an innate craving to be top of the heap might be suggesting to her that the position of wife and hostess to a rising young Labour MP would satisfy her trendy radicalism and her social ambitions at the same time. Would she be pleased, he wondered, if they married and he lost his seat at the next General Election? Would she be happy if they went back to Yorkshire and she became wife of a writer on the *Yorkshire Post*? You never knew how much these things counted with women, thought Endell. In rare cases girls of eighteen married repulsive old millionaires, or countesses ran off with gypsies – but elsewhere the edges were blurred and a man could never be sure whether it was his power, his money, his status, or just himself, to which the woman was attracted. Nevertheless, it would be annoying if Harriet had sent the photographer to Meakin Street and would get, tomorrow morning, a set of glossy 10 × 8s showing him walking into the pub with Molly Flanders. But – to hell with it, he thought, tired of the intricacies and uncertainties of private life. On impulse he said, "Look – I'm off to a meeting with the Borough Surveyor. Could you sit through an hour of housing plans and have dinner with me afterwards? We still haven't talked about the landlord."

Molly said "Yes." Of course.

They felt comfortable together, Joe Endell and Molly. It was as if, although they were excited by each other's presences, they had known each other for years.

Molly got interested by the housing plans. She said afterwards, in the cafe where they had gone for a meal, "Don't let him put up any more of those tower blocks – people won't want to live in them. They only suit single people with jobs who don't need gardens or somewhere for the kids to play. And they're not the people on the housing list."

Endell said, "They save space."

"They can't save much," said Molly. "They have to put big spaces round them so they look landscaped. Ordinary people would rather have a little patch of grass and flowers to themselves than a great big bit of landscaping. And what happens when the lifts break down and people start throwing old prams away all over the landscaping?"

"They're comfortable, convenient and decent," Endell said. "That's what people want."

"That's what the people who make the plans want – and the councillors who think they're wonderful," Molly said. "But half the councillors were brought up in places like Meakin Street and they hate them like my mum does. But there's worse ways to live. The other half just want the working classes tucked away on bits of old derelict ground where they won't interfere with the prices of the other property. Look at where they're building this lot – there's the railway lines on one side, the gasworks on the other and over to the north is the graveyard. Speaks for itself, doesn't it?"

Endell became annoyed. He believed in the destruction of the old slums, where many were still living without bathrooms. He believed in good, modern housing for families. He saw in Molly an example of the kind of woman who held progress back. He as good as told her she was operating against her own class interests. Molly said staunchly, "Look, Joe Endell, I bet I've lived in more places than you have in the course of a short career. I bet you come from some nice, detached house in the suburbs, with an apple tree in the garden. You may have the information and the brains, but I've got the experience. My mum's just achieved her life's ambition and moved out to the suburbs to a little house with a bit of garden. If you offered a flat on the nineteenth floor for nothing with all the furniture thrown in free, she'd laugh at you. It's not what she wants. It's not what I want. I wouldn't go there if you paid me. Aren't you in the business of giving people what they want?"

Endell told her, "Not when they don't know what they want really."

"Ooh," said Molly. "What makes you think you know what they want better than they do? You're nothing but a – an élitist." She was pleased to have found the word, which she had picked up over Christmas while listening to her relations.

Endell was still annoyed with her. He told her, "I don't think you know what you're talking about."

"All right," Molly said. "But I bet I'm right about your house with the garden, when you were a kid."

He owned up to a comfortable middle-class childhood in the suburbs of Leeds. His father was a doctor. His mother was a local councillor and the governor of a school. In turn Molly summarized her life for Endell. She added, "I'm thinking now, at my age, that it's time to get a grip on things. Up to now I haven't done much of the steering – I've just hurtled from one crisis to another. I mean – take you. You've followed a steady course. Admittedly you had a lot on your side. A middle-class family – just being a man – but I can see not everybody's carried on like me. Take Cissie Messiter – she had a far worse home than me and now she's got a good job and everything. She's never got in all the messes I got into."

"She probably doesn't look like you," Endell said frankly.

"Classic, isn't it?" Molly said. "Golden hair – and she's ruined. Then ruined again – and again – and again. It won't do. That's why I can't stand the idea of the *Daily Mirror* dragging it all up."

Endell, leaning forward over a plate of sponge pudding, said, "There's marriage. Ever thought of taking up with a steady, respectable chap – something like a Labour MP, for example?"

Molly laughed. "Nice for him," she said. "Do wonders for a man in the public eye, wouldn't it? A jailbird for a wife? A woman with a record of consorting with known criminals. He wouldn't stay an MP for long. What I would like," she continued, "is another pudding. The problem is, George Messiter has got the appetite of a wolf. So's Josephine. I haven't the heart to deny them because they're growing but I haven't seen seconds for a long time. I'm lucky to get firsts."

Endell, who had spoken quickly, on impulse, was relieved that she had not taken his remark about marriage seriously. He did not know why he had made it. After he had done so his first thought was of how angry Harriet would be. His second, how wonderful it would be to go and vote at the House of Commons and then go home with Molly Flanders.

I paid my half of the bill, dropped Joe off at the House of Commons and went home. But I knew it was all a technicality really. That's a thing you do know. I had to have Joe Endell. It was suddenly all I wanted. I wanted to feel his arms round me, I wanted to make love to him and, more than that, I wanted him to be there. I loved him, even his stupidity, even the fact that he talked about marriage without really knowing he loved me. But I had to try to get rid of him. For one thing, I really wanted – part of me really wanted – just to make it come out right for me by myself, without some Bridges getting me into trouble, without some Nedermann offering help, at a price, without threatening men like Arnie coming round – even without perfectly decent blokes, like Endell, changing things for me. But that was a dying impulse, really, and at the back of my mind I knew it. The real reason why I wanted to hold him off was what I'd told him – a woman with a record like mine could only be a handicap to a man in public life. Joe Endell had a clean sheet – no scandal, political or personal, unless you count an early marriage, which failed, no children and the ex-wife remarried and settled in New Zealand. If he got mixed up with me I'd be anything from a disadvantage to a disaster in his life. In short, to coin a phrase, I didn't want to leave him but I thought he ought to go. And I knew that if I didn't get rid of him fast I wouldn't be able to part with him later. My weakness is, I'm greedy. I knew I couldn't trust myself to say "no" forever.

When Molly got home that evening the house was quiet and Ivy was sitting in her coat on the sofa. She had her feet up. "I've done a bit of tidying," she reported, "and I'm just waiting for my mini-cab. I can get the last train from Victoria. Help yourself to a cup of coffee if you want one – it's standing on the table."

"Thanks, mum," Molly said, sitting down. "You've done wonders."

"Josephine's staying round at her friend's. I've phoned to make sure she's really there and she is. Also, I've had a word with Shirley and I've told her she's got to make her own arrangements. I've told her she can't stop here with you any longer – it isn't fair. There isn't room. And I've told her Sid and me can't take her in either. There isn't room there, either. She said it wasn't fair because I spent all those years looking after Josephine. Well she's right but Sid and me are getting older and there was only one of Josie. I didn't like to tell her straight but the idea of her drooping about the place while I get to grips with those two hooligans of boys is just like a nightmare."

Molly said, "But what's she going to do?"

"I don't know," said Ivy. "She's got to decide. I expect she'll go back to that Brian. She hasn't got a lot of choice. She'll have to work for her escape."

"Oh, God," said Molly.

"It's easier to get in than out," declared Ivy. "Like prison. That's what women don't understand. She's either going to have to bolt and leave her children behind or set her lips and get on with it until she's formed a better plan for getting out than just turning up at her sister's and dumping herself and the kids on you. Like I say – it was better for you because I was younger and it only meant Josephine –"

"I don't know how to help her," Molly said.

"You can't," Ivy told her. "And even you've had your wings clipped," Ivy observed, with mingled regret and satisfaction. "Anyway, while you're in the trade of getting respectable, the woman at the corner shop told me that snooty pair who bought our house are moving out. It's up for sale. Why don't you see if you can get a mortgage? Time you owned your own home."

"I've got enough to cope with," Molly said, "without putting a mortgage round my neck. I'd never get one anyway."

"Sid'll probably back you," Ivy told her. She stood up and went to the window. "Where's that cab?" she demanded. She was plainly in an impatient mood, brought on by once again, as she saw it, being hauled in to sort out her daughters' problems. "He'll offer Shirley a bit of help if she gets herself organized. God knows, none of us want to see her stuck with that Brian. The wedding was bad enough – all that praying and them watching us to make sure we weren't drinking too much as if we were a bunch of alcoholics. I'll never forget them standing there with their faces as long as fiddles and these glasses of lemonade in their hands. They thought I was crying because of losing Shirley. It wasn't that – I suddenly saw what her life would be," Ivy said. "What's all this about that MP?"

"What's all what?" asked Molly.

"I wouldn't want you mixed up with any of that lot," said her mother. "They're the worst – gambling drink, one wife in the constituency and one in London. They're like sailors – a wife in every port. Half of them make Johnnie Bridges look like a plaster angel."

"How do you know all this?" asked Molly.

"Jack," said her mother succinctly. Then the doorbell rang, she got into her mini-cab and left.

The next day Shirley also packed up and left for Greenford, looking more depressed than ever. "Ivy's right, you know," Molly said. "It's only a case of planning your escape better next time. It's just that no one can think what to do to help you." But Shirley only cried and Molly only felt more guilty.

In March Molly passed her tests very well and got a job with the managing director of a firm of dress shops. She ordered *The Times* and began to study the political news, with particular reference to Joe Endell. The photographs of Molly and Endell never appeared in the *Daily Mirror*. Molly believed this was the result of her angry conversation with the features editor, and her threats of taking legal action. The chief reason, though, was the conversation between Endell and Harriet, in which he, without putting the matter into words, implied that if she did not make an honest effort to stop the publicity, he would not see her any more. Harriet backed off. Her lack of enthusiasm and Molly's phone call deterred the news editor. Harriet, however, was resentful and suspicious. She filed the photographs carefully with her other information about Molly Flanders' past. And Endell, disliking what she had done, and his own part in stopping her, began to see less of Harriet. It seemed almost accidental. He was always busy, she hardly less so. Their schedules often conflicted. But Harriet was under no illusions. "It's that little tart, Flanders," she reported to her best friend. "And there isn't anything I can do about it because he doesn't know what he's doing himself."

Molly was in the Marquis of Zetland with Sid one evening when Endell strolled in. He sat down with them for a little while. They talked about Jack, whom Endell had met at the weekend. "There's a bye-election pending over in Battersea, and it's no secret now that they're putting up Jack. Safe seat, too."

"Then he can put up big skyscrapers all over Battersea," Molly remarked sourly.

"She's a bit of a reactionary, isn't she?" Endell said to her father.

"One thing you can say for skyscrapers," Sid remarked neutrally, "when the roof leaks only one family gets wet."

"How's the job?" Endell asked Molly.

"I'm leaving," she replied.

"After a month?" exclaimed Sid. "That's no way to go on. I've been in the same job over thirty years. Through the Blitz."

"Well, Hitler wasn't a married man who kept on grabbing you all the time and saying why not come out to dinner because his wife's got no sparkle," replied Molly. This was the reason for her sourness. An honest working life was beginning to resemble the days when she was fending off Arnie Rose. She was disillusioned.

Endell was outraged. "Can't you stop him?" he demanded.

"He's the boss," said Molly. "He thinks I'm one of the perks that goes with the job. What annoys me is that he's a driver – first he corners me by the filing cabinet in the outer office, then he starts demanding the thousands of letters he's wanted typed. He doesn't see the joke."

"Hit him with something and walk out," Sid told her. "Then phone head office."

"That's what I'm going to do," Molly said. "Then I'll find a job with a woman boss."

"That's my girl," said Sid. "Never lets anything get her down for long," he remarked to Endell. Then, standing up, he told them, "I'm going back to the delights of Beckenham, now." He left, shouting cheerios to his friends. "I'll bring you one of my home-grown cabbages next time," he told Ginger, who was behind the bar.

"Fancy a stroll along the canal?" Endell asked her.

"I've got to go home. Sid brought Josephine. She's all by herself," replied Molly.

"It's only eight-thirty," objected Endell. "She'll be watching TV. Come on – a breath of fresh air will do you good."

Molly yielded. She remembered leaving the pub with Johnnie

Bridges so long – more than ten years – ago.

Endell took her hand as they walked. She knew she should not let him do it. She remembered her Johnnie in 1953, in his sharp, gangster's suit. She remembered his overconfident smile – she had seen no need to hold back then, had not even considered it.

A cool breeze came across the canal. The branches overhanging the cemetery wall on the other side were already tinged slightly with green.

"I've got to tell you," said Endell. "Those pictures will be in the *Mirror* tomorrow – and more. I tried to stop it."

"Oh, fuck," said Molly, dropping his hand. "Oh, my God. Josephine'll have to face it out at school – I'll have trouble getting another job – and now it'll definitely have to be a woman. With all that I'll be fair game for any man boss – husband hanged, gangster's moll – what am I going to do?"

"It's worse than that," Endell told her. "I've got to tell you – I'm responsible. I mentioned you to my girlfriend – my ex-girlfriend – it was a long time ago, when I first met you. She works on the *Mirror*. I tried to stop her."

"Oh, sod it," Molly exclaimed. "You might be the people's friend, Joe Endell, but what good are you to me? God help this country if it's run by men who can't even stop their girlfriends from doing what they want. Didn't you tell her what it would do to me and my family, having all that raked up again? Don't tell me she couldn't have dreamed up something else to help her career."

"The trouble is," Endell said painfully, "she got angry when she saw the pictures. This is by way of a reprisal. Revenge."

"What?" Mary said. "What do you mean?" Then she understood. "Oh – you mean she thought there was something going on between you and me. Didn't you tell her there wasn't?"

"I tried," he said.

"Ivy was right," declared Molly.

"How?" asked Endell.

"Told me politicians were up to any game with women," retorted Molly.

"Hm," said Endell, uncertain of what strategy to adopt. He took her hand again and moved in front of her, to face her. "Let's go away," he said, "tomorrow – to France. I can arrange it. You shouldn't be going to your job anyway. You needn't see those pictures –"

Molly stared at him. She burst out, "We can't do it. You can't afford me." Then she flung her arms round his neck and kissed him. She meant to go immediately afterwards. Instead she stayed. Dropping her head towards Endell's shoulder – he was barely taller than she was – she said, "I can't hold out any longer. You'll have to take your chances."

"There isn't anything to worry about," he told her.

She pushed back the tuft of reddish brown hair which always stuck up on the top of his head and told him, "For a clever man, you're very stupid."

"I'm clever enough to get what I want," he said, kissing her again.

They sneaked in to Meakin Street, since Molly did not want to spend the night at his flat because of George and Josephine. By then George was lying flat out on his couch in the front room. Josephine had taken the mattress from George's bed and was asleep on the floor of his room. Endell and Molly, very quietly, made love. He was gentle and considerate, whispering to her to find out how she felt. Then they talked and laughed, then made love again. This time Molly said, "I'm not a lady, you know." And this time Endell, whose senses had been trained by another woman, was urgent, exultant and generous. He said, "I love you. I've loved you for a long time. I want you to marry me."

Molly feigned a greater sleepiness than she felt and murmured, "I love you, Joe." They muttered on for a little while but after he fell asleep Molly reflected that she could not marry him. And even felt that even if she had not known that her existence as his wife might damage him politically she might still have hesitated. A marriage might provide a more respectable background for her teenage daughter but did she really want to be married? It might make her Endell's in a way she did not want. And yet – she was happy.

Next morning Joe went out for the paper. He and Molly sat, each with their own copy, studying it. There was Molly, pregnant, in a black dress on the step at 19 Meakin Street just after Jim Flanders had been condemned to death – Molly in the nightclub snap with Johnnie Bridges and the Rose brothers – Molly and Steven Greene, both in evening dress, looking smart in their smart flat above the club in South Molton Street. There was Molly with Nedermann. There was a picture of one of Nedermann's slums. There was the story of Molly's imprisonment.

To her surprise when she looked at Endell across the table he was wiping away tears with a big blue handkerchief. "Joe!" she exclaimed. "What is it!" For a horrible moment she thought he was regretting that he would have to tell her they had to part. He said, "It's this picture of you in your teens, pregnant, after they sentenced that poor little bugger to death. It tells a story, that one."

"Don't start saying that's why I went to the bad," Molly said. "That was only part of it. I enjoyed being like I was — I liked the clothes, the bright lights and the excitement. Don't think I was happy before, shut up in that little flat with Jim — I wasn't. Pound to a penny, if he hadn't been hanged, I'd have skipped anyway."

"You don't look like skipping anywhere in that picture," Endell said. "You look puffy-faced and bewildered, like a child at a parents' funeral. All right — you wanted more than an early marriage and a baby you hadn't intended to have. But you didn't have much chance, really, did you?"

"Oh — it's nice of you to be kind about it," Molly said. "But no law stopped me from concentrating on my schooling, like Shirley. Or forced me to get myself in the club at fifteen years old. All right — if I'd been the daughter of a duke someone would have sorted it all out for me. But I was only a bus inspector's daughter, as the saying goes, and I wasn't careful enough."

"It's wrong," Endell said.

"Tends to happen, doesn't it?" replied Molly. "I don't mind — it's Josie I'm worried about. It won't help George with his friends, either."

"Take them out," advised Endell. "I'll get Sam Needham to bring a car round. We'll all go over to Ivy's."

"Haven't you got a car?" asked Molly.

"I keep on failing the test," sulked Endell.

"How many times?" asked Molly.

"Three," he lied.

"I'd have thought they'd pass you anyway," she said. "With you being an MP." Then she asked, "Shouldn't you be working on some papers, and that?"

He shook his head, "I'm in love," he pointed out. They were kissing in the kitchen, which was scattered with the mingled pages of two *Daily Mirrors*, when Josephine came in wearing her dressing-gown. She was chilly as she made herself a cup of tea and some toast. "I don't know what George is going to say about all this," she remarked to the grill. Then she asked, "Are you getting married?"

"That remains to be seen," Molly said with dignity. "And while you're making faces at your own mother I'm afraid there's worse." She pointed at the newspapers saying, "My glorious career." But

392

Josephine, pouncing on the papers, was not embarrassed. "Oh, look — there's me," she cried, pointing at the bulge in Molly's dress. "Ooh — Meakin Street — did you really know all these gangsters? What was Wendy Valentine really like?"

"Isn't this going to embarrass you at school?" asked Molly.

"Shouldn't think so," Josephine said. "It makes me look quite trendy. Have you got any of this jewellery left over?"

"You're eating it," Endell told her.

"I suppose it helps to be blonde," the girl said, with a look at her mother.

They all went over to Sid and Ivy's. Jack was there, by himself. He and his wife were getting on badly. Ivy was distraught. "There's Shirley — now there's Jack," she wailed at Molly and Endell. "Both marriages all over the place — where have we gone wrong? I suppose people won't put up with each other these days, like we had to. Too much choice, that's the problem."

"Can't have too much choice, Mrs Waterhouse," remarked Endell.

"Are you sure?" Ivy said grimly.

"I'd marry her like a shot, Mrs Waterhouse," Endell told her. "The problem is — she won't have me."

"Can't see why not," Ivy said comfortingly. "She'll change her mind in time."

"I am here," Molly reminded them.

"I'll talk to you later," Ivy said.

"Ask Jack, then," Molly said, as Jack and Sid came in from the garden.

"Ask what?" said Jack.

"Why I can't marry him," Molly said, nodding at Endell.

Jack considered. "Be tricky," he told his mother finally. "Very tricky. You see, no matter what pop stars do — no matter what they do next door — the public's still conservative about how MPs behave."

"Somebody organized this trip down memory lane," Sid remarked acutely, tapping the copy of the *Daily Mirror* under his arm. "Done it just to make sure there'd be a stink."

"A previous girlfriend," Endell admitted.

Sid offered him a beer. Josephine went angrily out of the room. "They're narrow-minded at that age," Ivy told her daughter. "Come on — I need some help with the dinner."

But in the kitchen she helped herself to a sherry and sat down heavily at the table.

393

"What a how-do-you-do, Molly," she said. "And I've already had Shirley on the phone, in tears, this morning."

"It's all right, mum," Molly said. "He's buying number 19. Your house'll be back in the family again. He'll live opposite me. Are you saying you can't be happy unless you're married?"

"That's the last thing I'd say," her mother replied.

Molly Endell

The new arrangement in Meakin Street worked well. Molly, officially sited at number 4, spent much of her time with Endell, across the street. George felt sufficiently mothered and sufficiently left alone to keep him happy. When Josephine was there she took on much of the task of caring for him. She recognized that different rules had to apply to poor George – he was almost incapable of looking after himself, required detailed instructions about how to cope with everyday life and was virtually helpless unless confronted with a mechanical problem. Almost incapable of finding his own socks, nevertheless he earned himself pocket money by fixing the neighbours' cars and motor bikes at low rates. Everything seemed simple, perhaps because Endell had the art of making things seem easy. When they went wrong he did not complain but worked out a way of making them come right the next time. He was not vain, nor fussy, and unencumbered by prejudices or set expectations. He worked hard, fell asleep anywhere, then got up and went on. Molly had accepted, as a fact of life, that in previous relationships she had to conform to a man's idea of what constituted a good woman. She had pandered to Johnnie Bridges' male gangster pride, she had attempted to live up to Nedermann's middle-European ideas of domesticity and she had been a silent naked Venus to Lord Clover while he poured out Cabinet secrets. She now found a relationship with a man which seemed to be without a rule book. She might rush back from work, feeling tired, to find herself cooking eggs and bacon for a minister of the government one day. On the next Joe would have made all the preparations for a dinner party that evening. The spare room at his house was almost continually occupied, sometimes by a refugee from Latin America, sometimes by a constituent on the run from a violent husband, sometimes by Josephine Flanders, or one of the many Endell relations, or an MP who had missed the train

397

back to his constituency on Friday night. The effect of living between two households and of the almost complete lack of privacy was offset by their continual conversation. Molly and Joe Endell talked all the time, interrupted each other, read things to each other, argued and agreed with each other. Molly, even at the hairdresser's on Saturday, often felt lonely for Joe, his shouting, chatting and general movement. She rushed home one day, hair still wet, and when she found him away, broke a couple of plates against the wall.

"What are you about?" demanded Joe, coming in.

"You weren't here," said Molly. "And I came back with my hair all wet to find you."

"I came to pick you up at the hairdresser's," Joe told her. "When I found you weren't there I was alarmed. Can you come to this strategy meeting tonight?"

"The election's years off," Molly objected.

"Not as long as you think," Endell said. "Coming? Anything to eat?"

"Cold meat," Molly said. "But Josephine sent George shopping and he's disappeared. She's gone off to find him. I'll make you a sandwich – I told Simon Tate I'd see him tonight. He's opened a restaurant in Chelsea. You could come on afterwards and we could have a meal."

"Right," Endell said, accepting the sandwich. "But I'd like you to have been there."

"It gets on my nerves – you keep on and on about the voters and the unions and the movement – and all you ever mean is the men. Look at Jack – his wife walked out because she was so fed up with making sandwiches for men discussing their own rights."

"There's equal pay –" Endell said.

"You know that's rubbish," Molly told him. "What's the point without paid maternity leave and crêches? How could I have managed without Ivy? And she had to give up her job to take care of Josie. You'll never convince me the Labour Party isn't just as keen to ignore women as anybody else. It's just another men's club, that's all. You want to keep us dependent on you – makes you feel safer."

"You want to have a baby," Endell said.

"Thinking about it. Thinking it means giving up my job," muttered Molly.

Once again Joe Endell made it easy. "I'm going to be a deputy parliamentary private secretary," he said. "I won't be able to manage without my own secretary. I might as well pay you as anybody else. That way the baby would fit in. Will you do it?"

"Which?" Molly asked. Then she said, "Yes."

"Upstairs, then," Endell said. "And we'll discuss your duties – I'm keen to get started."

They went upstairs. Later, as Molly put her clothes on she looked at Endell, whose tufty hair was rumpled, and told him, "I love you, Joe Endell, more than I've ever loved anyone in my life."

He grinned and was asleep.

In his sitting room above the restaurant in Chelsea, Molly told Simon Tate, "I'm happier than I've ever been before."

"So am I," he replied. "Isn't it nice?"

"What is it?" she asked. "The restaurant? Clive?"

"Well – I love the restaurant and I love Clive – when I look back at good old Frames it feels like a nightmare. Chinless wonders losing their socks and those bricklike gambler's faces – all overshadowed by the Roses, like a couple of ogres. Hard to believe either of us could stand it."

They were drinking brandy. "I suppose it had its good moments," she said. "I mean – we had a few laughs – when we had to call all that money in at short notice and Ephraim Wetherby threatened to kill himself over the phone, so we could hear the shot – and those constant problems in the Ladies' –"

"It was like Act III of a Lyceum drama in there some nights," he recalled. "Suicides, gynaecological crises – yes, I daresay you're right. But I was young –"

"And afraid of the police," Molly added. "It must have been like a shadow hanging over you all the time."

"That's it," he said. "It'll take years for that terror to wear off."

"Remember Steven Greene?" she said.

"He was a real victim," said Simon. "Let's drink to him – we can't do anything else for him." And they chatted, like two people who had survived bad times, sometimes laughing and sometimes sad. "She went up North, I heard," Molly said of Wendy Valentine. "I think they finished her. She'll find it hard to be normal again. Wherever she goes someone will find out who she is – anyway, that life's like being on drugs. It's hard to get off it – ordinary life seems so drab."

"All that left a lot of wreckage about," Simon agreed. Nevertheless, talking about those old times chilled Molly. Simon had known her in the old, mad days, when shifts and changes took place rapidly. Now, wrapped in love and contentment, like someone in a thick fur coat, she could not bear to even remember that might change. They had seen hard times together, she and Simon, and he was a reminder of the fact that nothing, or practically nothing, lasts forever.

They all ate together at a corner table in the restaurant after most of the customers had gone home. As they left Simon kissed her and said, conventionally enough, "Look after yourself, Molly." And, as he said it, her spine tingled with apprehension. She grabbed the keys from Endell on the pavement and said, without any explanation, "I'm going to drive, Joe." Endell looked annoyed, for now that he had finally passed the test his abilities as a driver were one of the few things he prided himself upon. Nevertheless, he got in the passenger seat without protest and Molly drove home.

I was delighted when I learned of Molly's happiness with Joe Endell. It was a delight perhaps marred by a little left-over jealousy about her but considerably increased by what might seem a rather odd feeling – that she had, somehow, not let me down. It can't be said that her previous choices of partner reflected much credit on her. Yet here she was, thoroughly happy, with a genuinely decent man and carrying out her duties as the near-wife of an MP very seriously. It made me feel less of a fool for having tried to defend her and to persuade my father and the others to see her as a normal human being, as we were ourselves, not just as a tart and a shocking liability. Now, here she was, respectably connected with a member of the government, "almost one of us" (as one of us might have put it) and it seemed to prove to me that I was right to have thought about her as I had done. At all events, Joe Endell was an honest man about whom, even in his gossipy world, very little scandal ever spread. If anything he had a reputation for an unpolitical degree of candour and incorruptibility which his colleagues must secretly have felt to be unprofessional. However, it worked – or rather, he did. It was felt he might become deputy Minister of Education after the 1971 election – the Conservative party put a stop to that, obviously, by winning the election. Even so, he still held his seat with a loss of only fifty votes. He was sea-green, Endell, protected from calumny by his own innocence, which he maintained vigorously, and from failure by a gift for intelligent hard work. Even his choice of a wife, which he seems to have made in a pub, after meeting the lady only three times – and on two of those occasions she was apparently a hopeless derelict – was one of the soundest decisions he ever made. No wonder I felt a little jealous. Endell had done what I might have done – asked Molly to marry me – but he had done it without qualms or doubt. And the result had been satisfactory. It made me feel cowardly, or unintelligent, or both. But I knew such feelings to be idiotic. I was perfectly happy myself in my private life. Before Endell and Molly married my wife had given birth to our second child. I was content – I suppose few people are immune to these small, wistful feelings on occasion.

In fact they lived their curious domestic life together for about seven years. They must have married just before, or just after, Molly conceived their child. By that time their union was fairly well known. Inside the constituency Molly's past misdemeanours were put down to youthful folly, prompted by the terrible death of her first husband. Perhaps her past even helped a little – people felt she was human, and could sympathize with a good many of their problems. She got away with it, in fact, because she was obviously ingenuous. She was energetic. She was enthusiastic. She was attractive and happy and kind. So, inside the constituency the marriage was mostly greeted favourably and outside it attracted only a few comments.

During the years she spent with Endell Molly was very obviously happy and one might have been forgiven for thinking that, for once in her life, happiness could last.

1974

Joe Endell sat contentedly by an open fire in Meakin Street with his feet on the fender. Some Yorkshire instinct had led him to have the fireplace opened up and the chimney swept in the autumn saying, "Hard times a-coming, Molly dear. You'll thank me later, I'm sure." By the light of a battery-operated lamp he chortled, wrote a speech and predicted the downfall of the government. "Lucky you're having the baby in June. At worst there'll be enough daylight to have it by. At best it'll be born the child of a Deputy Minister of the Crown."

"As long as it's all right," Molly replied. "I don't care." She felt better during this pregnancy, in her thirty-seventh year, than she had as Jim Flanders' reluctant, teenage bride. "But I must say, Joe," she said, looking up from her typewriter, "that I think you could try to trace your parents. It might be nice, now."

"It might not," said Joe Endell.

"Afraid you'll find out your dad was hanged for murder?" enquired Molly. "Or your mother was a tart? Don't worry. None of that's harmed Josie. No – honestly – aren't you ever curious?"

"No," Endell said shortly.

Molly, still typing, said, "Seriously, Joe, do you think all this gloating about Heath's disaster with the unions is a good idea? It's a bit boring."

Endell nodded. "Get that draft plan from upstairs," he said. "I'll use that, then concentrate on a rational future. Oh – well," he said, looking at her slightly tired face. "I'll get it. You sit there and take your bit into the future."

Molly sat in the dark room, which was lit only by the fire and the two low-powered lamps. She had raised the matter of trying to trace Joe's real parents before but he had always resisted. He told her that only the present and the future mattered to him. He had said, rightly, she thought, that his real parents were the mother and father who had reared him. Nevertheless, Molly imagined she detected, in his firm tones, some leftover traces from the doubts of childhood and adolescence. She spoke about this to Evelyn Endell, Joe's mother. "I know," Evelyn had said. "He doesn't want to think about it – I suggested it once before and he told me to leave the matter alone. Quite bluntly, really, for Joe. I wanted to do it anyway, years ago, but Fred felt it would be unwise. He said that he'd come in contact with a case once, in his own practice, where the patients had suddenly found out, by accident, that the real mother of their adopted daughter had been a prostitute. They'd virtually locked the girl up from the age of eleven. To conquer the bad blood, you see. And his idea was that if we found anything bad about Joe's parents we might be the same – not so extreme, if you see what I mean, but that it might colour our attitudes when he became difficult in adolescence, or at a time of crisis. I thought Fred might be right, so I let the idea drop."

They were sitting on the Endells' very green lawn, outside the house on the Lancashire coast. At the bottom of the garden there was a drop, then a long beach and then the sea began. Molly said, "I still think it's a bit peculiar. It was the one thing he never told me about himself. You had to tell me in the end. He never talks about it – and he hasn't got any memories before he came to live here. He was about five, you say. He must remember something – children do."

"What do you remember?" Evelyn Endell asked.

"Being on the train when I was evacuated," Molly said. "Oh, no," she suddenly recalled. "I remember Ivy giving me an egg, in an egg cup every day, after Jack went to school. We only had one egg cup. And it was a secret. That must be why I remember it. Ivy told me never to tell anybody I had that egg."

"I should think so," her mother-in-law said. "In wartime. Every day? Did you keep chickens?"

"In Meakin Street?" Molly exclaimed. "There was hardly room for a cat. What do you remember?"

"I think," said Evelyn Endell, "it was being on my father's horse, riding through the hills. The weather sometimes made the small roads impassable in those days – he must have had a call to an outlying farm and decided to take the horse across country. I remember the sky being very dark and a lot of wind. Then I remember being propped in a chair with a blanket over me, in front of the fire, drinking warm milk. My mother told me years later that she must have been in labour with my brother, which meant I was only about two and a half. Of course, it was typical of my father to leave my mother in the hands of a midwife while he went off to see another patient. Fred's exactly the same. Doctor's families always go short of medical attention. But I think that must be my earliest memory. People do vary – some people genuinely can't recall much of their early years. Others can remember being two, or even younger."

"It's the odd things you remember, I suppose," said Molly. "Out-of-the-ordinary things, like your ride – or my egg. But Joe must have had plenty of events – the orphanage, coming here – I don't understand it."

"Fred says it might be perfectly natural or it might be a buried trauma," said Evelyn. "He says, let sleeping dogs lie. There was only one point where he did begin to worry and that was when Joe got so angry about his father's money – Fred's father, that is." Seeing Molly's blank expression she said, "The inheritance – you know."

"I don't," Molly told her. "I don't think so, anyway."

"Oh," said Evelyn Endell. "Well – it was years ago, when Fred's father died. He was very rich, you see. He'd made his fortune in the '20s and '30s, running what started as a smallish firm making goods out of steel – light engineering – but he moved over to making arms. I agreed with Joe, really, or I could certainly see his point of view – Fred's father was trading with anyone who wanted arms and in those days there were no restrictions – he was a good friend of Basil Zaharoff's – I daresay if we knew the whole truth about who Fred's father had dealt with and what the consequences had been we'd all be shocked." She paused, "I suppose it might have looked different at the time, in the middle of the Depression."

"I daresay," said Molly. "Still – what happened with Joe?"

"Harold Endell, Fred's father, died," Evelyn told her. "He left half his money to Fred and the rest to be divided among the three grandchildren. This would have been almost twenty years ago. Joe'd just started work on the *Yorkshire Post*. And he refused the money, which was about £100,000, because he said he wouldn't take money from that source. Guns, you see. That was when Fred began to wonder if this fierce reaction he had didn't have something to do with rejecting the family because he couldn't face the thought of being adopted – you know the sort of thing –"

"Sounds far more like Joe's convictions than Joe's traumas," observed Molly. "Arms trading and big sums of capital – no wonder he went up in the air."

"He was so young," said Evelyn Endell. "We had no idea he was going to stick to his convictions. And I don't think parents take their children's political views all that seriously, do you? They always think they're going to grow out of them. All Fred could see was a young fool, daft enough to turn his back on a fortune." She looked at Molly. "Has he never mentioned any of this to you?" she asked.

"You know what he's like," Molly said. "What's over's over, where Joe's concerned. It's always tomorrow and the next day with him."

"That's why I think you shouldn't encourage him to explore the past," Evelyn Endell said bluntly. "I hope you don't mind —?"

Molly shook her head. "'Course not. You're his mother. You've known him a long time."

"It's just that you're so happy," she said earnestly. "Could you ask for any more?"

Molly shook her head and smiled. "Not a thing," she said. "Not a single thing. Leave the past in the past, that's the best idea."

The sea, out of sight, was rising. The sky, as they spoke, had darkened. "Oh dear," Mrs Endell said, looking up. "It's going to rain. Shall we go in?"

They walked back in silence to the house. Molly's instinct told her all was not well. Joe had been uneasy since they came, although here everything was the same as always. The only difference was that before they arrived she had told him she might be expecting their child. He had been so happy that he had cried. He had hugged her and said, "That was all I needed. All I wanted." And then came his nervousness. Molly told herself that it was probably quite normal for a man approaching forty, who had never been a father before, to feel strange about the event. And yet the explanation did not satisfy her.

By the time it came to leave Joe had a bad headache. He sat beside her in the passenger seat, looking white and strained. After the sedatives he had taken had put him to sleep, Mary clicked on the car radio. She turned it down and bowled along. She began to sing, in French, the tune which was playing, the sad, nostalgic little song she had learned first in her dreams and then in prison. As the song ended Joe woke up. Molly, glancing at him, saw that he looked drawn and quite wild-eyed. Turning her attention back to the road she said, in alarm, "Are you all right, Joe? Shall I find somewhere to pull up?"

He said, in a whisper, "It's all right — I had a bad dream. It must be the stuff dad gave me."

Molly drove on anxiously until she saw that he had fallen into a relaxed sleep.

But only a few weeks later he had a nightmare which woke him, screaming and shouting. She sat up and stared down at the sweating face. His expression of terror faded. He tried to smile. "I dreamed that Edward Heath won the election," he said.

As the election campaign got under way the nightmares ceased. They travelled up and down the country. Mary felt well and happy.

At four in the morning on 4th March 1974 Joe and Sam Needham, with Molly, left the house of another MP in Hampstead, sure of a Labour victory.

They decided to go to Transport House for a short while, to join in the celebration. Since Sam Needham had drunk several whiskies and Molly, in the sixth month of her pregnancy, was tired, Joe Endell, always enthusiastic about driving, volunteered to take the wheel. It occurred to Molly, as she got into the back seat, that Joe, who had just fought an election campaign, must be as tired as she was. Also, although she seldom liked to express the thought to herself, he was not a good driver. Nevertheless, as he drove off smoothly through the near-empty streets, she forgot her anxiety and even found herself dozing. She woke, briefly, thinking she heard a lion roar as they went past Regent's Park and, later, glimpsed the trees on the other side of the broad street as they drove down Park Lane. Lying low in her seat she heard Sam say, "Great night – great night, eh, Joe?" As she gazed up at the glimmering street lights they were passing she thought contentedly that in a few months she and Joe would have their child. She was in a half-dream when she heard Sam cry, "Joe – look out!" and at the same moment the car skidded, juddered, then skidded again. She was still terrified by the speed of the skid when a huge crash sent her jolting forward. She found herself hanging breathlessly over the seat in front, feeling, at that moment, no pain, but only shock. Alas for her, she did not lose consciousness. She was able to hear Sam saying dizzily, "Joe – Molly – are you all right? Joe? Joe!" She could hear voices outside the car and the insistent blaring of a horn close by.

"Joe?" she said. As her head cleared she saw his round head, with its reddish hair, slumped over the wheel. He was motionless.

Now, someone wrenched open the door in front. A man's voice said, "Don't move him – oh, God." Sam Needham muttered, "Lady in the back – get her out first." Another voice, more official-sounding, said, "How many in here? Are you hurt? Can you get out, madam?"

Helped from the car, she was taken to stand on the pavement where she stood looking at the four crashed cars blocking the left-hand side of Piccadilly, thinking that she must go to find Joe. Sam, beside her, said, "Are you all right, Molly? An ambulance is coming." Molly pulled away from the policeman's supporting arm and started to go to the car. "Joe's still in there," she explained to him. "It's better if you don't," said the policeman. "Wait for the ambulance." As Sam said, "No, Molly," she stepped off the kerb and walked to the car. Someone tried to stop her as she walked past the police cars, with their revolving lights. "It's my husband," she said.

She stood looking through the open car door at Joe Endell's peaceful face, now back against the high seat rest. It was only when she looked down and took in the red patch on the unmoving front of his shirt that she began to think he might be dead. Even then she did not believe it.

Indeed, as she crouched over him in the ambulance on the short trip to St George's Hospital asking, over and over again, "Is he dead? Tell me if he's all right. Is he dead?" she still did not really believe the answer might be, "Yes. Your husband is dead." And none of the ambulancemen, at that moment, dared tell her the truth.

She was released from hospital after three days, during which she behaved like a model patient. Her ribs were heavily bruised, but otherwise she was all right. She told Sid and Ivy, and everyone else, that she was going to be discharged a day later and went back to empty Meakin Street alone, in a taxi, having assured the hospital staff that her mother would be waiting for her. Her intention was quite clear. There was no point in living now that Joe was dead. She was going to kill herself.

As soon as she reached the house she went upstairs, without looking round, took a full bottle of codeine from the bathroom cabinet and, without a single tear, swallowed them all. She lay down on the bed, saying to herself, over and over, "Joe. Joe. Joe." She knew that she would never be able to love anyone again so much. Pagan, as only the city bred can be, she still believed she would see Joe again after she died and that was all she wanted, even if it was only for a moment or two. She knew in any case that she could not go on without Joe. She did not for a second consider that Joe's child made, or ever could make, any difference to all this. She was drifting, still tearless, towards her death, when Ivy foiled her.

At five that evening Ivy had telephoned the hospital, wanting to speak to Molly. Hearing she had left she immediately rang Meakin Street. Getting no reply she tried only once more before calling a cab. Sid, coming out of the living room, asked her what she was doing. "Our Mary's left the hospital," she told him, adding, with certainty, "I think she's going to make away with herself."

Sid looked at her, and said, "I'm coming with you."

"I loved Joe Endell," Ivy said to him in the cab. "He was like a son – he felt like a son to me."

Sid kicked in the lock at 19 Meakin Street. Half an hour later Molly was back in hospital.

She had no notion of how she passed the next few months. Her grief after Joe's death was absolute. She barely spoke or moved. She did eat, for the coming child was making its demands. Ivy looked after her at Beckenham, and grew more and more worried as the months passed and Molly lay motionless in bed, often moaning to herself, like an animal. The mound which was her child grew steadily under the bedclothes. Ivy became exhausted with anxiety and overwork.

This was the second time that her daughter had carried a child in terrible circumstances. It would be the second child born in tragedy, following the death of the father.

Two months after Joe's death she was talking to Isabel Allaun, who had come to express her sympathy.

"I'm afraid for the baby after she has it," Ivy told her. "It's not just her health. I'm afraid the shock of labour may disturb her mind worse. The doctor says leave her alone and she'll come out of it when the baby's born. He says it'll give her something to think about. The trouble is, all she says is she'll never love anybody like she loved Joe – the trouble is, I daresay it's true. I can't quarrel with her about it." She paused. "The doctor might be right," she added. "She might pull herself together when the baby's born – but there was a girl once, years ago, near where we used to live. She was like Molly. Her husband got killed on a building site before she had their baby. Three weeks after she had it she killed it – smothered it in the cradle. They let her off – said her mind was disturbed." She paused and looked at Isabel, who nodded. Ivy thought that this fierce opponent, whom she had once seen as in competition with her for her child, seemed very much reduced. She was shrunken and lined. The hands on which her jewelled rings still glittered were wrinkled and clawlike.

She said, "My dear, I'm so worried – I was dreadfully shocked when I saw her. She'll have to be made to get up – and very soon."

"I can't make her," Ivy said. "We've all tried – we've threatened and cajoled and pleaded. Nothing makes any difference. I've felt downright cruel from time to time. In fact there've been times when I could have dragged her out of bed out of sheer fury. I'm getting another doctor. Let's hope he can do something. Otherwise I'm afraid she'll end up in a mental hospital."

"In normal circumstances I'd invite her to stay," Isabel Allaun said. "But, quite honestly, at the moment nothing is as it should be. She's better here." She leaned back and added, "How sad it is. Poor Mary. She was such a lovely child, so pretty and spirited. One would have predicted less ill fortune for her. And now – a widow for the second time." She paused and then said, "Of course – the gypsy predicted it. Isn't that curious?"

"What gypsy?" Ivy asked.

"She probably never told you – I expect she forgot all about it. When she was quite a small child, living with us at Framlingham, my housekeeper, Mrs Gates, took her to a fortune teller, a gypsy, at a fair they used to have on the common. The woman produced the usual jumble of rubbish but I'm sure she said something about two husbands. And – what was it? – strange blood?"

Ivy said, very quickly, "I've never been superstitious. It's all rubbish and it does harm to those who listen."

"Of course," said Lady Allaun. "You're perfectly right. It's foolish of me to mention it. You have enough to worry about without nonsense like that." She stood up and said, "I must go or I'll miss the train. Thank you for letting me come. And I'm very sorry to find Mary as she is – I'll try to think if there's anything I can do to help."

After the narrow figure had gone down the path Ivy went back into the house and sat down wearily. She wondered what Isabel had meant by saying that nothing was as it should be at Allaun Towers. Sir Frederick had died two years ago. And she had not once mentioned her son, Tom. But the defeat, if it was a defeat, of an ancient enemy did not please her. She just thought, "Who'd be a woman, getting on in years, with all these problems?"

So she took a cup of tea and a slice of cake up to the helpless invalid who was her daughter. Molly, sitting up in bed, seized the cup and drank the contents in two gulps. She gobbled the cake, holding it in both hands, close to her mouth, like a child. Some of the tea spilled on her nightdress. There were crumbs on the sheets and blankets. Then she howled, staring at Ivy all the while. Then, as Ivy took the cup from the bed, where it lay on its side, she ceased to moan and put her hand, in horror, over her mouth. "I'll see you in a minute, Molly," Ivy said and, holding the cup, went out. She closed the door behind her and leaned against it, feeling that she had no strength left, that she might easily slide down the floor outside the bedroom and stay there, unable to get up. She wondered how long she could go on coping with her mad daughter, whether what she was doing even helped Molly, whether Molly would be able to look after the child when it was born. The image of a mad mother killing her child came to her so strongly that, now, she gasped. Then she breathed deeply and went slowly down-stairs with the cup. "Better if it died at birth," she thought to herself. "I can't take over another baby – not again."

Downstairs, in the kitchen, she felt a fierce resentment of Molly, of Endell, who had fathered a child and killed himself, of Sid and the doctor who persisted, as if they could not bear to examine the truth, in saying everything would be all right with Molly and the baby after the birth. "Who'd be a woman," she said to herself. "Men retire. But this lot is never-ending."

But in the event Isabel Allaun did change things, although uninten-tionally.

Tom Allaun and Charlie Markham were at the tables at Frames a week later. "Heard anything of Molly?" Charlie asked his cousin. He leaned back in a chair, a bit drunk. The years had not treated him unkindly. His thickset frame, which tended to run to fat, was still reasonably firm. His cheeks were still ruddy and his blue eyes clear. He looked what he was – a self-indulgent, entrepreneurial businessman, not too scrupulous in his dealings with women or business associates, but still in control of his situation. He had now been divorced twice and was paying indifferent court to a wealthy divorcee who, in her turn, was hesitating about whether to marry him or not. His cousin Tom, however, was in better shape, for he exercised carefully, watched his diet and drank sparingly. Nevertheless, superficially he remained a less attractive character than Charlie. He had not Charlie's expansive air. His eyes were less direct and his mouth had narrowed. Shaking his head at the croupier to indicate that they were not betting, he told

Charlie, "Molly's in a bad way. Got a bun in the oven, of course. Due in a few months. Ma went to see her and apparently she's right off her trolley and may stay like it. Looks as if it may come down to head-shrinkers and loony bins."

"Oh, God," Charlie said. "What a tragedy – she was a cracker in her time. What a goer she was." He was not prepared to admit that Molly had rejected him. Nor that in many ways he had been thoroughly frightened of her.

Tom, jealous of his cousin's success with Molly, said, "Well – not any more."

But Simon Tate, who had come in to look after the club as a favour that evening because both managers were away, had been listening to the conversation. He turned round abruptly, went upstairs to the office and telephoned Ivy.

He appeared in Beckenham next day. Ivy said, "I hope to God you can help."

"I'll try," he told her and went straight upstairs to the room where Molly lay. She lay on her side, a hump, under blankets, in the bed. Simon drew the curtains back. "I've got a lovely lunch waiting for you – all booked and champagne in a bucket. Just time to get dressed and get in the car."

"I can't," she said.

"Come on, Molly," he told her. "I've driven a long way to collect you. Don't disappoint me." She responded by trembling and crying, saying, "I can't. You can't make me. I can't."

He attacked her then, telling her, "Don't you dare lie about there saying, 'I can't and I won't.' Have you looked at your mother recently? I don't suppose so. You're killing her – she looks ill. Ill with the work of looking after you, a healthy woman. Do you want to bury her, next?"

Molly, to block out his voice, pulled the blankets over her head and moaned. Simon pulled back the covers, revealing the swollen face, pale with months of indoor life, the swollen body in an old blue nightdress, the pale, puffy legs. Molly screamed at seeing what Simon, a homosexual, could not help seeing – a swelling, termite queen. She tried to pull the covers over herself. Seizing a cruel advantage Simon said, "Not a pretty sight. Not pretty at all. I suppose you think Joe would have liked to see you in this condition? You don't have to look as horrible as this."

"Leave me alone. Leave me alone," she cried.

Simon stepped back and stared down at her. "Damn you, Molly," he said deliberately. "Damn you. You've tried to kill yourself and you failed. You haven't tried again, I notice. I expect your poor mother and father have taken the razor blades and the aspirin out of the bathroom – but there are plenty of ways. I haven't heard you've tried to jump out of the window – hang yourself with a dressing-gown cord – no, part of you wants to stay alive. So stay alive if that's what you want. But don't half-kill your parents and probably harm your child while you're doing it. If you're going to live – live, do it properly. Why do you think Joe loved you? Because you were alive, properly alive, alive and bloody kicking. Like he was – like the child will be, if you give it any chance at all. You've got to get up. You've got to go on. You've got to fight. You've no alternative, so you might as well put a good face on it – I'm going down now. If you're not downstairs, and ready, in ten minutes I'm leaving."

Downstairs, he sat in the front room with Ivy. Because they were both timing Molly, and because the matter was critical, Ivy began to speak in the flat, sombre tones of someone with an important statement to make. She said, "There's something I ought to tell her. Something I should have told her long ago. Perhaps it would make a difference. But I'm afraid. It could make it all worse."

Simon stared at her. "What do you mean?" he asked.

Ivy continued, sounding more normal now. "If she doesn't come downstairs in ten minutes I'm going up to tell her. It's the right time – I'll do it."

"Are you sure?" said Simon, leaning forward. "Why don't you tell me – perhaps I can help."

But Ivy, with her eyes on the hands of the gilt clock on the mantelpiece, just told him, "I've got a funny feeling. She ought to know now."

"I'll make a cup of tea," Simon declared. "Or would you like a drink?" He thought privately that the strain of looking after Molly was beginning to tell on her mother. They had coffee. They both sipped, tried to talk, with their eyes returning frequently to the clock. But before the ten minutes had elapsed Molly opened the door and came in. She was wearing a patterned dress in red and purple, with a yoke. She wore shoes and stockings. She had put lipstick on her pale mouth. She walked across the room shakily, saying to Simon, "I can't walk very well."

"The car's outside," he said.

He thought at first it was like having lunch with a ghost. Pale, speaking in a whisper, eating practically nothing, Molly sat opposite him. He began to be afraid that the effort of making her come was pointless, that she would just go home and sink back into the same state. She said, "I'm sorry, Simon. Sorry to be so strange. I just feel confused."

He nodded, "You're going to need practice."

"I can't forget Joe," she told him. "It might be like being an amputee – you keep on thinking you've got a leg, or an arm. All the sensations are there. Then you have to remind yourself you really haven't got a leg. Then you feel this terrible sadness. It goes on and on. It's like a constant pain." She added, "I know I'll never feel like I did with Joe. I've known a few men but I never felt like that before and I don't suppose many women ever do. This isn't just widow's talk – I wanted to live with him for a long time and die before he did, so I didn't have to lose him. He's gone, though, and that's a fact. He's dead and I have to go on."

"You'll have his child," Simon told her.

"I don't care about that," Molly said. "People think I ought to – but I don't. At the moment it's just something that's going to happen. I wish it wasn't, that's the truth."

"I expect you'll feel different when it's born," Simon said encouragingly.

Molly smiled at him, knowing he was out of his depth. "That's what they tell me," she said, "but I don't know any more about this than you do. I tell you this – I hope I can feel something for the child because if I don't, I don't know what'll happen to either of us."

She looked braver now. She put her hand on his and told him, "I'm grateful to you, Simon, for trying to help. I've been lucky. Ivy's put up with me, and Sid, and people have been very kind. Maybe kinder than I deserved. I owe you all a lot."

"All we want is to see you on your feet again, Molly," Simon said and then, glancing across the restaurant added, "Oh – bugger it!"

Molly turned her head and saw Tom Allaun advancing across the carpet.

"Surprise!" Tom said, coming to the table. "Molly – it's lovely to see you. How are you?"

"All right," Molly told him. "Thank you for your note, Tom, after Joe died. It was thoughtful of you to write."

"I was very upset when I saw the news," Tom said. Simon looked at him doubtfully. He had never trusted Tom but his sympathy and friendship for Molly seemed genuine. The coffee was brought and Simon had no alternative but to wave at a chair and say, unenthusiastically, "Why don't you sit down?" And Tom did.

"Mother wanted you to come to Framlingham," he told Molly. "But Mrs Gates hasn't been too good – and this and that – she said in the circumstances we couldn't look after you properly. She felt your mother was the best person."

"Well – I won't need looking after for too much longer," Molly told him. "I'll get back home and have the baby." She looked tired as she spoke. Neither of the men was convinced when she said, trying to sound cheerful, "Fresh start."

"Forgive me, Molly," Tom asked, "but we've known each other a long time – how's the money? Will you be able to manage?"

"I own the house – there's a pension for MP's widows," Molly said. "I can get a part-time job later if I want to. Josephine's independent – finished university and got herself a job. There aren't any problems. Joe even left me some money and life insurance – I haven't thought about that, yet."

"I'm glad there won't be too many practical problems," Tom assured her.

In the end he drove her home. He was kind, tactful and sympathetic. He asked her to go to the theatre with him later on in the week and Molly, surprised but pleased at his kindness, accepted. There were further outings. He helped her to move back to Meakin Street. He had, now, an easy manner. He was a gifted chatter about little things they saw, about films, about what they watched on TV. Mary, coming out of a long period of silence and depression, found him consoling. He was also quietly domesticated, a maker of cups of tea, a washer-up, a creator of snacks and small comforts. She was, however, surprised when he suggested that he should be present at the birth of the child.

"In the labour ward?" she exclaimed. "Whatever for? You'd probably faint."

"I'm very cool in these situations," he told her. "I'd love to be there. And you might be quite grateful in the end. And, of course, if you asked me to go at any point, naturally, I'd disappear."

"It's gruesome," Ivy declared roundly when Molly told her Tom's plan. "In my opinion men have got no place in a situation like that. It's just a fad and women'll soon realize they're better off alone when they're having a baby. But Tom isn't even the child's father. He's no relation at all – it's revolting. Imagine how he's going to see you, Molly, with your legs everywhere and sweat pouring down your face. I can't think why he wants to come. It's ghoulish, that's what."

Simon, when she told him, said "What?" in a tone of horror. Then, looking at her sternly, he told her, "Look – you don't know enough about Tom."

"I know he's been kind to me," Molly said. She was bending over painfully to put a casserole in the oven. "How could I have managed – sitting here on my own at night, thinking about Joe."

She thought of Tom, bending over her chair to wipe away the tears, comforting her, cheering her up. "He wants to do it," she told him. "It's not much to ask. I'd be glad of someone standing by when the nurses start to nag me. In any case," she admitted, "I'm afraid. I've no one to turn to. Having a baby isn't much fun at the best of times. If I start thinking about Joe being dead how am I going to manage? The pain'll be worse. I won't be able to help myself."

"I suppose so," Simon agreed grudgingly. "But it's a bit weird, you must admit. I don't understand it."

"You don't have to," Molly said.

Thus it was Tom who stayed at Meakin Street as the time for the birth approached, Tom who drove her to the hospital and Tom who talked to her in the early stages of labour, who mopped her brow and wetted her lips as the pain grew intense, who stood beside her, holding her hand and encouraging her as her body stretched and contorted in its efforts to produce the child.

It was Tom the doctor addressed first as he held up a large male baby. "What a whopper," he said. "There must be giants in your family."

And Tom, disconcertingly, replied, "Future light heavyweight champion of Britain, there." For some reason Molly was horrified by this exchange of remarks and cried, holding out her arms, "Give him to me."

For months she had seen the baby as an unpleasant physical problem and a source of future pain. Now she had him, he was real. He was half hers, half Joe's, and she loved him. When she had Josephine she had been young, and stunned. This time she was able to understand what had happened, imagine a future with a child. The nurse had some difficulty in prising the baby away in order to wash him and cut the umbilical cord. She ignored Tom completely.

Nevertheless, visitors who came to see Molly and the new baby at Meakin Street were surprised to find Tom in attendance. He did not help with the care of the child, but he did assist in other ways, although, it must be admitted, by that stage Molly was paying for everything and his attentions, though assiduous, confined themselves to the less serious forms of house-keeping. Cissie Messiter was severe when she arrived unexpectedly one morning and found Molly cleaning the bathroom, while Tom sat downstairs finishing his breakfast. Taking the cloth from Molly and finishing the cleaning of the bath she puffed philosophically, "I suppose he's better than post-natal depression."

Six weeks later Tom was still in the house. "I don't like it," Sid told Sam Needham in the pub. "I don't like the way he's hanging about. What's he waiting for?"

"I reckon," Sam said, "he's waiting for what you and I think he's waiting for."

"It makes me feel queasy," Sid answered. "But what can I do – what can any of us do? He's been very good to her. And she seems to need him."

"I just hope she doesn't do anything stupid while she's still in a state," Sam replied.

But Molly did.

Molly Allaun

Looking back I can see all those faces which were covered in smiles when Joe and me said we were tying the knot at last, going pinched when they heard the news about Tom and me. Then there'd be a sort of choking sound while the person bit back what they were going to say first, like "No!" or "For God's sake think again." Then would come the nearly polite remarks, like "Are you sure you know what you're doing?" "Isn't it a bit soon?" All that.

Tom won't mind me saying it was madness. Hard to say who was the most stupid – him or me. To be honest, it was probably him, just because he hadn't lost his husband and had a baby in the last six months, so he should have known better. I should have known better myself but I suppose I was in a desperate state, with no idea how to manage, or who I was, even. And I wanted the safety of Allaun Towers for the boy and even for Josephine to come to when she wanted. I thought I could learn to love Tom – after all, I knew I'd loved all the men I'd lived with, in different ways. So, I thought, why not Tom? I already depended on him for gentleness and comfort.

I little knew, that's all I can say – I little knew what I was letting myself in for. Of course, it might have been different if I'd once clapped eyes on Charlie Markham during the courtship. One glance at Charlie and memories would have come flooding back. More than that, once Charlie and Tom were together there was no doubt about what Tom was. But Charlie had been primed to stay out of the way – the cat and the fox split up so's not to arouse Pinnochio's suspicions. Seven months after Joe's death, there I was at the altar again. What a wedding – what a reception – and, oh dear, what a honeymoon.

The only truly cheerful face at the wedding breakfast at the Savoy was Isabel Allaun's. Enjoying the pleasure of seeing her son married at last

423

and the sense of being returned to an atmosphere she had long missed, where waiters in tailcoats presented silver trays on which stood shining glasses of champagne, she glittered.

"Such a pity your son couldn't come," she said to Ivy. She had already met Shirley and Brian and their sons, but Shirley's slightly depressed air and Brian's obvious disapproval had not made a good impression on her. She privately thought that Jack Waterhouse, now an MP, even if a Labour MP, might be more socially poised and generally acceptable.

"Jack had to go abroad," Ivy told her new relative by marriage. She did not say that Jack had made sure he would be abroad, seeing the hasty marriage of his sister into the upper classes as a double betrayal of Joe Endell and everything he had stood for.

"What a pity," Isabel said. "Never mind. He'll be able to see the photographs." "And don't bother to order any of the photographs for me, either," Jack had told Ivy dourly.

"Are you feeling all right, Ivy?" Simon Tate said, coming past. He saw she was very pale. "Shall I get Sid?" Simon was keeping an eye on Ivy. "He didn't turn up at that restaurant by accident," he had told her. "He phoned and my secretary said where I was and who I was with. He deliberately came along to pick her off."

"I'm fine," Ivy said, standing there in the crush and feeling faint. Sam Needham, like Jack, had refused to attend. "I've got nothing against Molly," he had said. "Only I think at the moment she's out of her mind."

"Such a happy outcome," Isabel Allaun said to Ivy. And Ivy wondered why Isabel should be so delighted that her son had married working-class Mary Waterhouse. Feeling dizzier and dizzier she looked round for Sid, but saw his back going through the door, just as Charlie Markham, who had been best man, stood up to speak. "I was afraid my cousin Tom would never marry," he said, "but now he has a wife, an old childhood friend, and with her he gains a child – wife and family, all in one –"

Ivy looked at the door through which Sid had gone, hoping he would return soon. She turned her head, searching for a chair. Horror engulfed her, and blackness. Simon Tate put his arm round her in time and helped her to a chair.

Molly, standing behind the cake, with Charlie, saw her mother start to collapse. She turned anxiously to Tom, who was laughing at one of Charlie's jokes. Sid was supposed to have made a short speech, but he had disappeared. Charlie completed his remarks, there was clapping, cries of "Speech," directed at Tom, who turned to Molly and brushed her lips with his. Together they cut the cake. As the steel went through the white icing Molly felt Tom's hand over hers on the knife. His palm was cold as ice.

I knew then, with Sid missing, and Ivy passing out and Charlie making his jovial, jolly-good-chap remarks, that I was done for. I should have turned and run but honestly I couldn't believe I'd have made such a mistake. I was used to making mistakes about what to do but not to making mistakes about what I felt. If my instincts had told me Tom was generous, kind and loving, I knew they had to be right. I should have thought then of the small betraying details – that washer that was always going to be put on the dripping tap, and never was, the way he'd never offered me more than a few caresses, which I thought was because he was shy about the fact I was a recent widow and I'd just had a baby. I might have been more curious if I hadn't been hiding things myself, like how important it was to me to see my child grow up at Framlingham with a live father, and not a dead one, and how much I needed to get a new identity, now Joe was gone. In fact that was what I didn't really understand myself. The trouble was we were both after things which mattered a lot to us, but which we weren't telling each other about. What a start to a marriage.

Eventually, the guests disappeared. Tom and Molly planned spending the night at the hotel and going to Framlingham in the morning. Sid and Ivy were to take care of the baby for a week and then drive to Kent.

Molly, left in the room with Tom and Charlie, said goodbye to the last of the guests and looked unhappily at the cake, with a section cut out of it, the confetti on the floor and the empty plates and glasses. She missed the baby, already. It had seemed appropriate to settle in at Framlingham without the child, but now she regretted she had agreed to the plan. She swallowed, then smiled at Tom. "Happy?" she asked him.

He nodded and smiled back at her. It was a smile which came a fraction too late. Charlie said, "Don't let's stand here among the remains of the marriage feast. Come on – I'll drink a toast to you in the bar."

They spent the afternoon there. Tom got drunker and drunker. Molly found that she felt better if she was not sober. The scene disconcerted even Charlie, who bent towards Tom as he ordered yet another round of drinks and said something to him in a low voice. Molly, a bit drunk, did not see him muttering into his cousin's ear. She did catch the expression of anger on Tom's face, which disappeared as he said to Molly, "You must be feeling very tired. Shall we go upstairs so that you can rest?"

She nodded. She had the idea that, once upstairs, Tom would make love to her. She wanted, now, to feel a body close to hers. She wanted the passion, the intimacy, the release. But in the suite upstairs Tom led her past the huge arrangement of flowers on the table, the long window looking out on to the Thames and, dropping her hand in the bedroom doorway said, "I'll run you a bath, shall I?"

"No thank you," Molly said. "I'll just lie down." Tom kissed her lightly on the lips and said, "Sleep well, then."

He went out, shutting the bedroom door. Molly, slightly bewildered, full of champagne and brandy, decided that perhaps she should rest. She lay down and slept. She woke at six, alone, desperately missing Joe Endell. Tom was not in the other room. She fell on to the sofa and cried. "Is it a mistake?" she said to herself. Then aloud, "Is it a mistake?" But she thought of Allaun Towers, the red bricks glowing in the sunshine. She thought of the pasture-land, full of grazing cattle, the lake and the trees. "He'll have all that, the way I did," she thought, imagining her healthy boy learning to walk on the lawn in front of the house, pushing his way through corn taller than he was, learning to row on the lake. She thought that he, without a father, and she, without Joe, would have something for themselves. She told herself that Tom must have got bored, as he sat there, waiting for her to wake up. She told herself that he was over forty, that he had never been married before, that he was bound to feel strange and uncertain with her. She told herself that she should not have decided to sleep in the first place. And yet, said a voice inside her, he suggested it. He led you to the room and shut the door. Tact, said another voice. It was tact, kindness, good manners. Why should he want a drunken scramble on the bed in the middle of the afternoon as a consummation of the marriage?

Glumly, she ordered coffee, and later, whisky. She watched TV and quelled a strong impulse to leave. I must give this a chance, she whispered to herself. She remembered Tom helping, Tom being kind, and drank more. At ten Charlie Markham rang up, sounding embarrassed. "Sorry, Moll," he said, "Tom's here – turned up unexpectedly and joined a small party I'm having here." He paused. "Trouble is," he said, "Tom's passed out now. I'm bringing him back."

"Thanks, Charlie," Molly said glumly.

"Case of a belated stag party, I think," Charlie told her. "He would sit at home last night – well – I'm on my way, then."

"Thanks, Charlie," Molly said again. She bit her lip and tried to control her rage. Charlie's effort at kindness made the whole matter seem worse. Together they put Tom to bed. Charlie looked at the defeated bride and the drunken groom with pity, which he tried to conceal. He accepted Molly's offer of a drink and sat down saying, "Weddings are bloody awful things if you ask me. Best forgotten once they're over."

"Yes, Charlie," Molly agreed, but she felt bewildered. She was alarmed by Charlie Markham's sympathy. She had never known him to be kind before. "He'll have a sore head for Framlingham tomorrow," Charlie said. "Don't be too hard on him in the morning."

"No, I won't," Molly said. "Thanks again, Charlie. Come and visit us when we're properly settled in."

"Looking forward to it," he said, getting up. "I haven't been there for years. Good luck, Moll." He kissed her on the cheek, and left.

After he had gone Molly sat and ached for Joe Endell. She pined for the baby. At the same time she felt very alarmed. She had a bath and leapt out of it quickly, as though responding to an emergency. She was half asleep in front of the television wearing the blue, embroidered dressing-gown she had bought before she married Tom, when at last he came in. He looked pale. He was carrying his jacket. He shut the door behind him with care and asked, "What's the time."

"Eleven-thirty," replied his new wife. "Are you all right?"

"As to that – I can't say," he told her in a slurred voice. Then he added, "Sick," and went unsteadily to the bathroom.

When he came out he said, "Been sick – sorry," and sat down.

"I've ordered some coffee and sandwiches," Molly told him. "Is that what you want?"

"Anything – anything," he said, shaking his head. "Oh Lord – on our wedding night. Sorry, Molly. I'm not much of a man."

"I'm looking forward to Framlingham," Molly said. "Perhaps this hotel wasn't a good idea."

Tom looked at her cautiously. "It's not exactly what it was," he told her. She had the impression he thought he was being cunning. He had a sloppy, sly smile on his face, which he thought he was concealing.

"What do you mean?" asked Molly.

"The old place – not what it was. Death duties," he said. "Never mind – we'll soon pull it all together." He stared at her, still with the same silly expression on his face. The waiter brought in a trolley. When he had gone Molly said, "You'd better have some coffee and some food." This she gave him. She was engulfed by a kind of despair. She knew everything was amiss – leaning, toppling, not to be relied on. She watched Tom eating the sandwiches. At one point he looked up and said, "We'd better have a chat," and then went back to the plate. He then drank a cup of coffee and stared at her. "Death duties," he said. "And one thing and another. These places don't keep themselves the way they used to – even in the old days they were generally financed from some rubber plantation or plenty of shares. Dad never got back to what he was before World War II – never had a business head anyway. Mother's the same, just carrying on in the same old way – no idea of reality. Same's true of me, I wouldn't wonder. Charlie says so –"

"What are you talking about?" Molly asked. "Do you mean the house has got to be sold?"

"Sold?" he said. "Sold? It's mortgaged to the hilt. Two mortgages. Never mind, Molly, we'll sort it out between us." He shut his eyes and dozed.

Molly poured herself a cup of coffee and thought. At least, she thought, she had an explanation for Tom's behaviour. He was ashamed that he hadn't told her the facts about the situation she would meet at Framlingham. Well, all right, she decided. Perhaps she could get a job – Mrs Gates could mind the baby while she worked. They could work something out. In a way, it was a relief to have something to think about other than the uncertainties of this unhappy wedding night.

Tom opened his eyes. He muttered something at her just as she said, "Tom – I've been thinking –" Then she said, "Sorry – what did you say?"

"You first," he said.

"I was thinking – if I got a job and Mrs Gates looked after the baby, that would help, wouldn't it?"

"What's this about jobs?" he demanded. "I asked you what you'd got." He added, "Sorry to put it so bluntly – but we ought to talk about it now we're married. Pour me another cup of coffee, will you – there's a good girl."

She got up and poured the coffee, took it to him and smoothed the hair back from his brow, saying, "Poor old Tom." And then could not help imagining that he moved his head a fraction so as to shake off her hand. "Well?" he asked.

She sat down on the sofa, near his chair and told him, "I don't really know what you're talking about. If you mean, how much money have I got – well, a few hundred saved and Joe's insurance – and the house, I suppose. Why do you want to know?"

"Because you're my wife. Because we have to make a few plans," he said, as if stating the obvious. "Come along, Molly – you're behaving as if you're drunk yourself and as it happens you're not and neither am I, now."

Molly stared at him in horror. "This is shocking," she declared. "We've only been married five minutes and you want to see my accounts – you're checking the money poor Joe left on his insurance. It wasn't much – only two thousand pounds. He planned to make it more after the baby was born –"

"Oh, my God," Tom said in disgust. "Come off it, Molly. Where's old Endell's money?"

"What –?" said Molly and then understood suddenly. "He wouldn't take it," she said. "He didn't like the source. He disapproved of inherited wealth, too, you see," she explained. "That's why he couldn't take it."

Tom was staring at her with an expression on his face which Molly, in a sudden moment of terror herself, recognized as fear. He said, slowly, "You're having me on –" and then, flinging himself back in his chair, "You're not! You're not! He refused to take the money – Endell refused it? That's true isn't it?"

Molly felt exhausted. The constant repetition of Joe's name, the idea that his child was with Sid and Ivy, far away and the shocking knowledge which now came to her – that Tom had married her believing her to be a rich widow – made her feel weak. She passed her hand, now, across her own brow and told him, "Tom – I don't believe what's happening – I don't feel very well."

But Tom, with a cry, jumped to his feet and swept the coffee pot, milk jug, cups – the whole tray – from the small table they stood on.

"Christ! This is a fine sod's opera for me!" And taking a few steps towards Molly he thrust his face down at her and said loudly, "You kept your secret well, I'll say that for you."

The sheer menace of his behaviour revived her. She was outraged – although later, she was to look back on that moment, the last when, it seemed to her, Tom demonstrated any passion at all, with some nostalgia. In fact it is probable that if he had not shown such energy in his venom she would have left on the spot. However, she leaped to her feet and cried, "Don't be so bloody stupid, Tom. I never hid anything from you. I didn't know you thought I was rich. You never even mentioned Joe's grandfather. If you had I'd soon have put you right. I never deceived you into marriage – anyway, what a rotten way to want to marry. As it happened I thought you loved me. And I thought I loved you. But if it's money you're after you'll have to look elsewhere. I'll go home – you can divorce me – then you can start looking around again for another heiress – a real one, this time."

Fully intending, at that moment, to leave, she ran into the bedroom and started pulling the few clothes she had brought with her from the hangers in the wardrobe.

Tom ran after her and grabbed her arm. "Molly – Molly," he said urgently. "I'm sorry. We're good friends – we love each other. Nothing's lost."

He put his arms round her. She moved back. "It's no good, Tom," she said. "Let's face facts. You wanted my fortune to put the roof back on the house and a smile on Isabel's face. I wanted your house and your position for me and the child. We only wanted each other a little bit and now there's no money for you, and no house for me, unless I want a leaky roof in the country – let's call it a day. We've no one to blame but ourselves." As she spoke she was cramming her wedding suit into the case. She turned round and looked at him. "Best to cut our losses," she muttered. She moved over towards the bathroom door and said, "I'll leave now – and pay the bill, for evidence. We can get an annulment."

Tom, standing in the bedroom said, "I wanted the boy."

"You what?" Molly asked, appearing in the bathroom door with her spongebag. "You wanted the boy, did you say?"

Tom nodded, looking embarrassed. He got his next words out with difficulty. "The place needs an heir."

"What!" cried Molly. "My son! God, Tom, that's disgusting. Why couldn't you have an heir of your own, if you want one so badly?" She

430

paused, scarcely able to believe, even now, what he had said. She said finally, "It's so old-fashioned."

"You said it was what you wanted," he said. "You said it."

"I wanted the fresh air," Molly told him indignantly. "Not a falling-down house and a crummy title. I wanted him to have the childhood I had – in the fields and that –" She sniffed. Her rage was evaporating. It left behind a feeling of stale loss. She bit her lip and put her spongebag on top of the case. Very slowly, she knelt down and started to lock the catches. As she did so, a tear plopped on the blue surface.

"Don't cry, Molly," Tom said behind her.

She turned round and stood up. They looked at each other. Both were wondering whether they might not be better off in a friendly alliance than alone.

Tom said, "Perhaps we can work something out."

Molly said, "What's in it for you? Without me you can start hunting again."

"I still need an heir," he told her.

"What's stopping you from having one of your own?" she said bluntly.

"I don't think I'm the type," he said.

She stared at him. "What on earth do you mean, Tom –?" She realized, then, what he must mean. "Oh, God," she said. "Why didn't you tell me? Why didn't I guess?"

"It's not as bad as that," he said.

"What about the girl you were engaged to?" she asked.

"What I say – it's not as bad as that," he told her.

Molly walked into the other room and flung herself into a chair. Tom had thought – and she guessed that Charlie had reassured him – that Molly, the girl they had tormented in a semi-sexual way in childhood, would be able to stir Tom's frail manhood to life. She had not guessed what he was like, probably because the courtship and marriage had been overshadowed by her grief for Joe and her love for the new child. Now she saw that things were worse than she had imagined. But, she told herself, how do you expect Tom to want you, when you know you don't want him?

Tom had followed her in. He, too, sat down. She realized he was waiting for her decision. She said, "I should have known all this. Why did you propose, Tom?"

"It could have worked," said Tom. "I just handled it badly." He seemed to be reproaching himself for manoeuvring wrongly.

"That wouldn't supply me with a vast fortune," Molly told him. "So there we are – I've got no money but I've got the boy, which you want. You've got no money but you've got the house, which I want. Well, well." Tom sat down, looking exhausted. He passed his hand over his brow. She asked, "Why don't you just sell the house? Even if it's mortgaged you'd get something."

"No one wants to buy it," Tom said.

"Turn it into a hotel – or flats," Molly said.

"Bank won't fund it," Tom said. "There's £5,000 a year from a trust fund we can't touch and on that we have to live and keep the place up. Mother can't bear the idea of what's happened –"

"She's going to be disappointed," Molly told him unsympathetically.

Tom said, "Molly – I'm too tired to talk about all this any more."

Molly suppressed her irritability. She thought they should decide what to do then and there. But he added, "I must get some sleep. You can have the bed if you like. We can discuss it in the morning."

But Molly went back to Meakin Street, to the cold bed she had once shared with Joe Endell and lay there, awake, all night, missing him sorely and trying to work out what to do. And thought, as she made herself a cup of tea at dawn and drank it in the room where she and Joe used to sit, that she did not want to stay in Meakin Street, with all its memories of old happiness, that, equally, she did not want a replacement for Joe but that she did want to bring her son up in the country, at Framlingham. She could rent Meakin Street, she thought, then she could get a part-time job and, who knew, perhaps she could work out some way of rescuing matters at Allaun Towers. As for Tom – she liked him. She could not expect to love him as she had loved Joe and did not want to. She lay on the sofa at Meakin Street and said to herself, "Joe – Joe. What am I going to do?"

And thought she heard him say, as if his voice were part of the thin, grey light coming through the windows, "Take the boy to Framlingham."

On the road to Kent next morning she and Tom chatted in their old way, as if there had been no marriage, no revelations and no early morning reconciliation. Tom showed an intermittent desire to bring up the old issue but Molly refused to talk about it. Her mind was set on the future. All she said was, "Let's give it a try, Tom. We've nothing to lose."

He was not pleased when he discovered that she was reluctant to sell the house in Meakin Street.

"I don't want to sell and the rent will come in handy," she told him.

"A drop in the bucket," muttered Tom.

"Cheer up," she said. "I've got £200 in my bag. When that runs out you can start complaining. Anyway," she added, "I'm looking forward to seeing Mrs Gates again and showing her the baby."

He said nothing. Into the silence Molly said, "Cheer up, Tom. Let's try for a fresh start."

Even so, her heart sank as they drove through the rusting gates which were now, it seemed, permanently open. They went up the long drive under the overhanging, untrimmed boughs of the trees. It felt gloomy. Although it was not yet September Molly, spotting one brown leaf on a tree, was reminded that soon it would be autumn.

Their first sight of the house was not encouraging. In the fierce August sun it was possible to see the missing tiles on the lower parts of the roof. The guttering was broken in places and long stains, made by water, marred the brickwork of the house. Some of the attic windows were broken. The paint around the windows was cracked and old. In the bright light a long jagged crack could be seen running from the eaves to the top of the front door.

Isabel Allaun stood on the steps to greet them. Her face, in the bright light, looked drawn. She led them in. Here, too, the evidence of neglect was all too plain. In the hall the paintwork was dingy and the marble squares of the floor were not entirely clean. Mrs Gates, Molly remembered, had spent an hour, every week, on her hands and knees washing them with some special substance she made up – was it vinegar, or soda, she wondered vaguely. At any rate, it had smelled a lot and made Mrs Gates very irritable. The staircarpet running up the wooden stairs was threadbare. The dragons at the bottom of the banisters were undusted. They went along the passage into the sitting room, where sun streamed through the windows, exposing worn patches in the upholstery of the chairs.

"I'll make some tea," said Isabel Allaun to her daughter-in-law.

Tom sat down. Molly opened one of the long windows which led to the lawn. She stepped out, enjoying the brilliant sunshine, walked down through the tangled shrubbery and across to the lake. It was low, now, and scummy. Dried-out reeds and long grass stood round the edges. Then she turned round and went back to the house. After the wedding, the long night of argument with Tom, and lonely reflection at Meakin Street, she was exhausted. She sighed as she crossed the lawn. It was the place she had loved best as a child but, now she came to it as an adult, everything seemed different. She wondered, again, whether she should have come here. And yet, neglected as it was, the house still had its big, high rooms, the air outside was still pure, birds still nested under the eaves. As she stepped back through the window Isabel Allaun came in with a tea tray.

"Tom!" she said sharply.

He got up to take the tray, asking, "Where's Mrs Gates?"

Molly had been about to ask the same question. "She's been ill for a week," Isabel said. "She had something like a slight stroke – the doctor wasn't sure. He wanted to move her to the cottage hospital but she didn't want to go. She's in her flat over the stables. Vera Harker's coming in twice a day to help."

Molly said, "Oh – I'll go to see her straight away."

"No tea?" enquired Isabel.

But Molly refused and anxiously took the path past the vegetable garden, which she saw had only a few straggling peas leaning on crooked sticks in it, and crossed the mossy flagstones into the stable block. It was surrounded by four walls. On one side stood the five stables and, above them, a hayloft and a set of small rooms where the groom and his wife must once have lived. The last horse had gone before Molly arrived as a child so that all she remembered of the rooms was bare boards and some tattered lithographs pinned to the wall of ladies with piled up hair and bare shoulders. What was Mrs Gates doing there now, she wondered, as she climbed the wooden steps up from the yard and pulled up the latch of the wooden door at the top. How ill was she and why wasn't she still living in the house?

She saw why as soon as she was inside. The small sitting room was panelled with the same dark wood she remembered from childhood but it had been restored, cleaned and freshly varnished. The paintwork in the little room was bright. The small fireplace was tidy and the brass fire irons shone. She smiled, recognizing that Mrs Gates had retreated from the deterioration at the big house and created a little snug for herself here. "Isn't it lovely?" she said to the elderly woman sitting in her chair with a rug over her knees.

"Mary," said the old woman in a tired voice. "I've been waiting for you."

"Well, I'm here now," she said. "Want a cup of tea?"

"Vera's coming," Mrs Gates told her. "Let her do it. You remember Vera – her brother Fred pushed you into a bramble bush once and she was the one who pulled you out."

"Can't say I do remember," Molly said, pulling up a chair and sitting down – Mrs Gates was speaking to the child she had been. She felt as if she had never left.

"You were scratched to smithereens," Mrs Gates said.

"I daresay," Molly replied. "But how are you, that's the question?" She studied the other woman carefully. Of course she knew that Mrs Gates would look older but she had not been prepared for her being so much thinner. She had always been a heavy woman, pinafore bursting round her bust and hips and legs like thick saplings. Now her face was thinner and more drawn. Her hands, on the blanket, looked frail and wasted. And she seemed very weary.

"I'm not so bad," Mrs Gates replied, cheerfully enough. "I'm just tired. I need a little rest."

"I'm not surprised," Molly said. "That place is enough to wear anyone out. As soon as you're well enough I'll take you to London in the car. Ivy wants you to come and stay – she told me to tell you this time she wouldn't take no for an answer."

"I don't know how they'd get on without me," Mrs Gates said. "Still – as you're here –"

"That's just it," agreed Molly. "I'm here. After all, you trained me up. Now you can profit by it. Anyway, my baby's coming down here soon. And I want you at the christening." Yet she felt uneasy as she looked at the old woman and, as Mrs Gates looked back at her, knew that she, too, doubted how soon she would be better.

"My Josie's coming, too," she said. "I bet you never thought I'd turn up here again, with all my offspring."

Looking into Mrs Gates's eyes she realized she was taking the jovial tone of someone visiting a sick person who assumes that the patient has, due to their illness, become an idiot.

Mrs Gates said, "I knew you'd come. Though I never thought it would be because you'd married Tom."

Molly noticed that she did not congratulate her and was relieved. "Sitting here," she said, "the past seems as plain to me as yesterday – maybe plainer. That's how I knew, you see – the gypsy. She told you such things – and they've come true, some of them. My goodness, though," she said, staring from the window as if she could see the

435

house, which she could not, for the windows faced out, over the lake towards the trees and the tip of the church spire. "My goodness, though, this place has gone down. All cracked and broken, all collapsing." She closed her eyes, then, and seemed to doze.

Molly sat there a little longer, listening to the ticking of the wooden clock she had so admired as a child, studying the toby jug, the plaster cat and the little statue of the pink and white lady in the old-fashioned dress which stood on this mantelpiece as they had stood on Mrs Gates's old mantelpiece in her attic back at the house. She gazed again at Mrs Gates's peaceful, lined face. Then she stood up and tiptoed across the carpet and down the narrow wooden stairs to the yard.

There she met a plump woman of about her own age. She had a wicker basket in her hand. "Lady Allaun?" asked the woman. For a moment Molly wondered where Isabel was. Then remembered she was Lady Allaun. She nodded, studying the other woman's features to see if she recognized a face from childhood. She did not.

She asked, "Did we go to school together?"

The woman said, "I wouldn't have recognized you and I don't suppose you recognize me."

"Can't say that I do," Molly said. Glancing up at Mrs Gates's window she added, "She's asleep now. I haven't really had time to find out what's the matter with her. She looks very ill to me – worse than they said."

"That's right," said the woman, Vera Harker. "The doctor wanted her to go to hospital. She's been waiting for you." Molly was startled.

"I hope I can do some good," she said. "I've been wondering if she should be alone at night."

"I'll stay," Vera Harker said promptly. "I've got my nightie in this basket."

Molly looked at her, wanting to ask how ill she thought Mrs Gates was. Vera Harker looked back. Molly did not ask the question but her heart sank.

Mrs Harker went up to the house to telephone her family and tell them she was staying. Molly sat on the wooden mounting block, and looked through the stable entrance to the vegetable garden and the corner of the house. The bricks of the vegetable garden wall and the house were reddening as the sun went down. Now she remembered Vera Harker. They always taunted her by saying her granny was a gypsy. She denied it but all the children knew it was true. She and Vera used to tag along after the big boys when they went out scrumping apples from the neighbouring orchards. We got chased by a big black dog, once, she thought, as she wandered back to the house. She was not looking forward to going inside again. At least I'm here for Mrs Gates, in case she dies, she told herself. This was the first time she had actually admitted the possibility of Mrs Gates's death but it had been there all the time – and she had read it in Vera Harker's eyes.

She did not go directly into the sitting room but, as if she were a child again, wandered through the house. As a child, she enjoyed the sweep of the big staircase and the huge, sparsely furnished rooms. As an adult, she observed the deterioration. It was not evident at first, for plainly Mrs Gates had cleaned everything that could be cleaned and mended everything that could be mended. But half the lights were out of action, one lavatory would not flush and five or six other minor defects made the mended tears in the faded curtains and the rows of shining pans in the kitchen look like a full-hearted effort to check continual decay. She wondered why Tom had not tried to do some repairs and then, knowing she did not want to be detected on the prowl by Isabel, went downstairs. She found them looking through an old photograph album. "I thought you'd like to see it," said her mother-in-law. "Such a pity there was hardly any film when you were here in the war. Look, Tom – there you are stepping on the Bishop's foot at Charlie's sister's christening." Molly, who had just seen wet walls and leaking cisterns, conquered a surge of irritation at this nostalgic search through the family albums. She went over to look through the pictures. It only made her more despondent. Allaun Towers was too expensive. The sale of the house in Meakin Street would not produce enough money to restore it and even then there would be nothing on which to keep it up. Once there had been a gardener who kept the lawn on which they picnicked in these snapshots, there had been servants to tend the rooms in which the people here were photographed in evening dress, drinking cocktails. Now both money and help were lacking.

Meanwhile, Isabel pointed out there was nothing to eat in the house because of Mrs Gates's illness. Molly made omelettes and she and Tom spent the night in the large bed in which his parents had once slept. Since Isabel had made a point of the efforts she had made to remove her effects from the room – "It's more suitable for you," she had said, "now there are two of you" – there was no question of not using the room. Molly and Tom undressed embarrassedly, Tom taking off his clothes and putting on his pyjamas in the dressing room which led from the main bedroom. They got into bed. Molly instantly declared herself to be exhausted. Tom agreed that he was, too. Having, so she thought, declared that she was not expecting him to make love to her, Molly thought that at least they might talk. There seemed to be much to discuss. She was hoping he might give her some idea of what his plans for the future were – instead he went straight to sleep. She remembered that even while they had been at Meakin Street he had been preoccupied with getting a night's undisturbed rest. Now she realized that what she had seen as the small change of conversation – "I must get some sleep," "I had nightmares all night long" – was, to him, the discussion of a crucial affair. In consequence Molly lay awake, worrying about Mrs Gates and wondering what to do about the house, the money and herself and her child. Had she really heard Joe's voice telling her to bring the child to Framlingham? Would the real Joe have advised her to stay, or go back to London as fast as possible?

She got up early next morning. The sun was shining and she strolled in the garden, sat drinking her tea on the still-dewy lawn, then leaned, half-dozing, against the apple tree in the kitchen garden. Scarlet pimpernels grew all over the parched earth. She reflected dreamily that Tom or Isabel could at least have grown some vegetables. But for the row of declining peas there was no sign of cultivation of the humped rows of earth where plants had once grown. She even remembered where Benson used to put the potatoes, remembered dropping the old, wrinkled seed potatoes into the trench and helping him to cover them over. She shut her eyes, recalling the long days of childhood, when time stopped, her small bed under the eaves, being woken at dawn by the wagtails nesting there in the guttering below the roof, the taste of an apple picked from the branch you were sitting on and the lane to school in autumn, when the hedgerows were going gold and brown and the air was thin and misty –

"Lady Allaun," came a voice from behind the garden wall. She glanced up and saw Vera Harker, and caught a curious glance. Vera saw no bride, just a tired woman in her thirties sitting under a tree in the early morning.

"You'd better call me Mary again," she said. "Or better than that – Molly. That's what they call me in London. No point in standing on ceremony. I remembered suddenly when we had to run away from Mr

Crewe's dog. How's Mrs Gates this morning?"

"I don't like to leave her alone too long," Vera Harker said. "But I've got to go and get the children off to school."

"I'll go," Molly said. "Will you get something for her lunch in the village? I'll give you the money when you get back." A thought crossed her mind. "Who's paying you for all this?" she asked.

Mrs Harker looked embarrassed and said, "Lady Allaun said she'd give me a sum – I don't like to charge at all, you understand –"

"We'd better talk about it when you come back," Molly told her. At some point she or Tom would have to reveal to Isabel that Molly had not come to Allaun Towers with a vast fortune. For all she knew Vera Harker's wages were guaranteed by this imaginary sum of money. She said, "Do you think you could come back at about twelve?" Then she hurried off to see Mrs Gates.

"The doctor'll be along later," called Mrs Harker.

Molly climbed the wooden stairs into the flat above the stables. Mrs Gates lay in the bedroom in her big bed with the carved wooden headboard. Her face was grey above snow-white sheets. She was asleep, or so Molly thought. By the side of the bed was a photograph in a silver frame, of Tom and Charlie, with herself standing in front on a summer day, on the lawn in front of the house. Even if Tom looked a little sulky they were all healthy; bare-legged, bright-eyed – Charlie was holding his treasured cricket bat. The other photograph, in another silver frame, showed a tall man, in an old-fashioned suit and a plump, smiling woman in a floral dress who held a baby in long, white clothes. Mrs Gates, thought Molly, and the absconding Mr Gates, and the baby which died.

She sat quietly on a chair near the bed and waited. On the mantelpiece a pink pottery clock ticked. She heard the birds singing. Later came the voices of Tom and Isabel, in the distance. Then the voices faded. The clock ticked on.

"Do you remember," said a faint voice from the bed, "that gypsy, Urania Heron?" Mrs Gates's eyes were still shut.

Molly said, in a low voice, "No – I don't."

"She was Queen of the Gypsies, so they said," came the murmur from the grey face on the pillow.

"Did they?" said Molly.

"She was famous for telling the future – she said you'd be here when I died. I never guessed that would come true."

"Now," said Molly in alarm, although some of the alarm was

assumed, "don't you go thinking what I think you're thinking. You've had a slight stroke, that's all. You're tired."

"Perhaps," said Mrs Gates, "but I'm seventy-one now. My mother died at fifty."

"Get over this," Molly told her. "And you can be semi-retired. Light jobs."

Mrs Gates said nothing. Perhaps she was asleep. The doctor came and spent five minutes with her. In the room outside he said to Molly, "Her heart's tired. There's nothing I can tell you." He looked uneasy. If Molly had spoken with a middle-class accent he could have accepted her as the lady of the house, in attendance on her old nanny. As it was, he could not make out what was happening.

"She looked after me when I was evacuated here – she was very kind to me," Molly told him.

"Oh," he said, and it was clear that the news of Tom's marriage to the former Mary Waterhouse was already in circulation. "It's lucky you're here," he said.

"You don't know what's going to happen, then?" she asked.

He shook his head. "Just make her as comfortable as you can," he told her.

After he had gone Molly went back into the bedroom and sat down again. She dozed off in her chair and awoke in the hot, silent room, thinking she had heard music in a dream. Mrs Gates was awake and looking at her.

"Oh," said Molly in confusion. "I dropped off – is there anything you want – cup of tea?"

"Chamber pot," Mrs Gates said. It was frightening, helping the old lady on to the chamber pot and supporting her while she used it. Afterwards Mrs Gates was exhausted. Molly came back from emptying the pot and sat down again. Then she heard her say, "She said that you'd marry three times – but that two would be no true marriages."

"She was wrong in that," Molly said, guessing she was again talking about the gypsy.

"She told me after, one marriage to end at a rope's end."

"Good God," Molly exclaimed.

"For children – a girl and a boy – unnatural fruit – a wrong deed but not done wrongly. Close to a fortune, close to a kingdom –" She said a little more but her voice was too faint to catch the words.

"Never mind all that," said Molly, impressed in spite of herself by

440

the gypsy's warning about a husband dying by hanging. "You rest, now. I want you fresh for your lunch or you won't eat it." But dull prickles went up and down her spine. Unnatural fruit? A kingdom? She felt uneasy. As the latch on the door went up she left the room. Vera Harker said, "I brought some fish – the fishman came today. And there's a calf's foot here. I'll make a broth."

Molly hurried back to the house deciding that if Tom had not told Isabel she was poor then she must do it, if only to work out who was paying Vera Harker. But as soon as she entered the sitting room she realized the bad news had already been delivered. Isabel was sitting, reading a book. When Molly came in she looked up stonily and then went back to her reading.

"Isabel," Molly said, sitting down. "How much are you paying Mrs Harker for what she's doing?"

"I hardly think that that's any affair of yours," said her mother-in-law.

"I thought you might like me to pay her," Molly said mildly.

"I don't see any necessity for that," Isabel said coldly.

"It's obvious there are difficulties," Molly said, trying to tailor her remarks to suit Isabel. "I'm living here now – I'd like to help." Then, dropping any effort at diplomacy she said, "I know both of you thought I was rich – and now you know I'm not. But if we all pull together I'm sure we can get out of the mess."

In response to this Isabel simply put her book down on the table next to her and said, "I find this a disturbing conversation, Molly. Tom's wife is Tom's wife. You need not enquire about the wages of people I have asked to help us. You need not discuss your resources, or lack of them, with me. I must go and see about lunch."

Snubbed, Molly stood there in the middle of the sitting room, for a moment almost convinced that she had been rude and vulgar in attempting to discuss money with her mother-in-law. Then she looked at the cracked paint around the window panes. Money had to be discussed. Then she realized that Isabel had not asked about Mrs Gates. She made a face at the door through which Isabel had gone, as if she were still a child. Then she went upstairs, had a bath, changed her clothes and took a basket down to the village. She bought some food for the evening and packets of seeds at the village stores. She left an order for more supplies and said that she would drive down for them next day. She knew quite well that the old woman behind the counter was the aunt of a girl she had been at school with. She did not

441

acknowledge the fact and, by acting briskly, like someone in a hurry, prevented the woman from starting to chat. She walked the long lane back to the house with her basket, wishing now that she had taken the car. When she arrived there was no sound in the house. Isabel must be resting. She had not seen Tom all day. She made a cup of tea in the kitchen and carried it outside. Then she went back to the stables. Vera Harker was sitting in a chair, reading a women's magazine. A small pile of material lay on the floor at her feet. She put the magazine down when Molly came in. "There's not much I can do," she explained. "I don't want to wake her."

"Did she eat any lunch?" Molly asked.

"I can't even get her to drink anything," Mrs Harker said.

"I think she ought to be in hospital," said Molly, the urban woman. Mrs Harker, country bred and still in the tradition of people dying in their own beds, said, "Perhaps you're right."

"Well," said Molly, 'can you drop a note in at the doctor's this afternoon? I think he should come again. I'll stay here."

The other woman got up. "I'll get the doctor to run me back in the evening," she said. She tucked the half made-up material into a large chintz bag and then waited while Molly wrote a note to the doctor and left.

The afternoon was hotter than the morning. Molly sat, sometimes beside Mrs Gates and sometimes in the room outside. As she watched the motionless face of the sleeping woman it seemed, somehow, to be sinking in. She studied the movements of her chest as she breathed in and out. It was like watching a newborn child, but at the same time she seemed to be waiting for something. Nothing in the room changed. Nothing changed in the condition of the sick woman but, gradually, she felt the room filling with an atmosphere which frightened her. She shooed a fly out of the window. Then she went into the other room and found, in a chest under the window, a small collection of books. Among them was the old copy of Perrault's fairy tales she had been given as a child. In the flyleaf she read her own name, written in careful printing. Mary Waterhouse, Allaun Towers, Framlingham, Kent. She sat, reading the book, by the bed.

At about six o'clock she became alarmed. Mrs Gates had hardly stirred all afternoon. When she bathed her face she muttered something, said "Mary" and then seemed to fall asleep again. Molly wondered if she should not ask the doctor to call sooner or even get an ambulance to collect Mrs Gates and take her to hospital. She thought of consulting Isabel, but decided she would not be helpful. Instead she decided to leave the flat for a little while. She walked, thinking, down to the neglected verge of the lake and sat on the dried-up bank in a cloud of midges, watching two dragonflies swoop over the water. The five or six large oaks which had stood on the opposite bank had been felled. Only the stumps stood there. There had been an effort to plant some saplings to replace them but only three or four had survived. The others stood with their leaves brown and drooping in the still-hot air. The lake, which had once been so fresh, was low, now, and scummy. The verges around it, which had once been green, were dried-up and neglected. It seemed like a place where bad deeds, acts born of anger and misery, might be done. This was the place to which she had been going to lead her son on his early toddles, would have shown him the wild ducks which alighted there in autumn. This place had been going to nourish him. She had lost Joe, the only man with whom she had shared a love based on gaiety, equality and hope. The house, the lake, the grounds where she had been a child, were supposed to compensate her son for the loss. Now everything seemed irredeemably corrupted, and that, in some way, took Joe further and further from her. Already she felt the house and its occupants, which she had seen as a present she could give her child, to be burdens settling on her shoulders. What a bargain, she thought wryly, to swap mourning a dead husband for nursing a dying woman and sleeping in a collapsing house with an impotent man.

The birds were beginning to roost in the clumps of trees beyond the lake. She had still not decided whether to call the doctor or an ambulance to Mrs Gates but, she thought, when she entered the room again she would see, with fresh eyes, exactly what she looked like.

When she went back into the room Mrs Gates was trying to struggle up into a sitting position.

"Here – here," Molly cried in alarm. "Let me help you." She pulled her up against a pile of pillows. She put a glass of water to her lips. Mrs Gates drank some.

"I was looking for you," she said, leaning back on her pillows.

"You were asleep. I just stepped out for a breath of air," Molly said. "Would you like a cup of tea, now?"

But she could see from the grey face and the distanced look that Mrs Gates did not want anything. The strange, heavy atmosphere in the room was stronger but now it was not fear Molly felt. It was more like awe. She said, "I don't suppose I ever thanked you enough for taking care of me when I was a child. You have to be older to appreciate properly the sacrifice it is. It can't have been easy, being landed with a small child, right in the middle of a war."

"It made me young again," Mrs Gates said, with an effort. "I never felt young after you left. I didn't feel old – I just didn't feel young."

"It did a lot for me," Molly said. "You did a lot for me."

"Everything's sadly altered here," Mrs Gates said. "You'll put the place on its feet again."

Molly could not reveal that she had not yet decided to stay. She said, "I'll do my best," and wished it did not sound so much like a pledge. Mrs Gates's face had tightened. She was in pain.

"My chest's very tight," she told Molly.

"I'll lie you down," Molly said, in a panic.

"Better – propped up," the old woman said. Molly did not know what to do. She did not want to leave her alone but she could see now that she ought to get help. She thought desperately, too, that Tom or Isabel ought to be here with her.

"The doctor'll be here soon," she said, studying Mrs Gates closely. "Then he might say we should get you into hospital where they'll make you more comfortable."

"It's a bit better now," said Mrs Gates. Her face had relaxed and she seemed to be breathing easily. Molly took her hand and, trying to conceal her anxiety, told her, "I'll stay with you all the time until the doctor comes."

"I'd like to lie down," Mrs Gates murmured. Molly took away the pillows and helped her to lie down. She sat beside her, holding her hand.

"Take – my things – bits and pieces," she whispered. "There's no one else."

Molly swallowed and said, "Not yet, please God."

Then Mrs Gates's breathing got worse and Molly held her hand and said, "Don't be frightened. The doctor will be here soon."

Mrs Gates looked at her and relaxed. She closed her eyes. The breathing got worse until rasping breaths were filling the room. But still Molly did not dare to leave her to call for help. Her breath stopped, then started again. Molly hauled her up, propped her against the pillows and bathed the sweat from her face. She gave her sips of water.

Finally she said, "I must go – I've got to get an ambulance."

"Don't leave me," Mrs Gates said. She spoke with difficulty but her

444

tone was assured. Molly thought she knew how close she was to death. She knew Molly would not leave her and so, as one corner of Molly's brain protested, what a mess, what a mess, where is someone to help me? yet another concentrated on the laboured breathing and the livid face and prompted her to speak phrases she scarcely knew she had in her. "I remember when you used to let me help you hang out the washing on windy days. Do you remember how I used to hold on to the bottom of the sheets while you pegged the tops on the line? Then we'd stand back and watch the wind take them and say they looked like the sails of ships. In a way I was happier then than I've ever been." Then an instinct would urge her to be silent, to let Mrs Gates rest. Then she would say, "I'm looking forward to having the baby here. Perhaps you'll be well enough, then, to hold him. It must be a long time since there's been a baby in this house. It'll be nice." Mrs Gates said, in a very low voice, "I – hope – so." The heaviness of the atmosphere grew in the room. It began to darken. And then, finally, the old woman gave two great, convulsive gasps – and was still. Her head lay at an odd angle on the pillow, looking towards Molly. Molly heard herself groaning aloud into the empty room. As she did so she settled, with calm hands, the grey head on the pillows. Even then she was not sure that Mrs Gates was dead. She only knew that a crisis had come. But as the doctor came in, followed closely by Vera Harker, she was saying, "Oh – my God. Oh – my God."

"Molly?" came Vera Harker's voice behind her. She stood up. "I think she might be dead," Molly heard herself saying.

"Go with Mrs Harker, Lady Allaun," said the doctor.

In the other room, Vera Harker stooped down and took a bottle of brandy from the sideboard. Molly's teeth rattled against the glass as she drank. She sat down suddenly in a chair. "Do you think she's dead?" she asked the other woman.

"It might be a mercy," Mrs Harker said. "I don't think she'd ever have got out of that bed again. She was an active woman. She wouldn't have wanted to end up bedridden." She paused and said, "And she hasn't been alone."

"It's peculiar, isn't it?" she said. "She told me a creepy story about how a gypsy foretold I'd be there when she died – years ago, during the war."

"She told me that," Vera Harker said. "Before you came."

The doctor came into the room and said, "Lady Allaun –" and paused.

"She's dead?" Molly said.

He nodded. "I expect Sir Thomas will be making the arrangements?" he asked.

Molly found herself, even at that moment, wondering if Tom could, or would, ring the undertaker. But she said, "Of course."

There was a silence. "You'd better go up to the house," Vera Harker said.

She obviously knew the proper thing to do. Molly said, "Yes. We'll go up to the house."

They went in through the open kitchen door to find Isabel peeling potatoes with determination but little expertise.

Molly said, "Isabel —"

At the same moment she had asked, "How's Mrs Gates —?" but broke off when she saw from the faces of the others that the news was serious.

"Isabel — I'm afraid she's dead," Molly told her. She went to her mother-in-law and took her arm. "It was quite peaceful. I was there all the time."

Isabel said, "Oh, my dear. If only I'd known how serious it was —"

"Is Tom in the house?" Molly asked.

"Poor Mrs Gates," continued Isabel. "Her loyalty — she was above praise."

"I think we'd better find Tom," Molly insisted.

"He's gone to London," Isabel said. "Surely he told you — really, he's so forgetful. And now, when we need him —"

"Never mind," the doctor said. "It's a pity but he's not indispensable. I'm afraid I need to make out the death certificate —"

"I suppose we'd better go into the library," Molly said. She turned to Vera Harker, "Do we need a nurse?"

"I think Mrs Twining would like to come. She was away on a visit but she should be back now," Mrs Harker said. "I'll phone her."

Molly said to the doctor, "Follow me."

"You must sit down, Lady Allaun," Mrs Harker said to Isabel, taking her arm. "Let me help you." Molly felt grateful. When Joe had died she had made none of the arrangements. Now she was glad of the presence of Vera Harker, who knew what was appropriate and sensible.

The library was musty. The books were in bad condition. The doctor, looking at the fading spines said, "Are you interested in books, Lady Allaun?"

"I can't say I am," Molly told him. "But I suppose we shall have to do something about all this."

"Well – if you decide to get rid of any I'd like to look at them," he told her. "I'm a bit of a collector. In fact, if you need any advice –"

"I'll remember," Molly said, clearing a space on the dusty desk. He opened his bag and took out a form. "I'm putting the cause of death down as a coronary attack," he said. "Her heart had been giving anxiety for several years."

"I didn't know," she said.

He looked at her shrewdly and completed the form. "There we are," he said.

When he had gone Molly wandered into the kitchen where she found Vera Harker with the teapot in front of her. "I hope you don't mind," she said. "I'm waiting for Elizabeth Twining."

"Of course not," Molly responded. "I'll help myself, if you don't mind." Looking round the kitchen, and finding the ranks of old saucepans still gleaming, the flagstones on the floor impeccable, she uttered that old valedictory for the working-class woman, "She worked hard all her life."

"All her life," Vera Harker said. "They don't make them like that any more."

"Good job, too," Molly said, spoiling the tribute. In fact, she thought in grief and rage, this place had gobbled Mrs Gates up. No husband, child dead – and the Allauns. She had washed the ugly chandelier in the sitting room, piece by clinking piece, she had scrubbed the kitchen flags on her hands and knees, laundered the heavy sheets and pegged them out on the line. She had ironed, washed and cooked but nothing was her own, only the little pink porcelain lady, the clocks and the bed she slept in. And what of the children she had tended – Tom, weak, absent when she died, Charlie, bluff and brutal, and she, who had stepped so often and so heedlessly into the street without looking that her life had come to resemble one huge traffic accident? Had all that been worthwhile? All that work?

"She saw it as duty and self-respect," Mrs Harker continued.

Molly said bitterly, looking at the scrubbed surface of the big pine kitchen table, "They should put this up as her tombstone." And thought to herself, "I can beat this house. I'll do it for her sake, to prevent all her work from going to waste." And she stared fiercely at Vera Harker, who, already disconcerted by the turn the conversation had taken, dropped her eyes, wondering what new follies were about

447

to begin at Allaun Towers under the aegis of this new and inappropriate mistress.

But there is a point, after a death, when people feel a kind of energy, a determination to get back at death and make it concede that its victory over life is, after all, only a draw. As the months wore on at Allaun Towers and summer gave way to autumn Molly, if she looked back at that moment of resolution at all, felt only slightly ashamed and embarrassed. Nevertheless, as events later proved, the moment had not been completely meaningless.

There was a sudden flurry of interest in the fate of Mary Waterhouse around the time of her marriage. Those who needed to know what was happening to her had their own family problems and this for some reason seemed to focus attention on her. There was only moderate enthusiasm for her marriage to Joe Endell because although it settled her it did put her into the hands of a notable radical, and a man living in areas where he might hear gossip – a dangerous combination. When he died it was rather a relief but, of course, it meant she was on the loose again. Then came the marriage to Tom Allaun and it was felt that all concerned could breath normally again. A decent future for Molly and the child lay ahead. And although no one stated it, one of the greatest advantages of her new position was that it would keep her away from London. No more prison sentences, vagrancy or taking up with shady characters. It is embedded deeply in the English psyche – this notion that life in the country is purer and more wholesome than life in the town. The country is like a kind of lay monastery to which people go to redeem themselves and avoid the temptations of the world.

It was my wife, Corrie, who poured cold water on these illusions. She pointed out that bringing Molly's son up as a landless peer might be worse than letting him grow up in the city and learn an honest job. And she added that, from what she knew of her, anyone who imagined that Molly Allaun was going to spend the rest of her life living quietly in the country as a gentlewoman in reduced circumstances, married to a gentleman of no capacities and uncertain sexual orientation, must be stark, staring mad. I told her that Molly was now a woman of thirty-eight, not a girl of twenty. She had presumably seen enough trouble to make her want no more. And, in addition, she had a young child to bring up.

Corrie said, "You underestimate women, Bert. You always have. They're capable of anything, you know – anything. It's a crippling disadvantage men have got – not realizing that women are exactly like themselves – just as likely to be heroines or bank robbers, saints or hypocrites. You'll all have to wake up one day. But if you want that woman to keep quiet the first thing to do is to get her some money. If she's too poor she'll get desperate. And you know what she's like when she's desperate. She's been in a thousand situations where her most proper response would have been to have shouted 'Alas, cruel world,' and jumped off a bridge. Instead she thinks of something – she's like a dreadful child left alone in a room for one minute – the kind who can always think of something to do like opening the bird-cage or cutting off all their own hair. Your job is to stop Molly Allaun from having any ideas at all. Can't something financial be arranged?"

"I don't see how," I said. "And I don't think they'd do it."

"These things were better organized in the old days," Corrie remarked. "There were pensions and grants – you might have to put up with spies in your household or even the slight prospect of an accident – but that wasn't too big a price to pay for all the rest. Poor Molly," she added, severely, "has only had the spies."

We were sitting alone, over tea, in our house in the country. The fire had been lit. The winds of early autumn were hissing through the trees outside. I was annoyed by Corrie's last remark. She had never overtly criticized my involvement with Molly Waterhouse. I think many of the charges she might have made about my part in the affair were bitten back because of her slight resentment of the ancient hold Molly had on my affections. Wise women do not even discuss these things. But this time, it seemed, her pity for the woman had overcome both a tiny jealousy and her feeling that it was not quite right for her to interfere. Corrie was indignant and her indignation stung me – all the more so, I suppose, because I was sensitive about the whole business.

"I did my duty," I said, in my own defence. "I did what they asked."

"Only obeying orders," she said. "I'm sorry, Bert. I can't stand being associated with this situation – where people pry and spy and worry about the consequences, but never do anything to help. It seems so wrong."

"I know," I said. "I'm not sure what the alternative was, though."

"Have you got the file still – the one upstairs?" she demanded suddenly. I was alarmed. It even seemed possible she was contemplating action.

449

"Of course not," I told her. "That file was not mine to take."

"But you took it, Bert, and copied every page," she pointed out. "I found it all in a blue file in the attic when I was getting out the old christening dress for Laura's child."

"Well, yes," I admitted, "I did copy it. I took it with me when I left." For I had, a few years before, taken over my father-in-law's firm after his death. And I must admit I was relieved to be able to go without fuss.

"You were angry," she told me. "But why are you pretending you haven't got the papers – do you think even I can't be trusted?"

"It's partly just a conditioned reaction," I told her. "I inherited the secret from my father. I've kept it so long –"

"Then why did you copy the papers?" she asked. "I suppose you realize that if we were burgled they could end up on a dump, in a field – it's almost asking for trouble –"

"I didn't think of that," I said.

She leaned back in her chair and said, "Bert – I believe your attitude is ambiguous. On the one hand you can't even tell me, your wife, that you have the copies. On the other hand, you deliberately make another copy and leave it in a very unsecret secret place. An attic, for heaven's sake, where any curious person, any burglar, looks first." And she added cruelly, "It's like some horrible case history where a man is trying to conceal and reveal his trauma to an analyst. In any case," she went on, having crippled me with the observation in which I felt there was some justice, "I'd like to read the papers."

"I can't do that," I protested.

"They're in my attic. You put them there. I could have read them at any time during the last few years," she pointed out.

I could not deny this. In a way I could not refuse to let her read the documents. And yet it disconcerted me to think of my wife, the mother of my three children, rummaging in the attic for my records, my memories of Mary Waterhouse, my past. It was almost as if she had coolly announced that she wanted to read my old love letters from another woman. And yet I realized that Corrie was a tactful and sensible woman, perfectly aware of my old tender feelings – the feelings which had begun when I was a silly young man, virtually an adolescent boy. And I knew she would not mock me about them. It seems strange, I imagine, for a grown man to make such a fuss about a pile of old documents. But, remember, the secrets considered important by one generation seem absurd to the next, which, in turn, is keeping secret the kind of information quite openly presented by the previous generation. And remember, too, the story those papers hid. I was putting highly confidential information which, strictly speaking, I should not have had available, into my wife's hands. To be candid, at that moment I thought what a fool I'd been to copy the papers and store them.

Just how considerable the secret was I don't think even I realized, as she sat down and said comfortably, "There's a couple of hours till dinner time – and it's a casserole, already in the oven." She opened the cardboard cover of the file and began to read. Only minutes later she said, "Good Lord – I didn't realize it gave chapter and verse to this extent."

I had been looking into the fire and feeling slightly gloomy, like a child standing by while his father reads his school report. I reassessed the whole affair in my mind. There is something about the sudden production of old documents – letters, invitations, photographs – which does not always tend to pleasant nostalgia. Sometimes they can induce feelings of self-reproach, "To think I never saw him again before he died" or just self-contempt – "What a fool I was." And in nine cases out of ten it's impossible to do anything about it – the past is gone, and that's that. In this particular case the fact that half the revelations were not mine at all, but belonged to the main actors in the affair, seemed to make it worse, rather than better. So when Corrie remarked on how specific all the information was I just agreed sourly. "Oh yes," I said, "there isn't anything there which wouldn't stand up in court."

" 'Abbé des Frères Chrétiens'," she read. " 'Poulaye-sur-Bois. Loire.' He writes a steady hand for an old gentleman – oh, well, perhaps he was a young gentleman when he made this deposition."

"He was," I said. "That was probably why he got mixed up in the affair in the first place."

"Could still be alive," she said.

"I doubt it," I told her.

"A wedding photograph!" she exclaimed. "You didn't tell me there was a photograph."

"I didn't tell you anything," I pointed out.

"But a photograph!" she said again.

"Village photographer," I explained. "My father went over a few years after it happened and got all the information, including the photograph. And the negative."

"Where's that?" she asked.

"Handed over," I told her.

"I wonder what they did with it?"

"I don't suppose they had an enlargement made for the family album," I said.

"They look a happy couple," she said, studying the old picture closely.

"I often thought that," I said. "I doubt if either was really ever so happy again." My wife looked at me sadly, and said, "What a tragedy."

"A mess-up from start to finish," I told her. "Lies, concealments – no justice done. It's damned depressing."

Corrie, now sobered, went on reading. She looked up again and asked me sharply, "What happened to the other one?"

"Dead," I told her.

"It doesn't say so here," she said.

"Everybody else died," I said. "Read the reports for yourself."

"I have – there isn't any mention of a child."

Meanwhile the wind came up stronger. Corrie read on and on. The wind howled round the house and down the chimney, making the fire flicker to and fro. I sat on for a while, watching Corrie read the records of the old crimes, lies, concealments and evasions to which I had made myself an accomplice in the name of service. It began to make me nervous. The wind seemed to be howling old screams at me, or old accusations, I didn't know which. As Corrie read, I also seemed to hear her own mental commentary on the whole affair. I suppose this may have been one of the reasons why I was not very pleased when she asked me to read the files – there is something about the attitude of a firm-minded and sensible woman which can throw a cold and unkind light on the activities of men working according to established precedents and moral standards. In the light of pragmatism many male activities look like folly. In the end, unable to sit and watch her any more, I retreated to the dining room where I sat looking at a film on the television and wishing there were someone in the house other than just the two of us.

She was silent as we ate our dinner. Finally I said, "What did you think about it all?"

She looked at me rather soberly and said, "In the end I wondered how they dared involve you so deeply. Or your father. Even after you left they've called you in for an opinion, or that's what it looks like now."

"It's a long tradition," I said. I thought the discussion was finished but that night, in bed, she said, "Bert – I've got a feeling the matter hasn't ended. Do you think that boy could still be alive?" I imagine I responded as people do in such circumstances, by saying, "Let's go to sleep," or "Can we talk about it in the morning?" But she persisted, "This could burst, like a boil, at any moment." And here I remember saying, "Corrie – I don't think I appreciate your choice of words at this time of night. Shall we go to sleep now?" I distinctly remember her reply coming at me through a fog of sleep, "It seems to me that you've been asleep half your life." At the time I thought she was just being unpleasant – in retrospect, I realize she was in some ways right.

At about the same time Molly Allaun and her other mother-in-law, Joe Endell's mother, were sitting on a rug by the lake with the pram containing the baby, who had been named Frederick, after his grandfather.

"Clouding over," said Evelyn, looking up.

"It's nice of you to come all this way to see me and the baby. I could have come to you."

"It's easier for me to come here,' Evelyn Endell said. "And it makes a break to come to Kent."

She had probably wanted to see where and how her grandchild was being brought up. Molly said, "I'm sorry conditions are so rough. It's worse since Mrs Gates died. I don't think Isabel realized how much of the work she was doing."

"I don't suppose she did," Evelyn agreed drily.

"It might come down to going back to Meakin Street," Molly said. She did not add that it might be a question of going there alone, without Tom.

"Pity, though," her former mother-in-law said ruefully. "This is a lovely place. A child couldn't ask for a better spot to grow up in." Then she opened her large buff handbag, which lay beside her on the bank and said, "I hope this won't upset you – I thought of sending it and decided to give it all to you myself." She pulled out a big brown envelope and told Molly, "It's all Joe's papers. Everything. I've made copies. I thought you'd like to have them for the boy, when he's older. There's school reports and his first article for the local paper – oh – and all sorts."

"Oh, thank you," Molly said, taking the envelope. "Thank you,

Evelyn." Overwhelmed for a moment by her own sorrow she remembered a little later that this was Joe's mother, wiped her eyes with the back of her hand and said, "At least I had his son — before he died. At least we've got that."

Mrs Endell blew her nose and said, "That's right."

"I'll never forget him," Molly said. "I'll never get over it. I married too soon — mostly for the child's sake." It was a confession she did not want to make but she thought she owed it to Joe's mother.

"I know that," Evelyn Endell said. "No one who'd seen you and Joe together would think otherwise. I'll be honest — Fred was angry at first. I told him I was convinced you were doing it for the best. Now I hope you're happy. A child needs a happy home."

"I'll do my best," Molly said.

"I'm sure you will," Evelyn said. "And if you have to bring Fred up in Meakin Street it won't hurt him. And it'll certainly be logical because I don't suppose you knew Joe was born near Meakin Street. I don't think I told you."

"What — round there?" Molly said in astonishment. "I can't believe it. How did he come to drift so far north?"

"You read it — it's in the envelope," Evelyn told her. "We adopted him from an orphanage in London. He was rescued from a bombed building. I don't know what can have happened to him before we got him but the account from the orphanage is heart-breaking." She put her hand on Molly's arm. "I had it in mind to tell you more about all this when we were talking about it before. But I'd always known there was something locked up in Joe which had to come out in its own good time. I thought a happy marriage would release it in the end. I was afraid you'd press him too soon. I think if he'd lived to see his child it would have helped. When a child is born we relive the past. You see, what I didn't want was for Joe to have to face whatever it was he never thought about — what must have happened when he was a child — before he was ready. It's not as if he was miserable or unfulfilled."

"Oh, no," Molly said. "He wasn't that."

The two women sat quietly side by side in the last sunshine of the year. Overhead, flocks of birds flew south. Then the baby cried in his pram and they wheeled him back to the house.

Molly did not open the brown envelope. She put it in a drawer in the bedroom and left it there. Indeed, for a while she almost forgot about it. It had been a hard time for her and she knew at heart that harder times lay ahead.

After Mrs Gates died Sid and Ivy had driven down with the child. Then came the funeral. The baby had been christened a week later. This had meant arranging two gatherings at the house, one for the mourners after Mrs Gates's funeral and one for the family after the christening. Molly had been relieved, although she felt guilty about it, that the Endells had not been able to come at that time. They would have stayed several days and been uncomfortable in the over-strained household.

After the christening she said grimly to Ivy, "I've spent the last month watching a woman die and her coffin lowered into the ground and my baby christened and I've spent the rest of the time cleaning this house and cooking. It's been a funny honeymoon."

"I wouldn't call it funny," remarked Ivy. They were standing, for some reason, in the library. She looked at the space on the ceiling where a piece of plaster moulding had fallen off and said, "This lot is going to take a bit of sorting out. Sid'll help you. It's no good asking Jack to do his storm trooper act on the premises – he's too busy these days."

"He's still too annoyed about the marriage," Molly said.

"He'll get over it," Ivy said. She looked at Molly and added, seemingly irrelevantly, "Well, thank goodness you've still got Meakin Street."

The next day Molly decided she had better sort out Mrs Gates's possessions. While the baby slept in his pram in the yard, she went sombrely through the orderly cupboards and drawers in the flat above the stable. Isabel and Tom had not offered their help with the task. Both had the useful knack of silence when situations demanding action arose. This meant that, on the whole, they were never seen to refuse responsibility while, on the other hand, they were seldom forced to accept it. It must have been this habit of keeping still in a crisis, thought Molly, which had enabled them to ignore so many warning voices. It was more explicable in Isabel's case – she had not been reared to expect change and action – but in Tom's it seemed more of a mystery. He had a degree in law, though a poor one, and had had a job in a stockbroking firm run by an old friend of Sir Frederick's. He had also been employed by a legal firm. Both jobs had ended mysteriously. Now Charlie Markham had secured him a place in a small firm of lawyers used occasionally by his companies.

Tom went to London on Tuesdays, returning to Framlingham on Friday nights. The salary was low but that Tom was employed at all was a relief to Molly — so, unfortunately, was the fact that Tom so rarely shared her bed. The marriage was consummated now. On the night of the christening Tom, affectionate, and primed with champagne, had met a ready response in Molly, who felt that her child was now the child of the house. Tom, who had before been unable to sustain an erection, managed it at last. For a few moments, as they began to make love, Molly was filled with joy and relief, not so much with pleasure at the action, as with what it might mean for the future. But few genuine loves have begun on this desperate basis. Tom, above her, laboured effortfully, his face tormented. He came after a short time leaving Molly unsatisfied. Tom, evidently rather pleased, fell asleep. His attempt to make love to her the following night failed. Molly was left beside him with her uneasy thoughts telling herself that he had failed her and suspecting, in her heart of hearts, that she had failed him. She did not love Tom, she did not want him particularly, except as a physical release. But she knew that the marriage, a commercial transaction, could have been saved by sex and now she knew that, without a miracle, it would not be. A bleak life, involving much hard domestic work and loneliness, began. Only the baby, large, cheerful and thriving, consoled her.

Now it was autumn and, as she took Mrs Gates's clothes from the drawers, she saw a cloud of leaves blowing past the window and wondered how hard it would be to face the long, dark winter in Framlingham.

Her money was running down also. "Get out," she told herself, "cut your losses and get out of here." Abandoning the piles of blouses and brown stockings she stood up and went into the other room. She opened the small bureau which stood in the corner of the room, in case there was information in there about a relative of whom no one knew, or some matter of business which would have to be tackled by the Allauns. There were letters there — some apparently from Mrs Gates's husband, Andy, written while they were courting, some from her father, written from the front during the First World War. In an old envelope was a marriage certificate from Dover, dated 1927. A child's death certificate, dated three years later. In the cupboard at the bottom there was a biscuit tin containing old photographs. Women with bustles and men in frock coats stared out, straightfaced, from the pictures. Unknown babies lay in long robes in women's arms. Two bright girls in long white dresses and straw hats stood, arms entwined, on a beach. Apart from that there was little in the desk but some old bills, newspaper cuttings about the end of the war, an envelope containing a lock of fair hair. Molly wondered whose it was – perhaps, she thought, it might even be her own. She could not face throwing away the relics of someone's life. She shut the desk and turned round as she heard voices on the stairs. Vera Harker came in with Elizabeth Twining. "Oh," Molly said, "Mrs Twining. I'm so relieved to see you. I've been trying to sort everything out – I was hoping you'd be able to find a use for –" She gestured round her. "And the photographs – I don't know who they are."

The two women looked at her without pity. Their glances seemed to tell her that they had faced this situation before and dealt with the realities following death. Vera Harker softened. She said, "At least you tried." They stood in the room, full of little piles of clothing. She pulled an envelope out of her basket. She said, "She wanted you to have this. The day before you came she made me get a form from the Post Office. She had some savings – she wanted half to go to Elizabeth and half to you. Said you'd need it – to make sure you spent it on yourself or the boy. 'Make sure she keeps it for herself, for her and the child,' she said."

Molly was concerned. "Isn't there anybody else – closer?"

"Five hundred and fourteen pounds in there," Vera Harker told her. "You'd better count it in front of us. I didn't fancy the responsibility but she was in a bad way – I couldn't refuse." Molly hesitated. "She wanted you to have it," Elizabeth Twining said.

"But was she – did she know what she was doing?" Molly asked.

"Oh yes," Vera Harker told her. "She said what was to happen to the clocks and her other bits and pieces. I told her not to be so morbid but it wasn't any good. She was set on dying, that's my opinion."

Molly took the envelope and counted the money out. "Don't you forget, Mary, she said it was for you," Elizabeth Twining told her. And Molly, who was thinking of leaving Framlingham as soon as she could, felt guilty.

"I ought to do something with this," she said, half to herself. Instead, she put it in the biscuit tin on top of the photographs and shut the tin in the cupboard.

"Go back and have a lie down," advised Elizabeth Twining. "You look all in. Go on," she said to Vera Harker. "Give it to her."

What Vera Harker produced, a little shyly, from her basket was a comical scarecrow doll, about a foot long, dressed in patchwork rags, with hair made of real straw. Molly was touched, and very taken with the doll. It had an engaging, silly grin and eyeballs made of green buttons.

"Don't thank me," Vera Harker said. "I'm forever making them. There aren't enough children in the village to give them to. The whole place is fed up with them."

"Don't listen to her," Elizabeth said, "they're famous for miles around — there's all sorts — scarecrows and pretty ladies and funny old men, and dogs and cats. She ought to sell them, that's what I tell her. Lou Gates used to say she should get herself a market stall at Hale Market —"

"Who'd buy those?" interrupted Vera Harker. "They're only old scraps."

"I've never seen anything like it," Molly said, impressed. "How did you invent it?"

"Just came to me as I went along," the other woman told her. "Well all this praise and flattery's cheered me up good and proper. Now you go along and Elizabeth and me'll sort this lot out."

And Molly departed, holding the scarecrow doll.

After giving the baby his bottle she went upstairs to put him in his cot, to find Tom lying on the bed in their bedroom.

"Aren't you well?" she asked.

"I decided to take the afternoon off," he told her. "It got tedious."

Molly, feeling bitter about the time she had spent trying to look at Mrs Gates's things without crying, said, "Well, life does, from time to time."

"I don't want you to leave, Molly," he said. He must have been lying there, thinking about his life, she thought. It was odd that the silent Tom had spoken at last. She said in reply, "I don't know why you want me to stay. You don't really like me, or so it seems. There's nothing between us — not even as much as there was when we were living at Meakin Street."

He looked at her pitifully. "I'm not used to being a husband," he told her. "I don't think I'm very good at it. I'd like you to stay." He burst out, "I can't take a winter here, with mother."

And Molly thought that she might as well stay a little longer. She did not want to remake her life again, after this botched attempt. She said, "I'll stay. Maybe not for ever. But I'll stay. But we might both feel easier if I slept alone. I don't sleep well when you're here — and I worry about Fred disturbing you. I'll move back into my old room, on the corner of the house. I always loved it." But Tom was afraid of his mother's questions. "Just say the baby disturbs you all night long and you're going mad," Molly said. "She'll accept that. She doesn't want to ask too many questions."

"Sometimes I think I'm going mad," he said.

"This is all impossible," Molly said, sitting beside him. "I've seen and been in some rotten situations but this seems one of the worst. There's a lock on it – and no key. You should get rid of this place – it's dragged you down, over the years. You should just walk away and leave it to rot."

"It's mother," he said.

"You'd have to be firm," Molly said. She gazed out of the window. "It's criminal – cutting down the oaks."

"I know," Tom said.

"Anyway, I just made up my mind. I'll try to make a bit of money for Christmas."

"How?" asked Tom, alarmed.

"I'm going to work with Vera Harker," she said. "I can't leave Fred but I can do that."

That evening she went to see Vera and looked at all the toys – the knitted harlequin, the fat red velveteen man with yellow hair and surprised button blue eyes, the terrier dog, the squashy black and white cat, the pretty ladies in their full skirts, petticoats and little removable shoes. She persuaded Vera and her mother to let her borrow the toys to take to London next day. "I'll try to get some orders," she said. "It could mean a nice little sum for all of us before Christmas."

The two women were cautious. Harker, who worked for a market gardener, put down his paper and said, "Good luck to you. I've told her time and again those were too good to give away."

"If I get too many orders would anybody else help?" Molly asked Vera.

"You'll be lucky to get *one*," Vera said. This was her right as the creator of the toys.

"There won't be a woman here who won't help, just before Christmas," Vera's mother said. "It's a slack time for work."

And so, next day Molly put all the toys in the back of the car with the baby and got a large order from a large, smart toyshop. She returned to Framlingham with material, thread and buttons and told the women, "They cost three pounds to make and they're giving us seven – that's an average price – and they want a hundred in all. That's for

459

Christmas, so we have to do them in six weeks. But I want them in two lots because if they sell them out before Christmas they might take more. And even if they don't, someone else may. I'm taking a pound on each and the rest of the profit goes to the woman who makes the toy. Can you get about eight or nine other women to help?"

She was using Mrs Gates's legacy as stake money. The women did not hesitate. As autumn wore on Molly was touring the village every day, checking on progress and submitting the other women's toys to Vera for approval. "I can't sew," she explained apologetically. "But it looks as if I can sell."

A fortnight later she was back at the shop with her consignment. The department manager was reluctant to display and sell them early. "We could use up space and spoil their freshness," he said. Molly, desperate, went to three stores. The last one gave her an order for a hundred and fifty toys, but only if they were half the size. Molly, knowing that the cost of the materials would be higher in proportion, nevertheless agreed. Vera, slightly horrified by having the challenge thrust on her at short notice, worked out patterns and prototypes. Molly, who knew that Vera's creative pleasure was diminishing as trade increased, said, "Leave the others to make them, Vera. You sit and think about another one. Have you thought of a footballer – then people can buy one for quite a big boy without thinking they're turning him into a cissie. You know what people are like – they won't get anything cuddly for the boys after they're about three. But they still want something to take to bed with them at night." Vera's stocky footballer was, if anything, outclassed by her gangling cricketer in cap and long scarf.

"You're a genius, Vera," she told her. "They're witty – these. It must all be locked up inside you."

"I've always been a quiet sort of a woman," Vera said. "My dad and mum brought us up to be quiet, on account of us being nine, all in one small cottage. She used to look at you, did Mum, and say if Lady Allaun wanted to take in a child she could have looked closer to home. Quite bitter, she was, when you came round calling for me in your little white socks and starched dress. I suppose a lot gets locked up in you when the family's big and the money's short."

Throughout October Molly added up the bills for the materials used, and badgered the women through a flu epidemic which hit nearly all of them or their families. They were grateful to her but she knew few of them liked her. To them she was a fast-talking Cockney, using their labour to make money, someone who, in spite of having been an evacuee and having a dubious past, had managed to manoeuvre her way into becoming Lady Allaun.

"The old gypsy said she was to marry three times," reported tall, thin, Clarisse Smith to plump Vera Harker, when she brought round ten knitted harlequins and columbines, "now that's true enough, isn't it. But the child – unnatural fruit – and the marriages no true marriages – what sort of a thing is that, said to a child of six? Must be something in it."

"Means rubbish, I should say," retorted Vera, examining columbine's hat and picking at a loose stitch. "Whoever listens to gypsies? Only if you want an upset and something to worry you."

With a glance at Vera Harker's mother, who was quietly sewing on a footballer's scarf in her chair by the fire, Clarisse said, "Well, some of it came true, didn't it?"

"Said she'd make her fortune, too," remarked the old lady. "If I remember right. So let's believe that and get on with the work."

"Unnatural fruit, though – makes your blood run cold," said Clarisse.

"Well, the boy looks natural enough," Vera said. "Mum's right – let's get on with it. I'll soon have enough to pay for my freezer."

"I don't know about the marriage, though," her mother remarked treacherously. "You want your blood to run cold, take a look in her husband's eyes. I'm glad none of mine ever took up with him, that's all, title or no title."

Vera said, "I don't remember him ever come round courting me. He ever come knocking on your door, Clarisse?"

By Christmas Molly had made a hundred and fifty pounds, which took them through a quiet Christmas Day and paid some bills. By then she was too busy working out a plan to keep trade going after the Christmas boom to think very much about the sombre quality of the Christmas cheer or remember very much that this was her first Christmas without Joe. She just exhausted herself with calculations about the toy trade, with cooking and putting up decorations and caring for the child. She had decided, without realizing it, to look for no more happiness. For the time being, at any rate, she had to concentrate on survival.

The months after Christmas were grim. The income from the Allaun's unbreakable trust fund did little more than keep up the interest payments on the heavy mortgages. The farms, even the better pictures in the house and some of the silver, had been sold off years before. Tom's income was small because in effect he was more legal clerk than solicitor. Molly's earnings were soon gone and soon she was attacking the dwindling sum which had been Joe Endell's life insurance. The Twinings were kind and tactful – Elizabeth brought eggs from the hens, a few apples she had been clearing out of the loft, unwanted vegetables from the garden, always making the point that if Molly did not accept the gifts they would be thrown away. Her husband sent his grandson over to do heavy digging in the vegetable garden and give Molly tips on what would and would not grow. The boy, Rob, was more sceptical.

"I might get some hens," she told the boy one day.

He looked at her shrewdly. "I should concentrate on business," he said.

In the meantime, Molly, saying nothing to the Allauns, wrote to Sam Needham and asked him if he could recommend a tenant for Meakin Street. He, about to marry, suggested himself. Molly wrote back and offered him the house – she knew that Tom and Isabel very much wanted her to sell her house to finance Allaun Towers. She had noticed that Isabel had hung on to her rings, the last items of any real value in the house and did not propose to sell her own house to mend the roof at Framlingham, while Isabel's hands still flashed with their old sparkle. These rings were plainly vital to Isabel's conception of herself as a well-off country gentlewoman, as were the trips up to Town, as she described them. There she visited old friends, to whom she was able to misrepresent her situation. "My daughter-in-law is a keen gardener", for example, would bring to mind the vision of a lady in a straw hat cutting roses but not Molly's mud-stricken battles with the kitchen garden in a high wind, while Fred lay rawly in his pram in a thick hat and mittens, his nose running. The friends, no doubt, retaliated by shining a glamorous light over their own affairs. But although these outings revived Isabel, Molly, furious and intolerant, could not bear her evening remarks: "I had such a nice time I forgot I had a train to catch and had to take a taxi to the station." "We went to a matinée – it was quite like the old days."

After these conversations Molly would lie in her room fuming with rage and trying to do the impossible calculations for a household where no one was quite candid about income and expenditure, money came from different sources into different hands and no one person was responsible for what was spent. Meanwhile Vera Harker, Clarisse and the others had tasted blood.

They were keen to keep the toy business going and continue to earn as they had before Christmas. But Molly knew the shop and the store she had dealt with were reluctant to offer more orders until the spring and her efforts to find other customers had been unsuccessful, except for one order, for fifty toys. She had to decide whether it was worth carrying on and hoping for better times, as the year progressed. March was cold and blustery. The orders had still not arrived, if they ever would. She had the idea Tom and his job were about to part company. The house had been freezing for six months except for small areas around the sitting room fire and kitchen stove and both Molly and the child had severe colds. She was lying in bed, slightly feverish, listening to the unfriendly wind howling round the corner of the house and huddling the baby under the bed covers to keep them both warm, when Charlie Markham walked in wearing country tweeds.

"Ho," he said, startled and deterred by the sight of Molly, red-nosed in a grey sweater, flat on her back in bed beside the large, snuffling baby. "Well, well. Isabel said you were ill when she let me in – I thought I'd just slip over and make my New Year visit to the family."

"Come here ratting every March, do you, Charlie?" Molly said, annoyed at being caught looking so demoralized by a smartly dressed Charlie Markham. "You're in luck. There's one creeping into the kitchen at night."

"Don't take on, Molly," remarked Charlie. "I'm a visitor – and you can't see many of those. I've brought a bottle of Gordon's from Simon Tate. And I did a sweep at Fortnum's before I set off. And Simon's sent his christening present for little Fred, here."

"Oh," Molly said, encouraged. "Well, you go down into the kitchen and keep warm. Put the kettle on, if you can find it. I'll be down in a minute."

As she scuffled into her grey flannel trousers and combed her dried-up hair hopelessly before the mirror, she thought that Charlie was right. Any visitor was welcome, even if he would turn nasty as Charlie probably would.

By the time she had changed the baby's nappy Charlie had already made the tea. She settled Fred in the pram by the kitchen range and said, "Where's Isabel?"

"She said she was going up for a rest – she'd see me later," Charlie told her. "It's the cold – it's enervating."

"Fucking country life," declared Molly. "Look at me – my hair's dried, my hands are all cracked and wrinkled – I'm coming apart at the seams." She coughed.

Charlie ignored all this and asked, "What are those big parcels in the hall?"

Molly explained to him that they contained an order for toys. She told him she was trying to decide whether to continue, which might mean expansion, or put a stop to the business. If it expanded she might have to get several electric sewing machines. Charlie, though unsympathetic, was sensible, and because she had no one else to talk to she told him that she was trying to decide whether to go back to London or not.

"At the moment," she said, "the money from the toys and the rent from Meakin Street and everything else are just going into shoring the collapse. It just keeps it all ticking over for a bit longer."

"Can't see you getting any money out of a bank on the basis of what you have here," Charlie said. He cut himself another slice of the cake he had brought. In his suit, collar and tie, chewing happily on the cake, he looked like a large schoolboy.

"I suppose you were the joker who told Tom I was a wealthy heiress," Molly challenged him. "I hope you're satisfied."

Charlie had obviously heard about this from Tom. He said coolly, "Do me a little justice, Molly. I wouldn't say anything like that without checking. It was a rumour at Frames, where some of the older clientele still take an interest in your affairs. I think Tate started it – he thought it was true and he didn't realize anyone would be mad enough to believe it and act accordingly. I didn't know what he was thinking."

"You wanted him married to me, though," Molly said.

Charlie frowned at her. "I take it," he said, "that Tom isn't giving every satisfaction, matrimonially speaking?"

"You know damn well he isn't," exclaimed Molly. "And you could have bloody warned me."

"How did I know?" Charlie said. "He was all right with his other girlfriend, the one he nearly married. Or, I suppose he was. It sounded all right. And, be reasonable, Molly – I thought you were old enough to know what was what. I just wanted to see him settled. How was I supposed to know that he thought you were a millionaire and you'd not – well," he said impatiently, "I never thought you'd let the bells ring out before you'd run him up the course – got a rough idea of his form, so to speak."

"I was rattled," Molly told him. "I'd just lost Joe – I'd just had a baby –"

Charlie said unsentimentally, "Water under the bridge, now. But, quite honestly, Moll, I don't think you're giving him a chance. You're a handsome woman underneath the chilblains but are you really trying? I mean, you're getting rough and tough, you're all bills and invoices and with Tom being a wee bit frail – I mean, it's not all that encouraging –"

"There isn't a lot of scope here for lying on sofas in nothing but a light spray of Diorissimo," Molly said in annoyance.

"Yes, well," Charlie said evasively, "well – that may be true but after all, I'm Tom's cousin – not that I don't see your point of view – on the other hand, you took on a man you didn't love, I think you'll admit that, and poor old Tom, not robust at the best of times, has to compete with Endell's ghost and Endell's child – boy child, just to make it worse – a man would have to be Tarzan –"

"And Tom certainly isn't Tarzan," Molly said philosophically. "Still – there it is. It's a disaster."

"Things could perk up," Charlie said, "in the summer –"

"Shut up, Charlie," Molly said emphatically. She knew part of him was enjoying the collapse. "The fact is, you shouldn't have encouraged Tom – you should have warned me. You didn't stop either of us from making bloody fools of ourselves –"

"Look," said Charlie. "I'm opening the gin – I just want to say this before Isabel comes down –" He unscrewed the cap from the bottle of gin. Molly found some tonic. He lifted his glass to her. "It's this," he said. "I'm not plunging on the Allauns, family or no family. I already got Tom a job, which he messed up, then jettisoned, then I had to make embarrassing explanations. Now he's doing it again and I've had enough. But you seem to be thinking. The toys are nice. If you ever come up with a sound idea and want capital I'll give it my earnest consideration."

Molly was stunned by this. Charlie, hooligan and sado-masochist, was sitting there offering her money. She asked, "Can you do that – I mean, have you got the power?"

"Power?" Charlie said, "I'm on the board of a twenty million pound group of companies. I'm the director of three." He handed her a piece of pasteboard and said, "Tuck that in your bra in case you need it. And not a word to anybody else here."

"Right," Molly said, taking the card and hiding it in a tureen on the top shelf of the cupboard. "Why me?" she asked.

"Blood's thicker than water," Charlie told her.

"I don't believe you," Molly said.

He leaned forward. "Your rather eccentric career has taught you a lot. You're up against it now. I've got a feeling that your lessons in the hard school of life – under teachers like the Rose brothers, and poor old Ferenc Nedermann, etc, etc – will stand you in good stead. And anyway," he told her, "I've always been fond – very fond – of you, Mollikins. I've thought of you with yearning many times – now I realize our little fracas that time –" His hand was now on her knee.

"Charlie," Molly said quickly. "It's bleeding cold in this place. It's enough to put off a sailor who's been at sea for three months. And on top of that, I hear Isabel's feet on the stairs."

"Fair enough," Charlie said and, as Isabel came into the kitchen he added, in a bonhomous, nephewly voice, "Tea's ready, Aunt Isabel. And cake. Sit down, do."

And ten minutes later Tom came back early from London and they all sat chatting in the warm kitchen. Not long after it was time for drinks. Out came the gin again and a bottle of whisky and the Allauns all had a glass or two and began to enjoy themselves. They ate supper in the kitchen and later Charlie went back to London.

It had not been a bad day but Molly, still slightly fevered, lay in bed that night, with the baby breathing stertorously in his cot beside her, and thought about the future. It was not likely that Charlie Markham would run about holding board meetings in order to find the capital for her plan to convert the old stable block into a toy factory. The scheme was too chancey, and unlikely, even if it succeeded, to bring in high profits. Instinct also told her that it was men who had all the money and that they were less likely to invest readily in a woman's business, making items connected with women. I'd have to tell them I was digging for oil in the lake, she thought, or making artificial rhinocerous horn or a chemical cure for death or working on transistorized robots – any bit of rubbish that would get them out of the nursery and into a man's world, anything which would create a fantasy – triumph over nature – fast fortunes – huge sexual potency – immortality. If I stay with the toys, she brooded, no one will back me until it's so successful I don't need the money. I need a project, thought Molly Allaun, a bright idea – and she fell into uneasy dreams and woke in the cold room to a baby's cry and an Aga which had gone out overnight.

But a fortnight later the sun came out at last, throwing a slightly warmer light over Allaun Towers and its affairs. Molly felt better, packed up the baby and went to see Ivy in Beckenham. She had been ill and even now, when she said she was better, Molly thought she looked frighteningly grey and weak.

"Have you seen the doctor?" she asked anxiously.

"For flu? What can they do for flu?" Ivy demanded.

"For a check-up," Molly suggested.

"Check-up? Rubbishy things," said Ivy. "I'm not some nervy executive suffering from too many business lunches. It's just the end of winter. Be better when the sun shines."

"You're obstinate," Molly told her. "I'm going to tell Sid."

"I expect I'm getting old," Ivy said, coughing and lighting another cigarette.

"Sixty-one?" Molly said. "In California you'd just be getting married again."

"Well, this isn't California," said her mother. "Thank God. You're all on your feet, one way and another, you and Jack and Shirley. That's the chief thing. And four grandchildren – six, if you count the little blackies – I'm not complaining. Not that I'm cheering either. Jack's marriage has gone for a Burton and Shirley's on the phone all the time complaining. She seems to be doing all right with her accountancy, though." Ivy laughed. "She's made the family pay for that course or they'd never have let her go. But they got all excited about having their own free accountant when she's finished – and putting her out to work for other people – so they did it as an investment. But my idea is that the minute she's qualified she'll take the children and go."

Molly was marching the child round the kitchen holding his arms up as he paced forward. She said "Phew" and sat down. The baby struggled off her lap and set off across the room at a fast crawl. "He's very active," Ivy said. "Still, at least he doesn't keep climbing up, like Josephine did. She was climbing up from the moment she could move. I'll never forget her and kitchen dresser falling down together. I thought she'd been killed, but she was lying underneath it, laughing." She sighed, "I had some energy in those days. I couldn't do it now. Still, he looks very well. It must be the country air."

"It's kill or cure," Molly said. "I've never been so cold in my life. It can't have been as cold as that when I was a kid. It must have been though – there was fuel rationing."

"I expect they got round that all right," Ivy said. "People in the country always do. Anyway, I can't imagine Mrs Gates letting you get cold. That woman wouldn't have left a splinter in your finger for more than two minutes. She was one of the good ones. They don't make them like that any more."

"She never got anything for her pains," Molly said. "Dead child, hard work – and dies in the stables. She might have been alone if I hadn't been there. Isabel wasn't worrying. She said she had no idea that it was so serious – that was afterwards – but I wonder. She's a world expert in not letting herself know the truth."

"You could always go back to Meakin Street," said her mother.

"Don't think I haven't thought of it," Molly said. "But after all, I let it to Sam. He'd go, I expect, if I asked him to, but it isn't fair. Anyway, I'm all right as long as I know it's there. But I don't fancy it – too many memories of Joe and all the thoughts of how badly I've managed everything – and then what do I do? Work? – What do I do with Fred? Go on Social Security? You know what that's like for a woman. Not enough money to go round – you can't work because they don't let you and there you are on your own, pinching and scraping and then you start brooding and the next thing, it's Valium – you're half conscious all day. If you're one of the lucky ones you get a knock on the door and lo and behold it's Johnnie Bridges or his double. And he knows, and you know, you've no right to anything decent in your position, so then the trouble starts. And unless he starts keeping you you're penniless because they cut off the Social Security. I'm better off as I am."

"Maybe," said her mother.

"I can't go till Easter, anyway," Molly said. "George Messiter's finished his course and got a job. But Cissie rang up and said he was looking peaky and could he come on holiday for a week. He can fix a few items while he's there – why don't you and Sid come, too? It'd do you good. Country air," she said encouragingly. "I'd like to see you looking better."

Ivy said, "I'll talk to Sid. Let's give this baby an early tea. We'll have time to get to Bromley and buy you a dress before you go. You need perking up. You may be living in the country but there's no need to let everything go to pot."

"I left everything in the attic at Meakin Street," Molly told her.

"If you wanted to become a nun why did you get married again?" Ivy said tartly. "Honestly, Molly, I think you sold poor Tom Allaun a pig in a poke there. You don't seem to care about yourself any more."

"There isn't any money, Mum," Molly told her. "And it's been so bloody cold in that house –"

"Well, you look like a man," her mother told her. "Those terrible trousers and that sweater – you've got to do something."

"I'll go and boil an egg for Fred," declared Molly, getting up.

In the kitchen, putting water into a saucepan, Molly stared at the flooding tap and thought about the days in Meakin Street with Joe. She heard the thump, thump, thump as Fred approached down the hall, heard Ivy saying from the sitting room door, "That's right, Freddie. Keep on going. Find Mum."

The door opened and the boy's head came through, a little above floor level. His broad mouth smiled and his blue eyes shone.

"He's a lovely little boy," said Ivy, coming in after him.

Molly put the egg into boiling water and felt a wave of sadness flood over her. "I wish Joe could have seen him," she said.

Her mother did not reply. She only said, "Well – you need a dress – that's what. Life must go on."

But Molly, for some reason, could not find a dress to buy. "What do I wear," she demanded of her mother, "if I'm going to dress up as a mother, housekeeper, gardener, cottage industry promoter and sole support of two decayed aristocrats? Because," she added, voicing her greatest fear, "I think Tom's losing his job."

"Those bastards," said Ivy, startling the girl who was bringing up another dress for them to look at. "Are they mad, or what? You're too weak with them, Molly."

"It was only my greed," said Molly. "And wanting too much for Fred."

"Well then, nothing's too good for Freddie, is it, then?" said the indulgent grandmother, leaning over the child's pushchair.

"Yes," said the rosy child, looking up at her.

Ivy stared at him. "Am I hearing things?" she said, amazed.

"I heard it," Molly told her. "Yes, Fred – yes," she said encouragingly.

"Are you wanting anything?" asked the girl.

"Yes," Fred said.

"I don't believe it," exclaimed Ivy. She said to the girl, "He's nine months old."

"Maybe he's just mumbling," the girl said. "You don't want a dress, really, do you?"

"No – we'd better go home," said Molly. "I'm sorry."

Ivy said, "Fred's made our day anyway. Clever boy," she told him. "Say 'yes' for your granny –"

"Come on, Mum," Molly urged. "We're blocking the place up here and my feet ache. Let's go."

"Yes," remarked the clever boy.

Isabel Allaun was not very pleased at the prospect of an Easter visit from Sid and Ivy Waterhouse and the son of their old friend. She could, however, put up no real objection. In the end she decided to take up a long-standing invitation of a friend who lived in Hove. After insisting that Tom should take a day off work to drive her there, since it was more impressive to drive up with an attentive son than a weary-looking daughter-in-law, she left just before Sid, Ivy and George arrived.

"You can tell she was brought up a lady," Ivy remarked dourly in the kitchen, as she unwrapped the fish she had brought, "because she's so polite."

"Sid says where do you keep the spades and stuff?" said George. "He reckons we can get started on the garden before dinner."

"There's a shed over there," Molly said, pointing in the direction of the kitchen door. George, now twenty-two, had grown to the height of six feet two but he was very thin and pale. He now wore glasses.

After they had gone out Ivy said, "I doubt if George is going to be much help. He's so vague – he never seems to know where he is. The only time he seems to come to life is if you give him some mechanical problem to solve. He did wonders with our central heating. He's a car mechanic now. Here – I never had time for a proper look round the house at the christening – show me."

Molly and her mother toured the house, from the cellars, where pools of water lay on the floor, through the big, high, faded rooms on the ground floor, where plaster came down to powder the carpets all the time, and on to the upper floors, where faint squares of old wallpapers showed where pictures once hung. Glancing at the aging carpets, patchy velvet curtains and neglected furniture Ivy said, "This was a handsome place, once."

Upstairs in the attics there were large patches of damp on the ceilings, and on the floors below. There were mildewed trunks, a rusting train set and heaps of mouldering books. A black silk umbrella, now in rags, lay across an upholstered stool covered in white pock-marks. A starling, when they came in, fluttered up from a pile of clothing with a strip of material in its mouth.

"Collecting for a nest," said Ivy. "Comes in here and then flies out the window. Clever birds, starlings. But what a shocking waste." She was burrowing into the clothes. "Look at this," she exclaimed. "Molyneux – look at that label. Criminal, isn't it – you could sell this today if it hadn't been left to moulder." She straightened up and looked round. "What a pity – to have had so much – and now look at it." She stared at Molly. "It'll cost a bloody fortune to get all this back into repair again. Why don't they turn it into flats?"

"Too heavily mortgaged. The bank won't lend the money," Molly said.

"I can't believe that," Ivy said.

"That's what Tom tells me – maybe Allauns can't face the risk –"

"Can't face anything, it seems to me. No common sense. I should get out, Molly, before you get like them and just sit there on the sinking ship, not doing anything about it. You've got Fred to think of, after all."

"Can't see what difference it makes to him," Molly told her mother sulkily. "I expect he'd rather be here than stuck in a nursery in London all day long." She was developing a sense, as the months went by, that she did not want to leave. She kept the toy-making business moving, holding its own although there was no progress. Somehow she had the superstitious feeling that if she just clung on, the right answer would arrive without her looking for it.

Sid, Tom, George and Molly went down to the pub that night, leaving Ivy babysitting. The pub, which she remembered as being full of oak beams, with wooden tables and chairs and bare boards on the floor, was smarter now, carpeted, with a juke box. She recalled wandering home at twilight, as a child, hearing the sound of the piano, the men's voices inside, coming out into the street.

Under the influence of a few ciders George began to talk. "She reckons I spend too much time on my cycle, and trekking oil into the house," he said of his sister. "She's very houseproud, Cissie."

"Riding a bike?" said Molly.

"No – it's – it's an invention, like," he told her. "It's lighter and stronger than other bikes and you can rig up a motor on it when you want it, and take it off when you don't. It's a little motor, so you can even take it with you." He stopped, finding nothing else to say about it. "I'm just tinkering with it, really," he said. "Trouble is, I'm in trouble with my boss."

"Working on it in the firm's time?" suggested Sid.

"A bit – and using a few spare bits and pieces – it's that he resents the interest, really. One of my mates at the garage, Wayne, he got interested in it, too. The boss hates the garage, really, hates motors, hates his wife – Wayne reckons he just can't stand anybody else having something they like doing."

"I can't see the use of it, frankly," Tom said. "I mean – if you want a bike, you get a bike. If you want a motor scooter you get one of those."

"Be cheaper than a moped," Molly said. "And you could buy the bike first and then save up for the engine. Or you could have cycling holidays and just use the motor for really steep hills. Does it work?" she asked George.

"Me and Wayne are working on a few modifications," he told her. "Maybe Tom's right. I don't reckon we could get the speed above fifteen miles an hour – not without making the engine heavier." He stared in the direction of two labourers drinking beer in the corner. He said, "I'd like to use electricity."

"Said the mad inventor," added Sid.

"Can you go back to London at the weekend and get Wayne and the bike? If I pay your fares?" Molly asked.

George stared at her wonderingly – but she saw convoys of the bicycles, painted red, green, silver, gold, violet, climbing hills with their little engines chugging. "Wayne can stay the weekend," she added. "I want to see the bike."

"All right, Molly," said George, who was accustomed to taking orders from women, who usually knew best.

Tom gaped at Molly and then looked furious. Sid looked at his daughter carefully. He looked at George. Then, discouraged, he looked into his beer.

That evening Tom came into Molly's room and said, "What possessed you to ask that boy to get his friend down here? Without asking me or Isabel, either. It seems high-handed – and extremely odd. I'm wondering if you're in your right mind?"

"I may not be," Molly said, sitting wearily at the dressing table in her old dressing-gown. She glanced at Tom, standing in the doorway. "I want to do something, Tom," she said. "I want you to lay off me for a bit. Will you?"

"Why should I if you don't tell me what you're up to?" he asked.

"Tom," she said. "Is your job all right?"

"I'm quite touched at your showing an interest," he said. "There hasn't been much of that. The procedure's up to now been to send me off in the morning to earn the money and let me in at night after I've done it – and, since you ask me, no, the job is not all right. I'm on the verge of resigning. The senior partner dislikes me and the other solicitor is an incompetent. I've asked for more money and been refused and I don't think I can stand it any longer."

Molly, without bothering to sift the story for the rights and wrongs of the situation, just said, "I thought so. If you don't mind, Tom, I'm going to bed. I'm dog tired and Fred's waking at six these days. Wayne's only staying over the weekend and he'll be on his way home by the time you get back with Isabel." Tom, at a disadvantage because of his confession, went to bed and said nothing more about the visit until Saturday morning. Wayne had arrived on his motor bike earlier but Tom had not seen him. He was very big, and black. Molly secretly hoped he would not, by a mischance, run into Isabel.

That morning Wayne and George got up early and went to the stables. George was hammering some parts on to the prototype cycle while Wayne worked on the engine, which was standing on the old mounting block. A transistor radio on the wall played heavy rock — Fred was sitting in his pushchair, watching, with a chocolate biscuit in one hand and a spanner in the other. There was a smear of oil on his cheek.

Tom arrived and, seeing all this, turned round at the yard entrance and went straight back to the house, where Molly was rolling out pastry.

"What in God's name's going on?" he demanded. "Are you trying to convert this place into a slum?"

"Two lads fixing up a bike in the stables, hundreds of yards from the house?" she asked. "What's wrong with that?"

She went on rolling the pastry, knowing perfectly well that this had nothing to do with the argument. It was the class, and in one case, the colour of the young men to which Tom was objecting. It was the fact that the household, that weekend, consisted of her mother, her father, a lad from Meakin Street and his black friend. Tom felt swamped — and ignored because he didn't know what she was up to.

"It starts as a visit from your mother," declared Tom, "and ends up with all the hooligans in London banging and shouting. And Fred's out there with oil and chocolate all over his face. You'll have to tell them to go."

"Wayne's going tomorrow anyway," wheedled Molly. She did not want to reveal her plans to Tom before she had checked that they might work. But she needed his cooperation because otherwise she would not see the bike in action. And she did not want a confrontation, which she would win, proving what they both knew – that Tom Allaun was not master in his own home.

"Honestly, Tom," she said. "They're only young men – hardly more than boys. Don't make me make them go. At least Isabel's not being disturbed. Please let them stay, Tom."

"All right," he said, "but I'm going to Sebastian Hodges' and when I come back after lunch tomorrow I expect to find George's friend gone and the house at peace again."

"Thank you, Tom," Molly said humbly. So, she thought, after he had left, she had got her way with placatory behaviour. As she made a rabbit pie from two rabbits she wondered whether if she made Tom feel more powerful he would turn into a normal husband and father. After all, Charlie Markham had told her she was too domineering, energetic and forthright.

"Mum," she said, as Ivy came into the kitchen. "Do you think I'm being fair to Tom? Do you think I'm too bossy and tough?"

"I suppose you could try to boost his ego a bit," Ivy said without interest.

"It'd take a bit of doing," Molly said. "And while I'm fainting and wheedling him into doing things I could be doing something myself –"

"Well. Try to see it as a challenge," advised her mother. "Make making Tom more manly be your task in life." Then she spoilt it by laughing.

"Quicker to get some wool and large needles and knit yourself another one," Sid observed as he came in from the garden.

"Sid!" Ivy reproved. But Sid had just turned over about an eighth of an acre of kitchen garden. After lunch he was planning to patch up the wall behind the lavatory cistern upstairs. He was beginning to wish he had gone off on the angling party with his friends in Beckenham. Here, he had not even found time to unpack his fishing tackle.

Nevertheless, the weekend passed happily enough. Sid did get out his fishing tackle in the end. Ivy tacked up some fresh rents in the curtains and gave the sitting room carpet a good clean while George and Wayne worked on the bike in the stable yard, continuing after dark by lighting some lanterns they found and put into order. In the end as twilight fell on Sunday evening they were ready for a test run. Molly knew that Isabel would be back shortly but was too excited to halt the experiment.

"It'll have to be up and down the drive," Wayne told her. She, Sid and Ivy assembled on the step in front of the house and watched.

"Will it work?" called Molly nervously to the two men who were bending over the bike in the half circle of gravel in front of the house.

As she spoke, George jumped, then went back to making adjustments. Wayne called back, "Might do."

The cycle standing between the two of them was small, with an unpainted frame which was dented in places. The engine in the poor light was a bulge, rather like an udder, set on the frame just in front of the bicycle chain. The handlebars were rather wide in order, George said, to balance the machine.

In fact from the front it looked rather like a small longhorn steer. Molly wondered whether, even if it worked, purchasers would find the bike's slightly odd appearance appealing. It certainly lacked streamlining.

Now George sat on the machine, one foot on the ground. He revved the little engine, which choked, and died. Molly set her teeth and told herself not to worry. Suddenly George was off, careering down the drive in the twilight. He disappeared under the trees. In the silence of the country evening they heard him cut the motor. He came back up the lawn, pedalling. He switched the motor on again and came towards them, ploughing up the turf. From the corner of her eye Molly saw a taxi coming up the drive beside him. Raising one hand above his head he shouted, "She made it!" Wayne, both arms raised, cried, "Yeah!" Then, as George got closer and closer he shouted, "Cut the engine, man." George did. He braked and fell off in the gravel in front of the taxi.

Isabel Allaun got out. "What is this?" she asked Molly. "And where's Tom? He was supposed to collect me at four." Upstairs the baby began to wail. George got up, holding his arm. Molly said, "Didn't Tom come?"

Isabel stared first at Wayne, then at George, and then back at Wayne again.

"This place is a bear garden," she said. "Perhaps you'd like to tell me what's happening, Molly – inside the house." She took Molly by the arm and began to steer her through the front door past Sid and Ivy, whom she did not acknowledge. Molly resisted. "You'd better pay the taxi driver, Isabel," she said. "And I'm going upstairs to see to Fred."

"The taxi's on account," Isabel told her. "And I'm sure your mother will look after the baby." The pressure on Molly's arm continued. She withstood it. Turning to George and Wayne she said, "Why don't you two go down to the pub for a celebratory drink?"

475

"And we'll join you," said Ivy, who was furious. Once inside, with the baby settled down, Molly poured Isabel a drink, apologized for the disorderly scene in front of the house and said nothing of her plans. She felt nervous, but assured. She considered she might get some capital from Charlie Markham for the development of the little bike. It worked. It used only a small amount of petrol. It offered the rider the choice of pedal power or motor power at will. It would be cheap to produce and, she suddenly thought, even its odd appearance would not necessarily count against it. If it was not smart it was, at least, original, almost as if it competed against, rather than trying to copy, the world of streamlining and excessive horse power. But she knew that if she revealed her plans to try and put it into production Isabel would, in her present mood, obstruct her. She needed the use of the stables and the yard in front of them.

She also needed to keep hold of any money Charlie could raise for her — if she told Isabel her plans there would be builders in the house renovating and restoring, clothes and furnishings would be purchased before she had even got George to plan the workshop. It would happen in the least blatant and nicest possible way — but it would happen and bills would start arriving before the money had been banked.

The lack of explanations made Isabel even angrier. Not long after Tom arrived, also in a temper. Isabel was accusing him of leaving Hove only fifteen minutes after he should have arrived to collect her. During the discussion which followed Molly set the table for supper in the dining room and cycled down to the pub to meet the others. She hoped that by the time they all trooped back for the meal some of the animus would have evaporated.

She sat down with a drink and told George and Wayne that she had a source of possible capital and that if she could get backing she would be happy to fund them to make a proper prototype of the bicycle and then put it into production.

"I'm sure there's enough room to build another workshop on the other side of the yard," she said. "Or use it for warehousing. It'd only be small at first but I'd like to try it. If it works, we could expand."

George instinctively looked at Wayne. "What do you think?" he asked.

"I'd give it a go," Wayne replied. "I'm sick of that garage."

"It'd have to be a partnership," Molly said. "Low wages and a share of the profits — all drawn up by lawyers."

"You have to make the decision yourself," Wayne said to George. "It's your machine –"

"I don't know where they'd live," Ivy said. "They can't live up there."

"There's a few people round here who could do with lodgers," Molly said.

"Like me?" Wayne asked.

"The vicar'd take you in," Molly grinned. "To provide an example of racial tolerance – there's a couple of empty cottages to let, too – it's not a problem."

"George?" Wayne asked. "– Listen – I don't want to bully you into this –"

George, who had been staring dreamily in front of him said, "What? What, Wayne?"

"Do you want to do it, man?" Wayne said patiently.

"Of course I do," George said, as if he were surprised to be asked. "If we get a cottage we can store some of the parts in one of the rooms. Storing enough frames'll be a problem."

"If I get the money," Molly said. She bought a round of drinks and said, "Well – to the Messiter."

They lifted their glasses to the grinning George and all repeated, "The Messiter."

"You going to have some explaining to do to the people over there," Wayne said, nodding in the direction of Allaun Towers.

Molly told him, "They'll do it if there's money in it."

That evening, after supper had been eaten in a chilly atmosphere – Wayne had set off home on his motor bike before the meal – Molly telephoned Charlie Markham and arranged to see him in London in two days' time. Then she put down the receiver and, reassured that no one in the house had overheard the call, went upstairs to lie down. It had been a long day. She was experiencing, now, the fatigue which accompanies a new venture.

The baby was asleep in his cot near a lighted lamp. She lay beside him in half-darkness, wondering whether she would get the money from Charlie and whether, if she did, the experiment stood any chance of success. She had now involved two other people, George and Wayne. She was moving in territory she did not understand. Charlie had been right about one thing, though, she reflected – she had witnessed the manoeuvrings of men like Ferenc Nedermann, had observed the hard attitudes of professional criminals like the Roses and had learned from what she saw. She had watched Joe Endell at work, steering committees, looking at the problems of his constituents, making deals and she had learned from that, too. She knew a lot – but, she thought, had never done anything herself.

She must have drifted into a doze for suddenly she was back in the prison laundry, surrounded by huge, steaming drums, full of sheets and dresses. She had been hauling out long, boiling strips of sheets, all tangled together, when she saw, through the cloudy atmosphere, a familiar face. The woman standing beside the wardress walked into the middle of the room and greeted her in a low voice, "Hullo, Moll. I heard you was here."

She recognized Peggy Jones, larger and fatter than she had been the last time she had seen her standing on a corner in Soho. Peggy started hauling at the sheets, in order to avoid the wardress's eye. Obviously she had been here before.

"What are you in for?" asked Molly.

"The usual," Peggy responded calmly. "Prostitution. Not the first time – don't suppose it's the last."

"Come along, girls," the wardress called. "Stop talking."

In a way Molly almost resented the arrival of Peggy Jones. She had insulated herself as far as possible from the prison.

She went through her days, from the unlocking of the doors in the morning to the locking up at night, in a carefully maintained state of semi-consciousness. She took no notice of the insults of the other women or the occasional brutalities of the staff. She made no friends and tried to make no enemies. She looked no one in the eye and spoke only when she was spoken to. She did not know, at night, who screamed, or why. She kept herself from her own distress and that of the others. She was rewarded by relative peace and the maximum remission of sentence. She was punished by not being able to leave the state she had created when she walked from the prison door, free. But Peggy's brief stay in the gaol took her, for a time, out of voluntary numbness. One day they were both sitting at the back of a large room where other women were watching TV and Peggy began to talk about her short spell as an evacuee at the Rectory in Framlingham. "Half of us should never have gone," she told Molly. "Half of us were home a year later, Blitz or no Blitz. I wish my Mum had never sent me, though. That woman – Mrs Templeton – she still haunts me. Thank God I was with Cissie. I don't know what would have happened to me if she hadn't been like she was." Her big, round face was suddenly sad as a

478

child's. "She wouldn't have sent me, I don't think, my mum, if it hadn't have been for that house in Meakin Street going – the one next to Tom Totteridge's stables, where we used to live. Course, mum wanted me out of the way because she was making a fortune off the GIs. But I reckon that bombsite next door kept on nagging at her."

"What happened?" asked Molly.

"Didn't they tell you?" Peggy said in astonishment. "About how old Tom saved them poor little children. You see, there was a direct hit on that house, in the early morning, and only old Tom out on the street, because he wouldn't ever take any notice of the sirens. So he's clopping up Meakin Street with his horse and cart when, whoomph, there's a bomb – and bang goes the house next to the stables. So the horse shies and there's dust everywhere and by the time he's got the horse under control some of the dust has settled and he can see the house is on fire, right up the back. And above the sound of the crackling there's this horrible screaming sound. So old Tom just runs up the street, into the house, where it isn't burning, and right up the stairs, which he thinks are going to give way at any moment – there's no roof, all the back rooms are on fire. He opens a door, there's flames everywhere – and on the bed, there's this dead woman.

"And underneath there's a boy, still alive. He's the one who's screaming. So old Tom grabs him and beats him out, because his shirt's on fire and then –" Here Peggy paused and a woman turned round and said, "Keep it down, for Christ's sake – you're interfering with the sound." "Then," said Peggy, "he realizes. Under the boy there's another kid. So he picks them both up and he runs – just as he gets to the front door the whole staircase collapses."

"God Almighty," Molly said. "I never thought of old Tom as a hero."

"Nor me," Peggy said. "He was a dirty old man."

"What happened to the children?" Molly asked.

"Dunno," Peggy said, with a characteristic lapse of interest and concentration. After a little while she added, "Hadn't of been for that I'd never've been sent away."

Molly awoke and shook her head, finding it hard to remember she was at Framlingham, in the bedroom she had slept in as a child, that her son lay in a cot beside her. She had forgotten about her meeting with Peggy in prison. It was part of the time she wanted to forget. She could almost smell the prison smell. She gazed, blinking, into the lamp, thinking that Sid and Ivy and George were downstairs in the drawing

479

room with the Allauns and that she should go and mediate between them. She put her legs over the edge of the bed and stood up wearily. But as if she had planned to do it, her hand reached out for the top drawer of the tallboy beside the window. She opened the drawer and took out the fat buff envelope Vera Endell had given her six months earlier. She took the first sheet, which had a letterhead – St Barnabas's Orphanage, Kilburn, London. The date was September 21st 1940. It was a doctor's report. The small precise hand had written, "The boy now called Joseph was apparently brought to the orphanage and left in the care of the nuns by an itinerant street trader named Thomas Frederick Totteridge of Meakin Street, London W. He appears to be about six years old. He was found hiding under a burning bed in a bombed house in Meakin Street from which the body of a woman, presumably the mother, was later recovered. His burns, on the left arm and left side, are not serious and are responding to treatment. But he is suffering from shock. He moves very little and does not speak, although he appears to hear and understand what is said to him. The owners of the house were killed in the raid and neighbours state that the woman believed to be Joseph's mother had moved into the house as a lodger only a short time before.

"The police have been notified and advertisements have been placed in newspapers all over the country in an attempt to find the boy's friends or relatives. The discovery of someone familiar with him would probably help his mental state. I do not believe him to be mentally sub-normal." The doctor's signature followed the report.

St Barnabas's Orphanage, Routledge Street, thought Molly, putting the paper down carefully on the top of the tallboy. She had seen the noticeboard outside the high-walled building often as a child – and shuddered, imagining being an orphan penned up in there, in the charge of frightening women in long black habits and funny headdresses. And that was where Joe had begun his life. Not begun – that was somewhere else. And she turned the pages which followed eagerly but found no more information about Joe's origins. There were further reports from the doctor. A fortnight after his arrival at the orphanage the boy was responding better to the nuns who were taking care of him. But he still did not speak and would not make friends with the other children. His burns were healing. But he had not been claimed. The doctor commented also, evidently with some surprise, that he looked as if he could read to a fairly high standard. He had entered the room where the boy was sitting by a window and watched him turning the page of *Gulliver's Travels* which he appeared to be reading and understanding. A later report was more encouraging. The boy had begun to speak but, it added, he never apparently asked about his mother and father, or referred to the bombing. And the reports got briefer as the busy doctor began to include the child on the record sheets with the other children at the orphanage. The next papers, eight months later, began the story of Joe's adoption. And, after that, the record of an ordinary boy growing up in a secure home in the north of England, away from the bombing. There was the programme of a brass band concert – Joe Endell, cornet. There were school reports, exam results, a cutting from a local paper, with a photograph of a young man with a grin and big ears, who had won an exhibition to an Oxford College. There was an article from the *Yorkshire Post* by-lined Joe Endell, "Can We Save Our Railway History?" Molly, wearier still by now, put all the papers back in the big envelope and again hid it under a pile of nightdresses. She couldn't understand why Joe had never spoken of all this to her. Had he forgotten his entire life up to the age of six? – it seemed unlikely. Had he been too scarred to speak of it? Perhaps that was it – or perhaps he had once been unable to speak of the past and, even when the trauma had gone, the habit of silence remained. She could not reconcile the outward-looking, enthusiastic man he had been with the idea of a man badly damaged by the past. And now, she thought, glancing across at the sleeping child who lay with his arms above his head in the position of a footballer who had just scored – now there was Fred, grandchild of a woman killed in a back room in Meakin Street and a missing father, perhaps a serviceman. What peculiar combination of circumstances had prevented anyone from coming forward to ask what had happened to him? Had the woman run away from home so no one knew where she was? Had the father been killed in action? Perhaps, she thought, there was no father as such. No father, no relatives – what would have brought a woman and child with no connections in the world to a top bedroom in Meakin Street in the early part of the war? Or had she been a refugee from Europe, a fugitive without friends or relatives? There was no way now, Molly thought, of ever finding out who Joe really was. Now, she thought, she had better go downstairs to keep her son's living relatives from quarrelling. But on her way downstairs she wondered why she had never heard the story of Tom Totteridge's rescue. Hadn't Sid and Ivy heard about it? Peggy Jones had. And what about the other child Peggy had mentioned? She resolved to ask her parents what they knew about the story, now part of their grandchild's history. But the sound of raised voices from the sitting room drove this idea from her head and sent her hurrying forward. When she got into the room she found that George had begun, naively, to talk about Molly's plans for converting the stables. When she came in Isabel and Tom stared at her in horror and disbelief. Ivy's face wore a look of resignation. George looked blank and it was Sid who broke the silence by saying, as she walked into the room, "George has been talking about your plan to turn the stables into a workshop-cum-factory. I think you've got a bit of explaining to do."

"Tom – Isabel," Molly said, sitting down. "The point is I have to raise the money first. That's why I haven't mentioned it. Unless I can get the backing nothing will happen anyway. I thought there was no point in dragging the whole thing over the coals till I had finance."

"I should have thought the first thing to do was discuss it with me," Isabel said. "Because without my permission no amount of money will help. And that permission I do not give. I can't imagine how you can ever have thought I would. You actually plan to turn my stables into a bicycle factory – quite honestly, I still don't believe it. It's a fantasy. I think you must be mad!"

"But it could work," Molly said. "The bike's unique. People would want it. And there's what – sixty or seventy square yards of disused space and buildings we could make a start in – it isn't a stupid idea, if you stop to think about it."

Isabel said, "You come here, and within six months you're planning to use my land and my buildings, without any consultation at all – I still can't believe it. It's the most outrageously impudent thing I ever heard. You must believe me to be so old and so foolish that you can do what you like. Let me tell you now – you're wrong."

"I'm sorry Isabel," Molly said. "As I said, my main idea was not to start talking about something that might not be going to happen."

"And where's this money supposed to be coming from anyway?" demanded Isabel. "If you're thinking of the bank you're wasting your time."

"I wasn't thinking of the bank," Molly told her.

"Where then?" Isabel demanded. Molly was silent. But Isabel was now curious and becoming interested in the new source of capital Molly appeared to have discovered.

"I asked you where you were thinking of getting financial backing," Isabel said again.

"I'd rather not say at present," Molly answered.

"Really," Isabel Allaun said in a tone of pure rage. "Really – I see. You're prepared to make plans to convert my stables, fill the grounds with noise and dirt and labourers, without any consultation at all – but when I ask you a simple question I'm denied a reply. It's quite unbearable."

Tom said, "Come on, Molly, what have you got in mind?"

It seemed even more impossible to reveal to Tom that she was in collusion with his cousin than it was to tell Isabel her nephew was involved. And she knew that once she told them she was seeing Charlie they would start watching her like thieves hanging about in an alley waiting for a likely prospect to come down the street.

At that moment, as the silence following Tom's question became intolerable, Sid stood up and said, "Come on, Molly. I'd like a word with you in private."

In the library, where he led her, he looked round at the shelves of neglected books and the dust, and said, "This is a gloomy spot for a chat, I must say."

"Well?" said Molly, standing her ground in front of the closed door.

"Well," Sid asked, "where are you going to get the money for this mad scheme?"

"It's not a mad scheme – not that mad, anyway," Molly said.

"Don't sulk at me," Sid told her. "All right – it's not mad – it's just half mad. But what I asked is where you're expecting to get the cash from? My worry is, you're planning to sell your house. I don't think that's a good idea."

"I'm going to Charlie Markham," Molly said bluntly. "He offered me backing when he was down here – if I had a good idea and if I didn't let Isabel or Tom know what I was doing."

"Charlie Markham," said Sid. "After the way you've talked about him all these years."

"This is business," Molly said. "He's got money to invest and I've got a proposition."

Sid sat down in the big cracked leather armchair by the fireplace. A smile spread over his face. He said, "My God, Molly. You've got a nerve and all."

"Shut up, Dad," Molly cried. "Somebody's got to do something round here – and don't start bloody laughing at me. I'm not confident. I don't need any help but I don't need people acting incredulous either."

Her father said, "I don't know anything about whether this plan will work or not. I suppose this Charlie can tell you that – but you're taking a big risk with George and Wayne – they're giving up their jobs."

"Oh, Dad," Molly said. "They don't care. They can always get other jobs working on cars. If it all falls through no one will be much worse off – but at least we'll have had a try."

"Maybe," Sid said. "But you can see my point of view – you've got no capital, you're a woman going into business – and worse than that it's something you don't know anything about –"

Molly felt discouraged. She knew that what he said was true but she didn't want to listen to him. He spotted her expression. "All right," he said, "but I can't see how you can get away with not telling your mother-in-law. It's a bit high-handed to take over her premises without telling her –"

Now Ivy burst in. "What's going on?" she asked. "Am I a leper or something? Not good enough to be told what's happening?"

Molly told her quickly what they had been talking about.

"Oh my God," said Ivy. "You must be raving mad. This place is a lunatic asylum. I knew it'd contaminate you in the end. If you want a decent life why don't you get back to Meakin Street and find yourself a job?"

"Thanks a lot," Molly said. "Thank you very much indeed, Mum." And she walked out of the room and back into the sitting room. If, she thought, her own parents were chipping at her, George was unable to understand what was going on and Tom and Isabel were in a temper already, there seemed no point at all in keeping her secret. She sat down and said bluntly to Isabel, "I'm going to Charlie Markham to try to raise some money."

"Ha!" exclaimed Tom. "You'll be lucky. Blood from a stone, that'd be. Whatever gave you the idea he'd help?"

Molly did not say that his cousin had made the offer. She told him, "Charlie's in the business of making money – if he thinks it'll produce a profit he'll invest."

Isabel stood up. "I'm going to bed," she said. "I think we've all discussed this quite enough for tonight." She turned in the doorway and asked, "Have you arranged to see Charlie?"

"Tuesday," Molly told her.

And Isabel went out. "Having lunch with him?" asked Tom. "Yes," Molly said. "I can manage Tuesday," Tom assured her. "I think I'd rather do it by myself," Molly replied. "Two heads are better than one," Tom told her, "and, after all, you're a woman. You're not used to dealing with operators like Charlie M." "I'll be going alone," said Molly. "I think it's better."

He came into her room late that night, rather drunk, and woke her by leaning over the bed and saying, "I want you in my room." Molly was frightened. She knew that her new plans had changed matters between them. Her refusal to let him come to the lunch with Charlie Markham only confirmed her lack of faith in him.

She said, "Not tonight, Tom. Let's pick a better time."

"Get up," he said, and grasped the top of her arm.

And so she allowed him to wrestle her through the doorway of her bedroom, resisting only as much as she knew she must in order to inflame his feelings. She submitted, in the big, cold bedroom, to his tearing off her nightdress. She even pulled away from him as he pushed her towards the bed, feigning terror and anticipation. She was half-convinced by her own performance – he was, after all, stronger than her. Tom entered her quickly and, almost immediately, his erection failed. He took a handful of her hair and pulled it. He bit her shoulder. She raked at his back with her nails. Then he stared down at her with hatred and flung himself from her body, "Cow," she heard him mutter. Then, wearily, "Woman? I don't think so." She had little trouble in crying. Through her tears she said, "Tom – please, Tom." It was partly that she wanted to redeem his failure by her humility – partly that she felt genuinely upset. Each failure, not just sexual but emotional, reminded her of what she once had, and what she and Tom would never find. She tried to rouse him and succeeded only, it seemed, in sickening him, and herself, more.

She cried again and said, "Tom – cry. It could save us."

"There's nothing to cry about," he said bitterly. He lay, naked, with his legs wide apart.

She said, "This can't go on."

Reaching for a cigarette from the bedside table he lit it and puffed out smoke.

"Why did I marry you?" he said.

"You wanted what I once was, or seemed to be," she said. "And Fred – and all the rest of it. Maybe you thought a fast tart, all blonde hair and curves – was what you wanted. I suppose you thought if I was what everybody had always wanted, I'd be what you wanted, too. What do you want to do?"

"Do?" he said, getting up and putting on his dressing-gown. "What do you mean – do?"

"I either go or we face facts," Molly said. "There's very little chance now that we can have a proper marriage. So either I leave and we get divorced and you find somebody else or I stay and we accept each other for what we are. If I take up with someone – I won't push it in your face. Same applies to you. Just keep it out of the way. I don't care if it's a boy or a girl – I'll just wish you well. It's no good protesting, Tom," she said, seeing him about to challenge what she said. "I saw you looking at Wayne yesterday. You fancied him. Wayne knew it, too. All I'm saying is, let's tell the truth, be as happy as we can, and whatever we do, don't make a big fuss about it. Then maybe we can be friends, if nothing else."

"I can't see what either of us gains by your staying," Tom said.

"I need the use of the premises," Molly told him bluntly. "And the name might do no harm. Lady Allaun sounds respectable."

"And me?" he asked.

"A cut of the profits, if any – and your freedom," she said. "At worst you lose nothing."

She felt, now, stunned with fatigue. Her arms and legs were like lead, her eyes closed continually. She could not be sure if she had spoken, or just thought she had. Tom said, "What financial arrangements were you thinking of exactly?"

"Ten per cent to you and five to Isabel," she muttered.

"I'll get it drawn up if you settle things with Charlie," he said.

Molly was asleep. He nudged her. "Yes?" he asked.

"Yes," Molly told him.

Shirley declared later that it was unfortunate that Molly had learned everything she knew about contracts from Ferenc Nedermann, to whom a contract was chiefly a gesture of moderate goodwill and, otherwise, an item, like a net, as valuable for its holes as its more solid parts.

Nevertheless, she signed.

It must have been at almost exactly this time that I was invited to tea by my former employer. This was not unusual but I had an instinct, which became stronger after I arrived, that she had some purpose in mind. But I couldn't imagine what it might be so I settled down to enjoy the occasion. There was a poet there, I remember, who had little to say for himself and a very pleasant professor of biochemistry. In fact I had got up to leave and was on my way out when someone came up to me and asked if I would be good enough to go into another room and examine some letters on which my hostess would like an opinion. Old they indeed were – they proved to be to the Abbess of Whitby from her brother. I was certainly interested although I could not give a firm opinion about their authenticity on the spot. It was when the door opened behind me that I realized the letters might have been a pretext to detain me, which my hostess admitted saying, as I stood there still holding the ancient documents, "Quite simply, I'm trying to clear the ground a little for the coming celebrations – and my mind suddenly turned to Mary Waterhouse. I wondered if you had any news of her."

"None at all," I said. "As far as I know she's still living quietly in the country with her husband. There may have been changes, of course."

"It seems to me," she said, "that anything which keeps her out of the newspapers is a gain. But I'd be interested to know the details of her situation."

"I'll find out," I said. And remembering what Corrie had said, I added, "I imagine they're still short of money and that often leads people to change things for themselves." I could see that although she was quite composed she was not altogether easy in her mind.

She said, "You've never been pleased by how this matter was handled, have you? Be frank with me."

I demurred, hesitated and finally admitted that the tactics used had not seemed to me to be very efficient or even to lead in the general direction of a solution. But I added that I didn't know what I would have recommended anyone to do at the outset of the business – and that it was not always a bad idea to tackle a problem by doing as little as possible and letting it disappear of its own accord.

I went home thoughtfully to my wife, unsure whether my answer had been true, or only diplomatic. Corrie's attitude was more forthright. "Wait till she finds out about the boy," she said, rather vindictively, I thought.

I said firmly, "Corrie – there is no boy. The boy is dead. The rest is a figment of our over-heated imagination."

"Just wait," she said.

If Charlie Markham hadn't suggested we should meet for dinner as well as lunch I'd probably have had too little time to go and look up

Peggy Jones. Because I'd spent the morning seeing shops about the toys, then shown him, over lunch, the drawings and some figures to prove the bike would be profitable if he got the backing. And he'd said he was going to talk to some people that afternoon and see what he could do, so why didn't we meet for dinner that night and see what he'd come up with? I should've known better – too much speed in these things is always a bit suspicious – there's a difference between not hanging about and the sudden production of contracts and che-quebooks, like a conjurer bringing a rabbit out of a hat. But I fell for it – being like a babe in arms in the ways of that world. This left me with the afternoon free, so I went to see Peggy. I walked straight out of the restaurant after seeing Charlie that lunchtime and got a cab to the Rose and Crown in Kilburn High Road.

It was nearly closing time when I arrived but the bar was still crowded . . .

"I'm looking for Peggy Jones," Molly told the barmaid. "Know where she is?"

The barmaid, as might have been expected, was cautious. Molly, in her fur jacket and boots, did not look like a policewoman, but might have been. "We grew up in the same street," Molly explained. "Off Wattenblath Street. I'm trying to find her. I wondered if you knew her address."

The manager had been listening from a little way off.

"Joe Endell's widow, aren't you," he said. "A shocking loss – please accept my condolences."

It was no time to explain that she had remarried. Molly said, "Thank you."

"Looking for Peggy? It's Murchison Street – in the phone book. You could give her a call."

So within fifteen minutes Peggy was coming through the pub door, looking round for Molly. She, who had always been plump, was now thin. Her eyes were heavily outlined with black and her skirt was short. She wore high-heeled pumps. She looked clearly what she was, an ageing prostitute but, Molly thought, she seemed contented. "Molly! Lady Allaun, eh? Come up in the world!" she cried, sitting down. Molly went to the bar and was served rather sulkily by the manager, who pointed out that he would be serving no more drinks and the pub would shut soon. She suspected he had been speaking to someone who

488

had heard about her quick re-marriage and had, in consequence, lost sympathy for her.

"Well," Peggy said, "Cheers, Moll. You're looking sharp these days."

"It's not as good as all that, Peg," Molly said. "I'm barely keeping my end up."

"Don't let them get you down," Peggy said. "That's right, isn't it? Still, don't tell me you're short of a bob or two." She paused, suddenly seeming to lose her concentration. Then said, "You're not here for nothing, are you? What d'you want?"

"Nothing much," Molly told her. "Only a bit of information."

"Ah," Peggy said, becoming cautious. "Depends what, doesn't it?"

"Nothing incriminating," Molly said. "Would I get you into trouble?"

"You've got yourself in enough," Peggy stated flatly. "Still, never mind. My horoscope said it'd be a wonderful year for me."

"Has it?" asked Molly.

"Got myself a new flat – three piece suite, red velvet – and a gold clock in a glass case," Peggy told her.

"That's nice," said Molly.

"They tell you it gets harder when you get older," Peggy said. "But it's not true – a lot of the punters like an older woman. They feel more comfortable. You get more regulars."

"I'll tell you what I want to know," Molly said. "It's about that story you told me in the nick – how Tom Totteridge did a rescue at that house in Meakin Street during the war."

"Oh – yeah," Peggy said. "Course, it was Mum told me. I never knew anything about it." She paused. "Funny, isn't it," she said. "You're a lady and I'm on the game."

"There's less difference than you'd think," Molly said.

Peggy looked at her. "Can't be the same," she said decidedly.

"Well – what did she tell you – your Mum?" asked Molly, becoming impatient.

Peggy hailed the barmaid, who was emptying the ashtrays at the next table. "Send up a couple of drinks, love?" she suggested.

"We're closed," said the woman.

"This lady's an aristocrat," Peggy claimed. The woman looked at Molly. "I don't care if she's the Empress Josephine," she said.

"Come on, darling," coaxed Peggy.

"Wait till we shut," said the woman.

Molly, who had spent the morning discussing orders for funny scarecrows and cuddly foxes with the toy buyers of two London stores and the middle of the day talking about frames and horse power to Charlie Markham, suppressed her impatience. It seemed slightly fantastic here – as Peggy watched the pub doors being shut by the manager and she, Molly, wondered whether Charlie would raise twenty thousand pounds for her in the course of an afternoon she was also trying to unbury a secret over thirty years old. As if she guessed the nature of Molly's thoughts Peggy said, "I don't remember – it was a long time ago. And it was mum's story – and old Tom's – but they never talked about it a lot. He didn't dare wait for the proper people to come because he knew the house could collapse. And there was this terrible crying, right over the noise of the house burning and bits falling to the ground. London was a lot quieter in those days, wasn't it? When we were kids the mornings were like living in the country. Except for the odd bus – people didn't have cars so much. You got a car?" she asked.

Molly nodded. "What happened?" she said, so that Peggy would not lose sight of the story again.

"He had to get them out before the stairs collapsed, see," she said. "So he did – could have been killed himself, of course. He picked them up, rushed downstairs, put them on the cart – and straight to the nuns. He couldn't think what else to do with them. I reckon he didn't want to mess about going to the police and making long reports. See – these air raids were his opportunity – stuff all over the place and plenty of time to pick it up if you got there first. He left £15,000, you know. Old Tom, who never had a decent pair of trousers to his name. He was going to leave it to the horse but, of course, the horse died first."

"Well," Molly said, "what about the children?"

"Seems he asked the boy who he was but he couldn't speak. Too shocked. It was the girl who'd been screaming and crying. He was lying on top of her but her face was free. Right under the bed they were with the bed on fire and their dead mother lying on it. Let's hope they never knew how bad it was."

"I wonder?" Molly said. "You see – it looks as if the boy was Joe Endell – my husband. So the sister may be alive somewhere. No reason why not – she'd still be quite a young woman."

"I wouldn't go looking for her," Peggy said. "You never know what you'll find when you start that lark. I had a baby once, years and years ago. I don't want to find her now and I hope to God she never finds me.

Let the past stay buried, that's what mum used to say." She grinned. "Course, that was when I asked who my dad was. You're an angel, Harry," she said to the manager as he came up with two glasses.

"Well, that's your lot," he said, "if you'll pardon my bluntness. But some of us have got things to do this afternoon."

Peggy looked at Molly. "No — I wouldn't dig about for missing relatives," she said. "Not unless they've got something to leave you. Still, it's all a funny mystery, isn't it." She sighed, drank her gin and said, "I used to think I was somebody else's kid. I suppose we all do. You know — left in a basket with a note pinned to my nightie — 'Please take care of my child. I will return.' And then this posh lady turns up years later and takes you to live in luxury in her house and you meet this handsome rich fellow — things would have been a lot different if that had happened — no punters, no fines — oh Christ, Moll, don't things turn out different to what you expected, eh? Oh, God — look at the time," she said in alarm, glancing at the clock above the bar. "I've got someone coming at four."

"I'll run you back in a cab," Molly said. "I've got nothing to do so I'm going to get my hair done."

"Funny, though," Peggy said when they were outside in the crowded street, waiting for a taxi to appear. "Funny old Tom hardly ever talked about his rescue. You'd think he'd have made more of it — I mean, he risked his life. He was a hero — and he wasn't the sort to shut up about a thing like that." She paused. "He only mentioned it when he was drunk."

"Could be he took something out of that room besides the children," Molly said waving a taxi to a stop. "Something valuable — jewellery or money the woman had in a drawer. So he didn't want any investigations in case it came out."

"I expect you're right," Peggy said as she climbed in. "There was plenty of people not like what they say in the papers these days. Our finest hour, and all that. I know it was my mum's — she used to come home with big rolls of notes tucked in the top of her stockings."

In the hairdresser's Molly began to shake as the man cut her hair. It must have been the wine at lunchtime and the drinks in the pub, she thought. It must be nerves about the result of Charlie's attempts to raise money for her. But when the hairdresser asked her if she was cold she responded automatically, "I was thinking about the Blitz."

"That's a strange thing to be worrying about now," he told her, masking his distaste at her ancient memories as he tried to make her look like Joan Crawford.

Later she went to a film, and slept. Later still she was sitting in the restaurant. She looked up at the waiter and pointed at the menu and said, "That one. And a green salad. I'll start with whitebait." She had been talking to Charlie about the Roses. She now said, "Small fry shouldn't get mixed up with sharks. In the end they get eaten."

"Well, all that's over now," Charlie said. "Let's pour the wine and talk about the present. The man I spoke to this afternoon is keen to lay off some money against tax. If you start a company on a proper basis he'll buy in."

"How much?" asked Molly.

"Twenty, twenty-five thousand," Charlie informed her.

"What percentage?" Molly insisted.

"Sixty-five," he said. "The point is that this way you get all the advantages of being associated with the group."

Molly put down her glass and looked at the plate of tiny fish the waiter had just put in front of her. She looked hard at Charlie and said, "I've got George and Wayne, and there'll be others. How am I going to look after them if I'm being pushed by someone who owns two-thirds of the business? How do I look after myself? This geezer can manipulate the company, the staff, me, right out of the way whenever he feels like it. What happens if he complicates his life too much and he goes under –" Then she looked at Charlie, picked up her fork and ate some fish. "It's you, Charlie, isn't it? This financial mystery man?"

He did not reply. Her heart sank. He was her only source of capital.

Charlie said, "All right, Molly. It's me and a man called Adrian Trelawney. He's another member of the board of the group of companies I work with, the Lauderdale Group. He and I talked and we decided that it was worth expanding, investing something in your idea. But you can't expect us to sign you a cheque and leave it at that."

"In case I hand it all over to Johnnie Bridges?" Molly said angrily. "Because you can't trust a woman with money if there's a man about? That is what the Roses used to think."

Charlie, ignoring this, told her, "Our point of view is that you have a good idea and absolutely no track record – I don't mean to be insulting, Molly, but you must see that's true."

"Then Lauderdale plunges," Molly declared fiercely. "And my bike goes under with it. Or it gets sacrificed first to save the situation because we're small and there's none of your mates, only a woman and a couple of youngsters involved."

"Don't be ridiculous, Molly," Charlie said. Once again he was the older boy, tormenting her. "Lauderdale's as sound as a nut. Your difficulty is that all your experience of the world comes from the back streets of London."

"Big or small it's always the same," said Molly. "Only big's worse because if there's trouble they dump you – or else you all go down on the big liner together." She paused and then, trying to sound more certain than she felt, said, "There's another way of doing this. A small independent company's the way. If you and Trelawney are so interested you can take out fifty percent between you. No Lauderdale Group of companies, no fiddling about on the stock exchange – just three people putting up money to start a business."

"Where would your money come from?" Charlie asked.

"I'll get £10,000," Molly said. "And you two can put in twenty-five between you – that's because I'll be supplying the premises."

"How will you get hold of it?" Charlie said.

"That's my business," Molly replied. She was planning to take out a massive mortgage on Meakin Street, if she could, but she was not going to tell Charlie that because she felt it might put her at a disadvantage. Now she felt sick but she picked up her fork and began to eat. A moment or two later she began to feel better. She realized that, no matter what the terms, she had her money. She realized that Charlie had not disagreed with her, which meant he would go ahead. She smiled and raised her glass.

"To the future," she said.

Charlie smiled back broadly, "To you," he said. "I never imagined that you and I would ever be business partners."

"There's a woman over there who keeps on staring at me," said Molly.

"It's my ex-wife, Caroline," Charlie told her. "I saw her when we came in. I took this seat deliberately so that after I'd waved at her I didn't have to look at her any more."

"I've got to, though," Molly said. "She's very nice-looking."

"Not quite so nice-natured," Charlie said. "She's got a violent temper. The stuff I've seen her throw would surprise you. Even a television. She's astonishingly strong."

"Provoked, I daresay," remarked Molly.

"All water under the bridge now," said Charlie. "She was number 2.

Now number 3's left me. I expect she feels quite pleased about that."

"Where did the last one go to?" enquired Molly.

"Rome – with a Roman," said Charlie tersely. "A month ago."

"She might come back," Molly said.

"I don't know if I want her to," he said. "No – that's a lie. I'd have her back like a shot. She wasn't very old – had a French mother – I thought she'd keep me going in my old age with tisanes and showing me her new pairs of shoes. I gave her everything she said she wanted. Cost a packet, I can tell you. There's no future in it – women prefer your Johnnie Bridges who knock them about and steal their handbags. I wonder why that is?"

"You're free, in a way, when you don't have to be nice all the time to your bread and butter," reflected Molly. "At least it's a voluntary association –" she said. "And it's more interesting than sitting about being handed everything on a plate – boredom's more powerful and dangerous than anyone thinks."

"That Roman had a twelve-inch prick," Charlie remarked. "I think that might have had something to do with it."

"You could be right," Molly said.

"A chap shouldn't say this to another chap's wife," Charlie said, "particularly when that other chap is a close relative – but would you consider coming home tonight with a lonely old bachelor?"

"Last time you chased me round the room with a whip," said Molly, who had been considering it.

"I was young and uncertain in those days," said Charlie. "There won't be any repetition."

"You're on," said Molly.

"Better than sitting in Fitzcrumbling Towers, worrying about the mortgage," Charlie said. "Waiter – bring some champagne."

But Molly was not slow to see that the bedroom of the large flat opposite Hyde Park which Charlie occupied still carried the black and red colours and the vaguely sinister air of the room where he had terrorized her so many years ago. The effect was muted, but still present. Nevertheless, the two of them made love carefully and fell asleep feeling cheerful. In the morning Molly rang Sam Needham and said, "Sam – I've got a business arrangement I'd like Dick Richards to help me with –" and Sam cut her off quickly.

"Molly," he said, "there's bad news. Isabel rang last night in case you were here – couldn't get any reply at your hotel –"

"What is it?" cried Molly, thinking of her child.

"It's Ivy," he said. "She's very ill. Sid rang Framlingham to tell you."

"What's happened?"

"She collapsed – the news is very bad, Molly. She'll pull round but –"

"What is it?" she said. "You'd better tell me, Sam."

"Cancer," he said.

"She was weakening – I told her to go to the doctor."

"I'm sorry, Molly."

"Thanks, Sam, I'll go straight there," she said.

She took a taxi to where her car was parked and drove to Beckenham. She did not really believe, yet, in Ivy's illness. As she pushed the doorbell she could hear the sound of a vacuum cleaner. Ivy answered the door with her head tied up in a scarf and the nozzle of the cleaner in her hand.

"Mum!" cried Molly. "What are you doing? You shouldn't be –"

"Where have you been?" Ivy said, opening the door more widely so that she could get in. She turned off the vacuum. "This is all Sid's fault. I rang Isabel to tell you not to come."

As they walked through the passageway she remarked, "You've had your hair done – nice."

To this Molly, following her, replied, "You ought to have someone in to clean."

They sat down in the sitting room, which smelt of fresh furniture polish. Molly looked at her mother's pale, thin face and said, "What happened?"

"Where were you?" Ivy asked.

"Never mind – what happened?" Molly repeated.

"I've got it – all right?" Ivy said defiantly. "I've had the tests. I'm booked for an operation. I've had a small collapse, that's all. The doctor said it was only to be expected."

Sid came in saying, "Hullo, Molly. We've had a nice game trying to find you."

She said, "Then I do a mercy dash and find her hoovering away at the floor."

"They're sending a woman – the Council," he said. "That's why she's all over the place. She doesn't want the cleaner to come in and find the place all dirty. She's going to treat her like an honoured guest."

"I'm still here," Ivy said. "You don't have to talk about me as if I was a dog just because I'm ill."

495

"I'm going to make some coffee," said Molly. Sid followed her out.

"She shouldn't be up and doing," Molly said.

"Tell her that," Sid told her.

"What does the doctor say?" she demanded. "It's in her glands," Sid said. "They're going to cut it out. Then there'll be treatment –"

But, as they stood staring at each other, each knew how doubtful the other felt.

"That's good," said Molly.

She turned to make the coffee. As she did so she murmured, "Oh, dad."

"I'll tell you what I told Jack and Shirley," he said roughly as he put milk and sugar on a tea tray. "And that's that I don't want any long faces round here. It won't help anybody if we all start moaning and groaning."

"Is she frightened?" Molly asked.

"Sometimes – she doesn't say much," Sid said.

"She's got to have some help here," Molly told him.

"That's where I wish we were back in Meakin Street," he said. "The women there helped each other out more. We could do with Lil Messiter now. I'd do it, Molly, you know that. But she's kept me out of the kitchen so long and now everything I do is wrong. It only irritates her."

"Vi Hutton'd come for a fortnight – give her a rest," Molly said. She was talking about Jack's former mother-in-law.

"They're in the middle of a divorce now," Sid told her. "I don't know what Vi thinks –"

So Molly rang up. "She's coming," Molly reported. "I said I'd go and pick her up. But she won't leave unless you go and fix on her window locks. She doesn't want to get broken into while she's away. She says she's had them six weeks and none of her sons will do it – they keep on saying they'll get round to it later."

"Fair enough," Sid told her.

Ivy, now in her nightdress, said, "I can see I'm never to be consulted about anything."

"No harm in Vi coming to stay," Sid said placidly. "You two have been planning it for years. And she always makes you laugh. I'll have to lay in a stock of vodka and tomato juice. Vi can't half knock back the Bloody Marys."

"She's looking forward to it, really," Sid said as they drove through the streets to East London.

Molly, in the passenger seat, was overcome with horror. She felt death all round her. Her courage fled.

"You all right Molly?" asked her father.

"It's a shock," she said.

"It hit me very hard, at first," he told her. "But I had to realize it didn't help."

Molly just nodded. "Hard, though," she said, "being normal all the time."

They stopped at a pub and ate sandwiches and drank beer, looking out over the wide, slow-moving river. Molly's eyes followed a tug downriver.

"Do you remember how this river used to be?" asked Sid. "Full of traffic? And the docks, with ships queueing to unload, and the wharves covered in goods — it's all gone now. I sometimes wonder what's happening to this city. It's all office blocks. There's no real trade. I get depressed every time I come down here and see the gulls flying over the empty docks and the old warehouses falling to pieces. What do you do with a place where there's no trade? It seems useless."

"Better ask Jack," Molly said. There was a silence. She said, "I've not been much of a daughter. I want her to see me make something of my life."

"Never mind about that," Sid said. "At least you've cheered her up. More than Shirley. In her heart of hearts she always thought you'd got out — got free. Not that she'd admit it."

"Out of what?" asked Molly.

"Responsibility — a home, kids, struggling along. You know what women are like — always grumbling. To their way of thinking all women ought to be the Queen and it's only the cruel hand of fate which gave them homes and husbands who take a drop too much and kids who get into trouble. One of them sods off and it's 'Good luck to her — wish I had the courage.' If the man does it, it's 'The rotten bastard'. They're all the same. Whatever you've done or not done, it's Shirley who makes Ivy feel depressed. Course, now she's worried about our Jack. He's taken up with some woman who works for ITV. Ivy doesn't like it." He put his glass down. Molly went to the bar and got him another drink. When she came back he said, "On the other hand, if you've got any bad news for her I should keep it to yourself."

So she told him about her meeting with Charlie Markham. He said doubtfully, "It *sounds* all right, Molly." And added, "Don't you forget

I've still got a pair of hands and I'm used to engines. I wouldn't mind having a go if you need a bit of help."

"I'll get in touch with you if I'm stuck," promised Molly.

She began the conversion of the stables in the following week. She had raised the loan on Meakin Street house without difficulty. Tom remarked, as the workmen came in, that he would not spend too much on the strength of Charlie Markham's promises if he were in charge of the business, but Molly, encouraged that Isabel was making no objections, took no notice. However, the following week Charlie was solidly unavailable when she telephoned and, when she finally ran him to earth, he told her that some problems had come up and that they should meet as soon as possible. Molly, nervously, got in the car and drove up to London. On the way she reflected that she was in debt now and if the other two backed out she would either have to find more financing or sell off the house in Meakin Street to cover her losses. In the restaurant that evening he told her, "Trelawney's doubtful. He doesn't really see himself putting up independent financing for a small company. For one thing, it's too complicated. For another, it doesn't help sufficiently with his tax problem. The whole idea was to absorb some of the profits from Lauderdale. He still wants a subsidiary company and not an independent one."

Molly stared at him in discouragement. The evening had started badly for, as Charlie lifted his whisky to his lips at the bar, she had seen him, suddenly, as too heavy, too lined, too stale. He was, she thought, permanently depressed. He seemed to see no good in the world. He was all right when he was good-humoured and tolerant of his own despair but, when all that was stripped away, he was a sad, aggressive man whose battles with a world he mistrusted seemed to make it worse for him, rather than better. And after that it was no surprise to find out that he and Trelawney were still trying to get control of the business. She said as much. "Obviously," she told him, "you want your share to be under the Lauderdale umbrella. That way, if it starts to rain you don't get wet. You can probably write it all off. What about my bit?"

"We could arrange that for you," Charlie said, but she was not sure if she believed him. "That's not the point. You want to run a market stall here. Lauderdale gives you, eventually, the possibility of expansion, fresh financing when this lot comes to an end – can't you see the advantages? You've got the mentality of a seaside landlady, Molly, and you can't operate like that in business."

"We've had this discussion before, Charlie," she said. "There's no

498

point in going over it all again. I don't trust large companies and I don't trust people with money and no real responsibility —"

"Sit down and eat your dinner," he said. "Here comes the wine."

"No, thanks, Charlie," she told him.

"I can't sit here eating by myself," he protested. "For God's sake, just sit down and be civil, Molly. It won't kill you."

But she did not sit down. "Look, Charlie," she said, "I'll buy you some fish and chips or an Indian take-away and we can have it at your place. That'd be nice. As for the rest, if you won't help, I'll just push as hard as I can to get the prototype bike ready and then see what I can do elsewhere."

As she spoke he was signalling to the waiter but she saw an expression of alarm cross his face. He soon controlled it but she realized that his idea had been to buy into the company cheaply and safely and he was worried now he saw his chance slipping away. Foolishly, she pressed her advantage, "George Messiter's got another idea, too. My guess is he's a natural inventor, like you used to get years ago, like George Stephenson and the kettle and Darwin and the apple and all that — with Wayne to do the practical stuff and steady him down generally he could do all sorts of things."

Charlie said, "Well, of course, if that's your attitude —" and waited for her reply.

And Molly said, "Well, it is, Charlie."

He was not in a good mood as they ate curry by candlelight on his dining room table. It's only a bike, thought Molly. He's on the board of a company worth millions of pounds. He's on the waiting list for a brand new Rolls Royce. So why is he so sulky? He got up when they had finished and came behind her chair. He pinched her breast and said, "Up to beddy-byes, then?"

"Ouch," protested Molly. "That hurt." As his arms went round her in bed she felt his body, chill and stiff against hers. It's coming from his brain and his heart, she thought, and tried to warm him, console him.

"Molly," he said afterwards. "You're wonderful."

"You're not so bad yourself," she said, but felt a reserve towards him she could not understand.

During the following week the trees grew greener and the new grass began to spring at Framlingham. The baby showed signs of being about to stand up and walk. He cried, " 'Ay' 'Ay' " at Wayne when he threatened to walk past him in the yard without noticing. Molly, paying a wage to Vera Harker and the other women, knew there was a shortage of orders for the toys for the summer and begrudged them the fifty percent of profits she had guaranteed. She was still paying George, Wayne and two other workmen for the conversion of the stables and ordering in the equipment they would need to get the prototype Messiter bicycle ready. Funds were low, and getting lower, while gracious living began at Allaun Towers. Isabel was improving their standard of living by putting in large orders for food and wine at the high-class grocer's in the town. The arrival of their green van on two successive days made Molly's heart sink. She wrote cheque after cheque and felt she was bleeding to death.

At the beginning of the following week the telephone rang as she was carefully beating the faded grey tracery of the upholstery of the drawing room chairs, which she dared not attack too vigorously for fear of damaging the old fabric. It was Shirley, at the station three miles away, asking for a car to be sent to pick her up.

"Are the children with you?" asked Molly.

Shirley, in a muffled voice, said, "Yes."

"Oh, God," said Molly, putting down the duster and going out to the yard to collect Fred.

Her sister was crying when she arrived. The boys, Brian and Kevin, were now ten and eight years old. They were still as pale, and as thin, as ever. The older looked bewildered and the younger truculent. Three suitcases stood beside Shirley on the steps of the station.

"You can stay a week," Molly told her sister bluntly as they ate a scratch lunch of sandwiches and cups of tea in the kitchen. "You can see what it's like here – workmen everywhere, I'm in hock to get a business started. It's being done on a mortgage on Meakin Street – I've got a young child and a tricky mother-in-law."

Shirley said, "I don't know where else to go – Ivy's ill, Jack's in a small flat and his girlfriend doesn't want the disturbance – but I couldn't stay, Molly. I've been on Valium for three years."

"I've got six weeks before they bring the axe down on me," Molly told her. "I'm right on the edge, Shirl, and that's a fact."

"Ivy was always there to bale you out and take care of Josephine when you needed it," Shirley went on as if she had not heard.

"I'm sorry," Molly told her.

Brian staggered in with a bucket and said, "Which is the hot tap?"

"The one with the red nozzle," Molly said. "Why can't you use the tap in the yard?"

"Allan wants hot," said the boy. He added, as he heaved the bucket into the sink, "He's giving Kev and me fifty pence a day to be helpers."

"He's nice, Allan," Molly told her sister as she closed the door behind the boy and his bucket.

Shirley began to cry. "It's a lovely place," she said. "If only there was room. That family's ruined my boys – I want them to get healthy and normal."

A worse incident then occurred. The telephone rang. Molly listened to what Charlie Markham had to say and then, wordlessly, put the phone back on the cradle. She ran out, through the front door into the yard. "Wayne!" she cried. "Wayne! I've got to talk to you."

Wayne, up on the roof putting on tiles with the other workmen, looked down at her. Without saying anything he came down the ladder and said, "Is it about George?"

A watery sunshine filled the yard. She looked at him and said, "You knew?"

"Mr Markham rang up while you was out, once. He wanted to speak to George – make a date to see him. I told him not to go. But he went. I knew it was no good. So – what happened?"

"He bought him," Molly said flatly. "He's signed him up. I suppose he's offered him a big salary and all the facilities he wants. Job as a designer, he says – that means he'll work for Charlie and whatever he develops he won't get a penny for. You know that, Wayne, don't you? It seems George is trying to get you on the team, too."

"That Markham won't want me," Wayne said. "To him I'm just the black guy, all muscle, no brain. Anyway, I don't want to work for him. Minute I heard about him I knew who he was. You shouldn't blame George, Molly," he said earnestly. "He doesn't understand anything. He doesn't know who anybody is. All he wants is a workshop and the chance to get along with his work. About all the rest – he's like a kid. He believes what people tell him – like I told you, I said not to go and see that man."

Molly stared up at the half-tiled roof above her and thought, they'll have to stop work at the end of the week. She said to Wayne, "Can you tell Allan and his mate to stop work at the end of the week. Tell them I'm laying them off with two weeks' pay. I can't face telling them."

"You done your best," Wayne said. Molly walked across the yard and back into the house telling herself that she was a fool. She'd been a fool to start the conversion without a proper financial basis. She'd been a fool not to have guessed what Charlie Markham, faced with an obstinate woman blocking his path, would do next. Her legs weakened once she was inside. She sat down heavily at the kitchen table and put her head in her hands.

"What's the matter?" asked Shirley.

"Charlie Markham's sold me out," her sister told her.

"What happened?" said Shirley.

Molly told her briefly in a flat voice, thinking that Shirley, blowing her nose on a sodden handkerchief, was not capable of taking much interest in what she said.

Wayne came in. "Told them?" she asked.

"No – I thought it over and I didn't tell them. I want you to come to London with me and talk to George."

"What's the point – he's signed," Molly said despondently. "He saw his chance – and took it."

"That means nothing," Wayne told her. "He's only signed a piece of paper – he's got no money. He's done no work. What will they do to him if he says he changed his mind? They can't kill him. What you going to do now? Just sit there and let that fat man trash you?"

Molly, seeing her choice as a day discharging the workers and staring at Shirley's tear-stained face, or a day in London taking some action, decided on the latter. At worst, she thought, she could go round to Charlie's flat and break his windows with a brick.

In the train she said, "Maybe George'll be better off with Charlie – he'll get everything he wants."

"Man like George?" Wayne said sceptically. "He'll be a racehorse they feed till it starts losing – then –" and he made a gun out of his fingers and pulled an imaginary trigger. "Least we can do for him," he said, "is go and see what kind of paper he signed."

George was at the garage in West London, collecting up his things. Molly stood in the pale sunshine reading George's contract as she leaned against a crashed van. A little further off George was saying, "I'm talking to Mr Markham about a job for you, Wayne," and Wayne was saying, "Forget it, man. I rather have the old job back here."

As Molly read she couldn't help remembering poor bewildered George, youngest of a poor family, helping his drunken mother upstairs at night. This was the boy to whom Charlie Markham had offered seven thousand pounds a year and full facilities for two years, with no mention of a royalty fee on any innovations he might create. Molly felt angrier still. She took the contract back to George. She said, "I can't stop you but you ought to get this re-negotiated. If you come up with anything they just take it and exploit it. You get nothing. They can milk you dry for two years and then throw you out on your ear. Can you see what I'm talking about, George?"

"Yes – course," said George.

"He don't," Wayne told her.

Wayne was quite relaxed. Molly had a feeling that in this situation, where George was too embarrassed to look at her and she was furious with George, Wayne was under control. And yet he had reason to be angry with George himself, since George had signed up with Charlie Markham without including him in the deal.

Molly shrugged. "Look, George," she said, "I'm not complaining because you tried to do the best for yourself. I'm complaining because you didn't even warn me. And I'm complaining because what you've got here is a rotten deal. Charlie's skinning you – or he will if he gets the chance."

"Cissie said to sign," muttered George.

"Of course she bloody well did," Molly said furiously. "Because your father and mother between them knocked all the stuffing out of both of you. So now all you can do is tuck yourself safely away under the wing of something called the Lauderdale Group of Companies because no matter how badly you get robbed, that way at least you feel safe. And all I can say is I hope it keeps fine for you. Because to people like that, George Messiter, you're just a bit of meat for their mincer."

There was a silence. George, hearing nothing but her angry voice, looked at the ground. She said to Wayne, "Try to talk to him," and walked out of the yard.

She got back in the car feeling exhausted and had to stop on the way back. She sat in a copse near a lay-by and tried to breathe steadily. She now had two mortgaged homes to her credit, a heap of bills she could pay, but only just, and a set of half-converted stables. She would have to cancel the order for one of the lathes. The other had arrived that morning and would have to be resold quickly, probably at a loss. She lay back on the damp earth and wished she could go to sleep, here, and not wake up for a long time. But, she thought sitting up, she had promised to be back before supper time to collect Fred from Vera Harker. It was no good, she thought. The toy business would never keep the place going. She would have to go back to London, get a job, take a room somewhere until Sam moved out of Meakin Street, put Fred in a nursery and go out to work to pay back her mortgage. She arrived at Framlingham exhausted, dreading Isabel, who would have returned and found out that Shirley was staying, dreading Tom's face when she told him that Charlie had tricked her, dreading Shirley and her tears.

As she drew up in front of the house Shirley appeared on the steps, not weeping, as Molly expected, but pirouetting on the steps, one hand extending the skirt of a brightly-coloured dress.

Molly got out of the car and recognized the material. The green bodice of the dress was the scarecrow toy's trousers. The various colours in the skirt came from the doll, the fox and the parrot. She observed two other things – the dress was very stylish and Shirley had cut up the toy materials to make herself a dress. Oh God, thought Molly, there's no end to the selfishness and stupidity of these people – the Markhams, the Allauns and the Shirley-fuck-ing Waterhouses. And this, in her tiredness and depression, she said, adding, "I'm going upstairs now, to put Fred to bed. When I come down I'll give you all one last, final pint of blood. Then I'll be off – that do for you?"

She walked past Shirley up the steps, holding the child. Shirley said behind her, "What's the matter, Moll? I thought you'd be pleased."

"I'm not your husband," Molly said flatly as she crossed the hall. "Though you seem to think I can double for him on a bad day. I'm not delighted when you show me you've made yourself a pretty dress, out of stock."

Shirley ran after her, up the stairs. "You stupid bitch," she cried. "I've done all this out of the offcuts – stuff you couldn't use. I've looked through that rubbish in the desk in the library you call your accounts. You're overstocked and those women are still producing stuff you can't sell. You can sell these."

Molly turned round. The bodice of the dress tucked loosely into the longish, brightly coloured skirt, which had a jagged hem. The effect was that of a jumble of expensive rags. Her mood was slow to yield but she said, "Maybe you're right. Come upstairs."

As she put Fred in the bath she said, "I'm sorry, Shirley. I can see you're right. How many more can you get out of the offcuts?"

"Only a couple," her sister said. "But unless you can get some more orders you might as well use the material you've got on these. It wouldn't be too hard to get some orders."

"Think so?" asked Molly.

"It's worth a try," Shirley told her. "I can sort out your accounts, too."

"I'm grateful, Shirl," Molly said. "But you can see Charlie's done for me. I've had to put Meakin Street in pawn to pay for these conversions and all I can do now is pay my debts and clear off. You can stay till it's over, if it suits you, but remember, we're both homeless now."

As she pulled Fred from the bath she heard Isabel behind her in the doorway. "I can't say this is any more than I expected."

"What you expected, Isabel, was a small fortune brought by me, and an heir to the throne here, also brought by me. Well, I've done my best, and now I'm leaving, so you can put that in your pipe and smoke it."

"I imagine that in future you will not be using the name Allaun," Isabel said. "After all, you've several others to choose from."

"Don't worry about that," Molly said. "I'll be forgetting all this as soon as I can." She walked past Isabel and into her bedroom. She dressed the child for bed and put him in his cot in the room next to hers. There was a connecting door and, as she entered the other room, she could hear the low buzz of Shirley and Isabel, talking on the landing. She lay down on her own bed reflecting that if she had a flat, a room of her own, at least she and the child could live separate lives, away from the continual sense of feet on the stairs, chats on the landing, silences as one person entered a room occupied by others. And she slept, hearing the French song Madeleine, the whore, had sung to her in prison. She could pick out some of the words, although she did not know what they meant. The song went on, in her dream, making her feel warm and safe and at home. Then she saw the old Meakin Street, still with its gas lamps and the little, faded houses and, coming towards her in fog was a figure, Joe Endell. There was someone beside him. She could not see who it was but she knew she loved the person.

The fog swirled and she could see neither of them, although the song went on. She awoke, consoled, and looked up at the large, corniced ceiling above her head. She looked at the fading wallpaper of the room, at the dying light coming through her windows and at the trees beyond. And she knew then she was not safe, not safe at all and nor was her child.

Some hard times lay ahead, she guessed, though no worse than for many others and a good deal better than for some. The Allauns would spiral down until one person offered Tom another job and another presented Isabel with a cottage in the country. They would be looked after, in some way, but the chances were that she, Mary Waterhouse, would not. She hadn't got the right connections. Shirley came in with a cup of tea. "You'd better stay where you are, Molly," she said. "I'll bring your dinner up."

"I've got to get up and talk to the bank manager," Molly said.

"He's coming tomorrow afternoon," said Shirley. "He phoned while you were away and I told him he'd better come here for a conference. Don't get up, Molly. Tom's home and he's heard the news. I dread you meeting him in this mood."

"He's gloating, I suppose," Molly said gloomily.

"No – no –" Shirley cried in alarm but Molly, jumping up and struggling into her skirt cried, "I'll see him in hell, first. I'll tell him what's what."

"Don't be such a silly fool –" her sister called out as Molly went pounding down the stairs and into the drawing room, where Tom was sitting having a drink.

"I've heard the bad news –" he began lugubriously.

"Well, you can put that glass down while you're talking to me," Molly said. "I doubt if it's your first drink and I expect I'll be paying for it too."

"I was about to say I was sorry," Tom told her, putting his glass on the table. "Suppose I pour you one and we sit down and talk rationally."

"Rational conversation won't help now," said Molly. "Some help and support might have done. You couldn't manage that, though, could you? Or even an opinion? Standing about making faces was all you could manage while I've been struggling."

"Try to remember that you prevented me from coming to have lunch with you when you met Charlie," Tom said. "You would try to manage it all alone."

"Because I couldn't stand the idea of you hanging about having a free lunch while I did all the work," said Molly. Isabel Allaun came into the room, tried to speak and then sat down as Molly rushed on. "If you'd come, Charlie wouldn't have offered anything. Because he mistrusts you. As it happens it would have been better if he hadn't offered anything – then he couldn't have gone behind my back and shopped me. But, Tom Allaun, if you were anything like a man – and I'm not talking about sex – he wouldn't have dared do all that. He wouldn't have dared buy up George like that – he did it because I'm a woman, and because there's no one to stand up for me except a man he despises. So don't you dare sit there pulling faces and condoling with me – I'll tell you this – at least I tried, which is a damn sight more

506

than you've ever done. I'm leaving you and you can go on sitting there like Cinderella and wait for another Princess Charming to bail you out."

She slammed out of the room and went into the kitchen. Shirley was stirring salt into a dish in the oven. "Thank God I made a casserole," she remarked, as Molly rummaged in the pantry. "At least it won't spoil while all this is going on."

Molly, holding out the half bottle of brandy she had found on the kitchen shelf, said, "Have some?"

"No thanks," said Shirley. "I'll stay sober and ready to catch Fred when he gets out of his cot and threatens to fall downstairs."

"I'm sorry about this, Shirley," Molly said.

"I dunno," Shirley said. "It reminds me of Meakin Street. Anyway, you're right. The Allauns haven't done anything but complain about the noise and the inconvenience – and those grocers' bills in the kitchen drawer are ridiculous."

Tom came in saying, "I know you're upset, Molly –"

"Sod off, Tom," she said. "Talking won't improve anything."

He looked at her and stood for a moment. Then he went out. Molly sat down, drank some brandy, topped up her glass and jumped up again. "I've had an idea," she said. Shirley sniffed and went to the back door to call for Brian and Kevin. They might as well have some supper before another row broke out, she thought.

In the meanwhile Molly was in the drawing room saying to Isabel, "So why don't you get planning permission, convert the stables into flats, use the foundations opposite to build more flats, or little maisonettes, sell the lot and when you've done it you can pay me back for the work I've already done?"

"Would you pour me a small whisky and water?" asked Isabel. "I'm feeling remarkably tired." She said, as Molly brought her the drink, "Yes – I think that's an excellent idea. And since the bank manager's coming tomorrow I think we should both put it to him and let him look at the stables. And if he agrees to lend me the money then I shall have you to thank for starting the work and indicating the possibilities. You may have been misguided to trust Charlie Markham and I confess I've always been dubious about the whole scheme. But you tried, and that's something. And I'm furious with Charles. I've telephoned his mother and explained what he's done and I've told her I'd be glad if she'd tell him he's no longer welcome here. You are, after all, Tom's wife and I think he's treated you unfairly."

Molly was surprised and impressed. "Thanks Isabel. I didn't expect you to stick up for me," she said. "I'll be leaving shortly."

At this point Isabel bowed her head a little, gracefully acknowledging the decision. Molly turned her head to conceal an involuntary smile. They must both know, she thought, that Molly, as Tom's wife, had a claim to the house – and Isabel must be hoping, discreetly, that the idea had not occurred to Molly. She said, "Isabel – do you know this tune?" And she hummed the song which had come, yet again, into her dream. Isabel said, "Yes – yes – I think I do. I can't remember what it is." She hummed the tune to herself, faltering, then correcting it.

"That's right," said Molly. "What is it? I hear it sometimes in my dreams."

"In your dreams?" Isabel asked. "But where in the world – it's well before your time. It comes from the thirties." She repeated, "In your dreams?" Then said, "It's cold, Molly, please put those two large logs on the fire."

She stared at Molly, as if she were framing a question to ask her, then said, "I don't know – life's strange – who would have thought we two would be sitting here now, after all these years." She paused, asking now, "You don't even know any French, do you?"

"No," Molly said, and began to think of Peggy's story about Joe Endell's rescue from the bombed house. And what shall I do now, Joe? She interrupted her thought to herself. Isabel's cool voice was asking, "What are you thinking of doing?"

"Paying up, leaving here, putting Fred in a nursery and getting a job," Molly said stoutly, resisting the temptation to assure Isabel that she would make no claims on Tom or the house. She wanted nothing but she felt she was not big-hearted enough to put Isabel out of her misery.

"You were trying to save an impossible situation," Isabel said. "It *was* impossible, you know, once it became plain that you had no fortune."

"It might have been possible, without Charlie Markham," Molly said.

"Even so –" said Isabel. "In any case, you were optimistic if you expected Charlie to play fair."

"I didn't expect him to be as dirty as that," Molly said.

"In my experience," remarked Isabel Allaun, "people change very little after they grow up. Charlie was quite a nasty little boy and he's grown up to become quite a nasty man." She sighed and said, "Molly –

I wonder if you'd pour me another small whisky." She said, as Molly did so, "I think matters would have been less serious if Fred had not died. He would have held things together a little better. Tom's not had the experience –" Her voice trailed away. Molly handed her the whisky. Isabel was being friendly now that she was going, Molly thought. Not entirely truthful – when had she ever been? – but she was showing some candour. "I've always regretted the way you were bundled off at the end of the war," she said. "It was largely my fault – I've had to admit that to myself. He wanted to adopt you – Fred – and I believe I was a bit jealous, for Tom's sake of course. I expect we were all a bit mad, then. It had been a long war – we were all tired out."

"All forgiven and forgotten now," Molly said, hoping to cut her mother-in-law short. The apologies and explanations were too easy. Some of them had the ring of a rehearsed cadenza – as if Isabel had gone over the events, explaining them to herself many times in private.

"Frederick was so strange at the time," she said. "The war had exhausted him. It was almost as if he could talk to no one but you. Looking back on what he must have been feeling, I can see now how natural that was, but it was hard, then, to understand. I may have acted hastily, I think perhaps I did."

Molly helped herself to some more brandy. It was too late – it was all too late. Isabel's attempts to explain the past, excuse herself from any guilt, work out where it all went wrong, were pointless now. She was relieved when Shirley came in saying, "Everyone's in bed what ought to be in bed."

"Please help yourself to a drink," Isabel said. "We're planted in our chairs, chatting. That song," she said to Molly, "quite suddenly I've remembered it – every word. Isn't it extraordinary how that sort of thing happens? You hear one phrase of a tune and half an hour later you've remembered the whole song and all the words."

"How does it go?" Molly asked.

"Les plaisirs et les ennuies –

Sont evanouiées," Isabel sang in a clear voice, younger than her years.

"Comme les vents dans les champs

De mon pays

Then there's some more, I've forgotten – then it goes something like," – and she sang again, "Tous comme les vents dans les blés de mon pays. It's just one of those cabaret songs of the thirties," she explained.

"You know, about lost love and how it's all gone by like the wind across the fields in the singer's native land, or region."

"Well, well," said Molly. "I wonder why I'd hear a song in my dreams in a language I don't even understand."

Isabel said, "Another mystery."

"I suppose no one will ever want anything to eat?" Shirley asked.

Molly shrugged. Shirley said, "I'll turn the oven down."

By the time she returned Tom was back, saying, "I've been drowning my sorrows in the pub."

"We're discussing the future," his mother told him.

"Well, I'll join in," said Tom, making a bold dash at the whisky.

"Seems to me we've all got different plans to discuss," Molly observed. "You've got to think about turning the stables into flats, Shirley and I have to think about accommodation in London for ourselves and our children. I suppose we could share, Shirl?" she suggested.

"I don't know why you don't sell Meakin Street and settle here permanently," said Isabel. "We're a family, after all." Molly giggled, although she realized immediately afterwards that she was drunker than she thought. The notion of Isabel, her homosexual son, herself and her child by Joe Endell constituting a family made her laugh.

Shirley said firmly, "I don't know that that would be in Molly's best interests, Lady Allaun."

"And why not?" Isabel asked.

"Because from what I've seen the money Molly got by selling the house would be soon gone in this household," Shirley replied primly. Molly tried not to laugh again.

"I think you should hold your tongue," Isabel said.

"I speak as a sister but also as a trained accountant," Shirley said. "That's if I've passed my exams, which I don't know yet."

"Are you a trained accountant?" asked Molly.

"That was why I ran away. I'd just finished the final exams when they made me man the bacon cutter eight hours a day, as well as do the housework and the children," Shirley explained plaintively. "Then I nearly cut my finger off on it and they still made me go on doing it. Then Brian was complaining about the state of the house but every time I put my hand in hot water the cut opened again. So I might be a badly-treated wife or I might be a qualified accountant. It remains to be seen."

"None of that excuses what you've just said, in my opinion," Isabel said. "I think it's time I went to bed."

"Oh, no, stay, Isabel," Molly said. She was beginning to enjoy the random nature of a conversation held by four such different people, in the middle of a collection of catastrophes.

"Thank you, but I'm going," Isabel said. "I'm extremely tired. I don't relish your sister's presence in a family discussion and I think if she hadn't the tact to leave the room she could at least have refrained from comment."

"Phew," said Shirley, after she had gone. Molly stared at the carpet and began to feel sour. She remembered dancing at the Dorchester till dawn, riding about in big cars and being given big jewels by men. She remembered rushing back from clubs in the darkness with Johnnie Bridges, falling into bed with him and making love till dawn. Wicked days, she thought, associating with gangsters, slumlords and villains of every kind. Now all she wanted to do was start a bicycle factory and this honest wish had been denied her. Who's the idiot, she thought, Molly Waterhouse, gangster's moll, or Lady Allaun, failed bike shop owner?

She looked at Tom nastily and said, "You'll have to get another wife to help you out. This place is falling to pieces."

"You should talk," retorted Tom in the same tone. "You've lived off men all your life."

"I'm a woman," Molly pointed out. "It's expected of me. They queued to do it. Anyway, you had better chances than I did. You could have been a famous barrister, or a doctor, or anything. It doesn't matter anyway. Facts are facts. This place is falling to bits and I'm leaving and I don't care."

"That's the trouble," said Tom. "You don't care. Live here when it's easy, when you're a kid. When it's harder you bale out fast."

"It was one of your lot – Charlie – sold out Molly," Shirley said. "Not one of ours."

"It was one of yours – George – who agreed to be bought," Tom said. "Trust you to drag class hatred into it, as if things weren't bad enough."

"What does it all matter now?" Molly said wearily.

"I'm going up," Tom said, yawning.

"What a shocking pair," Shirley said, after he had left the room. "To think it's us that's supposed to be common."

"I don't care," said Molly. "I've got a life to lead and a child to keep and I should never have got mixed up with all this in the first place. It hasn't made me forget Joe – just remember him worse. I think if I can get out of here I'll remember him more happily. I should never have tried to change things. I should have sat in Meakin Street crying my eyes out and occasionally trying to do myself in and getting stomach pumped. It was a dream – trying to get back in a dream. It's been a half-dream all my life, this – the house, the countryside, the life you could lead. Like security. Then I got here by a trick, sort of, and it was real – all falling to pieces, Mrs Gates dying in the stables, not a dream, more like a nightmare. The house gone rotten and the people inside gone rotten with it. I don't care – I'll be glad to get out of here."

"You're entitled to something – a divorce settlement –" Shirley said.

"I wouldn't take a sodding, rotting brick from the wall," Molly declared. "I should never have married Tom. It was part of the dream."

"You going to bed?" asked Shirley.

"No. I'll just sit here," Molly told her.

"Never mind, Moll. Never mind," said Shirley.

After Shirley had gone Molly sat on and saw the dawn come up over the lawn where the starlings still hopped as they had on those summer mornings when she had come there with her precious skipping rope to skip and skip and skip. Now, above her, she felt the whole house crack and groan under the weight of years of neglect. Then she went to bed, as the early light came in between the cracks of the faded curtains in her room.

The next day she began, wearily, to assemble her things in a corner of the bedroom. In the afternoon, as she drank tea in the drawing room with the bank manager, she was saying, "I shall have to ask you to keep the loan going for me while I make arrangements to pay it –" when she saw, past his head, through the long windows, a hunched figure coming up the drive with something on its back. And as the banker, James Davidson, said, "I shall try, Lady Allaun, but I can't agree to do it entirely on my own responsibility," Molly realized that the figure was Wayne and that he was carrying the bicycle frame.

"Excuse me," she said, jumping up. "There's something peculiar going on outside." She crossed the room. "He's got the whole bike on his back," she said.

Davidson was at her side. "Oh – so that's the bicycle," he said. As she opened the window to go out she glimpsed Davidson's face. He was fascinated.

"Come and have a look," she said, stepping out. "Though it can't be too good, if he's carrying it, instead of it carrying him."

Wayne dropped the bike on the grass and straightened up.

"Hullo," Molly said. "What are you doing here, with that? Come inside and have some tea."

"I'll have a wash in the kitchen first," he said. "I've walked seven, eight miles with it. Your phone's out of order," he told her.

"Did it break down?" asked Molly.

"No," he said tiredly. "We had a democratic discussion and decided it was the bike's turn to ride."

He turned round and trudged off to the kitchen.

Davidson was still on the lawn. He had righted the cycle. "Nice and light," he said. "Unless you have to carry it. Something's happened to the back wheel."

Molly knelt on the grass. "The engine's about four pounds," she said. "And it looks as if it slipped its pins and hit the back wheel. They were worrying about whether the pins were strong enough to hold it over roads."

"Where's the engine?" wondered Davidson.

"In that bag over his shoulder, I expect," Molly said.

"Small as that?" Davidson said.

"That's the whole point," Molly told him. "When you want it you've got fifteen to twenty miles an hour – when you don't you can put it on a shelf or in a suitcase, carry it about. If you look," she pointed out, "you can see where the pins keeping it in place sheared through. I must need a bigger pin or a stronger alloy." She bit her lip thoughtfully.

She stood up. "Never mind," she said, "that's not my problem now."

"Well, well," said Davidson, following her in reluctantly. "I can see now why your competitor wanted it. Very handy little item – it would suit all sorts of people. It's got a rather attractive appearance too, if it had a coat of paint."

"I had this dream of fleets of them, all painted gold, green and silver and purple, swooping up and down hills together," Molly told him. "Like a fleet on the ocean. Would have made a lovely ad on TV."

Davidson looked at her in surprise. He nodded.

"I'll go and make a fresh pot," she said. And to Wayne, as he came in, "Help yourself to cake. This gentleman's Mr James Davidson, the bank manager – we're just having an inquest – and this," she said to

Davidson, "is Wayne Edwards, my former business partner."

"That's what —" Wayne said as she went out to the kitchen. She did not hear the rest but as she boiled the kettle she had a sudden instinct he had brought good news. She stood impatiently, waiting for the kettle to boil, and wondering what had happened.

When she went back Wayne was talking about the Messiter to James Davidson. "The old engines on the old motorized bike had got too conventional," he was saying. "There was no reason why they should be so heavy, and stuck on the side like that. It meant you had to have a heavy frame, and compensate for the weight on that side. With the new alloys you didn't need all that. George just started thinking how to do it different — George can do that. He just looks at a problem and forgets how anyone else thought about it, or done it before." He turned to Molly and said, "He's on the train — George. We tried to phone."

"I didn't pay the bill," Molly said frankly. "And I knew no one else would."

"Better get it put back on, then," Wayne said. "Because George tore up that agreement with Mr Markham. He wants to come back."

Molly had been wondering if that was what had happened but now could not believe it. Wayne looked awkward, "All right, is it?"

Molly nodded. "It's all right if Mr Davidson says it's all right."

"You'd better come in tomorrow with your costings and plans," said Davidson. "How much would you plan to sell the machines for — have you thought about it?"

Still stunned, Molly said, "Not much. What do you think?" asked Molly. "As a potential customer?"

"Given that the reliability was proved, the petrol consumption reasonable and the length of life of the machine no less than ten years," Davidson said, "I'd guess about one hundred and fifty pounds."

"All that?" Wayne said in astonishment.

"What do they cost to make?" Davidson asked.

"About sixty-five," Wayne told him.

"Add your labour, plant costs, distribution costs, advertising — you can't afford to sell them for any less and make a profit enough to expand on," Davidson said. "That's guesswork, of course. It depends on how many you make. It'll have to be worked out in detail." He hesitated, "If you go forward," he told Molly, "I foresee a difficult year or two for you. I should advise you to think deeply about whether you want to continue."

Wayne, too, was looking at her. And Molly, as usual, said, "Yes. Yes – I'll do it."

"Well – there's no point in going on with our other discussions," said Davidson. "Goodbye, Lady Allaun. Shall we saw three o'clock, at the bank?"

"Certainly, Mr Davidson," she said.

When he had gone she fell into a chair and said, "He was thrilled, Davidson – you could tell. Pour yourself a cup of tea, Wayne. What's been going on? Is George serious? Why's he backed out?"

"I had a go at him. And it seems he told Cissie why you thought Mr Markham was on the fiddle. And Cissie said she changed her mind and you were right. Seems she said you'd be fair and she had confidence in the family you come from."

"But can I rely on him to stand firm now?" Molly asked. "I mean, suppose we get finance and get started – then George is got at by somebody else?"

Wayne shrugged. "You better put him under contract," he said.

"We'll have to draw up an agreement," Molly said. "But I'm not tying him up like a runaway slave."

"He needs a nice, sensible woman," Wayne said.

"Maybe Shirley'll take a fancy to him," Molly said. "And I'd better get her now. Whether she passed her exams or not she's the only accountant we've got and we're not going to find another one before three o'clock tomorrow. We've got to make this look good." She paused. "Isabel's going to be really fed up when she finds out she's not going to be able to turn those stables into nice maisonettes."

"Can she refuse to go along with it?" asked Wayne, in alarm.

"She won't," said Molly, convinced that the threat of her divorce from Tom, accompanied by a claim on the property, would persuade Isabel to accept the continuing of the work on the stables. She started to shout, "Shirley! Shirl! Get your calculator – we're back in business!"

And so the career of Molly Waterhouse began again on that late spring afternoon.

In the summer of 1978 we had spent a week in the Loire with an old friend of my wife's and it was as we were driving on after the visit that I noticed, on the long, dusty white road, a little French signpost reading Poulaye-sur-Bois. At first the name did not register. Then I remembered it but I drove on, faster, if anything, than before. Corrie, who was sitting beside me, said, "If you turn right and right again we can have lunch at Poulaye-sur-Bois."

"Are you sure?" I asked. "Is there any point?"

"The Michelin," she said, finding the pages, "describes it as a pretty village with a picturesque abbey, sited on a hill, among woods. Part of the abbey dates from the fourteenth century and the Hotel de Ville has one star."

We had spent the past year dealing with the problems of a family of three teenage children. This had led, in the end, to a feeling between us, never expressed, that we, our marriage, our family, had all failed. All the love and efforts of the past had been futile and not worthwhile. I knew that these doubts are part of the business of bringing up a family. Nevertheless I had been very keen to get Corrie away from the scene and try to reunite our lives and feelings. Now, I did not want to argue with her about visiting Poulaye-sur-Bois. In fact, her desire to go there quite amused me. I knew, of course, that she had always disliked my involvement in the affair of Mary Waterhouse. She had never quite told me what it was that she most mistrusted about it but I had a clear impression that she saw me, in that context, as the equivalent of a doctor running an abortion clinic or the director of a not-quite-honest company. I thought this attitude unfair but, unfortunately, I also knew that she was usually right and just in her reactions. So, as I turned right, then right again, for Poulaye-sur-Bois I smiled privately at the idea that high-minded Corrie's rejection of a situation she found thoroughly unsavoury had been subsumed by ordinary, common or garden feminine curiosity. I should have known better.

We pulled up in the square and got out of the car. Around the square were small, old houses. Opposite us, under trees, were the tables of the Hotel de Ville. We sat down gratefully and began to talk to the patron about what to eat. "And we'd love to see the abbey. Is it up there?" asked Corrie, pointing past the car to a gap between two old houses, on the other side of the square, where a footpath evidently led upwards, between trees.

"That's it," he told us. "You can't see it from here because of the trees. But we can see the rooftop of the abbey, above the trees, from our upstairs windows." He added that the building was no longer an abbey, although the chapel attached to it was still open, Poulaye-sur-Bois having no other church – the other had been burned down many years before and never rebuilt. At that point the hotelier's elderly mother, in black dress and black stockings, came out of the restaurant and said that if we wanted to see the abbey she would have to telephone the curé's housekeeper, who was in charge of the keys. We protested a little about the amount of effort involved – she or the housekeeper would then have to come with us up the steep slope to the abbey – but she was proud of the place and insistent that we must see it if we wanted to.

Sure enough, after we had finished our meal a sturdy looking sixty-year-old, also in black dress and stockings, pedalled into the square and approached us. Parking her bicycle and refusing our offers of coffee or a drink she led us, with a springy step, across the square, between the houses and up a steep path through trees until we came out into a small clearing. The abbey, a low building built of dark stone, stood in front of us. The elderly woman, whose black-stockinged legs had taken her up the path in front of us like a goat, went up the step in front of the massive wooden doors, studded with big brass studs, and, producing a large key from her pocket, opened the door. Before us lay a large square of overgrown grass. The monastery buildings formed a square around this. The cloisters lay opposite, beyond the large dry fountain in the middle of the grass. All was silent. There was a smell of herbs and hot stone. So we went, Corrie and I, through the cloisters into the ancient, once-whitewashed refectory, into the little stone cubicles where the brothers had once slept. Through the slit windows of the cubicles we could see the overgrown remnants of the vegetable garden, the beds marked now only by the different patches or lines of weeds and grass which grew there. Inside, in the silence, the noise of crickets was loud in the long grass. Then we turned and walked out of the cloisters to the dried-up fountain. I declared that we must next see the chapel, the door of which lay outside the abbey proper beyond the main building. But Corrie, in that kind of female, ruthless, to-the-point attack which often embarrasses the men who witness it, asked, "Et l'Abbe Benoit, Madame, est-il toujours en vie?"

The woman gazed at us and some kind of comprehension came into her face. She knew something, even if it was only that there was something to know. She answered that the Abbé Benoit was indeed still alive and, having retired when the abbey closed, was now living with her employer, the curé, who was a relative of his. Corrie, still determined and obviously fascinated by talking to a woman who actually looked after the Abbé, asked her whether he was in good health. The curé's housekeeper replied that although the Abbé was almost eighty years old he was, in fact, very fit for his age. And my wife remarked confidently that she was very glad to hear this. She added that she did not know the Abbé personally but had heard of him from friends. The best of women, I have noticed, are very good at making strange things seem ordinary, when it suits them. They can get amazing concessions and acceptance for the most bizarre propositions, just by casting an air of normality over everything. On the other hand, although men may be deceived and find themselves suddenly accepting the existence of a lover or agreeing to move house, just because a woman had made it seem like the most ordinary thing in the world, other women are less easily deceived. That was what happened here. I saw the curé's housekeeper's black eyes take in Corrie's shoes, her clothes, her face. Her eyes rested for a moment on me and then she said, in French, of course, "The old English lady goes to mass every Sunday." This, I could see, stopped Corrie in her tracks completely. An ace had been carelessly thrown on the table. For my part I was quite bewildered. I could not see what they were talking about. The woman went on, "Are you looking for her?" And Corrie, mastering her features, said, "We must be back in England tomorrow. Is she still well?" And the woman said, "Oh, yes. Considering her age. This is a very healthy place to live." I simply stood there, wondering who they were talking about, and why. That is to say, I could not accept the truth I was hearing. And finally we went to see the chapel, small, with thick stone walls, five, six hundred years old. As we left, Corrie turned in the bright doorway and looked into the darkness to where the red light burned at the altar. "A light which burns for six hundred years must have shed itself on many strange sights," she said poetically to the housekeeper.

The housekeeper appreciated this, replying, in the same vein, "And over many secrets."

I was thoroughly relieved to be getting into the car, saying goodbye to the woman, giving her money for the church and waving farewell to the landlord of the Hotel de Ville who came out in his apron to say goodbye. The visit had been too much for me. During Corrie's conversation with the old Frenchwoman I had felt like a man standing with his dog, while the dog reacts to sounds which he, the dog's owner, cannot hear and feels anxious about — is the noise that of a man with a revolver coming closer and ready to shoot or is it just a rabbit in a faraway bush? We drove for a mile in silence, while I tried to remember that we were on holiday, that we were going home. Corrie spoke first.

"Well, well," she said. "I wonder who else knows about all this?"

"I don't know," I said.

"You mean — you don't understand?" she asked.

"I understand perfectly well," I said. "I just wish we'd never gone there." I recalled the dry fountain, the smell of herbs, the sound of the crickets in the garden.

"Why do you wish we'd not gone?" she said.

"Because we're meddling in matters which have nothing to do with us," I told her.

"And are you so sure they haven't?" she said angrily.

"I don't know what you mean," I said.

She told me. After that I drove on in silence. Then I asked her what she expected me to do about all this. She said it was none of her business, that decision was mine. I said, very well then, supposing the decision was hers, what would she do? And she said, "Go and see Molly. What else?"

"Perhaps. I'd better think about it," I said. But when we returned to England events in the family began to claim all our time again. I did not go to see Molly.

1979

Those three or four years after George and Wayne came back went in a whirl. I didn't realize it at the time – you never do until later – but I'm surprised now at what I did and how I managed to cope with it all. I wouldn't do it again, that's for certain. I was sailing close to the wind all the time. The books wouldn't have borne close examination, nor the premises, nor the workforce. I had no plans for the future except not to go bankrupt and to keep on paying the wages. The CBI sent a smooth chap down a couple of years ago to write me up. A Celebration of British Industry, it was going to be called – a celebration of British infamy, Josie said, when she heard about it. I must have been mad to agree because when he came and started asking questions I couldn't remember anything. Half the records, at least, were creations of Shirley's and she told me there was no way she was going to get the microfiches of the real records out of the Swiss bank where she'd put them. It was a sod's opera, she said. There was enough in those records to put us all in jail nine times over. In the end I had to send the chap packing and he was only too glad to go. I heard they called off the project and no wonder. I daresay all these few celebrated British industrialists he was going to interview had the same story behind them – it's like the old days when they called you a pirate until you started to do well and then you became a British merchantman. And I started up in business just in time to establish something before it got tougher and tougher so don't tell me anyone who started after, and survived, could have done any different. As for me, half my employees were on the dole or social security back in the old balmy days before the recession of the late '70s and '80s. You could call me a pioneer in the business of cash in hand and no questions asked. I made sure I never had to pay any insurance stamps, even for the ones who weren't getting unemployment or pensions from the state – I never even paid a stamp myself until they caught up with me in 1981. I broke fire regulations, planning regulations, I defrauded the Inland Revenue, took cash payments where I could and paid bills and wages in cash as often as possible. I bribed planning officers, I talked my way round the health and safety regulations, I had four companies operating, at one time, each with a different bank account and then I was playing silly buggers with two bank accounts in the names of Shirley and Tom Allaun. Half the time I didn't know what regulations I was breaking – I just kept on running. In the end these things go by their own momentum – you feel as if you're in a car with no brakes and you just keep on steering and hoping you don't crash into anything. The only rules I stuck to were mine – I had to pay the wages and I had to pay the suppliers. Apart from that Houdini had nothing on me and I'll never know how I got away with it. Later, I think blind eyes were turned. They needed me. I even think they liked me.

We got the Messiter prototype sorted out fairly quickly and the next spring, just as the money was running out badly, we had a first batch of 2,000 bikes ready for sale. I had everybody working, even Sid, the weekend we were due to get the bikes out. I had Tom, of all people, loading them on the lorry. But the problem was we had to expand immediately because then we needed warehousing for spare parts, a proper office to handle orders and all that. I told Isabel I was going to put prefabricated factory buildings on the front lawn. She nearly went mad – in the end I had to buy the bottom field, past the lake, from the Twinings and a nice price they charged for it, too. Then I had to pay the council officer to look the other way while I put up the buildings. But in the end Framlingham got too complicated. Housing was difficult for the labour I brought in and that wasn't going to get any better. The locals didn't take to Wayne's team, which was nine black kids, and they wouldn't let them in the local disco so there was a fight and the police were called – it'd all have improved in the long run, the way it did between us evacuees and the local kids, but I could see that expanding any more in Framlingham would bring in more strangers, make the housing problem worse and we'd have culture-shock, mixed marriages and God knows what while I was turning the village into something like a small industrial town. They couldn't really take a lot more and I was already getting too much attention from the West Kent Preservation Society. I could see myself with all these preservers, interested parties and nosey-parkers breathing down my neck and then goodbye privacy and my tolerant relationship with the local council and the fact that half the workforce was drawing benefit of one kind or another and a lot of the wages were paid out in cash – dirty notes which never saw a tax officer from the moment when somebody paid me (and probably hadn't seen one before that) right to the day when they were put down on a three piece suite. Don't forget that all the while the women were hard at it with electric sewing machines leased to them by the firm. The toys kept going and we were making a lot of dresses – I had put Vera Harker in charge of the whole operation and before long she was running up to London in a Mini, having lunch with the buyer at Harrods. You never know what people can do until you ask them to do it. Anyway, what with one thing and another I thought I'd better move some of the operation back to the smoke. I knew the landscape and the language there. It's easier to fiddle where you aren't the only one doing it – you aren't so conspicuous. So I left the spares business, which was going to expand anyway, down there and turned one side of the stable block over to George for Research and Development. As a matter of fact I thought after he'd developed the Messiter, George had shot his bolt – he certainly spent a few years sitting on his bum or fiddling about on a lathe and getting no results – I little knew what was going through his head or what it would mean for all of us. I just thought he needed a rest and maybe he'd come up with a new mousetrap in due course.

So I got a crumbling old engineering works in about an acre of spare ground beside the railway lines at the end of Wattenblath Street. I could remember when it was quite a thriving little business, turning out enamel sink bowls and basins and all sort of drums – they used to stand about outside and sometimes we'd nip over the fencing and kick them, to make a noise and run away. Anyway, with plastics and so forth they changed over to making cheap toys and novelties and mugs with names on them and all that, so by the time I got there the staff was four old men and one of them was the boss. But it was a building and land which I got for a song and because of previous use the regulations about noise and preserving the amenities didn't bother me. The other advantage was I knew a few of the Town Hall officers, through Joe. Wayne started the work on the place and I reckoned that we could treble our output over the next year and that was as fast as I wanted to go. The beauty of the situation was that what with the constantly rising price of petrol, plus the fashion for bikes, plus transport strikes, we never had any problem selling the bikes. But I had to keep the costs low so I used nearly all part-timers, which meant I could cut down on the facilities and I paid as much cash as possible and one little skinny girl, you'll never believe it, was paid to do nothing else but stroll around making sure there weren't any snoops about snooping. The rest of the time she kept a complicated rota to make sure the labour was diving in and out at irregular intervals so no one could keep a proper check – it was diabolical. I lived in terror of a really bad accident, apart from anything else. I did everything I could about safety but there'll always be one silly bugger with a hangover or she's had a row with the old man and they'll be the ones who drag you down when they cut a finger off. It was a farce, all right – I had school-leavers, pregnant women and old men working there and I argued that as long as people were working, getting a bit of training and getting paid then I wasn't doing any harm. If they were collecting from the state at the same time, well, they would have been anyway, so why worry. No one was any worse off and a lot were a bit better off. I started a small garment factory not far off, too, and got a girl with three children in to manage the outworkers. What I did was employ three women and a lad full-time and all the rest was sweated labour. The factory was more for warehousing and distribution than actual production. Again, I couldn't see the harm in it. I was keeping people in work and paying what I could and the main sufferer was me, because I was never out of debt and I wonder I ever slept a wink, with all the worries. Of course, when Jack got to hear about it he was furious.

It must have been 1979, because he'd nearly lost his seat in the election and I was over in Beckenham because Ivy's first operation hadn't been successful and she'd just come out of hospital after the other one. She thought it would be all right, did Ivy, but I don't think Sid was so confident and nor were the rest of us. Anyway, we both arrived to visit Mum at the same time and we were having a cup of tea in the kitchen afterwards, with Sid, when I realized Jack was giving me funny looks. By this time Jack was well and truly divorced from Pat and he'd married this woman from the TV company and he'd got a small baby called Jasper which his wife, as they say, wasn't letting interfere with her career. I liked him better when he was living with Pat, whether she was a dogmatic Communist or not, and I sometimes had her and the kids down at Framlingham for a break because her problem was that Jack had interfered with her career, in fact she'd never had one, because he had, and now she was having to turn to with nothing but twelve years of being acting unpaid secretary and tea lady to a gang of political activists, all men, behind her. In the end she got started in a little East End print shop with a few other women, so it worked out all right, but at the time, because I stayed friendly with her, it created tension between me and Jack, because his new wife didn't like it. So at first I thought that was why he was acting funny.

Finally, I said, "What are all those funny looks about?" and he denied it, the way people do, and I asked Sid, who told us both to shut up because Ivy was ill upstairs and then Jack said, "I don't want to drag it all up while Ivy's not too good."

"No need for a row," I said. "If it's because you think I'm seeing too much of Pat – well, I've known her a long time and I can't switch loyalties every time you get married again."

He just looked uncomfortable and said, "It isn't that at all."

"It's the business," Sid said. "That's what he's making all these faces about. And if you want my opinion, Jack," – not that any of the Waterhouses ever did want each other's opinions but they were sure to get them anyway – "If you want my opinion," said Sid. "I think you shouldn't interfere. Molly's doing the best she can and she's got a boy to keep."

"The old cry through the ages," said Jack. "It's not an excuse for non-union labour. That's not what we've been fighting for all these years. It's employers like Molly who are eroding all the others struggled and fought for."

And I told him I couldn't afford to use union labour. I told him the truth – if I did, I'd go out of business. It'd put a third on the price of the bikes and I'd lose sales. I said, "And moreover I can't afford the tax and insurance either. I can't afford to run proper canteens, observe full fire regulations and I can't afford proper rest breaks. That's why I use so many part-timers. They can eat and rest in their own time. On mine, they're working."

"Sweated labour," he said.

"They sweat in my time – they can have a bath in their own," I told him. "I'm sorry, Jack, but it works. I use local labour – they don't have to come fifteen miles to work. They don't have to do a full day. They like it and I like it. You can call them blacklegs if you like. I call them people who want a job. It's better for the women too. They don't get so flogged out looking after their homes and families and doing a full day's work as well. If they can get it. They even mind each other's kids, some of them. While one's on shift she looks after the kids – then the other one takes over. The government isn't going to build nurseries for them and I can't afford it – so that works, too."

527

"Meanwhile sister Shirley's fudging the books so it looks as if you've got a third of the workers you really have and you're greasing palms everywhere and fiddling the income tax," he said.

"Shirley's been offered double her wages by two other companies," I said. "She's in demand. What are you going to do – turn us in?"

He dodged that issue and said, "It's the principle I'm complaining about. You're part of a system that's keeping down negotiated wages. Your business is being run on the state – your workers are drawing benefits and not declaring them, you're not covering their contributions towards the National Health or the pension scheme. You're not paying fair tax. You're taking out but you're putting nothing back. If everyone were like you, we'd be put back a hundred years –"

"I'm keeping people in work," I told him. "In a few years' time I'll be in the export market."

"Nice for you," he said. "But it doesn't do much for the rest of us."

"I don't know about that," I said. "I know it's embarrassing for you, in case they catch me and Shirley and you end up with two sisters on trial. But they won't catch us, not if I'm quick. All I've got to do is build up sufficiently and I can go straight. Live in a world where a bribe is called an honorarium and all that. In the meanwhile don't think I'm going to take on your great pork-fed trades unionists. I'm employing the working-class end of the working class – unemployed kids, women, pensioners – all the people your aristocratic unionists can't or won't help and protect. And what's more, I always shall, as much as I can. Why not? They're the likes of me."

"Condescend to pay some tax?" asked Jack.

"Yes," I said, "I'll club up with the rest of you for nuclear bases and a million a year for the Royal Family and fact-finding tours for civil servants and MPs –"

"The roads you walk on, the hospitals you're ill in, the schools you send your children to –"

"That's enough," Sid said. "I'm tired."

"I'm right though, aren't I, Dad?" Jack said.

"I daresay you are, Jack," Sid told him. "Only I wonder if it's going to be any good being right, soon. Things are changing."

"Some things never change," Jack said.

"All right, Oliver Cromwell," said Sid. He looked tired. We were all tired. Jack had just come through an election campaign. I was working long hours. And we all knew that Ivy was dying. In the end Jack and me didn't have the energy to go on with the quarrel.

Ivy did not rally after the second operation, which was followed by a second course of long radiation treatment. The family, beguiled by ambiguous statements from doctors, specialists and nursing staff, and confused by information and misinformation picked up from newspapers, radio and TV and other people, lived between hope and fear and all the hopes and fears were different – they hoped that Ivy would recover or that she would die swiftly and without pain. They feared a pathetic partial recovery, and a long drawn-out death. They feared that she knew she was dying. They feared that she did not know. In fact Ivy both knew and did not know just as children know and do not know that Father Christmas is really their own parents.

Fortunately, she felt no pain until the end. The effect of the illness was just to make her weaker and weaker and to introduce her, by degrees, to a world the family did not know. One day she would be tired and rambling, the next, in the grip of a strangeness no one understood. Then perhaps she would be her old self, ill but worrying about Sid, complaining about the repairs to the washing machine, taking tablets – Ivy Waterhouse, tired and ill, but her old self again. And those close to her went in, and out, of the world of the living with her.

Sid Waterhouse did what so many do in that situation – he became a hero. He ran the house and put up with Ivy's irritability at his incompetence. He resisted all efforts to appoint a housekeeper and only grudgingly accepted the council's home help. Sid was patient, thoughtful and he kept his fears and his grief to himself. During the final year of the illness Ivy was having radiation therapy and drugs together. She became thin, her hair fell out and then started to grow again. Sid's shoulders began to bow. His expression set in a curious way – he began to look patient and gentle, serious. Molly, watching him one day, remembered the face from childhood, when he would come in from work and sit down, tired, and help Shirley build her bricks into a big house, or help her re-dress the doll she had just stripped. Sometimes she would sit on his knee while he read her the comic strips in the *Daily Mirror* – Garth, Molly suddenly recalled, had been Shirley's favourite.

Ivy's illness affected Jack worst – or at least, it led him to behave worse. While Molly and Shirley went frequently to Beckenham, bringing things to take Ivy's fancy – special soaps, or flowers, or titbits for her to eat – and also tended to bring cooked foods so that Sid would have less to do, Jack came less often, and never without his wife, Helena, who made Ivy feel uncomfortable. "She makes me feel common," was how she put it to Shirley who replied, "Well, Mum. You are, to her – we all are." And Ivy said to this that they might be but it was wrong to make them feel it. But Shirley confided to Molly that she thought Helena had spent so long doing programmes on the unfortunate – the poor, people with crippling diseases, the parents of children in care – that she was treating her mother-in-law as if she were the subject of one of her programmes. "She's like a social worker," Shirley reported. "She keeps on asking Ivy how she feels and I know she means 'Tell me how you feel about dying.' Of course Ivy just stares at her – she knows there's something wrong but she can't work out what it is."

"It's all problems these days," Molly said. "You know – everything in life turns itself into a problem – how to adjust to marriage, how to get over an abortion – Helena says Ivy's got to come to terms with death. So all the time she's there she's secretly trying to find out what progress she's made. No wonder Ivy feels uncomfortable."

"I hope they let me die in peace," Shirley said. "The whole time she's here she's looking like one of those relations who come round to spy out what they can get when the last breath leaves your body. Only she's getting it beforehand – information, a human problem. She's ghoulish. I wish Jack'd leave her behind when he comes."

"He's too frightened to come by himself," Molly said. "It's different for you and me – women can take these things."

Josephine came in on her last words. She was now a tall, beautiful woman of twenty-eight. She lived in Kensington with an actor who was more out of work than in it and seemed to do very little when he was unemployed. Josephine herself was away a great deal. She had a job which involved collating and editing material on the third world for a Sunday newspaper. She was in touch with radical groups all over the world and Molly was always afraid that her bold daughter would end up in jail in Bolivia, South Africa or Thailand. All Ivy ever said was, "What did you expect? Did you expect her to settle down in the civil service – she's your daughter, after all."

"She does it all for arguments," Molly protested. "Like exposing multi-nationals or women's rights – I never had a principle in my life. Wouldn't know one if it jumped up and bit me."

"Now you know what it's like," Ivy said in a satisfied voice. "Sitting in bed at night and wondering what your daughter's up to now. Mind you," she added, "I don't like the sound of the fellow she's living with. He's doing nothing while she's racing round these famines and wars."

"I hope Fred goes into a bank," replied Molly.

1980

In April, Josephine's wedding to James Kingsbury took place. Molly gave a party at Allaun Towers where, over the years, a precarious prosperity had been built up from the old ruins, though there was never a moment when Molly felt easy about the future. Nevertheless, as a hundred and twenty guests filled the drawing room, the dining room or walked outside, where a marquee had been erected on the lawn, the situation looked respectable enough. The day was bright. Waiters on the lawn carried trays of champagne. Everyone came – actors and journalists, friends of the bride and groom, the men and women from the Framlingham factories and Evelyn and Frederick Endell, who had always been fond of their step-grandchild. Simon Tate came, accompanied by Arnold Rose – "He insisted, Molly," Simon told her unhappily. Jack's first wife, Pat, came with her two adopted children and a sober-looking official from the Docker's Union. Jack and Helena came with Jasper in a carrycot. There was a political argument at the back of the marquee between the two men in which Pat's husband-to-be accused Jack of going soft on the real issues. Molly saw Jack's face, which reflected apprehension about whether personal and political issues might get confused and lead to a fight, so she brought up Arnie Rose to talk to them. The atmosphere did not lighten for Arnie himself looked apprehensive. "Opinion in the police is beginning to turn against them now," Simon said to her. "The Rose brothers are done for."

"I hope no one's going to get arrested here today," Molly said. Beside her Richard Mayhew, who had been best man at the wedding, looked amused and said, "It'd add some drama to the proceedings." Molly looked at him. He was six or seven years younger than she was. She had not met him until James Kingsbury, Josephine's husband, introduced them just before the wedding. He was tall and had dark hair, a lock of which fell into very blue eyes, and Molly, who had not been in love for years, thought he looked more like a film star than a playwright and TV scriptwriter, which he was.

She smiled at him and said, "I'm praying nothing will happen – would you like another drink?"

"Not for the moment," he said.

"I think I'd better just pop in and see how my mother is," Molly said.

He came with her and they all sat by the drawing room sofa, where Ivy had been since early in the party.

"Lovely do," Ivy said to Isabel. There were groups all over the room, chatting. "Mind you, I thought Josie's face was a bit set during the wedding."

"Nerves, I expect," said Richard Mayhew. "I've been terrified, both times."

"I don't know," Ivy said. "Everybody gets married so much, these days."

Molly, who knew her daughter would not stay with her husband, said, "Oh, well – things have just changed, Mum."

"The men aren't what they once were," Isabel said. She was very grand in her navy silk suit. The rings still flashed on her fingers. She added, in an undertone, "I can't say the bridegroom looks much of a protector."

"She'll be looking after him," Ivy muttered back.

"All right until she has a child," Isabel Allaun said.

"If," Ivy said darkly.

"How are you, sweetheart?" came Charlie Markham's voice behind Molly. He ruffled her hair.

"Charlie!" exclaimed Molly.

"Tom invited me," he explained. "I thought – 'Good Heavens, Charlie. Surely you don't believe Molly's the sort to hold a grudge?'"

"I'm not too sure," Molly replied truthfully. "Still, now you're here, what about a drink?"

"I knew you'd forgiven me, really," Charlie said.

"Come over here," she said. "There's a buffet. Mum – Isabel – do you want anything?"

"I'll look after Ivy, dear," Isabel said kindly.

"Well, Charlie – this is Richard Mayhew – Charles Markham, an old and unsuccessful business competitor –" Molly explained as they walked away. "I see Lauderdale's taking a dive."

"I was lucky enough to get out in time," Charlie said. "Severed my connection a year ago."

"Typical," remarked Molly.

"I've been sneaking round the premises," Charlie said, stopping at the table and helping himself to a drink. "Looks very promising. Mind you this is the second shock I've had today –"

"What?" asked Molly in alarm.

"Well, the first is coming across Arnie and Norman Rose. Now, secondly, I find this isn't champagne. You want to have a word in the kitchen."

"Oh – the buggers," cried Molly. Richard Mayhew followed her to the kitchen.

"Did he say Arnie *and* Norman?" enquired Molly.

She picked up a bottle and examined it. "Thought only Arnie was here," she said to herself.

"If this is a Bollinger," Richard Mayhew said to the head waiter, "then I'm a Dutchman."

"A terrible mistake," said the head waiter.

Outside Frederick Endell, Sid Waterhouse and their five-year-old grandson, Frederick Allaun, were walking by the lake. From the edge of the lawn Molly saw his bright face.

In the drawing room, Isabel looked into the eyes of her old friend and enemy, Ivy Waterhouse, and said, "You should tell her."

"I mean to," Ivy said.

"You're ill, you know," Isabel said.

"Why do you think I'm thinking about it now?" Ivy said.

Isabel looked up sharply and said, "Tom – will you get us some more wine?"

Tom, near the sofa talking to a friend of the groom's, said, "Yes, mother," and turned back to the other man.

"Now," said Isabel sharply.

Tom, sulky, took the empty glasses.

Simon Tate surveyed the marquee, the guests, the waiters in their black coats and said, "What a success story, Molly. Marquees on the lawn. I say this – you never cease to surprise me."

"All right if it doesn't come on to rain," Molly replied. "And all that glitters, Simon, is not gold. Here –" she said, struck by the thought. "Why is Norman here? You only brought Arnie."

"He came under his own steam," Simon said. "And, between

ourselves, you'd better hope he and Arnie leave under it."

"Why –?" Molly said. "But if the cops are after them what are they doing here? Why aren't they in South America?"

"Because they think they're all right," Simon said. "The people prepared to give evidence against them haven't told them yet." He looked alarmed and said, "For God's sake don't tell them I told you. Or anybody."

"Hope they don't catch them here," Molly said. "It'll spoil the day."

Josephine, in the library, was telling her old friend, Barbara, "I think I'm going to Latin America for three months."

"You're not," exclaimed Barbara. "Just as you've got married."

"Too good to turn down," Josephine said.

"What does James say?" asked her friend.

"He doesn't know," said the bride.

On the marbled tiles of the hall, under the portrait of Sir Joshua Biggs, Simon Tate said to Jack Waterhouse, "Who's that fellow Tom Allaun's been chatting to all afternoon?"

"Actor friend of the groom's," Jack said. "There's another who's been trailing my sister about."

As Tom Allaun and the other man came through the hall they heard Tom say, "I'll show you the lake."

"I think it's love," said Simon.

"Does Molly know?" asked her brother.

"Just as well if he gets on with it," Simon said.

While in London policemen were staking out the homes of Arnold and Norman Rose, waiting for them to return. Arnie, at Framlingham, was puffing on a cigar and saying, "Good luck to you, Josie. And what are your plans now?"

"I'm going to Latin America," Josephine told him.

"Nice place for a honeymoon," Arnie Rose told her.

Josephine nodded.

By six o'clock Josephine and her new husband were on their way back to Kensington. Arnold and Norman Rose, in two limousines, were driving home into the hands of the police. Jack Waterhouse was sitting beside his wife, who was driving, thinking regretfully about his ex-wife and their two adopted children. His wife, Helena, knew what he was thinking and felt sad and angry.

And, as they travelled away from the wedding, Tom Allaun and his actor were together on Framlingham Station, waiting for the train. Beside the lake they had looked from the water to each other. The actor, Donald, had suddenly grasped Tom's upper arm and, as the other man started and trembled slightly, he said, "I want you to come back to London with me." And Tom had said nothing but merely nodded.

So an hour later, at five, just as Molly was waving off some departing guests, he had come up to her and, standing close, said awkwardly in a low voice, "I'm going to London. With Donald Jacobson. I'm sorry. It means you'll have to clear up without my help." Molly, who had retained the fixed smile on her face which she had adopted for the farewells, turned, suddenly sober, and told him, "All right, Tom. I can't say I blame you."

Tom had noticed her with Richard Mayhew so for a little while the couple stared, wearily charitable, perhaps even wishing each other happiness, until their gazes broke and Tom said, "I'll just go up and get my bag, then."

"All right, Tom," Molly said. "Do you mind going out the back way?"

He was surprised for a moment, until he saw another knot of people approaching to say goodbye. He nodded, then, saying, "Quite right. Might as well preserve the amenities."

"Story of our marriage, isn't it?" remarked Molly.

In the meanwhile, as the newly-married couple, the other guests, and even the bride's stepfather departed, Ivy Waterhouse lay resting on the specially prepared couch in the library. She looked out on to the piece of grass beyond the kitchen, watching the odd guests drift to and fro. Evelyn Endell brought her some tea and bread and butter saying, "They're all going now. Why don't I take your shoes off?" As she did so she asked, "Shall I stay while you have your tea? Or are you too tired for company?"

"Can I tell you something?" Ivy asked. "I want you to tell me what Molly will think."

"Of course," Evelyn said, drawing a chair close to the couch so that she could hear Ivy's weary voice. To give her a little time she said, "It's been a lovely day. And so nice to see that Josephine's grown into such a lovely woman. And Fred — oh, isn't he lovely? So handsome — whoever would have thought he would be like that?"

Ivy drank some tea. Her eyes rested on the round and sensible face of

Joe Endell's mother. "It was Isabel said I should tell you," she remarked.

Evelyn looked at her. "Are you sure," she asked, "that you should be talking and not just resting?"

"I'm weak, Evelyn," Ivy pointed out, "but I'm not rambling. I'm in my right mind."

The sun was low outside the window. Ivy said, "It's so nice here – the sun behind those trees far away. Just coming into bud." Then she said, "This concerns you in a way, Evelyn, with Molly being Fred's mother. You see," and she paused, "it's a hard thing to say because I've kept it locked up so long. She's not my daughter – Molly. She's sort of adopted."

"What are you saying!" cried Evelyn. "Where did she come from?"

Ivy, still looking out into the trees, said, "I'll tell you."

Fragments of the day continued. Sid Waterhouse and Fred Endell were gratefully drinking glasses of foaming beer in the kitchen while their grandson ate scrambled eggs at the kitchen table. Molly and Simon Tate were eating plates of chicken in the dining room while George Messiter, who had no head for strong drink, lay on the settle under the window with his eyes closed. On the lawn men were packing up the marquee. And Molly, with her feet on a chair said, "It's better if Tom goes. It's been a dog's life here for him." Richard Mayhew came in and said, "I'd advise you to count the undrunk bottles of champagne. They're hauling the stuff out at great speed." And Sam Needham came in, saying, "It's on the news – the police have picked up Norman and Arnie Rose."

But in the library Evelyn Endell was staring in horror at her friend, Ivy.

Molly was never told about the conversation between the two women. She was very busy, from then on, with the production of the Messiter. She was, moreover, in love with Richard Mayhew. And perhaps the main reason why she heard nothing about what had taken place in the library on Josephine's wedding day, was that from then on everything was overshadowed by the fact of her mother's approaching death.

Ivy no longer lived in the neat little house in Beckenham. Her home was now one room at a hospice which stood in wooded grounds a few miles away. The room, at an angle in the building, had windows on two sides which looked out into trees, now shedding their leaves. Ivy, very thin now, was afflicted, not by pain but by the incessant struggle of a body being fought down into death by an internal enemy. She was a country in civil war, where heroic last-ditch battles were staving off inevitable defeat. There were times when they all, even Sid, wished that she could die peacefully without the battles her own body was putting up and the reinforcements of trying medical treatment. But they recognized that as long as Ivy needed to maintain the fiction, which she did not herself really believe, that she was in hospital receiving treatment and not in a clinic, waiting to die, all these routines must go on.

Molly was sitting by her mother as she slept one afternoon, sadly remembering the old energetic set of the heavily-lipsticked lips, the heap of bleached hair and the often-terrifying vigour she had injected into her life when she was younger. And it was as she recalled the vicious tongue, the sharp blows about the head, the sudden, erratic kindnesses of hard-pressed Ivy in her slum, that her mother opened her faded eyes and said quietly, "Mary – I'm very ill."

"I know, Mum," Molly said, looking down at the gaunt face, which seemed to have no flesh on it. Ivy's eyes roamed the ceiling, then turned on her daughter. "Is Sid here?" she asked.

"He'll be here in a little while," she said. "Half an hour."

"He said I ought to tell you," she said. "Or he would himself. He wanted to – years ago – but I wouldn't let him. I'd been keeping it a secret so long –"

"Never mind, Mum," Molly said, wondering if perhaps the drugs her mother was being given were affecting her brain. "Never mind –"

A nurse put her head round the door. "Bedsores," she said boldly, willing Molly out of the room.

"Not now," Ivy said faintly.

"Five minutes," said the nurse, setting her pan on the bedside table.

"I'll come back, Mum," Molly said. Her mother's eyes followed her to the door.

Downstairs she rather guiltily got out her calculator and started doing some figures. She did not need the calculator for the sums were engraved on her brain. She had to expand again and she had to do it more legitimately this time. She must have a proper factory on the Atlantic coast. There were orders, now, from the USA. As they produced more Messiters the repairs, spare part business and distribution grew more complicated. They were outgrowing the premises in London and Framlingham. And she knew it would be impossible to stand still – they must either grow, or fade. And she had over five hundred people working for her now. She had found a factory, near Liverpool, and because it had gone out in a recent shower of bankruptcies the price was not high. But, again, she would have to pledge everything, borrow everything she possibly could, to start up. Would there be housing for the workers, if they decided to move with the business? Could they make enough in the first year even to cover the interest payments? And enough in the second to bite into the loan? And enough in the third and fourth to see the business profitable? And even if they could, was the venture worthwhile? Sometimes she thought she would rather leave things as they were or just persuade the other major shareholders – George, Wayne, her sister, Tom and Isabel Allaun – to sell up, take their money and run. The now-familiar figures jolted in front of her eyes. In the end, she thought, it was not an exclusively financial decision she was making – it was personal. The others wanted her to go ahead. Shirley was cautiously optimistic. But she alone had to decide whether she was prepared for further struggle.

She stood up and went back to Ivy. Slowly taking the stairs she thought, "And then there's the dress shops down in Covent Garden – the little brass and clockshop –" "If you hadn't this to do you'd be taking in stray kittens," Tom Allaun had said to her sourly while they were having coffee in a coffee shop in the West End after their visit to the lawyer. He was talking about the clockshop with the little brass foundry at the back, where she had installed an apprentice to the proprietor, who was an old man. "Oh," she said, "it looks stupid now. This ramshackle collection of businesses – outworkers, old clockmenders. But look at the alternatives – great big companies with top-heavy managements, shareholders, union interventions – they're like dinosaurs most of them. They eat too much, their brains are too small and they won't survive the hard times. I'm flexible – maybe that'll save us in the end. You don't have to worry, Tom. You're a lawyer and crime's one thing we won't be short of in the years to come."

Tom nodded. He and Molly were getting a divorce. He was living with his lover in a small flat in Lambeth. He was applying himself to the new job he had obtained. The couple had a large Airedale dog called Mr Brown – sometimes Molly envied them their happiness and quietude. Her own life sometimes seemed like a badly-tied parcel going through the post with a label on it bearing an address no one could quite make out. She asked Tom, "Is it all right if I go on using the name after the divorce? It's good for the export trade. The Americans love a lord."

"Of course I don't mind," he said. He glanced at his watch, "I'd better be getting back." He looked at her and said uneasily, "You're looking well. I hope you're happy."

"I'm happy," she said. "I can tell you are."

They parted, he to go back to work and she to go down to Framlingham.

She remembered this as she mounted the polished stairs to the room on the first floor where her mother lay. She and Tom might have separated to go on different journeys, she thought, but there would be no more for Ivy, except the one which took her out of the world. Her mother lay flat in bed with her eyes closed. The nurse's five minutes would have tired her. As Molly sat down she asked, "Mary? Is Sid here yet?"

"No, Mum," she said. "He'll be along in about fifteen minutes."

"I thought it was nearly time," Ivy said, in her weak voice.

There was something in her face which alarmed Molly. She said, "I'll ring up just to make sure he's on his way."

"Don't disturb him," she said faintly.

Molly went to telephone Sid. She said, "Haven't you left? Mum wants you."

"I was on my way out," he said. And immediately asked, "Is she worse?"

"I don't know – she keeps asking for you," Molly told him.

"I'm on my way," he said.

Molly went back to Ivy's room and sat down. "Sid's on his way," she said.

Ivy sighed. "On his way," she muttered. Then she said, "That thing I wanted to tell you –"

Molly said, "Yes."

"Prop me up," Ivy asked. The tired voice was urgent.

Molly very carefully drew her frail body up the bed. She could feel Ivy's sharp elbows and shoulder blades. She was secretly afraid that she might break one of her bones. Finally Ivy was propped up against two pillows, resting against a frame at the top of the bed. She shook her head in bewilderment at her own frailty. She turned her head towards Molly and said, "I'll say it straight out. You're not my daughter."

"Mum?" said Molly. She stared at the wasted face. It must be a delusion brought on by the drugs she was being given, she thought. But what a horrible fantasy. She felt hurt that now, at the last moment, Ivy's brain had produced a dream, a nightmare, in which she rejected her.

Ivy nodded her head slightly from the pillow. "You think I'm losing my mind," she said. "But it's true."

Molly, not knowing what to think, drew a deep breath and answered, "If it is true it doesn't matter. You've been my mother – a good mother. That's what really matters."

"I hope so," Ivy said. "I've tried. But sometimes, with what's happened to you, I thought you could have had a better life somewhere else."

"I'm all right. I'm fine," said Molly in bewilderment. At that moment it did not really seem to matter whether Ivy had adopted her or not. The present was too important. Every moment took Ivy closer towards a mystery – Molly felt it now, hovering about her. She knew Sid had felt it, and Shirley. There was little room, here, for the past or the future. Time had stopped. She said, "Don't worry, Mum. I'm content with everything. Tell me what you like but don't tire yourself. Mothers are the people who bring you up – you were Josie's mother too, most of the time. You took her in when I was fit for nothing. You saved her."

"She's a lovely girl," Ivy said.

"Thanks to you," her daughter said.

"I don't think you believe me, Mary," her mother said, and it may have been the way in which she persistently called her by her old name, the name she had had as a child, which made Molly wonder if what she said was true. Ivy said, "Tom Totteridge found you in a bombed building and on the way down the street Sid met him. He had you on the cart. He just took you up in his arms and handed you down, a little girl, with golden curls, all filthy from the fire. There wasn't anybody about."

Molly gazed at her mother in horror. "Sid brought you home to me. I'd lost my baby, on account of the bombing. A bomb landed nearby and blew me over. I got up and started to come home but I fell down in the street – a man had to carry me to hospital. The roads were all blocked. And then I nearly died and after that I think I went a bit mad. I kept on hitting Jackie, poor little mite, and in the end they had to take him away from me. He stayed with my sister. I wanted a girl, see, and

544

this baby would have been a girl. I was beside myself. I didn't know what I was doing. And they didn't have these drugs in those days. They couldn't do anything for you. Old Tom knew how I was. He found me in the street one day, crying, and brought me home. He saw Sid, that early morning when there was nobody about – I suppose he thought it'd help." She paused, "After that I was all right. At first I thought you was mine, the little girl I wanted. Then I came round and I knew you weren't." She was staring forward now, talking as if to herself. "But no one came forward to claim the other one. So I kept you."

Molly's head spun. The other one. Oh, God – the other one, she thought. And remembered what Peggy Jones had said in the Kilburn pub. "It was the girl who'd been screaming and crying. . . he was lying on top of her but her face was free . . . the bed on fire and their dead mother lying on it . . . he asked the boy who he was but he couldn't speak." She murmured Peggy's words, "Let's hope they never knew how bad it was." Ivy, very tired, asked, "Who?"

"The children," Molly answered, scarcely knowing what she was saying. She knew she must respond to her mother's story without telling her the whole truth. How could Ivy ever forgive herself for what happened later? And yet she could not think what to say, how to act. Ivy had told her the secret she had kept for so many years – now she must keep the secret beyond the secret. The atmosphere in the room was heavy now, full of death. Molly herself struggled to get some air into her own lungs. Finally she said, quietly, "Thanks for telling me, Mum. But, like I say, I'm still your child. The past is still the same –" and then, trying not to cry she said, "it doesn't matter. It doesn't matter. What difference does it make?" And added, "You saved me from the orphanage – it was the same as the way you saved Josie –"

She knew she was tiring Ivy, who lay leaning against the pillows, after her confession, as if she were completely exhausted, her eyes open and unblinking. Molly felt the contrast between her own human vitality and her mother's body, from which the spark of life had almost gone. And Ivy lay back, drugged and dying, seeing Lil Messiter walking up Meakin Street towards her. It was a sunny day and Lil was wearing a cotton dress with flowers on it. "Hullo, Lil," said Ivy. Molly leaned forward in her chair to catch the mumbled words but she could hear nothing. Lil smiled at Ivy. "Hullo, Lil," she said again.

The door opened. Molly turned at the sound and put her finger to her lips. Then she shook her head, sadly. And she mouthed at him, "She told me – about you getting me off Tom Totteridge's cart." She smiled. "Nice bargain off a rag-and-bone man. Tell her when she wakes up — it doesn't matter." She stood up and kissed him and left the room quietly. But Sid was behind her in the corridor, "I told her," he said. "Told her time and again you should know. She was like a madwoman on the subject — a madwoman, I'm telling you. Like she was with the Flanders' when Jim died. That was when it all came back to her — You should have known before."

"Doesn't make any difference, does it, Dad?" Molly said. "Children are who you bring up, that's right, isn't it? Doesn't matter where you get them from — it's who you bring up."

He nodded at her and said, "I'd better get back inside."

Molly walked swiftly down the corridor. She saw the nurse who had attended to her mother earlier.

Molly said, "She's looking very weak. Can you tell me anything?"

"She's happy," said the nurse. "That's the chief thing."

Molly asked her directly, "How long will it be?"

"You can never tell," said the nurse in her professional voice. "The main thing is that she's happy and comfortable —" But there must have been something in Molly's expression which commanded a less brisk approach. She broke off and said, "Not long now."

"Is it days?" asked Molly.

She hesitated. "I don't think it will be days," she told her.

"Thanks," Molly said.

She met her brother Jack coming through the swing doors into the reception area. He looked at her in fear as if she might be bringing the news of Ivy's death.

"Hullo, Jack," she said. "I thought you weren't coming till tomorrow."

"I had an impulse," he said. "I came straight on from a meeting. How is she?"

"Pretty bad," Molly told him. "I talked to the nurse — she said it would be soon. Not even a few days, she said."

Jack sighed. "I must have known it," he said. "Are you going to ring Shirley?"

"No point yet," said his sister. "Do you want to come and have a cup of tea? Sid's up there and she's half asleep."

They sat in two chairs and drank their cups of tea. Jack looked hopeless. Molly said, "She's in no pain."

"Going though, isn't she?" Jack said. He burst out, "What did she do to us? We're a restless lot, aren't we? You've been married too many times and now you're making bikes. I'm in the House of Commons waiting for the revolution – even Shirl's married to a Chinese, now, and she was the quiet one. Why aren't we living quietly in nice semis with steady jobs?"

"Well," said Molly. "It's partly Ivy but it's partly that we were the revolution – we were post-war kids. We had all this free orange juice and opportunities. Not that Ivy didn't stir us up – it must have been all that yelling and screaming."

"Must be some funny genes somewhere," Jack said.

"Speak for yourself," said Molly. "I've got news for you. I'm not your sister. Added to that, you're not my brother. They picked me off a bomb site and took me in."

Jack looked at her, wondering if she were trying to make a joke. "Ivy told me just now," she said.

"It's a fantasy," Jack said. His face fell. "Just a minute," he said. "That's right. I was staying with Auntie Win. They told me I had a new sister. When I came back there you were. I can remember you now – you were standing up sucking your thumb."

"Didn't you ask why I wasn't a baby?" asked Molly.

"I might have done," Jack told her. "They clouted me for my pains. I was only a small kid – I seem to remember saying 'Why isn't she a proper baby?' and Sid belting me." He looked vague. "I wonder if that really happened?" he asked himself, then said, as if she had accused him of something, "You know I've got no childhood memories, Moll. I went through half the Blitz and I can't remember a thing. I can dimly remember being locked in the coal cellar by myself and thinking I'd never be let out. But, even then, Ivy swears she never did it to me so I don't know if it really happened." He said, "Do you want another cup of tea?"

When he went to get the tea Molly sat and stared at a couple in the corner. They spoke quietly to each other. The woman said something, angrily, to the man. Jack came back and put the tea on the table between them. "I must say, Molly," he told her. "It's a ridiculous story. I could be expected to forget but what about the others? Are you telling me they picked you up and brought you home and no one knew? What about the other people in the street? What happened to the baby Ivy was expecting? I still think she's made the whole thing up. It's dreadful – like dredging something out of her subconscious – frightening."

"It doesn't matter anyway," Molly told him. "I believe it – you don't have to. You see," she said, "it happened in a war. The men were away fighting. The women had jobs and kids and the whole place was being bombed to smithereens. And Ivy miscarried – she was off her head – that's why they gave me to her, like you give a new doll to a sick child, so I daresay anyone who knew would shut up about it, for Ivy's sake. You know what they were like in Meakin Street. The neighbours could be nasty but they had their limits, like never letting on anything to the landlord, or the police – maybe this was one of the things where they'd stick by you and what with that and the confusion I suppose a lot went by the board." She thought for a moment and said, "I bet that was why Mum let Elizabeth Flanders treat her like that after Jim died. She was afraid Elizabeth would lose her head and make a scene, blaming me, and shout out in front of the neighbours that nobody knew where I came from."

"I don't know what to think," her brother said. "I don't know what scares me more – the way Ivy's having delusions or the way you're believing her." He studied her closely, as if checking her for signs of instability.

"Doesn't matter, Jack," she said. Her attitude seemed to satisfy him that she was, indeed, not responding normally. He evidently decided that she was under too much strain for he patted her arm and said, "Do you want to come back with me to Pimlico – drive back to Kent in the morning?"

"It's all right," said Molly. "I'm fixed up in London for the night."

He nodded and stood up. "I'll go and see Mum, then," he said.

Molly, who had no arrangements to spend the night in London but dreaded her sister-in-law's sympathy, took a chance and telephoned Sam Needham, who offered her a bed.

And so Molly was in bed at 19 Meakin Street, where she had grown up, where she had lived with Joe Endell and conceived his child, when the telephone rang at three thirty and Sid told her Ivy was dead.

She had fallen asleep knowing that in all probability Joe had been her own brother. For if Ivy's tale was true – and it was corroborated by what Peggy Jones had said, and by the papers Evelyn Endell had left her – then both she and Joe had been found in the burning house at the top of Meakin Street and although she could not assume that they had been brother and sister it was very likely. The thought, strangely enough, did not worry her. If she still felt she was the child of Sid and Ivy Waterhouse, no matter who her real parents were, then, by the same inner logic, she felt she was the sister of Jack and Shirley and not of Joe Endell. The rest was a technicality, a bit of the past which had no real meaning. The important thing had been her marriage to Joe, not the birth certificate which connected them. Thinking this she fell quite peacefully asleep until the telephone rang in the hall and woke instantly, knowing what she was going to hear.

Sid sounded quite calm. He said only, "She's gone, Molly."

"Oh, Dad. Dad," she said.

"It was quite peaceful," he said. "She came out of the coma she was in and she knew what was happening – I think she did. She sent you all her love and she said goodbye –"

Molly stared at the telephone, the digital phone book which lay beside it, the pair of gloves on top.

"It's not fair, Dad," she said. It was still hard to realize Ivy was really dead. You won't see her any more, she told herself. It's all wiped out now, the body and the whole person. She said, "Shall I come? Do you want to come here?"

"I'm tired," he said. "I'm going home to sleep for a few hours. When I've phoned Jack."

"I'll come over early in the morning," said Molly.

"I'm glad it's happened now," he told her. "She was worn out. The fight had gone on too long. It had to happen. I'm glad, for her sake, it's over. It's not a shock – I faced it already, over and over, in my mind."

"She's released, now," Molly said. "I'll see you in the morning, Dad."

Now she sat down in the sitting room and breathed heavily in and out, as if she herself had been threatened with death. And she felt empty. She could not even cry.

They took Ivy back to the West London Cemetery for the burial. It was a cold November day. There was not a leaf on the trees as they drove through mean, drizzling streets. Richard Mayhew sat in the car with Molly and put his arm round her. Fred sat opposite her, very close to Josephine.

Miles and miles of tombstones surrounded them as Ivy's coffin was lowered into the grave. They all walked away, knowing they were abandoning her, alone in the ground.

Halfway down the path Molly caught up with Sam Needham and his wife. "Thank you for coming," she said.

"We suddenly thought we wanted to," he said. "She was a good

549

woman, your mother. It wasn't easy to bring up children in Meakin Street."

"That's the point," Molly said on impulse. "She did that but before she died she told me I wasn't her daughter. She said an old man found me in a bombed building and took me to her and Sid."

He paused and said, "I heard a story like that from an old lady once – but I thought it was about Joe –" His voice trailed off. He stared at her. A sharp wind hit them, bringing tears to Molly's eyes.

"That's the trouble," she said, "I think there might have been two of us."

Sam took this in. His face altered. "Oh, Christ Almighty," he said. Then he looked at his wife, who seemed not to be listening. In a low voice he said to Molly, "Better keep quiet about this. I'll make enquiries but are you sure you want to –"

"Yes," Molly said firmly. "I've got a feeling – it was like Ivy's last message to me. She wants me to find out what there is to know."

"All right," he said quietly. "There might be a couple of people who know something." And, as Jack and Helena came up with Richard Mayhew he said to Jack, "Hope you didn't mind us coming on impulse, Jack. Your Mum will be missed."

"We're going off to get something to eat now," Jack told him. "Will you come?"

It did not help that the ceremony had been so small for later Molly woke up in bed at Framlingham and wept, thinking that they had shunted Ivy away quickly and left her behind. In the end she got out of bed, rather than wake Richard, who lay peacefully asleep with his rather long, dark hair spread out on the pillow. She felt very far away from him. He was five years younger than she was but, she could not help thinking, fifteen years younger than her in experience. It was funny, she thought, that he was meant to be a playwright and ought to understand things – yet someone much younger like Josephine or Wayne seemed to have more grasp of real life. How could he understand about Ivy, she wondered, going downstairs in the darkness? He had spent his life at schools, universities and then mixing with the people he had met in those places. He couldn't understand Ivy, who had had almost no education, who had spent her life dealing with circumstances beyond her control, whose only epitaph at the end seemed to be that she had clung on, reared her children, looked after Sid and caused no tragedy or disgrace to herself or the family. Yet, poor and encumbered, she had taken in another woman's child, scraped up money for food, smacked her, cleaned up, shouted, worried and loved. And she, the greatest complainer of them all, had never complained about that, or felt hard done by nor, even when Molly's life was at its worst, had she allowed herself to declare that Molly's behaviour was not her responsibility, since the girl must have bad blood in her. And after Molly came her daughter – Ivy had spent years of her life providing cough mixture, clean clothes and meals for a girl who was not her child, and her daughter, who was not her granddaughter. She had been good, Ivy, her daughter decided. She had no halo, her expression was rarely placid or saintly but she must have been good, or why should she have done what she did? Richard didn't seem to see things that way, thought Molly and, as the wind roared round Allaun Towers, she sat and wept for her mother.

Two small grey-haired old ladies, arm in arm, helped each other up the hill to the chapel of the abbey of Poulaye-sur-Bois. One of them, smelling woodsmoke on the chill, early air, suddenly remembered a still-smoking house, the back a pile of broken, blackened bricks in the yard, the parlour full of sodden, black furniture, the staircase collapsed, remembered being lifted from the iron bedstead upstairs under a shattered roof, open to the blue, calm sky. The old woman breathed the clear air of France, took in the acridity of smoke, remembered the foul stink of a burning slum and the terror of war.

Molly, still hesitating about opening the big factory up North, was looking up at the London sky through the holes in another roof and said, "Cost too much to repair, Mr Donelly, with labour costs the way they are. And it'd take someone with bigger resources than me to put this neighbourhood on its feet. Look at it."

From the upper window of the ruined factory, where once they had made parts for mangles, vacuum cleaners, railway trolleys and lifts, they could see, opposite, small terraced houses, backed by the giant skyscrapers of the council estate behind. Five of the houses opposite were shops. Only two of the big windows of the lower storeys were lighted on this dark, November afternoon. In one there were displays of disposable nappies and cameras. In the other, displays of bottles of wine and spirits. The off-licence window was covered by heavy wire mesh. There was no one in the street.

She said, "Sorry – but who could tackle it? No shops, council flats full of hooligans and vandals – would you want to live here if you had kids or you were old? You'd be locking yourself in here at six at night and never opening the front door. And if you had premises here you'd have constant trouble and you couldn't leave your car in the street. You'd spend a fortune in guard dogs."

Donnelly, a short man in a striped shirt, said in his upper-class voice, "You've done it in other places, Lady Allaun."

"Yes," she said. "But what happened here was a disaster. Two thousand jobs lost by the tyre factory shutting – everything else goes with it. I can't reclaim the area by opening up on a small scale."

A woman came along with a child in a pushchair. She turned into the chemist's. "The woman's frightened, you see," she said. She sighed, "This neighbourhood's too big to fight. It needs GEC or a big power station opening up –"

He said, "I don't think this situation is permanent."

As she stood beside him in the window she felt tired. The country seemed to be lying under a dark cloud of inertia, as it had once lain under the dark cloud of its own factory smoke. Sometimes she felt the despair pulling her down with it. The presence of thoughtless optimists like Donnelly did not help.

She said simply, "There's a lot of misery about," and turned to walk out.

Donnelly came behind. She could feel his admiring regard on her back. She was collecting, she knew, more admiration these days, as one of the few expanding industrialists, than she had as Mary Waterhouse, murderer's widow, Mary Flanders, gangster's moll – the world, she thought, forgot quickly when it wanted to.

As they got in the car she said, "I'm sorry to have wasted your time – I had a feeling it might be like this. I had to see for myself."

"Not at all, Lady Allaun," Donnelly said politely.

"Could you drop me off at the end of Meakin Street?" she asked.

They needed a West End office, Shirley had said. No business could run from Framlingham, where the telephone connections were unreliable and clients had either to be met in London, or drag themselves to Kent in order to do business on a personal level. Molly responded sharply that she had seen enough West End offices at God knew how many thousands of pounds a year per square foot, crammed with men in suits exerting executive privileges and typists tending potted plants. She added that such a building could ruin any business.

So they had turned the ground floor at Meakin Street, with an extension at the back, into a small but efficient set of offices and retained the upstairs as a small flat. Shirley and her new husband, Ferdinand Wong, lived a few miles away. Wayne, who had married a local girl, lived very smartly in a purpose-built house just outside Framlingham. Any racist feeling there might have been once about the marriage had been subdued in the face of Wayne's income and position as manager at Framlingham and was probably now forgotten. His children went to the village nursery because, as Molly had told him, "When we came here, with no nighties or knickers and our heads full of nits, we were as black as you as far as the locals were concerned. But it all blew over for us, just like it will for your kids." Because of the other black workers who had married and moved to Framlingham, sociologists from Sussex University had come down to study racial tension in the village, and gone back concluding that villages were different from cities since the worst incident reported had been the attack by one of the black workers' wives on the manager of the small supermarket, who was a Bengali.

Molly, who had insisted on being dropped outside the Marquis of Zetland, walked slowly up Meakin Street towards the house. She had seen Donnelly's respectful appreciation, even as she got out. She was in her middle forties now, unlined, tall and strong. She wore a blue suit with a wide skirt, boots and a knitted pink hat like a beret. And, as she walked to the house through the afternoon gloom, thinking "It'll have to be Liverpool," she saw Johnnie Bridges waiting for her in the rain, outside the front door, heard him saying, "Moll." That night she had been the barmaid at the Marquis of Zetland. Now, with the computers inside, waiting for her, she felt the whole weight of Allaun Towers, the businesses, the family responsibilities, pressing down on her. "You chose it," she told herself.

Inside she said to the man behind the desk. "Anything up?"

"Nothing much," he said. "Only there's a man called Sam Needham waiting upstairs. Said he was an old friend. The Liverpool people want to talk to you urgently."

"I'll see Sam first," she said, and ran upstairs.

"Sam!" she said, going into the sitting room, which overlooked Meakin Street. "Is that a cup of tea?"

"Freshly brewed," he told her.

"Wonderful to see you," she said. "What do you think of the office?"

"They should have you at Transport House," he said. "I see brother Jack's shadow Minister of Defence."

"Don't talk to me about that lot," Molly said. "They're forever standing in the way of good, dodgy businessmen and women and then whining about industrial collapse." She handed Sam a cup of tea. "We'll never agree on that," Sam told her. "All you are is a capitalist. I don't deny you do your best but if you don't conform to the regulations no one else will. There's a fine line between benevolent capitalism and exploitation. Anyway, I came here to give you a shock."

"Impossible," declared Molly, sitting down. "But you can try."

"It's about the kids in that bombing," he said. "I talked to an old lady in the council home – she heard a story from Lil Messiter when she was drunk. Lil was, I mean. And what she heard was that the old rag-and-bone man did meet Sid in the street and give him a little girl. And there was another child, a boy, which he took round to the orphanage."

Molly, opening a packet of biscuits, said, "The people who lived in the street must have known this, some of them. Why didn't I ever find out?"

"Search me," Sam Needham said, taking a biscuit. "I suppose there was a lot going on in people's lives, then. And you got evacuated not all that time after, so when you and Jackie came back everyone forgot you weren't brother and sister. After all, there were men coming back from the war, there'd been bombing and moves and evacuations –"

"Yes, and after that, everything was gone over with a toothcomb," Molly said. "Who's baby was born ten months after the old man went away on active service – who'd acquired a pair of vases from somewhere they shouldn't – it went down to the last tin of black market corned beef and who'd been spotted in a pub up West with a GI. So why wasn't I included?"

"I expect you were," Sam said. "Only behind Ivy's back. You know what she could be like when she was roused."

Molly ate a biscuit and said, "I wonder who my Mum was? I suppose I could find out."

"The old woman said she was alive when they took her to hospital," Sam said.

Molly put the biscuit down. She stared at Sam. "Now you have shocked me," she said. "She could still be alive." She was silent for a moment. "Oh, my God," she said finally.

Sam Needham shook his head. "Don't start digging about, Molly."

554

he told her. "Think of the damage you could do. If she's alive she'll have good reason not to try to find you. And – well, God, Molly – supposing she confirmed you and Joe were brother and sister. Think what that means for Fred."

"I've thought," Molly said. "And I don't care. Why should I? Why should I? It was all a mistake. It makes no difference. What hospital did they take the woman to?"

"St Mary's," Sam said, "but I asked one of the members to see if you'd be allowed to see the records and the answer is no – there aren't any records. They hit the annexe they were kept in with a doodlebug in 1944. The whole lot went up – records stretching back ten or twenty years. There'll be no record of the woman's admission or what happened to her. She must have died afterwards, somehow. Be reasonable, Molly – she would have looked for her children if she'd lived. Once the police had started checking they'd have found Joe first and then you."

"Poor woman – no husband, no relations – no name," Molly said. "I wonder what it was all about?"

"There's one thing that will surprise you," Sam said. "The old lady said that Lil reckoned Ivy was sent money right up to when you went to Framlingham. Notes – in an envelope. No message. She thought it must be for you. She used to get you food on the black market with it. She reckoned it helped you and made everybody else's rations go further."

"I don't believe it," said Molly, eating biscuits. Now she remembered the illicit eggs Ivy used to give her.

"Apparently after that Ivy got suspicious and thought taking the money could lead to trouble. She got this suspicion – perhaps it came from crime, or she'd be asked to account for it one day. So when the payments started up again after the war she took to sending the envelopes back with "not known" written on the outside. But, you see, she was right when she assumed it was for you. Because the payments stopped when you went away and began again when you came back. Funny, isn't it? It must have been some guilty father, maybe a married man, trying to salve his conscience. Or maybe just a charitable eccentric who'd heard how Ivy took you in."

"You know as well as I do, Sam," Molly said, "that charitable eccentrics were in short supply round Meakin Street in those days. That street could've kept an army of them in charity, only funnily enough, all we ever got was the Salvation Army, when we were in luck.

I reckon somebody involved knew what happened." She paused. "I expect you're right about the guilty dad. I suppose she didn't say where the envelopes came from – the old lady?"

Sam shook his head. "If there'd been anything special about them I daresay Ivy would've traced the sender. It wouldn't be like her not to."

"Well," Molly said. "It may stay as one of the great unsolved mysteries of all time. I'm certainly not going to start a hue and cry straight away. I'll write it all down for Fred, when he's older."

"Best thing," said Sam. He stood up and put his cup on the table. "Thanks for the tea," he said. "I'd better push off – we're picking candidates for the council elections this evening."

"Thanks, Sam," Molly said. "Keep your mouth shut about all this, won't you?"

"Of course," he told her. He added, "I still miss Joe."

"So do I," said Molly. "I've never found out how to replace him."

Well, thought Molly, as she sat there alone for a moment. I've no kith and no kin and I've changed my name so often now I don't even know what that is. If Mary Waterhouse wasn't even Mary Waterhouse, then Molly Flanders, Molly Endell and Molly Allaun seemed even less her names than they had been before. It's enough to drive a woman mad, all this, she thought to herself, and went downstairs to dictate letters and examine the previous weeks' accounts, already scrutinized and annotated by her accountants, Shirley and Ferdinand Wong.

Later Richard Mayhew came in for supper. He had been at a rehearsal of his play at a theatre in Hammersmith. He was irritable and she was distracted. He told her about the botched rehearsal and then, as she said nothing, asked her, "Is something the matter?"

Sniffing, she said, "I suddenly wanted a slice of Ivy's bread pudding."

"Oh, my God," he said.

But Molly was thinking that somewhere she could have brothers and sisters, uncles and aunts, nieces and nephews, a whole tribe of them. The guilty father might still be alive somewhere. Not just my relations but Joe's and Fred's, she thought.

He said, "Get Shirley to make you some – Ivy must have handed her secret recipe down to someone. Then you can eat it or put a lump in each pocket to weigh you down when you jump in the canal." He was growing tired of her lack of energy.

He's gone off me, she thought, and I'm not surprised, because I think I've gone off him.

He had telephoned her the day after Josephine's reception and asked her if she would like to see his play, which was on at a theatre in Shaftesbury Avenue, and have supper afterwards. Molly had gone, although she found the play literally incomprehensible. There seemed to be a large cast of people flinging themselves in and out of a drawing room in a country house in the thirties, making remarks about others she had never heard of.

In the ladies room during the interval, she looked at the programme notes and read what his play was meant to be about. Embarrassedly, she rejoined Richard Mayhew and was obliged to tell him she really could not understand his play. "I'm very uneducated," she said. "I don't know who all these people are – the thinkers, I mean. But I can see the audience is enjoying it."

And he had smiled at her, turning his black-fringed blue eyes on her and said, "I'm sorry – I'm afraid I'm writing for a rather small number of people."

In the star's dressing room afterwards she had said, "Nice play, isn't it?" and the old actor had turned his ruined, drunken face to her and said, "Absolute pretentious rubbish, my dear." It was Christopher Wylie, she knew suddenly. She had not recognized him on stage, just as, she thought, he did not recognize her now.

"What are you in it for, then?" she asked, very amused, her mind going back to the old days.

"I'm keeping eight people," he told her, accepting a thick wad of notes from his dresser. "Second favourite came in at twelve to one," he said. At this moment in came Richard Mayhew, tall and slender, laughing. "If you ever get tired of him, my dear," he said to Molly, "remember, there are compensations to making an old man happy." Molly burst out laughing. She slapped him on the shoulder and said, "I'll remember."

Eating supper after the play with Richard Mayhew, Molly asked, "It's left-wing politics you're interested in?" It was more politeness than anything else – she was still amused by the encounter with Christopher Wylie.

"Roughly speaking," he said.

"Well what I was wondering," she said, "was how all those well-off people could come along and laugh and applaud. You see, where I come from there's working class, and they're Labour, like Jack, and there's upper class, and they're Conservatives. But these people dress Conservative and support Labour – don't they realize it's people like them who'll get hit in the redistribution of property and higher taxes and all that?"

"I don't think I can answer that," Richard Mayhew had told her. "But didn't you meet a lot of people like that while your husband, Joe, was an MP?"

"No," said Molly. "I didn't." She thought these were the kind of people Joe Endell had gone out of his way to avoid.

But the affair had begun gloriously. Indeed, for a fortnight, in early summer, Molly had forgotten the firm, the long-delayed question of whether to move to Liverpool or not, and had basked in the joys of long nights in bed with Richard and long days in the sunshine, meeting his friends, going to plays, relishing the irresponsible sense of being in love, in someone else's world. It was as she had gradually to resume her normal occupations, had met Fred from his camping holiday and taken him back to Framlingham, where Isabel had told her about the new window frames upstairs, which were beginning not to fit, had gone down to the warehouse in what had been Twining's field and noticed that sixty frames had been stacked outside for too long, because a consignment intended for Leeds had somehow not been despatched – it had been as these realities had to be dealt with that she had felt the first twinges of doubt about the affair with Richard Mayhew. He was giving up his flat in London so that they could live together at Framlingham. She began to think of the wife and children he had in Hove and wondered who, and what, they were. She quelled her doubts and went ahead. Now finding herself uneasily playing the successful woman, proprietor of a country house where weekend parties were given for artistic people. Isabel enjoyed it and Richard revelled in it.

She had begun the new factory in Liverpool only six months before and found the strain of constant entertaining tiring. Now she was relieved to be leaving for a weekend in Scotland, saying cheerfully as she skewered her hat on with a hatpin she had found in a cardboard box in Ivy's dressing table, "There's no doubt about it – I'm like Lazarus, rising from the dead, time and time again." She cocked her head on one side, gave herself a charming smile of encouragement and said wonderingly, "How do you do it, Lady Allaun? So beautiful, and so carefree, while all the time you've got a new factory in Liverpool about to be halted because of a strike and you're only a hundred thousand pounds in hock and if you don't sort it all out they'll soon be selling you up lock, stock and barrel."

"I don't know how you can face going to this place in Aberdeen," he said to her now.

"Be a nice outing for Fred," she said, ignoring his sulky tone.

"Well, I hope you enjoy the company of those who are bringing the country to ruin," he said.

"I'm getting used to left-wing denunciation," responded Molly. "It's water off a duck's back, now."

Looking at his handsome, gloomy face on the pillow she reflected that a smile from the face of a face-grinder of the poor might be cheering after the sad, puritanical expressions of Richard and her brother, Jack.

"Anyway," she told Richard, "there's a man there who might give me cut-rate on the new model bike engines if I put in a big enough order. So I suppose I'm going there partly for trade, as well as pleasure. That must make me a double villain. Still, that's nothing new."

"You're still keeping on those bucket-shops. Still employing black-leg labour – I don't believe it," her brother Jack had told her, only a few days before. "Even now you've opened the new factory you're still expanding these places."

"Look at the date on your calender," Molly said sourly, "October 1982. There's three million and over out of work. What's your answer? One thing's certain – *your* job's safe. When they start laying off MPs, amalgamating constituencies and so forth, come and call me a sweatshop owner."

"I suppose you're the Victorian dream the government has in its heart," Jack said.

"I hate politicians' dreams," Molly said. "I never have any myself."

"You're just a rudimentary economic organism," her brother said. "You adapt and survive."

"Like a rat, you mean," said Molly.

They were walking by the lake in the late sunshine. Saplings, surrounded by protective mesh fences, grew opposite.

"I'm a liar," Molly said. "This place was my dream – once."

Jack nodded. Fred, very blonde and ruddy in the face, came running up. "Richard just arrived," he said. "I'm going down to the village to play football."

"I hope he's in a good mood," Molly said, as they walked back to the house. "Don't start a political argument, will you?"

"All right," Jack agreed. "I suppose it's his artistic temperament which makes him so stroppy."

"Yes, and your political temperament," she said.

Now she went downstairs to make some coffee. Fred was in the kitchen, eating cornflakes. He was washed, dressed and packed. He was looking forward to the flight to Aberdeen. So was Molly, but felt gloomy about Richard. The affair had now lasted nine months. On their first night together she believed he was bringing back the body Johnnie Bridges had found, and lost. It was not the body which had been with Joe Endell, where sex had been confused in her mind with Joe himself, with their life, with the vibrant optimism and love he exuded. She had slept with Joe for twenty, thirty, a hundred reasons – to be close to him, to express love for him, to talk to him in another way. Their bed had been like a private club for them, in a world where otherwise there was little privacy. But with Richard, as with Johnnie, sexual feeling did not lead to any real ease between them. At first she had not understood this – but this morning, as she made the coffee, carried it up to the bedroom and sat beside the bed, still in her hat, drinking it with him, she understood clearly that they would never go any further together. He could give no more now, only take from her.

She sat under her hat, feeling glad to be going away, on her way to Scotland thinking about the new factory.

Before she opened it, George had been alarmed. "I'm not going up there," he had said. "They're savages."

Wayne, no keener than George on transplanting himself, had been more philosophical. "He thinks civilization stops north of Watford," he said. "So do you, really, Molly. But they brought us from Africa to the West Indies to cut cane and from the West Indies to London to work on the buses, so I guess we're easily moved."

There was some justice in the charge that Molly resisted the idea of leaving the South of England. But she said, "Thank God someone'll go. There's no point in bothering if I have to employ some gin-drinking overcharging manager, or a bright, ambitious lad full of ideas about how things have always been done, plus a pack of shop stewards who'll make sure even that doesn't happen. Give me all that, and we'll be out of business in three months. It makes my heart sink, all of it. I'm not sure I'm up to being the manager of a large British company. I don't think I've got the guts."

Shirley, who had come into the flat at Meakin Street where the matter was being discussed, had shrugged off her fur coat and said, "If you've any sense you'll go public. Start the factory and sell shares. Otherwise you'll be raising loans everywhere."

"Christ!" exclaimed Molly. "Now I've got the bureaucrats running a big factory, and the strikes on the shop floor and to crown all, a pack of shareholders to satisfy. You and that Chinaman must be secretly conspiring against me to make me bankrupt and put me in a mental home. It feels bad, Shirl, I'm telling you. It won't work. It's an idea that includes every fuck-up industrial system I ever heard of. Lazy managers, union trouble and a company owned by outsiders wanting fast dividends. Let's have a nice big board with plenty of lords and generals on it to finish the joke. Let's go one better – ask Charlie Markham if he's free to join. Then he can make a bundle on the side without giving a stuff what happens to the place." She added, "What's more I've had the housekeeper at Framlingham on the phone again. She reckons she's been looking after Brian and Kevin solidly for ten days and she's wondering when you're going to make an appearance."

"If you think this is any time to discuss who's putting the baked beans on the table," Shirley said loudly, "then I don't. All I know is that the strain of working this lot out is telling on Ferdinand and me, who, by the way, doesn't like being called a Chinaman, especially by his sister-in-law, and I'm telling you neither of us can go on keeping you out of trouble for ever. Put at least some of the business on a decent footing or we're clearing out."

"Clear out, then, you disloyal cow," Molly yelled at her sister.

"I'm going – don't worry," said Shirley and, picking up her coat, she left.

"Oh God," Molly said to Wayne. She hit her head with her hand. "Oh God – I'm done for if Shirley goes. She and Wong are the only ones who can make sense of it all."

"Trouble is, some of what you said is right."

"Trouble is, I can't go back and I don't want to go forward," Molly said.

"In that situation," Wayne told her, "you have to think of something else."

"Or you," Molly pointed out. "If you're going to be managing the place you've got to tell me what you want."

Wayne stared at her. "Give everybody a piece of the action," he said. "Best way to pull the team together is to make it pay to work."

Molly picked up the phone and dialled Shirley's number. No one was there. She said into the answering machine, "Wayne says we should think about a form of co-ownership, Shirl. Can you and me and Wong – and Wayne," she said, glancing at him "meet to discuss this."

Shirley rang next day and screamed, "It's never been tried – not properly. Start from stratch on an untried basis and the confusion'll be shocking. This isn't a solution – it's a cop-out –"

Molly's heart sank. There was some conversation in the background and Ferdinand Wong was on the line. "Get up there and talk it over with the union, Molly," he said. Then Shirley was back, "I'm coming with you," she said angrily, "to make sure you don't commit us to some stupid deal."

And now, before the scheme had even begun, a transport strike threatened.

Worry, worry worry, she thought, cheerfully applying scent in the now elegant bedroom at Allaun Towers. All plus a sulking lover. Leaving him half-asleep in bed she went downstairs and as she was drinking another cup of coffee, it crossed her mind that perhaps the situation between herself and Richard was not really his fault. Perhaps, over the months since she had met him, she had been too preoccupied with the business. He, the only child of devoted parents, was not used to taking second place to a bicycle factory. He might well be thinking of the actress, stage manager, script editor, who would understand his work, discuss it with him, perhaps marry him and make a home with him. She ran upstairs and kissed him, saying, "I'll ring you up when I get there." Nevertheless it was a pleasure to get out of the house where she felt disapproved of and take the shuttle to Aberdeen with Fred. Molly was very excited, perhaps more so than her son, who had regularly had holidays abroad with his grandparents. A chauffeur met them at the airport and drove over roads, and finally on little more than lanes, to the imposing house where they were to stay.

"Highland cattle," exclaimed Fred, looking on to a rugged field.

"Mr Monteith likes to keep some of them," the chauffeur said. "I hear there are two calves expected. Maybe you'll be here when a calf is born."

"I can help," he said. "I've done it before."

"I don't think," said the man, "that anyone but the vet and the head cowman will be let near the cow when she gives birth."

But as they arrived in front of the house a boy rushed through the garden, crying to Fred, "Come quickly, father says, and you can see the calf born." Turning to Molly he remembered, "Father says will you excuse him. One of the cows is calving."

"Right," said Molly, and as the two boys raced away she made her way up the steps. Donald Monteith's wife, Jessica, was in the hall when she arrived. Molly stared at the stags' heads mounted on the walls with incredulity.

"I'll show you to your room first," Jessica Monteith said. She was a tall woman with pale red hair. As they went upstairs she said, "I take it Willy found your son."

"They both dashed off," Molly said. "Is Willy your son?"

"Yes," Jessica said and as they reached a landing over which hung a large painting she walked a little way along a corridor and opened the door of Molly's room.

"We're in the drawing room. Do come down when you're ready," she said. "Your son will be upstairs in the nurseries, in the room next to Willy's. I'm sure he'll enjoy himself – all the toys are there."

After she had gone Molly stared upwards in amazement. The ceiling was painted all over, with men and women in eighteenth-century versions of Roman clothes. There were bulls and goats and swans. From the window she could see, beyond the garden, hills rising. And as she watched she saw two figures, her hostess's son and her own, running up through the grass. Halfway up they bent over, examining something. Molly combed her hair, washed her hands and put on fresh make-up. She left her hat on the bed and went downstairs. There were six people in the vast room, where logs burned in a huge grate. The walls were pale, a grand piano stood at the other end of the room. A great vase of pale lilies stood on a table. Windows on one side looked over the garden and out on to the hillside.

Donald Monteith, in tweeds, said, "It's not a beautiful house, architecturally, but we've lived here a long time and we come here whenever we can. Partly because I'm a sportsman when I get the chance."

Molly, who knew he spent most of his time between the City of London and Miami said, "Nice to have somewhere to go. What about the calf?"

"False alarm," he said, looking disappointed.

There were two other couples in the room, the Floyds and the Jamiesons. Mary Floyd, small, dark and pretty, said, "You live in Kent, Lady Allaun?"

"Sometimes," she said. "But I have to be in London a lot, too. The problem is that there are factories in both spots."

"Quite schizophrenic," said Mrs Floyd. Molly saw in her eyes that mixture of anger and pleading women frequently offered her. They felt

563

they had no reason to regret their lives, which were led around their homes and marriages, yet they wondered if they might be doing something else.

"Yes, it can be," Molly said to her dryly, thinking of her £100,000 debt and the threatened transport strike which would put her out of action.

"You're such a busy woman –" Harold Jamieson said, coming up to her with an odd look on his face, half afraid, half challenging. She knew he was remembering that her life with men had been a shambles and that half her business operations were dubious if not actually illicit. Well, she thought, she couldn't deny it. She looked at him, in his London suit, caught a glimpse of Donald Monteith, in his tweeds, and suddenly recognized Arnold and Norman Rose, standing with their glasses in their hands, at the bar of a drinking club in London. She smiled rather broadly and said to Jamieson, "I just make money selling bikes and I offer jobs to a few people and luckily, so far, I've never had to fire anybody yet – or only for pinching."

Jamieson, who had just closed a spares factory in Middlesborough and made 200 workers redundant, said "I pray you never have to. It's not a pleasant experience."

"On either side," Molly said.

"Let me get you another drink, Molly," Jessica said. But glancing at the doorway, where a woman in a green overall stood, she said, "Oh – well, lunch is ready."

She sat next to little Colin Floyd who said enthusiastically, "I've been wanting to meet you. I think this whole Messiter business has been a tour de force. I don't know how you've managed it."

He was a handsome little man, chief shareholder and managing director of a thriving electronics firm. She said, "I'm not out of the wood yet. I'm pretty worried about this transport strike."

"Aren't we all?" he told her. "It's easier for the Monteiths of this world. They have big interests abroad which cushion them. I'm a British businessman working exclusively in Britain. I have to deal with the many vagaries of British life. Still, cheer up, the strike may not happen."

"I've decided that if it does," Molly said in an undertone, "I'm getting the workforce to ride the buggers to the docks. They'll call me a strike-breaker, it'll embarrass my brother Jack no end – he's an MP – but my idea is that it's like the old notice in the pub. 'We have agreed with the bank that we will not cash cheques if they will not sell

564

beer.' See, if the unions don't interfere with me I won't interfere with them. The problem is, will the workers do it?"

"That's always the problem here, it seems to me," said Caroline Jamieson feelingly. "No wonder money's flooding out of the country. Are you interested in opera?" she asked Molly.

"Not much, I'm afraid," Molly said. "I've seen a lot of plays recently." For a little while they discussed the plays running in the West End until Monteith boomed across the table, "More wine for the Boadicea of British industry," and Molly said, "The trouble is, Boadicea got beaten."

"Well, my dear, I'm sure that won't happen to you," he said.

Colin Floyd turned to Monteith and said, "You know I've got a craving for a round of golf. I don't suppose there's a course near here."

"Straight in the car after lunch," Monteith said instantly. "What a remarkable thing – I was thinking along those lines myself." He pushed his glass back. "That's enough of that then. Did you bring your clubs?" he asked Floyd.

"Well, it just so happens that I did," Floyd told him.

"Good man," said his host. "Just the thing to put the ulcers on the run. Jamieson?"

"Try to leave me behind," said the red-faced man. And bang goes my chance of cornering you in the library or attacking you in the conservatory, thought Molly Allaun. Well, I'll nobble you yet.

So that afternoon Molly splashed and swam with the two boys in the water under the green dome of the swimming pool. Then Willy took her on a tour of the farm with its clean hay-filled byres, containing clean, fluffy cattle, and its neatly painted chicken huts outside which fat hens scratched in well swept runs. It looked almost like a farm set up for city children to visit on educational trips. Fred talked knowledgably with the farm manager and, carrying home two eggs from the hens, they all went back, the boys discussing their trips to Disneyland as they walked through the darkening formal garden where chill misty air hung over the clipped bushes and trees, which had been trimmed into the shapes of birds and crowns. Over supper upstairs in the attic rooms Fred decided that he would stay for a week or two. "Gavin will be needing help with the pheasant chicks," Willy said importantly.

"You haven't been invited and you have to go to school," Molly said. "And I'm afraid I can't spare the time to stay here with you."

There were ten more guests for dinner. They all sat round a big table in candlelight. Next to Molly was Colin Floyd. On her other side she had a neighbour of the Monteiths, Sir Graham Keyes. Molly, by now getting the shrewd impression that none of this dream of loch and glen was without commercial underpinnings of skyscraper and Concorde to New York, was not surprised to find the industrialist buried beneath the laird. "What am I doing here?" she thought in amazement, sitting in the light of candles in old silver sconces, with portraits of the Monteiths, one dating from the seventeenth century, on the walls around her. Glancing about her at the women's jewels, winking in the candlelight, and the solid faces of the men, she felt almost frightened, noticing that here all was not as it seemed, catching, occasionally, the gamblers' expressions, watchful eyes in seemingly relaxed faces. And the room filled suddenly, in her mind's eye, with the figures of the unemployed and hopeless, in their anoraks, faded overcoats, cheap shoes and old sneakers. They leaned against the walls of the room and against the old paintings. They were pale. I must be mad, she thought, hauling her attention back to Graham Keyes. He said, "There's only one flaw to my land – the moor's just enough tracks for cycles and it's just steep enough to make bicycling difficult unless you've legs like a marathon runner. So do you know what they do?"

Molly laughed and said, "They get little power-driven cycles –"

"Which scare the pheasants all over the place," he said. "I tried to ban them but, do you know, my gamekeeper caught two poachers the other day and that's what they were using – quick and easily man-oeuvred in the lanes, you see."

"I'm sorry," Molly said. She added, "I had a dream last night that they were soundless, sort of floating through the air."

"What's that?" he asked, "wish fulfilment or woman's intuition?"

"I don't know," she said. "What's your guess for the coming years – floating bikes?"

"Who knows?" he said and leaning across the table said, "Barnabas – what's your horoscope-Johnny give you as a prediction for the coming years? Lady Allaun would like to know."

"Wouldn't we all?" said Jessica Monteith.

The man opposite drank from his claret glass and said jovially, "He advises me to make sure I'm wearing clean underwear in case I'm run over crossing Piccadilly Circus and taken to hospital. Listen, Keyes, I don't pay a man five hundred guineas a year to tell you the future – just me."

Colin Floyd said, "Good God – you give him that? Is he worth it?"

"He is to me," he said.

"I just can't see you sitting in a flat in Cricklewood while some tatty character gazes into a crystal ball," Keyes said.

"Cricklewood?" the man called Barnabas replied. "He lives in Belgravia."

But Molly, drifting back into the dream where the room was filled with silent, watchful faces of the poor, began to think nothing was real, not the candles, the plates, the women's jewellery – nothing seemed substantial. Something's going to happen, said a voice in her head, and as she tried to contend with the expectation running through her, for no reason, she realized that Colin Floyd had broken off his sentence and that Jessica Monteith was standing at the table, trying to catch her eye while the other women had left and were drifting to the door. She realized that something Isabel had told her about was happening – the ladies were withdrawing.

In the drawing room Jessica told her, "It's absurd – we actually don't do it in London. Just while we're here. That's because half the time in London the guests are from America or other places where the custom died out, or never existed. The men are supposed to swap racing tips or whatever they do while we talk about our children and household management. I believe they sit there telling dirty jokes. I know we do, sometimes. Actually, it's rather fun, I think."

Feeling bullied, Molly said, "It's like what professional criminals do when they're planning their next job. They say, 'Why don't you girls step upstairs and try on each other's clothes while we talk some man's talk.' And the women all go out of the room."

There was a silence, broken fairly quickly by Jessica, who said, "Well, actually I think it's rather a nice old custom being maintained."

But she saw she had made the women feel gloomy and excluded, as if their dresses and jewels had suddenly become burkhas and leather nose pieces. Before she could make amends Jessica said into the small silence, "I was expecting Bert Precious, but he had to stay in London today. He's coming up by the shuttle tomorrow morning."

Graham Keyes' wife asked, "Is Corrie coming, too?"

"Oh no," Jessica said. "She's still in Canada."

"Looking after her father?" enquired the other.

"I gather he died," Jessica said. "But I think it was what happened to their son which drove them apart. So very sad."

"There's no reason for it," the other woman said. "Corrie and Bert

567

did everything parents could. It was exactly the same with the Fellowes family – devoted parents, a lovely, bright girl – such a useless tragedy."

"I blame the pushers," Mary Floyd said angrily. "They're responsible. And I just don't believe that enough's being done to track them down."

Molly felt removed again. She still saw, outside these windows, which were curtained, the crowd on the hillside. As she sat in the room with the other women, who talked of their friends and places she had never been to, she felt the gulf between herself and the other women to be very great. How could it be otherwise? It was not even a matter of background but of how she now led her life. She must seem to them very tough, almost freakish, doing the job most of them left to husbands, brothers and fathers.

Jessica moved across the room and turned on a lamp. "So peaceful here, isn't it?" she said, smiling at the silent Molly.

"Oh yes," she agreed, "very peaceful."

"These old houses are unique," Mary Floyd said. "It's partly the sense of one family having lived here for hundreds of years. Just imagine – one day, in due course, Willy will be living her with his wife and children."

"Yes," said Jessica, but Molly had the idea that small Mary Floyd's ebullience, born of what looked like a united marriage, did not strike all the women as being appropriate. Second wives themselves, some of them, they all knew that divorce and the birth of new children would result in their own evictions and the disinheriting of their children. Quite a nervy world, thought Molly, who in that sense had never had anything to lose.

And, again, came the sense of change coming, almost excitement which made it hard to concentrate, until, later, the men came in looking cheerful, and drunker than they had been at dinner. Jessica went over to her husband and put her arm through his. "You said not long," she told him. "And look how you've kept us waiting."

"We've bored each other sufficiently now," he said. "We join you with great relief." But Molly reflected that as they sat over the port they might well have been talking business. She badly wanted to talk to Jamieson about her bicycle engine but was beginning to realize that here was a world where men talked business and exchanged tips in clubs, changing rooms, after the ladies had left the dinner table – anywhere women were not admitted. But she was fighting, still, through the strange, dreamy state she had entered. After chatting for about half an hour she declared herself to be rather tired and went up to bed.

Lying in the silence, between linen sheets, she soon went to sleep. She awoke with the clear voice singing to her in French – "Comme le vent dans les blés de mon pays."

Next day she stood right at the top of the windy hill behind the house with Colin Floyd. On the other side of the hill the voices of the two boys came to them in gusts on the breeze.

"Phew," she said, for it had been a somewhat steep scramble. "Isn't it lovely?"

Floyd, also breathing hard, said, "Yes – perfect."

They sat on the grass in silence looking across the valley, where the house lay, and over the hills opposite. Down the valley, in a small plantation of firs, lay the waters of the loch.

"There must have been a farm here for hundreds of years, even before they built the house," Floyd said. "It makes me think how much I'd like to own a country house – but, of course, you do."

"I married into a collapse and turned it into a bicycle factory," Molly told him. "I'm not the sort you can trust to respect the past. I couldn't afford it, for one thing."

Floyd laughed. They sat watching the two boys, who were shooting at each other from behind hillocks.

Floyd stood up. "Bert!" he called, waving. "Bert! Is that you?"

The lean figure in a greenish tweed suit stopped on the path and waved. As he toiled up Molly saw he had a long, pale face and very large, hazel eyes. His eyebrows were strongly marked, although his hair was light brown. "Bert Precious," explained Floyd as he came up. "An old friend. Do you know him?"

"No," said Molly.

As he got to the top he grinned at Floyd and shook his hand. In some ways, she thought, it was a clown's face, long and mobile, expressing innocence. She felt she might have met him somewhere, but was not sure. He looked at her and smiled broadly as if, she thought, they really did know each other.

"Do you know Molly Allaun?" asked Floyd. "Molly – Herbert Precious."

Bert Precious was getting his breath back. "Phew," he said, "I'm out of condition. Is it wet on the ground?"

"Not very," Floyd said.

"Then – excuse me," he said, and sat down. He looked up at her. "I think we met once, at Frames Club," he told her.

"Ah," Molly said. "I met a lot of people then."

"I expect you did," he said drily.

She laughed and said, pointing upwards, "I know I'll never rest until I've got to the top of that higher hill, there."

"Come on, then," said Bert Precious, scrambling to his feet.

"Count me out," said Colin Floyd, sitting down.

So together Molly and Bert scrambled over rocks and rough ground to the top of the windy hill. They found the two boys playing there.

Bert looked at Frederick Allaun consideringly and said, "He looks rather like you."

Molly said, "I always think he looks like his father. Especially in the photographs when Joe was a boy."

She had not thought for some time about Fred's parentage, or her own, or Joe's. Now she did, and the notion made her grave. At the same time she saw Bert's eyes appraising her son and herself. "Perhaps you and your husband were alike," he said.

"Perhaps," Molly said, trying to throw off serious thoughts. But she said to herself – "Liker than we should have been." "Isn't it wonderful?" she said, taking in the large view and the huge, blue sky above them. When she looked at Bert, who was standing at her side, she noticed he was looking at her, and not at the view. Meanwhile the two boys, who had been playing a complicated game of cowboys and Indians, Scots and English, were shooting each other and falling over. Suddenly, with a cry, Fred fell over the edge of the hill. Molly and Bert both ran forward. The boy lay a few feet below, laughing into their alarmed faces.

"Ha, ha," said Molly. "Very funny I must say."

She turned to Bert but his face was still. She had learned the day before that his eldest child, a son, had died of a drug overdose two years before. She said suddenly, "Come on. We'd better go. It's time for lunch." They walked down the hill, with Colin Floyd. And Molly felt an internal stillness, as if there were a pause in time. She did not put it to herself that she was going to fall in love with this tall, long-faced man, whose features completely failed to conceal the movement of his thoughts and emotions. She did not tell herself this but part of her knew it was going to happen.

They walked across the formal garden, past the pool and the low hedges surrounding geometrical flower beds. Looking at a tree shaped like a peacock Bert shook his head. "Funny notion," he said, half to himself, "a French garden in Aberdeen."

They sat together at lunch, which was an informal meal with no placings. Jessica Monteith was not far off, next to Fred, who sat by his mother.

As he and Jessica talked she discovered that he was short of money. He spoke of selling his house and moving to a cheaper one. She discovered that his two remaining children, a fifteen-year-old son and a thirteen-year-old daughter, lived with him and that a daily housekeeper was in charge. She had the impression of a sad life which he accepted, barely knowing how sad it was, for he was not self-conscious. It also began to dawn on her that Jessica Monteith had her eye on him.

"The next time I'm in London, in a fortnight's time," she said, "I shall arrive on your step and sort you out, just as I did the last time."

"The last time you came the housekeeper resigned," Bert protested. "I had to talk to her for an hour to persuade her to stay. I should be very pleased to see you, as indeed I always am, but I'd be equally pleased if you decided you didn't want to count the sheets or look in the refrigerator. Your company is always welcome and quite enough in itself, Jessica. Don't think me ungrateful."

"Honestly, Bert," protested Jessica. "I don't know how you manage at all. And with the children at day schools — As a woman who's brought up a daughter, don't you agree, Molly?"

"I'm afraid I didn't bring her up. My mother did," Molly said. "I don't think I know enough about it."

"Well, you must all come and stay with us Bert, *en famille*, very soon. We'll be here for ages — what about Easter?" Jessica pressed.

"Simon and Anne are going to Canada at Easter," Bert said.

"Come alone then," Jessica said promptly. "Otherwise you'll be glooming about the house alone being bossed by that morbid woman you employ. Absolutely no good at all."

Bert Precious said, consideringly, "Thank you, Jessica. I'll certainly think about it. Then asked, "Donald! You think we can get a boat out and row to the island in the middle of the loch this afternoon?"

"If Ian'll let you," his host said. "Whenever I want one it's laid up for repairs or being repainted. But if you can get one, then do."

"I like rowing," Bert said to Molly. "Do you feel like taking the boys for a row — you'll let Willy come, won't you, Jessica?"

"I'll come as well," Jessica declared. "I hope you row well."

"No," he said. "Wear a mackintosh and gumboots."

"I'll bail," said Molly.

"You can swim, can't you?" Jessica asked her. "If you can't it really isn't safe."

Molly wondered if she was riding shotgun for her absent friend, Bert's wife, or if, as she supposed, Jessica had a fancy for him herself. She said, "I can swim."

"I've got certificates," Fred announced.

"All's well, then," said Jessica.

Molly had suspected Bert's claim to be a poor rower was a gentlemanly stance but once they were in the boat she realized that he had spoken nothing but the truth. The water with which he spattered them was ice cold, straight down to the loch from the hills. The wind was chilly. She finally cried, "Blimey! I can't stand this. These boys are drenched, Bert. Why don't I row?"

"Come and take an oar," he suggested.

Molly walked towards him across the lurching boat and sat down beside him. Sid, during their outings on the Serpentine and the occasional seaside holiday, had been a fussy oarsman, insisting on accuracy and correct strokes. They weaved across the loch until they arrived at the fir-fringed lochside. Fred jumped out in his gumboots to pull the boat in.

Molly jumped out saying, "Isn't it nice?" Jessica, whose approach to the expedition was more temperate, said, "It's a tiny island. You can walk to the other side in five minutes."

"I'm going to find Andy's grave," Willy cried out alarmingly. Fred ran after him into the trees.

"Who's Andy?" asked Bert.

"An old dog Willy remembers. We always bury the dogs on the island," she replied.

"Better than Meakin Street, where I grew up," Molly said. "People used to throw them in the canal."

The two boys came out of the woods and the grassy bank they stood on was full of the music of a tango.

"Willy!" protested Jessica. "Did you bring your radio with you?"

The boys were dancing in their gumboots. Bert Precious took Molly in his arms and they tangoed on the grass. He bent her over and gave her a kiss on the cheek. He straightened up and bowed and turned to Jessica. "Will you dance?" he asked.

"My card is full but I can make space for you," she answered.

As they moved off in the dance Jessica shot her a black look. This jockeying for a position with Bert Precious was the same as the rivalries between the girls in the old drinking clubs she had gone to with Johnnie Bridges, thought Molly. But the women had been younger and the price of failure higher – back behind the counter of a shop or straight on to the streets.

But as Jessica and Bert danced the music stopped, and the voice of the announcer took over. "So much for history, now for something closer –" The strange voice sang, "This town is coming like a ghost town – can't go on no more –"

"Turn that off, Willy," Jessica said impatiently. Molly, on the edge of the loch, was returned to the boarded up shops, the neglected look of much of her native city. She thought of the threatened haulage strike and said, "Can you walk right round the loch?"

"If you don't mind balancing," Jessica told her.

"I can balance," Molly said, still thinking of the haulage strike. If the first consignment of Messiters for the American market missed the boat because they couldn't get the machines to the docks the bikes would not be on the market for another two months. The lack of projected profits could mean no more credit from the bank. Materials could not be ordered – the factory could be almost at a standstill for eight weeks.

And so they all set off to walk round the loch. Sometimes they were on broad strips of grass, sometimes edging over the roots of trees close to the water. Molly slipped and got her foot wet. She said, "It's a shame it's too cold for swimming." To one side of them the clear water stretched away to the other side. On the other were thick pines, their needles littering the ground.

They sat down on the grass near the boat. The boys were among the trees. "Fred's enjoying this so much," Molly said to Jessica. "And so am I."

"It's very nice for Willy," Jessica said, "he gets rather lonely in the holidays."

"Good Lord," said Bert Precious, as the rain began. "That was quick. I wonder – is it just a shower?"

"Hardly any such thing here," Jessica told him. "Once it starts it persists, usually."

"Better all jump in then," Bert said. "I'll get the boys." Jessica and Molly stood in the drizzling rain until he came out of the woods with the two reluctant boys. They were protesting. "We were busy building a camp."

"Well, we don't want to have to come and sit in it for two hours till the rain stops," Molly said. "Hop in the boat."

Fred insisted on rowing them back, with Willy at the other oar. The rain poured down. Jessica put on a headscarf. Molly's hair dripped down her neck. They lurched back to the other shore and set off, drenched, back to the house. Going through the garden Jessica said to Bert, "Do you remember we looked for *Les Memoirs de Montespan* when you were here last – it turned up in one of the guests' bedrooms. Come to the library and I'll show it to you."

Molly went upstairs and lay down on her immaculate green satin bedcover. He's a married man, she said. Never mind if his wife's in Canada pretending to look after her dead father – she's doing that because their child died, and because a drug death always looks like a suicide, and when there's a suicide people blame themselves, particularly the parents, if it's a child. So if you butt in you're interfering with a married man, a grieving wife, two guilty parents – so what sort of a shit does that make you? Plus, she said to herself, Bert Precious is a gentleman, a real one, maybe the last one left in England. He's not Charlie Markham, or even old Monteith. He'll respect his marriage vows as far as he's able. Get mixed up with him and he'll take it hard. And just because you haven't had a holiday for years, she warned herself, don't start acting like a secretary on a two-week break in Torremolinos – you're too old for that lark. She told herself, too, that she had a bicycle factory to think of.

She stood up, changed her damp skirt, combed her hair, put on fresh lipstick and went downstairs. She stood in the entrance to the billiard room, watching Jamieson and Colin Floyd play. The game was ending. "All I can say, James, is damn you," remarked Floyd cheerfully, putting his cue on the table.

Jamieson lifted his cue, spotting Molly in the doorway.

"Fancy a game?" he said. "I'll give you some points."

"I'll take them," said Molly, advancing.

She was quite good, though not as good as he was. After a clever shot of hers he asked, "How did you learn all this?"

"It's true, what they say," Molly told him. "It's the sign of a misspent youth. I used to hang round a dubious snooker hall in the Edgware Road as a teenager. In winklepickers and a tight skirt," she added, to make the picture clearer. "Mostly, the lads used to play and us girls would hang around giggling and trying to attract their attention. But sometimes my boyfriend would wheedle me in for a few games. A year like that," she concluded, "and you were well away — some of those boys were dedicated, like saints." And the one that got me in on the games was hanged by the neck until he was dead, she added to herself.

"I see it all," Jamieson said. "You were the girl I used to wish I knew while I was sitting in the taxi with my luggage on the way back to school." He trickily potted six balls in succession. Molly said, "You're almost as good as Lester O'Dowd at Arthur's, Edgware Road, and that's a compliment."

As she bent over the billiard table he asked, "Tell me — have you ever thought of using our engines in the Messiters?"

Mary carefully potted her ball. At last, she thought, at last. She moved round the table for her next shot.

"It's crossed my mind," she said. "More than once." Her next shot went astray.

"Good," Jamieson said. "I'm moving in for the kill now. You can forget about Lester O'Dowd."

And at this point he began to win the game in dead earnest. At one point he put up his head and said, "We'll talk about this business in detail later, if you agree. I have to think in terms of whether it's worth retooling."

"My designer guesses it is," Molly told him. "That's to say, my accountant made the guess, after talking to the designer . . ."

"Messiter?" Jamieson said, "I hear he's not too well."

Molly, trying to produce a resistance to Jamieson's game, thought hard. She did not know if George was well or not. He had spent two years almost exclusively working on a project he would say very little about. Wayne, down at Framlingham, was, with his wife, virtually George's minder. George now lived with them because, as Wayne's wife said, "He's like a baby." The profitless two years were explained by his friend as research likely to lead somewhere. But plainly the word was out that George Messiter had shot his bolt, was, perhaps, unbalanced.

She straightened up and said frankly to Jamieson, "I don't know. He's a funny man. I have to let him go his own way but — I don't know —"

"You've got to watch these design Johnnies," Jamieson said, "or they'll have you believing reading the racing results is a creative pause.

– Well played!" he exclaimed, as Molly cannoned two balls into two separate pockets.

"Don't know how I did that," she muttered, going for her next shot and then missing it. As she unbent she said, "I think that George is all right."

She wandered, later, in the formal gardens outside the house, while the two boys watched TV with Mrs Mooney. Bert, so far as she knew, was still in the library with Jessica. She pictured them with their heads together over the French book, shrugged, sat on a bench in a small box maze on the outermost edge of the garden, near where the moors began. Bert Precious came round the corner, sat down beside her and took her in his arms. He kissed her. Molly drew back. "You've been reading French books, haven't you?" she said. "That's right," he said, and kissed her again. She stared into the very pale, long face, looked into his almond eyes and said, "Oh, Bert. Bert."

He said, "Corrie won't come back to me, Molly. I'm very lonely. I want you," and he stressed the *you* slightly. She put her arms round him. He murmured, "There's an old country house tradition known as the rest before dinner –" They went, side by side, round the house to the kitchen entrance. The back stairs took them up to the corridor leading to Molly's room. She said, "You've done this before."

"Only as a young man," he told her. Later she leaned on one elbow, staring at the sleeping face on the pillow beneath her. It was tranquil. Indeed, his face was usually calm. It must have been the candour of his eyes which gave him the open, responsive look he bore. Then she got up, bathed quickly and quietly in the bathroom next door and put on her dinner dress. She slipped upstairs to have supper with the boys. Mrs Mooney, who was looking after them, was talking about her grandfather, the most famous poacher in the county. "But since what he did was wrong," she said portentously, perhaps for the benefit of the two young members of the landlord class eating custard in front of her, "wrong and against the law, he finally went to prison. For six months."

"Can I take Fred off to see the blackbird's nest?" Willy said. "Can we go nesting?"

"It's too dark," Mrs Mooney said.

"Let us just go out and look up at it in the tree – you can see it when the drawing room lights are on," he said.

"Straight down, and straight back," Mrs Mooney said.

"Nesting tomorrow?" said Willy.

"That depends on your mothers," Mrs Mooney said. The boys raced off.

Molly had a cup of tea and said, "Poaching being a thing of the past round here, of course?"

Mrs Mooney looked at her cautiously, then gave her jolly laugh. "What do you think?" she said, "there's more than ever."

"Mr Monteith says they're using my bikes to get them to the spot," Molly said.

"Aye," Mrs Mooney said. "They're handy, you see. They can go over rough country and down narrow lanes. Well – it's hard enough to manage, these days. There's no work out here, none in the town – people are getting poorer. We're going back to the days my mother can remember, when folk saw little meat, just bacon sometimes and a rabbit or two for the pot.

"But the problem now's that the men from the towns are out poaching on a big scale. A whole sheep, twenty pheasants taken while they're sleeping, with flashlights – it annoys the landlords and it makes the gamekeepers very angry – they're that much more keen to catch anybody. And sometimes, when they do get someone, they're none too gentle."

"Poaching here – mugging in the cities. It's the same thing," Molly said.

"You and yours, though, will be all right," Mrs Mooney said politely.

"If I keep going," said Molly.

"So long as the bairns are all right," the woman said.

"Some will be," said Molly.

"We could all do with some work hereabouts," Mrs Mooney said. She looked at Molly shyly.

Molly shook her head. "Can't Mr Monteith do anything – ?"

Mrs Mooney said, "That's not what he's thinking about."

"I suppose not," Molly said. She stood up and said, feeling embarrassed, "I'd better go and put my face on."

She took the narrower stairs down from the attics to the carpeted floor of the passageway to her room. He could do something, surely, she thought. I hope they poach his salmon and pinch his pheasants – and she opened the door of her room to find Bert gone. Her heart sank. Perhaps he'd just got carried away and now regretted it. Felt guilty, perhaps. She sat on the bed, feeling joy ebbing. She wanted him now, more than anything. The door opened and in he came, dressed in a shirt and evening trousers, carrying two martinis. He kissed her and handed her one. "I've seen this at the pictures," she said. "You in evening clothes, coming in and kissing the nape of my neck while I'm putting on my diamonds." He sat on the bed and looked at her, as she powdered her face in front of the dressing-table mirror. He said, "I ought to tell you about Corrie."

"Oh, don't get embarrassed, Bert," she said. "It's all right. I know the situation. If you want to back out just say so."

"She's seen a solicitor about a divorce," he said, "but I don't think she's made up her mind."

"Has she got another man?" asked Molly.

"I don't suppose so," he said. "She's just less decided about this than she thinks she is. And if she wants to return I shall – well, I shan't quarrel with her. She's my wife – the mother of my children. I owe her some loyalty."

"Ah, well, Bert," Molly said, sitting there, with her lipstick in her hand, "nothing you say surprises me." She told him that she lived with Richard Mayhew, adding that she thought there were discontents on both sides. And then she sat beside him and asked, "You haven't told me everything."

He stared at her, opened his mouth to speak and then said, "I think I have."

"Oh," said Molly. "I suddenly had the feeling there was something you weren't telling me." And of course there was and he knew it – the fact that he had witnessed her history over the past forty-five years, that he knew in some respects more about her than she did herself. She stared at both their feet, hers in tights and his ending in shiny black shoes. She said, "I don't want anything from you. Just what you can spare. To be honest, I even wondered if I had time to fit you in."

"Oh, I'll fit in all right," he said, deliberately mistaking her meaning. As he pushed her backwards on to the bed she muttered "– late for dinner."

"Plenty of time," murmured Sir Herbert, unbuttoning her black pearl buttons.

"It wouldn't be easy to let you go," Molly said seriously, as they lay in disorder among their clothes.

Equally sombrely he said, "It wouldn't be easy to go."

Molly managed to arrive in time to join the others as they went into the dining room. Bert took his place after they were all sitting down, murmuring to Jessica, "Terribly sorry – lost cuff-link, as usual."

"And where did you eventually find it, Bert?" enquired Jessica, who was sitting beside him.

"Under the bed," he replied.

"Of course – where else?" Jessica said in the same even tone. Molly, who was far away on the other side of the table, did not see or hear what passed but she caught a glance from Jessica. As she looked at Bert she felt a little weak. A silly smile spread over her face, which she tried to remove as she turned her eyes on Mary Floyd, who was speaking.

There were twenty at dinner that night and she watched Mrs Mooney handing the dishes round, still with the same air of contentment. What's it all about, thought Molly to herself – these factories, that white elephant of a house in the country, Isabel – the whole lot? Why don't I go and live a small life, with Fred, with Bert, in peace? But then she wondered if Mrs Mooney's placid manner was really all it seemed or just the expression her employers liked her to wear. And reflected that a lot of people relied on her to keep going. And thought that perhaps even if she had a simple life she would not be plump, contented and placid but bored and fed up. Jamieson turned to her and said, "You're smiling."

"I was just wishing for love in a cottage – me," she said.

Jamieson did not laugh. "I don't suppose you're the only one here thinking that. But not many of us would last more than six months."

Even by candlelight she saw that the healthy and generally good-looking faces were closed. Mouths opened in laughter, expressions were attentive, amused, interested. Molly, taking meat from the platter Mrs Mooney offered her, watched her go on to the next guest. Even if her placid good cheer was partly assumed when dealing with employers, it was still an honest face. She wondered if she, Molly, looked like the others – as if she were thinking too many thoughts at once, as if her face had been marked by the complicated life she led. And she looked across at Bert again. He was listening to something Jessica was saying and she could read kindness, attention, and discomfort on his face. That discomfort would be because Jessica was probably saying something spiteful or hinting at a secret and it was embarrassing for him to sense her misery and anger. I think he's too good for me, thought Molly. I'm afraid that's what'll ruin everything between us. Suddenly she remembered the letter she had received from Pentonville a week earlier. "Write to me, Molly dear," Arnie Rose had written. "It's a dump but I can have as many letters as I like. Or a tape. Be nice to hear

579

how you're getting along." It was funny, she thought, that terrible man, Arnie Rose, suddenly wanting a penfriend. She had tried to make a tape but the memory of having been tricked and sent to gaol by Arnie made her tone less than friendly. In the end she had dictated a cheerful-sounding letter to her secretary and sent off a food hamper and some fresh blank tapes, hoping that if Arnie started the conversational ball rolling she would be able to follow it up. There was no point in holding a grudge now the man was faced with dragging out the rest of his life in a top security prison wing. She said to Mary Floyd, "You won't believe this but I've only been abroad once – to Paris. My son's been all over the world, virtually – but I've been rooted here." It had been with Johnnie, she remembered, recalling an unexpected snowfall over the Jardins de Luxembourg, the big bed with the big bolster at the hotel, the oysters, the wine, she'd been dizzy with love. She pulled herself back from memory, saying, "I know everybody needs a break from time to time," she said. "I don't know why I never get one. That's why it's so marvellous being here –" She'd been in love then, she thought, and now she was again. She stole one of her rationed glances at Bert. She was waiting for evening, when she and Bert would go upstairs separately and then be together again. She had been drinking too fast and felt muzzy. Dinner seemed to have gone on for ever and even now, she noticed with horror, they were only just getting to the dessert. She refused some mousse, drank water and thought that it would be hours before they could go to bed.

She was relieved to be called from the drawing room after dinner. "What's up?" she asked her sister Shirley.

"Sorry to disturb your posh weekend," Shirley said. "Thought I'd better tell you – the Liverpool transport men are starting a wildcat strike and the electricians up the factory have come out in sympathy. Wayne's talking to them now – that's why he asked me to ring you. He wants ideas, instructions from you. If you've got any," her sister added. "You know the position – we've got a week to polish off the consignment and get it to the docks. We can't do either of those things with no electricians and no transport."

"Tell him to do practically nothing," Molly said. "Tell the whole factory we're coming in on Monday and I want a meeting – with everybody."

"Listen," said Shirley, "Wong wants us to line up some blackleg labour and work at night, with heavy security round the factory in case anyone sneaks in."

"I don't want to do that," Molly said.

"Well I really don't think that you're going to get very far appealing to our electricians," Shirley said. "I'll come up on Monday then, shall I?"

"And Wong too," said Molly. "I'll see you both in the office about twelve."

"What's happening?" said Shirley acutely. "You sound very – I don't know what. Love – that's it. You've met a bloke."

"Mind your own business, Shirl," Molly said affectionately.

Because she and Bert had spent the night talking and making love, Molly after breakfast retreated to the stone balcony outside the library. Here, in the sharp air, sitting in the pale April sunshine, and looking over the garden and on to the moors beyond, she fell into a doze, through which the voices of men in the library came to her only dimly. "Never could stand the woman – Maria Johnson, poor girl – incredible, I don't believe it – talking of abdication – Maria Johnson."

But all the time Molly was feeling, through her doze, the mixture of languor and suspense lovers know at the beginning of a happy love affair. She wondered if it would be possible to live with Bert. The contrast between this new life, and the old one, with its fierce concentration on business, its responsibilities for so many others, was too great – she could never, surely, lead both lives at the same time. But would he want her? And would his wife return? And she sighed, and drifted into a deeper doze, hearing somehow, "Maria Johnson, Maria Johnson," in her ears until some lover's instinct awoke her. She heard the library door open and Bert Precious's voice saying, "Is the front part of an *Observer* in here? Jessica wants it."

Then came Donald Monteith's voice, "Bert's the man who'll know all about this. Here, Bert, tell us all about Maria Johnson. Did she ever exist?"

There was a silence, interrupted by another man. "Leave him alone, Donald. His lips are sealed."

Bert said stiffly, "It's really not my story to tell."

"Good God, Bert," came Monteith's voice, sounding impatient. "It's all old history now. Better to get it all out in the open."

And Molly, only wanting to spare Bert what sounded like an embarrassing moment, got up and walked in saying, "I've just woken up – did you say something about an *Observer*? I've got one."

Bert was looking at her in amazement but said, "Come with me

581

then, and give it to Jessica. I told her you wanted to see the pictures and she said she'd take you round."

Later she and Bert were sitting on the hill above the loch. "I love you, Molly," he told her. "But I've little to give." He seemed, she thought, too sad.

"What do I want?" she asked him. "If you mean marriage – don't you think I know I've done that too often? As long as we can be happy –" and she gazed at him, but his expression did not lighten. He said slowly, "Perhaps there's something I should tell you –" and she hated his reluctance and the sense that he was carrying some kind of shame. She took his arm and said, "Tell me nothing. I don't need to know anything." But she thought perhaps he wanted a confession forced from him while she just wanted to be happy. They might have very little time together, she thought, and she did not want to spoil it. She was too old, now, to believe that she, or he, could live for very long in a world of permanence.

As they lay back on the grass she said, "I'm afraid I've got to start very early tomorrow for Liverpool."

"Ah," he said sadly. "Will you still want to see me when you get back to London?"

She turned her head to look at him, "Do you think I wouldn't?"

"I thought perhaps I might be just a holiday romance," he said, looking pleased with himself.

"I thought I might be," she said.

"I'm not that kind," he told her.

"Well, neither am I," she said. "Just because I've got a bad reputation – it always seems much worse than I am." She paused, "I suppose everybody thinks that. We all think we're innocent."

"Fates are made partly by circumstances," he said.

"And partly by choice," she said.

"Choices are made by circumstances too," he said. He was looking at the pale blue sky. His mood had again darkened.

"Oh," she said, feeling impatient about the whole, sad discussion. "Who you are depends on what you choose. No point in denying it. Anyway, if people couldn't believe that they'd hang themselves. There'd be no point in carrying on."

"You're an optimist," he said.

"Where would I be if I wasn't?" she asked. "People whose lives are all mapped out like yours can afford a little bit of gloom and melancholy. It'd be a luxury for me." She knew positively that he was talking about a subject which had nothing to do with her. She thought she had better ask him what he had been about to tell her earlier. "Is this to do with what you were going to tell me just now?" she asked.

"In a way," he said. "There's a pub in the village. They open up for you if they know you. It's a few miles – can you walk it?"

"I'd go ten," Molly said. "On the way you tell me what you were going to tell me."

"I don't think I can," he said.

Molly, bewildered, shrugged and stood up. "I'll tell you about my strike, then," she said. She was beginning to feel very gloomy. She had not expected a lifetime of careless happiness but she was disconcerted by Bert's sudden withdrawal, so much like the attitude of a man who does not want to break the news that he is leaving one woman for another. She wished now she had listened at first, when he was prepared to speak. They kissed by the big trunk of a pine tree and she thought it was all right again.

"A drink, then lunch, then a screw in the afternoon," she told him.

"That's known as a siesta," he told her.

"Not where I come from," said she.

They were let into the little dark pub opposite the church, where the door was promptly bolted behind them. In the dim light created because the shutters had been closed Molly sipped her beer, tried not to make a face and said, "What was all that about in the library? You sounded upset when Donald Monteith asked you about that woman – Maria somebody."

He glanced at two men sitting at the bar, drinking their illicit, Sunday beer and told her, "I can't really talk about it, Molly." He paused. "I really can't. Not now."

"Somebody else's secret?" suggested Molly.

He sighed and said, "That's right – somebody else's secret." But he seemed so depressed by what he was thinking that Molly said, "I expect it's all over and done with now. Not your fault is it? Come on – don't let it play on your mind – don't spoil the day. Drink up your horrible beer and I'll get you another one."

The sensations of an adulterous husband, facing a cheerful and unsuspecting wife, must be nothing compared with the shame I felt, as Molly tried to cheer me up, and I sat in that dark pub wondering what on earth to do. If I didn't tell her what I knew of her, that I'd been following her almost all her life, I'd be deceiving her in a terrifying way. If I did tell her, what would she do? She might cause a massive scandal. She would certainly believe I had betrayed her. Like many a man in my position, I didn't want to be truthful because I couldn't face her rage or her rejection. Basically I was just going on, hoping we could go on loving each other, hoping that the deception in which I was involved would somehow make no difference. It was pathetic and, looking back, I'm still horrified by my own stupidity. Naturally, after that, things changed between us. Chiefly because of my own feelings – I may have been a villain, but I can't say I was an effective one. I lost a lot more than I gained, that day, because of my dutiful, cowardly silence.

And so the couple walked back to the house through pines, still holding hands as they passed under the stiff arms of the trees but each keeping their secrets. For it was Molly who knew that Joe Endell had been her brother and Herbert Precious who knew about their mother and father. And like all secrets, these began to cause restraints between them. Bert Precious began to think of his wife and children and Molly of her coming visit to Liverpool. Bert thought of his dead son and Molly of his absent wife. They went back into the house together, but slightly apart. That night it was again as if there were no secrets between them but it was fortunate that the next day they had to part, for whether Bert Precious spoke out or not, either way the relationship was doomed.

In the half-built canteen of the factory Molly looked at the two hundred and fifty faces in front of her, stood up and said, "I haven't got a lot to say – but I have to say this. I don't want to be the boss here for the sake of it. I've begged, borrowed and stolen to found this factory so that I can get a living from it. And you're here to get a living from it too, so we're in agreement over that. Now, I never started this because I wanted it to run the old way – I'd hold the whip hand over you, you'd fight me back and in the end I'd automate and get rid of the lot of you. So we have to think of another way to keep this place open. This is my proposal – I'm going to hand you fifty percent of the shares and, of course, you get a share of the profits accordingly. If there are any – and that's up to all of us. There'll be a proper set-out of all the terms and clauses for everybody tomorrow. I'll need your answer to the proposition in twenty-four hours – because we have to get this strike out of the way and what you're going to have to do, if this transport strike goes on, is ride these bikes down to the docks to get them on the ship which'll be taking them to the States. You can do that, strike or no strike, because you own the bikes and if they don't get to the market the firm could go bust. If they do get there, in a year or two you'll be drawing dividends. But if you accept the proposal, bear this in mind – you'll have to pull your weight because once this bit of news gets out, my credit's shot. There isn't any bank in this country which won't be very cautious when they hear this is a firm half-owned by the workforce. I don't believe they'll extend any more credit. There's a huge loan out on this place and they've got to be paid back what's owed and you're the men and women who've got to do it. Along with the ideas for the new scheme you'll get a full balance sheet. My sister here, and her husband, the firm's accountants, will be here tomorrow to answer all the questions." She added, "I meant to do this all along but I thought I'd better get the firm on an even keel first – but I'm beginning to see that as long as you can go along striking on me, because you don't understand what's going on, and I'm fuming away treating you like naughty kids – well, we may never get on an even keel in the first place.

"We're going away to get our proposals together now. There'll be copies available when you arrive at work tomorrow. You can take all day to talk it over, with Shirley, Lee here, your shop stewards, husbands, wives – I don't care. Turn the place into a public meeting if you need to – but let me have an answer by midday Tuesday."

And after this brief and serious address, she walked out of the silent canteen, wondering what thoughts were going through the heads of the men and women in overalls who sat there. She knew her timing was wrong. The scheme should have been started earlier. Jack would see it as a way of breaking a strike. And probably it was, thought Molly, but what other choice could she make? Together with Wayne, Shirley, Lee and the firm's lawyers they roughed out the proposals. Then Molly, very tired, and Fred, who was very bored by now, got a car and drove back to Framlingham. They both slept most of the way, arriving at breakfast time, although no one was up.

There was a scatter of garden catalogues and blueprints in the drawing room, so she deduced that the plan Richard and Isabel had concocted, to restore the old walled rose garden at the back of the house, was now being put into operation. Whether it was memory of

585

the carefree weekend with Bert Precious or the thought of the anxieties connected with the decision about the Messiter factory in Liverpool, Molly felt a surge of resentment. As she left the bright catalogues and the plans for the beds and replanting of the garden and went into the kitchen she thought, "I need a wife here, not a couple of garden designers." Gloomily, she cooked eggs and bacon and wished herself back at Meakin Street, remembering the way the mist had hung round the old gas street lamps when she had been a child, remembering Ivy in her apron on the pavement yelling at the children to come in out of the street and get their tea, remembering Joe Endell, who had started there with her their jolly mealtimes, with take-home curries, and documents all over the table, and a couple of friends laughing about the day in Parliament. She found her eyes filling unaccountably with tears – it was the prospect of some happiness with Bert Precious, it was for Joe Endell, it was the workload and the worries about the factory, it was her overdraft and the knowledge that she was going to have to pay for the roses, the garden walls, the construction of a pool. "It isn't good enough," she thought, as she cooked the breakfast.

After she and Fred had eaten their eggs and bacon, in order to avoid the arrival of Charles and Isabel, who were getting up, and the housekeeper who would be coming in from the village shortly, Molly and Fred went out to look at the rose garden. It lay behind old brick walls. They forced through the archway, which was blocked with brambles, and stood in the longish grass, for the path was overgrown and lost, and looked into the choked pond, in the middle of which was a broken statue. The roses, untended for years, dropped, grew along the ground, climbed the walls.

"I like it how it is," said Molly's son. "It's spooky and if they clear it all up we won't be able to play properly here any more."

Molly nodded. She, too, was fond of the old garden, rioting untended roses in summer, brown and grey in winter. She liked it, she did not want it ordered, for people to stroll round and admire. The whole business felt like the last straw. She dealt, day by day, with mundane problems, like ferrying material to outworkers who were drawing the dole and could not take in consignments of fabrics without attracting the attention of malicious neighbours who might betray them to the DHSS, she dealt with gigantic problems, like how to set up worker management at a factory over two hundred and fifty miles away, with very few precedents to go on. It seemed to her that her revolutionary lover and her mother-in-law had nothing better to do than rearrange the flower beds. In spite of their different ideologies, both were trying to recreate the same dream. Here am I, she thought, tens of thousands in debt and everything pawned in the hopes of healthy trade over the next few years and they're here talking about fountains and rose gardens. Even Fred's got more sense than that. She sat down on a slightly rotting wooden bench and thought. There had been a message from Bert in the pile of letters and notes of telephone calls waiting for her when she got back. Yet now she was, somehow, not telephoning him at his house in London. She had not rung him while she had been in Liverpool. It was partly the sense of being under strain, as though she did not want him to see her workaday personality – the Molly Allaun waiting for negotiations in Liverpool to end and losing her temper about plans for a garden. But as she sat there, watching a starling tug at some old grass caught in the thorns at the foot of a sprawling briar rose, she seemed to feel mysteries and evasions surrounding the situation. She imagined, now, banalities involving a long-standing mistress, some peculiar upper-class connection with the secret service, even bouts of mental instability, schizophrenia, perhaps. None of these fantasies seemed to make any sense when she thought of the man who was supposed to be involved in them. On the other hand, she still felt there was something less than straightforward going on and, at present, she realized, she could not cope with any personal situation which was not clear as glass, outstanding as an elephant in Oxford Street. There had also been a message from her daughter, taken down by Isabel, on the heap. It had read, "Josephine has left her husband and gone to Peru – how sad. It sounds as if she may have number 2 lined up! Isabel."

Molly thought to herself, would Bert really fancy today's Molly – harassed family woman, stressed businesswoman and hater of rose gardens?

On the following day, as she waited at Framlingham for the call from Liverpool to tell her if the workforce was prepared to go ahead with the new scheme, she opened a short letter from Herbert Precious. There were, he said, things he felt he had to tell her. He could not put them in writing. Would she meet him very soon, so that they could talk? Molly, in a fit of impatience, wondering why any practical person could not either pick up the phone and discuss the matter, whatever it was or, if writing, not outline the problem, wrote a brief reply saying she had no time for mysteries, that she would always treasure the time they had spent together but she felt their chances of permanent happiness were very small. She stepped out in the brisk spring air, to put the letter into the postbox in the lane herself, feeling that she had been sensible. She regretted it later but argued to herself that it was only natural to feel regrets – it did not mean she had done the wrong thing.

Nevertheless, she expected some response, even a short note from Bert saying that he regretted her decision. When none came, Molly shrugged and thought that she had always sensed mysteries in the affair, reflected that perhaps she had never understood him in the first place, then shed a tear and got on with her life. She could not know how much it had cost him to decide to reveal everything to her and how pleased he was to have a breathing space where he could, he imagined, organize matters so that his information caused as little trouble as possible. And only a day after her note arrived he had a telephone call from his wife saying that she was planning to return. The end result was that he solved his problem by the age-old human device of doing nothing and letting events decide for him.

Whether Corrie Precious returned because of a change of heart, or because Jessica Monteith had lost no time in writing to her about his affair with Molly, or just to attend Prince Charles's wedding, her husband did not know. Neither, he thought, did she. But, true to her nature, when she came back she not only took up the reins in the sense of seizing the keys to the linen cupboard and redecorating the attic, so to speak, but made a genuine effort to heal the breach in the marriage, started during years of matrimonial business and horribly widened by the death of their son. Her efforts calmed a tired and disillusioned husband, worried about an income badly affected by inflation and uncertain of what he wanted for the future. It was not for nothing, after all, that he was devoted to those two strong-minded women, his wife Corrie and his old passion, Molly Allaun. Nevertheless, a patched-up marriage where the issues are not brought out into the open is not always wholly comfortable. It was fortunate that at this stage he was offered a job by his cousin, Monsignor Paul Fitch, who told him that an archivist was needed in the vast, uncatalogued cellars of the Vatican. He was offered this post because he had, after all, a first-class degree in history, had written a thesis, much praised, on Rome's dealings with the barbarian hordes of the eighth to tenth centuries, had considerable skill in Latin and, in large measure, because of his guaranteed discretion. He was also to act as a counter-weight to the ecclesiastical team working on the massive project. And so it was that Herbert Precious's history of keeping his mouth shut and showing loyalty to his employers was partly responsible for getting a job more suited to his temperament than anything else he had so far done. Additional advantages were that it paid well and got him out of the country a great deal. This did not really suit Corrie, who was looking forward to the sale of the big house in Hyde Park Gate left to him by his father and going to a more modest place, where she could keep house on a smaller scale and enjoy a greater state of intimacy with her husband. Nevertheless, if Bert would be happier commuting to the Vatican and spending years in the dusty caves, examining the correspondence of Ghengis Khan with the incumbent Pope or cataloguing the scandals of Alexander VI, then she would not complain. At the same time she had many hard thoughts about Molly Allaun, whose picture had recently been in all the papers, and on TV, riding in front of a column of Messiters to Liverpool docks, and waving cheerfully at the motorcycle policeman riding beside her. This provided much useful publicity for the firm, in Europe and the United States, but to Corrie it seemed unfair, as the chairman of this thriving company, showing a lot of still-shapely leg, rode her little scarlet bike through the streets, followed by a hundred other such machines.

To Corrie's mind, Molly looked too young and too successful, considering the life she had led. In fact Molly was putting a good face on a worrying financial situation, and a complicated industrial position, for the part-ownership of the factory by the workers was so far causing confusion while the details were sorted out. She was also having a fierce family quarrel with her brother Jack who said that the whole manoeuvre would only be interpreted in Britain and outside it as a bit of clever strike-breaking by a management hostile to the rights of workers. But Corrie knew none of this and, if she had, might not have been consoled by it.

In the meanwhile, Molly was also worrying about the order book. Home demand held up, was, in fact, improving, but that alone would not keep the factory on its feet. She needed a much larger export business to make it profitable and an export business is not built overnight. A year after the opening she was still just paying the suppliers, the wages and the interest on the loan. She was surreptitiously feeding profits from the small businesses in London to the Messiter factory. And as they proceeded with the untested worker participation scheme she began to wish she had listened to Shirley and somehow suffered through the strike without putting the scheme forward at that time. "It's not that it won't prove itself in the long run," Shirley said. "It just causes hiccups at the moment – and hiccups are what we don't need."

"Sometimes," Molly had replied, untruthfully, "I wake up in the middle of the night and wish I was back in the nick again."

At the same time her daughter was covering the riots in Los Angeles and her new future son-in-law was, as she reported to her sister furiously, "just sitting on his bum all day in Hammersmith, calling meetings to discuss the future of the community."

"Well he's – er – a community worker, isn't he?" Shirley had replied, looking at her sister wryly. Molly, seeing the point, had burst into laughter. "I think you're right," she said. "Josie's got another one – I ought to get him down to Framlingham so he can join the famous Framlingham Rose Garden and Pension Scheme."

"Thank God I'm married to a Chinaman," was her sister's comment.

Molly often thought weakly that she should end her relationship with Richard Mayhew but like many a tired tycoon, she could not face disturbance. She was paying for stability and supposed vaguely that as long as Richard and Fred were happy laying bricks and digging in peat she should be grateful. Philosophically, she endured a life of mingled business anxieties and domestic impatience, telling herself that things would somehow change. They always did.

1985

"What are you doing down South, Wayne?" Molly shouted. "You're supposed to be up North. I thought we had a complete smash-up on the front frame side? Have you sorted it out?"

"Never mind that," he said grimly. "Get yourself down here."

"What's happened?" she cried.

In the Meakin Street office her assistant stared at her.

"Nothing to worry about," Wayne told her. "It's something George did. I don't even want to talk about it now."

"What? On the phone?" she said, recognizing the voice of someone who thinks others may be listening in. "Is it an emergency?"

"Not the sort you mean," he said. "Why don't you get down here?"

"OK," she said. "I'm coming. What happened about that front frame assembly?"

"Kennedy's in charge," Wayne said dourly. "He wants to participate."

"Maybe you're right," she said.

Somehow she expected signs, when she arrived, that there was a crisis afoot. Instead the house was the same, shrouded now in mist which stood a foot high on the ground as she pulled up outside. Putting her head in the drawing room door she found Isabel by the fire.

"They're out in the stables," she said. "They're extremely excited about something. Fred refused to go to school this morning."

Molly ran down the corridor to the kitchen. As she passed the long, large mirror in the hall she saw, in the old frame, a middle-aged woman, pale hair flying, and remembered her image as a little girl, caught in the same mirror, running to the kitchen. She ran through the mist to the old stable entrance and into the room where George worked. The walls were banked with instruments and there was a long formica and enamel workbench in the centre. George, in a baggy old brown suit, his long legs extended under the bench, was asleep. Beside his head, on the shiny surface of the workbench, was a round, glittering object, the size of a football, with a flattened top.

Wayne stood beside him, holding a mug of tea. He said, "I turned round to make him a cuppa and the next thing I knew he was like that. He's been up for the best part of a week."

Molly studied the silver globe on the workbench and said, "That's it, is it? It works?"

Wayne nodded. Fred came in and paused in the entrance, seeing George asleep. Molly thought, if it works we'll all be rich. We can employ thousands of people. We can dictate our terms. She looked at Wayne, who read her eyes. He nodded. "He's cracked it," he said. "I knew he would."

She was almost too nervous to ask Wayne to hook up the new engine for a demonstration. It had been years, now, since George had told her that he was working on a scheme to power the Messiters electrically. Even Molly knew that to do this would mean a battery about half the size of the bike itself, but he told her he would not be thinking of using batteries, but, instead, energy stored by a flywheel working inside the new engine. There were, he said, three problems, the first concerned having a material for the flywheel resilient enough to stand the friction it created for itself in motion, and the second involved safety – if the flywheel broke loose while the bike was moving it would burst through the casing and then anything else in its way with the velocity of a bullet. The third was simply to achieve enough power and conduct it, without increasing the weight of the Messiter. In progress reports she learned over the years that George had decided on laminated steel, that he had solved the problem of energy storage, that he had decided that, to reduce wear and tear on the flywheel, he was mounting it in a cylinder, in a vacuum. As time went on he had worked out the best remodelling of the Messiter to allow the new engine to function properly – the chief problem was now how to ensure that if the drum containing the flywheel broke open and the flywheel came off its mounting, the result would not be a dangerous projectile. A too-heavy casing would be safe but would make the machine heavy. One which was too light might be dangerous. As all this had gone on Molly had sometimes followed it with scepticism, sometimes she had forgotten about it completely. She had admired the way George had solved problem after problem but she was not sure that ultimately he could produce independent electrical power for the bikes. Now, it seemed, he had. She looked down at the tousled head, asleep beside the new power source and said, "Did he solve the safety problem?"

"He's using two casings," Wayne said. "The interior one is resin-impregnated glass fibre and the exterior's laminated steel. It's impossible for both cases to crack right open in normal circumstances – even a bullet wouldn't produce cracking. Only a bomb'd smash it and if that happened you wouldn't bother about a flywheel screaming past your ear."

"So the power's running from that casing, which we've got mounted in the same position as the other engine, through to the back wheel?" she said.

"He'd like to alter the shape of the bike but I said, 'Leave it,'" Wayne told her. "He reckons, get rid of the pushbike design, forget the pedals and chain – all it needs is two bars for the rider's feet – and I told him, stick to the old design for now. Maybe people like new things to look like the old ones for a bit, maybe the old design is more practical than you know – all that's for later. The point is – he did it."

"Aren't you going to hook it up, Mum?" said Fred, still in the doorway. He came in.

"Haven't we got a bike to mount it on?" demanded Molly, still trying to put off the moment when she had to believe George had managed to work out a way of producing enough power from a silver globe the size of a football to take a small machine up the road at 15 mph.

"Have to fix it up tomorrow," Wayne told her. "It's too dark to play around out there now, anyway." He added, "Molly – do you want to see this or not?"

Molly picked up the engine and handed it to him. "It must weigh three pounds," she said. George, as she picked it up, had stirred and woken. His eyes went to Wayne, who linked the engine up to a control panel on the wall and said to Molly, "Watch the needle on the panel over there."

Molly watched as the static needle arced steadily across the face of the dial. Fred, in the corner, raised his hands above his head and shouted "Yeah!" Molly put her hand on George's head and found herself saying, "My God, George. Your mother would've been so proud of you."

His eyes were red as he looked up at her. "I don't know what to say," she said. "I'm speechless. I can't believe you did it."

"Wait till tomorrow – you can ride it," George said.

595

"Come in the house and have something to eat, George," she told him. "Then I'm driving you home. I want you to get some sleep."

They all walked out. She was about to shut the door when she turned and said, "Christ! Don't leave that thing in here!"

"What's the matter?" George asked.

"It's worth bloody millions," Molly told him. "So are your plans and notes. They've got to go in a safe place till you've taken out the patents."

"Oh – yes," George said vaguely. "Well – where are we going to put it all?"

"I've got a safe in my room," declared Fred. "I got it off a boy at school whose father's a lawyer. He was putting in a new one. It cost me fifteen quid."

"I hope you haven't forgotten the combination," Molly said. They carried the engine and some of the drawings back to the house and locked them in the safe in Fred's room.

They ate in silence. Molly produced a bottle of champagne but there was something in George's pale, thin face, in his air of complete exhaustion which inhibited a real celebration. In the end she got up saying, "Congratulations, George, and thanks. I'll see you in the morning." She turned in the doorway and said, "Better say nothing about all this – till we've thought what to do."

Fred had gone upstairs to his room. Molly joined Isabel in the drawing room. She was watching a soap opera on TV and Molly sat down silently, wondering what Wayne and George were saying to each other. She began to realize what a lonely life George must have been leading in Framlingham since Wayne and his wife had moved north. He was lodging in the village with a niece of Vera Harker's. He had no interests and, it always seemed, no close relationships. Cissie came down for a week occasionally to visit him and that was all. From now on he would be wealthy and she wondered what he would do with his money – nothing, perhaps. It seemed sad. She waited until the programme was over and asked, "Where's Richard?"

"Oh," Isabel said, "didn't he tell you? He went away suddenly to see a film producer in Berlin – about a script." Molly nodded.

"Anything the matter?" asked Isabel.

"No," said Molly.

"I thought you looked rather preoccupied," Isabel said.

"No," Molly told her. "Just thinking about something."

"I'm sure he said he would leave a message for you at the office in London," Isabel said.

"It's not that," Molly said. Isabel looked a little disconcerted. Molly supposed that if she and Richard parted the rose garden plan would be spoiled. And Isabel got on well with Richard. She would be lonely without him. Then, somehow feeling she was interrupting Isabel's viewing she stood up and said, "I think I'll go and read in the library." She could hear George and Wayne talking in the dining room where they had eaten, and the sound of the TV and even Fred's record player, coming faintly from upstairs. She lay by herself on the sofa in the library, staring at the dark windows and letting thoughts run round her head. If she were to exploit the new engine she would need a great deal more capital. It would mean a new factory, or factories. And after she had thought that she began to wonder about the wider implications of George's discovery. Her musings made her sit bolt upright, groaning aloud, "Oh, my God – is it true?" She slept very little that night, was up at dawn and had cooked Fred's breakfast too early. "What I'm thinking, Mum," he said, surveying his dried-up sausages, "is you'd better get another safe somewhere else for all that stuff. I don't want my room turned over by agents from Dallas just as I've got all my tapes organized."

Molly nodded numbly at him. "There's such a thing as industrial espionage, you know," he informed her.

"I've heard about it, Fred," she said.

"Give Isabel a shock, see," he said. "Arabs sneaking round the house trying to get in to steal the plans. Can we have security guards?" he added hopefully.

"And Alsatian dogs?" she said.

He nodded with enthusiasm. "What a world you kids are growing up in," she said. But she was impressed that Fred had come spontaneously to the same conclusions as herself. George did not see the new engine in this way and Wayne, if he saw it, had said nothing. She had reminded them to take the engine from the workshop. But Fred had followed her line of reasoning on from that point. Now she told him, "If we have to take precautions some of them might not be much fun for you."

"I don't mind having a minder," he told her.

George and Wayne arrived before half past eight. Molly stood in a corner of the workshop while they mounted the engine on the new Messiter. "If it comes off, what happens?" Molly asked. "It lies on the ground," Wayne told her. By eleven thirty she was sitting on a stool, dozing, when Wayne said, "Molly – do you want first ride?"

"George first," she said.

"I've had one," George said. "When I thought the casing was dodgy. I had to prove it worked –"

"I'll get on," said Molly. She gripped the handlebars and wheeled it into the yard. "You've got to keep controlling the speed with this," said George showing her the lever on the handlebars. "It controls the output of power. But it's sluggish so while you're doing it, left for less power, right for more, keep your other hand on the braking system on the other side. If you have to stop quickly you can't cut the power fast enough so you have to rely more on braking than with the petrol-driven engine."

Molly thought she would drive through the entrance to the yard, along the narrow path to the area in front of the house, then take the machine down the drive to the road beyond. George gave her a push, she turned on the engine, pedalled a little and, before she reached the entrance to the stable yard felt the machine begin to pull. She found she was careering through the entrance and turned the handlebar on the left. As he had said, the response was sluggish. She had reached the semi-circle of gravel in front of the house before the bike slowed down. She went smoothly along the drive, hearing only the crunching of the gravel beneath the wheels. She turned into the road and travelled through the misty air, so silently and so effortlessly that she felt she was flying. She half expected the little bicycle to take off under her and sail into the air. Making a half-circle, rather recklessly, to get back on to the other side of the road she found the machine turned sharply and was in danger of being hit by a car which had swept round a bend further up. She sailed on, with the fields on one side and the wall of Allaun Towers on the other, quite unwilling to go back. She dismounted outside the house and said, "It's really fun – George – it's really fun. There are a lot of other things about it but – I can't explain it. I can't see anyone not wanting one of these. You feel like a kid when you've first learned to use roller skates. Or ride a bike, for that matter." She looked affectionately at the little bike and, discharging these thoughts, said, "It looks dirt cheap to produce. What I haven't got is figures for the small modifications to the frame and the different brakes and so on. Any idea, Wayne? I humbly ask – I don't expect anyone to tell me these things."

"Sorry, Molly," he said. "But it wasn't strictly necessary. Fact is, these would come cheaper than the old petrol engines, if the materials involved don't suddenly leap up in price. Course – there's testing."

"We'll have to do at least 10,000 miles," Molly said. "And in different climates, too." She handed the bike back to Wayne and said, "Lock it up."

"What is this?" Wayne asked.

"At the moment," she said, "it's my son, Fred. He'd give anything for a go –" She looked at George and said, "George – you put him on the unsafe one."

"I found him on it," said George. She watched Wayne taking away the new Messiter and told him, "I'd give anything to have that."

"When we've finished with it," he said. He was beginning to look proud of himself.

Inside, over coffee in the dining room she said, "Here's the problem – no, here are the problems. First – I've got to work out in my own mind whether I've got the nerve, or the capital, to develop it. Second – well, the second's a question. Would it drive a car – this engine?"

"Nothing to stop it," George said. "The principle'd be exactly the same. They were working on something like it in the States in 1981–2. There was a hitch. I couldn't see –"

"That's the problem," Molly said. "From the moment you apply for a patent you're in trouble, George. I think you'll get offered money for this. I think if you phoned any big motor manufacturer now they'd offer you a few million. Either to develop it themselves or to secure the patent so they could wait until they wanted to develop it – or suppress it."

Wayne was smoking a thin cigar. "I thought about that," he said. Some rooks cawed in the trees nearby. "That's got to be your decision, George." Molly told him. The front door banged. "And another thing," she said, "give us one of them cigars, Wayne. The trouble is, you're in danger, George – we all are."

George looked at Wayne. Wayne nodded.

"Chuck us the matches," she said. Richard Mayhew put his head round the door. "So's he," she said, pointing at him. "Hullo, Richard," she said brightly. "Back quick from Berlin?"

"Wouldn't mind a cup of coffee," he said.

"Get it yourself," said Molly. "We've got a bit of a problem."

He shrugged and answered, "OK. I'll see you later."

"Fred saw it, you see," she told the others when he had gone. "He took it for granted he'd need a minder. You know there's more kidnaps these days. We've got to imagine we've got an engine which can drive cars, trucks — anything. Conservationists cheer — what are all the others going to say and do? There's billions of pounds at stake here — do you see what I mean?"

George said, "Yes," in a slightly doubtful voice. Wayne said, "I'm going to ring my wife and tell her to be careful."

"You mean people might try to get the plans?" George said. Molly could have cried. Poor Lil — she had not lived to see her brilliant child fulfil himself. She had not lived, either, to see him remain a brilliant child.

"Look," she said, "George — supposing you'd been a stagecoach operator when they invented railway trains. What would you have done?"

"Gone into steam," he replied humourlessly.

"Never mind," she said. "I think you'd better take out this patent and disappear. You can go down to stay with Sid in Ramsgate. And while you have a seaside holiday, which, God knows, you need, the rest of us'll have to be careful. We'll have to have security men — Wayne, when you ring your wife tell her she's going to have to share her life with a couple of ex-coppers. I'll have to stay here for a bit and live with a few of the same. Isabel'll go spare but I can't help that. Meanwhile I've got to decide if I can handle going into this business and you've got to decide, George, if you'd like to sell off the idea and go into a wealthy retirement. Is it all right if I ring Sid and tell him to expect you?"

George nodded. Her urgency was beginning to affect him. Molly took another of Wayne's cheroots and said, "I didn't expect this." Wayne went out to the telephone. "God knows why we haven't got a handset in here," muttered Molly. "We'll have to get some technology in this place." She looked at George, who said, "You're right, you know — it's a pity Mum isn't alive. I could've done a lot for her. She had a rotten hard life."

"Don't I know it," Molly said. "Time you got married yourself, George. That's what she'd've liked." But, she thought, please God, to a sensible widow not a blonde tart after his money.

Wayne came back. "How did she take the news?" Molly asked. He laughed, "Like usually — told me she wished she married a local farmer's boy. Then she says make sure the guys're good-looking."

"You make sure to get ugly ones," Molly said sympathetically.

"You could get government backing for this," Wayne told her.

"Money got selling off hospitals," Molly said.

"You need backing, Molly," he warned her.

"There's got to be a better way," she said. And went out to ring the security firm.

The day went on quickly. George left in a car for Ramsgate. The lawyer came from London. Wayne was collected by the security men who would stay in his house in Liverpool and went back up north. Molly made some brief explanations to Isabel, who took the news that the house was to be heavily guarded very well.

Richard Mayhew, however, said that he would find it unbearable to live in an armed camp and left an hour later to stay with a friend in London. She and Isabel were eating a sandwich together in the dining room when the telephone rang. Herbert Precious said that he had something important to say to her and asked her if she would meet him in London as soon as possible. Molly, now unable to pause, agreed to drive up immediately. She told Isabel she would be back before ten that night and as she drove out into the main road, crossed the security men driving in with a couple of Alsatian dogs in the car behind a grille. As she went to London she knew she must begin to see beyond present emergencies and work out what to do, but she now felt very fatigued. Her doctor had told her almost a year ago, when she visited him with a minor throat infection, that she should try to lead a calmer life. "It's all right," she had said, "I'm the sort that thrives on stress." And he, the quiet country GP who had attended Mrs Gates at her death, had said, "Even your sort can't go on forever. There's a kind of battle fatigue I've seen in people who live as you do. In the end they do collapse – it surprises everyone, but they do. It doesn't need to happen if only you live sensibly. Take proper holidays, for example." Of course she had taken no notice but now the conversation came back to her. Why had she automatically agreed to go to Meakin Street to meet Bert, when she had, half an hour before, been turning Allaun Towers into a fortress? Was she simply running too fast herself, unable to work out what was important and what was not? Bert's voice had sounded urgent, she thought, not like someone about to make a declaration of love – and why should he, after all this time? He had sounded more like someone with urgent business to discuss. Perhaps, she thought, Tom Allaun was in trouble. But her secret hope was that Corrie Precious had fallen in love and run away to Trinidad for at that moment, tired and with urgent decisions to make, she felt urgently that all she wanted was a peaceful, loving life with Bert. But, "No such luck for you, Mary

Waterhouse," said a voice inside her head. "Pull yourself together, gel – count your blessings and think what's happening to everybody else." This was not difficult as the frozen, darkening countryside gave way first to the suburbs, where houses, a long way back from the street, had lighted windows and people moving about inside, then to the city, where the streets were almost empty except for small bands of young men, walking about. In the wide, inner city thoroughfares some shops had already put tawdry Christmas displays in their windows, many of which were protected by mesh grilles. Other shops were boarded up, showing "For Sale" signs.

She went on, through Parliament Square. There was a police cordon blocking off Piccadilly and Regent Street. Ambulances and police cars stood with their red and blue lights revolving. She made a detour and got to Meakin Street. By now it was completely dark. She opened the door with her keys and knew that Bert Precious was there already.

"Sir Herbert Precious –" the office manager began.

Molly nodded. She said, on impulse, "You and Tony and Sarah can go home now."

As he protested she said, "Take whatever it is home with you and do it." The office manager glanced at the ceiling. She said, "A friend – very harmless."

As she walked up the stairs she heard her own voice saying, "Very harmless." She did not believe it.

There he was, stretched out in a chair. She could not help smiling at him but his own face was serious. Feeling even more alarmed she offered him a drink and as she looked through the cupboard in the kitchen, finding only gin and Armagnac, wondered what was going on. Had Corrie died – surely Bert wasn't the kind to bring his bereavement instantly to her doorstep? Did he need a loan? She could not believe he would summon her to London to ask for money. No contingency she could think of, indeed, no area of life she could think of, seemed to fit the urgent summons. Carrying the Armagnac and two glasses back into the room where he sat, she poured him a drink and handed it to him. As she did so she said, "How are you, Bert? I've wanted to know but I decided, with Corrie back, that the less seen of me the better."

"I've missed you, Molly," he said distantly. He paused. "The situation is – that is, there's something I have to tell you."

Molly, growing increasingly apprehensive, said, "Well, spit it out then. I can't stand people creeping round bad news."

"It's not bad news,' he said. "Your instincts were quite right, when you said in your letter you felt everything wasn't quite out in the open."

"Special Branch," Molly declared instantly. "You're Special Branch, aren't you, Bert? Is this something to do with Josephine? Will you kindly get on with it? Tell me what's going on."

"It's not that," he said. "It's not an immediate crisis. It's connected with your family."

Molly sat silently, thinking, somehow he's found out that Joe was my brother. He's breaking it to me. But as she sat there she heard the little, tuneful voice of a woman singing the French song about cornfields and loss. I'm going mad, she thought.

"My part in all this may make you angry," he said.

"Damn all this," she burst out. "What's going to make me angry is you beating about the bush." Unable to control herself any longer she said, "I think I know anyway – you've been poking about and you found out about Joe."

"Joe?" he said, staring at her. "It's not Joe. What is it about Joe?" She stared at him, saying grimly, "You first."

He said, "I have to ask you, Molly – have you ever had any inkling that Sid and Ivy were not your parents?"

Did it, didn't I? Molly thought angrily to herself. Told him what he didn't know while he tells me what I do. She said, "I know they're not. Ivy told me before she died." A sudden thought struck her. "Do you know who they really were? My parents?"

"I've orders to tell you," he said.

"Whose orders?" she asked.

"Orders from Her Majesty the Queen."

"You must be joking," Molly said.

"I'd like to hear about Joe," he said.

"I'd like to hear why the Queen's taking an interest in me," she retorted.

Molly just wished she did not feel so weary and that the voice in her head would stop singing. It made her want to cry. To cover it she said, "All right – what I thought you'd come to say is that you'd somehow found out Joe Endell might have been my brother. We were both rescued from the same bombed building and perhaps the poor woman was our mother. Course, we didn't know when we got married. Joe never knew. But if you think I care, I don't. I loved Joe and he loved me and that was all there was to it. All I want is for my son not to find out while he's young. It could upset him at his age – I want to tell him myself, when he's older. I don't want him haunted in his teens, thinking there's something horrible about his birth." She looked at Bert Precious, sitting opposite her in the silent room, and jumped up instantly. "My God!" she cried. "Is something the matter with you?" She stared into his pale face and put her arms round him. "Are you ill? Can I get you anything?" For a moment she thought perhaps he had lost his balance. Perhaps the summons, the story about the Queen, were part of the madness. He looked up at her and said, "Oh, God, Molly. This may be worse than we thought."

Through the weariness Molly felt some anger rising. She said, "Are you all right? Drink your Armagnac." She handed him the glass and stood back. She said, "There isn't a lot you can tell a woman like me that'll shock her. I've seen more trouble than you've had hot dinners. Now, will you say what you came here to say?"

And he told her. "You were born in France in 1936 at a house in Poulaye-sur-Bois in the Loire area. Your mother was Maria Johnson and your father Edward, then Prince of Wales."

Molly said, "What? Have you gone mad?"

Sir Herbert, drawing a deep breath said, "You'll have to judge for yourself." And he told of the marriage of a seduced girl from an old English Catholic family to the youthful Prince of Wales. He told her of the secret ceremony conducted by the Abbot at Poulaye, of the birth, six months after the wedding, of a boy, her brother, of the birth, two years later, before the abdication of the new king, of the girl, who was to become, by a series of accidents, Mary Waterhouse. "She agreed," Bert Precious said, "to stay in France quietly and cause no trouble. You have to remember what girls were like in those days – they were trained to be obedient to God, their husbands and their sovereign. And the young David was at least two of those things to her. And she came from a family which boasted a martyr burned at Smithfield for adhering to Catholicism and had suffered all sorts of penalties –"

"You can spare me the history lessons, Bert," said Molly grimly. "I can see the poor girl for myself – silly young man, girl's pregnant, hole-in-corner ceremony he's not man enough to stand by when it comes to it. Just take me on to the bit where I come in."

But Herbert Precious proceeded firmly as if, and this was true, he had often planned how to tell her the story. "The girl, Maria Johnson, continued to live in France in retirement. Perhaps she hoped that one day her husband would acknowledge her. Perhaps she was just resigned. But France fell and at this point her parents took a hand. They went to the King and asked for help in getting their daughter and her children away from the Germans. Apparently they'd been urging her to leave for some time, but she'd refused to leave because of the undertaking she'd given that she would never go back to England and never let anyone know her secret. She was a very honourable girl – she'd only been in France, where she met the Prince of Wales, because she'd refused to be present at Court and told her family she had a vocation. They'd sent her away to live with an aunt to think it over."

Herbert Precious glanced at Molly, who was sitting very straight in her chair. Her face was calm and stern and he felt, at that moment, somewhat afraid of her. He continued, "The whole thing must have come as a terrible shock to a young king, who had never expected to become a king, and who now ruled a country at war and threatened with invasion. But he rallied quickly – almost straight away an expeditionary force of eight men was put together. They landed in France at night and made their way to Poulaye-sur-Bois. And they found that Maria and the children had just gone. The maid told them that she had made her own arrangements for escape and left a few days earlier with a manservant. And she said that the man could fly a plane. Obviously there was no point in eight men blundering round occupied France, especially with the story they might tell if they were captured and tortured. So they returned. Then a fortnight later there was a report that a light plane had been seen to land in Kent, at dusk, and been found by a labourer empty next morning in a field. Naturally, the fear was that the plane had landed Germans. It was the Queen who sent my father to Kent to see what he could find out. And he discovered that a strange man and woman, with two children, had bought tickets to London on the morning the plane had been discovered. It was a small country station. They had attracted attention. But they were gone. There was no trace of them – the Johnsons were frantic. They couldn't understand why their daughter, if the woman at the station was their daughter, hadn't got in touch with them."

"They didn't give her much protection, did they?" said Molly calmly. "Not after they'd got her married off."

Sir Herbert said, "I don't know why she didn't go to them. In any case, they put her on the wanted list, along with the spies and aliens who hadn't turned up at the police station to register – and a month later an intelligent policeman spotted a woman and her children in a

London street. The hunt was up. They found out that documents and ration books had been issued to a Maria Lavalle, née Johnson, who had escaped from France to England in a plane. She'd been interviewed, naturally, but the men who saw her were quite convinced by her story and the whole matter got lost in the bureaucratic confusion of the times – she got her ration books and went off. So my father went to the address she'd given."

"Guess where?" Molly said, in the same flat tone she had used all along. She was beginning to frighten Herbert Precious more and more. What was she thinking? How could she sit there so calmly, as if showing no interest in the story? And what, in God's name, would she do when he got to the end, when it became plain her mother was probably still alive?

He said, "He got to Meakin Street too late. It was a ruin. He found out where the ambulance had taken the woman but she was gone. He even found out what had happened to one of the children – you." He paused, waiting for her to do or say something, but all she said was, "Joe had been taken to the orphanage."

Herbert Precious said, "So it seems. A pity no one thought to make enquiries."

"Would have saved some incest," Molly said. "If anyone had liked to interfere. In case their names got into it."

"Be reasonable, Molly," said Bert. "At first you were a lot better off in Meakin Street. The country was expecting an invasion. You stood a chance of surviving in Meakin Street – what do you think would have happened to the Royal Family if Hitler had taken over? And they didn't need a royal scandal at that moment – bad for national morale."

"Didn't need it then and didn't need it afterwards," Molly told him.

"The longer a secret's kept the harder it becomes to tell it," he said.

"Good reason for not keeping them in the first place, isn't it?" she said. Now she leaned back in her chair. "That's it then, is it? That's the lot. You've been told you can say your piece and you've said it and it's over?"

"One more thing," he said uncomfortably.

"I thought there would be," she remarked.

He stared at her, almost as if he was trying to pacify her. "Your mother's probably alive, in France, at the place where you were born. She was alive and well three months ago. She survived the bombing, thinking you were both dead, I suppose, you and Joe, or so unnerved she wasn't able to think at all. At some point she must have gone back

606

to France." He paused and said, "I still don't understand why she never asked anyone for help. Both her parents were dead by the end of the war, of course. Her father was on a corvette on the Russian convoys. Her mother died of pneumonia in 1944."

"Does she know I'm alive?" asked Molly.

Bert Precious said, "No. You see, we – I, didn't know she was alive herself until a few years ago."

Molly's neutrality began, now, to melt. She found she was angry. "You could have sent us all a telegram," she said. "I don't understand how you could keep this under your hat for so long and now, suddenly, for no reason –" She broke off. She felt bitter – bitter that so much information about her own life had been kept from her for so long, while others watched and watched, spying on her all the time. She felt bitter that while she had loved Bert he had been keeping this secret.

She asked, "While we were together, in Scotland, you knew all this, didn't you? Even that my own mother was alive. And you never told me. You never told me."

She became angrier and angrier. She stood up saying, "God – it's disgusting! The whole bloody thing's disgusting!" She was choking now. "It's the worst – the worst bloody bit of treachery I've ever heard of. The whole situation's been false from beginning to end. I've known gangsters, pimps – I thought I'd seen everything. But it's what they say, isn't it, the worst crimes are done by people in clean collars. That's you, isn't it, Bert, the dirty man in the clean collar."

He sat silently under her reproaches. "I don't like it," she said in a calmer voice, "I don't like you being a spy – that's treachery if you like – and it's worse because you got into bed with a woman you've been watching on the sly since she was – what – fifteen, twenty – and your father before you. I've been part of your family's living, Bert, practically from when I was born. Me, Mary Waterhouse, from Meakin Street, a nice little earner for the Precious family of gentlemen. There's no difference between you and Arnie Rose, or Charlie Markham. They thrive by getting to the top of the heap and standing on people not as determined and crafty as they are – so do you, only you do it in white breeches. I don't know how you can sit there, Bert. You should be dropping through the floor with shame." She frowned, "And why now, that's what I ask myself? Why, after all these years, have you decided to come clean? It didn't trouble you before – what's new? Course, now no one can point the finger at the guilty father – that's one thing. Then again, it wouldn't be nice to leave a nasty mess for the next generation. That's right, isn't it? The scandal's just about old enough to be like history – some king's mistress or some secret treaty signed hundreds of years ago – so it doesn't matter if it comes out." She paused, "Ah – you've got the contract in your pocket, haven't you, Bert? I sign it, swearing eternal secrecy out of patriotism. You carry it back and get the grateful thanks of your monarch. Arise, Duke of Banana and Lord Warden of the Swamps. Thanks," she added, "I'm signing nothing."

Even in her anger she was able to think of Joe Endell. He would have laughed, she decided, but thinking of Joe and what he would have said and thought introduced another set of propositions. She looked at Bert Precious who sat there, she decided, rather like a spider waiting for a fly he felt too embarrassed to catch, and then stood up, walked up to him, pushed her face in his and said, "You bastard. You're sitting there, hoping I'll sign quickly without realizing what this is all about. My Fred's legitimate – Joe and me were legitimate. We're not bastards – I'll leave that to you. We're more than a bleeding scandal – we're contenders. That's right, isn't it, Bert? You don't want a pledge of secrecy – you want an abdication." She looked at him. "They should have sent somebody else, Bert. You're not a dealer – you've let me think for too long. A real fixer would have had all this sewn up by now. Been in a taxi on the way back to the palace. You're too slow and too scrupulous. That's one good thing – maybe you aren't quite as bad as Arnie Rose, after all."

"Molly," he said with some difficulty. "Fred is not a legitimate child. You and Joe were not entitled to marry, any more than you would have been if one of you were already married."

"Try that one, Bert," Molly said. "Just try it. And if you do we'll see what the courts have to say about it. Years ago, when I didn't know nothing from nothing, I might have fallen for all this stuff. But I've been around too long and you try to turn my son into a bastard and I'll take the whole bleeding thing to the European Courts of Justice if I have to –"

"That wasn't what I meant," he told her.

"I know what you meant – I know what you're doing. Running with the hare and hunting with the hounds. You've been involved in a racket for years – you know it – it shows on your face, the way you're sitting – I'm embarrassed for you, Bert."

"Molly," he said, leaning forward. "It's quite true that this situation ought to be regularized. It'd only be a formality. No one is going to try to make your son a bastard. No one has any malice against you. Everyone, not just myself, regrets the pain and muddle."

"But only one of us is going through the bloody mincer – that's right, isn't it?" she said. "And only one of us is having the wool pulled over their eyes – that's right, too, isn't it? I'm asking myself all the time what Joe Endell would have thought – how he'd have seen this. I can't work out the rights and wrongs of it all but I know he'd have been disgusted. I don't think he'd have stayed in this room to argue." She stood up. "I wouldn't have stayed if I hadn't've had some feeling for you. You say my real mother's at this place in France – where did you say?"

"Poulaye-sur-Bois," he told her. "Please don't go there until something's resolved, Molly."

"Blood's thicker than water when it comes to rights, isn't it? Not when it comes to feelings?" she said.

"I'm suggesting a meeting," he said, "with some advisers –"

"Plan One fails," she said. "The punter won't sign. Try Plan Two – call a meeting and blind her with science. Experts, generals and law lords. What it boils down to," she said slowly, "is that I'm legitimate. I suppose I put the monarchy in a funny position. I could make a claim."

She felt dreadful. She paced the room now. "Hundreds of years ago you'd have jumped me in Meakin Street on a dark night and bludgeoned me to death. As it is, I'm alive. When was the abdication?" she asked.

"At the end of 1936," he told her.

"Ah – so he still had his rights when I was born. Also Joe," she said.

"You're a Catholic," he said. "You were christened."

"So what?" she said. "What difference does that make?" He was silent. She thought. "Catholics can't come to the throne?" she suggested. Bert Precious nodded.

"So that's the area we're in," she said slowly. "You lot are actually wondering, aren't you?" She ceased her wandering up and down and said, "Oh, Bert, Bert. What a rotten business. That poor woman, always hoping he'd come back – she must've done or she wouldn't have been mad enough to have me, after he took up with the other woman, Mrs Simpson, if that was her name. Then having to escape to England and there's a bomb and she thinks her children are dead – why didn't she get some help? She must've been in a shocking state for years, always waiting for him to turn up, never making any claims, even though she was the real wife – oh, my God, it makes you ill to think of it. For two pins I'd fight, if only because of that. See some justice done."

"You must take time to think," he advised.

"It's all coming up – past, present, future," Molly said. "I don't understand anything. I've got a mother alive, but Ivy was my real mother. My father was some kind of ex-King but Sid Waterhouse is my real father. What do I want with these others? Even my children don't feel like my children any more. They're like claimants to a throne – do people like that have to live like this – half like people and half like some kind of function, ninth in line and hereditary guardian of the Welsh Marches – all that? I came in here as Molly Allaun, woman, mother and bike factory proprietor – and now who am I? Somebody you never told me about – somebody else's daughter – oh, God, Bert – I'm so tired. On the way up to London I was working out I'd been tired for years –"

"You do realize, Molly, you need never have any more anxieties about money," he told her.

"Nice, Bert – nice," she said wearily. "Hold out the bribe when the victim begins to cry with tiredness. What happens? I sign – then I'm allowed on the payroll with the others? Look, Bert, in all this confusion one thing stands out – I don't want anything to do with it. Not a thing. I have to keep quiet for Fred's sake. A boy in his teens doesn't want incest thrown in his face. I've got no ambitions to queen it over this ramshackle place – four million out of work – country sold off to greedy men and foreigners – the shame'd kill me. I don't fancy driving through Brixton, or Corby or Leeds or Glasgow, thinking, "Goody, goody. These slums and this misery are mine, all mine. Aren't I lucky?" I tell you this – if you'd sat there and asked me, as if it was just an idle question, whether I'd rather be who you say I am or just be Sid and Ivy Waterhouse's daughter and Joe Endell's widow I'd soon've told you where you could stuff your crown and orb. No," she said, staring at him intently, "you can't believe it, can you? You and your family were born with flexible knees and a dutiful smile on your faces. Your greatest pleasure is respecting your betters, isn't it? Well – you have, Bert, you have, but just think – while you've been respecting them you haven't respected me. You've kept me in ignorance of who my parents were for over forty years. I've struggled and I've suffered and I've been to prison. You let me marry Joe Endell, which I doubt if I'd've done if I'd had the information you've been keeping from me. And you've been spying on me, Bert, and writing things down. And you've been watching me like a hawk, I bet, in case I got in too much disgrace or in case I found out what I should have been told in the first place. That's your respect, Bert. Respect for them – not for me, not even for yourself. No wonder you think I ought to feel honoured to be included. They've made you feel so inferior so, naturally, I'm even more inferior. I ought to feel pleased about getting elevated. I'm not. It's disgusting."

He came to life and said, "Molly, I can't listen to any more of this rubbish. I've tried to be reasonable. You have to understand that all this arose because no one knew what to do – it all happened at the wrong time –" Then he sighed and said, "This is insupportable. You're right – my position's ridiculous. I'd better go. Before I do, will you give me your promise that you won't do anything until we've had a chance to talk again?"

"The old racket," she said tiredly. "Don't move till I tell you to – then I find out you've used the time to get organized."

"Why do you take this attitude?" he asked. "No one wants to trap you."

All Molly said, wearily, was, "Get out, Bert. I can't stand any more."

After he had gone she sat still for a few moments, trying to work out what had happened. She telephoned her brother, Jack, at the House of Commons and told him what Herbert Precious had said. He listened, without interrupting and then said, "Molly – you sound ill – I'm coming round."

"Don't come, Jack," she told him. "I'm too tired. I never felt so tired. I want to get some sleep."

"Phone me if you need me," he said. "Don't do anything yet. Let me think about it, too." He was sounding more and more shaken as he took in what had happened. "What a bloody mess," he said. "How could they do it? How?"

"I don't know," she said wearily. "I don't know anything." And then said, "There's a bit more." She told him, then, about George Messiter's discovery. Jack said, "Oh, my God, Molly. It's all too much. Look – get some sleep and I'll be round first thing. Are you all right?"

She told him she was, then put all the telephones on to record messages and went to bed. As she slept she could hear the first ringing of phones in the flat and downstairs in the offices. She woke at one o'clock in the morning and lay awake, realizing she could not go back to Framlingham next day. Richard would have recovered from his fit of sensibility about the presence of the guards and both he and Isabel would be waiting, half-flattered by the importance of living in a guarded camp, excited by the secret discovery which made it necessary and able to indulge in princely sulks about the inconveniences of the situation. Any hint of her dealings with Herbert Precious would interest them more and she, exhausted as she was, felt she could not face the need to make decisions surrounded by curious witnesses looking for information. Any hint of a coming industrial fortune, or of royal connections, would lead Richard to abandon the actress she was fairly sure he saw in London and take over the position of the bookish young squire of Framlingham in dead earnest. Meanwhile Isabel would start the cellar to attic search for her missing pearls.

She usually conducted this when a particularly grandiose fit overtook her. Molly, who knew the pearls had probably been stolen at Josephine's wedding, had ceased to be sorry about the loss and now dreaded the hunt.

No, she thought, as she lay on the big, brass-knobbed bed that night, she could not go to Framlingham next day. She felt as if she were in a great sea, where the waters were slowly being sucked back and back, forming a huge tidal wave in the distance which would soon speed towards her, break and engulf her completely.

In the short while before she slept again she was blackberrying in the lanes and down the hedges of the fields in Framlingham.

Jack was beside her in his thick boots, pushing back the pungent brambles under a hot sun. She could feel the heat, the stickiness of the fruit on her purple fingers, the itch of the scratches on her legs and arms and the little prickings of the bramble spikes in her fingers.

Then, there she was, dancing at the Roxy Ballroom with Jim Flanders, while the coloured lights went round and round, feeling the rough material of his jacket against her bare shoulders and arms, smelling her own heavily scented face powder and the sickly spray which they sometimes wafted into the ballroom on crowded nights. The band played as she swung round and round in Jim's arms. Then out, shivering into the wet city streets, eating chips from the bag as they walked home together, arms right round each other, dizzy with the lights and the music.

There was fog in all the windows the day Jim was hanged, Johnnie Bridges was kissing her on the canal bank where the greenish water lay sluggish under the wall overhung by trees, she was sitting on the sofa talking quietly to Steven Greene at night, Ferenc Nedermann lay on the bed, dead, with his eyes open, Joe Endell was bounding up Meakin

Street towards her with a big file held across his chest and, on top, a bunch of chrysanthemums. Josephine lay like a goblin, screaming in her cot, Mrs Gates trickled golden syrup on to her porridge in the shape of a wobbling M, George Messiter lay asleep with his head on the bench, next to the silver globe which was his new engine, corks popped, a baby cried, Ivy said, "You can't have everything."

The film went on running. At one moment she was making love to Johnnie Bridges in the bed she now lay on, then standing cold by Steven Greene's grave. There were flames everywhere, the woman's voice sang in French, the nurse in the gleaming corridor said, "It won't be long, now," and she was searching Sid's pockets for sweets on Friday night when he came in from work, the boughs on the trees above the canal wall swayed. Am I dreaming or dying, she wondered, before she fell asleep.

She woke again quite early and could not think of anything but evading the return to Framlingham. She rang her office manager at home and told him not to come to work – she asked him to tell the others. She rang Framlingham and spoke, guiltily, to Fred. She told him that she would be back fairly soon, but could not say when. Exhausted by the effort of seeming to be in charge she lay down, quite frightened by her own behaviour, but giving way to an animal sense of needing to lie low and undisturbed. And so she sat in the little sitting room at Meakin Street, doing nothing. She lay on her bed watching the sparrows fly in and out of the bare branches of the sycamore tree which was growing, unwanted and unencouraged, in the yard at the back of the house. The doorbell rang and she did not answer it. She had forgotten Jack was supposed to be coming. The telephones rang and cut off as messages were put on the recording machine. Molly was not happy as the telephones rang more frequently. She was nagged by the thought that she had decisions to make, and constantly pushed the thoughts to the back of her head. On the second day of all this she thought, "I'm going mad" and did not care. She slept, had uneasy dreams, sat remembering the clang of the doors in Holloway, the popping of the corks at the Dorchester and the sound of Lord Clover's voice, taking her through Cabinet meetings while she lay, naked and unmoving, on a fur cover on the bed in Highgate. During this time she did not bathe, dress or comb her hair. She ate very little and never felt hungry. Sometimes she muttered to herself, "Too much has happened." On the third day, as the ringing of the doorbell grew insistent and the telephones took more and more messages, Molly, making herself a cup of tea and hearing all the bells thought, "No – no – shut up." But something inside her told her that it was over. That evening someone put a thumb on the bell and left it there and from above she heard Shirley shouting, "Molly! I know you're in there! Answer the door! If you don't I'm calling the others and we're going to break it in. Come on – don't be a stupid bitch. Open up now or we'll smash the lock."

Her sister surveyed her dressing-gown and tousled hair as she stood in the doorway. She looked carefully at her face, decided all was well and walked in. "Are you all right?" she asked. Molly nodded.

"Jack told me," Shirley said. "We thought we'd leave you alone for a bit, if it was what you wanted. But then they started telling me you'd done yourself in," she said. "Wanted to get the police to break in – I said you weren't the type. But I thought I'd come and take a look at you."

"I wish you hadn't," muttered Molly.

"I wish I hadn't," Shirley said. "I don't like what I see. But you've picked a silly way to try and have a holiday. Want a cup of tea?"

Upstairs, looking at the unwashed dishes and packets open in the kitchen, she said, "What a rats' nest." Turning round from filling the kettle she said, "You've been pushing yourself too hard for years. Now it's all this royal family carry-on. And George Messiter's discovery which is probably a lot more important. That's why you came here and fell to pieces. Personally I don't think Jack's a lot of use. He doesn't seem to know what he thinks. Still –" she said, with the air of a person staying away from worrying subjects during a visit to a patient in hospital, "Never mind all that. What are you taking the aspirin for?" She looked at the open bottle on the kitchen counter.

"Headache," said Molly. "Everybody gets them." She added, "No need to treat me like a mental patient, Shirl."

"You might as well let me," Shirley said. "You know it's all waiting for you out there." As she poured out the tea she said, "Look – do you really want to go away for a bit? On a holiday – even a week or two's rest at a clinic – whatever you want. We can keep everything going. No one's indispensable, you know."

Molly was conscious, although she did not want to be, that Shirley and the others had decided they would take over for her if they had to. But she knew she could not accept the offer. With an effort she said, "I think I'm going to have to keep on going." And put her hand to her brow, where she felt a stab of pain. "Headache?" Shirley said. "That's your body threatening you, Molly. I'm going to get a doctor."

"Shut up, Shirley," Molly said, knowing that Ivy Waterhouse had taken over her sister's mind and was now in complete control. That being so, there was nothing she, Molly, could do to stop her.

"Might as well give in," Shirley told her, with the telephone in her hand. All she said on the telephone was, "Dr Bleasdale – she'll see you." A plan had been made beforehand.

"Well, then, Shirley," Molly said encouragingly. "That's settled – I'll let him in when he comes. You can go now."

Shirley shook her head grimly. "I'm here – and I'm stopping," she said.

"I only want to be left alone," Molly said in a tired voice.

"Treat me as a buffer between you and the rest of the world," Shirley said. "Get into bed and have a sleep till Dr Bleasdale comes."

Molly could hear her downstairs, running through the recorded messages and making return calls. A little later she was upstairs again, asking what she wanted for supper. The doctor, she thought, could not be any worse than her sister, with her energetic and bossy air. But he was. He appeared disappointed to find the capable industrialist laid low. After examining her he said, with an air of mild reproach, "The problem appears to be that you've been overdoing it. I'll make an appointment for you to have a thorough overhaul, but for now I'll leave a prescription for some tablets."

After he had gone Molly screwed up the prescription and threw it across the room. "Overhaul," she said. "What does he think I am – an old car? Where did you dig him up from?"

"He's my own doctor," she said.

"I don't need someone about who expects me to be well so they can feel better about life," she said.

Shirley shrugged patiently. Molly went to sleep. Next day she sent for another doctor. Molly refused to see him. "Even an animal's allowed to lie down in a bit of straw on its own when it wants to," she told her sister. "Why don't you piss off – get the district nurse to look in on me from time to time."

She heard the doctor, in the hall, use the words, "nursing home". Later she listened to Shirley arguing with Herbert Precious, who was evidently on the doorstep. "It's you and your crooked tricks which've triggered all this, that's what I think," she was saying. "And now you come bothering her – you're the last person she needs at this time."

She heard Herbert Precious reply something and Shirley say, in a hostile voice, "All right – I'm listening." Then came more mumbling and Molly went to sleep again. She thought Shirley must be dosing her food with tranquillizers. She dreamed of Johnnie Bridges and woke up crying. "First love, I suppose," she thought. She dozed and dreamed of Mrs Gates.

Later, Shirley brought Herbert Precious's flowers, and Fred in. "Are you feeling better, Mum?" he asked timidly. She had almost never been ill.

"Quite a lot," she said and made Shirley promise she would do nothing if she would take him to a film before he went back to Framlingham. Before he left she scanned his face to see if it bore the marks of sickness or insanity – they said that children of incest were often sickly or mad.

Isabel stood in the doorway saying, "Richard was so disappointed they won't let him see you."

"Doctor's orders," Molly said shortly.

"While I'm in town I'll put in an order for Christmas at Harrods," Isabel said. "I'm assuming I'm in charge this Christmas." Molly turned her head away.

"Do you think it would be a good idea to have a brace of wild ducks?" she said.

"Wild ducks," Molly said.

"They might as well supply the tree."

"I don't feel very well," Molly said.

"Oh, my dear, I'm so sorry," Isabel said. "I'll leave you to rest," she said and left the room.

Seconds later Shirley put her head round the door, mouthing the words, "I couldn't stop her from coming up." It was too much, though, and Molly felt her eyes filling with tears. Before they had found her she had been dry-eyed. Now she could not stop crying.

She heard Shirley, whom she knew to be growing threadbare, talking to her husband downstairs. "George is getting persistent. He wonders how long he is supposed to stay in Ramsgate – I don't know what to tell him."

"Tell him to stay there," Ferdinand Wong remarked. He came into the room where Molly lay, bringing roses. Molly looked at him suspiciously. He sat down and said, "I'm cooking a meal tonight – chicken, mushrooms, all sorts of good things. Then, I'm sure you'll agree it's right, I'll take Shirley home. She's very tired and you need to think."

"I need a holiday," Molly said.

"Yes," he agreed calmly. "I don't think you can have one. Do you?"

She shook her head. "I don't know who I am," she said.

"Does anyone?" he asked.

"Come to give me some oriental philosophy?" she said.

He said, "No – yes. Yes. Perhaps I have. I've come," he said clearly, "to offer you any help I can give, knowing that when the moment comes you'll recover but not knowing when that moment will be. If it is now, then my help will be useful. If not, then you'll be angry."

He seemed to expect nothing from her, not help, not strength and certainly no decisions. She became calmer immediately.

She asked, "Ferdinand – is Shirley putting tablets in my food or drink?"

"Not any more," he told her calmly. She knew that he had persuaded her sister not to do it.

Then she said, "I was worn out when all this happened. And for all these years there's been more and more stuff about who I wasn't, who Joe was – then it all comes to a head when Bert Precious tells me his news. I've changed my name so often –" she was crying now. "How can you know who you are anyway, when you're Waterhouse, Flanders, Endell, Allaun – then your mother says you're not her and your father's child –"

"Herbert Precious offered to go with you to France to see your mother," Wong told her quietly.

"Not with him," she said, shaking her head.

"I think you're right," he said.

Downstairs, Wong said to Shirley, "She has had no inner life since I've known her. Probably not for years. Your sister is naturally active and worldly but even she needs time to rest and contemplate for a little while. All human beings do."

Shirley stared at her husband. He had been impatient and worried about the neglects and delays caused by Molly's shutting herself up at Meakin Street. He had, in fact, been creeping in late at night to listen to the phone messages, open the post and do his best to stall on issues demanding Molly's personal attention so that suppliers, and customers, did not find out what was happening and Wayne could go on running the factory. The tangles in the illicit businesses were becoming very great – the factory itself would be in a mess if Molly did not either get back to work or hand over full authority to someone else. Shirley found it strange that her husband was suddenly thinking about what afflicted Molly.

"She's always been a doer, not a thinker," she pointed out. "I'm not cheered up if she's in a state of contemplation. It's not natural to her — it usually means there's something wrong."

"She needs to be as she is now," he said.

"I don't care what you say," Shirley told him. "She's never had any worries about her identity up to now. I think it's all a load of clichés covering up a nervous breakdown. You know as well as I do we need a decision about when she's going to pull herself together. It's got to be soon. Apart from the day-to-day business there's George stuck down in Ramsgate with his invention and Allaun Towers under siege conditions, Christmas coming on —"

"In the meanwhile," Wong said, "you're coming home."

"What about Molly!" cried her sister.

"She's better off alone," Wong said.

Shirley looked at him. "There's times," she said, "when you act really Chinese."

"Do as I say," he said implacably.

After Shirley had gone, Molly turned to dreaming. Days drifted by as she sat in the little house, in the little street thinking of the past, which had now become strange for her because she realized her past was only partly private — that from her birth on she had been part of history. And sometimes she thought of nothing at all. She dragged about the house in her dressing-gown, scarcely eating, in a state halfway between sleeping and waking. One day she fell on the stairs and lay, with a bruised shoulder aching, crying, "Oh Joe, Joe. I wish you were here." All that answered her was the hollow echo of her own voice. She called out "Ivy! Ivy!" Again there was no answer. She lay there on the stairs at Meakin Street, not bothering to rise. She said, "Joe," again, in a doubtful tone. And still there was no one. The stairs were hard and the smell of the stair carpet began to offend her nostrils. She went upstairs and lay down, sobbing.

The next day she got up and went out. Jack Waterhouse was horrified when he met his sister in the hall at the House of Commons. She was pale, gaunt and untidy. He wondered if she had gone mad. "Don't worry," she said to him as he came towards her, looking very alarmed. "I'm all right. I just wanted to talk something over with you."

They sat in a draughty office which belonged to three other MPs. Molly drank two cups of coffee and ate half a packet of biscuits. Spitting crumbs she outlined her idea. Jack, half appalled, wondered again if she was mad. He thought for a moment, then said, "It's fair, I suppose. If anything in this business could ever be fair now. You'll sign the renunciation, of course?"

"Sign?" said Molly. "Sign? Never. I'll never give away my rights."

"Christ, Molly – you're mad," Jack exclaimed. "Your rights? What are you talking about? The only rights you should want are the ordinary rights of a citizen in a democratic society." He stared at her. "I thought you were talking about blackmail redeemed by the fact that it looked like rough justice –"

"I hate signing things," said Molly. "When I have to sign anything I feel as if I'm signing in my own blood. Just think, Jack Waterhouse, your great-aunt Rosie, Sid's favourite auntie, his Mum's twin sister, died of double pneumonia brought on by malnutrition in the winter of 1927. And because they couldn't afford to call the doctor. Those days are coming back – rickets are back, people are getting ill because they're out of work and they don't get the right food to eat and they can't afford warmth in their houses. Don't talk to me about justice, rough or smooth. Don't talk to me about blackmail or justice. The world we've living in is hard and getting harder."

"All right, all right," he said holding up his hands in surrender. "I can't argue it."

Until she decided to produce her *Confessions* Molly never made it generally known how she found the capital to start the Messiter Electric Car company (MEC). Ferdinand and Shirley Wong knew, of course, because it was they who calculated how much she would have received in Civil List payments, as a member of the royal family from the time of her birth to the year 1985. Sir Herbert Precious guessed where the money came from and no one minded his guessing but, equally, no one confirmed the guess as truth. Ferdinand Wong, becoming enthusiastic once the calculations were made, suggested charging interest on the money, but Molly rejected the idea. Several million pounds, she said, was all she needed to set up a new firm to exploit the electric motor on a modest scale. After that, she said, the business would have to earn its own living in the world just as, she supposed, they all would.

Her interview with the Queen at Buckingham Palace was less frosty than she had thought it might have been for Her Majesty was more than gracious. She was obviously realistic, and, Molly claimed later –

much later – to Herbert Precious, appeared relieved the matter was out in the open, pleased to make a donation to British industry and, Molly said, not entirely unamused by this original ending to fifty years of family shame and anxiety. What did not please her was Molly's refusal to sign papers of renunciation but, as Molly also reported, she thought the Queen half expected her to refuse. At any rate, the meeting was as pleasant as it could be in the circumstances and the two negotiators parted on cordial terms. "You couldn't," as Molly said, "have asked for a nicer person, or cousin."

And so it happened. Starting with the manufacture of electric cycles the Messiter company gradually expanded into fuelless cars and, later, other vehicles. By 1990 one car in ten bought in Britain, and one in a hundred elsewhere, was a Messiter. Gradually other companies followed suit. Throughout the bleakness of the late '80s and early '90s the Messiter company survived, pursuing a policy of worker management and profit-sharing which appeared to operate smoothly. Indeed, when the ferocity of governments in the early years of the company was over, and the wobbling of the governments which succeeded them ended, the industrial example of the Messiter company appeared very much in keeping with the new times. So, indeed, did the product. Neither the management nor the vehicles were exciting, tension-producing, aggressive, glamorous, noisy or smelly. In this manner the company survived eight years of economic swings, mounting social violence and repression and the strains of a deeply divided society at home without losing either its viability or, too often, its conscience. The proprietor, Molly, née Waterhouse, later Flanders and Endell, finally Allaun, although mysteriously unhonoured by the Queen's Award for Industry or any other kind of official recognition, earned herself at least a footnote, and perhaps more, in the industrial history of Great Britain.

For the rest, events went on as they might have been expected to. Isabel Allaun lived to be ninety years old, desolated, at first, when Molly's lover Richard Mayhew left Framlingham for good but much consoled when her son Tom and his lover came back to live in a cottage in the village, although she was never able to acknowledge the real relationship between them. Shirley and Ferdinand Wong stayed on as directors of MEC – Shirley had twin daughters and the family ended as a large one, containing the couple, their children and his old parents, whom he was able to bring over from Hong Kong before the British lease on the island ran out. Josephine, twice divorced, married an amiable garage proprietor called Joe Marks and was happy, working for Amnesty and leaving for Bogota, Thailand or Prague when her husband's large previous family of children threatened to descend. Jack Waterhouse, who lost his seat in Parliament, took a job at the research department of Transport House and returned to his first wife, Pat who left her husband for him. Sid Waterhouse died, peacefully, one summer day, between the runner beans and the lettuces in his garden at Ramsgate. And Molly's son, Fred, told of his unnatural birth when he was eighteen and about to leave for a kibbutz in Israel for a year, refused to believe it, left the country and then phoned from Jerusalem to say that he did believe it and that, having seen at close quarters how time and chance had dealt with the Jews, he thought that royal birth and incest made no difference at all. Molly failed to see the reasoning but was relieved that her confidence in her son's natural good sense and healthy ego had been justified. Fred came back minus two fingers on his left hand, which he lost on the Lebanese border. "Not fit now," he said, "to wave out of the window of a state coach."

1996

As the last tape ends Sir Herbert sits in the silence of his ivory and blue sitting room in London.

Molly's last words linger in the room. "I suppose the proper ending to my story's really me finding my real mother at last and with her finding me and seeing Fred and knowing when she died she'd leave something behind. Yes – that's the real end, I suppose – Life goes on – that'd be the moral of it all."

"Oh, my God," the infuriated Sir Herbert exclaims into his empty room. The final addition of this piece of homespun philosophy, delivered in Molly's ever-lively tones, is more than he can stomach, after all the unnecessary and embarrassing revelations she has insisted on making. It's just about the last straw, he thinks – absolutely the last. And what's to be done about it all? There's enough material buried in Molly's story for a hundred TV, magazine and newspaper investigations – enough to topple a government, a company, even the monarchy itself, once the threads start to be pulled out, once the unravellings begin!

He stares blindly, tiredly, desperately at his large black and white cat, which is tapping indignantly at the window, waiting to be let in. Behind the cat stretched the garden, sunny in the afternoon light. He gazes at the great chestnut tree, standing very still in the middle of the lawn. The solid mass of leaves are still dark green but interspersed among them, and visible at the ends of the branches, some are yellowing, preparing to drop. He glances across the room at the big grandfather clock in its blue alcove, sees that it is four o'clock, sighs, gets up and opens the window. In springs the cat and begins to rub round his legs. "If only Joe Endell had lived," he sighs in a sudden access of pity for Molly, and, behind it, lies the thought that if Endell had lived, perhaps the problem of Molly's memoirs would never have arisen.

The telephone rings loudly in the quiet room. It is, most likely, thinks Sir Herbert, either his sovereign ringing to enquire about Molly's story, or Molly herself asking for an opinion. Showing a good turn of speed for a man of his age, Sir Herbert is swiftly away from the telephone, the cat and the room, and out in the hall collecting his coat and then in the street hailing a taxi.

As he leans back in the seat he enjoys driving through the noisy, tatty, brightly-coloured, jibber-jabbering streets of London, on to the peace of the gentlemen's club to which he belongs.

Perhaps it is rightly in France where we should leave Molly, as she and her son walk across the flagstones of the courtyard to the big grey house, ring the heavy doorbell and see before them in the doorway the bent figure of the old maid who has been her mother's constant companion during so many years of exile.

Or perhaps we should leave her as she and the tall boy walk down the drive and turn to wave back at the two small, grey figures who stand there, light, bent and frail as if, like leaves ready to blow away, they are only insecurely placed on the heavy flagstones where they stand. Behind them looms the house, all wreathed in mist, a complicated, massive pattern of stone crenellations, buttresses and bays. One of the figures, her mother's, slowly lifts her arm, then links it to the supporting arm of the old servant. Both women turn and begin to walk slowly up the steps of the house, while Molly and Fred continue down the drive, past the misty trees and lawns on either side of them. They go through the gates to the car which will take them to the airport.